DATE DUE

NO 1 '00			
OC 18 02			
NO 1 '02			
AG 5 '04			
JE 1 0 '09			

THE OUTSIDER

RICHARD WRIGHT

WITH AN INTRODUCTION BY MARYEMMA GRAHAM

THE RESTORED TEXT ESTABLISHED BY THE LIBRARY OF AMERICA

THE OUTSIDER

HarperPerennial
A Division of HarperCollins*Publishers*

A hardcover edition of *The Outsider* was originally published in 1953 by Harper & Brothers. A paperback edition was published in 1965 by Perennial Library and reissued in 1989. The text as restored by The Library of America was published in 1991 in a volume entitled *Richard Wright: Later Works* which also included *Black Boy (American Hunger)*.

HarperCollins books may be purchased for educational, business, or sales promotional use. For information, please write: Special Markets Department, HarperCollins Publishers, Inc., 10 East 53rd Street, New York, NY 10022.

First HarperPerennial edition published 1993.

ISBN: 0-06-081248-6

94 95 96 97 OPM 10 9 8 7 6 5 4 3

For Rachel
my daughter who was born on foreign soil

ARNOLD RAMPERSAD
WROTE THE NOTES FOR THIS VOLUME

Contents

Introduction to the HarperPerennial Edition

The Outsider is Richard Wright's second installment in a story of epic proportions, a complex master narrative designed to show American racism in raw and ugly terms. The kind of racism that Wright knew and experienced, a racism from which most black people of his own time could not escape, remained the central element in his fiction. Stories of American racism and economic injustice told in the way Wright preferred to tell them have all but gone out of fashion. Ironically, however, it is precisely Wright's "fictions" which are coming to life for us today: The stories of Bigger Thomas (in his earlier book *Native Son*) and Cross Damon bear an uncanny resemblance to many contemporary cases of street crime and violence; and the media's often thoughtless exploitation of the negative and sensational aspects and perceptions of black communities is probably even more frequent in real life today than in Wright's world of fiction.

There is also a prophetic note in Wright's construction of the criminal mind as intelligent, introspective, and transformative. As a number of critics have noted, Cross Damon is a good example of Wright's attempt to cast light upon the revolutionary potential of the average black person: Cross is articulate and assertive, and engages in actions—up to and including murder—that represent explosive acts of resistance sparked by his refusal to be dominated or to let others be dominated by political ideologies or social forces.

The Outsider appeared in 1953 during the height of McCarthyism in the United States and the advent of the

Cold War in Europe, two events which had a significant bearing on its initial reception. The year before, Ralph Ellison had published *Invisible Man*, a highly acclaimed novel which made apparent the extremely symbolic nature of racism and its peculiar effect on the individual psyche. And in the same year, Algerian psychiatrist Frantz Fanon published his influential study, *The Wretched of the Earth*, which examined the psychological oppression heaped on the masses of African people as a result of French colonialism. Seen within this context, Wright's first exile novel takes on a significance which must be carefully assessed.

Early critics saw *The Outsider* as Wright's attempt to become "universal," to move outside the racial paradigm. They suggested an important shift in Wright's ideological and aesthetic sensibilities had occurred, one that linked him more closely with French existentialism than with African-American writers. This opinion served a useful purpose in a sense, for it shielded Wright from some of his critics who would tend to characterize him as an "ex-Communist and rabble-rouser" who had been a serious critic of American race relations. According to this interpretation, Cross Damon symbolizes modern man, whose existential dilemma is manifested through an internal rather than an external conflict. Sensitive and intelligent, Cross denies his racial identity and feels free to act upon the world in order to invest it with meaning. In doing so, he accepts a great deal of responsibility and displays divine or demonic power (as the name "Damon" suggests) in the new life he has created for himself as Lionel Lane. Such actions on the part of an individual come at great cost, however; for Cross Damon, the price is his death, the cause and meaning of which he struggles to understand. This existential analysis was accepted by and large due to the similarities between Wright's novel and *The Chips Are Down*, a novel by Jean Paul Sartre, a leading French intellectual and proponent of existentialism whom Wright had come to know in Paris.

Unfortunately, we do not have the benefit of Wright's own expressed ideas concerning the conception and meaning of *The Outsider*, as we do for *Native Son*. (Ever conscious that his work be fully understood and correctly represented, and especially in response to hostile reviewers, Wright wrote "How Bigger Was Born," which is now regularly included in the text edition of his most famous novel.) In the absence of these kinds of insights, the fully restored text of *The Outsider*, presented to us by the Library of America as Wright wished it to be, is an important milestone in literary studies. This source becomes the single most important evidence needed for examining a novel that won greater acceptance for Wright within the European community, and, at the same time, placed him outside the tradition of African-American writing with which he had been most identified.

When we study Wright in order to develop an ideological and artistic map of African-American literature, he is all too often identified primarily in terms of his early works, the impact of which on the subsequent literature is viewed to be both liberating and inhibiting. In other words, modern black literature is defined on the one hand as one that derives from Wright's school of "protest fiction" or, on the other hand, one that seeks to write against that tradition. The latter trend is said to be represented by James Baldwin and Ralph Ellison and more recently by the work of African-American women writers in general. The career Wright started after his move to Paris was, many critics contend, not only a mistake, but also was marked by a decline in his literary abilities, beginning with the publication of *The Outsider*, a book which records Wright's disillusionment with communism.[1]

Revisiting *The Outsider* serves an invaluable function for examining Wright from a different perspective, especially in the wake of communism's collapse as a world power and in our own post–Cold War era. First, we need to make these epochal developments central to our contemporary reading of Wright's novel. Equally important is the need to uncover more of the complicated connection between the life and the work of a great writer who was above all concerned with questions of oppression and resistance and the relationship between domination and the oppositional strategies that form the individual and social practices of black people.

Toni Morrison's fiction helps us to reconstruct history in texts which resemble meditations more than novels. Her works involve a complicated network of associations and imagery which challenge the reader's sensibilities and linguistic acumen. Unlike Morrison, Richard Wright's fiction as essay critique was concerned primarily with his own present and with framing the contradictions posed by racism and the responses it created. Training himself to perceive experience in intellectual terms so as to understand it rationally, Wright's greatest strength derived from his ability to symbolically appropriate the culture of violence, exploitation, and terror which was firmly planted in his own consciousness by the time he left the South at nineteen.

The books that best capture the meaning of southern racism and brutality and the consequences in the urban

---

[1] Robert Bone, James Baldwin, Warren French, Horace Cayton, Arna Bontemps, J. Saunders Redding, and most recently, Andrew Delbanco in *The New Republic* (March 1992: 28–33) have all held this position.

North are generally understood to be *Uncle Tom's Children* and *Native Son*, respectively, books Wright wrote at a relatively young age and which established his career as a major writer. In these works, Wright engaged the discourse on racism by focusing on physical poverty and extreme methods of social control in the form of violence against blacks and their consequent counterviolence or ultimate death. Wright portrays the heinous crimes committed against black people with power and passion no writer had ever been able to do.

Wright's most memorable character in this regard is Bigger Thomas, a black gang member living on Chicago's South Side who is responsible for the deaths of two women and is psychologically transformed by his acts of violent resistance. He comes to fully accept the deaths he has caused as an act of empowerment, as a definition of his identity when he says, "What I killed for, I *am*." Likewise, the episodes in the lives of black people which Wright selects for *Uncle Tom's Children* develop their own characters who variously resist and rebel, making the necessary choices that sustain them, even if on a limited basis. But Wright's emphasis on rebellious violence, his characters' seemingly blatant disregard for human relationships and lack of remorse, do not satisfy many a contemporary reader accustomed to more subtle ways in which blacks and other subordinated groups locate and interpret their resistance/accommodation to and/or transformation of the dominant culture.

By creating a text of his own life in the autobiographical *Black Boy*, Wright became a paradigmatic statement of the black intellectual's struggle to resist domination and become an agent of transformation. In that remarkable and now well-known life story of a difficult and repressive childhood and adolescence, Wright told how he learned systematically to "be natural, to be real, to be myself," he says, only ". . . in rejection, rebellion and aggression." Wright's success owed much to his own genius, his penetrating vision, and his active involvement in powerful ideological, social, and political movements during the 1930s—Marxism and communism. And although Wright became disenchanted with the Communist party in the United States, he remained a Marxist with a revolutionary vision of societal change, continuing his activist commitments throughout his life.

Thus, Wright's early writing, like his life, is paradigmatic, that is, broadly representative of black life. It recounts the journey from slavery and a disenfranchised existence in the agricultural South into the cities, both South and North, where dreams were shattered and hopes denied. This is the centerpiece around which most of us have been taught to frame Wright's contribution to American culture and from which his fictional texts extend.

The events surrounding the creation and publication of *The Outsider* are little known. The book generated nothing like the response his first novel had, and some critics even suggested Wright had sold out to a more cosmopolitan, European way of life. Nothing, however, could be further from the truth. It is worth pausing over the events that transpired between the publication of *Native Son* and *The Outsider*, if we are to understand the critical role Wright's "flight" from the United States played in enlarging and expanding his master narrative of American racism. Wright moved quickly to consolidate his personal life and to pursue an active writing career in the wake of the unprecedented success of the first book by a black American to receive national acclaim and its enthusiastic acceptance by both white and black—even if somewhat reluctant—audiences. Another book, *12,000,000 Black Voices*, was published along with "The Man Who Lived Underground," in which he first treated more explicit existential themes. *Native Son* opened on Broadway while Wright continually wrote autobiographical articles, radio programs, and film scripts.

Wright's continuing political interests and his race relations work made him even more visible as a writer and spokesperson. Various offices in national writers' organizations and peace groups such as the League of American Writers and the American Peace Mobilization, as well as local organizing in Harlem, were part of a steady regimen of anti-racist activity.

A key moment in his literary career came when he went to speak at Fisk University in Nashville at the invitation of Horace Cayton. Here in the South, talking to other young people at a prestigious, historically black institution, Wright felt more confident than ever that he should make his personal story public.

The Fisk visit bridged an important gap between Wright and the black intellectual community. He had not grown up with this group in the South; he was introduced to it only after he moved to Chicago, and was often alienated from this class of individuals, according to biographers. Nevertheless, intense interactions with black intellectuals usually occurred at key junctures in his life and provided critical support for his projects. There was, for example, the work that came out of the black Southside Writers Group, which Wright organized in Chicago, to provide an opportunity for black writers to critique each other's work. Active in this group were Arna Bontemps, Frank Marshall Davis, Theodore Ward, and Margaret Walker, among others. From this experience came "Blueprint for Negro Writing," written in 1937, perhaps the clearest and most powerful statement about the role and function of African-American literature ever to be written. There Wright began a close friendship with Margaret Walker, a native southerner and writer like himself. Unlike Wright, Walker had come to Chicago to complete college.[2] It was she who sent Wright clippings on the Robert Nixon case, upon which he based the story of *Native Son*.

After the autobiography which had been inspired by the Fisk visit, Wright provided a long introduction to *Black Metropolis* by his friend Horace Cayton and St. Clair Drake. This book was to become the classic study of black urban life in the United States.

It was during these years that Wright became more and more interested in psychoanalysis, especially the psychology of oppression and violence. He continued to read extensively on the subject and helped to found the LeFargue Clinic as a free psychiatric clinic in Harlem. It bears mentioning here that the large volumes of mail from or about black prisoners generated by *Native Son* could only have stimulated this interest; it also created a direct relationship between Wright and the black prison community, which was unusual for writers of his time. For example, Wright had championed the cause of Clinton Brewer, a convicted murderer, who had become a talented musician during his incarceration. Seeing the possibility of rehabilitation, Wright got Brewer's music recorded and arranged for his release, although Brewer was apprehended for a second murder shortly thereafter.

Wright's forays into crime psychology and the interest he maintained in young black males as the target prison population suggests a dynamic in Wright's own psyche which is frequently ignored. His identification with this aspect of the black community not only served

---

[2]See Allison Davis's chapter on Wright in *Leadership, Love, and Aggression*, (New York: Harcourt, 1983), for a discussion of Wright's relationship to the traditional black middle class.

the purposes of his fiction, but also reflected his desire to gain deeper insight into the one process which could give objective meaning to the lives of black people as the "wretched of the earth." The physical prison in the real world was not unlike the symbolic prisons Wright created in his fiction.

Wright tried writing a story about the Brewer case, just as *Native Son* had been based on the Robert Nixon case in Chicago. But Wright had taken this kind of story as far as it could go within his current thinking. The experiences of his middle years—personal, political, and intellectual—required a different aesthetic response.

Wright's move to Paris provided an appropriate context for this change to take place. The decision to leave the United States seems to have been based on several things: his break with the Communist party, which he had made official by publishing "I Tried to Be a Communist" in *Atlantic Monthly* in 1944, thus cutting ties of long standing; his need to find a less hostile environment to live in with his wife and growing family; and the warm reception and contacts he had made on his earlier visit to Europe.

By moving to Paris, however, Wright was departing for the first time from the archetypal migration pattern that characterized the lives of most black people of his time. He had moved from Mississippi to Memphis and then on to Chicago and New York. This trek provided him with the objective basis for bringing to consciousness effects of the particular class and racial phenomena he had experienced. On the other hand, the move to Paris provided an environment where he could become a world-class intellectual, where the issues of race and class could take on greater significance as he became more knowledgeable about the independence movements in colonial countries and developed friendships with those who would play leading roles in the anti-colonial movements in their respective homelands. Wright did not write about Paris, nor did he speak French fluently. But Paris gave him something he didn't have: a view (vision) of the black experience and of the colonized world from an international perspective. His anti-racism became more solidly anti-imperialism; his interest in black people in the United States became a Pan-African and Third World interest.

Wright's contacts with West Indian and African intellectuals brought him in touch with *Presence Africaine*, an important magazine founded in 1946 which promoted racial and Pan-African solidarity, especially the ideas of the Negritude literary movement espoused in the works of its founding members, Leopold Senghor, Aime Cesaire, and Alioune Diop. Good friendships developed with George Padmore and C. L. R. James, two black revolutionaries who, like Wright, had been members of the Communist party.

His friendships with Gertrude Stein, Jean Paul Sartre, Simone de Beauvoir, and Albert Camus exposed Wright to the core of French existentialism. The intensity of the African-American experience gave both meaning and expression to this philosophy, which provided another window through which he could see the inhumanity and negative consequences of racism and oppression. Like his conversion to Marxism, Wright accepted existentialism as an ideology that could be developed for and applied to those who were oppressed.

The Outsider must be seen against this background of anti-colonialism, anti-fascism, and anti-racism, sentiments all shaped by Cold War politics and Wright's own personal experiences in organized political movements. In looking both backward and forward in terms of Wright's career, *The Outsider* marks a critical turning point. Speaking about her father, Julia Wright suggests that *The Outsider* broke a silence, embodying "new inflections, greater maturity, and the texture of alien psychological, emotional, and cultural roots."[3] But why the silence? Just what is the "old" Wright in this novel? And what indeed is the "new"?

The silence is perhaps easiest to explain. Wright had come to Paris as an ex-Communist, openly critical of the Party. He found himself under attack by the very people who had promoted his early works throughout the world. This, combined with being a black American in a strange land, could understandably make him quieter and more reflective than usual. If we read *The Outsider* in this way, as a book which emerges after an important period of growth and change in Wright's life, a book in which Wright is speaking directly to us out of his own experience, we can see in it a kind of evolution of the author's vision and craft.

The Outsider shares with Wright's earlier works a basic structure and theme: a series of graphic and dramatic reproductions of a race- and class-based system of oppression, where the code words "rich" and "white" are synonymous with the dominant cultural values. Depictions of powerless individuals abound and the struggle to gain power supplies most of the narrative line. The five-part structure of *The Outsider*, though slightly extended from that of *Native Son*, frames the familiar tale: Highly motivated and intelligent, Cross Damon sees his ambitions thwarted as the boundaries of his existence become dictated by others (his mother, his wife Gladys, his job at the Post Office, and his girlfriend, Dot); he becomes alienated from his family and friends; a freak accident on a Chicago "L" train leaves him with a

[3]Private correspondence, 2 October 1992.

choice: He can either set himself free by claiming a new identity or turn himself in as a survivor of the wreck. He chooses the former, finally taking on the identity of Lionel Lane, whose name he takes from a grave. This sets in motion a series of interrelated events. After assuming a variety of masks—comic Negro, defender of human rights, black intellectual—Cross meets a black West Indian worker who invites him to meet fellow Communists.

Cross immediately falls in love with Eva Blount, a white artist and wife of Gil Blount, Party Central Committee member. Cross becomes increasingly critical of the Party the more they try to recruit him, finding their attitudes racist and condescending. He is especially scornful of Gil, who followed orders to marry Eva so that the Party could benefit from her talents. Cross's murders of Gil Blount, to free Eva, and Jack Hilton, another leading Party member, add to the murders he has already committed. His confession to Eva drives her to suicide. In the end, Cross is free to go, for Ely Houston, a disabled (hunchback) district attorney, thinks that permitting Cross to live according to the rules he himself has created is appropriate punishment. In the final scene in the book, Cross had been found out by the Communists as well; and he dies from a bullet wound inflicted by an assassin, pleading his own innocence, understanding and accepting what he has done in terms no one can understand except Ely Houston.

The central image in the story is the "outsiderness" of Cross Damon, represented by Wright as an extreme case. His "alienation from himself and society is complete," says Robert Coles. "Damon is racially outside (a black man living outside of a dominant white racist society), spiritually outside (an atheist living outside of Christianized Western society), materially outside (a postal worker who is deeply in debt), and emotionally outside (involved in a marriage-family situation which he abhors)."[4] In short, Wright had made a grown-up Bigger Thomas, and one whose characteristics are as uncommon in contemporary society as Coles would have us believe. Cross Damon may have occurred to Wright as an outsider but he presents us with an inside view of some of the problematic aspects of working class and black existence.

This reconfiguration of a black protagonist suggests several things: first, that Wright was deepening his analysis of modern racism through the useful prism of philosophical existentialism; second, that he was very conscious of framing the character in a way so as to make Cross distinct from Bigger; and third, that Wright intended for the reader to understand Cross through the questioning of his own condition and motivations.

Cross Damon, like Bigger Thomas, is introduced to us as an individual powerless to act, inevitably trapped within images that others have constructed of him and obliged to destroy that which devalues him. But the enemy is not so easily identified as being white people as it is in *Native Son*. The novel forces the reader to see a complex of issues pertaining to Cross's relationships with a number of people, both black and white. More fully aware of his subjective reactions, Cross seeks to understand and analyze each experience and relationship in light of an entire social, political, and ideological system. In his extreme self-consciousness, Cross signifies for Wright the black intellectual without privilege. Rooted in neither the black middle class nor the conventional folk culture of the rural South, this prototype

---

[4]Robert Coles, "Richard Wright's *The Outsider*: A Novel in Transition," *Modern Language Studies* 13 (1983): 58–59.

of the black worker – intellectual is a mirror of Wright's perceived self-identity. Wright wanted "to demystify the ideology of Left and Right for his readers," according to John Reilly. "He created a protagonist formed out of his own experience. . . . Wright provided Damon with the insights of the author."[5]

Wright's disillusionment with the Communist party plays an important part in the overall plot. But it is not sufficient to see *The Outsider* as a transcription of this one moment in Wright's life. It is perhaps more correct to say that Wright reached a new understanding about the meaning of his own independence, a moment of immense personal and historical significance. Just as he had always created texts that brought to consciousness the particular effects of cultural and social phenomena, reflecting various stages of his own understanding of the world, Wright in *The Outsider* found a literary equivalent for his expanded consciousness, broader political concerns, and intellectual perspectives.

If this literary equivalent appeared more ambivalent than his previous fiction, it is important to remember that Wright's protagonists can always be seen from two perspectives—the way they are seen by others and the way they wish themselves to be seen. This kind of double vision or ambivalence is what Du Bois called "double consciousness," one of the central themes in African-American literature. It is this theme that Wright expands upon in *The Outsider*. By putting Cross in charge of his own fate, the ambivalence or double consciousness is intensified. The ambivalence is doubleedged, however. Not only does Cross expose the contradictory attitudes that whites have of him as an

    [5]John Reilly, "Richard Wright and the Art of Non-fiction: Stepping Out on the State of the World, *Callaloo* 9, no. 3:510.

intelligent black person, but he is also as ambivalent about the new self he has created as he is about the old self that he has rejected.

The problem of audience also complicated Wright's presentation of Cross Damon. Wright had been much clearer about the two audiences for whom he was writing in *Native Son*. "I would tell Communists how common people felt, and I would tell common people of the self-sacrifice of Communists who strove for unity among them," he commented in *American Hunger*. Now Wright's audience—or at least his understanding of it—was a world that was more diffuse, more complex. And this world was undergoing sweeping changes involving left and right. The dramatic tension created in *The Outsider* stems from being in a state of emotional and intellectual turmoil, an in-between stage both for Wright's character and for black people as a whole.

For other reasons, Wright had to move beyond the image of *Black Boy* and *Native Son* as well. Having failed to convince his publishers to publish the entire manuscript he had submitted as the original autobiography, Wright accepted the shortened version, which became *Black Boy*. One critic has suggested that in agreeing to a generic designation, Wright was indeed acknowledging the "reductive manner in which all black men are perceived by a racist society." But this is also a "synonym, an external mark for the title of the second book, *American Hunger*, designating the inner affliction suffered by all blacks."[6]

Cross Damon's story became the expression of that inner affliction, the difficulty of making choices when faced with the full range of possibilities of human

[6]Jan Mohamed, in Abdul R. Jan Mohamed and David Lloyd, eds., *Nature and Context of Minority Discourse* (New York: Oxford University Press, 1990)

knowledge. Although the story of Wright's own turbulent coming of age represented a striking contrast to that of Bigger Thomas, whom racism transforms into a symbol of its own defeat, both are images of black men as "boys."

The Outsider went further in exploring the meaning of freedom, unrestricted and non-ideologized. Presenting Cross Damon as someone who is an oppressed victim, Wright also gave him the possibility of becoming the agent of his own liberation in a way different from Bigger Thomas. If freedom for Bigger meant the ability to act decisively, to kill that which was killing him, for Cross Damon it meant escape from all repressive structures, including the ideology of communism which is integrally woven into Damon's life and death. While Bigger kills for survival, Cross kills to permit transformation.

Many of the restored sections of the present text heighten the contradictions we see within Cross's consciousness at the same time that they give us further insight into his character. While he is certainly psychotic, he is also compassionate and demonstrates a strong moral sense regarding the exploitation of others. In an important scene which was deleted from earlier editions, Cross attempts to intervene in a real estate scam that his landlady, Hattie Turner, has become involved in. Although it is Hattie's own greed that gets her into the situation, Cross recognizes that she too is being exploited and exposes the two men who are trying to cheat her. The restoration of this scene is crucial because it gives us a glimpse into Cross's relationships with other black people, especially another woman, for reasons other than his own self-interest.

Although Damon is guilty of physical violence, he presents an occasion for seeing another kind of violence, perhaps more dangerous and deadly. Prefiguring the debates in a variety of disciplines as well as the historical events of the 1960s, Cross's world is characterized by what may be called symbolic violence, or various ways in which authority and power over his life become the domain of others. He has a dead-end, low-paying job at the Post Office which requires that he stop taking his evening classes and undergo the humiliation of borrowing money on a regular basis. In addition to having to confront the racist insults and paternalism of his white superiors, Cross finds that his personal business—his girlfriend's pregnancy and his wife's complaints—is public information in the Postmaster's office. In the end, he is regarded as just another "colored boy" who can't get his act together. Cross experiences these forms of domination which are equally as terrifying as physical violence or coercion. His desire to escape from this domination is also symbolized through violence; Cross understands that a symbolic death, perceived as real to others, can give him an opportunity for a new life, one that he himself can control, one that will not be subjected to the domination of others. But this is also precisely the moment when Cross first perceives of himself as a criminal (105).

Cross's articulation of issues of domination, violence, and victimization makes him a uniquely crafted individual and contributes to Wright's importance in changing the direction of literature which sought to interpret social and psychological phenomena.

In the early sections of the book, Cross is aware that victimization can stimulate violent aspects of one's character, and he engages in violent actions as an effective means for releasing himself from the control of others. Thus, Cross is growing increasingly aware of the way violence can be used against him as well as the way he can employ it for his own ends. He traps Gladys by pretending insanity and abusing her, hoping she will want to divorce him; in turn, he is trapped by his girlfriend Dot, a minor, who falsely accuses him of the violent act of rape, hoping to coerce him into child support. These examples further problematize the meaning of violence. For once violence—ideological, symbolic, or physical—is understood to be an acceptable tool of domination, then the categories of "resistance" and "accommodation" are not what they appear to be.

In the latter portion of the book, and especially in the restored sections, Cross's resistance to the power and authority of others becomes stronger as does his desire to become the agent for the liberation of others. He refers to his acts as "ethical murder" but decides he cannot confess, and is obliged to "lie, to dodge, to blend with the changing hues of the foliage . . ." (311). He queries Menti, a Communist functionary who has been discharged to spy on him, "But . . . don't you feel that you've got some value that's yours and yours alone?" (372) Such instances are telling, for we realize that Cross's actions are inspired by his desire to empower himself and others.

Because of the death-rebirth symbolism and the moral tone which Cross adopts, many critics have chosen to read this story as Wright's attempt to reinscribe a politically corrupt world with a moral message. Just as Cross Damon, himself demonic, is born again, so too must the ideas of humankind be grounded in morality. I would prefer to read Wright's presentation of the complex social world in which Cross Damon lives and the psychological state that breeds his criminality as a cautionary tale about the excesses of individuality and the dangers of human alienation. In the end, Cross has no appropriate context in which to give meaning to his actions, other than one he himself has created.

By demonstrating the consequences of human alienation—irrational, irresponsible murder and death—in a racist society, Wright highlights the inadequacy of interpretations which privilege individualism, even at the risk of being self-critical. Cross's fatal flaw is ultimately his individualism. When carried to its logical conclusion, he has nothing left.

If for no other reason, therefore, reading a book like *The Outsider* is a challenge to our understanding of the past. And it demands that we reassimilate into the critical present a writer whose fiction articulates moments of discovery and change which have profoundly affected the way we construct the political discourses of our own day and time.

If the dominant theme in twentieth-century literature is the search for identity, then Wright reinterprets this theme for his own work by electing to have his characters search for their freedom in ways as complex and ironic as the history of racism itself. It is this that forms the crux of Wright's stories from the beginning of his career to the very end. Moving inside and outside of the realities of people's lives becomes an abundant source for writers of fiction. When these realities are complicated by a carefully woven blend of historical fact and knowledge about domination—social, cultural, ideological, or otherwise—the results can be explosive, as they were for Wright.

This then is the context for revisiting *The Outsider*—a novel in which we see inscribed Wright's increasing desire to explore human reactions to oppression and domination and to find a way perhaps to mirror his own feelings of marginality, the spiritual exile of Paris, and the alienation from the land and the people of his birth.

MARYEMMA GRAHAM
NORTHEASTERN UNIVERSITY

Cruelty has a Human Heart,
And Jealousy a Human Face;
Terror the Human Form Divine,
And Secrecy the Human Dress.
                    —WILLIAM BLAKE

Mark me, and be astonished,
And lay your hand upon your mouth.
                    —JOB

THE OUTSIDER

BOOK ONE

DREAD

Dread is an alien power which lays hold of an individual, and yet one cannot tear oneself away, nor has a will to do so; for one fears what one desires.

— KIERKEGAARD

FROM AN INVISIBLE February sky a shimmering curtain of snowflakes fluttered down upon Chicago. It was five o'clock in the morning and still dark. On a South Side street four masculine figures moved slowly forward shoulder to shoulder and the sound of their feet tramping and sloshing in the melting snow echoed loudly. The men were warmly dressed and wore mufflers about their throats. The brims of their hats, encrusted with snow, were pulled down at rakish tilts over their eyes. Behind turned-up overcoat collars their gruff voices exploded in jokes, laughter, and shouts. They jostled one another with rude affection and their hot breaths projected gusts of vapor on to the chilled morning air. One of the men threw out an arm and grabbed a companion about the neck and crooned:

"Booker, let me rest this tired old body on you, hunh?"

"Hell, naw! Stand on your own two big flat feet, Cross!" Booker, a short, black man protested with a laugh.

The man called Cross turned and flung his arm about

I

the shoulders of a big, fat, black man and said, "Then how about you, Joe?"

"Look, Crossy, I'm tired too," Joe defended himself, shying off. "Why pick on me?"

" 'Cause you're soft as a mattress and can stand it," Cross explained.

"If you're cold, it's your own damn hard luck," Joe said. "You don't take care of yourself. Me, I ain't never cold. I know how come you're always so cold, Cross. You drink too much. Don't eat enough. Don't sleep. But, *me* . . . Ha-ha! I eat and sleep as much as I can. And my good old fat helps to keep me warm. Ain't that right, Pink?"

The man called Pink did not reply at once; he was reddish in color and older than the other three.

"Cross," Pink said seriously, "you ought to take some vitamins or something. Man, you *couldn't* be cold now. Hell, we just left that steamy Post Office *twenty* minutes ago."

Cross swiftly pulled the glove off his right hand and, grabbing Pink's shoulder, rammed his bare fingers down the collar of Pink's neck.

"How do they feel, Pink?" Cross demanded.

"Jeeesus! Your fingers're cold as *snakes*!" Pink gasped, his eyes lit with concern. "They ought to call you *Mr. Death*!"

"I just need some alcohol," Cross confessed grimly. "My old engine won't run without it."

"You better quit that bottle, Cross," Joe, the big, fat, black man warned. "When you start *living* on alcohol, you're traveling a road that ain't got no turning. You been hitting that bottle heavy for a month now. Better let up, boy."

"Man, whiskey ain't never hurt nobody," Pink said; he broke into song:

If the ocean was whiskey
And I was a duck
I'd dive right in
And never come up

A rich, rolling laughter erupted and died away over the snow-blanketed sidewalks.

"Crossy, how come you're drinking so much these days?" Booker asked in a tone free of moral objections.

"My soul needs it," Cross mumbled.

"Makes you feel better, hunh?" Booker asked.

"No. Makes me feel *less*," Cross corrected him.

"But how about your liver?" Joe demanded.

"My liver's in the death house," Cross admitted.

"Say, Pinkie, remember when Crossy used to be the life of the gang?" Joe asked. "Now he just swills and every word he says is a gripe."

"We all have blue days," Pink said.

"*Pink* has *blue* days," Cross's tongue played softly with the words.

They tossed wild laughter amidst the milling flakes of snow. All of them laughed except Cross whose lips shaped themselves into an ambiguous smile whose meaning might have been a jeering at or a participation in the merriment. He was tall but slightly built with a smooth, brown and yellow skin, and his body moved as though it had more nervous energy than it could contain.

"Aw, leave Cross alone," Pink said.

"Thanks, pal," Cross muttered.

Joe suddenly paused amid the flakes of dancing snow, laughing hysterically, slapping his thighs, sending blasts of steam on to the frigid air. The sheen of a street lamp sharply etched his ebony face.

"What's the matter, Joe?" Booker asked.

"Oh, God," Joe gasped, his fat cheeks trembling and tears gleaming at the corners of his eyes.

"All right; share the damn joke," Pink said.

The three men confronted Joe and waited for his mirth to subside.

"Today I heard somebody say the damndest thing about Cross—" Joe went off into another spasm of mirth, bending over, coughing, spluttering, sending tiny flecks of spittle into the run-away snowflakes. Joe finally straightened and placed a brotherly hand upon Cross's shoulder. "Now, listen, if I tell what I heard, you won't be mad, will you?"

"I don't give a damn what you heard," Cross muttered.

Tiny crystals trembled whitely between their dark faces. The shoulders of their overcoats were laced with icy filigrees; dapples of moisture glowed diamondlike on their eyebrows where the heat of their blood was melting the snow.

"Well, spill it, man," Pink urged impatiently.

Joe sobered only to give way to so much laughter that Pink and Booker joined in and laughed so infectiously that even Cross surrendered to the contagion and chuckled.

"Somebody said," Joe began, "that Cross was trying to imitate the United States' Government. They said the trouble with Cross was his four A's. *Alcohol. Abortions. Automobiles.* And *alimony.*" Joe laughed so violently that his eyes were buried in fat and the pearly gleam of his white teeth vied with the translucence of the snow. Jerking out his words, he continued: "They called C-cross the Q-q-quadruple-A Program! Said that the best thing for Cross w-was to plow h-himself under . . ."

Cross stood aloof as the others bent double with their giggles. Cross did not resent what had been said; it was as though they were laughing at the foibles of an absent man who was well-known to him. He smiled, admitting to himself that the analogy was not badly put, that it fitted the snarled facts of his life pretty aptly, and that he could not have summed up his situation any better himself. The more Pink, Joe, and Booker guffawed, the longer Cross retained his nervous, ambiguous smile. Finally the laughter died and Joe, putting his arm about Cross's shoulder, promised consolingly: "Goddammit, Crossy, I'm gonna buy you a drink. Hell, I'm gonna buy you *two* damn drinks. You need 'em."

Still chuckling, they trudged on through the snow to a corner tavern whose neon sign dimly identified it as: THE SALTY DOG. They pushed through the door and went in. Cross followed solemnly, his hands dug into his overcoat pockets, a cigarette stub glowing in his lips. He sat with the others in a booth and looked at them with quiet eyes and an enigmatic smile. A short, fat, brown proprietor with a bald head and a grey goatee called to them from behind the bar: "Same old thing, boys?"

"Same old thing, Doc," Joe and Pink chorused.

"Crossy, what's the trouble?" Booker asked softly.

"You *know* what's wrong with 'im," Joe insisted. "His Quadruple-A Program's got 'im down."

They laughed again. Doc sat four whiskies before them and, at the sight of the little glasses of pale brown fluid, they grew sober, almost dignified; each took up his glass daintily and threw back his head and tossed the liquor down his throat.

"One of these days, Doc," Cross said, sighing and smacking his lips, "we're going to fool you. We're going to swallow the glasses too."

"Atta boy!" Joe approved.

"The spirit moved 'im at last," Booker commented.

"Crossy," Joe said, "you're losing your touch. Remember the time you used to pull them crazy stunts?" Joe turned to the others for confirmation. "When Cross first came to work in the Post Office, he was a nonstop riot, a real killer-diller. Early in the evening, when the rush hour was on, he used to—we were working on the 11th floor then—lift up the window, run his hand in his pocket and toss out every cent of silver he had. Just throw it all out of the window to the street. And then he'd lean out and watch the commotion of all them little antlike folks down there going wild, scrambling and scratching and clawing after them few pieces of money and then, when the money was all gone, they'd stand looking up to the window of the 11th floor with their mouths hanging open like fishes out of water. And Cross'd be laughing to beat all hell. And Cross'd say that them folks was praying when their faces were turned up like that, waiting for more money to fall. Ha-ha!

"Remember when two men jumped at the same time for the same quarter that Cross had tossed out? They dived toward each other and they butted head on and knocked each other out, cold? They just lay there, like a truck had hit 'em, and all the other folks crowded round, looking and wondering what had happened. They had to send the riot cars full of cops to break up the mob and take the two dopes who had been diving for the quarter to jail. Ha-ha! Honest to God, I thought I'd die laughing. Cross said that that was the only time he ever felt like God. Ha-ha!"

They laughed musingly, their eyes resting on Cross's face which carried a detached smile.

"Remember that wild gag he pulled at Christmas time in 19—?" Joe frowned thoughtfully and the others waited. "When the hell was that now? Oh, yes! It was in 1945. I'll never forget it. Cross bought a batch of magazines, *Harper's*, *Atlantic Monthly*, *Collier's*, *Ladies' Home Journal*, and clipped out those ads that say you can send your friends a year's subscription as a Christmas gift. Well, Cross signed 'em and sent 'em to his friends. But he didn't sign 'em with *his* name, see? He signed 'em with the names of friends of people he was sending the subscriptions to. He sent me one and it was signed by my wife. Ha-ha! Was she mad? But in the end, she really paid for it. Crossy sent one to James Harden and signed it with my name. Ha-ha! Christmas morning Harden calls me up and starts thanking me for the gift-subscription I'd sent 'im to *Harper's*. I didn't know what the hell Harden was talking about, and I was so 'shamed I sat right down and sent *Harper's* a check! Man, the whole South Side was in a dither that Christmas morning. Folks was thanking other folks for presents the others didn't know nothing about. And Crossy was listening and watching and saying nothing. Lord, it was a mess! Cross, how in God's name did you dream up such stuff? Any man who can do things like that is a man standing *outside* of the world! Know what I mean? Like somebody outside of your window was looking into your house and poking out his tongue at you." Joe went into a gale of laughter; then he pointed to Cross's smiling face. "Look at 'im, will you? He sits there, smiling, not saying a word, not letting on he used to pull stunts like that."

They laughed, looking at Cross with tenderness in their eyes.

"Say, remember all them big, deep books he used to read and tell us about?" Joe asked looking from Cross to the others. "He used to use so many big words I thought he'd choke! Every time I saw 'im, he had a batch of books under his arm."

"But what I couldn't understand," Pink recalled, "was why Cross wouldn't believe anything in the books he read. One time he was all hepped-up over one writer and the next time he was through with 'im and was gone on to another."

"And the books in Cross's room!" Booker exclaimed. "I went to see 'im one day when he was sick, and I could hardly get into the door! Big books, little books, books piled everywhere! He even had books in bed with 'im."

Their heads tilted back with laughter; Cross smiled without rancor.

"I told 'im," Booker continued, " 'Crossy, you better find a gal to sleep with you, 'cause them books can't keep you warm!' Man, in the clothes closet: books. In the bathroom: books. Under the bed: books. I said, 'Crossy, you ain't got no 'flu germs; you got book-worms!' "

They clapped their hands with laughter; Cross smiled and looked off.

"Cross, you ain't never said how come you was read-ing all them books," Joe pointed out.

"I was looking for something," Cross said quietly.

"What?" Pink asked.

"I don't know," Cross confessed gloomily.

"Did you find it?" Joe asked.

"No."

Joe, Pink, and Booker howled with delight.

"In those days Cross's mind was like a little mouse, running every which way— Say, Cross, how many books you got in your room?"

"I don't know," Cross mumbled.

"I wished I had a dollar for every book you got," Joe sighed. "Now, honest, Crossy, how come you don't read no more?"

"I've put away childish things," Cross said.

"Aw, be yourself, man," Booker said.

"I am what I am," Cross said. "I'm sparing you guys a lot. I'm not going to bother you with my troubles."

"Can't we help you any, Cross?" Joe asked seriously.

"Lay off, guys," Cross said, frowning for the first time. "I'm all right." He turned and beckoned to Doc. "Bring me a bottle, Doc!"

"Don't drink any more, Cross," Pink begged.

"Ain't you gonna eat some breakfast?" Booker asked.

"Whiskey ain't no good on an empty stomach," Joe reminded him.

"It's my stomach," Cross said.

"Aw, leave 'im alone," Booker said.

"But a man who drinks ought to eat," Joe insisted.

"Eating's all you think about, Joe," Cross growled.

"Hell, you got to eat to live!" Joe shouted with authoritative rudeness. "And you better stop drinking and eat and sleep some." Joe suddenly laughed and began a game of make-believe, imitating a baby's crying: "Awwwww—Awwww—Awwww—!" He altered his tone. "Now, what the little baby wants?" He bawled out the answer: "The bottle, the bottle, the *whiskey* bottle, Mama!"

Laughter seethed and Cross joined in to show his appreciation.

"Leave 'im alone," Booker said. "He knows his own mind."

"If he keeps up that drinking, he won't have no mind left," Joe said emphatically. "And it'll kill 'im."

"All right," Cross said darkly. "Do I want to live forever?"

"You're nuts," Joe said.

"It pleases me," Cross said without anger.

"Okay," Joe said.

"Sure; it's okay," Cross said, opening the bottle and taking a long swig.

"Wheeew," Joe whistled. "You can't *drink* like that, boy!"

"I *am*," Cross said calmly.

"You gonna finish that bottle today?" Booker asked softly.

"Maybe. How do I know?"

"Ain't you gonna sleep?"

"If I can."

"'If I can'," jeered Joe. "Stop drinking and you *can* sleep."

"I wouldn't sleep at all then," Cross said.

"What's *eating* you, Cross?" Pink implored softly. "We've been your friends for six years. Spill it. We'll help you—"

"Skip it," Cross said. "Am I complaining? You signed for my last loan and that took care of my Quadruple-A debts. That's enough."

They laughed at how Cross could laugh at himself.

"There're some things a man must do alone," Cross added.

The three men looked silently at Cross. He knew that they liked him, but he felt that they were outside of his life, that there was nothing that they could do that would make any difference. Now more than ever he knew that he was alone and that his problem was one of a relationship of himself to himself.

"We ain't your mama and your papa," Joe sighed, forcing a sad smile. "We can't hold your hand, Big Boy. And you're a big boy, you know."

"Yes, I'm a big boy," Cross smiled bitterly.

"It's between you and Your Maker, your problem," Joe said.

"Lucky Joe," Cross murmured in a tone of envy.

"What do you mean?" Joe asked.

Cross rose, smiled widely for the first time, pointed his finger into Joe's fat, black, round face, and intoned: " 'And God made man in His own image . . .' "

Pink and Booker yelled with laughter. Joe passed his hand caressingly and self-consciously over his black face and looked puzzled. Cross demanded in a mockingly serious voice: "Did God really make *that* face? Is He guilty of *that*? If He did, then He was walking in His sleep!" Cross shook with laughter. "To blame God for making Joe is to degrade the very concept of God!"

Pink and Booker leaped to their feet and grabbed Joe about the waist.

"Did God really make you, Joe?" Pink demanded.

"Was God absent-minded when He cooked you up, Joe?" Booker asked.

Joe forced a smile, but underneath he was a little disturbed. Then he protested: "God made me, all right. He made my soul and He made my *body* too."

"But why did He make your body so *fat*, Joe?" Cross asked.

"I just ate too much and got fat," Joe replied sheepishly.

"But *God* gave you your appetite," Pink told him.

"And the body reflects the soul," Cross clenched it.

"Wow!" Pink screamed, covering his mouth with his hand. "I'm going home 'fore I laugh myself to death!"

They all rose except Cross; he still sat and smiled up at Joe.

"Go home and get some shut-eye, Cross," Joe advised him.

"God won't let me sleep," Cross said.

"God ain't got *nothing* to do with it!" Joe pronounced.

"Then who keeps me awake all day long?" Cross wanted to know.

"You, yourself," Joe said.

"Maybe you're right," Cross conceded.

"So long," Pink said.

"See you, Crossy," Joe said.

" 'Bye, now," Booker said.

"So long," Cross mumbled, not looking at them as they filed out.

"Some guys," Doc said from behind the bar.

"Yeah; *some* guys," Cross repeated, staring at the floor.

Yeah; it was time to sleep. He felt dead. How long could he last like this? His eyes suddenly clouded with displeasure. He had promised to see Dot this morning, but he didn't want to talk to her, much less see her . . . That was all he needed: seeing Dot and having one of those long, hysterical, weeping arguments. He knew what Dot wanted to ask and the answer was no and it would always be no! Oh, *damn* that Dot! But if he didn't call her, she'd soon be coming to his room and they'd argue all day long. And that was the last thing he wanted. Yes; he'd better call her; he'd tell her he was sick, feeling too bad to see her. He rose, jammed the whiskey bottle into his overcoat pocket, went into the telephone booth, dropped a coin into the slot and dialed. Almost at once Dot's voice sang over the wire: "How are you, darling?"

She was waiting in the hallway by the phone, he thought.

"I feel like hell," he growled.

"Have you eaten breakfast?"

"Naw; I just left the Post Office—"

"But honey, you got off from work at *four* o'clock and now it's nearly *six*. You've had plenty of time to eat."

"I was in a bar," he told her.

"Oh, God, Cross! You must stop *drinking*!"

"Do you think I can with what I've got on my mind?"

"Come over right *now*, hunh? I'll cook your breakfast—"

"Naw."

"Why?"

"I don't want to."

"You're mean! And you promised you'd see me this morning—"

"But I don't feel like it. I'm exhausted."

"You mean you're too *drunk*!" she said savagely.

"So?"

"Oh, God, Cross! Why did I ever get mixed up with you?"

"I've told you how to get *unmixed* with me, haven't I?"

"Don't you say that to me again!"

"I *am* saying it!"

"Listen, come here now! I want to talk to you!"

"I'm tired, I tell you!"

"I don't care! You come over *now*!"

"You're crazy, Dot! Do you think you can make people do things they don't want to do?" he asked her earnestly.

He heard her suck in her breath and when her voice came over the wire again it was so shrill that he had to hold the receiver away from his ear.

"If you *don't* see me this morning, you'll be *sorry*! You hear? Whatever happens'll be *your* fault! You can't treat me this way! I won't *let* you! You hear? I said I won't *let* you! You made me a promise and I want you to keep it! Now, come over here. I've got something to tell you—"

"Dot—"

"No; no; let me talk—"

"Listen, Dot—"

"I said let *me* talk!"

"Oh, Goddammit, Dot!"

"Don't cuss me! Oh, God, don't cuss me when I'm like this! Can't you understand? Have a little pity—" Her voice caught in her throat. "I'll *kill* myself—"

"Dot— Don't go on like that—"

"You don't think I'll kill myself, but I will—"

"You're crazy!"

"I'll get you for that!" she shouted. "I *will*!"

"If you keep shouting at me, I'll hang up!"

"I *will* shout at you!"

He hesitated, then slammed the receiver on to the hook. Damn her! He was trembling. He'd not wanted to call her because he'd known that it'd go like this and he'd be unnerved for the rest of the day. He fumbled for the bottle and took a deep swallow. Yes; he had to get some sleep or go mad. He went out of the telephone booth and waved good-bye to Doc and kept on out of the door and walked along the snow-piled sidewalks. He caught a trolley and rode standing on the platform, swaying as much from the rocking of the car as from the influence of alcohol. He alighted in front of his apartment building, groped for his key, and let himself in. Fifteen minutes later he was undressed and in bed. He was so tired that he could scarcely feel the sensations of his body and he could not relax. He stared wakefully in the semi-darkness and wondered what he could do about Dot . . .

What a messy life he was living! It was crazy; it was killing him; it was senseless; and he was a fool to go on living it. What a stinking botch he'd made out of everything he had touched! Why? He didn't know. I could be teaching school, he told himself. He'd dropped out of the university right after he'd married Gladys and after that nothing had gone right.

He lay still, his bloodshot eyes staring blankly before him, and drifted into dreams of his problems, compulsively living out dialogues, summing up emotional scenes with his mother, reliving the reactions of his wife, Dot, and his friends. Repeatedly he chided himself to go to sleep, but it did no good, for he was hungry for these waking visions that depicted his dilemmas, yet he knew that such brooding did not help; in fact, he was wasting his waning strength, for into these unreal dramas he was putting the whole of his ardent being. The long hours of the day dragged on.

He twisted on his crumpled bed, reshaped his lumpy pillow until his head nestled into it exactly right; and, for the hundredth time, he closed his eyes and lay still, trying to purge his mind of anxiety, beseeching sleep. He felt his numbed limbs slowly shedding tension and for a moment he floated toward a world of dreams, see-sawing softly between sleeping and waking. Then, convulsively, his entire body jerked rigidly to stem a fearful feeling of falling through space. His rebellious nerves twanged with a terror that his mind sought desperately to deny. He shook his head, his body seething with hate against himself and the world.

He checked his watch: two o'clock. A grey day showed through the curtained window and from the snowy street rose the din of traffic. Today was like yesterday and he knew that tomorrow would be the same. And it had been like this now for many months. Each morning he'd come from work and crawl wearily into bed and toss for hours, yearning for the mercy of a sleep that was not his and at last he realized that his search for surcease was hopeless. He sighed, stood, crossed to the dresser and took another pull from the bottle. At six o'clock he'd report to work and for eight long hours he'd sway upon his feet, drugged with fatigue, straining against collapse, sorting mail like a sleepwalker. He moistened his lips with his tongue. He had not eaten all day and, as the alcohol deadened the raw nerves of his twitching stomach, he thought: I'll do it now; I'll end this farce . . . He hunched determinedly forward and his crinkled pyjamas bagged about his gaunt body and the muscles of his neck bulged. He'd not crawl like a coward through stupid days; to act quickly was the simplest way of jumping through a jungle of problems that plagued him from within and from without. A momentary dizziness swamped him; his throat tightened; his vision blurred; his chest heaved and he was defenseless against despair. He sprang to the dresser and yanked open a drawer and pulled forth his gun. Trembling, feeling the cold blue steel touching his sweaty palm, he lifted the glinting barrel to his right temple, then paused. His feelings were like tumbling dice . . . He wilted, cursed, his breath expiring through parted lips. Choked with self-hate, he flung himself on the bed and buried his face in his hands.

Broken thus in will, he relaxed for the first time in weeks; he could rest only when he was too drained of energy to fret further. At length he lifted his head and the fingers of his right hand pressed nervously against his lower lip, then tapped his knee as though to still the writhing of his spirit. He was despairingly aware of his body as an alien and despised object over which he had no power, a burden that was always cheating him of the fruits of his thought, mocking him with its stubborn and supine solidity.

Claimed at last by the needs of the hour, he proceeded to bathe and dress. Again he drank from the bottle and was grateful for the sense of depression caused by the alcohol which made him feel less of pleasure, pain, anxiety, and hope. Could he get through the night without collapsing? Suddenly he was filled with an idea: *He would take the gun with him!* And if the pressure from within or without became too great he would use it; his gun would be his final protection against the world as well as against himself . . . And if he was ever so unlucky as to be found sprawled from nervous collapse upon some frozen sidewalk or upon the floor of the Post Office, it would be manfully better to let others see a bloody hole gaping in his temple than to present to the eyes of strangers a mass of black flesh stricken by stupor. His decision renewed his courage; if he had not thought of the gun, he doubted if he could have gone to work.

He pulled on his overcoat and stood hesitantly by the door; he knew now that even the gun sagging in his pocket did not convince him that he was fit to work. During the past month he had been absent so often on excuses of illness that he did not dare telephone and report himself on the sick list. He would master his tricky sensations; he would force himself to carry on till he dropped. He usually found that he did not really collapse even when he had the consciousness of being about to pitch forward on his face . . .

He yearned to talk to someone; he felt his mere telling his story would have helped. But to whom could he talk? To his mother? No; she would only assure him that he was reaping the wages of sin and his sense of dread would deepen. Could he talk to his wife with whom he was not living? God, no! She'd laugh bitterly and say, "I told you so!" There was Dot, his sweetheart, but she was not capable of understanding anything. Moreover, she was partly the cause of his present state. And there was not a single man to whom he cared to confess the nightmare that was his life. He had sharp need of a confidant, and yet he knew that if he had had an ideal confidant before whom he could lay his whole story, he would have instantly regretted it, would have murdered his confidant the moment after he had confided to him his shame. How could he have gone on living knowing that someone else knew how things were with him? Cross was proud.

His hand touched the doorknob and the telephone shrilled. Now, who in hell could that be? Was it Dot? Or Gladys? He turned the doorknob and the telephone rang again. Hell! Anger flashed through him at some vague someone who was trying to snatch him from his futile wrestling with his problem, trying to pry him loose from the only thing that made his life possess meaning even though it made him suffer. Impatiently he picked up the receiver.

"Cross? Is that you?" It was his mother's quavering, high-pitched voice singing uncertainly over the wire.

"How are you, Ma?"

"Fine, Cross, I reckon," she said querulously, like those who are over sixty and who feel uncommonly well but are too superstitious to admit it. "Can I see you, Cross? Sometime today . . . ?"

He bridled, trying to slap away the clutch of his mother's wrinkled hand as it reached invisibly for him.

"Anything wrong, Ma?"

"I want to see you," she said, evading his question.

His teeth clamped; he did not want to see her, certainly not now with this mood of bleak dread in him.

"Ma, I'm trying to sleep," he lied, speaking reprovingly.

Silence. He felt he had hurt her and he grew angry. He waited for her to speak further, but only the metallic hum of the line came to his ear.

"Ma," he called softly. "You're still there?"

"Yes, Cross." A note of firm patience in her voice frightened him.

"What is it, Ma? I work nights and I've got to get some rest."

Again silence.

"Is it about money?" he asked, trying to hasten it.

Another silence; then his mother's voice came clearly: "Cross, that Dot girl was just by here to see me . . ."

Her tone, charged and precise, was filled with a multitude of accusations that evoked a vast, hot void in him. His mother was still talking, but he did not hear her. His eyes darted like those of a bayed animal. Oh, God! *Why had Dot done that?* He had not kept his promise to see her this morning and she had gotten into a panic; that was it. But she had sworn to consult him before acting on her own, and now . . . His life was a delicate bridge spanning a gaping chasm and hostile hands were heaping heavy loads upon that bridge and it was about to crack and crash downward.

"What did you say, Ma?" He pretended that he had not heard.

How much did she know? Perhaps everything! That crazy Dot! He could wring her neck for this! She had no right to tell tales to his mother! Women had no sense of . . .

"You *know* what I'm talking about, boy," his mother scolded him sternly. "That girl's in trouble—"

"*Who* are you talking about, Ma?" He still stalled for time.

"Stop acting foolish, Cross! That girl's blaming *you*—"

"Blaming me for what?" he asked. He knew that he was acting silly, but he could not easily change his attitude now.

"She's in a family way, Cross," his mother spoke boldly, a woman lodging woman's ancient complaint against man. "And she says it's *you*! She's worried sick.

She had to talk to somebody, so she came to me. Son, what have you done?" There came the sound of a sob being choked back. "You're married. You've three children. What're you going to do?"

"Just a sec. Somebody's at the door," he lied for respite.

Like always, he had doubled his burdens; he heard his mother's tirades and at the same time he pretended that he was not reacting to them, and this dual set of responses made him frantic. That harebrained Dot! Trying to save herself and ruining me, the only one who can save her . . . Dot's panic had made her deal him a dirty blow. He brought the receiver to his mouth.

"Is she still there, Ma?" His tone of voice confessed that he now knew what it was all about.

"Hunh? No; she's gone," his mother said. "She's gone to see Gladys . . . Cross, that girl's young, a child. She can get you into serious trouble . . ."

Dot was talking to his wife! This was the end! The void in him grew hotter. A widening circle of people were becoming acquainted with his difficulties. He knew that Gladys would do her damndest now; she would be merciless. Her knowing about Dot would redouble her hate for him. She would bare the details of his private blunderings before the domestic courts . . . He had to try to stop her. But could he? Maybe it was already too late?

"I'll be right over," he said, hanging up abruptly.

He took another drink and went out of the door. As he descended the stairs, his mother's scolding intensified his mood of self-loathing, a mood that had been his longer than he could recall, a mood that had been growing deeper with the increasing complexity of the events of his life. He knew himself too well not to realize the meaning of what he was feeling; yet his self-knowledge, born of a habit of incessant reflection, did not enable him to escape the morass in which his feelings were bogged. His insight merely augmented his emotional conflicts. He was aware, intimately and bitterly, that his dread had been his mother's first fateful gift to him. He had been born of her not only physically but emotionally too. The only psychological difference between them was that he was aware of having received this dark gift from her at a time when he was too young to reject it, and she had given it to him in a period of her life when her intense grief over the death of her husband had rendered her incapable of realizing the full import of what she had been doing. And he could never speak to her about this difference in emotional similarity; he could only pretend that it did not exist, for not only did his deep love of her forbid it, but he did not possess enough emotional detachment from her for that to happen. As her son, he was much too far from her and at the same time much too close, much too warm toward her and much too cold. To keep her life from crushing his own, he had slain the sense of her in his heart and at the same time had clung frantically to his memory of that sense. His feelings for her were widely distant: flight and embrace . . .

From the vestibule he stepped into a frozen world lit by a lemon-colored sun whose glare sparkled on mounds of ice. The snow had stopped and the sky stretched pale and blue; the air was dry and bitter cold. The sun disclosed in sharp detail the red brick buildings, glinted on the slow moving trolleys, and cast into the windowpanes liquid reflections that stung his eyes. His shoulders hunched forward and he shivered and clenched his teeth to keep them from chattering, his breath steaming against the freezing air.

He was conscious of himself as a frail object which

had to protect itself against a pending threat of annihilation. This frigid world was suggestively like the one which his mother, without her having known it, had created for him to live in when he had been a child. Though she had loved him, she had tainted his budding feelings with a fierce devotion born of her fear of a life that had baffled and wounded her. His first coherent memories had condensed themselves into an image of a young woman whose hysterically loving presence had made his imagination conscious of an invisible God—Whose secret grace granted him life—hovering oppressively in space above him. His adolescent fantasies had symbolically telescoped this God into an awful face shaped in the form of a huge and crushing NO, a terrifying face which had, for a reason he could never learn, created him, had given him a part of Himself, and yet had threateningly demanded that he vigilantly deny another part of himself which He too had paradoxically given him. This God's NO-FACE had evoked in his pliable boy's body an aching sense of pleasure by admonishing him to shun pleasure as the tempting doorway opening blackly on to hell; had too early awakened in him a sharp sense of sex by thunderingly denouncing sex as the sin leading to eternal damnation; had posited in him an unbridled hunger for the sensual by branding all sensuality as the monstrous death from which there was no resurrection; had made him instinctively choose to love himself over and against all others because he felt himself menaced by a mysterious God Whose love seemed somehow like hate. Mother love had cleaved him in twain: a wayward sensibility that distrusted itself, a consciousness that was conscious of itself. Despite this, his sensibilities had not been repressed by God's fearful negations as represented by his mother; indeed, his sense of life had been so heightened that desire boiled in him to a degree that made him afraid. Afraid of what? Nothing exactly, precisely . . . And this constituted his sense of dread.

As he neared his mother's rooming house, he could already feel the form of her indictment, could divine the morally charged words she would hurl at him. And he knew that his reaction would be one of sullen and guilty anger. Why, then, was he going to see her? Because he really wanted her to rail at him, denounce him, and he would suffer, feel his hurt again, and, in doing so, would know intuitively that somewhere in the depths of his raw wound lay the blood of his salvation or the pus of his disaster. This obscure knowledge had stayed his finger on the trigger of the gun whose barrel had touched his temple this morning . . .

He entered a dilapidated building, went down a dark hallway and tapped upon a door. Sounds of muffled movement came to him; the door opened and framed his mother's solemnly lined face, the white hair pulled severely back from a wide forehead, a gnarled right hand holding a woolen shawl about stooped shoulders. Her mouth was a tight, flat slit and her eyes peered through cloudy spectacles.

"Hi, Ma."

Without answering, she widened the door and he walked past her into a tiny, shabby room that smelt of a sweetish odor of decaying flesh that seemed to cling to the aged who are slowly dying while still living.

He noticed, as he did each time he visited her, that she appeared to have shrunken a bit more; and he knew that it was her chronic fretting, her always tearing at her emotions that was whitening the hairs of her head, deepening the lines in her face, and accentuating the stoop of her back. His mother could no more relax than he could. Like me, she's using up herself too fast, and she's just a little over sixty . . . If she cared for herself more, judged life less severely, time would deal easier with her . . . Why were some people fated, like Job, to live a never-ending debate between themselves and their sense of what they believed life should be? Why did some hearts feel insulted at being alive, humiliated at the terms of existence? It was as though one felt that one had been promised something and when that promise had not been kept, one felt a sense of loss that made life intolerable; it was as though one was angry, but did not know toward what or whom the anger should be directed; it was as though one felt betrayed, but could never determine the manner of the betrayal. And this was what was making his mother old before her time . . .

He smoked, looked about vacantly, avoiding her accusing eyes, and was already fighting down a feeling of defensive guilt. She turned and began rummaging aimlessly in a dresser drawer and he knew that she was deliberately making him wait before she spoke, attempting to reduce him again to the status of a fearfully impressionable child. Before pronouncing her condemnations, she would make him feel that she was weighing him in the scales of her drastic judgment and was finding, to her horror, that he was a self-centered libertine ruthlessly ridden by this lust for pleasure, an irresponsible wastrel thoughtlessly squandering his life's substance. And afterwards he would listen with a face masked in indifference and he would know that she was right; but he would also know that there was nothing that neither he nor she could do about it, that there was no cure for his malady, and, above all, that this dilemma was the meaning of his life.

Long ago, in his fourteenth year, while standing waiting for her preachments, he had demanded to know why she always pinioned him in solitude before handing down her moral laws, and she had replied that it was to make him develop the habit of reflecting deeply, that he knew as well as she when he had done wrong and she wanted to teach him to be his own judge. Anger now rose in him and he sought for some way to make her feel it. He grew suddenly resentful of the rickety furniture of the room. It's her own damn fault if she lives like this . . . She could be living comfortably with Gladys . . .

Yet, even as he thought it, he knew that he was wrong. Gladys and his mother hated each other; once, when they had lived together during the early days of his marriage, Gladys and his mother had vied for female dominance in the home and it had ended with his mother's packing and leaving, declaring that she preferred to live alone rather than with a wilful daughter-in-law who did not respect her.

"Why do you insist on living like this?" he broke the ice.

"We're not going to talk about how *I'm* living," she countered.

"No matter. But why do you live like this?" he asked again.

"And why do you live as *you're* living?" she demanded bitterly turning to him. "You're drinking again. I can *smell* it."

"Not much," he said; his voice was clipped but controlled.

Her right hand dabbed clumsily at a tear on her wrinkled cheek. She slid into a chair and cried, her withered lips twisting, her false teeth wobbling loosely in shrunken gums.

"You've started spoiling little girls, taking advantage of children . . . Son, can't you *control* yourself? Where's all this leading you? Why in God's name do you lie to a little girl like Dot and seduce her?"

"I didn't lie—"

"You *did*!" she blazed. "You let her hope for what you couldn't do, and that's lying. I'm no fool! If you didn't lie to her, that's worse. Then she's just a little whore. And if she's a whore, why did you take up with her? Cross, it's easy to fool a young girl. If you're proud of this cheap trick, you've fallen lower than I thought you had."

She had done it; she had evoked in him that shameful mood of guilt born of desire and fear of desire. He knew that she was not lamenting for him alone, but for her own betrayed maidenhood, for how she had once been so treacherously beguiled into trusting surrender; she was blaming him somehow for its having gone wrong, confusedly seeking his masculine sympathy for her sexually blighted life! Goddamn her! Hadn't she no sense of shame? He imagined himself rising and with a single sweep of his palm slapping her to the floor. And in the same instant a poignant pity for her seized him. Poor, lost, lonely woman clinging for salvation to a son who she knew was as lost as she was. He was too close to her and too far from her; much too warm toward her and much too cold. If only he understood her less! But he was cut off from that; he was anchored in a knowledge that offended him. And this image of his mother's incestuously-tinged longings would linger with him for days and he could curse her for it, and finally he would curse himself for living in a crazy world that he could not set right.

"Promising a child and knowing you don't mean it," she sobbed in despair. "How can men *do* that?"

He knew that now she was reliving her own experience, grieving over the thwarted hopes that had driven her into the arms of religion for the sake of her sanity. And he? Where could he be driven? Nowhere. His mother was lucky; she had a refuge, even if that refuge was only an illusion. But he could only get out of this world or stay in it and bear it. His anger waxed as he saw that she had a balm, however delusory, and he had none. And yet *she* was complaining to *him*! If she knew what he lived each day, she would be horrified. But his mother was convinced that he was hardhearted, that he was withholding his help out of selfish malice. An ironic smile stole across his lips.

"You can laugh!" she stormed at him. "But God'll punish you! He *will*! You'll see before you die! You'll weep! God is a just God! And He's a hard and jealous God! If you mock Him, He'll show you His Power!"

He shuddered and again projected his pity out upon her, then his pity recoiled back upon himself, for he knew that she would never understand him. A second later he pushed even this self-pity from him, realizing that it too was useless, would only depress him.

"I'm sorry, Ma," he sighed.

"Sorry for what?" she railed. "You can't undo what you've done. You've sinned, Cross, and it's to God you must confess with a contrite heart. Even if that girl gets rid of her child, she'll be forever hurt. She'll remember what you promised—"

"But I didn't *promise* her anything," he protested.

"Oh, stop lying," she said. "You *did*! You promised by the way you *acted* . . ."

A hopeless silence rose between them. Through the years his mother had related to him how, when she had been a country school teacher in a tiny southern community, she had met his father during the early days of the First World War. A Negro regiment had been camped nearby and excitement was everywhere. Her heart was ready and full of love. They first met at a church dance and he had straightaway declared his love. In her romantic eyes he was a huge boy going away to die on some distant battlefield and her heart had gone impulsively out to him, and finally her body also.

They married a month after they met and his regiment moved northward. She followed, feeling glad that she was giving him her life. But she soon learned that there were other girls foolish enough to look at him through romantic eyes and give him their hearts and bodies too. She finally upbraided him and he was cynical and defiant; then, more to avoid her than from motives of patriotism, he had, after returning from France, joined the army as a regular soldier. She trailed him dismally from army camp to army camp, begging for an understanding. Instead, the gap grew wider. Even before her son was born in 1924, she knew that she was only in his way, a worrisome wife. It was then that she took her sorrow and her infant son to God in copious tears. A year later she learned that somewhere in the reaches of Harlem, in a dirty, vacant lot at midnight, the police had found him lying wounded. He had been in a drunken street brawl, had lain unconscious in sub-zero weather, and had died a day later in an army hospital . . .

With Cross in her arms, she had returned South and resumed her teaching, but her real profession was a constant rehearsal in her memory of her tiny but pathetic drama, a continuous clutching of it to her heart in the form of a blend of complaint and accusation.

Cross looked at her; tears were still streaming on her cheeks.

"Son, can't you deny yourself sometimes and not hurt others?" she begged of him humbly; she was again, in the evening of her life, supplicating the fateful world of man. "You're destroying yourself. I know you believe only in your own pleasure, but must you hurt other people? If you feel you can't master yourself, then take your problem to God. He'll teach you how to live with others before it's too late. Life is a promise, son; God promised it to us and we must promise it to others. Without that promise, life's nothing . . . Oh, God, to think that at twenty-six you're lost . . . What're you going to do, Cross?"

He stood and gazed solemnly down at her.

"I don't know, Ma."

"Is it really over between you and Gladys?"

"Yeah. There's nothing there."

"Why?"

"I don't know. We can't make it."

"But your children? They *need* you . . . Cross, you can lose your job. Gladys can ruin you, and so can that girl. A wronged woman is a hard woman, Cross."

On wobbly legs he waited for her to grow quiet; he was frantic to see Gladys.

"To think I named you Cross after the Cross of Jesus," she sighed.

"I got to go," he said brusquely. The longer he stayed the more she would bewail the past and grate her heart as well as his nerves. "You need anything, Ma?"

"I need to know that you've found God, Cross," she whispered. "For months now everything I've heard about you is bad."

"I'll—" He felt the need to be kind. "See you tomorrow, hunh?"

"And pray, son."

He went out of the door quickly to escape this fountain of emotion that made him feel guilty. He had to see Gladys and attempt to arrange a roughshod compromise to curb any rashness she might be contemplating as a result of Dot's crazy visit. But the thought of Gladys made him quail; he knew that she would grasp eagerly upon his predicament and turn it against him, would try to use it to hold him at her mercy. Goddammit, if necessary, he would threaten to throw up his job . . . That ought to make her think a little. After all, the only thing Gladys really wanted was money.

Of all the mad things on earth, the maddest was Dot's talking to Gladys. Damn . . . He paused in the snow and stared. He ought to see Dot *first* and learn what had happened between her and Gladys. And he would give Dot the dressing down of her life! Didn't she know that Gladys was her enemy, that she would never befriend her, would do all in her power to humiliate her? Yes; instinct should have warned Dot not to reveal her plight to the wife of the man she claimed to love. He stopped at a street corner and looked at his watch. He had three hours before reporting to work; he had to hurry.

The sun had waned and already a touch of darkness was in the sky. It was growing rapidly colder and an icy wind swept through the streets. Hunger and emotional tension had drained him; he had to eat to stave off that incessant grinding in his stomach. He saw a dingy lunchstand with a sweaty plate glass window. He'd grab a bite to eat . . . He turned, crossed the ice-packed pavement, pushed through a narrow doorway and saw a crowd of working class Negroes and heard babbling voices. He perched himself atop a high stool and propped his elbows upon a greasy counter.

"A hamburger and a cup of coffee," he told the girl who came toward him.

"Right," she sang out.

The girl turned to prepare his order and his eyes, trained by habit, followed the jellylike sway of her sloping hips. At once his imagination began a reconstruction of the contours of her body, using the clues of her plump arms, her protruding breasts, the gently curving shape of her legs, and the width of her buttocks. Through the bluish haze of tobacco smoke and amidst the hub of laughter coming from the rear of the cafe, his senses dreamily seized upon woman as body of woman, not the girl standing by the steam table, but just woman as an image of a body and he drifted toward a state of desire, his consciousness stirring vaguely with desire for desire. His feelings, set off by the sight of the girl, now turned inward, then they projected themselves outwardly again, not so much upon the girl but in a seeking for a girl, to an image that fetched him toward something to embrace as desirable: woman as body of woman . . . The girl came toward him now and he looked fully at her; she slid the plate with the hamburger to him and he saw her face: hard, with small reddish eyes; a full, coarsely formed mouth; huge cheek bones that slanted to a stubborn chin; sullen lips . . . An intractable bitch, he thought. He sighed as the girl's too-solid reality eroded his deepening mood of desire for the desirable: woman as body of woman . . .

He munched his hamburger and fell into a melancholy brooding upon the mysterious movements of his consciousness. What was this thing of desire that haunted him? It seems that I just desire desire, he told himself. And there's no apparent end or meaning to it . . . And then there came to his mind the memory of the many sultry, smoky nights when he had been drunk with his friends in cheap dives and had seen girls like this. And, on those times, like today, a drive toward desire had risen imperiously in him and he had been just drunk enough for this desire for desire to hold fast to itself in spite of the girl's blatant ugliness and he had

sordidly bargained with her and had had her; and, like
now, in the end, he had recoiled from her in self-disgust
while lying beside her in bed just as he had recoiled a
moment ago from this one without ever having gone to
bed with her. On those drunken occasions he had gone
back alone to his empty room to reflect moodily upon
the obscurity of what he had been seeking when he had
wanted the girl. Surely it had not been *that* girl he had
so ardently wanted. No. But, yes, it had been the girl
and it had *not* been the girl; he saw clearly that he had
wanted the girl because his desire-impulse had pointed
to her; but after having had her, desire was still not satisfied, still sought to encompass something within desire
and hold it steady, to possess it, to become one with it.
And that's impossible, he told himself. One's crazy to
try to do it . . . Yet, he did try, and his trying seemed to
be the essence of living. And marriage, could he build a
marriage upon desire? Should one give pledges, make
promises, swear vows the sacredness of which depended
upon such running sands of feelings as desires . . . ?

And what about his desire for Dot? Although she was
carrying his child, his desire for her had already gone
. . . God in Heaven! What could he do? When he had
been a child he had thought that life was a solidly organized affair, but when he had grown up he had found
that it had the disorganized character of a nightmare.
What crazy fool had thought up these forms of human
relations? Or had men and women just drifted blindly
through the centuries into such emotional arrangements? He was convinced that an idiot could have conceived of better ways of establishing emotional alliances,
and men must have felt uneasy about it too, for they
had sought to make desire and passion stable by subjecting them to legal contracts! If human emotions fail to
remain constant, then draft laws stipulating that that

which will not remain constant *must* remain constant
. . . As he brooded over the problem of desire a quiet
sense of awe drenched him. Moods like these were the
nearest he ever came to religious feelings.

He jerked to attention as a wave of guffaws rose from
the crowd of Negroes in the rear of the cafe. Most of
them were young and they were bent double with
mirth. A tall Negro lifted his voice with loud authority
over the rolling laughter.

"Where there's lots of rumors, there's bound to be
some truth in 'em," he pronounced.

"You mean to tell me you believe Flying Saucers are
real?" a short, brown boy demanded with indignation.
"You got better sense than *that*!"

Cross had heard a hundred such arguments in bars
and cafes and he was primed to relax and listen to yet
another one, to see to what heights of fantasy it would
soar.

"I say these white folks is hiding something," the tall
Negro maintained, "and what they're hiding *scares* 'em!"

"And what're they hiding?" the waitress asked.

"Things they don't want *you* to know," the tall Negro
said cryptically.

Teasing laughter full of suspense went from man to
man. Cross could feel that they wanted to believe this
high mystery, but they needed more fantastic facts before their beliefs could jell. Their attitude was one of
laughing scepticism underscored with seriousness.

"Know what they found in one of them Flying Saucers?" the tall man demanded. "One of 'em was full of
little men, about two feet high, with skin like peach
fuzz—"

A waterfall of laughter showered in the cafe. Men
rose and stomped their feet, tossed back their heads, and
bellowed.

"But what the white folks so scared about?" someone asked. "Little men can't hurt nobody."

Silence. All eyes were turned expectantly to the face of the tall man.

"THEM LITTLE MEN THE WHITE FOLKS FOUND IN THEM SAUCERS WAS COLORED MEN AND THEY WAS FROM MARS!" the tall man spoke in deep solemn tones. "That's why they hushed up the story. They didn't want the world to know that the rest of the universe is colored! Most of the folks on this earth is colored, and if the white folks knew that the other worlds was full of colored folks who wanted to come down here, what the hell chance would the white folks have?"

Screams of approval, leaping from chairs, and clapping of hands.

"You ought to be shot to think of a thing like that!"

"It fits in with the way white folks act!"

Laughter died slowly. The men wiped their mouths with the backs of their hands, gazing at one another with sly joy.

"But it *could* be true," a man said soberly. "White folks in America, France, England, and Italy are the scaredest folks that ever lived on this earth. They're scareda Reds, Chinese, Indians, Africans, *everybody*."

"But how come you reckon they so scared?" an elderly man asked.

" 'Cause they're guilty," the tall man explained. "And guilty folks are *scared* folks! For four hundred years these white folks done made everybody on earth feel like they ain't human, like they're outsiders. They done kicked 'em around and called 'em names . . . What's a Chinese to a white man? Chink-Chink Chinaman with pigtails down his back and he ain't fit for nothing but to cook and wash clothes. What's a Hindoo to a white man? A nigger who's in love with ghosts, who kisses cows and makes pets of vipers. What's a black man to a white man? An ape made by God to cut wood and draw water, and with an inborn yen to rape white girls. A Mexican? A greasy, stinking rascal who ought to be worked to death and then shot. A Jew? A Christ-killer, a cheat, a rat. A Japanese? A monkey with a yellow skin . . . Now our colored brothers are visiting us from Mars and Jupiter and the white folks is sweating in a panic—"

Negroes rolled in laughter, feeling that the powerful white world had been lowered to their own humble plane by the magic of comic words. One black boy danced ecstatically, then, holding his hands over his mouth as though he felt it unseemly to vent his savage mirth indoors, ran out of the cafe, leaving the door open. Upon the snowy sidewalk he screamed and howled and flapped his arms in the icy wind. For a moment he paused, then ran back to the door and, gasping for breath, said:

"Man, that's sure cool!" He lifted his eyes to the grey sky. "You colored brothers on Mars, come on down here and help us!"

Cross found himself joining in the laughter. His heart went out to these rejected men whose rebel laughter banished self-murder from his thoughts. If only he could lose himself in that kind of living! Were there not somewhere in this world rebels with whom he could feel at home, men who were outsiders not because they had been born black and poor, but because they had thought their way through the many veils of illusion? But where were they? How could one find them?

It was time to go. Amidst a tidal wave of laughter he paid his check and went out, passing the black boy on the sidewalk and looking back several times to see other

Negroes leave the cafe to join the black boy laughing in the white snow. Their peals reached his ears for half a block.

Yes, he had to see Dot. The thought made tension rise in him and he went into a bar and had a double whiskey. When he came out a bluish mist hung in the air and the sun was a faint red ball. The outlines of the buildings were beginning to blur. A freezing wind stung his face. He found a taxi and climbed in.

"5743 Indiana," he told the driver.

Underneath all he had felt that day, Dot had rested as a kind of uneasy undertow, a slow black tide that would not be gainsaid. And, now that he was going to have it out with her, he flinched with fear at the hurt she would sustain. It had been six months ago that she had first floated into his mind as just another image of desire, woman as body of woman; but, for reasons which he had not foreseen, she had clung to him and he had clung to her and slowly she had come to mean more to him than just a woman's body. Now that the moment of what she so melodramatically liked to refer to as the "payoff" was at hand, he did not like it. What bothered him most was that he knew that he had to betray her, and this betrayal was not springing from any innate perversity in him, but from the very complexity of his relations with Gladys. There was no way out but to hurt her, and he was convinced that she knew it. He had helped her with money, advice, sharing with her his life; but it seemed that these gifts enraged her. She had said that they were not enough and he knew that, as a woman, she was right. Dot was so close to what she wanted in life, that is, to marry him, that its impossibility drove her almost out of her mind.

In her struggle for legal possession of him, Cross knew that she was in the end counting heavily upon his weakness to carry her through. Yes, he was weak, but he knew that he was weak, and that made a difference. He also knew more about the turnings and twistings of her mind than she knew he knew, and this knowledge gave him an ironic insight into her that he did not relish. How could he ever make her know that, though he gave forth the appearance of weakness, that this weakness was really a kind of strength of not wanting to hurt others. His own experience had shown him that he was cold-bloodedly brutal when trapped in situations involving his self-respect. All his life he had been plagued by being caught in relations where others had tried to take advantage of him because they had thought him supine and gullible; and when he had finally confronted them with the fact that he knew that they were playing him, they had hated him with a redoubled fury for his having deceived them! And he dreaded that happening with Dot.

He had never tried to conceal from Dot his situation; he had been transparently honest with her from the beginning; he had told her everything and if she had any illusions, they were of her own making. And what saddened him to inward tears was that he suspected that Dot had allowed herself to become impregnated in order to test the strength of their attachment, hoping that he would be so moved and harassed by her passionate appeals that he would find some way of breaking legally with Gladys and marrying her. And he knew that freedom was the last thing on earth that Gladys would ever grant him. Dot's just young and romantic enough to try such a fool thing, he thought bitterly.

He had met her, of all the places in a teeming city, in the liquor section of the South Center Department Store one Saturday morning last spring. There had been a widely advertised sale of Jamaica rum and long lines of

people had queued up to buy at the unheard of rate of
two bottles of rum for three dollars. The store had been
jammed with milling crowds. He had taken his place at
the end of a long queue and a moment later he had been
aware that a young, willowy slip of a tall yellow girl had
fallen in directly behind him. It was warm; he was without a coat and his shirt sleeves were rolled up past his
elbows. He sniffed the perfume she wore, then gave her
a quick survey; she was uncommonly pretty and was
wearing a sheer pink print dress that showed the shape
of her body with disturbing distinctness. She looks
sweet, he thought. He glanced at her, trying to catch
her eye; but the jostling crowd so distracted him that he
forgot her until a few minutes later, when, all at once,
he felt his naked elbow touching something yieldingly
soft behind him. He looked around and she smiled
shyly; a soft lump rose in his throat. Good God, what a
gal! And so *young* . . . Did she know that his elbow was
touching her left breast? If she did, she gave no out-
ward sign; she still had that vague, sweet smile that
could mean anything: coyness or just simple self-
consciousness. Why, she's just a child, he thought with a
twinge of shame. He looked at her again, feeling his
elbow still touching her breast; she smiled and looked
off, yet she did not try to move away. She knows . . .
But really, would a young girl with a face so sensitive
and finely chiselled allow him to do that to her in public? Was she alone or was that man behind her her husband? The image of woman as body of woman filled
him and his head felt pleasantly giddy. He was determined to know if she knew that his bare elbow was tan-
talizingly touching the tip of her breast. Perhaps she's so
excited about the rum that she does not feel it . . . But
his knowledge of the erotic made him feel that that was
impossible. He sensed in her a quality of quiet waiting

and it made him feel that she *did* know and did not
mind, was even welcoming it. The line inched forward.
The metallic ringing of cash registers sang out over the
crowd. Traffic clanged through the streets outside. And
all around was bubbling a cacophony of voices. He was
now so near the counter that he could see the towering
rows of bottles of dark yellow rum. Slowly, so slowly
that no one could notice anything, he moved his bare
elbow to and fro across the tip of her breast, realizing
with sensual astonishment: She's not wearing a brassiere! Desire surged softly through him. Out of the corner of his eye he could see that she had not moved; she
was staring steadily ahead, holding her purse primly in
front of her. He tried it again; she did not move or
seem aware that she was being touched at all; her face
was sweet, composed, solemn, angel-like in its purity
and remoteness from erotic passion. Was she aware or
was she not? He had to know; it obsessed him. She
could, of course, abruptly leave the line to indicate her
disgust; or she could, if she were the hysterical breed,
yell out that he was molesting her. But he did not believe that she would . . . Was she playing the same
game that he was playing? And who was she? Again he
moved his naked elbow across her left breast, caressing
it, gently indenting the soft, surrendering flesh under
the sheer cloth of her dress as much as he dared, and,
this time, he knew that she knew, for he felt the tip of
her loose breast gradually hardening, growing delicately
into a pointed, taut nipple. He gazed at her directly
now, but still she did not look at him; and her face was
as passive and serene as a summer landscape. The line
shortened and he fondled her breast with his elbow and
she made no move to withdraw her body; instead, as
the line snaked forward, she managed to keep her breast
where his elbow could touch it. He was now certain

that the man behind her was not her husband, did not know her. Finally he turned to her and smiled, still touching her breast, and said:

"It's a long time, hunh, to wait for two bottles of rum?"

"It's awful," she said, and they both laughed.

"You like rum?" he asked.

"Now, what do you think?" she countered teasingly.

"What do you make with it? Cuba Libres or Rum Punches?"

"Both," she said.

"You live around here?"

"Naw. Up near 37th Street."

He looked at her openly now, as a man looks at a woman he likes and wants.

"You *couldn't* be over sixteen," he ventured.

"You're wrong. I'm seventeen," she corrected him.

They had spoken in low tones, as though both were conspiring to keep secret the erotic link that was springing up between them. He noticed that she was trembling slightly and he knew that she was being claimed by a state he knew well: dread. This was perhaps the first time she had ever let herself be caressed in this manner and he must not frighten her. He cast about for something to say to let her know that, though he was after her, he was also a gentleman and that she need not be afraid of him, that she could rely on him for discreetness and good sense. It was then that he saw a Wendell Phillips High School pin on the collar of her dress.

"When did you get your sheepskin?" he asked her.

"Last June," she answered readily.

"Phillips was my school, too," he told her.

"Really?" she asked. She smiled broadly, relaxing completely for the first time.

They were at the counter now and he paid for his

rum and stood aside, waiting for her. When she left the
counter, he said:

"Here. Let me help you carry that."

"Thank you," she said with a charming degree of hesitation; then she allowed him to take her bottles.

They walked out of the store together, making small
talk. She told him that she lived with her mother and a
younger brother; but her mother was a terror, depriving
her of all freedom. She said that she was thinking seriously of leaving home and living with Myrtle, a girl
friend . . . During the first five minutes he had let her
know that he was not free, that he worked in the Post
Office, that he was married but not living with his wife.
They passed a movie house and he asked her if she liked
movies and she said yes. He invited her to see a show
with him that afternoon and she demurred modestly. She
doesn't want to seem too *forward*, he thought; and he
laughed out loud about it when he was alone in his room.

"But you can call me sometimes, if you want to," she
said, and she gave him her telephone number.

That was how it had begun. She had known from the
beginning that he was not free and she had told him
that it did not really matter for the time being. In their
relationship he had found her a passionate child achingly hungry for emotional experience. Of an afternoon
she would come to his room with the most disconcert-
ing directness he had ever known in a woman. He
would try to talk to her and as he talked he could tell
that she was not listening; she was pulling off her dress,
stripping down her nylon stockings, stepping out of her
nylon slip and panties . . . And afterwards he would
stare at her unbelievingly as she would stomp her foot
and tell him with a childlike seriousness that was all the
more serious because it was so childlike: "I never want
to make love with anybody but you."

"You'll live and learn," he had told her, yawning.

"Don't *say* that," she had protested with sudden fury, and he realized with a sense of dismay that what had taken place was to her sacred.

But that did not prevent some nuance of perversity in him from trying to make her admit that she had been conscious of his elbow caressing her breast that warm, spring Saturday morning in the liquor store, but she would never confess it, would exhibit feelings of shame and indignation whenever he mentioned it; but beneath her ardent denials was a furtive sense of erotic pleasure. He was amused by the manner in which she balanced her moral notions with her emotional hungers. Under his questioning she would pause in her dressing and stare at him with wide, hurt eyes and exclaim:

"How can you *say* that? You sure have a *filthy* imagination!"

"But, Dot, dammit, you *knew*! I *swear* you did—"

"Do you think I'd let anybody do *that* to me in public?" she asked, her voice ringing with genuine incredulity.

"But you *did*, Dot!"

"I *didn't*!"

Tears would roll down her cheeks and he would take her in his arms and soothe her; but she never got angry about it. And until the end she would never concede that that morning was the first time that she had ever felt so keen a sensual pleasure. But Cross was certain of it and it made him marvel that she could deny it with such passionate consistency.

His bond with her grew deeper with the passing days, for it was with her that, for the first time in his life, he found himself talking freely, emptying out of his soul the dammed up waters of reflection and brooding thought. He told her of his morbidly tangled yet profound relation with his mother; he told her how, when he had been twenty-one years of age, he had naïvely been sucked into a stupid marriage with Gladys; and he confessed to her his incurable melancholy stemming from his mulling over his emotions. He never quite knew how much of what he told her she understood, but she always listened patiently, now and then timidly venturing a detached question or two, but never commending or blaming. He came at last to believe that she accepted the kind of talk in which he indulged as a mysterious part of a man's equipment, along with his sexual organs. But the mere fact that she listened to his analytical tirades had been a boon to him beyond his deepest hopes.

And now he had to hurt her. And what would she do? Once he had toyed with trying to find possible friends of his with whom she could fall in love; he had once even spoken to her in glowing terms of a man who worked with him on the job. And he had been amazed when she had turned to look at him and demanded:

"Are you trying to pawn me off on somebody?"

To hear her speak like that had so shamed him that he had never tried it again. Then, one Sunday evening over dinner in a crowded restaurant, she told him that she was carrying his child. His stupefication had been such that the food stuck in his throat. Later, in his room, she had wildly resisted his suggestion that she abort the child and it had maddened him. The scenes of emotional conflict that took place the following month had frayed him almost to madness.

He had just left one woman, his mother, who, in an outpouring, had hurled at him her life draped in the dark hues of complaint and accusation, had tried futilely to rouse compassion in him by dramatizing the forlorn nature of her abandoned plight; now he was on his way to struggle with yet another woman. And after Dot there loomed the formidable figure of his wife.

"Okay, Buddy; here you are," the taxi driver told him as the cab swerved to a curb hidden by snowflakes.

He paid, ran up the steps, pushed the bell of Dot's apartment three times, the signal they agreed upon when he was calling to see her. The buzzer was so long in answering that he thought that surely she was not in. Where could she be? He rang again and was about to leave when the buzzer suddenly responded in a long blast of sound that would not stop. He opened the vestibule door, feeling that something was wrong. He heard the buzzer still emitting its tinny throb long after he had passed the second floor. She must be upset or something . . . When he reached the door of Dot's apartment, he saw Myrtle, Dot's girl friend, looking at him with a face as devoid of expression as she could make it. Myrtle was a tall, dark girl with a handsome face and sardonic eyes. Cross slowed his movements, sensing knowledge of a crisis behind Myrtle's reserved manner.

"Hi," he greeted her.

Without answering, she caught hold of his arm and drew him forcibly into the hallway of the apartment.

"Where's Dot?" he asked, trying to keep his voice calm.

"In bed," she said flatly.

"What's happened?"

"*You* ought to be asking . . . All hell's broke loose, that's all."

"What do you mean? I want to see Dot."

"You can't now," she said with an air of petty satisfaction.

He started for Dot's bedroom and Myrtle held him back.

"The *doctor's* in there," she whispered fiercely.

"The doctor? Why? Tell me what's happening!"

"You *men*!" She curled her lips in scorn. "How much do you think a poor girl can stand?"

"Okay. You can can that," he told her roughly, unable to suppress hot resentment. "Dot can talk to me like that, but *you* can't!"

He had never liked her and she did not like him and the way she was now acting was something he had known she would do if she ever had gotten the chance; now she had it and was doing it. One instinct told him to ignore her, but she had cut too deeply into his bleeding feelings for him to leave off. He stood glaring at her, his fingers trembling.

"Look, I'm Dot's best friend, see?" she shot at him. "I'm taking care of her, trying to repair the damage you've done. I can say what I damn well like . . ."

"Not to *me*," Cross said.

"And why not?" she flipped at him.

"Because I don't sleep with you," he told her brutally, looking her straight in the eyes.

An anger so intense burned in Myrtle's face that her large eyes shrank in size.

"You dirty sonofabitch," she said in an even, low tone.

"Thanks," he said.

He opened the door of Dot's room and peered in.

"Who is it?" a loud masculine voice called out to him as he stood uncertainly.

It was the doctor who had yelled; Cross could see his back bent over Dot's bed. Dot was lying with her face to the wall.

"It's me, honey. Cross."

"Please, please, don't come in now, Cross."

"Will you be kind enough to wait outside until I'm through here?" the doctor asked brusquely. "What happens after I'm gone is your business . . ."

Cross shut the door and turned to see the smirk on Myrtle's face.

"What happened?"

"I ought to spit right in your face for what you said to me," she said forming her lips as though about to spew something through them. "What she ever saw in your sullen heart, God only knows!"

"I'm sorry," he relented to get information. "But why don't you tell me what's happened?"

"Yeah, *sorry* . . . Men are always *sorry*," she derided him openly, keeping her voice low and charging it with hate.

"For Christ's sake!" he exploded. "Now's no time to carry on like that! Tell me what happened."

"Wait and she'll tell you," Myrtle said and went into the kitchen, closing the door behind her.

Cross sat and fumed. How crazy women could be sometimes . . . What did she think she was gaining by throwing dramatic fits? He looked up as she came briskly out of the kitchen, opened the door of the hall closet, took out her coat and put it on. She paused, not looking directly at him. The muscles of Cross's body tightened; he could have kicked her right through the brick wall into the snowdrifts piled outside.

"I've got to go down to the drugstore and get a prescription filled," she said matter-of-factly. "I'm leaving a hypodermic needle and a syringe boiling in a pan on the gas stove. Turn out the fire under it in two or three minutes, will you?" She shot him a sidelong glance. "You ought to be able to do *that* now."

"You can go to hell," he growled at her.

"I'd gladly go, if only I could take you along with me," she snapped at him and pulled the door shut behind her so violently that it sounded like a rifle shot.

His nerves twitched in protest, then he was conscious that the droning murmur of the doctor's voice in the bedroom had ceased and he heard Dot's distressed voice ringing out:

"Oh, Cross! What was that?"

Before he could reply the doctor had opened the door and was glaring at him.

"The girl slammed the door," Cross told the doctor sheepishly.

"This child's a nervous wreck," the doctor said, throwing up his hands in despair. "She's got to be kept quiet."

Cross huddled forward in his chair. The doctor went back into Dot's room, drawing the door shut.

Once more the masculine murmur of the doctor's voice resumed. What was he saying to her? And what had she told him? He was convinced that he was under discussion and it made him feel deprived of his humanity, converted into a condemned object, exposed to the baleful gaze of a million eyes. He crept softly to the door, cocked his head and listened, but he could not distinguish any words. Now and then he could hear Dot's silvery voice rising in a melody of complaint, of protest. Goddamn . . . Why had she called in that doctor without telling him? If she'd only trust me . . . But he knew that her trusting him would not get her what she wanted; he was in no position to marry her. All right; suppose Dot was in trouble? Did that justify her subjecting him to shame? The South Side was a small community and if Dot had revealed their relations to this doctor, their predicament would be on the lips of a thousand gossiping men and women in a day's time . . .

He had a hot impulse to rise and flee the apartment and disappear forever . . . What had he to lose by throwing up this fool's game? His job? It was not worth a damn, so mortgaged was he with debt. He really had nothing to lose. What a stupid situation for an intelligent man to find himself in! What greater shame was there for a man than to walk the streets cringing with fear of grasping women whose destructive strokes were draped in the guise of whimpers and accusations? Somehow he would shake loose from this and never in all his life let himself be caught again . . .

He was already supporting Dot, but she could, if she wanted to be brutal about it, compel him, at the behest of a court of law, to support the child after it was born. He knew that she would do such only if she were certain that he would never marry her. Had Gladys told her that a divorce was impossible? More than likely she had . . .

He ought to leave *now* . . . But he sat, hating himself. He yearned to roll himself into a tight little black ball and fling himself away as far as his strength would allow. But, no; there were his small sons, Cross, Junior, Peter, and Robert, whom he loved and did not want to leave. He would regain his influence over Dot; all was not lost. Dot had gone berserk because he had broken his promise to see her this morning and now he would have to be with her constantly to bring her around. Above all, he had to persuade her to abort the child for her sake, his sake . . .

A gurgle of water sounded in the kitchen. That pot that Myrtle had told him to look after! He ran and turned out the gas just in time, for there were but a few bubbles left in the pan.

The telephone rang. He entered the hallway and stood uncertainly.

"Shall I answer it, Dot?" he called through the door.

"Yes, please," Dot answered weakly.

He picked up the receiver.

"Dot? Is that you?" It was the voice of a woman speaking with breathless eagerness.

"No, this is not she," he said.

"Who's speaking?" the voice was cautious now, but still urgent.

"Just a friend," Cross said, disguising his tone. He was always afraid of Gladys' trapping him in Dot's apartment.

"Is this Mr. Damon?"

"No," he lied, hoping that his voice would not carry to Dot's room. "I'm a friend of Myrtle."

"Won't you please call Dot to the phone?"

"I'm afraid she can't come. She's in bed. The doctor's with her. Who's this?"

"Mary, a friend of Dot. Listen, tell Dot I've found her a lawyer. He's a whizz. She's to call me as soon as possible."

"I see." His eyes widened.

"Tell her that she'll have to act fast to tie up Damon—"

"I'll tell her." He struggled to keep his voice normal. There was a hesitating silence.

"*Who's* this speaking?" Fear was in the voice.

"Brown's the name," he lied.

"Oh . . . For a moment I had the feeling you were Dot's friend, that Damon man," the voice sighed with relief.

"Oh, no. I wouldn't want to be in his shoes—"

"Nothing's seriously wrong with Dot, I hope?"

"No. She just needs some rest."

"Tell Dot that she's got to hang on to her birth certificate; it's her quickest way of proving that she's under sixteen. My lawyer says that as long as she's not sixteen, Damon's guilty of rape. Now, Dot's birthday comes in June, and that gives her four months of grace."

Cross felt a red horizon of danger closing in about him.

"What did you say?"

"Explain this to Dot," the voice spoke distinctly. "Wait a minute."

He held his breath as a faint rustle of paper came over the wire.

"I got it," the voice was edged with satisfaction. "I copied it down as my lawyer read it to me this morning. Here it is: '. . . Every male person of the age of seventeen years and upwards who shall have carnal knowledge of any female person under the age of sixteen years and not his wife, either with or without her consent shall be adjudged guilty of the crime of rape . . .' You know what *carnal* means, don't you?"

"Yes," Cross breathed; he felt wrapped in a nightmare.

"'. . . Every person convicted of the crime of rape shall be imprisoned in a penitentiary for a term of not less than one year and may extend to life . . .' You got that?"

"Yes."

"Now, this Damon's married, so he *can't* marry Dot and wriggle out that way," the voice went on in a tone of hard triumph. "So if Dot doesn't get mushy, she's got Damon where she wants him."

"I see," Cross said. "But are you sure Dot's *under* sixteen?"

"I've seen her birth certificate," the voice assured him.

"I'll tell her," Cross promised heavily.

"Good-by."

" 'Bye."

He hung up, swayed a bit, then sat. Dot was a minor? How was that possible? He was certain that she had told him that she was seventeen. Jesus . . . Could this be true? He had been honest with her and she had tricked him! Yet, in casting back his mind, he remembered that he had often felt that she was younger than she had claimed. How in God's name had he stumbled into a situation of such deadly seriousness? He sat hunched over in the chair, too stunned to move. If ever, now was the time to act upon the impulse of flight. He had about fifty dollars in his pocket. He ought to buy a railroad ticket for as long a journey as the money would cover, and vanish. There was no doubt now but that Dot had made up her mind, and from now on he had to regard her as his enemy. Longing for a drink, he rummaged in the kitchen and found an inch of gin in a bottle and drained it.

The hall door lock clicked and Myrtle entered without glancing at him. Yes; she was in on this too. Her knowledge of his being a potential convict was what had made her so bold in sassing him. He glared at her as she pulled off her coat and went into the kitchen and returned with a tray; she went into Dot's room, closing the door behind her. That bitch . . . His talk with Dot would be decisive; either she called off the lawyer or he would drop her and let her do her worst. He had a last weapon, his gun, and it would change things and leave her dismayed . . .

At last the doctor emerged, leaving Dot's door open this time. Moving methodically, the doctor placed his black bag on a chair and proceeded to get into his overcoat. He pulled on his hat and looked at Cross with cold eyes. Abruptly he grabbed his bag and went unaided out of the door. Yes; Dot had identified him to the doctor. Cross felt sick and cheap.

On his tongue was a storm of reproaches he wanted to hurl at Dot, but he checked himself. To lose his temper would be playing into her hands, giving her an opportunity to wallow in an emotional scene. He walked slowly into the room and saw Dot lying with her face to the wall. Myrtle sat huddled on a side of the bed with her head bent forward, her body shaking; she was weeping. The hypodermic needle and the syringe lay on the tray at the foot of the bed. A medicinal odor hung in the air.

"Myrtle, what the hell's eating you?" he demanded.

As he had expected, they had been waiting for this signal; both women started to berate him at once. It was Dot's voice that won out.

"Please, Cross, in the name of God," Dot begged, without turning to look at him. "Be gentle with Myrtle. She's been waiting on me night and day. She's all I got. Don't insult her."

"I'm not insulting anybody——"

Myrtle jerked upright, her limbs trembling and her face wet with tears.

"You did! And what have I ever done to you?"

"You started slashing at me the moment I got into this apartment," he charged her.

"But can't you see what's happening?" Myrtle blazed at him. "This poor child's half out of her mind . . . Try to be *human*!"

"That's the trouble," he almost hissed. "I'm simply too *damned* human."

"If I was Dot, I wouldn't take this off you for a single minute," Myrtle burst out in a torrent of rage. "Oh, boy, I'd have you in a way that you'd never forget!"

"Do you think I don't know that?"

"I'd get your money, your job, and throw you smack into jail!"

"Oh, Myrtle, no . . ." Dot protested.

Yes, Myrtle was going further than Dot wanted. Cross looked at the two of them. When he spoke he was not smiling, but there was a note of hard irony in his voice that was worse than laughter.

"Yeah, I know. I'm just a big, bad, black brute. Pushing little girls around. Taking advantage of the helpless. Spoiling innocent children. I've no feelings. I'm just having a damn grand time and making others suffer." He summed up their case for them and then sat on the edge of the bed beside Myrtle.

"You're a man and you can't dodge your responsibilities," Myrtle told him wailingly.

"I'm not responsible to *you* for anything," Cross told her. "And I don't like your meddling. Now, get the hell out of here and let me talk to Dot."

"You are a *real* bastard," Myrtle said. "You ought to marry Dot, but I pity her spending a lifetime with you."

"Don't worry," he taunted her. "I'm not going to spend a lifetime with *you*."

"Cross, for God's sake," Dot whimpered. "Don't be that way."

"That's the only way he can be," Myrtle said.

"Get out of here, Myrtle," Cross told her again.

There was silence. He stood his ground. He was determined to wreck their rehearsed appeal to him. He felt that instinct was guiding them, prompting their attitudes and the strategy of their attacks. Both of them were weeping now and he made no move. He would let their tears flow futilely for awhile; they would see that he was not to be easily overcome.

"You're lucky that it's Dot you're dealing with instead of me," Myrtle said. Weeping, she stood and walked from the room.

Cross heard the door close behind his back. He could almost see the little wheels turning in the brains of both girls as they planned their next move. Men had to consult together for concerted action; women simply gravitated together spontaneously, motivated by their situation in life as women. They knew without prior consultation the most effective assaults. Cross was conscious of their consciousness. He knew them as women better than they knew him as man.

"Dot, I want to talk to you," he began. "Are you up to it, or should I come back in the morning?"

Dot lay without moving. He knew that she was debating. Finally she slowly turned over and faced him, the mass of her tumbling brown tresses framing an oval of face delicate and demure. God, but she's really beautiful . . . Her deep brown eyes were haunted, empty. She lifted her head an inch from the damp pillow and then let it fall again, as though she was too weak to bear the strain of holding it erect. She managed a wan smile. What an actress! How do they learn it? Is it instinct?

"I'm sorry, Cross," she whispered.

And he was truly sorry too. He wanted in that instant to take her in his arms and comfort her, but he knew that she would at once take advantage of it, would exploit it, would try to wring out of a simple act of compassion a promise of marriage. Goddamn! He reined in his feelings. She was gazing toward the window and the thought shot through his mind: She's about to switch her tactics . . . His eyes traveled along the slight outlines of her body stretching under the blanket; she was so tiny and yet somehow so strong, this girl. Woman as body of woman was not in his consciousness now, but there was rolling teasingly through his memory a memory of it. He did not really want to hurt her, but what was he to do? How could he avoid it?

"Dot, let's start from the beginning," he commenced. "Are you going to do what I suggested?"

"What do you mean, Cross?" she hedged, sparring for time, her eyes swimming helplessly at him.

"About the child," he told her. "I've got it all arranged."

She leapt to a sitting position. Her body rocked to and fro; she clenched her fists and shook them at him, her mouth gaping in protest.

"No, no, no!" she pealed hysterically. "Don't ask me *that* again! Please, Cross, if you do—"

"I *am* asking you," he said. "There's nothing else I can do."

She sprang from the bed in her nylon gown and screamed, then ran on bare, scampering feet across the room to the window. He walked toward her, calmly. The door burst open and Myrtle stood staring at them with parted lips and tense eyes.

"If you ask me that again, I'll jump out of the window! I swear I will! I swear, I swear . . ." Dot sobbed, clawing blindly at the window latch.

"Oh, God!" Myrtle exclaimed, grabbing Dot with both arms. "Darling, don't! You don't know what you are doing!" She looked beseechingly at Cross who stood near Dot. Cross had not budged; he regarded Dot coldly. "Please, Cross, help me to get her back to bed . . ."

"Get back in bed, Dot," Cross said in a detached voice; he still did not touch her.

Dot sobbed brokenly, clinging convulsively to Myrtle. Then she slid heavily to the wooden floor, resting on her bare knees. The nylon gown was pulled taut across the curves of her firm, yellow thighs and through the sheer white translucence of the tissue he could see

the dark smudge of her pubic hair. She beat her knees
frantically with her fists, violently shaking her head,
tears oozing from her eyes, her body rocking back and
forth. She keened: "No, no! I'll *never* kill my child! I'll
die first! You can't make me *murder* . . . ! It's my child
and I'll keep it and love it like I love my own life . . . !
Oh, God, don't let this happen to me!" She gulped for
breath and fell prone to the floor, her body jerking with
nervous spasms.

"Help me, Cross," Myrtle begged, struggling
with Dot.

He did not move; he stood looking silently at both of
them. Myrtle stood over Dot, looking from him to Dot.
Yes, she's trying to weigh how much influence this is
having on me, he thought. A woman's business is emotion and her trade is carried on in cash of tears . . . He
would help to keep Dot from leaping out of the window, but that was all he was prepared to do at the moment. And, besides, he was not convinced that she
would leap.

"Come, darling," Myrtle coaxed, lifting Dot.

Dot allowed herself finally to be led back to the bed.
Myrtle eased her upon it and Dot sat and sobbed with
tears streaming through the fingers of her hands which
covered her face.

"I won't kill my child," Dot took up the refrain. "I
won't . . ."

"Darling, get in bed," Myrtle cooed. "The doctor said
you had to be careful. You're not well, you know."

Cross knew that these words were aimed at him.
When Dot was once more in bed, Myrtle turned to him.

"Why do you treat her like that?" she demanded.
"The doctor said—"

"Leave me alone!" he shouted; he did not relent; he
could not.

"I never dreamed anyone like you existed," Myrtle said.

"You know better now," he said tersely.

Myrtle ran from the room. Cross sat on the edge of the bed and tenderly touched Dot's shaking shoulder.

"Dot," he began, "try to listen calmly. This may be the last time I can talk to you like this—"

"Don't say that, Cross. You're going to leave me?" she asked.

"I don't know what I'm going to do," he said.

Dot lay very still. Cross heard an "L" train thundering past outside. Night was falling and a dark blue sheen of sky stood at the windowpane.

"You promised not to tell anybody about this without first telling me," he began.

"Oh, Cross, I *had* to tell the doctor," she said in a rush of words. "I was so nervous and he kept asking me what was the matter—"

"I'm not talking about *that*!"

Dot's eyes showed helpless bewilderment. He knew that her pretended naïveté was particularly dangerous, for in it was a pathetic appeal for love that his heart yearned to answer. He knew that her deception stemmed from her craving for security and that she was expecting him, if he ever caught her in it, to forgive her.

"Don't you know that if you destroy me, you're hurting yourself?" he asked her. "This calling in a lawyer—"

"Oh, Cross!" she wailed. "I didn't! You don't *understand*!"

"I understand more than you think," he told her.

She flung herself into his arms and clutched him frantically. All grief and despair vanished from her face as quickly as a summer rain, and he could not help but marvel at the weapons of a woman when she fought.

Her volatile emotions altered with dialectical suddenness, changing into their opposites, disappearing, hiding under new guises.

"Mary phoned and told me to tell you that she had a lawyer for you," he told her.

"That was Mary on the phone a while back?" she asked with wide eyes.

"Yes."

Dot sighed with such relief that Cross wondered if she had other plots cooking . . .

"Oh, Mary . . . She's crazy," Dot explained it away in a childlike voice. "I don't have to obey her, Cross. The lawyer was her idea."

He would now try to see what was really on her mind.

"Dot, how old are you?" he asked her softly.

She did not look at him; her eyes were steadily before her and yet he knew that she knew that he was staring at her and waiting for an answer.

"Did you hear what I asked you, Dot?" he demanded.

She still did not answer or look at him. Well, he would wait her out. He had been intimately tender with this girl and now he had caught her acting most cruelly against him. What excuse would she give? Then he guessed her strategy; she would give none. She would just be a helpless, hard-put-upon, suffering woman playing her oldest and strongest role.

"Dot, I'm talking to you," he said. "How old are you?"

The knowledge of the criminal threat she held over him stood between them like an invisible wall. She still could not turn to look at him; then she bent suddenly forward, covered her face with her hands and sobbed.

"I don't know what to do," she gulped.

She had failed to answer; instead, she had let him see

the emotional dilemma in which she was caught, let him glimpse the terrible weapon she held in her hand, let him surmise how reluctantly she would use it, but use it she would.

"Look, Dot, you can haul me before a court and get me convicted, but I swear to you that I'll find some way out, you hear?" he warned her. "You lied to me. You told me you were seventeen. You led me to this crime, if you call it a crime. Now, how old are you?"

"I'll be sixteen in June," she breathed, not looking at him.

Cross sighed. "Why did you lie to me?"

"I wanted you," she whispered, her eyelashes nestling against her cheeks.

"And now you want me put into jail for ten, maybe twenty years?"

Myrtle entered and lifted the tray from the bed.

"Darling, I'll never do that to you," Dot said sweetly, too sweetly.

"If you do, you'll never win," he warned her solemnly.

"Maybe Superman'll kill himself and escape everybody?" Myrtle gave forth a brittle laugh. "You *could* run off to South America, too."

She went briskly through the door and Cross balled his fingers in fury. He turned again to Dot.

"Look, start with Ma. Why did you go to her?"

Again Dot became too weak to talk; through tears she groped blindly for Cross's hand and gripped it.

"I was wild— Even my mother won't speak to me," she whimpered.

"Your mother? Does *she* know?" he demanded, amazed.

She gave him a look that begged forgiveness. She had not kept her word. He would never be dumb enough to trust anybody again. Dot's face suddenly brightened with joy.

"Your mother's wonderful," she sang.

Goddammit! Wouldn't Dot ever learn that these assumed poses would never work.

"I understand now why you love her so," Dot floated on warmly. "She has such a *noble* face . . . . And she's *for* us, Crossy. She hates Gladys; she didn't tell me so, but I can feel it. She says your children are beautiful! Oh, Crossy, I'd love to take care of them. I *would!*"

She's out of her mind . . . Did she think that she could take away another woman's children? Were there no limits to her vanity? Dot turned and looked yearningly at him.

"The children, yours and mine, could all be together—"

"Did Gladys tell you that?" he asked with soft irony.

Dot's eyes narrowed as she conjured up the image of Gladys. "She hates me; she hates you— God, she's *awful!*"

"Look, Dot, I'm going to tell you the lay of the land, then you must let your common sense guide you. Gladys will not let me go; her keeping me is her revenge on me for leaving her. Let's live together and ride this out. Or, get rid of the child—"

Dot sat up and looked at him; she had changed.

"Cross, you *got* to get a divorce," she pronounced.

"*Somebody* has to give way in this," he insisted.

"I won't kill the child," she said simply.

She was telling him that she would not let go of the hold she had upon him, no matter what. He stood up.

"I don't give a damn," he muttered. "I couldn't care less—"

"Then, why do you blame me for getting a lawyer?" she demanded.

"I'm not talking to you. I'm talking to myself, about myself," he said.

His eyes were hot and vacant. He was in a rage.

"You're threatening me with jail to make me get a divorce my wife won't give," the words growled out of him.

"Pull off your coat, honey," she seemed to relent.

"Naw; I got to go," he said. "I've got to see Gladys and try to undo some of the harm you've done."

"Aren't you going to tell me *something*?" she begged.

"*You* tell me what to tell you!" he shouted.

Myrtle came in and stood by the bed, and asked, "What did you decide about Dot, Cross?"

"Nothing," he told her bluntly.

"Wouldn't your wife take some money?"

"Sure; if I had it."

"Can't you borrow some?"

"I'm already up to my neck in debt."

"Give her monthly payments—"

"And what'll be left for Dot, then? I'm paying for the car—"

"Sell it," Myrtle suggested.

"I haven't got the car to sell. Gladys has it and she's hanging on to it and I've got to keep up the payments," he explained.

"Well, it's your funeral," Myrtle said. "You can't expect Dot to sit here and not defend herself; can you?"

"All right; put me in jail, if you want to," he spoke through tight lips.

He turned abruptly and walked out. He was so spent that he felt that he was floating down the steps. Through the night's mist the street lamps gleamed dully. He tramped over snow-carpeted sidewalks without knowing it. He had to see Gladys, but he did not know what he would say to her. He paused and rubbed his hand over his eyes. If those who were pressing him knew how little he felt himself as a real being, they would recoil in horror; he felt unreal, scarcely alive. How long could he go on like this? Shame flooded him as he recalled his attempt with the gun. He could not even do *that* . . .

He stopped at a street corner and waited for a south-bound trolley. The snow enforced a hush over the city, muffling the sounds of traffic and the footsteps of pass-ersby. Above him an invisible plane droned through the night sky. Icy wind flapped his overcoat and he turned his back to it to escape its knifelike pain on his face. His eyes caught a scrap of paper whirling uncertainly on currents of wind; he watched it rise, veer, hover, then vanish aimlessly around a corner. A clanging trolley heaved into view and he approached the tracks and sprang upon the trolley when it slowed to a stop. He paid and sat in the rear of the car and closed his eyes and leaned his head against a sweaty windowpane.

Dread was deep in him now; he had to tackle Gladys and he did not know how. The tussle between them had been so long and bitter that there was not much room left for jockeying. Over the years they had hurled at each other every curse word they knew and he felt that his present visit would be by far the most exacting. He had not seen her for more than three months; he made his payments to her by sending a check through the mails every two weeks. His not seeing her had made him forego his joy in seeing his sons and he missed them acutely, but Gladys had so adroitly managed their part-ing that she had extorted his not seeing the children as part of the price he had to pay for his being rid of her. After the terrible scene the last time he had seen her, he had told her that he did not intend to come again, and, in his black mood, he had given her the right to tell the children any damn thing she chose. And Gladys had seized literally upon his words and had written a special delivery letter to his mother informing her that he had disowned his children, branding him an unnatural monster. His mother had summoned him, had upbraided him, wept and prayed.

His head lolled as the trolley jolted through the snowy night streets and his mind drifted back to the time he had been attending day classes at the University of Chicago, majoring in philosophy and working the nightshift in the Post Office. In those days he had not had much time for fun and had been constantly hankering for relaxation. His mother had been in the South, living in the house that she had bought through her lifelong and morbid frugality, and he had been a lonely young man hankering after pleasure in a big city. A stream of her pious letters had urged him to marry, but he had ignored her naïve moralizing and had remained single. Ideas had been his only sustained passion, but he knew that his love of them had that same sensual basis that drew him achingly to the sight of a girl's body swinging in a tight skirt along a sunny street.

He had been more than ready for Gladys when she had first risen on his horizon. He had congratulated himself on having tumbled upon a naïve girl who was gratefully receiving his amorous attentions, and it was not until long afterwards that he had discovered that she had waited patiently while he had gropingly strayed into her domain, and then she had quietly closed the trap door over him. If some ironic enemy had been intending to tangle him in an ill-suited marriage, his self-enforced abstinence could not have better prepared him for her. She had been living in his South Side rooming house and he had spoken to her only casually. A registered nurse, quiet, perhaps more than a little repressed and with maybe a tendency toward the hysterical, she was soft-spoken, brown-skinned, and well-made. Sometimes he had seen her in her handsome nurse's uniform and he had admitted that she looked distinctively attractive in it.

Early one rainy autumn afternoon five years ago he had gone down into the vestibule to go out to drive his Ford to work and had found her standing there, sheltering herself against the roaring downpour. He could see the edges of her white uniform showing around the hem of her coat. Surmising that she was trying to get to work, he had offered her a lift. Enroute he engaged her in a bantering conversation which had ended with her accepting an invitation to have a drink with him at the GOLDEN KEY the next afternoon.

That was how it began. The next afternoon—the rain was still falling—he sat waiting for her in a rear booth of the tavern, hunched over an unfinished drink. She presented herself a half hour late all done up in a smart, dark blue suit with a white silk blouse. A red silk scarf was tied over her head and flouncing over her whole body was a transparent, plastic raincoat. He helped her out of her coat and noticed that tiny drops of rain gleamed on her wide forehead and her pert nose. From her there drifted to him the odor of lilacs and autumn leaves . . .

As they drank they talked about themselves, their families, racial problems. He found that she had no settled tastes or convictions, and he was not a little flattered to discover that she was curious about his notions and had the good sense to defer to him when he told her something of importance. Years later Cross realized that she had had enough sagacity to clear ample psychological ground about her so that he could move in at ease and without knowing that she was luring him. Her feminine instinct placed him at once in the role of a strong and reliable man and encouraged him to play it; he found himself liking to talk to her.

He had already made up his mind to invite her to dinner when she suddenly lifted her left wrist and looked at her watch, wailing:

"Oh, God! It's almost six. I've got to go."

"I thought you were going to be free," he said disappointedly.

"You didn't ask me to be," she said quickly. "I've got to go to a cocktail party. You know, the white and colored nurses' associations are merged and if a colored member doesn't show up when she's invited, they might get the notion that we don't want to belong." She frowned and stared off. "Really, I feel out of place in a roomful of whites. I'm afraid I'll be the only spook there."

"Guess I'll catch up on my sleep," he yawned.

"If that's all you've got to do, come with me to the party. Then I'll have dinner with you. And I'd feel better if you were with me."

They hustled out of the bar and drove to the Loop. The party was paralyzingly dull, with Cross and Gladys standing huddled together at one end of a huge, buzzing roomful of people, holding their drinks self-consciously, watching the others. He was amazed at how uneasy Gladys was in the presence of whites. She's too conscious of her color, he thought.

"Look, buck up," he sought to put some backbone in her. "Don't let the mere existence of these people intimidate you."

"They think they're *something* and we're *nothing*," she snapped.

"It's up to us to make ourselves something," he argued. "A man creates himself . . ."

"You are a *man*," she said simply.

He understood now; it was the helplessness of dependence that made her fret so. Men made themselves and women were made only through men.

They had been there only half an hour when Gladys whispered to him: "Let's get to goddamn hell out of here. They make me sick!"

"Okay," he assented. "But whites don't scare me."

They went straight to a bar on the South Side where Gladys sulked bitterly. He studied her, wondering what memories lay under her mood. Through gentle questioning he stumbled upon it; she had attended a racially mixed school in her adolescence and the snubs and ostracism had branded her with a deep sense of not belonging and a yearning to have her status as an outsider cleared of shame. Her consciousness of being an outcast moved him toward her, enabled him to drape about her a net of tender compassion. Underneath sex and common interests flowed a profounder tide of identity.

After dinner they began to drink in earnest, then they danced in a far South Side night club and it was while holding her in his arms on the dance floor that desire for her leaped in him and it carried an extra urge to bind her to him and make her feel her humanity; he hungered for her as an image of woman as body of woman, but also as a woman of his own color who was longing to conquer the shame imposed upon her by her native land because of her social and racial origin. Gladys finally said that she wanted some fresh air and they went to a little bar on 47th Street where they drank some more. They got quite drunk.

"I ought to be getting in," Gladys said. "It's late."

"Okay. I'll put the car up and we'll walk home; is that all right?"

"Anything you do is all right," she said, her head lolling and her eyes a little glazed.

He took her arm and guided her wandering steps to the car; he kissed her when they were inside and she went limp. But when he attempted to caress her further, she resisted. He put the car in the garage, then walked beside her, his arm about her waist.

"I'm drunk, really drunk," she said as though talking to herself.

"I am too," he confessed, chuckling.

It was raining and she began to stumble. Giggling, they supported each other. It was after three o'clock in the morning and they were fairly floating. The rain began to fall in broad, steady sheets and Cross, who wore no hat, let his coat flop open.

"Honey, you're getting wet," she said.

"I don't feel it," he said.

"But you'll catch cold!"

"Naw!"

He suggested another drink when they were near the rooming house and she agreed. They had three each. In the vestibule of their building, he kissed her; then, on the landing leading to their rooms, he kissed her again in the stillness and darkness.

Nestling close to him, she mumbled as out of a dream: "I hate white people."

"Why?"

"They're mean."

"Did white people ever bother you?"

"Hell, naw! I wouldn't let 'em," she said belligerently.

"Then why do you hate 'em?"

" 'Cause they're *different* from me. I don't like 'em even to look at me. They make me self-conscious, that's why. Ain't that enough?"

"If you say so, baby. But, listen, *I'm* not white."

"That's what's so nice about it," she said drunkenly.

He led her to his room and when he switched on the light she had a fleeting moment of soberness and shook her head, taking an aimless step backward. He tried to kiss her again and she twisted out of reach.

He switched off the light and kissed her and she melted, letting her lips cling fully to his; he carried her to the bed and they slept together in their damp clothes, being too drunk to undress. It was the beginning of the unleashing of a mutual, silent, and intense passion. During the following week, Cross had her in his bed, on the floor, standing up, in the bathroom . . . She made no demands, imposed no conditions, set no limits; she simply clung to him and when she spoke at all on general topics it was about how good it was to have someone to be with when the whole world was white and she was colored; he could say nothing to her about her color consciousness because he did not know how to handle it. In time he grew to accept it along with her womanness.

Cross's drunken carousal in the rain gave him pneumonia and Gladys stayed home from her job to nurse him. Quietly and all the time avoiding discussing it, she took total charge of him, created a situation that spelled unconditional surrender. She straightened out his disordered room, sent his piles of soiled linen to the laundry, gave him his penicillin injections, cooked and brought up his food. He accepted it all meekly, gazing up at her in humble gratitude when his fever was over one hundred and four. He had never been so comfortably looked after in all his life.

The climax of their relationship came unexpectedly when the fat, black, religious landlady told Cross that, now that he was well, she could no longer permit Miss Dennis "actually living in your room like that.

You know it ain't decent. I want folks to respect my home".

He told Gladys and she wept; he held her in his arms till she quieted.

"What must people think of me?" she moaned.

"To hell with that landlady," Cross said.

"You think the others in the house feel the same way?"

"God, I don't know."

"I hope it doesn't get to my job . . ."

His head reeled. He had not thought of that.

"I don't want to leave you," she told him.

"So; it's settled."

"But what are we going to do?" her voice echoed with ringing meanings.

It was the first time he had thought of marriage and it frightened him. But could he abandon her like that? He felt that if he had said that he was through with her, she would have accepted it, humbly. And it made him feel guilty. Well, would he ever find anyone better than she? He studied her face for a moment, then said impulsively to her: "Let's get married."

She had wept again. They rented an apartment and were furnishing it when they were married. Gladys had definite ideas about the home and Cross, having none, deferred to her. She argued gently that the thing to do was to buy a house and they did, arranging for the payments to fall due monthly.

The advent of the birth of their first child, a son, Cross, Junior, marked the commencement of protracted trouble. After safely transporting Gladys, who was in violent labor, to the hospital, Cross went out with a picked group of his Post Office cronies—Pink, Joe, and Booker—to stage a celebration which ended for his cronies after seven guzzling hours, but which, for Cross, extended itself for two whole days and nights during which he managed to pick up—he never knew exactly where or how—a brown-skinned girl who encouraged him to continue his "bat" as long as he had money to spend.

As strenuously as he could try, he could never recall quite clearly as to how he had come to bring the girl home with him and he never saw her after that to inquire. He suspected that he had drunkenly decided to do it after his money had run out; he had confused recollections of being ejected from bars for nonpayment of drinks. Before his nonstop carousal, Gladys had tried to reach him by telephoning from the hospital, and worried, she had come home with the baby and a nurse to find Cross unshaven, bleary-eyed and in bed with what Gladys chose to call his "whore". Gladys' reaction had been so savage and intense that she had wept for days, refused food, sat in deep moods of depression. Finally she demanded of Cross despairingly: "Aren't you happy with me?"

"Sure," he had said lightly, not wanting to think about it.

"Where did you meet the girl?"

"In a bar, I think . . ." he said vaguely.

"How in God's name can you pick up a girl in a bar?"

In a nervous rage he had demanded: "Do *you* want to go? Or do you want *me* to go? I told you I was *drunk*, didn't I?"

Gladys resisted an explanation that enthroned the demonical as a motive for his actions; she sensed the presence of irrational forces that could trample her and her home.

Despite this they remained together, but the naturalness and trust that had characterized their earlier relationship were gone. Cross hoped that Gladys had written off that shameful episode as an unrepeatable aberration which she would forget. But whenever he drank she would fling it at him and, in the end, a slow, mounting resentment rose in him toward her. More and more she sulked and, as he suffered her nagging, he felt increasingly walled off from her; but the more he felt it the more he sought to hide it, and finally there crept into his dealings with her a weird quality of irony. It first manifested itself in an innocent question: How could he help Gladys? And the moment he asked himself that question he knew that he did not love her and perhaps had never loved her . . . She had become for him an object of compassion. He was now haunted by the idea of finding some way to make her hate him. Her hatred would be a way of squaring their relationship, of curing her of her love for him, of setting her free as well as himself.

One winter when Cross was ill, Gladys nursed him and tried to reestablish over him her old emotional authority. It resulted in another pregnancy from which there issued two more sons, twins this time, Peter and Robert. Gladys had been hopeful, but not for long. Expenses increased and Cross's salary was squeezed. Gladys now had her hands full while Cross worked extra hours to pull in more money. The house was bedlam, filled with shouting, tumbling children. Cross found it all but impossible to sleep during the day and he became so nervous that Gladys would flare at him: "What are you trying to do? Drive us all out so that you can fill the house with your whores?"

Dating from this period, a wave of self-loathing began to engulf Cross. Each time he realized how much he had lost control of his life, his self-hatred swelled threateningly. He knew himself too well to blame Gladys and he was scrupulous enough to let her know it, which baffled and tortured her all the more. She longed for some simple definition of their troubles that she could grasp. She thought that she was losing her physical appeal for him and she went, without telling him—and submitted to an extraordinarily expensive operation to have her breasts lifted! That more than anything else had depressed Cross, filled him with a compassion mingled with disgust. He had been so stunned by it that he could never discuss it with her.

One afternoon in a bar, dawdling over a drink, he recalled how stunned Gladys had been when she had come home from the hospital with Junior and had found him in bed with the girl. That fantastic happening had now become accepted as an "accident". Well, why could not another "accident" happen? One so fatal and unique that it would make her remember the last one as a guide by which to interpret it! He was far from planning anything overtly criminal; it was a complicated psychological attack whose consequences would clarify Gladys' feelings about him. But what on earth could that "accident" be? It would have to be so decisive that she would tell him to go and never come back. He would support her and the children, of course. He sipped his drink idly, turning his wish carefully over in his mind. His self-hate, his aversion for Gladys, his perpetual toying with his own feelings had resulted in there flashing into his mind a confoundingly luminous image. He had it! By God, this was it! It could flow from him as naturally as it could be embraced by her, and it was simple. Though the seed of the idea came from the time when he had brought the girl home, it had only psychological affinities with it. Could he carry it out? It would take cool nerve, insight, timing, and ruthless execution. What decided him was a cynical question: "If I fail, I'll be no worse off than I am now, will I?"

He finished his nightshift in the Post Office at four

o'clock in the morning; then, with his cronies, he went to the SALTY DOG, a bar around the corner from his house, for what they jokingly called a "daycap", since they slept during the day. At five o'clock he went home for breakfast which Gladys was preparing in the kitchen in her kimono. Afterwards he went directly to bed. But on *that* morning, he would not stop for his "daycap"; he would go back for his drink *after* he had done it. Such timing would make his actions seem more *normal*. Furthermore, his going back to have a drink with the boys would give him an alibi, in case he needed one. Above all, the children should be sound asleep when he did it; he did not want to disturb them in any way.

He decided upon a Friday morning to carry his plan into action. After he left work he detached himself unobtrusively from his friends and went directly home, arriving shortly after four o'clock. Gladys had just gone into the kitchen and was putting a pot of coffee on the gas stove. He walked in and advanced wordlessly upon her, his eyes fastened on her face.

"Oh, good morning, Cross," she said, glancing at the electric clock on the wall. "You're early, aren't you?"

He stood directly in front of her, his eyes unblinking and his face a blank mask.

"What's the matter?" she asked, backing away a step.

He reached forward and gave her a slap with his open palm, not hard, but stinging and with enough force to send her stumbling backwards into a corner.

"Cross!" her voice was not loud, but charged with shock.

Then for a moment she was still as stone, staring at him, her lips parted, her hands lifted to shield her face. She lay against the wall, her kimono open and showing her full breasts. The sound that came from her now seemed to coincide with her recognition of danger.

"No, no, no . . ." she spoke in low, clipped words, the inflection of her voice rising.

As he advanced toward her again, her mouth opened slowly and her chest heaved as she sucked in her breath to scream. He roughly seized both of her hands in his left hand and slapped her once more, then stood leering down at her with a twisted face.

"Oh, God!" she screamed. "Don't kill me, Cross!"

As if pulled by cables of steel, he whirled and walked from the kitchen and out of the front door, hearing Gladys sobbing. He had not uttered a single syllable and the whole assault had taken no more than a minute. When he reached the door of the bar, he stood a moment to collect himself. He saw his pals sitting in the rear; he eased himself toward them and sat down.

"Where did you go, Crossy?" big, fat Joe asked carelessly.

"I was making a phone call," he said, lighting a cigarette and controlling his hand to keep it from trembling.

They began arguing politics. He spoke with composure, glancing now and then at the clock on the wall, wondering what was happening at home. He was pleased that the children had not heard him. Would she call the police? He doubted it; she would wait and talk to him first. Would she tell the children? He did not think so. Would she go to see his mother? Maybe. Her mind must be in a turmoil . . . At five-thirty, he said casually: "Well, guys, I've got to cut out and get some shut-eye."

He rose and waved good-bye. Now was the test. If his abrupt, physical attack upon Gladys provoked an immediate storm of reaction, then it would go badly for him; but if she was frantically trying to find some explanation for it, then all might go well. The main strategy was not to let her settle upon any one reason for it, to keep her judgment torturingly uncertain. Everything depended upon how much pretended incredulity he could demonstrate, how much simulated surprise he could convincingly sustain. As he turned into the walk leading to the house, he had a bad moment; a surging impulse made him want to turn about and dodge it all. He shook it off, went to the front door, entered the hallway and went into the bathroom. That had always been his routine and he adhered to it now. As he washed he whistled a tune, not steadily, but in snatches, not like a man intentionally trying to create an impression of carefreeness, but like a man with nothing serious on his mind. There was not a sound of movement in the house. Where was Gladys? Had she funked and fled? No; she would not leave the children . . . He emerged from the bathroom and went into the kitchen; he knew that she was not there, but he had to act as though he expected to find her frying his bacon and eggs. On the gas stove a blue flame glowed under the coffee pot and the scent of burning metal assailed his nostrils. He went to the stove and saw that the coffee had evaporated from the pot and that the metal around the bottom gleamed red hot. He shut off the gas and looked over his shoulder. That meant that Gladys had quit the kitchen the moment he had left the house. That's *normal* . . .

"Gladys!" he called out quietly, questioningly.

There was no answer. He made for the bedroom, calling again: "Gladys!"

Silence. He opened the bedroom door and asked into the semi-gloom: "Gladys, aren't you up yet?"

Silence. He hesitated a second, then switched on the wall light. Gladys was huddled on the bed, her eyes black with fear. She was so immobile that at first he thought that maybe she was dead, had died of shock.

But, no; he could see her chest slowly rising and falling.

"What's the matter?" he asked softly.

She did not answer. Tears rolled down her cheeks and her fingers writhed.

"Didn't you know you left the coffee pot on the fire? All the water boiled out and it was red hot . . ."

She did not move.

"What's the matter? Are you ill?" he asked.

He walked toward her and she lunged violently backwards, falling from the bed to the floor, leaving one of her bedroom slippers on the quilt. He stopped, blinked his eyes in simulated bewilderment. He advanced upon her again and Gladys shook her head wildly.

"No, no, no . . . Don't hit me, Cross! *Don't* . . . *!*" she whimpered convulsively, barricading her face and head with her elbows.

He stared at her, his mouth drooping open in mock amazement. "What's the matter with you?"

"Cross," she sobbed. "I never thought you'd *hit* me."

He stepped away from her imperceptibly, as though stunned. "*Hit* you? What in the world are you talking about?"

He went to her and she shrank, burrowing herself against the wall. He caught hold of her shoulder and she lifted her eyes and stared at him and he returned her stare with make-believe astonishment until her eyes fell.

"What's the *matter*, Gladys! You're *shaking*! Here, let me put you to bed. I'll call a doctor . . ."

He was still holding onto her shoulder and felt a slight lessening of tension in her muscles. Trembling, she allowed him to lead her to the bed and push her gently upon it. She looked at him with eyes filled with shock.

"Lie down and keep still," he said hurriedly, feigning

deep anxiety. "I'll have the doctor here in a minute. If you felt like that, why didn't you phone me at the Post Office?"

Delicately he pulled the cover over her, went to the telephone at the bedside, picked it up, dialed the first letter and then glanced at her.

"No, no, no . . . No, Cross," she begged; her eyes were pools of bewilderment. She breathed uncertainly. Her gaze fell and her fingers fluttered.

"Now, listen, you'd better have the doctor take a look at you," he said, play-acting and pitching his voice to a tone of half-command and half-entreaty.

She began to sob again, burying her face in the pillow. He sat on the edge of the bed and patted her shoulder.

"Take it easy. Have you any pains? What's happened? Where are the children?"

She stared at him again, unable to believe the evidence of her senses. Her head rocked on its neck. Her mouth trembled and she had to move her lips several times before she could speak.

"Why did you do it?" she whimpered. Then she spoke fully, almost rising to a point of objectivity. "Do you hate me that much?"

"Do *what*?" he asked, replacing the receiver upon the hook of the transmitter. "*Hate* you? What *are* you talking about?"

"Oh, God!" she croaked. "You *know* what you did?"

Fear filled him for a second. She was in her crisis now; would she veer against him or would she still float in indecision?

"You're dreaming!" he shot at her. "Do you know what you are saying?"

"You hit me . . . You beat me . . . What *for*?" she asked insistently.

"*Beat* you?" he echoed, as though he had to repeat the word to believe in its reality. His face was the living personification of stupefied surprise. "You are out of your mind. Now, look here, be calm. Tell me what happened."

Her chest heaved, emptying her lungs; then she looked distractedly about the room like a rat searching for a hole. She was a tiny child hearing a grownup tell a tale that it did not believe, but it dared not challenge that tale because it had no way of successfully disputing it, feeling that its reasoning was not acceptable.

"Cross, you came into the kitchen and knocked me down," she explained in a low voice.

"You are crazy!" He stood and pretended to look suspiciously about the room. "*Who's* been here?"

"You!"

"Good Lord, you're wild!" He shook his head. "I *just* left the bar; I went there directly from work and had a drink, like always . . . Look, get hold of yourself." He wagged his head, aping bewilderment. "Have you been *drinking*?"

"Oh, Cross!"

"Listen, if you don't stop I'll call the doctor. You've got the children to look after," he copied tones of responsibility.

She stared at him, dumbfounded. Slowly, she shook her head. *Yes!* The idea was working in her mind. It was coming off much easier than he had thought. But he had to be firm and not retreat from his position.

"When do you think I hit you, Gladys?" he mimicked the compassion of one resolved to be lenient.

"I *didn't* imagine it," she whimpered.

It was working; she was beginning to wonder if what had happened had not been wiped from his memory. Silence followed. The restoration of normality must de-

pend upon *his* initiative; what had so mysteriously occurred must seem to have been swallowed up in his
mind as though it had never transpired; he must not in
any way grant it one whit of objective reality.

"Look, kid," he began kindly, "I know we are not
the loving couple one reads about in books. But you
mustn't let our troubles break you down. There's no
sense in brooding 'til you start imagining things. You
need a rest . . ."

She clutched his arm. "Cross, don't you *remember*
what you did?"

"Darling, really, I hate to say it, but you're *off*!"

"I'm sane, Cross," she said, unable to restrain her
tears.

She collected her senses; she was no longer physically
afraid; she was fearful of something more menacingly
dark than a slap.

"I don't know what's happened to you," he played his
role.

"Cross, you *remember* you hit me," she moaned.

"I *didn't*!" His face pretended to grow hard. "You're
mixed up . . . Tell me, *who's* been here?"

"Nobody," she breathed.

"Who *else* saw me come in here?"

"Nobody," she whispered, her eyes widening with
understanding.

"Look, Junior's coming," he spoke in a low, rapid
voice. "Brace up . . . You'll upset 'im."

"Is it possible?" she asked herself in a despairing
whisper.

She pulled herself unsteadily from the bed to the
dresser and began arranging her hair with palsied hands.
He could see her watching his reflection in the mirror;
he had to be careful. She had forgotten her bedroom
slipper on the quilt; he got it and held it out to her.

"Here; you better put it on," he said in a neutral voice.

"Oh," she said in confusion.

She obeyed him with movements charged with suppressed fear. But when he looked at her she glanced quickly away.

Junior, four years of age, came running in in his pyjamas. "I'm hungry," he sang, lifting an earnest, brown face to his father.

Cross swept the boy up in his arms and fondled him. Watching Cross out of the corners of her eyes, Gladys went hesitantly from the room to prepare breakfast. Cross burrowed his head playfully into Junior's stomach and the boy giggled. He was now certain that he could handle it. This was the beginning, the setup; next time would be the pay off.

During the following week, under the cover of anxious solicitude, Cross craftily urged Gladys to see a doctor and she politely refused. A few days later she timidly begged *him* to see a doctor, telling him that she was *certain* that what had happened was a recurrence of what he had done with the girl. In a tone of play-acting shock, looking her levelly in the eyes, he scoffed at her interpretation and assured her that he was absolutely sane. He now made it a rigorous rule never to refer to the "accident"; all mention of it had to come from her. And, as time went on, she found it more and more difficult to bring it up; but he knew that the thought of it was continuously hovering in the background of her mind.

One day, puckering up her lips and touching his cheek gently as she spoke—hoping by such a gesture to negate any hint that she thought him insane—she expressed concern that he might harm the children "while in one of your spells". He patted her shoulder and said soothingly: "Don't worry, darling. Everything's all right." She beseeched him to reduce his drinking, his smoking, to sleep more. She strove to keep more order in the house, chiding the children lovingly not to "make noise and get on poor papa's nerves".

He chose Easter Sunday morning for his next attack. He knew that nothing would be further from Gladys' mind then, for her attention would be involved in buying Easter egg coloring and arranging new clothes for the children's Easter outing. He worked the night of Easter Eve and went straight home and found Gladys alone in the kitchen; she whirled with fear as he came in, for she knew that he was as early as on that other fateful morning. Again he walked slowly toward her, wordlessly, his facial expression simulating dementia.

"No, no, no . . . !"

He slapped her resoundingly and she went down like a log.

"Junior!" she yelled. "Somebody help me!"

He stooped and slapped her once more, his face contorted in an imitation of rage; then he turned and rushed out, hurried to the bar and joined Joe, Pink and Booker who had not missed him this time. He sat coolly talking and drinking with them, but his mind was trying to picture what was happening at home. At a little past five he went back, let himself in with his key, and headed as usual to the bathroom to wash up. He lathered his hands and whistled softly. Suddenly he was still, hearing muffled footsteps moving haltingly along the hallway. What's she doing . . . ? Then all was quiet. He dried his face and hands and when he emerged he did not have to look for Gladys, for there she was at the door, confronting him with his gun, pointing it straight at his heart.

"Cross," she said heavily, struggling to manage her breathing, "I can't bear with you another minute. Pack your things and get out, *now*! You're crazy, a danger to yourself and others!"

He saw such craven fear in her face that he was afraid that she would lose control of herself and pull the trigger, causing him to die messily in a trap of his own devising.

"My God," his voice rang with sincerity. "Take it *easy* . . ."

His nervousness made Gladys step quickly away from him and wave the gun threateningly.

"If you come near me, I'll shoot!" she cried. "And I'll go free, for you're crazy!"

Her arm trembled and she reached toward him, the gun barrel coming within inches of his right temple.

"Gladys," he breathed, leaning weakly against a wall. "I can't get my clothes unless you let me pass."

"You're sick, Cross," she pronounced in neutral, distant tones.

Realizing that she was blocking his path, she stepped cautiously to one side. He went into the bedroom and began to pack. She waited in the doorway, still nervously clutching the gun.

"Gladys," he ventured to protest.

"Get out!" she ordered in a frenzy.

He packed a suitcase and stood looking at her out of the corners of his eyes. "I'll come back for the rest of my stuff later—"

"You let me know and I'll *send* you your things," she said. "Don't *ever* set foot in this house without *first* telling me, you hear! If you do, it'll be dangerous for you."

"I'll phone you," he mumbled.

She held open the front door, still brandishing the gun loosely in her shaking hand. He saw her legs wobbling; he walked over the threshold, sweating, fearing that he would stumble.

"See a doctor, Cross," she said, slamming the door.

On the sidewalk he paused and saw her peering at him from behind one of the lace window curtains in the living room, still grasping the gun. He walked on and filled his lungs with crisp morning air. It had worked without a hitch.

Cross roused himself on the jolting trolley, wiped a clear spot on the sweaty windowpane and saw that he had ridden past Gladys' place. Good God . . . He rushed to the front of the car and when it slowed he swung off. As he neared the house his steps faltered. He was doubtful if Gladys would help him, but his predicament was so knotty that he had to try, whatever the outcome. He mounted the steps and paused; his instincts warned him away from this Gladys whom he had made hate him too well. But he had to see her. He pushed the button of the doorbell and almost in the moment of his pushing it, the door flung open and Gladys stood before him, grim, erect. Out of a tightly organized face two deep-set eyes regarded him with composed hate.

"Hello, Gladys," he mumbled.

"I've been waiting for you," she said with placid irony. "I watched you creep up the walk like a doomed man. Are you scared of your home now?"

"I want to talk to you about something important," he told her.

A twisted smile played on Gladys' rouged lips. "I suppose it's about Miss Dorothy Powers, hunh?"

Anger flashed through him. No; he had to be calm.

"That's it, Gladys," he admitted, forcing a smile.

She stepped to one side and he moved gingerly into

the hallway, feeling for the first time intimidated by Gladys. He glanced about apprehensively, his body screaming for a drink to brace him for this ordeal.

"Where're the kids?" he asked to fill the gaping silence.

"I knew you were coming," she announced, "so I sent them for the afternoon to the house of a friend of mine." Her voice was a midnight bell tolling tidings of bad news to come.

He walked into the living room and sat. Gladys followed and stood at the other end of the room and regarded him with hostile eyes. He could feel that she was clamoring for an emotional scene. Well, he would refuse her any such satisfaction. He would be polite, bantering, if possible.

"A young lady visited you this morning, I think," he said, trying to rid his voice of anxiety.

"You mean that bitch you sent—!" The hot lava of hate leaped out.

"Gladys, I didn't send anybody here," he cut in quickly.

"Cross, for God's sake, why do you insist on being such a crawling coward? You *sent* her here—"

"I didn't, I tell you!"

"You're lying!"

"Gladys, I know how you feel about me—"

"You ought to," she spat at him. "Do you think you can walk over me? Well, you won't, ever! You sent that little whore here to beg me . . ."

He tried to stop listening. It was going worse than he thought. Well, if she wanted to blast Dot, let her. The main thing was the question of divorce.

"There is one thing, by God," she roared, "that you are going to do! You are going to *respect* me. You can't send a filthy, stinking little tart like that to talk to me.

You can be sure I gave your bitch a hot welcome, and she won't forget it, not soon!" Gladys groped for words, her mouth open. "And while I'm on it, let me settle one more question. You'll *not* get a divorce. For a rotten slut like her, *never*! That's the way I feel and I'm not ashamed of it! If you can be dirty, then so can I! Keep on living with her, but if she asks you to make her respectable, tell her you can't! Take your Dorothy and fuck her and let her give you a litter of bastards. That's all she's fit for, and you, too, it seems! Is that clear?"

Her hysterical tirade made him ashamed for her. The satisfaction she was deriving from it was obscene.

"Look, I'm not going to argue with your feelings," he clutched at words to stem the tide, striving to be judicious, balanced. "Let's arrange something. I'm supporting you and the children—"

"And by the living hell, you'll keep *on*!"

"Okay. I agree. But your welfare depends on my job—"

He jerked as she burst into a gale of cynical laughter. "So, you've been to the Post Office?" she asked. "They put the fear of God into you, hunh? That's why you came crawling to me . . ."

Cross froze. Had she already told the postal officials about the possibility of his being convicted of rape? He had come to bargain with her, but if she had already talked, the game was all but lost.

"What are you talking about?" he asked quietly.

"Cross, are you stupid?" There was a mocking pity in her tone. "I must protect myself . . . That little whore of yours had not been gone from here an hour before my lawyer and I had gone to the Post Office—"

"Why?"

He knew why she had gone, but he wanted to know how far she had gone. Maybe his job was already lost!

Gladys spoke quietly, as though she were a school teacher explaining a complicated problem to a dullard. She came to within a few feet of Cross and sat.

"Cross, you really cannot expect me to think of you and your troubles," she said. "You're intelligent and you know what you're doing. I had to act in my own defense. I went straight to the Postmaster and told him that your Miss Powers was about to charge you with rape—"

"Did she tell you that?" Cross asked, feeling that his chair was whirling him round.

"Of course she did," Gladys informed him with a smile. "Do you think she's informing you of her moves against you? The Postmaster knows, of course, that you cannot marry the girl . . . And if you are convicted, you're ruined. Now, the Postal Inspector has your case, see?"

Cross had no will to gainsay her; he knew that she was summing up his situation accurately.

"Cross, you must not be naïve," she continued. "There's nothing that Miss Powers can do but charge you, unless she's willing to live with you and bear your child . . . And I doubt if she loves you that much." She paused, lit a cigarette, eyeing Cross the while. "Now, there are some rather disagreeable things I must say to you." She lifted her left hand and with her right hand she pulled down the little finger of her left hand and said: "Number One: You're signing this house over to me at once. Number Two: You're signing over the car to me. Number Three: You're going to the Post Office tonight and borrow eight hundred dollars from the Postal Union on your salary. I've already made the arrangements with the Postal Inspector. He's okayed it. I want that money to clear the titles of both the house and the car." She stood, lifted her hand to bar his words. "I know you want to say no," she said. "But you can't. Cross, understand this: so far as I'm concerned, you're *through*! I'm squeezing you like a lemon. If you *don't* do what I'm asking, in the morning I shall keep an appointment with Miss Powers. She, *I*, and her lawyer will go to the 49th Street Police Station and I will help her bring charges against you. I'm not justifying my actions. I'm not apologizing, see? I'm just telling you. That's how things stand between us, Cross."

He was willing to sign over everything, but he did not want to borrow the money; it would mean indebtedness for him for two years to come. And he could use that money to try to bribe Dot . . .

"They may not let me have the money," he said.

"Mr. Dumb," she said scornfully, "if the Postal Union thought you were going to be indicted for rape, they'd not let you have the money, for you'd have no job. I led them to believe that the girl would abort the child, that you'd pay her off . . . I made sure with the Postmaster that your job was safe, and the Postal Union has been told that it's all right . . ."

"But the girl can *still* charge me," Cross protested without strength. "What game's this you're playing?"

"*My* game," Gladys said.

"The eight hundred dollars," he was pleading now, "could keep the girl and I could make payments to you—"

"I don't give a damn about that girl," she snapped. "What happens between you and her is your business!"

Gladys was using Dot to drag money from him and at the same time betraying Dot! Cross wanted to close his eyes and sleep this nightmare away.

"If you get eight hundred dollars, you'll not help the girl?"

"Hell, no! Why should I? Let that bitch rot!"

He was properly trapped. There was nothing more to say. This was a cold and vindictive Gladys created by him. He rose and moved toward the door.

"What's your answer?" she asked.

"Okay. I'll get the money. I'll phone you tonight."

"Oh, there's one other thing," she said, opening the door for him. "Is your life insurance paid up?"

"Hunh?" His voice sounded far away. "Yes; yes . . ."

"Have you changed the beneficiary?" she asked.

"No; why should I?"

"I just wanted to know," she said.

He felt as though he were already dead and was listening to her speak about him. He went out and did not glance back. He was so depressed that he was not aware of trampling through the deep snow. About him were sounds that had no meaning. When he came fully to himself, his feet were like two icy stumps. I must have fever . . . He paused and stared around him. He was tired. Oh, God, I got to get that money for Gladys . . . He looked about for a taxi. Oh, there's the "L" . . . He ran for the entrance, stumbled up the steps of the "L", fished a dime from his pocket, paid, and rushed to the platform just as a Loopbound train slid to a stop. He found a seat, fell into it, and sat hunched over, brooding.

His seeing Gladys had compounded his problems. If he obeyed her, he was lost; and if he did not obey her, he was lost. Yet, because he could not make up his mind to ditch it all, he had to follow her demands.

Before reaching Roosevelt Road the "L" dipped underground. Cross rose, swaying with the speed of the train, and traversed each coach until he came to the first car whose front window looked out upon a dim stretch of tunnel. He leaned his forehead against the glass and stared at the rushing ribbons of steel rails whose glinting surfaces vanished beneath his feet.

When his station arrived, he got off and went toward the Post Office, a mass of steel and stone with yellow windows glowing, a mass that rose sheerly toward an invisible sky. The night air was still; it had begun to grow a little warmer. It's going to snow again, he thought idly. Yes, he'd see about the loan right now, but he'd not work tonight. He hungered for sleep. He flashed his badge to the guard at the door and went inside. Where's that Postal Union office? Yes; there on the right . . . He pushed open the door and saw Finch, the union secretary, sitting quietly, his hat on, chewing an unlighted cigar and holding a deck of soiled playing cards in his hands. Cross approached Finch's desk and for a moment they stared at each other. He suddenly hated Finch's whiteness, not racially, but just because he was white and safe and calm and he was not.

"Damon, hunh?"

"Yes."

"I was waiting for you," Finch said. "Sit down."

Cross obeyed. He did not want to look at Finch; he knew that the man knew his troubles and it made him ashamed; instead, he stared stupidly at the pudgy, soft fingers as they shuffled the cards.

"You look like an accident going somewhere to happen," Finch commented.

"I'm under the weather," Cross confessed. "I want to renew that eight-hundred-dollar loan I had last year—"

"Oh, yes." Finch looked up. "Your wife's been in."

White fingers took the cigar from thin lips and a brown stream of tobacco juice spewed into a spittoon. Finch replaced the cigar, chewed it, and settled it carefully again in his jaw.

"You colored boys get into a lot of trouble on the South Side," Finch gave a superior smile. "You must have a hot time out there every day, hunh?"

Cross stiffened. His accepting Finch's sneering at his racial behavior was a kind of compound interest he had to pay on his loan.

"Is the loan possible?" Cross asked.

"The Postmaster said it's all right," Finch said, finally stacking the cards and flinging them to one side, as though ridding himself of something unpleasant. "Half of my time's spent taking care of you colored boys . . . What goes on on the South Side?"

Cross cleared his throat to control himself. "I don't know," he mumbled. "I'm offering my house as security—"

"I'm ahead of you, Damon," Finch said. "On the strength of your wife's plea, I've had the papers all drawn up. Boy, you've got a good wife. You ought to take care of her—"

"I do," Cross mumbled.

"If you did, you wouldn't be in this mess," Finch said. He pushed the contract toward Cross. "Here, sign . . ."

Cross signed clumsily, his nervousness letting a blob of ink smear blackly across the page. He fumbled with a blotter to soak it up.

"Let me do that," Finch said, taking the blotter from Cross. "Looks like a chicken with dirty feet ran over this contract." He handed Cross a carbon copy of the contract, then opened a drawer and pulled forth a sheaf of vouchers. "How do you want this? A check or cash?"

"Cash. I'd like the money tonight."

"Why not? It's your money."

Finch initialed a voucher for cash and flipped it at Cross.

"Okay. Get going," Finch said, yanking his thumb toward the door.

Cross stood and wanted to spit at the man. He edged forward and opened the door.

"Shut the door when you go out," Finch called, picking up his deck of cards and beginning to shuffle them again.

"Yes; of course," Cross said.

He pulled the door softly shut and sighed. Well, that was done. Then he stiffened. One of the Assistant Postmasters was bearing down upon him, his grey eyes intent on Cross's face.

"Damon, just a moment!"

"Yes, sir," Cross answered, waiting.

The Assistant Postmaster pointed a forefinger at Cross. "Damon, don't ever again come to this Post Office on an errand like this. If it hadn't been for your wife, I wouldn't touch this stink with a ten-foot pole. Look, you had one loan and paid it. Do the same with this. We're here to handle the mails, not emotional dramas. Now, this eight hundred ought to settle your little business, hunh?"

"Yes, sir," he lied; it would only settle the claim of Gladys, but it would not help him with Dot. "Let me explain, sir . . ."

"Don't tell me about it. I don't want to know."

"I'd like the night off, sir," Cross said. "I'll take it out of my vacation days."

"And what other service can I render you?" the Assistant Postmaster asked with mockery.

"I'm ill," Cross said peevishly.

"You look it," the Assistant Postmaster said. "Okay. Take it. But I know a guy called Damon who's going to find the Post Office a hard line to walk from this out."

Cross bit his lip, turned away and descended the stairs

to the cashier's office of the Postal Union and presented his voucher.

"Cash, eh?" the teller asked, smiling. "What're you going to do with all that money? Buy the Tribune Tower?"

Cross pretended that he had not heard. He pushed the pile of fifty-dollar bills into his wallet, sought a telephone booth and dialed Gladys.

"I got the money," he told her.

"I want it first thing in the morning," she said flatly.

"I'll bring it by at noon."

"All right."

He made for the exit, showed his badge to the guard and stepped into the street. It was snowing again; fat, white flakes drifted lazily down from a night sky. An "L" train rattled past overhead. He sighed, feeling relieved. He had to be careful and not let a pickpocket rob him of the money. He put his badge, the duplicate copy of the loan contract into the pocket of his overcoat and stuffed his wallet into his shirt, next to his skin. His job now was to head off Dot.

Diving into a subway, he paid his fare and, two minutes later, when a train roared up, walked into the first coach and sank into a seat, closing his eyes. The train pulled into motion; he opened his eyes and noticed that another Negro, shabbily dressed, of about his own color and build, was sitting across the aisle from him. The movement of the coach rocked some of the tension out of him, but not enough to let him relax. Restlessness made him rise and go to the front window and stand looking at the twin ribbons of steel rails sliding under the train. A moment later, when the train was streaking through the underground, darkness suddenly gouged his eyes and a clap of thunder smote his ears. He was spinning through space, his body smashing against steel; then he was aware of being lifted and brutally catapulted through black space and, while he was tossed, screams of men and women rent the black air.

Afterwards Cross remembered that when the lights had gone out he had involuntarily blinked his eyes, instinctively feeling that the cause of sudden darkness was some fault of the functioning of his pupils. About him were sounds of ripping metals and then something thumped against his head, sending him to sleep. How long he was unconscious, he did not know. When he was aware of himself again he realized that his body was in a vaguely upright position, but jammed between what seemed like two walls of steel. The right side of his skull was gripped by pain and something wet and warm trickled down a side of his face. His left leg was being wrenched and his right leg was pinioned, crushed to numbness between what seemed like two vices. He groaned. The words: *It's a subway wreck!* shaped themselves in his consciousness.

Abruptly the thunder ceased and the only sounds he heard were screams. In the blackness that walled itself before his eyes, Cross was afraid to move. *How badly am I hurt? Is it over?* He became aware that he was holding his head tucked down to dodge another attack of annihilation. Lifting his eyes he saw far ahead of him a jutting spray of blue electric sparks showering down from somewhere. He had to get out of this, now, NOW . . . Gingerly, he groped with his fingers and what he touched made him project in terms of images what his fingers felt and he screamed. He imagined he saw the profile of a human face drenched in blood. He snatched his hand away and wiped it dry upon his coat.

He breathed softly, listening: a viscous liquid was slowly falling drop by drop somewhere near him: the whimper of a woman seemed to be issuing from a half-conscious body: a quiet coughing seemed to be trying to dislodge something thick and wet from a sticky throat: an incessant grunt grew fainter and fainter until it was heard no more . . .

He was calm now, thinking. His lighter must be in his left pants' pocket. Twisting, he reached for it, felt it with the ends of his fingers. Yes! Purpose gripped him and, squeezing the tips of his fingers together, he caught hold of the lighter and slowly pulled it out. He pushed the lever and a bluish flame shed feeble light amid a welter of topsy-turvy forms. Lines zigzagged and solids floated in shadows, vanishing into meaninglessness; images dissolved into other images and his mind was full of a sense of shifting significances.

He saw that the seats of the train were above his head; the coach had reversed itself, twisted within the tube of the underground and he was standing on the shattered lights of the ceiling. Seats had ripped from the floor and had fallen to the ceiling where he stood.

Cross shut his eyes and bit his lips, his ears assailed by screams. He had to get out of here! He bent lower and looked; a white face with unblinking eyes was wedged at the level of his knees and beneath that face he could make out a dark pool of fluid that reflected the flickering flame of his lighter. He moved the flame over shards of glinting glass and saw again that window and the shower of blue electric sparks still sprinkling down . . . Yes; he had to get to that window . . . But his legs . . . He had to get them free . . . He bent and looked closer; his right leg was gripped between the steel wall of the coach and a seat that had tumbled from the floor to the ceiling. He pushed at the seat and it would not budge. Again he shoved his weight mightily at the seat. Why didn't it move? He stooped lower with the light and saw that the seat that jammed his leg to the wall was anchored in place by the man's head, which, in turn, was rammed by another seat. The man's face was fronting Cross.

Cross lifted the pressure of his finger from the lever and the flame went out. He thought: That man's head is keeping this seat from moving . . . Could he get that head out of his way? He pressed the lever again and looked. He could just reach the man's head with his right hand. Yes; he had to shove it out of the way. He held the lighter in his left hand, shut his eyes, and felt the palm of his right hand touching the yielding flesh of the man's face, expecting to hear a protest . . . He opened his eyes; no breath seemed to be coming from the nostrils or mouth. Cross shuddered. If the man was dead, then any action he took to free himself was right . . . He held his fingers to the man's parted lips and could feel no stir of air. For a few seconds he watched the man's chest and could detect no movement. The man's dead . . . But how could he get that head out of his way . . . ? Again he pushed his right hand with all of his strength against the face and it budged only a fraction of an inch. Goddamn . . . He panted with despair, regarding the man's head as an obstacle; it was no longer flesh and blood, but a rock, a chuck of wood to be whacked at until it was gone . . .

He searched vainly in the moving shadows for something to hold in his hand, hearing still the sounds of screams. He felt in his overcoat pocket; the gun was there. Yes . . . He pulled it out. Could he beat down that foolishly staring face belonging to that head pushing against the seat wedging his leg to the wall? He shut his eyes and lifted the gun by the barrel and brought down the butt, and, even though his eyes were closed, he could see the gun butt crashing into the defenseless face . . . Sweat broke out on his face and rivulets of water oozed from his armpits.

He opened his eyes; the bloody face had sunk only a few inches; the nostrils, teeth, chin and eyes were pulped and blackened. Cross sucked in his breath; a few more blows would dislodge it. He shut his eyes and hammered again and suddenly he heard a splashing thud and he knew that the head had given way, for his blows were now falling on air . . . He looked; the mangled face was on the floor; most of the flesh had been ripped away and it already appeared skeletonlike. He had done it; he could move his leg.

Now, he had to free his other leg. Peering with the lighter, he saw that his left leg was hooked under a fallen seat. With his right leg free, he hoisted himself up and saw that he would get loose if he could use his left leg as a ramrod to shove at the seat. Pricked by splinters of glass, he hauled himself upward and perched himself on the back of an overturned seat and, with his left foot, he gave a wild kick against the seat and it did not move. Bracing himself, he settled his heel against the back of the seat, eased his overcoat—which was hindering his movements—down a little from his shoulders, and shut his eyes and pushed against the seat. It fell away. Both of his legs were free. An awful stench filled his nostrils.

He looked toward the gutted window; the blue electric sparks were still falling. From somewhere came a banging of metal against metal, like an urgent warning. That window was the way out. He crept forward over the ceiling of the overturned coach, past twisted and bloody forms, crunching shattered electric bulbs under his feet, feeling his shoes slopping through sticky liquid. He moved on tiptoe, as though afraid of waking the sleeping dead. He reached the window and saw that a young woman's body had been crushed almost flat just beneath it. The girl was dead, but, if he was to get through that window, he had either the choice of standing upon her crushed body or remaining where he was. He stepped upon the body, feeling his shoes sinking into the lifeless flesh and seeing blood bubbling from the woman's mouth as his weight bore down on her bosom. He reached for the window, avoiding the jagged edges of glass. Outside the blue electric sparks rained down, emitting a ghostly light. He did not need his lighter now. He crawled through and lowered his feet to the ground. He had to be careful and not step upon any live wires or the third rail . . . His feet sought for gravel.

He stood for a moment, collecting himself. His head throbbed. When he moved his right leg it pained him. His body was clammy and was trembling. For a moment he felt as though he would lose consciousness, but he remained on his feet. Screams, more distant now, came to his ears. He moved forward in the bluish gloom. Yes, ahead of him were amber lights! He pushed on and could hear distant voices and they were not the voices of the wounded. He had been lucky. I'd better let a doctor look at me . . . He now realized how fantastically fortunate he had been; had he remained in his seat, he would have been crushed to death . . .

He picked his way catlike over wooden trestles and then stopped. His overcoat . . . ? Oh, God, he had left it somewhere back in that death-filled darkness, but he could not recall how it had gotten away from him. The gun was still in his pants' pocket. With stiff and sweaty fingers he lit a cigarette and walked on. From above ground he caught the faint wail of sirens and ahead of him he saw dim traces of light in the circular tunnel. Later he made out blurred, white uniforms and he knew that they were doctors and nurses.

He trudged past overturned coaches whose windows were gutted of glass. He could see doctors and nurses quite clearly now. He heard someone yell: "Here comes another one! He seems all right!"

They had seen him and were running to meet him. A doctor and a nurse caught hold of his arms.

"Are you all right?" the doctor asked.

"I guess so," he answered out of a daze.

"You are lucky," the nurse said.

"Get 'im to an ambulance," the doctor told the nurse. "I want to take a look back here."

The doctor hurried off into the tunnel of darkness, spotting his way with a flashlight.

"Can you walk all right?" the nurse asked him.

"Yeah."

"Does anything hurt you?"

"My leg, my right leg . . ."

"Come along, if you can manage," she said. "They'll see about it . . . What happened?"

"I don't know."

She led him toward a group of doctors and nurses who were congregated upon a subway station platform. He saw policemen pouring upon the underground tracks and heard someone shout: "Tell 'em the current's cut off!"

Cross felt hands lifting him on to the platform, and now another nurse had hold of his arm. About him was a babble of voices. He began to revive, feeling a little more like himself.

"I'm all right now," he told the nurse.

"But you must go to the hospital and be examined," the nurse told him. "Come. The ambulance is waiting."

She led him through a throng of policemen to the sidewalk where masses of excited people clogged the streets. The nurse tried to guide him through the crowd but they were brought to a standstill. A policeman saw them and attempted to help by clearing a path before them.

"That's one of 'em," Cross heard someone say. "But he doesn't seem hurt."

Cross could see the ambulances now; there were internes with stretchers rushing toward the subway station.

"You can get through now," the policeman said.

"Look," Cross told the nurse. "I'll go and get into an ambulance. I'm all right. Go back and help the others."

"Are you sure you're all right?" the nurse asked.

"Absolutely," Cross assured her.

She let go of him and he was alone. He felt fine. He started in the direction of the ambulances. The crowd ignored him. He looked down at his clothes; save for dried blood on his shoes, he was all right. His overcoat had protected him somewhat. He paused. Why in hell should he go to a hospital? He was not wounded, only bruised. What he wanted more than medicine was a good, stiff drink of whiskey. Were the doctors and nurses watching him? He looked around; they were not . . . And the policeman had disappeared. The hell with it . . . He crossed the street and peered at his dim reflection in the plate glass window of a clothing store. His eyes were muddy and his face was caked with dirt and dried blood. He mopped at his cheek with his coat sleeve, rubbing it clean. Otherwise, he looked quite normal. Some whiskey would fix me up, he told himself and went in search of a drink.

A fine snow was falling, hanging in the air like a delicate veil. He limped toward Roosevelt Road and found a second-rate bar that had sawdust on the floor and an odor of stale bread and beer. He was glad of the warmth that caressed his face; he had been too preoccupied to notice that he was half-frozen. But what happened to his overcoat? He ordered a double whiskey and thought back over the underground accident. Then he remembered that he must have lost his overcoat when he had climbed atop that overturned seat to free his leg. That was it; he had had to pull his arms out of the coat and had been in such a frenzy that he had forgotten to put it on again. Well, he would buy another one. An overcoat was indeed a small loss in such a holocaust. He fingered the lump at the right side of his head; it was sore, but not serious. A man sure needs luck, he told himself.

The bar was filled with foreign-born working men who did not find his disheveled clothing outlandish. Over his head a loud-speaker blared. He was leaning on his elbow when he heard the radio commentator announce:

Ladies and Gentlemen, we interrupt this program to bring you a special news bulletin. One half hour ago, a Southbound subway train crashed headlong into another Southbound train that had come to a standstill about six hundred yards from the Roosevelt Road Subway Station. The cause of the accident is being investigated. Access to the wrecked trains is difficult because debris has blocked the underground tubes and rescuers are having to cut their way through thick steel beams with acetylene torches. Although it is too early to give any details, it is feared that the loss of life has been heavy. In the immediate area all subway traffic has been suspended. Doctors and nurses have been rushed to the scene of the disaster. Keep tuned to this station for further details.

Cross smiled. How quick they were! Then suddenly he started so violently that the white man drinking next to him drew back in astonishment. *That money!* He shoved his hand into his shirt . . . *It was there!* Thank

God . . . He leaned weakly against the bar. If he had lost the eight hundred dollars, the only thing left for him would have been to jump into the Chicago River.

He paid his bill and hobbled back into the street where snow was still sifting down. Tomorrow at noon he had to see Gladys. And he'd go home now and wash up and then see Dot . . . He was hungry; yes, he'd first go to a South Side restaurant and have a decent meal. But he would not take a subway. Hell, no . . . He'd treat himself to something better this time. At a corner he limped into a taxi and called out: "47th and South Park."

He leaned back and wondered why his life had been spared. Or had it been? To say that he had been "spared" implied that some God was watching over him, and he did not believe that. It was simply the way the dice had rolled. He stretched out his right leg, testing it; the flesh was still sore to the touch, but he could keep on his feet. Funny, that morning he had been ready to blow his brains out, but when his body had been tossed about in that darkness, he had wanted to live.

His postal badge! The loan papers! They too were in the pocket of his overcoat. He'd have to report their being lost the first thing in the morning to the postal officials . . . The taxi swerved to a curb at 47th and South Park. He paid the driver, limped out, walked through tumbling snowflakes and entered Dug's, a small restaurant that served the kind of food he liked. He went into the men's room, washed himself and then examined his face in the mirror. Not bad . . . He looked as though he had been on a two-day drunk, that was all. He grinned, reentered the restaurant which was almost empty and ordered a steak, fried potatoes, coffee, and ice cream. He took a sip of water, listening to the radio that was going near the front window.

. . . This is John Harlan speaking. I'm broadcasting from the scene of the subway wreck at Roosevelt Road. It is snowing here and the visibility is rather bad. I have my microphone with me upon the "L" platform and I'm able to see directly down to the subway entrance where doctors, nurses, attendants, and policemen are working frantically to bring the wounded from the underground. The scene is being illuminated by huge spotlights attached to telephone poles. Beyond the subway entrance, stretching far into the street and blocking the traffic, is a crowd of more than five thousand people standing silently in the falling snow. They have been here for almost an hour waiting for news of friends or relatives believed to have been passengers on the ill-fated subway trains that collided with a heavy loss of life more than an hour ago . . .

I see the internes bringing out another victim. A body is on the stretcher. It is the body of a woman, it seems; yes, I can see her long brown hair . . . Wait a minute. I'll see if I can get the police to identify her for us.

So engrossed was Cross in listening that he did not see the waitress when she placed his food before him. They're acting like it's a baseball game, he thought with astonishment. He was glad now that he had walked so unceremoniously away from the accident. He surely would not have wanted anybody to blare out his name over the airways as a victim. He shrugged his shoulders. They'll give us a commercial soon, he thought. The radio commentator resumed:

The name of the last accident victim is: Mrs. Maybelle Broadman of 68 Green Street, Ravenswood Park. She is being taken directly to the Michael Reese Hospital . . .

Ladies and gentlemen, I see the internes coming out with another stretcher. I can't tell yet if the victim is a man or a woman, for the stretcher is completely covered. It's a man . . . I can tell by the blood-stained overcoat which is draped over the foot of the stretcher . . . That is the forty-fourth victim taken so far from the wreckage of underground trains. Just a minute; I'll try to get the identity of the last victim who was brought out . . .

In spite of himself, his interest was captured by the description of the happenings at the scene of the accident. As he waited for more news, he chewed and swallowed a mouthful of steak and lifted his cup of coffee to his lips.

Ladies and gentlemen, while we are endeavoring to establish the identity of the last man taken from the scene of the subway accident at Roosevelt Road, I'm going to ask one of the eyewitnesses, who was a passenger on the subway train, to say a few words about what he saw and felt when the disaster occurred. I have here at my side Mr. Glenn Williams, a salesman of 136 Rush Street, who escaped with but a few minor bruises. Mr. Williams, could you tell us what happened? Where were you on the train . . . ?

WELL, I WAS IN A COACH TOWARD THE MIDDLE OF THE TRAIN. EVERYTHING SEEMED TO BE GOING ALL RIGHT. I WAS READING THE EVENING PAPER. THE TRAIN WAS FULL. I WAS SEATED. I GUESS WE WERE ABOUT A MINUTE FROM THE ROOSEVELT ROAD STATION, WHERE I WAS TO GET OFF, WHEN A GREAT CRASH CAME AND ALL THE LIGHTS WENT OFF. I FELT MYSELF BEING KNOCKED OFF MY SEAT . . .

I must interrupt you, Mr. Williams. I'm sorry. Ladies and gentlemen, the police have just informed me of the identity of the last victim taken from the subway crash at Roosevelt Road. His name is Cross Damon, a 26-year-old postal clerk who lived at 244 East 57th Street on the South Side. Mr. Damon's body was crushed and mangled beyond recognition or hope of direct identification. His identity has been established, however, by his overcoat, private papers, and his post office badge . . . His body is being taken di-

rectly to the Cook County Morgue. Relatives must address
all inquiries there . . .

Now, Mr. Williams, will you kindly . . . ?

Cross was still holding the cup of coffee in his right
hand, his fingers tense upon the handle. He stared, stupefied. *What?* He half stood, then sat down again.
Good God! He . . . *dead?* He had a wild impulse to
laugh. The damn fools! They were really crazy! Well, it
was his overcoat that had led them wrong . . . Yes, that
was it. He ought to phone them right now! He looked
around the restaurant; except for himself, the place was
now empty of customers. That tall, black girl who had
been eating in the corner had gone . . . Dug, the proprietor who knew him, was not there. The waitress was
a new one and he did not know her and she did not
know him. He saw her watching him curiously. She
must think I'm loony, he thought.

"Is there anything wrong, sir?"

He did not answer. This was rich! *He was dead!* He
had to tell this to the gang at THE SALTY DOG, right
now! Old Doc Huggins would die laughing . . .

"Is the food all right, sir?"

"Hunh? Oh, yes. Look, what do I owe you?"

"Aren't you going to eat?"

"No. I've forgotten something. I got to go at
once . . ."

"Well, sir. It's one seventy-five. You see, even if you
don't eat, they had to prepare it. We can't serve that
food to anybody else, sir, you know. So you'll have to
pay . . ."

"That's all right. Here," he said, tossing her two one-
dollar bills.

He hurried out into the spinning snow and headed
for THE SALTY DOG. This was the damndest thing!
It was even more freakish than his having escaped alive

from the subway accident itself. When he reached the corner, some force jerked his body to an abrupt halt amidst the jumping snow. He was stunned and shaken by the power of an idea that took his breath away and left him standing open-mouthed like an idiot amid the crazy flakes.

He was dead . . . All right . . . Okay . . . Why the hell *not*? Why should he refute it? Why should he deny it? He, of all the people on earth, had a million reasons for being dead and staying dead! An intuitive sense of freedom flashed through his mind. Was there a slight chance here of his being able to start all over again? To live a new life? It would solve every problem he had if the world and all the people who knew him could think of him as dead . . . He felt dizzy as he tried to encompass the totality of the idea that had come so suddenly and unsought into his mind, for its implications ramified in so many directions that he could not grasp them all at once. Was it possible that he could somehow make this false account of his death become real? Could he pull off a thing like that? What did one do in a case like this? These questions made him feel that the world about him held countless dangers; he suddenly felt like a criminal, and he was grateful for the nervous flakes of snow which screened his face from the eyes of passersby. Oh, God . . . He had to sit down somewhere alone and think this thing out; it was too new, too odd, too complicated. How could he let them go on believing that he was dead? But suppose later they found out that the body that they had dragged from the wreckage was not his? What then? Well, could he not hide away for a few days until they had made up their minds? If they buried that body as the body of Cross Damon, then he was dead, really, legally, morally dead. Had any of his friends seen him since he had come up out of the sub-

way? No, not one. And no one had known him at the
subway station. No doubt that doctor and those nurses
had already, in their excitement, forgotten that they had
ever seen him. He was certain that no one he knew had
seen him in that dingy bar on Roosevelt Road. And if
he was really serious about this, then he ought not go
into THE SALTY DOG. What wild luck! And Dug
had not been in! And that waitress was new and could
not have known him from Adam . . . !

Then, if he was to do this thing, no one who knew
him must see him now . . . From this moment on he
had to vanish . . . Hide . . . Now! And his mother
must not see him . . . And Dot must not see him . . .
Gladys must be led to believe that he was dead . . . His
sons . . . ? Good God . . . Doing this meant leaving
them forever! Did he want to do that? He had to make
up his mind . . . Well, they were not close to him as it
was; so leaving them was merely making final and formal what had already happened. And how was Gladys
to live? Ah, she'd get his insurance money, ten thousand
dollars! His cheeks felt hot. Gladys would be taken care
of. And no doubt his old mother would now swallow
her pride and go and live with Gladys. And the stern
logic of Dot's position would force her to have the
child aborted . . . He trembled, looking about him in
the snow-scattered street, his eyes smouldering with excitement. A keen sensation of vitality invaded every cell
of his body and a slow, strange smile stole across his
lips. It was as though he was living out a daring dream.
If, after hiding away for a few days, they discovered that
that body was not his, why, he could always come forth
and say that the accident had wounded him in such a
way that he had temporarily lost his memory! That
would be his alibi . . . And were not such claims being
made every day? He had often read of cases of amnesia

. . . It might work. Why not? It was surely worth trying. What had he to lose? His job. It was already com-
promised by Dot's possible accusations against him.
And only tonight he had signed an obligation to pay a
debt that would take him two years to discharge . . .
And if he were dead, all of that would be at an end!

All right; what next? He could not plot or plan this
by talking it over with anybody. He would have to sit
down alone and figure this thing out carefully. And he
had to keep shy of those sections of the city where he
might meet people who knew him. Where could he go?
Yes, down around 22nd Street, the area of the bums and
whores and sporting houses . . . And he had eight hundred dollars in cash in his shirt next to his skin! Holy
Moses! It all made *sense*! This eight hundred dollars
would be his stake until he could launch himself anew
somewhere else . . . It all fitted . . . He would be a
damn fool if he did not try it. All of his life he had been
hankering after his personal freedom, and now freedom
was knocking at his door, begging him to come out. He
shivered in the cold. Yes, he had to go to his room and
get his clothes . . . But, no . . . Someone would surely
see him. He could not take that chance. Funny, it was
hard to think straight about this. He had to break right
now the chains of habit that bound him to the present.
And that was not easy. Each act of his consciousness
sought to drag him back to what he wanted to flee.

He had to act, NOW! Each second he stood here like
this made it more dangerous for him to do what he
wanted. Yet he remained standing as though some
power over which he had no control held him rooted.
His judgment told him to move on, and yet he stood.
Already he felt like the hunted. Waves of realization
rolled through him: he had to break with everything he
had ever known and create a new life. Could he do it? If

he could conceive of it, he should be able to do it. This thing suited his personality, his leanings. Yes, take a taxi to 22nd Street . . . No, the driver might remember him; the South Side was a small place. The subway . . . ? No, he might meet another postal clerk. He would walk over to State Street and take a trolley northward to 22nd Street. He was not likely to meet anybody in that direction.

At last he moved through the shaking flakes of snow. If it did not work, he could explain it all away. But, by God, it *had* to work. It was up to him to *make* it work. He was walking fast, caught up in a sense of drama, trying to work out a new destiny.

He recalled now the other Negro passenger on the train who had sat across the aisle opposite him; the man had been about his own general build, size, and color. What had happened was simple; they had mistaken that man's body for his own! The body had been so disfigured that direct identification had been impossible, and, when they had found his overcoat with his postal badge and the contract papers in the pocket, they had leaped to the conclusion that it was the body of Cross Damon. Would anyone demand that that body be subjected to further examination to determine if it was really his? The insurance company? But why would they do that unless somebody put the idea in their heads? Would Gladys? Hell, no . . . She would be content to get the ten thousand dollars of insurance money and probably some more money from the subway company. Dot? She would not know what to do. His mother? Poor Mama . . . She'll just think that God has finally paid me off, he mused.

He seethed with impatience; he was both scared and glad, yearning to find shelter before meeting anyone he knew. Anxiety now drove a sharp sense of distance between him and his environment. Already the world around him seemed to be withdrawing, and he could feel in his heart a certain pathos about it. There was no racial tone to his reactions; he was just a man, *any* man who had had an opportunity to flee and had seized upon it. He was afraid of his surroundings and he knew that his surroundings did not know that he was afraid. In a way, he was a criminal, not so much because of what he was doing, but because of what he was feeling. It was for much more than merely criminal reasons that he was fleeing to escape his identity, his old hateful consciousness. There was a kind of innocence that made him want to shape for himself the kind of life he felt he wanted, but he knew that that innocence was deeply forbidden. In a debate with himself that went on without words, he asked himself if one had the right to such an attitude? Well, he would see . . .

He took a northbound trolley on State Street and pushed his way apprehensively into the packed crowd and stood swaying. Was there anything in his manner that would attract attention? Could others tell that he was nervous, trying to hide a secret? How could one act normally when one was *trying* to act normally? He caught hold of a strap and, his shoulders jostling others, rocked with the motion of the trolley.

He began to see that this project of deception he had taken upon himself back there in the winging snow of the street was much bigger than he had realized. It was a supreme challenge that went straight to the very heart of life. What was he to do with himself? For years he had been longing for his own way to live and act, and now that it was almost his, all he could feel was an uncomfortable sense of looseness. What puzzled him most was that he could not think of concrete things to do. He was going to a cheap hotel in order to hide for a few days, but beyond that he had no ideas, no plans. He would have to imagine this thing out, dream it out, invent it, like a writer constructing a tale, he told himself grimly as he watched the blurred street lamps flash past the trolley's frosted window.

As he neared 22nd Street he edged forward through the crowd, keeping his head down to conceal his face. He swung off and shivered from the penetrating dampness that bit into his bones. He was still limping, thinking: I got to find a hotel now . . . But . . . Who was he? His name? Age? Occupation? He slowed his feet. It was not easy to break with one's life. It was not difficult to see that one was always much, much more than what one thought one was. His past? What was his past if he wanted to become another person? His past had come to him without his asking and almost without his knowing; at some moment in the welter of his spent days he had just simply awakened to the fact that he had a past, and that was all. Now, his past would have to be a deliberately constructed thing. And how did one go about that? If he went into a hotel they would ask him his name and he would not be able to say that he was Cross Damon, postal clerk . . . He stood still in the flood of falling snow. Question upon question bombarded him. Could he imagine a past that would fit in with his present personality? Was there more than one way in which one could account for one's self? His mind came to a standstill. If he could not figure out anything about the past, then maybe it was the future that must determine what and who he was to be . . . The whole hastily conceived project all but crumpled. Maybe this dream of a new life was too mad? But I ought to be able to do this, he told himself. He liked the nature of this dare; there was in it something that appealed to him deeply. Others took their lives for granted; he, he would have to mold his with a conscious aim. Why not? Was he not free to do so? That all men were free was the fondest and deepest conviction of his life. And his acting upon this wild plan would be but an expression of his perfect freedom. He would do with himself what he would, what he liked.

He did not have to decide every detail tonight; just enough had to be fabricated in order to get a hotel room without rousing too much suspicion. Later, he would go into it more thoroughly, casting about for who he was or what he wanted to be.

He went into an ill-lighted tavern that reeked of disinfectant and sat in a rear booth and listened to the radio pour forth a demonical jazz music that linked itself with his sense of homelessness. The strains of blue and sensual notes were akin to him not only by virtue of their having been created by black men, but because they had come out of the hearts of men who had been rejected and yet who still lived and shared the lives of their rejectors. Those notes possessed the frightened ecstasy of the unrepentant and sent his feelings tumbling and coagulating in a mood of joyful abandonment. The tavern was filled with a mixture of white and black sporting people and no one turned to look at him. He ordered a beer and sat hunched over it, wondering who he would be for the next four or five days until he left for, say, New York. To begin his new life he would relive something he knew well, something that would not tax too greatly his inventive powers. He would be a Negro who had just come up fresh from the Deep South looking for work. His name? Well . . . Charles . . . Charles what? Webb . . . Yes, that was good enough for the time being. Charles Webb . . . Yes, he had just got in from Memphis; he had had a hard time with whites down there and he was damn glad of being in the

North. What had he done in Memphis? He had been a porter in a drugstore . . . He repressed a smile. *He loved this!*

When he went out he bought a stack of newspapers to keep track of developments in the subway accident. He searched for a hotel, the cheaper and more disreputable the better. If there was the slightest doubt about his being dead, he would come forth with a story to square it all; but if all sailed smoothly, he was free.

He came finally to an eight-story hotel with tattered window shades and bare light bulbs burning in the lobby. The hotels in this district were so questionable that they rarely drew a color line. Next door was a liquor store in which he bought a bottle of whiskey. He entered the hotel and a short, fat white woman studied him appraisingly from behind a counter.

"I'm looking for a room," he said. "A single."

"For how long?"

"Maybe a week."

"You got any luggage?"

"No'm. Not with me."

"Then you have to pay in advance, you know."

"Oh, yes'm. I can do that. How much is it?"

"One-fifty a night. I'll put you on the top floor. But no noise in the room, see?"

"I don't make any noise," he told her.

"They all say that," she commented, sliding him a sheet of paper. "Here; fill that out."

He answered the questions, identifying himself as Charles Webb from Memphis. When he returned the form to her, she pointed to the bottle he had under his arm.

"Look," she said. "I don't care what you do in your room, but I don't want any trouble, see? Some people get drunk and hurt others."

"Lady, I never really hurt anybody in my life but my-self," he told her before he realized what he was saying.

The woman looked at him sharply; she opened her mouth to reply, but thought better of it. He knew that that had been a foolish thing to say; it was completely out of character. He had to be careful.

"Come on," the woman said, leading him down a narrow hallway to a skinny Negro with a small, black face who stood in a tiny elevator and eyed Cross sullenly.

"Take this man up to room 89, Buck. Here's the key," the woman ordered.

"Yes'm," Buck sang.

He rode up with Buck who weighed him with his eyes. Cross knew that a bundle of newspapers and a bottle of whiskey were not the normal accoutrements of a Negro migrant from Memphis. He would have to do better than this. Five minutes later he was settled in his garishly papered room which had the white lip of a stained sink jutting out. The floor was bare and dirty. He lay across the lumpy bed and sighed. His limbs ached from fatigue. The hard light of the bare electric bulb swinging from the smoky ceiling stung his eyes; he doubled a piece of newspaper and tied it about the bulb to reduce the glare. He opened the bottle and took a deep swig.

Undoubtedly Gladys had now heard about his being dead. How was she taking it? He was perversely curious to know if she was sorry. And, Good God, his poor old mother! She had always predicted that he would end up badly, but he had presented her with a morally clean way of dying, a way that would induce even in his enemies a feeling of forgiving compassion. And Dot . . . ? She would find out through the newspapers or over the radio. He could almost hear Myrtle telling Dot that she

had the worst luck of any girl in the whole round world
. . . He was foolishly toying with the idea of trying to
disguise his voice and calling Dot on the telephone
when he fell asleep . . .

Late the next morning, Cross awakened with a pale
winter sun falling full into his eyes. He lay without
moving, staring dully. Was this his room? Around him
was a low murmur of voices and the subdued music of
radios coming from other rooms. His body felt weak
and he could not quickly orientate himself. He swung
his feet to the floor, kicking over the whiskey bottle. For
a moment he watched the bubbling liquid flow; then he
righted the bottle, corked it, and the action helped to
bring back in his mind the events of last night. He had
quit, run off; *he was dead*.

He yearned for just one more glimpse of his mother,
his three sons; he hungered for just one last embrace
with Dot . . . But this was crazy. Either he went
through with this thing or he did not; it was all or nothing. He was being brought gradually to a comprehension of the force of habit in his and others' lives. He had
to break with others and, in breaking with them, he
would break with himself. He must sever all ties of
memory and sentimentality, blot out, above all, the in-
sidious tug of longing. Only the future must loom before him so magnetically that it could condition his
present and give him those hours and days out of which
he could build a new past. Yes, it would help him
greatly if he went to New York; other faces and circumstances would be a better setting out of which to forge
himself anew. But first he had to make sure that he was
dead . . .

He washed himself and mulled over his situation.
When a man had been born and bred with other men,
had shared and participated in their traditions, he was

not required of himself to conceive the total meaning or direction of his life; broad, basic definitions of his existence were already contained implicitly in the general scope of other men's hopes and fears; and, by living and acting with them—a living and acting he will have commenced long before he could have been able to give his real consent—, he will have assumed the responsibility for promises and pledges made for him and in his name by others. Now, depending only upon his lonely will, he saw that to map out his life entirely upon his own assumptions was a task that terrified him just to think of it, for he knew that he first had to know what he thought life was, had to know consciously all the multitude of assumptions which other men took for granted, and he did not know them and he knew that he did not know them. The question summed itself up: What's a man? He had unknowingly set himself a project of no less magnitude than contained in that awful question.

He looked through the newspapers, finding only more extended accounts of what he had heard last night on the radio. For the latest news he would have to buy today's papers. Yes; and the Negro weekly papers would be upon the newsstands in the Black Belt neighborhoods tonight or in the morning. They would tell the tale; they would carry detailed stories of all Negroes who had been involved in the accident.

He spent the morning shopping for an overcoat and other necessities in a poor West Side working class district where he was certain that he would not encounter any of his acquaintances. He prodded himself to be frugal, for he did not know what the coming days would bring. How would he spend his time? Yes; he would lay in a pile of good books . . . No. What the hell was he thinking of? Books? What he had before him was of far more interest than any book he would ever buy; it was out of realities such as this that books were made. He was full of excitement as he realized that eventually he would not only have to think and feel this out, but he would have to act and live it out.

The relationship of his consciousness to the world had become subtly altered in a way that nagged him uneasily because he could not define it. His break with the routine of his days had disturbed the tone and pitch of reality. His repudiation of his ties was as though his feelings had been water and those watery feelings had been projected by his desires out upon the surface of the world, like water upon pavements and roofs after a spring rain; and his loyalty to that world, like the sun, had brightened that world and made it glitter with meaning; and now, since last night, since he had broken all of the promises and pledges he had ever made, the water of meaning had begun to drain off the world, had begun to dry up and leave the look of things changed; and now he was seeing an alien and unjustifiable world completely different from him. It was no longer *his* world; it was just *a* world . . .

He bought a tiny radio and went back to his hotel room. He was so spent from yesterday's exertions that he slept again. In the late afternoon there was a soft tapping upon his door and he awakened in terror. Who was it? Had somebody tracked him down? Ought he answer? He tiptoed to the door in his stockinged feet and stooped and peered through the keyhole. It was a woman; he could see the falling folds of a polka dot dress. The landlady? The knock came again and he saw a tiny patch of white skin as the woman's hand fell to her side. She was white . . .

He made sure that his gun was handy, then scampered back to bed and called out sleepily: "Who is it?"

"May I speak to you a moment?"

It was a woman's voice. He hesitated, opened the door, and saw a young white girl of about eighteen standing before him.

"Gotta match?" she asked, lifting a cigarette to her mouth and keeping her eyes boldly on his face.

He caught on; she was selling herself. But was she safe? Was she stooling for the police?

"Sure," he said, taking out his lighter and holding the flame for her.

"You're new here," she said.

"Yeah," he said. "I got in last night."

"So I heard," she smiled.

"Seems like news travels pretty fast around here."

"Pretty fast for those who wanna find out things," she said.

She had black, curly hair, bluish-grey-green deep-set eyes, was about five feet two in height and seemed to weigh around a hundred and five or six pounds. Her breasts were ample, her legs large but shapely; her lips were full but over-rouged and she reeked of too much cheap perfume.

"Having fun in the city, Big Boy?" She arched her eyebrows as she spoke, then looked past him into the interior of his room.

Ought he bother with her? He wanted to, but his situation was too delicate for him to get mixed up with this fetching little tart. Yet he was suddenly hungry for her; she was woman as body of woman . . .

"I don't know anybody around here yet," he said.

"Are you stingy with that fire water?" she asked, nodding toward his whiskey bottle sitting on the night table.

"Naw," he laughed, making up his mind.

She entered slowly, glancing at him out of the corner of her eyes as she went past; he followed the movements of her body as she walked to the center of the room and sat, crossing her legs and tossing back her hair and letting her breasts take a more prominent place on her body. He closed the door and placed the bottle between them.

"What do they call you?" he asked, pouring her a drink.

"Jenny," she said. "You?"

"Charlie, just Good-Time Charlie," he said, laughing. He saw her looking appraisingly about the room. "Traveling light, hunh?"

"Just passing through," he said. "Heading west."

She sipped her drink, then rose and turned on his radio; dance music came and she stood moving rhythmically. He rose and made dance movements with her, holding her close to him, seeing in his mind the sloping curves of her body.

"Want to spend the afternoon with me?" he asked.

"Why not?"

"Look, baby, seeing this is not the Gold Coast, what do you want?"

"I got to pay my rent," she said flatly.

"The hell with that," he told her. "How much do you want? That's all I asked you."

"I want five," she said at last.

"I'll give you three," he countered.

"I said five, you piker—"

"I said three, and you can take it or leave it; I don't want to argue with you."

"Okay," she said, shrugging.

"Let's drink some more."

"Suits me."

When the dance music stopped she turned off the radio, pulled down the window shade, and rolled back the covers of the bed. Wordlessly, she began to undress and he wondered what she was thinking of. Clad in nylon panties, she came to him and held out her hand. Her breasts were firm and the nipples were pink.

"I'll take it now, baby," she said.

"But why *now*?" he demanded.

"Listen, I'm selling; you're buying. Pay now or nothing doing," she said. "I know how men feel when they get through."

Cross laughed; he liked her brassy manner. Nobody taught her that; sense of that order was derived only through experience. He handed her three one-dollar bills which she put into the pocket of her dress, looking at him solemnly as she did so. She pulled off her panties and climbed into bed and lay staring vacantly.

"They could paint this damn place," she said matter-of-factly.

"What?" he asked, surprised, looking vaguely around the room.

"They could paint that ceiling sometime," she repeated.

Cross studied her, then laughed. "Yes; I guess they could," he admitted.

"You're not from Memphis," she said suddenly.

He whirled and glared at her, a sense of hot danger leaping into his throat. Did she know something or was she merely guessing? Was he that bad an actor? If he had thought that she was spying on him, he would have grabbed the whiskey bottle and whacked her across the head with it and knocked her cold and run . . . Naw, she's just fishing, he told himself. But I got to be careful . . . So shaken were his feelings by sudden dread that he did not want to get into bed with her.

"How do you know?" he asked.

"You don't talk like it," she said, puffing at her cigarette.

He relaxed. It was true that his accent was not completely of the Deep South. He drew upon the bottle to stifle his anxiety and when he took her in his arms he did not recall the fear that had scalded him. She responded so mechanically and wearily that only sheer physical hunger kept him with her. The edge gone from his desire, he lay looking at her and wondering how a woman so young could have achieved so ravaged a sense of life. His loneliness was rekindled and he lit a cigarette and grumbled: "You could have at least tried a little."

"You're not from Memphis," she said with finality.

"You're dodging the point," he reminded her with anger in his voice. "I said that you could at least pretend when you're in bed."

"You think it's important?" She looked cynically at him. "What do you want for three dollars?"

"You agreed to the price," he said brusquely.

"Hell, that's nothing," she said casually, squinting her eyes against the smoke of her cigarette. "I might've done it for nothing. Why didn't you ask me?"

She was fishing around to know him and he did not want it. He washed and dressed while she still lolled in the nude on his bed, her eyes thoughtful. He should not act now with these girls as he used to; things were changed with him and he had to change too. And she was taking her own goddamn time about leaving. Resentment rose in him as he realized that he had made less impression on her physical feelings than if he had spat into the roaring waters of Niagara Falls . . .

"Haven't you got something to do?" he asked her.

"I can take a hint," she said pleasantly, rolling off the bed and getting into her panties.

"Be seeing you," she said after she had dressed.

"Not if I see you first."

"You'll be glad to see me if you're in a certain mood,"

she said; she touched him under the chin with her finger and left.

He lay on the bed, feeling spiteful toward even the scent of her perfume that lingered on in the room. He rose, opened the window wide, let in a blast of freezing air, and peered over the edge of the sill, his sight plunging downward eight floors to the street where tiny men and women moved like little black beetles in the white snow. I wouldn't like to fall down there, he thought aimlessly and turned back into the room, closing the window.

He went down for lunch and got the afternoon newspapers. The final list of the dead was over one hundred, making the accident the worst in Chicago's history. The mayor had appointed a committee to launch an investigation, for the cause of the tragedy was still obscure. The *Herald-Examiner* carried two full pages of photographs of some of the dead and Cross was pricked by a sense of the bizarre when he saw his own face staring back at him. He knew at once that Gladys had given that photograph to the newspapers, for she alone possessed the batch of old snaps from which it had been taken. By God, she really believes it, he thought with wry glee.

Then anxiousness seized him. If Jenny saw that photograph, would she not recognize him? He studied the photograph again; it showed him wearing football togs, sporting a mustache, and his face was much thinner and younger . . . No; Jenny wouldn't recognize him from that . . .

Early that evening the snow stopped falling and Chicago lay white and silent under huge drifts that made the streets almost impassable. Cross was glad, for it kept down the number of pedestrians and lessened his chances of being seen by anyone he knew. Near midnight he went to 35th Street and bought a batch of Negro weeklies and rushed back to his room, not daring to open them on the street or in the trolley. There, on the front pages, were big photographs of himself. His funeral had been set for Monday afternoon at 3 P.M. at the Church of the Good Shepherd. He laughed out loud. It was working like a charm! He wondered vaguely, while downing a drink, just how badly mangled his body was supposed to have been. Then he saw the answer; an odd item in the *Chicago Defender* reported:

> Subway officials stated that the body of Cross Damon had been so completely mangled that his remains had to be scooped up and wrapped in heavy cellophane before they could be placed in a coffin.

He giggled so long that tears came into his eyes.

A little after two o'clock that morning, when the snow-drenched streets were almost empty, he took a trolley to the neighborhood of his wife. He was afraid to loiter, for he was well-known in this area. From a distance of half a block he observed his home: lights were blazing in every window. She's got a plenty to do these days, he said to himself, repressing a desire to howl with laughter. But as the faces of his three sons rose before him, he sobered. He was never to see them again, except like this, from a distance. His eyes misted. They were his future self, and he had given up that future for a restricted but more intense future . . .

He went next to 37th and Indiana Avenue and crept into a snow-choked alleyway back of Dot's apartment building and figured out where her window would be. Yes, it was there, on the third floor . . . A light burned behind the shade. Was Dot really sorry? Had she wept over him? Or had her weeping been over her own state of unexpected abandonment? The light in her window went out suddenly and he wondered if she was going to bed. He hurried around to the street, watching like a cat for passersby, and secreted himself in a dark doorway opposite the entrance of the building in which she lived. Half an hour later he saw Dot and Myrtle come out, moving slowly through the snow and darkness with their heads and shoulders bent as under a weight of bewildered sorrow. He noticed that Myrtle was carrying a suitcase. Yes, Dot was no doubt on her way to see a doctor about the abortion. Only that could account for their having a suitcase with them. He could not have arranged things so neatly if he had really tried dying for real!

The next morning was Sunday and it was clear and cold, with a sharp, freezing wind sweeping in over the city from Lake Michigan. He felt driven to haunt the neighborhood of his mother. How was she taking his death? Her lonely plight saddened him more than anything else. She lived in an area that did not know him and he waited in a bar near a window to get a glimpse of her as she left for church. His overcoat was turned up about his chin and his hat was pulled low over his eyes. He smoked, toyed with a glass of beer, keeping his eyes hard upon the entrance of her house. True enough, at a quarter to eleven she came out, dressed in black, her face hidden by a veil, and picked her way gingerly over the deep snow toward her church some two blocks away. Cross felt hot tears stinging his cheeks for the first time since his childhood. He longed to run to her, fall on his knees in the snow and clasp her to him, begging forgiveness. His poor, sad, baffled old Mama . . . But if he went to her, she would collapse in the snow and might well die of the shock.

His worry that something might go wrong with his burial was what kept Cross awake the whole of the Sunday night before his funeral. Had there been no inquiries about the Negro's body that they had mistaken for his own? Who had that man been? Would his family come forward at the last moment and ask questions? Maybe his wife would claim the body? In fact, anybody's raising a question would endanger his whole plan. But perhaps no one had known that the Negro had been on the train. As he recalled now the man had seemed rather shabbily dressed. Perhaps the man's wife, if he had had a wife, thought that he had run off. Cross chided himself for worrying. In the minds of whites, what's one Negro more or less? If the rites went off without someone's raising a question, then he would consider the whole thing settled.

Monday morning was bright and cold; the temperature dipped to ten below zero. Gusts of wind swept in from Lake Michigan, setting up swirling eddies of powdered snow in the quiet streets. Cross stood moodily at his window and stared out at the frozen world, occupied with the question of how he was to spy on his burial. The *Chicago World* had reported that his body had been laid out at the Jefferson Resting Home and that "his postal colleagues and a host of friends" had sent numerous floral wreaths; his death had been referred to as a "great loss to the South Side community". He felt that if he could get a sneaking glimpse of Gladys and the funeral procession, he would feel certain in judging how soundly his death had been accepted. Spying upon the church was easy; he had, late one night, rented a top floor room in the building opposite the church, identifying himself to the old black landlady as John Clark, a student visiting Chicago as a tourist for a week. He had already made two visits to the room, bowing respectfully to the landlady, and had observed the church at leisure.

A little after ten that morning, just after he had re-turned from breakfast, Jenny came to see him and her manner was so friendly that one would have thought that she had known him for years. Cross was decidedly in no mood for her company, fearing that she might ask him where he was going when he was ready to leave to spy on his last rites.

"I got the blues today," he growled at her.

"Maybe I can cheer you up," she chirped, seating her-self even though he had not asked her to. There was something in her manner that warned him to be on guard. She had a mouthful of chewing gum.

"Nothing to drink this morning?" she asked.

"Empty pocket, empty bottle," he lied.

"What kind of work did you do in Memphis?" she asked.

"Why in hell do you want to know that?" he de-manded.

"Just curious, that's all," she answered innocently, chewing vigorously. "Something tells me you got some money."

"Yeah; I opened the safe with a bar of soap and got a million bucks," he joshed her. "Now tell me, are you working for the police?"

She paled. Her jaws stopped moving. Then she said: "Well, I never . . . !"

"Then why in hell do you keep on questioning me?"

"You *are* scared of something!" she exclaimed.

She had trapped him so neatly that he wanted to slap her. Yet he knew that it was he who had betrayed his fear and made her suspicious of him. He decided that she was honest; but honest or not, he could not use her. Her present attitude might be buttressed by good faith, but she was tough and if she found out that he had something to conceal, might she not blackmail him?

"Look— Why don't you tell Jenny about your troubles? Maybe we can team up together," she said seriously.

"Forget it, Jenny. You'll save yourself time."

"You're in no mood for talking today," she said, rising. "See you when you're feeling better."

She let herself out of the room and he sat brooding. Maybe he ought to play safe and move? Was Jenny stooling for the police? But he had no criminal record and even if the police should question him, there was nothing they could pin on him. He had only a day to wait; he would remain where he was. Later, after the descent of the catastrophe, he wondered why he had not acted upon his sense of foreboding and moved . . .

It was nearing two o'clock when Cross, filled with trepidation, took a trolley to the South Side. He found himself being irresistibly drawn to Gladys' home and, rashly, he boarded an "L" that passed in sight of the house and rode back and forth, snatching a quick glimpse of the front door each time the train sped past. He would ride a station past the house in one direction, get off, traverse the footbridge, and ride past the house again in the other direction to the station beyond it, get off again and return. It was not until nearly two-thirty that he saw any signs of life; the front door opened and Gladys and his mother—both dressed in deep black— came out upon the sidewalk and stood in the snow. Junior, Peter, and Robert followed, being led by a distant cousin of Gladys. Excited, Cross got off the train, concealed himself behind a billboard on the "L" platform, and saw a man garbed formally in black go up to Gladys, his mother, and the children, and tip his hat to them. No doubt the undertaker, Cross thought. His eyes lingered on his mother and his sons and, as they left, a light seemed to go out of the winter sky. He would never see them again . . .

His heart bubbled with hot panic when a voice sounded in his ear: "Do you know 'em?"

He spun and looked into the face of a young Negro dressed in the uniform of the "L" company. He had never seen the man before.

"No," he answered, relaxing.

"That's the family of a guy who was killed in the subway accident last week," the man spoke in a detached voice. "I reckon they must be going to the funeral."

"Oh," Cross said, keeping his face averted. "I read about that."

"Man, that guy wasn't nothing but meatballs and spaghetti when the subway got through with 'im," the man went on.

"What do you mean?" Cross asked.

"Brother, your blood is the tomato sauce. Your white guts is the spaghetti. And your flesh is the meat, see? You'd be surprised how like a plate of meatballs and spaghetti you look when you get minced up in one of those subway wrecks. Ha-ha-ha," the man laughed cynically.

An "L" train rolled to a stop and Cross hurried into it; he had seen and heard enough. He rushed to his rented room and sat at a window overlooking the church entrance. Fifteen minutes later the hearse arrived. There's Tom . . . ! Tom was his old friend from the Post Office and he was one of the pallbearers. And there was Frank . . . And Pinkie . . . And Booker . . . And Joe Thomas . . . He could not make out the others, for their faces were turned. He watched them lift the black coffin and march slowly into the church. The undertaker's assistants followed, carrying many wreaths of flowers inside. He saw the undertaker lead Gladys, his mother, and his three sons into the church. He opened the window a crack and caught an echo of a melancholy hymn . . . The service was so long that he wondered what the preacher could have found to say about him. He was certain, however, of one thing: whatever was being said had no relationship at all to him, his life, or the feelings he was supposed to have had.

An hour later the church doors opened and the crowd began to file out, first Gladys, then his mother; finally his three sons came, led by the preacher and the undertaker. Again he saw them sliding the black coffin into the hearse. Soon a long procession of black cars pulled off through the snow. It was over. He had witnessed a scene about which he could never in his life talk with anybody. And he *did* hanker to talk about it. When men shared normal experiences, they could talk about them without fear, but he had to hug this black secret to his heart.

The procession had gone and the church doors had shut. He had to go back to his hotel and prepare to catch a train for New York. But he did not move. He was empty, face to face with a sense of dread more intense than anything he had ever felt before. He was alone. He was not only without friends, their hopes, their fears, and loves, to buoy him up, but he was a man tossed back upon himself when that self meant only a hope of hope. The church across the street was still there, but somehow it had changed into a strange pile of white, lonely stone, as bleak and denuded of meaning as he was. And the snowy street, like the church, assumed a dumb, lifeless aspect. He lit a cigarette and sat on the edge of the bed and stared about the room. His movements were mechanical. The dingy walls seemed to loom over against him, asking wordlessly questions that he could not answer. Nothing made meaning; his life seemed to have turned into a static dream whose frozen images would remain unchanged throughout eternity.

He told himself that he was brooding too much; he had to get out of this room. On the snow-cushioned sidewalk, his legs led him to a taxi, but when he reached his hotel, he did not want to go in. Instead he ambled into a nearby bar, THE CAT'S PAW, and ordered a whiskey. He drank eleven shots before he could feel the influence of the alcohol. He ordered his twelfth and the bartender told him: "If I were you, I'd get some air."

"I can pay you," Cross told him.

"That ain't the point," the bartender said. "Get rid of what you've got, then I'll sell you some more." The bartender studied him. "Worried about something, eh?"

He paid and went out. He was not drunk; there was simply no purpose in him. When he finally entered the hotel, he met Jenny in the corridor near the door of his room. Because she had no meaning, she meant everything to him now.

"Speak of the devil," she greeted him, smiling.

"Hi," he breathed.

"Look, I got a bottle," she said, showing it to him. "How about it?"

"I don't mind."

He needed a drink. He felt her take hold of his hand and squeeze it.

"You're freezing," she said.

"Yeah."

He unlocked the door and let her go in; he followed, pulled off his coat and flopped on the bed.

"You're all in," she commented sympathetically.

"Tired," he said and closed his eyes.

"You must relax," she said.

He was silently grateful when he felt her cool, soft

hand moving slowly across his hot forehead. Her hand left him; he heard her pouring whiskey, felt the glass as she took his fingers and gently forced them about it. He pulled up and drank. She sat next to him on the bed, cradling her glass in her palms.

"Don't you want to know anything about me?" she asked him.

"Jenny, you don't understand," he said kindly.

"I'm a little better than you think I am," she said; she bent forward and fingered his ear.

"Maybe."

"You *could* do a lot worse than me, and maybe you *could* do a lot better. But whatever it is, it's not for keeps," she told him.

"What are you trying to say?"

"Take me with you," she said. "When you're tired of me, then dump me. I don't care. I want to get out of Chicago."

"I can't."

"Why?"

Her soft arm went around his neck and his nostrils were full of the scent of her hair; he drained his glass and a moment later he heard her ask: "What's the matter? If you talk about it, it'll be easier."

She searched for his mouth and kissed him. His world was a blur. He needed what she was trying to give him but he was afraid.

"Why do you bother about me?" he asked.

"'Cause I like you. Ain't that enough?"

"Guess so," he mumbled. He was alone, empty. "Give me another drink."

She poured the glasses full. He drank again, stood, swayed, tugged at his tie.

"What're you doing?"

"Going to bed . . ."

"Wait, I'll help you undress," she said. "You're three sheets to the wind."

His limbs were like rubber. She aided him in pulling off his clothes, rolled back the blanket and pushed him into bed. His eyes closed; he heard her moving about, pulling down the shade, locking the door. Then he felt the sensual smoothness of her skin as she slid into bed beside him. She blended her body with his and he could feel the tender spread of her fingers on his back. His senses were dreaming. He looked at her and she was not a dangerous girl; those deep, tranquil, bluish-grey-green eyes were dark and helpful now and the heat of her body was filling him with thankfulness.

"Can't you talk to me?" she asked him.

"You wouldn't understand."

"I would. Just *try*."

He laughed, took her face between his palms and stared at her, feeling foolishly proud of the irony of his life.

"I'm dead," he said.

Her lips parted in bewilderment and she pushed his hands roughly from her face. She looked off a second and then back to him.

"You're nuts," she said.

He wanted to tell her. He knew now that she was not working for the police, but for herself. She needed a man and had fastened her hope on him. If she had been well-known to him, he would never have had the impulse to tell her. But a strange girl was different and he would be leaving soon. Dammit, he had to tell somebody just to make sure that his situation was not a fantasy of his own mind. He was too much alone and it was insupportable.

"I'm in a funny fix," he began. "You remember that subway accident last week? Well, I was in it."

"You were hurt in it? Is that what's making you act so funny?"

"I wasn't really hurt," he continued, knowing that he ought not talk, but hearing the words spilling out in spite of himself. "Listen, they found a body down there all mangled and they think it's mine . . ."

"Are you *sure* you weren't hurt?" Her eyes were round with concern.

"No. I wasn't hurt," he went on, nettled that she was not believing him. "Today, just two hours ago, they buried that body thinking that it was mine . . ."

She pulled abruptly away from him, rose, walked across the room and got her cigarettes. She lit one and sat near him.

"Are you trying to shit me? Now, come on; tell me what you've done."

Cross buried his face in the pillow to stifle his laughter. She did not believe him. He knew that his story was wild, but he had not counted upon so much outright disbelief.

"This is funny," he chuckled.

"What's so goddamn funny?" she snapped at him.

"You asked me to tell you, now you don't believe me."

"If you had done something like that, you wouldn't tell me," she said.

"Why not?"

"Because the insurance companies would want to know about it," she explained. "And you're smarter than that."

He grew sober. Her intelligence was frightening.

"All right," he said, relieved. "I'm lying." He stood and got his bathrobe and struggled into it. "*I'm not dead, then.*"

"Where're you going?" she asked.

"Down the hall to see a man about a coffin," he said.

He lumbered into the corridor, feeling swamped by confusion. This damn girl was making him lose control of the project he had planned. I'm really crazy to talk to her, he reproached himself. He resolved that upon his return from the bathroom he was going to get dressed and get the hell out of the city as fast as a train could carry him. And from now on he would keep firm hold on himself. He turned a bend in the corridor, his head lowered in reflection; he drew in his breath sharply as he felt his body colliding with that of another man. Before his senses could register what was happening, he heard a familiar voice bursting in his ears and saw an old, familiar smile of incredulous astonishment spreading over a fat, black face.

"As I live and breathe! You're either Cross or his twin!"

Cross stared at the face and had the stupid desire to shake his head and make it vanish. He was looking into the eyes of a man he had known for six years! Like he, the man wore a bathrobe and had evidently just come from the bathroom. He was done for; there was no way out of this except . . . *He had to decide what to do quickly!* Tension made him hot as fire; he had to check a crazy impulse to wave his arm and try to sweep this man from sight and keep his freedom. It was big, fat, black Joe Thomas who stood in front of him, the same man he had seen acting as a pallbearer around his coffin earlier that afternoon!

"*Speak*, man! They say you're dead, but you ain't no ghost and I damn well *know* it! We just put your coffin in the ground, man! What the *hell* is this?" Joe's eyes were dancing in his fat, black face; he threw out his hands, hesitated, then clapped both of them on Cross's shoulders. "I got to *touch* you to believe it!" Joe's face was a mixture of fear and gladness. "They *all* think you're dead, and *here* you are in a cat house with the chippies! Good God Almighty! I feel weak . . ." Joe blinked, his lips hanging open. "I just came in here to knock off a piece of tail 'fore going to work— Hell, the whole town's talking 'bout how you died—" Joe rocked back on his heels and burst into a gale of hysterical laughter. "This is a new way to cover up cunt hunting! Oh, Jesus, this is hot!" Joe sobered for a moment; he was struggling with himself to adjust his mind to what his eyes saw. "But, *say* something! You *are* Cross, ain't you?"

"Yes," Cross heard himself speaking. "I'm Cross."

"Well, don't be ashamed of letting me catch you in a whorehouse, man," Joe said, blinking and trying to understand the strange expression that shrouded Cross's face. "Come on *in* here and let me *talk* to you." Joe grabbed Cross's hand and dragged him forward. He unlocked a door and pulled Cross inside a room. Cross's eyes darted about. The bed was unmade, the shades drawn, and a dim light glowed on the ceiling. Joe's clothing was flung pell-mell over the back of a chair. Cross's fingers ached to blot out this black man who grinned with bewilderment.

"Sit down, man," Joe spluttered. "Tell me what this *is* . . ."

Joe shut the door and Cross heard the click of the lock; that meant that no one could come in without warning; he was alone with Joe . . . Joe flopped on the bed, his eyes full on Cross, waiting for an explanation. Cross moved on cat's feet to the center of the room, noticing the window which had the exact position of the window in his room, that window through which he had peered only a few hours ago and looked at the distant, snow-drenched streets far below . . . He then stared at the almost empty whiskey bottle on the night table. Tension was so tight in him that he felt his skull would burst. Joe saw him gazing at the bottle.

"You want a drink, hunh? I scared you, didn't I?" Joe took the bottle and drained the whiskey into a glass. "This bottle's dead. But we've got another one on the way." He sat the bottle on the floor and handed the tumbler to Cross. "I reckon I'm about the last man on earth you ever expected to see, hunh?"

Cross emptied the glass with one swallow, and smiling tightly, said: "That's right, Joe."

"You *are* Cross!" Joe shouted and slapped his thighs. "For a minute, I thought maybe I was making a fool out of myself. God, I'm sweating—! Cross, you're the goddamndest man God ever made . . ."

Cross reached for the neck of the empty whiskey bottle and lifted it.

"Ain't no more whiskey in that bottle, man," Joe said. "I just sent Ruth down for another fifth. She'll be back in a minute. Sit down, man! Don't be scared . . . Lord, I can't get over this!"

"When's this Ruth coming back?" Cross asked quietly.

"In a minute," Joe said, a shadow of disquiet flickering over his face. He brightened quickly. "Say, who you're shacking up with in here? Bertha, Mamie, Della, or . . ."

"Jenny," Cross said.

"She's great!" Joe approved. "Boy, she can go when she feels like it. She's got some build . . ."

Joe went on talking and Cross stared at him. He had to do something. But what? This clown was tearing down his dream, smashing all he had so laboriously built up. And there he sat: fat, black, half-laughing and half-scared, with beads of sweat popping on his forehead, his black chest showing and his bare legs sprawled out from the bed, his blue silk bathrobe flowing around him . . .

"God, but you're sly, Cross," Joe went on. "Ain't you gonna tell me what happened? I didn't know you knew about this place. But there ain't no better place to get over the blues, is it? Kind of crummy here, but the gals are nice. Hell, man, if you ain't gonna say nothing, I'll tell 'em. They made a mistake in that damned church today. I'm gonna call up Pink. He'll die laughing . . ." Joe rose from the bed.

Cross grasped the neck of the bottle firmly; his arm trembled; his fingers gripped the bottle so hard that he thought the glass would crush in his palm. He lifted the bottle high in the air. Joe's lips moved soundlessly, his eyes black pools of mute protest. Joe was frozen, waiting, his lips open and about to utter a question and then Cross brought down the bottle with a crashing blow on Joe's head. Just before the blow landed Cross heard Joe utter in tones of deep amazement: "Say?" The bottle caught Joe on the temple, bursting from the force of the blow and Joe fell slowly backwards without having lifted a finger; he lay still, his thick lips hanging grotesquely open. Cross moved now with the speed of a panther. He let up the shade and a tide of greyish light swept into the room; he opened the window and a blast of freezing air turned his breath to steam. He turned and faced the inert form sprawled on the bed in its bathrobe. He grabbed Joe's right arm and slid his left arm under Joe's legs and lifted him as one would a sick child. He stood a moment, looking at Joe's black, quiet face, and then he looked at the open window. He struggled to the window with the body, hoisted it up and for a moment the body was poised in space. He pushed it through and shut the window at once, all in one swift, merciless movement. He turned back to the room, picked up the glass shards of whiskey bottle and opened the door. The corridor was empty. He went out and hurried to the bathroom and secreted the shards atop a tall, wooden cabinet. He examined himself minutely in the full mirror and saw no telltale signs except sweat on his face. He mopped his brow with the bottom of his bathrobe, then stood still, listening intently. He heard faint voices and the muffled music of radios. Time seemed to be flowing on normally. Through the window of the bathroom he could see that night was falling upon the frozen city. He headed for his room, feeling unsteady in his legs. He hesitated before going in, trying to control himself. Again he mopped sweat from his face, then opened the door of his room. Jenny still lay on the bed.

"I thought maybe you had flushed down the drain, you took so long," she said.

He sank into a chair, fighting down a wild, foolish impulse to tell her what he had done. She rose, smiling, and went to him; he pushed her violently away.

"What's the matter with you? You're trembling and wringing wet . . ." She paused and narrowed her eyes. "Say, are you on the needle or something . . . ?"

"Leave me alone," he muttered.

"I wonder what you're up to," she said, turning away uneasily.

A knock came at the door. Cross stiffened and felt he could not breathe. He would not have been too surprised if the door had opened and Joe had walked into the room. But he had tossed Joe out of that window; or had he? He struggled to sort reality from fantasy. The knock came again, louder this time.

"Aren't you going to answer it?" Jenny asked him.

"You answer it," Cross said.

"Jenny!" a woman's voice called through the door.

"Yeah?" Jenny answered, going to the door and opening it.

A tall, fleshy blonde woman stood in the doorway with a bottle of whiskey under her arm.

"Hello, Ruth," Jenny said. "What's the matter?"

"Sorry. Didn't mean to disturb you," the woman called Ruth said. Her eyes looked about the room, resting at last on Cross. "But Joe isn't here, is he?"

"No, honey," Jenny said, shrugging. "I haven't seen him."

Ruth's lips curled in scorn. "That black bastard's run out on me," she hissed. "If he's dumped me without paying, I'll kill him the next time I see him, so help me God! But I don't understand . . . All his clothes are still there."

"Oh, he'll come back," Jenny smiled. "He always does."

"He tried a new trick," Ruth blazed. "He sent me down for a bottle of liquor and took a powder." Ruth forced a smile for Cross. "I'm sorry to bother you with my troubles. But, you know, the fool left his clothes behind . . . You reckon he could be two-timing me? Maybe he's in some other room . . . ?"

"*Might* be," Jenny said, laughing at the possibility.

"I'll leave you now," Ruth said, her eyes baffled.

Jenny closed the door and turned to Cross, chuckling: "Ruth and her Joe. I do believe she's in love with him, but he doesn't give a damn about her."

"Who's Joe?" Cross asked listlessly.

"A colored postal clerk who comes here all the time," she told him as she sat on the bed again, her hands folded modestly over her pubic hair. "He's Ruth's star client; he even keeps his bathrobe and slippers in her room. God, he's a scream. Jet black, fat . . . A regular clown . . . Spends his money like water . . . Listen to this: He once told me . . ."

Cross was not listening though his eyes were on her face. He was wondering how Joe's body had fallen and where . . . Had it landed on the street? He wanted to open the window and look out, but he knew that would have aroused questions in Jenny's mind. He had done a horrible thing; he had killed so swiftly and brutally that he hardly recognized what he had done as he recalled it to his mind. It was he who had made that assault on Joe in that room; yes, he had done that to save himself. He heard Jenny laughing.

". . . don't you think so?" she was asking.

"I don't know," he mumbled.

"Hell, you're not even *listening*!" she said angrily. "At least Joe's a good sport!"

"Well, go to him," Cross told her, relishing his irony.

If Joe's body had landed on the street in the snow, then it would soon be seen by someone and there would be an outcry. But maybe it had dropped into a deep drift? He was excited by such a prospect. If that had happened, no one would see it for awhile . . . He blinked when Jenny rose from the bed and came to him; she caught his hand and pulled him to his feet. Gently, she forced him to the bed, climbed in with him and drew the covers over them.

"Charlie, what's the matter?" she asked in a whisper. "Talk to me . . ."

Maybe at any moment now a knock would come at the door and it would be about Joe. He heard footsteps pass in the corridor outside and wondered if it was Ruth still hunting for her Joe . . . He had had no choice; it had been either he or Joe. He had known it the moment he had looked into that fat, black, laughing face.

"Your body is trembling," Jenny whispered. "I wish I could *help* you!"

She was getting on his nerves. Why didn't she leave . . . ?

"You're always watching me, questioning me," he complained in a distant voice.

"You're too goddamn fucking suspicious!" she cursed him, curling her lips back over her teeth.

He looked at her; there was an animal-like quality in her that made him like her, and that quality showed most clearly when she was angry.

"Okay, baby, spill your story," he consented. "You've been wanting to talk to me. Now, I'm listening . . ."

He lifted himself on an elbow, his eyes on her face, but he was really seeking over the snowdrifts outside, looking for Joe's body.

"You sure are a great help," she complained, her anger vanishing. "I'll try— Look, Charlie, you're black and I'm white— That's what this goddamn country says, but it's the bunk, and you know it and I know it. They say it to keep us apart, don't they?"

He nodded, not quite understanding what she had said. Maybe he had made a mistake in killing Joe like that . . . ? God, he had planned to be free, and now he had killed . . .

". . . I'd bet a million dollars that I've lived a much harder life than you have. I grew up in the slums of a small rotten town in the middle of Kansas. My father was a drunkard and a socialist of a sort . . ."

He was conscious that the more she talked the better she talked. The gal's got some sense . . . But wouldn't they raid the hotel when they found Joe's body . . . ?

". . . he was always yelling about the rights of Negroes and fighting for the underdog. My mother was the janitor in the town school. If it hadn't been for her,

I wouldn't 've even learned to read and write. My mother really supported us, brought us up and nursed father when he had the D.T.'s. She was the only decent person I've ever known in my life . . . Surprised to hear *me* say things like that, hunh?"

He was looking at her, but was wondering what the police would say about finding Joe's body clad only in a bathrobe . . .

". . . and I spotted you as an educated guy after you'd said only two words. I respect education . . . It's too late for me to get one now, I reckon. But I want one; really, I do."

He nodded his head as she spoke, telling her that he was following her, but he was only reacting to the general sense of her words.

". . . everybody in our little town looked down on us. Me, my brothers and sisters, we were the drunkard's children, the scum of the earth. Then I got in trouble with a boy, got knocked up, and had to have an abortion. You wouldn't think it, Charlie, but 'til two years ago I didn't know where babies came from. Honest to Pete! I thought they came out of women's bowels . . . Isn't that crazy? But I know *now*. And how! But let me get back to the story. You're listening, aren't you? You're not bored?"

"Oh, no; go ahead," he said; he might be lost already. It was good that he had his gun; if the police found out about him, well, he would blow his brains out . . .

". . . and when I got knocked up, the whole town knew it. My father drove me out of the house. I lived in a dump for awhile, then got rid of the child. It was hell; I was sick with a fever of one hundred and four for three days. I thought I was a dead duck. Mama finally made father let me come back home. But just to walk down the street to the store to buy a loaf of bread was hell . . . When I passed people, they'd stop talking and just stare at me . . . I ran off and came to Chicago. The first week I worked in a Greek restaurant; like a dope, I went out with the Greek. He raped me . . ."

He wondered why she felt so deep a sense of inferiority; he was black, but he had never felt that humble in the face of life. And Joe? Maybe the sirens would start howling soon . . . ?

". . . sounds crazy, hunh? But I'm not asking for sympathy. The hell with it. I'm young. I'll fight, work. Now, why am I telling you all this? You said you were going west, didn't you? I want to go to California—"

"Movies?" he asked.

"Hell, no. I'm not pretty," she said.

Cross studied her face; she was much prettier than she thought.

"Then why California?"

"I just like the sunshine and want to be as far from Kansas and my family as I can get," she said. "Take me with you, won't you? I could be of some use, couldn't I? I don't care if you're colored. The hell with that crap—"

"Jenny," he began. "It won't work—"

"Why not? You can trust me."

"But my life— No. It won't work at all."

"I don't give a good goddamn *what* you've done," she said.

Cross smiled ruefully. She doesn't know what she's saying . . . "Look, baby, I like you. I believe you. But forget it, honey. It's too complicated to explain."

She stood and her face grew red and her eyes blazed with anger. Would he have to do something to keep her quiet? Was she going to threaten him and make him take her with him?

"Why am I so different?" she demanded. "Do you loathe me? What's wrong with me . . . ?" Tears welled in her eyes. "Only last week Pearl Bland got a ride to New York with a guy with dough," she said bitterly. "Me? I can't even get a *Negro* to trust me!" She bent to him and asked: "*Why?* Tell me why . . ."

"Come here, Jenny," he said.

He folded her in his arms. Good God, this child was bitter! In despair she began kissing him with passion, still weeping. He relaxed. Why not let her make him forget? He could not control the flow of events now anyway; he was probably already lost . . . Any minute the cops would be knocking on the door. What did he have to lose? He pressed his lips to Jenny's and this time he knew that she was allowing herself to be more of a woman because she wanted his trust. When the spasm was over he lay with his hand gently touching her face, mutely thanking her for the benediction that she had shed upon his distraught senses.

"Darling, what's your real name?" she asked him quietly.

The respite was over; he felt danger again. He had to shake this girl off him quickly. But, what about Joe? He had pushed Joe out of that window and time had flowed on as though nothing had happened. No one here knew his name or that he had known Joe. So, when they found Joe's body, there would be no thought of him in connection with his death. They might even think that Ruth had done it. He lay still, plotting. He would not hurt Jenny; killing her would be a sure way of putting the police on his trail. He would fool her and ditch her. She thought that he was heading west. All right; agree to take her, dump her at the last moment, and strike out for New York alone. Cunning was better than violence; he must not allow himself to be confronted again with the unexpected, as he had been with Joe . . .

"You really want to come with me?"

Her arms tightened about his neck in gratitude.

"Where're we going?" she asked.

"We'll take a bus to Denver, then later we'll go to the Far West," he said.

"But we have to have dough. How much have you got?"

"Leave that to me," he argued. "I'll get you to the West Coast, if you want to go."

"When do we leave?"

"Tonight." He rolled swiftly from the bed and began washing up. "I'll go down for the tickets now."

"I'll believe it when I see those tickets," she said, rising and commencing to dress also.

"You better start packing," he told her. "How much luggage have you got?"

"Just a suitcase." She studied him, then rubbed her fingers together. "I need some nylons and things . . ."

He gave her ten dollars.

"Aw, come on," she exploded. "Be a sport."

"I'll give you more tomorrow," he said. "Now, go." He pushed her out of the door, looked both ways in the corridor, then shut the door and locked it. He hurried to the window and opened it. A clear night sky sent a sheen over the snow-covered world. He stared down, searching for Joe's body. Ah . . . There it was, on that roof! He could see it lying straight out, a black mark on the white snow. The soft snow had no doubt cushioned its fall and the impact of the body on the roof had not been heard. He had time to get away before anyone discovered it. He closed the window and stood in the center of the room. Why had that damn fool come upon him at that time? But he could not think of Joe now; he had to plan how to ditch Jenny . . .

He rode down in the elevator with Buck who was grumbling: "Jesus! Why can't that bitch leave me alone?" He spoke to no one in particular. "She keeps yapping at me about Joe, Joe . . . What the hell do I care about Joe? It ain't my job to keep track of her damn men! These whores make me sick. Let a bobby pin get lost, and they come running to me."

"Don't let 'em break you down," Cross told him.

"You damn right I won't," Buck seethed with anger. "I don't do my day's work at night, like they do, flat on their backs. Man, a woman'd make a man jump out of a window; *she would*!"

Cross walked from the lobby on legs he did not feel. He knew that Buck knew nothing about how Joe had died, but his talking of jumping from a window had almost paralyzed him. His body was seized with ague and he felt so weak that he went into an alleyway and sank down upon an empty wooden soda water case under the spreading glare of a street lamp. He started when a door opened and an aproned man came out with a garbage can and dumped its contents near him; the man glanced curiously at Cross, then went back inside, slamming the door and bolting it securely. Cross rested his wrists on his knees and his eyes traveled without purpose over the steaming pile of refuse, the top of which was crowned with a mound of wet, black coffee grounds that gleamed in the light of the street lamp; some of the grounds spilled over a bloodstained Kotex which still retained the curving shape of having fitted tightly and recently against the lips of some vagina; there was a flattened grapefruit hull whose inner pulpy fibres held a gob of viscous phlegm; there was the part of a fried sausage with grease congealed white in the porous grains of meat; there was the crumpled cellophane wrapping from a pack of cigarettes glittering with tiny beads of moisture; there was a brass electric socket still holding its delicate filigreed web of wires even though its glass globe had been shattered; there was a bone from a piece of roast beef still holding traces of red and grey meat; there was a lemon rind molded to a light green color; there was a clump of cigarette butts whose ends were blackened and whose tips were stained red from the rouge of a woman's lips; there was a limp wad of lettuce whose leaves glistened with a fine film of oil; there was a clean piece of wood jutting out with a shining nail bent at the end of it; there were several egg shells showing bits of yellow yolk; there was the stump of a cigar bearing the marks of a man's teeth; and there was a clump of fluffy dust freshly gathered from some floor . . .

His blood felt chilled. He had to shake off this dead weight and move on. He pulled to his feet and took a cab to La Salle Street Railroad Station and went directly to the reservation window.

"Have you any sleeping accommodations for New York?"

"For tonight?" the clerk asked.

"For the earliest possible train," Cross said.

"Just a minute," the clerk said.

Cross waited nervously while the clerk telephoned.

"We have one, a lower 13," the clerk informed him.

"Okay. Fix it up. When does the train leave?"

"At six on track eight, sir."

He paid, received the tickets, then rushed by cab to the Greyhound Bus Terminal and bought two tickets to Denver. Back in the hotel, he settled his bill in full and rode up in the elevator to the eighth floor. Jenny was waiting for him at the door of his room with her suitcase. She smiled warmly, but there was nervousness in her manner. When they were inside, he handed her her ticket for the bus.

"Where's your ticket?" she asked suspiciously.

"Here," he said, showing it to her. He had thought that she would ask that; it was why he had bought two tickets. The extra money he had paid for his ticket was his insurance that she would believe in him long enough for him to take the six o'clock train to New York. When Joe's body was discovered or when any word was ever raised about the identification of that body found in the subway wreck, nothing of him must come into the mind of Jenny.

"You know where the Greyhound Bus Terminal is?" he asked.

"Sure."

"The bus leaves at eight. I've got to see some people; I'll be gone about an hour." He looked at his watch. "It's five now. I'll be back at six. We'll eat and then we're off. Now, give me your suitcase and I'll check it at the Bus Terminal."

With his suitcase and hers, he got into a cab, checked her suitcase at the Bus Terminal and then rode over to the La Salle Street Railroad Station. A porter guided him to his coach. He showed his reservation and ticket to the conductor, got on, and, when he was in his compartment, he locked the door.

He cursed softly: That damn fool Joe . . . ! And Jenny did not know how lucky she was. From now on he had to cope with this impulse of his to confide. If circumstances had been just a little different, he would have had to kill Jenny too, or give up the game. He had thought he was free. But was he? He was free from everything but himself. Loneliness had driven him to confess to Jenny, and fear could have made him kill her as he had killed Joe. He kept his fists tightly clenched as he waited impatiently for the train to pull out. At last he heard the distant calling:

"Alll aboooooard . . . !"

He stood at the window as the train began to move. A light snow was raining softly down upon the world. Two hours from now Jenny would be searching frantically for him at the bus station. And she would never know that he had done her the greatest favor of her life.

But what was he to do with this conflict of his? This urge to confide and the fear of the danger of confiding? The outside world had fallen away from him now and he was alone at the center of the world of the laws of his own feelings. And what was this world he was?

The dreary stretches of Chicago passed before his window; it was a dim, dead, dumb, sleeping city wrapped in a dream, a dream born of his frozen impulses. Could he awaken this world from its sleep? He recalled that pile of steaming garbage, the refuse the world had rejected; and he had rejected himself and was bowed, like that heap of garbage, under the weight of endurance and time.

As the train wheels clicked through the winter night, he knew where his sense of dread came from; it was from within himself, within the vast and mysterious world that was his and his alone, and yet not really known to him, a world that was his own and yet unknown. And it was into this strange but familiar world that he was now plunging . . .

BOOK TWO

DREAM

As silent as a mirror is believed
Realities plunge in silence by . . .
— HART CRANE

CROSS'S WORLD was now sunk in sleep and, in his compulsiveness to rouse it from its slumber, the moments of his life became a dream of anxiety. He had lied, killed, and fled to get shunt of his old hated consciousness and now he was dismayed to find it redoubled in its density and still with him. He had merely shifted his cares from without to within him, from that which he could deny to that which he could not. Imprisoned he was in a state of consciousness that was so infatuated by its own condition that it could not dominate itself; so swamped was he by himself with himself that he could not break forth from behind the bars of that self to claim himself.

During the nightmarish weeks that followed his heightened sensibilities became responsive beyond his control. His turbulent mind developed a million mental eyes that ceaselessly hunted down non-existent dangers; and his tense emotions started in terror at the most casual phrases falling from the lips of strangers.

He found that he had been deprived of the will to make decisions, that he had, by his flight, abandoned himself to be tossed and buffeted by the tyranny of daily minutia. Thrust thus back upon himself, his actions were snared in a web of self-love that made the images of his mind assume a hypnotic sway over his body that was more decisive than the food he ate to sustain himself.

The train had been plunging through the wintry night for some hours before his memory of the happenings of the last days in Chicago had dimmed in his consciousness enough for him to feel somewhat relaxed. Whenever he recalled the past there returned to him not only the mere constellations of events through which he had lived, but also a psychological grasp of the role that his desires, hates, hopes, or loves had played in them. What helped him most was that he possessed the lucky capacity of reducing and referring his memories to an intense and personal basis, and could, therefore, once he was emotionally free of the concrete context from which they had sprung, live with them without a too-crushing sense of guilt.

His memory of his relationship with Dot was not only a recollection of a man's sensual affair with a pretty girl whom he had forsaken in the trouble he had brought upon her; but, above all, Dot had been to him an alluring representation of a personal hunger which he had projected out of his heart upon her and, the two of them—Dot and what she subjectively meant to him—had been something he had not been able to cope with with satisfaction to himself and honor to her. There had been no element of sadism in his love for Dot, and he would have gladly, if such had been possible, taken upon himself in a spirit of atonement the hurt she had sustained. But who can reverse time? What was done was done and the only part of the past that he could alter was that portion lingering on in his melancholy heart. The mirage of desire that he had sought so

pathetically was still his to mull over in regretful recollection.

In breaking his life in two he had left his baffled
mother to fend for herself as best she could, but that
baleful gift of the sense of dread which she had, out of
her life's hysteria, conferred upon him in his childhood,
was still his beyond his right to surrender. More definitely than ever her fateful gift was shaping and toning
his hours even now on this fleeing train, was subtly
sculpturing the contours of his destiny, staining all the
future that he was to embrace even to that lonely grave
which he would some day have to fill alone.

His being quit of Gladys was infinitely more than his
shedding a vindictive wife; it was his inheritance to the
full of an insight into those quicksands of appalling
loneliness that had sucked him into her waiting arms in
the first place. He did not remember her in a way that
made him yearn to return to her; his memory assumed
the form of an intense appropriation of that intimate
part of himself which had seduced him into embracing
her, and toward that part of his being he had now a
change of heart of not wanting ever again to seek fulfill-
ment of desire in that direction.

He was, however, far from being resigned; an urge to
launch again into life was still strong in him. His sorrow
for Dot, his mother, and Gladys originated in his knowing that they had hoped for something from him which
he did not possess; his pity for them was his knowledge
of himself, a regret for his ever having allowed them to
build their dreams upon the mercurial instabilities of his
emotions.

His memory of the death of Joe was of greater simplicity. His killing of Joe had been dictated by his fear of
exposure, and he knew that what had happened with Joe
could happen again under conditions whose advent he

could not gainsay or choose. Given a situation of danger and the dreaded tension that went with it, his impulse to save himself would sweep him toward what horizons? He knew that his being able to reflect coolly upon this did not mean that he was free of it, that to see was not to control, that self-understanding was far short of self-mastery. He was afraid of himself.

Had they discovered Joe's body yet? Or would that snowdrift on the roof hide it for a few days longer? He would keep track by reading the Chicago newspapers . . . But he had no real fear of his ever being accused of killing Joe, for his relation to Joe had been twice removed and no apparent motive for his having killed him could be easily deduced. For days the Chicago police would no doubt sniff about aimlessly in the hotel corridors, accusing first this whore and that, and, in the end, they would probably mark it down either as suicide or death at the hands of parties unknown . . . Or maybe they'd conclude that his death had been accidental . . . ?

The next morning, as the train neared New York, he made his way apprehensively into the dining car for breakfast. He was afraid that his preoccupation with his burden of non-identity and his fear of sudden surprises would distract him to the point of robbing reality of its naturalness and innocence. The serried white faces floating above the tables about him were signs whose meanings he had to decipher in terms of wondering if they suspected him. Or could he find with them some basis of relationship to still the howling loneliness of his heart?

Seating himself circumspectly at a vacant table, he looked about for the waiter. Coming from the front of the dining car, grinning broadly, holding aloft in his right palm a tray of steaming food, was a short, nervous, brown-skinned man who winked smilingly at Cross and kept on looking at him as he passed. The waiter had given him an innocent, racially fraternal greeting common among Negroes and Cross knew that most whites never dreamed that their behavior towards Negroes had bred in them, especially when Negroes were in the presence of whites, a situationally defensive solidarity that possessed no validity save that occasioned by the latent pressure of white hostility. He idly observed the waiter's movements as the brown hand deftly placed succulent dishes under the impassive faces of whites. Having emptied his tray, the waiter turned, paused at Cross's table, dusted his napkin at imaginary bread crumbs on the white table cloth, and whispered: "How you, guy?"

"Fine," Cross answered. "And you?"

"Just dragging my black ass, serving these white sons-ofbitches," the waiter said in a sniggling whisper. "Be with you in a sec. I'm the only waiter in this car. My pal took sick and got off in Cleveland. So I got my hands full of white shit." The waiter clapped his hands over his mouth and widened his eyes at Cross in a sign-language laugh.

"Take your time," Cross told him. "I'm in no hurry."

"Wish these white monkeys felt like you do," the waiter whispered in appreciation. He handed Cross a folded newspaper. "Want the paper?"

"Thanks," Cross mumbled.

He gave Cross another wink and moved swiftly on between the crowded tables. Cross opened the paper and glanced at the headlines. Was there any news of Joe? It was not until he had reached the bottom of page four that he saw a small caption:

POSTAL CLERK'S BODY FOUND

He lowered the paper quickly, reading:

The almost nude body of a Negro postal clerk, Joe Thomas, 39, of 3433 St. Lawrence Avenue, was found dead early this morning on the near South Side by an emergency line repairman. The body was lying clad only in a bathrobe in a deep snowdrift atop the roof of a four-story dwelling.

The victim had apparently been drunk and it has not been determined if Thomas leaped, was pushed, or died from exposure.

That was all. Could they trace Joe's death to him? But how could they discover that he, Cross Damon, had been in the hotel? He felt safe. He looked through the moisture-streaked window at the sunny fields of snow glittering and turning slowly outside. The train rumbled on clicking wheels of steel. Ice-encrusted telegraph wires shot past, rising and dipping like strings plucked by invisible fingers. It was a normal world whose events flowed intelligibly and each object had a sharp, precise meaning. He looked in the direction of the waiter and was surprised to see the waiter looking at him, winking, smiling . . .

Out of a void, anxiety rose and captured his senses; he could feel the reality of the dining car falling away as alien powers claimed his consciousness, projecting menacing meanings upon the look of the world. He fought against it feebly, but in the end he succumbed, trembling and embracing what he dreaded. Was he being followed on this train? Was not that waiter being especially friendly to allay any fears he might have that he was being watched? Had not that waiter cursed the white folks with the idea of inducing in him a false notion of security? His grasp of reality became confounded . . .

He had no objective evidence that anything extraordinary was happening in the dining car, but this rational perception did not down his fear. His mood sought restlessly for proof to feed his beast of terror. Why was that tall white man staring at him? And why had he looked off when his eyes met his? In vain his mind protested this mood of delusive reference that was stealing his sanity away . . .

Passing to get another tray of food, the waiter again paused at Cross's table, grinning, whispering: "These white bastards think they're smart, hunh? But one of these days we'll show 'em, won't we, boy?"

The waiter knew and was teasing him! He had spotted him for the police and was so sure of himself that he could joke about it! Cross blinked and fought to control the sensations of his body; he had the illusion of something crawling over the surface of his skin. When the waiter finally came to take his order, he was so confused that he kept his eyes on the menu and mumbled what he wanted to eat. He was conscious of the irrational nature of what was transpiring, but he could not master it. His sensibilities clamored to believe in this delusion; his emotions needed the certainty of this transparent fantasy; yet, in the end, his mind was tough enough to cling to its anchorage in the hard ambiguities of normal reality. When his bacon and eggs came, he had no desire to eat. But would not that make him conspicuous? He picked up his knife and fork and forced himself, praying for this spell to pass.

He was loading his fork with a bit of bacon and a part of egg yolk when a stretch of black cloth appeared before him. He lifted his eyes and saw a Catholic priest: tall, heavy, florid of face, and with a white, turned-about collar.

"Good morning," the priest said, smiling.

"Good morning," Cross answered.

The priest sat down, then nodded toward the white landscape. "We've had a lot of snow."

"Yes."

"Did you sleep well?" the priest asked.

"Yes," Cross lied.

"I didn't," the priest said. "I can never sleep on trains. By the way, do you live in Harlem?"

"Yes."

Why was he being so closely questioned? The priest stared thoughtfully out of the window and Cross wondered what he was thinking . . . He gripped his knife and fork hard. Goddamn . . . He had to keep his head above this dangerous water and not go under. As the waiter passed, the priest caught hold of his arm and asked: "May I keep this seat for my friend? He'll be here in a moment."

"Certainly, sir," the waiter said and, when he was out of the range of the vision of the priest, he made a grimace with his lips to Cross.

Cross's anxieties now condensed themselves into an attitude of sullenness toward the priest. He disliked most strongly all men of religion because he felt that they could take for granted an interpretation of the world that his sense of life made impossible. The priest was secure and walked the earth with a divine mandate, while Cross's mere breathing was an act of audacity, a confounding wonder at the daily mystery of himself. He felt that the attitude of the priest was predicated upon a scheme of good and evil ordained by a God whom he was constrained out of love and fear to obey; and Cross therefore regarded him as a kind of dressed-up savage intimidated by totems and taboos that differed in kind but not in degree from those of the most primitive of peoples. Cross had to discover what was good or evil through his own actions which were more exacting than the edicts of any God because it was he alone who had to bear the brunt of their consequences with a sense of absoluteness made intolerable by knowing that this life of his was all he had and would ever have. For him there was no grace or mercy if he failed.

The waiter paused with a loaded tray at his table and said: "I'll be serving your coffee, next."

"Good," Cross mumbled.

He saw the waiter bend with a dead-pan face to serve a white woman who sat across the aisle from him.

"I'm sorry I had to make you wait, Ma'm," the waiter mumbled.

Cross watched the waiter place a tumbler of orange juice before the woman, then a platter of ham and poached eggs. The waiter was about to lift a silver pot of steaming coffee to fill her cup when the woman turned abruptly with her whole body, opening her mouth to speak. Cross saw the woman's plump, naked elbow describe a tiny, swift arc and collide with the coffee pot as it left the tray. There was a ringing clatter of metal and a brown spout of boiling coffee, emitting a cloud of vapor, splashed over the woman's bare arm and on to her bosom. The waiter's movements froze and the woman leaped to her feet and screamed, her face distorted with fury and pain.

"Nigger, you're burning me!" she yelled.

The waiter stood paralyzed, his mouth open. The woman's frantic eyes swept the dining car, then rested upon the table. In one flowing movement, she seized the handle of a silver water pitcher and raised it above her head, her eyes bulging and her darkly rouged lips curled in pain.

Cross was on his feet before he knew it and had traversed the aisle and was standing between the woman and the waiter, fronting the woman, blocking her action with his uplifted right hand which still clutched his napkin. The woman sighed and lowered her hand.

"You're not hitting me, nigger," the woman said quietly.

"You're not hitting anybody either," Cross said.

The priest rushed to the side of the woman, put his arm about her, then looked from Cross to the waiter. The dining car was full of the rumble of the train speeding over steel rails. In the middle of the car a tall, hard-faced man stood up and glared.

"What's the matter down there?" the man called.

"I'm sorry, lady," the waiter crooned in humility.

The woman pawed at her arm which gleamed a brick red where the coffee had scalded it. Steam still rose from her dress. She began to weep.

"I got something for that burn, Ma'm," the waiter found his tongue and ran toward the rear of the car. The tall, hard-faced man rushed to the side of the priest and now two men were holding the woman and looking at Cross. Cross's hand fell to his side. He was surprised to find that he was smiling; he had acted before he had known it. Another white woman came forward and took hold of the injured woman.

"Darling, I've got something in my purse for burns," the woman said and led her from sight, toward the women's lavatory. The waiter came running with a tube of salve and stood staring helplessly at the backs of the two retreating women.

"It wasn't my fault," he said, looking at the silent, thoughtful faces in the car. "She turned round—like this." He imitated the woman's movement. "And she knocked the pot out of my hand."

The train whistled a long, mournful blast and Cross could feel the centrifugal pull of its speed as it struck a stretch of curving track. He went to his seat and sat before his half-empty plate and stared out of the window. Low voices were murmuring in the car.

"It's a shame— Was she burnt badly?"

"But I *saw* her; she knocked the pot out of his hand . . ."

"What happened? Did somebody hit the woman?"

"Oh, no; it was an accident. It wasn't the waiter's fault."

Cross became aware that the priest had also sat and was staring at him; when their eyes met, the priest looked off toward the snow-filled fields. Cross realized that he had sprung without thinking to his feet to block the woman's tossing the pitcher into the waiter's face and he knew that the priest had leapt up to defend the woman. Both of them had acted before they had been fully conscious of what they had wanted to do. And now shame made them avoid each other's eyes.

"It's a strange world, isn't it?" Cross asked the priest softly.

The priest ruefully smiled his answer and nibbled thoughtfully at a slice of buttered toast.

The injured woman came briskly down the aisle with lips pursed and eyes glazed. The other woman followed.

"I'm going to report you," she told the waiter.

The waiter paused, stared, his lips hanging open in dismay. He shook his head and when he spoke his voice was so high-pitched that it was ludicrous.

"It wasn't my fault, Ma'm." It was a plea issuing from a soul that hated its shame and humility.

"You were careless and I'm going to sue," the woman said.

She tossed her blonde hair and flounced out of the car and another silence reigned. The waiter's face was a mask of distress and Cross chided himself upon ever having thought that he could have been spying on him.

"Oh, there you are!" a sonorous voice came from a hunched-back man who slid into the seat beside the priest.

"What kept you?" the priest asked.

"I went in the wrong direction looking for the diner," the man said, laughing and letting his eyes settle upon Cross's face.

Suddenly the priest beamed at Cross and spoke: "By the way, I'm Father Seldon and my friend here is District Attorney Ely Houston of New York City."

"How do you do?" Cross asked, full of fear, nodding to the hunchback. A District Attorney? *The* Ely Houston of whom he had heard? The celebrated crime-buster . . . ? At once his tensions began to deform the look of the world. Though the two white faces regarded him with friendliness, he projected out upon them an air of the sinister. Maybe the Chicago police had wired ahead and Houston had gotten on the train to apprehend him? How had they come to seat themselves *exactly* at his table? And he recalled that the priest had *expressly* asked the waiter to save the chair next to him for Houston . . . Was Houston armed? He imagined he could see a slight bulge under the man's right armpit and he mentally pictured a gun nestling there . . .

"You live in New York?" Houston asked.

"Yes."

Could this be a trap? He did not volunteer to tell his name and they did not ask him to do so. Would they think it odd that he had not identified himself?

"Mr. Houston and I are very much interested in your people," the priest said to Cross.

Cross knew exactly what the priest meant, but he allowed his eyebrows to lift in surprise. He did not want

to be drawn into any discussion with them, yet he did
not want to make them feel that he was afraid.

"*My* people? What do you mean?"

Father Seldon chewed industriously upon his mouthful of bacon and eggs and kept his eyes on his plate,
answering: "I mean the colored people—"

"Oh," Cross said, giving a play-acting laugh. "But
they were born that color. Nobody *colored* them."

Houston and the priest were startled for a moment,
then both of them laughed. Houston continued to ex-
amine Cross in a friendly manner; finally he nodded his
head affirmatively.

"That's good. I must remember it," Houston said.

"Well, Ely," Father Seldon said, turning and smiling
at Houston, "if you should ever run for the Senate,
you'd know how not to make a mistake before an audience in Harlem."

"I sure would," Houston admitted.

Cross was through eating and he wanted to go back
to his compartment. But he must not act too fast and
arouse unnecessary suspicions. He lingered on, studying
Houston closely. The man had a huge head of remark-
ably black, unruly hair; a long, strong, too-white face;
clear, wide-apart brown eyes; and a well-shaped mouth
that held always a hint of a smile at its corners. His
shoulders were Herculean with long arms that termi-
nated in huge hands with delicately strong fingers. The
hump on the back was prominent but not in any way as
noticeable as Cross would have thought it would be, so
naturally did it blend in with the man's general build.
Cross had not particularly noticed this deformity when
Houston had first sat down, but now he remembered
that Houston had moved forward to the table with a
motion that slightly resembled that of a creeping animal, holding his body still as he walked. He reminded

Cross of a giant, patiently waiting white spider whose temper was never ruffled but whose mental processes ground both fast and exceedingly fine. He had the impression of a man possessing stealthy reserves of physical and emotional strength, and he felt intuitively that this was exactly the kind of man whom he had to fear not only because he was a defender of the law, but because Houston had an ability to delve into life. He was afraid of this man and yet his fear made him want to know him.

"Where's your parish, Father?" Cross asked.

"In Harlem," Father Seldon said, obviously glad to speak of it. "We also operate a school for delinquent boys in Upstate New York. Maybe you've heard of it? The Sanctuary, it's called. We have about sixty Negro boys up there now."

"I see," Cross said.

Houston, whose deformity always made him seem hunched forward, now leaned even more over the table, dawdling his fork in his plate and speaking in a tone that made Cross know that he was expressing thoughts of deep interest to himself, thoughts touched and lighted by passion, almost.

"I'm profoundly interested in the psychological condition of the Negro in this country," Houston said. "Only a few people see and understand the complexity of this problem. And don't think that my interest is solely political. It's not; it was there long before I ever thought of entering politics." He smiled cryptically and let his eyes wander over the icy landscape flowing past the train's window. "My personal situation in life has given me a vantage point from which I've gained some insight into the problems of other excluded people."

Cross's impulses were at war. Was Houston raising the question of the Negro to mislead him before he was told that he was under arrest? Why did he not come right out with what he wanted? He had a foolish desire to reach forward and grab Houston's shoulder and say to him: All right; I know you're after me . . . Let's get it over with . . . His stomach muscles tightened as he checked himself. He knew that Houston, in identifying himself with Negroes, had been referring to his deformity. Houston was declaring himself to be an outsider like Cross and Cross was interested, but he kept his face passive to conceal it.

"The way Negroes were transported to this country and sold into slavery, then stripped of their tribal culture and held in bondage; and then allowed, so teasingly and over so long a period of time, to be sucked into our way of life is something which resembles the rise of all men from whatever it was we all came from," Houston said, the smile on his lips playful and knowing.

"I follow you," Cross said.

"Yes; I see you do," Houston smiled with satisfaction. "We are not now keeping the Negro on such a short chain and they are slowly entering into our culture. But that is not the end of this problem. It is the beginning . . ."

"What do you mean, Ely?" Father Seldon asked.

"I mean this," Houston hastened to explain. "Negroes, as they enter our culture, are going to inherit the problems we have, but with a difference. They are outsiders and they are going to *know* that they have these problems. They are going to be self-conscious; they are going to be gifted with a double vision, for, being Negroes, they are going to be both *inside* and *outside* of our culture at the same time. Every emotional and cultural convulsion that ever shook the heart and soul of Western man will shake them. Negroes will develop unique and specially defined psychological types. They will become psychological men, like the Jews . . . They will not only be Americans or Negroes; they will be centers of *knowing*, so to speak . . . The political, social, and psychological consequences of this will be enormous . . ."

"You are much too complicated, Ely," Father Seldon said. "The problem's bad enough without trying to make it into *everything*. All the colored people need is the right to jobs and living space."

"True," Houston said. "But their getting those elementary things is so long and drawn out that they must, while they wait, adjust themselves to living in a kind of No-Man's Land . . . Now, imagine a man inclined to think, to probe, to ask questions. Why, he'd be in a wonderful position to do so, would he not, if he were black and lived in America? A dreadful objectivity would be forced upon him."

"Oh, Ely, you're always climbing some rocky, goat track of speculation," Father Seldon protested. "Take the simple facts of life just as they are found—"

"That's what I'm doing," Houston said. "And when you look at them closely, those simple facts turn out to be not so simple."

"I think Mr. Houston's close to the truth," Cross said, pretending a smile, relishing an irony that came from his referring both to his own feelings that maybe Houston was trying to track him down and to the aptness of the man's remarks. "After many of the restraints have been lifted from the Negro's movements, and after certain psychological inhibitions have been overcome on his part, then the problem of the Negro in America really starts, not only for whites who will have to become acquainted with Negroes, but mainly for Negroes themselves. Perhaps not many Negroes, even, are aware of this today. But time will make them increasingly conscious of it. Once the Negro has won his so-called rights, he is going to be confronted with a truly knotty problem . . . Will he be able to settle down and live the normal, vulgar, day-to-day life of the average white American? Or will he still cling to his sense of outsidedness? For those who can see, this will be a wonderfully strange drama . . ."

"Right," Houston agreed by stabbing the air with his fork. "You're on the beam. Say, where did you go to school? Not that you learn things like that in school . . ."

"Fisk," Cross lied. He rose; this was getting too close. He had to go and hug his black secret. "I'm sorry, gentlemen," Cross smiled at them. "But I must leave. It's wonderful to talk like this."

"Well, sit down and talk," Houston said.

"No; really, I must go. I've a lot to do," Cross lied vaguely. "Good morning." He made his way nervously out of the dining car. Goddamn . . . He was frightened of that hunchback, that outsider who understood *too* much. Houston was a man crammed with guilty knowledge. What weird luck to encounter a kindred type to whom he wanted to talk and who wanted to talk to him. And this would be his life until he found himself an identity behind which he could hide.

The Pullman porter had made up his bed and he was alone; he sat and stared moodily out of the window. He who had a secret to hide loved talking! When one tried to conceal one's self, did not one make one's self conspicuous? And that seductive fear that always surged up in him, how was he to handle it? And why did he always yearn to embrace those delusive fantasies? What unearthly greed made him want to feed upon what he knew to be unreal? He could run away from Dot, Gladys, his mother, but he could not run away from this; it was he and he was it. A tapping came at the door and he rose in dread, his lips parting. Was it Houston? The tapping sounded again and he opened the door.

"Hey, guy," it was the waiter, holding a scared smile on his lips.

"Hello," Cross said, relieved.

"Can I speak to you a minute?"

"Sure; come on in."

The waiter came hesitantly into the compartment.

"Man, that bitch is raising hell," the waiter began. "She's gonna sue the company for damages, and she's saying it's all my fault. If she wins, it's my job." The waiter's eyes danced in his head.

"What're you going to do?" Cross asked.

"I got to get some witnesses," the waiter said. "You know, that priest won't witness for me. Can you feature that? Man, what can we do with these white folks?" He spoke in a low, nervous tone of voice charged with bitterness. "I'm gonna take it up with the union; they'll fight for me. But I got to have evidence, see?"

"Sure," Cross said.

"My name's Bob Hunter," the waiter said.

Cross knew that Hunter was waiting for him to give his name.

"Mine's Addison Jordan," Cross said, feeling that he was speaking out of a dream.

"Would you be a witness if that bitch makes trouble?"

"Sure," Cross said, beginning to hate the man.

"Give me your address and the union'll get in touch with you," Hunter said, taking a frayed address book from his pocket.

"It's 128 West 137th Street," Cross lied, never again wanting to look into Hunter's eyes. He could not explain his unavailability to this man, yet it was wrong to allow him to think that he had his help.

"Thanks," Hunter said, jotting down the address. "You don't live so far from me. Here; take my address. 142 West 144th. If you're ever up there, drop in and we can kill a bottle, hunh?"

"Sure," Cross agreed.

Hunter made him feel his impotence so keenly that he wanted to spit in his face. Hunter's manner of pronouncing certain words bothered Cross and Cross asked him: "Where were you born, Hunter?"

"Texas, man," Hunter said, eyeing Cross closely. "Why?"

"I don't know. Just curious, that's all."

"Say, you need any help with your bags?" Hunter asked.

"Oh, no," Cross said through clenched teeth. "I've only one suitcase."

"Just want to help you, man," Hunter smiled. "We colored folks got to stick together, don't we?"

"Oh, yes," Cross agreed with pretended heartiness.

"Good-bye, now," Hunter said, leaving and closing the door.

Christ Almighty! Hunter was believing that he had his help, that he would be a friend. He had made Hunter a promise that he could not keep, just as he had made his mother, his sons, Dot, Gladys, and Jenny promises that he could not keep . . . His nonidentity was making Hunter believe in the unreal. Cross sighed. He had to break out of this dream, or he would surely go mad. He had to be born again, come anew into the world. To live amidst others without an identity was intolerable. In a strict sense he was not really in the world; he was haunting it for his place, pleading for entrance into life . . . He sat and rested his head in his hands. He must eventually find Bob Hunter and try to square this deception. But why did he care about Bob Hunter?

No; it was not Hunter himself that bothered him; it was Hunter's delusive belief in him that he found offensive. He started as another knock came. Hunter again? If so, he'd explain to the man that he could not help him. He rose and opened the door.

"I'm not disturbing you, am I?" Houston asked him, smiling.

"Oh, no," Cross lied. His body seemed suddenly made of soft, melting wax. "Come in."

"Are you sure? I just wanted to talk a little," Houston said.

Houston's manner seemed sincere. Maybe he was wrong? As he talked to Houston, he would be waiting for the trap to be sprung. Houston sat and held out his pack of cigarettes. Cross took one and Houston held his lighter. Cross strove for nonchalance, meeting Houston's gaze with a smile. Houston studied Cross for some minutes. Why in hell doesn't he speak . . . ?

"It's not often that one meets someone who can grasp ideas," Houston began. "If I'm bothering you now, it's a little of your own fault; you ought not to have agreed with me in the dining car." Houston laughed. "You know, to get to the point, I've never had a chance to talk to Negroes like I'd like to. There's something about the Negro in America that almost hypnotizes me, really . . . By the way, quite frankly, talking about this problem does not bother you, does it?"

"Not at all," Cross said, grinding his teeth in anxiety.

"People are so tender-skinned these days," Houston went on. "Everybody's trying to be other than what they really are: something official, approved of, safe—"

"They are afraid," Cross said, suppressing his own fear.

"You strike me as being a man of pretty cool

judgment and having some insight into life," Houston said.

Cross wanted to laugh out loud. If the man only knew how lost and guilty and scared he was! How wrapped in anxiety . . . !

"I don't know," Cross said.

"Whenever I've tried to talk to most educated Negroes, I've felt a barrier," Houston continued. "I can understand why they feel constrained. They feel that I'm enjoying their humiliation. And many whites do enjoy talking to Negroes about this problem; it makes them feel superior and secure."

"That's all too true," Cross agreed.

"But this hump on my back ought to give me some licence," Houston argued. "I know what it means to be an object outside of the normal lives of men. I know how it feels to be stared at, to have some silly woman want to touch your hump for luck . . . When I was a child, I hated myself, cursed my ill-fortune; but now I'd not want to give up what my peculiar situation has taught me about life. This damned hump has given me more psychological knowledge than all the books I read at the university.

"My deformity made me free; it put me outside and made me feel as an outsider. It wasn't pleasant; hell, no. At first I felt inferior. But now I have to struggle with myself to keep from feeling superior to the people I meet . . . Do you understand what I mean?"

"I do," Cross said quietly.

"Some men are so placed in life by accident of race or birth or chance that what they see is terrifying," Houston said, carried away by his theme. "Life converts the lives of such men into something almost dreamlike. And I've often wondered why I could not detect this feeling of the outsider in the Negroes I've met. In America the

Negro is outside. Our laws and practices see to it that he stays outside . . . Or, am I mistaken in looking for this in Negroes, Mr. — ?"

"Addison Jordan's the name," Cross lied, murmuring softly. Was Houston spying on him? If he acted afraid, Houston would wonder why. The best policy would be to talk frankly, and when he spoke he was talking of himself, a self pushed away from him and described in abstract terms. "Yes, Mr. Houston, the Negro feels exactly what you are asking about. But he hides it. The American Negro, because of his social and economic situation, is a congenital coward. He's scared to reveal what he feels. He fears reprisals from his white neighbors." Cross was feeling how much he was hiding from Houston.

"But they ought to be able to talk to *me* without fear," Houston said with a note of pleading in his voice. "After all, in a psychological sense, I'm a brother to them."

"They're even afraid of you," Cross said, smiling, wondering if Houston too was being ironical.

Cross could feel that Houston sensed the quality of the demonical in him, and he could feel the same in Houston. But this man, of all men, must not get too close to him. He represented the law and the law condemned what he was and what he had done. Cross felt the hot breath of danger as Houston continued.

"My position's difficult," he said. "I feel outside of the lives of men. Yet my job demands that I enforce the law against the outsider who breaks that law."

"How do you manage it?" Cross asked with a constricted throat.

Houston laughed and did not answer.

"Do you have sympathy for those who break the laws of civilization?" Cross felt compelled to ask.

"In a way, yes," Houston confessed. "But it all depends upon *how* the laws are broken. My greatest sympathy is for those who feel that they have a *right* to break the law. But do you know that there are not many criminals who feel that? Most of them almost beg you to punish them. They would be lost without the law. The law's vengeance is what gives meaning to their lives." Houston paused and stared at the floor. "You asked something about civilization . . . Ha-ha-ha! Civilization," Houston repeated the word, letting it roll slowly on his tongue. He looked at Cross, smiled, then asked teasingly: "You call this *civilization*? I don't. This is a jungle. We pretend that we have law and order. But we don't, really. We have imposed a visible order, but hidden under that veneer of order the jungle still seethes."

"But why do you call it a jungle?" Cross asked. "Isn't it normal life and we've tried to hide it with order because it is too terrible, maybe?"

"Maybe," Houston admitted.

"Is not life exactly what it ought to be, in a certain sense? Isn't it only the naïve who find all of this baffling? If you've a notion of what man's heart is, wouldn't you say that maybe the whole effort of man on earth to build a civilization is simply man's frantic and frightened attempt to hide himself from himself? That there is a part of man that man wants to reject? That man wants to keep from knowing what he is? That he wants to protect himself from seeing that he is something awful? And that this 'awful' part of himself might not be as awful as he thinks, but he finds it too strange and he does not know what to do with it? We talk about what to do with the atom bomb . . . But man's heart, his spirit is the deadliest thing in creation. Are not all cultures and civilizations just screens which men have used to divide themselves, to put between that part of themselves which they are afraid of and that part of themselves which they wish, in their deep timidity, to try to preserve? Are not all of man's efforts at order an attempt to still man's fear of himself?"

"And what is man that he has to hide from himself?" Houston asked, smiling; there was a look of frightened delight in his eyes.

Involuntarily Cross drew in his breath and looked past Houston to the bleak landscape of snow sweeping past the train's window. The conversation was making him feel a sense of intense isolation, and, even though Houston was there in the compartment with him, for a moment he was unaware of it. He was man who had killed and fled, man who had broken all of his ties and was free . . .

"Maybe man is nothing in particular," Cross said gropingly. "Maybe that's the terror of it. Man may be just anything at all. And maybe man deep down suspects this, really knows this, kind of dreams that it is true; but at the same time he does not want really to know it? May not human life on this earth be a kind of frozen fear of man at what he could possibly be? And every move he makes, might not these moves be just to *hide* this awful fact? To twist it into something which he feels would make him rest and breathe a little easier? What man is is perhaps too much to be borne by man . . ."

Houston rose quickly; there was intense excitement in his face and Cross grew afraid. Maybe he had talked too much?

"Maybe my theory is too wild," Cross said with hasty self-deprecation.

"No," Houston pulled down the corners of his mouth. "I've had the same notion and I can't get rid of it." Houston looked directly at Cross and smiled. "I *knew* that this existed! By God, I knew that someday I'd hear this from your side of the fence. The Negro *has* to know this. How could he escape knowing it . . . ? He looks right at it every day of his life, every hour . . ." Houston paused, smiled cynically. "All my life I've been haunted by the notion that this life we live is a pretense, and all the more deadly because it is a pretense. And woe to the man who tries to reveal that pretense. *He* is the *criminal* . . ." He pulled deeply at his cigarette and laughed softly. " 'Man's nothing in particular'," he repeated Cross's words. "I think you're pretty close to something there, guy. It's not often that one meets somebody with whom one can talk, somebody who sees that deeply into things . . . Say, we seem to be getting into the city . . . Look, here's my card. Call me up sometimes and we can chat a little, eh? I'd love it."

"Sure," Cross said, rising and taking the card. "I'd be glad to."

Houston left, smiling, seemingly satisfied. Alone, Cross sat again and stared unseeingly at the dreary apartment-building landscape of the Bronx as it heaved into view. Of one thing he was certain: he could never see Houston again. It was Houston's job to bring him to justice. The man's mind seemed to find its recreation by delving directly into problems of consciousness like those that were possessing him. He felt like a bird veering and fluttering toward the wide, unblinking eyes of the crouching cat . . . He had to master himself; he had to steer clear of being always drawn toward that which he dreaded. And, intuitively, he knew that Houston was caught in the same psychological trap. That was why Houston was a District Attorney sworn to uphold a system of law in which he did not really believe. Houston was an impulsive criminal who protected himself against

himself by hunting down other criminals! How cleverly
the man had worked out his life, had balanced his emotional drives! He could experience vicariously all destructive furies of the murderer, the thief, the sadist,
without being held to accountability!

The train slowed and was passing 125th Street and
Cross looked down at the wintry drabness of Harlem, at
its rows of towering tenements, at black men and
women huddled in overcoats, trudging through snowy
streets. Well, here I am . . . I've made no promises . . .
I'm nobody . . . I'm responsible for nothing . . . He
sighed as the train slid into the underground, making
for Grand Central Station.

Half an hour later, Cross, lugging his heavy suitcase,
followed the crowd down the ramp toward the waiting
rooms. As he edged forward, his anxieties began to
mount. Care seemed to bring him these compulsive
moods which, when they first made their presence felt,
when they first declared their emotional authority, were
nothing definite. They simply rose seemingly out of nowhere and in defiance of his rational capacity and began
seeking their own object; failing to find it, they created it
out of what was at hand, anything . . . Cross knew that
this was himself acting, and that self was alien to him.

He passed the train's huge, sighing, black engine and
longed to become as uncaring and passively brutish as
that monster of steel and steam that lived on coal. But,
no; his was to feel all of these anxieties in his shivering
flesh. Goddamn! To swap the burden of this sorry consciousness for something else! To be a God who could
master feeling! If not that, then a towering rock that
could feel nothing at all! His life was becoming a tense
prayer interspersed with curses. He wondered if the
priest felt life as keenly as he did. Or had not the priest
become a priest precisely in order *not* to feel it?

Through the bars of the gate he saw crowds milling in the station; porters rushed to and fro; hand-trucks piled with luggage rolled toward the exits; he heard shouts of friends greeting friends. If his apprehensions were true, if Houston were playing a game, he could expect the police to accost him. When he was out of the gate, he saw Houston and Father Seldon smiling and waving at him and he smiled and waved back. He was still safe.

Twice before he had been in New York with Gladys on summer vacations and he knew his way about. He headed for the Grand Central subway station and took the shuttle to Times Square where he changed for a Harlem train and stood at the front window of the first coach with his back to the other passengers, his emotions reading a secret language in the red and amber and green lights that swept past in the noisy night of the underground. At 110th Street he began to wonder where he would get off. Such were now the tiny decisions that clogged his consciousness. He was *too* free! For no reason at all he rode past 110th Street and at 125th Street he decided to get off simply because it was one of the best known thoroughfares in Harlem. Standing uncertainly on the platform, he debated: Maybe 125th Street is *too* crowded; it's just possible I might meet somebody I know . . . He waited for a local and rode to 135th Street and got off and climbed the stairs to the upper world.

Loitering, holding his suitcase, his cheeks stinging from the icy wind, he pondered what direction to take to find a room. When he finally ambled forward, he avoided looking into the faces of the passersby, feeling instinctively that he did not have the right to do so. He was without a name, a past, a future; no promises or pledges bound him to those about him. He had to become human before he could mingle again with people.

Yet he needed those people and could become human only with them. Dimly he realized that his dilemma, though personal, bore the mark of the general. The lives of children, too, were subjected to this same necessity; they, too, could become human only by growing up with human beings . . .

He came to Seventh Avenue and walked up to 136th Street, turned left, looking for FOR RENT signs. At last he saw a brick house set well back from the sidewalk with shutters closed and it appealed to him. It was as though his doubt about his right to exist blended with the closed shutters and the distance the house was from the street. He mounted stone steps and rang the bell; the opening door disclosed a woman with a brown face,—a burning cigarette slanting across her chin made her seem sluttish at first—wearing a dark blue dressing gown. He saw the tip of a soiled brassiere struggling to keep her bulging breasts to the dimensions of modesty. She was about twenty-eight or thirty, had hard surfacy eyes that might have indicated that she was limited in her thinking. Woman as body of woman shot through his senses, but he pushed the impulse from him; he was in too much danger now to play around . . .

"What can I do for you?" she asked bluntly.

"You have a room for rent, I think," Cross said, a little taken aback by her abrupt manner. Yet he liked her. She was the kind of woman who would most likely take him for granted and not pry into his past; her attitude seemed to place her in the sane, ordinary events of Harlem life.

"Come on in if you want to see it," she said.

He stepped inside, sat his suitcase in a corner, and followed her down a hallway and up a flight of steps to a second floor. She trailed an odor of tobacco smoke.

She opened the door of a large room and threw him a defiant glance.

"There it is," she spoke flatly.

He sized her up as a naïve woman who had created about herself a hard-boiledness of manner to protect a too-believing nature that had been tramped on and abused by sundry men. In appearance, she was intensely feminine, seemingly ready to surrender in a yearning for a happiness which she was certain that she would be cheated out of in the end.

"How much is the rent?" he asked her.

"Ten dollars a week," she said.

"I'll take it."

"You don't have to decide right now," she told him; she seemed to be uncertain of herself.

"I want a room and here is one: large, airy, clean. I'll take it," he smiled at her, took out his wallet and gave her a ten-dollar bill.

"When do you want to move in?" she asked.

"I'm here," he said. "My bag's downstairs. It's simple."

Having identified himself as Addison Jordan, Cross, half an hour later, was lying on his bed, trying to plot out his life.

The weather continued bitterly cold. An icy wind swooped from a bleak sky, ripped against windowpanes, and clawed at passersby in the streets. Cross, overcome by a listlessness which he could not shake off, spent his days either lounging in his room or in the consoling shadows of movie houses. He was Mrs. Hattie Turner's only paying guest and he heard rather than saw her, slightly in her cups at times, stumbling around downstairs in her dining room or kitchen. He learned from a gossipy drugstore clerk that she was a widow who owned her own home, that she drank a little too much, and that she had recently begun to receive the attentions of two men. Most of the time he could hear her playing blues or jazz records whose wild rhythms wailed up to him through the thin flooring. His morbid mood was susceptible to the lonely melodies and, as he tapped his feet to the beat of the tunes, his sense of estrangement became accentuated and he felt more inclined than ever to avoid contact with reality.

The raucous blue-jazz welling up from downstairs was his only emotional home now and he listened with an appreciation he had never had before. He came to feel that this music was the rhythmic flauntings of guilty feelings, the syncopated outpourings of frightened joy existing in guises forbidden and despised by others. He sensed how Negroes had been made to live in but not of the land of their birth, how the injunctions of an alien Christianity and the strictures of white laws had evoked in them the very longings and desires that that religion and law had been designed to stifle. He realized that this blue-jazz was a rebel art blooming seditiously under the condemnations of a Protestant ethic just like his own consciousness had sprung conditioned to defiance from his relationship to his mother who had shrilly evoked in him exactly what she had so desperately tried to smother, had posited in him that which she loathed above all in the world by bringing it too insistently to his attention. Blue-jazz was the scornful gesture of men turned ecstatic in their state of rejection; it was the musical language of the satisfiedly amoral, the boastings of the contentedly lawless, the recreations of the innocently criminal . . . Cross smiled with depressed joy as he paced about his room, his ears full of the woeful happiness of the blues and the orgiastic culpability of jazz.

He had enough money to keep him for awhile, but his pile of dollars was dwindling fast. Each night he vowed that on the following morning he would do something practical about his problem of identity, but the morning found him ready with excuses for inaction. He avoided trying to justify his fear of activity, but in his heart he knew that to exert himself was to invite down upon him those spells of dread; so he remained inert, hoping that by blending his bleak mood with the empty hours he would elude his compulsions.

Of a morning or of an evening he would encounter Mrs. Turner in the downstairs hallway and they would exchange greetings. Whenever she asked him if he were comfortable, he would tell her that everything was all right in a tone of voice that sought to hold her off from him, for he sensed slumbering in her strained manner a nervousness whose content he did not want to know. Now and then he noticed two well-dressed Negroes coming to visit her, but they roused neither his interest nor jealousy.

When she did finally break in on his jealous solitude, it was with a naïve brusqueness that swept him before it and he was again acting with swift heartlessness to save himself. His anxiety rose when he noticed her staring at him. Inflamed, his dread sucked all innocent events into its greedy maw. Was she not suspicious about his background? Why did those two men come to see her? Why were they always *together*? Did not policemen act that way? Why was not Mrs. Turner more relaxed with him of late? He even wondered if she searched his suitcase when he was out . . .

On the morning of the day of the eruption, the coming storm was presaged by the brittle manner of Mrs. Turner who failed to return his greeting in the hallway. At noon she knocked on his door. He made sure that his gun was handy, then rose and opened the door. She stared at him blankly, embarrassed.

"God, I'm rattled today," she complained. "I came up here to say something, and now, for the life of me, I can't remember what it was." She tapped the knuckles of her hand against her forehead. "It'll come back to me in a minute. If it doesn't, then it couldn't've been so *very* important, could it? I'm silly." She forced a smile and left.

Cross was frantic. Had she come up to make sure that he was in his room? He ached to grab her and shake the truth out of her. He was certain that she had not forgotten the object of her errand; a mere failure of nerve had swamped her before she could speak. Quickly he packed his suitcase. Maybe she was trying to tempt him . . . ? Or maybe the cops were waiting downstairs? He sat on the side of the bed and sweated.

What stalled his fleeing was his recollection of past times when he had misread events under the hot promptings of anxiety. Was he wrong now? But too many unanswered questions stood between him and Mrs. Turner's nervousness. He fretted, listening for sounds in the house. No blue-jazz came up now, yet he knew that she was downstairs, alone. If the police cornered him in this room, what could he do? He looked out of the window upon a backyard whose deep snow gleamed bluish in the night. He could jump for it . . . He was suddenly alert, hearing slow footsteps on the upper stairs. Finally the sound of her heels tapped hesitantly along the hallway, then stopped at his door and all was quiet. He ran to the window, hoisted it, shivering in a stream of freezing air. He would never unlock that door until he was satisfied that she was alone. If the police were with her, they would have to bash in the door; meanwhile, he would leap out of the window . . . His suitcase? Hell, he'd just leave it . . .

She was standing quietly at his door. But why? He

fingered his gun and waited. At last there came the sound of a congested throat being cleared, then a light sigh. He stiffened as he heard Mrs. Turner's voice:

"Have you gone to bed yet?"

Why hadn't she knocked? And why hadn't she called him by his name? Perhaps she wasn't speaking to him? He decided not to answer. Then a timid rap came at his door.

"Are you sleeping?" she called loudly this time.

"Just a second," he said. He closed the window, adjusted his gun, turned the key, and opened the door cautiously, keeping his weight back of it to slam it shut. She was standing quietly with her back to him. He had opened the door so noiselessly that she was unaware that he was looking at her.

"Yes?"

She whirled, drawing in her breath, looking at him in blank fright.

"You scared me," she sighed, her hands flutteringly protecting her breasts. Then she laughed nervously. "I'm so jittery. I hate like hell to bother you."

A mute begging swam in her dark eyes and his dread vanished.

"What's the matter?" he asked.

"You've *got* to help me," she spoke as though she had debated for days on how to talk to him. "I need your advice about something terribly important."

"Come in," he said.

The dark blue dressing gown made her seem somehow naked, gave her an abandoned air that clothed her body in an appeal of sex. Cross fought shy of it. She moved to the center of the room, not looking at him. He left his door ajar as protection against any unexpected entry. Luckily, his packed suitcase was under the bed, out of sight. She seemed afraid of him; why? Was it the severe reserve that he had imposed upon himself that made her hesitate? He was poised, his feelings mobilized to react violently and suddenly in any direction.

"Mr.—" she looked helpfully at him. "*What's* your name? I must be going out of my mind." She sat and closed her eyes in confusion.

He smouldered. He knew it; she was fishing for information. Did she think that he was so naïve that he would inadvertently blurt out that he was Cross Damon? Yet, he was dubious; his mind believed her.

"Jordan's the name," he flung it at her and waited for her to challenge it.

"Oh, yes. Mr. *Jordan*, I've something to ask you—"

"What is it?"

"I'm in trouble and worried sick . . ."

Cross relaxed a bit. This silly woman . . . Suppose she had *his* trouble? She'd jump out of a window, he thought.

"Okay, Mrs. Turner. What's bothering you?"

"I'm not trying to be fresh— But if you call me Mrs. Turner again, I'll *scream*!" she protested in a sob of complaint.

"All right, Hattie," he relented. "I'll help you if I can."

His words produced a convulsion in her and she clapped her hands to her face and wept. He wanted to console her, but he was afraid of his gesture committing him to more than he knew. She wiped her eyes on the sleeve of her dressing gown and looked off.

"What do you want to tell me?" he asked her gently.

"Maybe I've waited too late to talk," she stammered. "And I don't know what to do . . ." A tremor went through her. "I'm scared I'm being cheated. Oh, why was I such a fool to believe them?" Her face darkened.

"If they cheat me, I'll *kill* them!" A crazy light lit her eyes.

"Who are you talking about?" Cross asked.

"They *call* themselves my friends." She was composed now and talked more coherently. "I'm a widow. My husband died six months ago. He left me this house. It's all I got . . . He was a good provider and took care of me. Now, I'm alone, and it's hell when you're a woman and all alone. I'm hounded by men running to me but for one reason: to steal this house. Every time I get to know a man, he's up to some lousy trick . . . I didn't know people were so *bad*." She wagged her head and swallowed, overcome with self-pity. "About a month ago I met two men. One's a real estate broker, Mr. White. The other's a plain-clothes detective, Mr. Mills . . ."

A wave of voluptuous dread engulfed him. He stood, flexed for action. She was pulling a crude confidence trick by pretending to be in trouble and winning his sympathy and trapping him for the police! She noticed his agitation.

"What's the matter? Oh, you'll like Mr. Mills—"

"He's on the police force?" he asked.

"Yes."

"Where's he now?"

"At home, I guess," she answered vaguely.

If she was really trying to deceive him, would she talk about a detective like that?

"How did you meet these men?"

She hung her head bashfully.

"Come on; tell me. How did you meet 'em?" he demanded.

"In a bar," she answered coyly; it had been modesty that had made her hesitate. "Well, they told me how to make some quick money—"

"You mean you're building a printing plant here?" he asked her; she was beginning to amuse him now.

"Oh, no! *That* would be wrong!" she protested, her eyes widening with shock. "They know an old, blind, sick man who wants to sell a $100,000 apartment building. Now, I can get an $8,000 mortgage on my house and they can persuade this old, sick man to sell me his building for $8,000— It's a beauty; I've seen it." Her eyes shone with hope.

"But why's he selling a $100,000 building for $8,000?" Cross asked, trying to make sense out of the picture.

"That's the point," she explained eagerly. "You see, they're friends of the old man. He's about to die; he's blind and'll sign what they ask. I'll get the $8,000 and they'll draw up the papers and the old man'll sign 'em. He'll be dead in a month and can't make trouble, see? Now, that's an attractive proposition to me." She added in a tone of regret: "Of course, I'm giving fifty percent to Mr. White and Mr. Mills."

"Hattie, you're joking," Cross accused her.

"But it's true," she swore. "Ask Mr. White or Mr. Mills if you don't believe me."

"I doubt if they'll talk to me," he said.

"That may be," she admitted. "They're *very* high class men."

Every time he thought that he was going mad, he met somebody else who had already gone mad, but in a nice, sweet sort of way.

"Don't touch a deal like that," he advised her.

"Why not? I'm alone and I need security—"

"But you've got your home—"

"But I want to *do* something! I don't read and I'm tired of listening to jazz all day." She brought her life's problem to him.

"Hattie," he spoke in a stilted manner to force the absurdity of her story upon her, "who's this sick, blind fool who signs strange papers, who's giving you a $100,000 apartment building for $8,000, and who's dying in a month so you'll have things clear?"

"You don't understand," she chided him gently; she was debating if Cross was intelligent enough to grasp the subtlety of her project. "It's not quite fair for the old man," she conceded. "But it's legal. Mr. White says so."

For days he had crept about the house with loaded gun, shaking in fear—all because of a woman with fantasies like these!

"How old are you, Hattie?"

"What's that got to do with it?" she asked indignantly.

Cross knew the game: the sick, blind man, together with White and Mills, had chosen Hattie who didn't like reading and who was tired of jazz as their sucker. Cross studied her full breasts, her plump thighs, her smooth arms . . . Her husband had protected her, but no one else ever would. Men would either want her money or her body, and no doubt they would take both.

"Do any of your friends know White or Mills?"

"No. They don't associate with people like me, Mr. Jordan."

"Hattie, you ever see Mills in the company of his fellow officers?"

"No," she answered readily. "He works alone on very important cases." What Cross was driving at finally hit her and she demanded: "Say, you act like Mr. Mills isn't a real person, like I'm making this up—"

"Oh, Mr. Mills is real, all right. Too real. Hattie, have you a lawyer?"

"No," she laughed gaily. "Mr. White calls 'em *liars!*"

"Hattie, these men are trying to cheat you," Cross told her.

Her eyes widened and she covered her mouth with her hand to smother words she wanted to speak but did not want to hear.

"You *think* so?"

"They're *crooks!*"

"Oh, Mr. Jordan, how *could* they be?"

He ought to leave right now and find another room. Was it his business if this woman wanted to lose her money? If he saved her now, she'd not rest until she had found others to deceive her. Hers was the kind of personality that bred the desire to cheat, and he was certain that, despite her tears of protest, she loved her role. Then why should he hinder her? If Hattie's life was what living was without the screen of civilization, why did he not leave her with it? But it was not for Hattie that he was worrying. What was happening to her made a mockery of his conception of life, offended him and he wanted to stop it.

"Don't see these men anymore," he told her. "And don't give them one damn red cent of your money, see?"

Hattie's mouth gaped open; she stood abruptly, looked wildly about her, then flopped weakly on the bed, shaking with sobs.

"I don't know," she wailed.

"Now, don't cry," he told her. "Everything's all right."

"Men are so *awful,*" she lamented.

"They tried to take you," he told her. "Now, you're wise. Break with 'em."

She turned on the bed and looked at him with stricken eyes and he wondered if she had already given them her money. Then suddenly he knew; she had given them her money and did not want to tell him, hoping that before she did, he would tell her something that would redeem the horror and undo her actions!

"What have I done?" she begged him meekly.

"You *didn't* give them your money?"

Her weeping took on a quality of laughter, high-pitched and painful. Cross wanted to kick her. How could anyone be so avariciously dumb? And could he help her now?

"You gave them the money? A check?"

"No," she gasped in reply. "Cash."

"But why cash? We could stop the payment of a check."

"They said deals went quicker with cash. They wanted to close the deal before the old man died . . ."

Had she a right to be alive? Was anybody bound to respect a creature like this?

"How old are you, Hattie?"

"You asked me before," she complained. "Why do you want to know? I'm twenty-nine."

She began talking in a whimper, reliving the events of the morning. "We took a taxi to Mr. White's office and signed the mortgage, then we went to my bank and got a certified check and I cashed it. We stopped and had a drink—"

"Who paid for the taxi?"

"Me. Why?"

"And the drinks?"

"Me. They said I was making the biggest profit. That's the way men do it. I want to be business-like and I did what they said." She dabbed softly at her eyes. "What can I *do* now?"

"Hattie, I want to ask you something and you must answer truthfully. I want you to understand what you've done, see?" he argued gently.

"Yes," she answered, looking at him with dark, placid eyes.

"You were trying to steal a building, weren't you?"

"But it was *legal*!" she defended herself.

"You're lying!" he shouted at her. "I asked you to tell the truth!"

She did not answer; it was odd how respectable she really was. The crime did not offend her; but the idea of it did.

"You don't have to talk to me," he said, rising. "I've been thinking of moving—"

She whirled and clutched him with both of her hands.

"Don't leave me! I need you, God knows— Don't be mad at me. I'll do anything you *say*!" She collapsed on the bed again.

"Hattie, you turned thief and while you were trying to steal from the blind man, they stole your $8,000. It's an old trick," he explained.

"I'll lose my *house*," she wailed. "What must I *do*?"

"Tell the police at once—"

"And I'll get my money back?"

"I doubt it. They're not so foolish to keep that money. That so-called blind man's got it. Mills and White are watching you to see if you get wise. When are you seeing Mills and White?"

"They're coming tonight."

"I'll talk to them," he said.

She rested quietly against him on the bed and he could feel the heavy, slow beat of her heart. He would try to scare those crooks into giving her her money back, and then he would move at once. He feared getting involved; it was possible that something would go wrong and he would be questioned by the police and his identity would come out. And under no conceivable conditions could he allow his fingerprints to be taken; if that happened, he was lost, for his prints were on file in the Post Office in Chicago and in Washington.

The doorbell rang and Hattie locked her arms about his neck.

"That's them now," she whispered.

"Let's go down," he said.

She rose and went to the mirror and began rearranging her hair, tucking stray curls into their accustomed niches. She turned to him and asked coyly:

"Do I look all right?"

"You're wonderful," he assured her.

"You're so kind to me," she said with eyes round with gratitude. "Come on."

He followed her down the stairs and was standing behind her when she opened the door.

"Good evening, my lady," a tall black man called.

"How are you, Mrs. Turner?" a short brown man boomed.

"Come in," Hattie said. When the men were in the hallway, Hattie gestured toward the tall black man and said:

"Mr. Jordan, this is Mr. White."

"How are you?" Cross asked.

"Fine," White said, eyeing Cross intently. "You're a friend of Mrs. Turner?"

"Sort of," Cross said, turning to the brown man. "And you're Mr. Mills, I take it?"

"That's right," Mills came out with a hearty voice; but his eyes were cold and watchful.

"Come into the living room and sit down, won't you?" Hattie asked them.

"We'd like to speak to you alone, if it's all right, Mrs. Turner," White said, smiling at Hattie.

"But Mr. Jordan wants to ask you some questions about my business," Hattie told them.

"I'm looking after her, gentlemen," Cross said.

There was a split-second silence. The eyes of White and Mills were directly on the face of Cross.

"Sure, sure," White said suddenly, entering the living room.

"Why not?" Mills said, following White in.

Cross knew that he had two tough men on his hands and he had no stomach for the job. White and Mills sat, their overcoats still on, their hats on their knees, their eyes never straying from Cross's face. Hattie stood in the doorway, demure and anxious. Cross lingered in the center of the room, cleared his throat and waded in.

"Let's get to the point," he began. "I'm wise to the game. You want to cough up her money and call it quits?"

"Who in hell are you?" White shot at him.

"Does it matter?" Cross countered.

"Are you interested in real estate?" Mills asked him.

Cross knew that Mills was asking if he would be *their* partner in cheating Hattie.

"No deals," Cross said. "Can we settle this between ourselves?" He found himself referring obliquely to the police long before he had wanted to. "Where's the money you took from her?"

White turned to Hattie and asked:

"Mrs. Turner, are you letting *him* horn in on this? He's after money, that's all! Is this the man who walked in one morning with a suitcase? Haven't we been fair with you? Are you out of your senses?"

Hattie blinked and Cross knew that she was already influenced by White's words.

"I don't want her money," Cross said. "I advised her to get a lawyer. Then she can make any deal she likes. Where's her money?"

"In a bank," Mills said flatly and laughed. "You think I carry money like that around on me at night?"

"When can you give her her money?" Cross demanded.

"If she wants to drop the deal," Mills said, "she can. She can have her money in four days—"

"She wants it now," Cross said. "Look, you were going to tell her that the blind man ran off with her money, or some such tale. And you're here tonight to see how she's feeling. Four days from now, you'll be in California . . ."

Mills rose and stood before him, his eyes hard and his lips flexed with anger. Cross grasped the gun in his pocket.

"Don't accuse me of being a thief," Mills warned. "I know a thing or two. I've got police connections here in Harlem—"

"You're no cop," Cross shot at him.

"No cop, hunh? Listen, I can have you put on ice 'til this deal is cleaned up! Now, get *wise!*"

Cross's ardor suddenly waned. Mills was no policeman, but he could slip a ten-dollar bill to a cop and he could be picked up and put in the Tombs for investigation. The police could always say that he resembled somebody they were looking for. His fingerprints would be taken . . . He looked at Hattie who was waiting for him to save her and he cursed himself. He would stall for time, coach Hattie to talk to the police, and then vanish. He plotted his next move, hating himself. He had to make Hattie think that he was not backing down and, at the same time, he had to appear to compromise with White and Mills.

"You can get her money in four days?" he asked, feeling that self-loathing would choke him.

White looked at Mills; they were uncertain.

"Sure," Mills said, trying to hide his surprise.

"Will you give her that in writing?" Cross asked.

"Sure; why not?" White agreed, but he was baffled. He took out his fountain pen and a sheet of paper and began writing.

"Oh, I'm so glad," Hattie sighed.

Cross dared not look at her. Mills backed off into a corner and stared appraisingly at Cross. Cross knew that the man was trying to figure him out.

"Why don't you come in on this deal with us?" Mills asked again.

"I'd feel safe then," Hattie said.

"No," Cross growled. He longed to be as far from this dopey Hattie and these wily crooks as space could take him.

"Are you on the level?" Mills asked.

"Are *you*?" Cross countered cynically.

Hattie suspected nothing. Of what use was pity? Did not pity only choke up your life and make it into something which others ought to pity? White handed him a slip of paper which he did not bother to read, for he knew that it was worthless; he handed the paper to Hattie and watched her eyes devour it.

"Thank you," she breathed.

"Is everything all right?" Mills asked.

"Of course," Hattie said, smiling sweetly.

"Well, I suppose we'll be getting on," White said.

"Yes," Mills said. "We're late now."

"I'll see you Thursday?" Hattie asked.

"Of course; good night," White said.

The door closed and Cross watched them rush down the steps to the sidewalk. They paused, looked back, all round them, then hailed a taxi and climbed in; the taxi, no doubt at their bidding, shot off wildly down the snow-covered street.

"They seemed to be in a hurry," Hattie sighed.

He saw her eyes grow thoughtful and he wondered what processes of ratiocination were transpiring in her brain.

"You think maybe they were honest after all?" she asked.

If one good smack on her chin could have awakened her to the truth, he would have given it. Instead he pushed her violently from him.

"Get away from me," he growled.

She backed off, trembling. "What's the matter? I don't understand you," she gasped. "You helped me, then you turn wild!"

He saw her bleak face and relented. What good was there in punishing this irresponsible creature?

"I'm sorry," he breathed.

She waited to see if danger had gone out of him, then she circled his waist with her plump arm and led him toward the stairs.

"Are you angry with me?"

"No."

"I could go for you," she crooned, regaining confidence and hugging him tightly. "You saved me. Say, how about a drink?"

"God, yes; I need one," he said.

"Go to your room. I'll bring up a bottle."

He was lying on his bed when she came with a bottle and two glasses. He had a big swig and felt the whiskey numbing his stomach; he felt better. He saw her moist, round, giving eyes.

"Why are you so blue?" she asked.

"I'm thinking," he said.

"About me?"

"How could anybody be with you and not think about you?"

She bent forward and kissed him. He smelt the odor of her hair and wondered what could one do with a woman like this but love her even when one did not love her? She was woman as body of woman for him now and he wanted her. He laid her on the bed and she struggled up.

"Wait," she murmured. "I'll be back in a minute."

She kissed him and went quickly out of the room. A moment later he heard water running in the bathroom. He leaped from the bed, grabbed his suitcase and softly groped his way out, tiptoeing. In the hallway he heard the sound of water still coming from the bathroom and he could see a light shining from beneath the sill. He crept down the stairs to the front door and paused; he opened it and saw a bluish haze hanging in the dim streets. It was late, far past midnight; the world was wrapped in silence. He scampered over the snow to the sidewalk with Hattie hovering as a poignant image in his mind. He reached Seventh Avenue, walked to Lexington and ducked into a subway, relieved that he was free, free to wrestle again with the tyranny of himself. The fear induced in him by the cheap threat of White and Mills drove home to him the unreal nature of his life; he was defenseless. He had to break out of this dream. Hattie was already the melancholy memory of a woman he had tried to help and failed. He felt that his fleeing was best for her, not the best that could be for her, but *his* best.

Cross's opportunistic rejection of his former life had been spurred by his shame at what a paltry man he had made of himself. What little external pressure had compelled him to this stance was also a part of that self which he had rejected, for he alone had been responsible for what he had done to Gladys and Dot. His consciousness of the color of his skin had played no role in it. Militating against racial consciousness in him were the general circumstances of his upbringing which had somewhat shielded him from the more barbaric forms of white racism; also the insistent claims of his own inner life had made him too concerned with himself to cast his lot wholeheartedly with Negroes in terms of racial struggle. Practically he was with them, but emotionally he was not of them. He felt keenly their sufferings and would have battled desperately for any Negro trapped in a racial conflict, but his character had been so shaped that his decisive life struggle was a personal fight for the realization of himself.

What really obsessed him was his nonidentity which negated his ability to relate himself to others. He realized that what was happening to him now had been buried implicitly all along in his past life, had slumbered there in the form of a habit of acute reflection, in the guise of a propensity toward a certain coldness in judging even those closest to him, in a manner of forgetting too quickly what had been a long time in or with him, all because none of it really interested him.

He had long yearned to be free of all responsibilities of a certain sort, but that did not imply that he had no capacity for responsibility in general. What irked him about his past responsibilities had been their dullness, their tenuity, their tendency simply to bore him. What he needed, demanded, was the hardest, the most awful responsibility, something that would test him and make him feel his worth. And his South Side Chicago environment had held forth no hope of his ever being able to find any such responsibility in it.

Where could he find such experiences, such spheres of existence? In the main he accepted the kind of world that the Bible claimed existed; but, for the sufferings, terrors, accidental births, and meaningless deaths of that world, he rejected the Biblical prescriptions of repentance, prayer, faith, and grace. He was persuaded that what started on this earth had to be rounded off and somehow finished here.

He had reckoned that his getting rid of the claims of others would have automatically opened up to him what he wanted, but it had merely launched him to live in the empty possibility of action whose spell, by purging reality of its aliveness, had bound him more securely in foolish drifting that he had experienced in all the past. The world became distant, opaque; he was not related to it and could find no way of becoming so.

It was this static dreamworld that had elicited from him those acts of compulsion, those futile attempts to coerce reality to his emotional demands. There was in him a need for a stabilization of his surroundings. The world of most men is given to them by their culture, and, in choosing to make his own world, Cross had chosen to do that which was more daringly dangerous than he had thought.

One walks along a street and strays unknowingly from one's path; one then looks up suddenly for those familiar landmarks of orientation, and, seeing none, one feels lost. Panic drapes the look of the world in strangeness, and the more one stares blankly at that world, the stranger it looks, the more hideously frightening it seems. There is then born in one a wild, hot wish to project out upon that alien world the world that one is seeking. This wish is a hunger for power, to be in command of one's self. Because Cross had lied, killed, and fled, it was to a sense of guilt that his heart leaped when he looked about him and felt his lostness . . .

Toward the ideology of Communism his attitude was ambivalent; he found as much in it to hate as to admire.

He knew the imperialistic wars of the Western World far too well to be snared into believing that Stalin was the historic essence of the Satanic; even if Stalin had personally eaten fifteen million human beings, it did not cancel the destructions of entire civilizations and the barbarous slaughter of countless millions by the arms of the Western World during the past four hundred years. Further, he was constrained by logic to accept Marxism as an intellectual instrument whose absence from the human mind would reduce the picture of the processes of modern industrial society to a meaningless ant heap. He was also compelled by facts to accept the Communist notion that one form of social consciousness, designated as bourgeois, had been outlived, but he emphatically spurned the slavish class consciousness with which the Communists sought to replace it. Above all he loathed the Communist attempt to destroy human subjectivity; for him, his subjectivity was the essence of his life, and for him to deny it was as impossible as it would have been for him to deny himself the right to live.

In his weighing of ideas, Fascism possessed the same vitally negative merit of Communism in sensing the imminent end of a system of economic domination in the Western World, but what revulsed him in the fascist doctrine was its boast that it needed no ideological justification for its desire to rule. Life was denuded of all meaning when a Hitler could kill millions of men by an efficiently scientific method of mass industrial extermination simply because he did not like the color of their skins or the shape of their nostrils.

All of these rejections, plus that of himself and his past, were behind the man Cross as he walked up the exit of the stairway of the 116th Street subway station the night he had fled from Hattie and started looking again for a room in which to hide and try to think out

his future. When he reached the sidewalk the weather
had turned to sleet and it was bitter cold. Lugging his
suitcase through the slush underfoot, he leaned against
the stinging wind and squinted his eyes, seeking a FOR
RENT sign. He was tired; it was after two o'clock in
the morning. Now and then he felt the pavement beneath his feet trembling from the rush of underground
trains. Ahead he saw faint blobs of traffic lights wink
from red to green and back again. Here and there a few
neon signs glowed, half lost in murkiness. He went into
a little bar that was almost empty and ordered a
whiskey.

As he sipped his drink, his eyes fell upon a series of
crude signs on the dingy walls. He smiled as he read: IF
YOU SPIT ON THE FLOOR AT HOME, YOU MAY DO SO
HERE. Under the wording was a drawing of a coarse-
faced man in a nicely furnished room reclining in an
easy chair; his legs were stretched out and his feet rested
upon a sofa. He was expectorating upon the floor, much
to the horror of his long-suffering wife who was on her
hands and knees with a scrub rag trying to keep the
floor clean.

Another sign read: NO PROFANITY IN HERE, PLEASE.
IF YOU DON'T BELIEVE IN GOD, THEN WHY DO YOU
CURSE HIM ALL THE TIME? Cross gave a silent laugh
and studied the drawing illustrating the philosophical
profundity of that question. There was a drunkard at a
bar with a half-filled bottle before him and he was represented as giving forth a string of vile oaths whose
meaning was conveyed by exclamation points, question
marks, and asterisks.

There was still another sign which read: DO NOT ASK
FOR MR. CREDIT. HE DIED A LONG TIME AGO AND WE
BURIED HIM. Under this drawing was the picture of a
neglected grave in a hideously dilapidated cemetery. En-

graved on the headstone was: MR. BROKE, BORN APRIL
1, 1949—DIED APRIL 2, 1949.

Cross wondered who thought up such legends. Oh,
yes . . . That image of the grave! That reminded him
that *he* was supposed to be dead! How fantastic it
seemed! How did his grave look? And where was it? He
did not even know the name of the cemetery . . . He
sighed and closed his eyes. Wonder what did Gladys en-
grave on my tombstone . . . ? He visualized big words
hewn into marble:

CROSS DAMON

1924——1950

In Loving Memory

Would Gladys say more than that? Hell, would she
even say *that* much . . . ? Perhaps she might; people
had a way of forgiving you when you were dead. And
why not? You could not hurt them then and maybe their
forgiving you was an expression of their joy at your being dead . . . ?

He downed his last drop of whiskey, then held his
breath, caught in the grip of a paralyzing idea. Good
God! Why in the name of all that was reasonable had he
not thought of it before? It was *too* easy, that's why. He
had often read about such things in newspapers; it had
been reliably reported that underground Communists
had established new identities by such methods. Why
not? It more than answered his problem. Sure; all he
had to do was to go to a cemetery and find the name of
a man born on his birthday or any birthday that would
make his present age and appearance seem normal!
Why, if he were clever about it, he could even have a
birth certificate! He had been pounding his brain for
days for a new identity, and all he had to do was go to a
graveyard and copy down a name. And there might be a

hell of a wide choice; he could even afford to be critical about whose name he took. First thing in the morning he would go. He was excited.

"Hey, another whiskey here," he called to the bartender. When he was being served, he asked: "Say, you know where a guy can find a room for rent in this neighborhood?"

The bartender pursed his lips, put down the whiskey bottle and stood thoughtfully.

"I know a Mrs. Crawford who lives up the street," the bartender told him. "She's been asking me to send her somebody. She's kind of old, but she's got a nice place. I lived there once myself, 'fore I got married."

Cross took down the number; he gulped his drink, thanked the bartender and was about to go when the door flew open and two Negro policemen entered. Dread froze him to his stool. One cop sat to one side of him and the other went to the end of the room and looked about the bar carefully, his eyes at last resting upon Cross's face. Cross scarcely breathed. Was this *it*? He kept his head down, hiding his features. Goddamn, why did he always have to have that suitcase with him? He looked up and saw one of the cops coldly examining the reflection of his face in the mirror opposite him. Yes, they were looking him over; there was no doubt about it. He slipped his hand slowly into his overcoat pocket and grasped the gun. Then he started violently.

"It's okay, Jerry. Set it up in the back," one of the cops boomed out.

"Right," the bartender said.

Both cops disappeared wordlessly into the rear and Cross felt his hot muscles relaxing. The bartender took a bottle of whiskey back to the cops. When he returned, Cross said in a whisper: "I thought they were raiding the joint."

"*Them?* Hell, naw. They want a drink. They're on duty this time of night and they're just making sure no spotters are about, that's all. Say, you gonna take that room?"

"Yeah, sure," Cross said. "Thanks a million."

Ten minutes later he was climbing dirty, smelly stairs to the door of Mrs. Crawford. He rang the bell, waited, then he heard an old woman's voice ask: "Who is it?"

Cross told her that Jerry, the bartender, had sent him for a room. She opened the door and peered at him. She was about sixty years old and had on a dressing gown. She'll be safe, Cross thought.

"Oh, you want a room? Kind of late, you know . . . Well, come in."

"I just got into the city," Cross lied.

"I see," she said, trudging slowly down the darkened hallway.

Mrs. Crawford was a brown-skinned, talkative, motherly, and slightly crippled old woman who was rather nervous at his sudden appearance.

"When did Jerry tell you 'bout this room?"

"A few minutes ago, Mrs. Crawford. I just left the bar," Cross assured her.

He accepted the room, paid his rent and an hour later he was in a warm bed and feeling more hopeful than he had felt in a long time. Soon he would have an identity. But what kind of man would he pretend to be? What kind of beliefs would he pretend to have? Would he pretend studiousness or gaiety? He would choose the kind of disposition that would make people like him and accept him. Was not that the way life was lived in this world? Didn't people select deliberately the types of personality that would get them the kind of attention that they thought would help them? He laughed silently on his bed, enjoying the insight into life that his outlandish position was giving him. He felt that at last he was beginning to grapple with his problem, was getting near its meaning.

The next morning near ten o'clock Cross was roused from sleep by the solicitously soft voice of Mrs. Crawford calling to him through the partly opened door.

"Good morning. Wouldn't you like a hot cup of coffee?" she asked, smiling shyly.

"I'd love some, Mrs. Crawford. Would you mind if I came out in my bathrobe?" he asked her.

"Come right along. Make yourself at home here, son," she said. "I've no dining room; you'll have to take it in the kitchen."

"That's all right with me," he told her.

He liked her and felt secure; she was homey. Unlike Hattie, her concerns were simple. He slipped into his bathrobe and lumbered into a spotlessly tiny kitchen.

"Hope I didn't wake you up too early," Mrs. Crawford mumbled.

"Not at all. I should have been up hours ago," Cross said, sipping black coffee and wondering about how to find a graveyard.

"That weather outdoors beats everything!" Mrs. Crawford exclaimed.

Through the fogged windowpane Cross could see a world of churning bits of snow and could hear the wind whimpering like a thing in agony as it tore past the corner of the building.

"Looks like we're in for it," Cross commented.

"A body needs something hot in the stomach first thing in the morning, especially on days like this," Mrs. Crawford proceeded to give her views on life.

She was skinny, brittle, fragile in her bone structure; her eyes were sunken, cloudy, weak.

"There's nothing better than a good cup of hot coffee," he agreed, feeling that this woman was lucky to have such elementary preoccupations.

"Planning to stay in Harlem long?"

"I don't know yet," he answered honestly.

"Where're you from, if you don't mind my asking?"

"Not at all; I'm from Maine," he lied, naming the first state that popped into his mind.

"Maine? Well, what do you know about that! Are many colored people up there?"

"Plenty," he continued lying, beginning to relish it.

"I didn't know that," Mrs. Crawford sighed over a world much too big and complex for her. "Well, you're young and you keep on the go," she philosophized. "Me, I'm old and I'm not too long for this life. I just pray and keep my house straight and wait for the Good Lord to call me home." Her voice was charged with courageous resignation.

"Oh, no! You'll be around for a long time yet," Cross spoke with make-believe sincerity. She looked as if she would die in two weeks. Malnutrition, maybe, he said to himself.

"The only thing I worry about is keeping up my insurance payments," the old woman went on, as though talking to herself. "I'll have just enough money to lay me away decently. I don't want a pack of strangers toting this old body of mine off to some Potter's Field. If I thought something like that would happen to me, why, I wouldn't be able to sleep at night. Before my poor husband died he bought us a little plot out in the Woodvale Cemetery. That's where my blessed husband's sleeping now. I'll be joining him soon, please God."

Cross's interest heightened. Woodvale Cemetery? And he was *looking* for a cemetery!

"Is Woodvale a nice cemetery?" he asked casually.

"It's simply *beautiful*," the old woman cried enthusiastically. "I'm so happy I'll be sleeping there till God calls me to rise from the dead." She paused and looked quizzically at Cross. "But son, you're young. How come you interested in cemeteries?"

"I was thinking about taking out some insurance," Cross explained. "I'm alone too and I've got to look out for myself. I may as well buy a plot somewhere . . ."

"You're wise," Mrs. Crawford approved. "Ain't too many young folks these days serious enough to worry about important things like that . . ." Her dim eyes shone. "Just a minute—I want to show you something." She rose and hobbled hurriedly out of the kitchen.

Poor woman, Cross thought. Mrs. Crawford returned with a huge bundle wrapped in thick brown paper. She placed it upon the kitchen floor and commenced to unwrap it. Cross saw a pile of filmy summer clothing, each piece of which was delicately folded in white tissue paper.

"This is what I'm going to wear," Mrs. Crawford said, looking at him appealingly. "Don't you think it's nice?"

"Yes; it's nice," Cross said, puzzled. "But where're you going to wear it?"

"When I pass to the other shore to meet Jesus, this is what they're going to dress me in," Mrs. Crawford told him sweetly.

Cross felt that he had blundered; he quickly bent forward and fingered the aged material. There was a pearl-handled fan made of large, colored feathers; there was a faded silk, cream-colored parasol; there was a long, tea-colored ruffled voile dress which had huge pleats and a décolleté neck-line; and there was a pair of fragile, high-heeled slippers. Cross noticed that she had even included a pair of nicely starched drawers and a pair of nylon stockings from which the price tags had not been removed. Christ Almighty! The woman was acting as though she was preparing to go to a cocktail party. He opened his mouth to tell her that her burial wardrobe was for summer and not this raging blizzard that held forth outdoors, but thought better of it. Yes, each time he thought that he was mad, he met someone else with a head full of sane, socially acceptable madness.

"Where is Woodvale?" he asked gently, sighing.

"Out near White Plains—"

"Is it a colored cemetery?" he asked.

"*Strictly* colored," Mrs. Crawford assured him. "And only the best colored folks are buried there. You'd be surprised at how well they keep those graves. Why, in the summertime, it's like a garden. I was lucky to get my plot when I did, for the prices have gone up something awful."

"You're right," Cross said, thinking that he would go out to White Plains at once. "Thanks for the coffee, Mrs. Crawford."

"'Twasn't nothing, young man," she told him.

Half an hour later Cross was hurrying toward the subway through the raging blizzard. He was grateful for the lack of visibility, for that would obscure him when he was pillaging the tombstones of the graveyard for names and dates. He asked himself musingly if anything could be wrong with his taking the name of a dead man for his own? Did not parents every day bestow the names of the dead upon their children? Well, instead of letting someone give him the name of a dead man, he would take one.

Arriving at White Plains, he inquired his way to the Woodvale Cemetery, which he had to reach by a long bus ride and then tramp almost a mile through deep snowdrifts. At last the cemetery came into view, veiled

by demonic snowflakes dancing crazily in the winter
wind. Myriads of white marble crosses and tombstones
stretched away in a white, shaking shroud. The huge,
iron gate was locked; no one was about. He climbed
over the fence and stood in the white silence with a feeling of unreality filling him. He went to the nearest grave
and peered at the inscription on the headstone: MARY
HAWKINS. The hell with her . . . He searched farther
and read: MAYBELLE SMITH. Shucks . . . Even people with the name of Smith have to die . . . He looked
at yet another which said: BESSIE ROUNDTREE.
Hell, were only women buried here? He walked a good
way into the cemetery, looking over his shoulder to
make certain that he was not being observed. He approached another batch of graves, bent and wiped
snowflakes from a slab of marble with his hand and
read: JAMES HOLIDAY—1934—1948. Hunh . . .
Cross was thoughtful. Only fourteen years old, just a
kid . . . He looked farther, reading: NEIL BROWN—
1870—1950. That old bugger had a long span, he commented. But he's not for me . . .

It was proving harder to find a good birth date and a
name than he thought. Snow was heaping up on the
crown of his hat and his feet ached with cold. He stood,
breathing gusts of vapor into the snowflakes that flitted
about his face and clogged his eyelids at times. Dammit,
he couldn't give up now. But an hour later he had not
found what he wanted; he had seen graves containing
young girls, old men, babies, middle-aged women, the
twin graves of husband and wife, of brother and sister,
all kinds of graves, white and eternally silent in the
shuddering snow. But all these dead seemed to have
died either too early or too late for him to use their
abandoned names . . . Hell, there *must* be some young
men here my age, he told himself bitterly, his teeth chat-

tering, his body shivering in an icy gale. Finally, when he discovered that he was examining the same graves twice, he found that he had somehow overlooked a plain, obscure grave whose cheap, wooden board at the head of the mound read: LIONEL LANE—1924, June 29th–1950, March 3rd . . . Ah, this was something like it. The guy had been buried only two days ago . . . He scraped the clinging snowflakes from the headboard and read the rest of the inscription:

Sleeping secure in the Faith of the Second Coming of Our Lord and Savior, Jesus Christ, Amen . . .

Awkwardly, Cross took out his pen and ripped off a bit of paper from his notebook and copied down the name and the date; he hesitated at the expression of sentiment regarding Jesus' second coming; but, what the hell, take it all down; it couldn't do any harm. Had this guy been widely known? Would it be wise for him to go to the Bureau of Vital Statistics and ask for a birth certificate in the name of Lionel Lane? What proofs of identity would the clerks ask of him? He would have to invent a good pretext . . . Well, he would try it. What had he to lose? After all, the identity he was seeking did not have to be foolproof; he wanted a mask of normality just airtight enough to enable him to start living again without too much fear. He would create his own past if he could find a respite of but a few weeks.

But if he wanted to assume Lionel Lane's name, should he not try to learn something about him? Where he had worked? How he had lived? Did he have a family? His ardor ebbed somewhat when he realized that he had not the remotest idea of how to find out about the man. Oh, there must be a caretaker somewhere around this cemetery who could tell him if Lane had belonged to a church, or the name of the funeral home from which he had been buried . . . He looked about in the sea of frightened snowflakes, full again of that old sense of dread and criminality. But there's nothing to be scared of . . . Find the caretaker and tell him that Lionel Lane had been an old pal of his, that he had just come from the army and had learned that poor Lionel was dead, and that he was searching for Lionel's folks . . .

Cross struggled through the snowdrifts back to the huge, iron gate and peered about for signs of life, a house . . . Nothing but silence and flurrying flakes of white. He was about to leave when he noticed on the gate a square, wooden plaque whose face was obscured by a thick layer of snow crystals. He cleaned the flakes away with his coat sleeve and read: Address all inquiries to Mr. Sloane, 6 Pine Road, White Plains . . .

More frozen than alive, he dragged himself out of the cemetery and tramped back to the street. When the bus rolled silently toward him out of the scudding swirls of whiteness and stopped, he stumbled on board and had difficulty getting his money out of his pocket, so frozen were his fingers.

"Looks like you came out of a deep-freeze," the bus driver said.

"You can say that again," Cross mumbled.

At the office of the Woodvale Cemetery in White Plains, Cross found a colored girl of about eighteen years chewing gum behind a typewriter. In reply to his plea to find the relatives of his "long lost pal", Lionel Lane, the girl said:

"You'd better come back this afternoon at four when Mr. Sloane's in, because I'm not allowed to give out information like that to anybody—"

"What harm could that do?" Cross asked. "My

friend's dead now. Come on, have a heart." Cross aped the sentiment of nostalgic distress. "I want to see his mother—"

"Why don't you try his pastor at his church?" the girl suggested.

"I don't know his church or his pastor—"

"And you say you were an old, dear friend of his, hunh?" the girl asked him in a light, taunting voice.

"But I never asked him about his religion—"

"He lived in Harlem," the girl said. "But that's all I can tell you. I'm sorry, but you'll have to see Mr. Sloane . . ." The girl resumed masticating her gum and turned back to her typewriter.

Though disappointed, he decided not to press her any further; he thanked her and left. If untoward events developed in the future, he did not want that girl to recall that a young man had been demanding details about Lionel Lane . . . Dammit, he had failed in his first essay. But perhaps he could phone the office later in the afternoon and pretend that he was . . . Whom could he pretend to be? He stood musing in the street amid the circling columns of snow, then he looked again at the scrap of paper upon which he had written the data he had taken from the wooden headboard of Lionel Lane's grave, rereading the words: Sleeping in the Faith of the Second Coming of our Lord and Savior, Jesus Christ, Amen . . . Where and when had he heard words like those before? They reminded him of something. *Yes!* Of course . . . That inscription expressed the cardinal article of faith of the Seventh Day Adventist Church! He had, in his childhood in the Deep South, met and known adherents of that denomination. True, it was a guess, but not at all a bad one. His task, now, was to find the Seventh Day Adventist Church from which Lane had been buried. The girl had said that Lane had lived in Harlem, and it would be safe to assume that the church was there . . .

During the subway ride to Harlem, he pondered over the difficulties involved in his quest. As the excitement wore off he realized that he was attempting a long shot gamble. For instance, he did not know if Lionel Lane had been born in the State of New York or not. Suppose it turned out that Lionel Lane had been born in, say, Ohio? What could he do then?

At 110th Street he got out of the subway, went into a drugstore and consulted a telephone directory. Ah . . . Here were three addresses of Seventh Day Adventist organizations in Harlem. One was on West 135th Street and another was on West 123rd Street; and there was still another organization called the Seventh Day Adventist Conference on West 150th Street . . . Yes, he'd call the Conference. He dialed and heard a suave, masculine voice answering:

"Hello."

"This is the Eastern Insurance Company," Cross lied smoothly. "I wonder if you'd be kind enough to give us some information, please?"

"Yes. What is it?"

"We are searching for the address of a man's family; the man, we believe, was buried from one of your Harlem churches about two or three days ago. The name is Lane, Lionel Lane. Could you tell us where his parents are living? Or do you know the last address of the deceased?"

"Just a moment, please."

Cross waited, looking uneasily over his shoulder at people shopping at the counter of the drugstore.

"We have no direct information here, sir. But I understand that there was a funeral three days ago at our

Ephesus Church at 101 West 123rd Street. Why don't you get in touch with Elder Wiggins there?"

"Thank you," Cross said.

He dialed Elder Wiggins and, still impersonating an insurance official, asked for the whereabouts of the Lane family.

"Oh, yes," the gentle, tired voice of a man came over the wire. "We held services for the Departed at our church last Thursday. But I cannot help you very much, sir. My secretary's not here for the moment. But I know that the Lane family lives in Newark, New Jersey. The Departed lived here in Harlem, I'm fairly certain. You see, the Departed was not himself a member of our church. His mother, Mrs. Mary Lane, is one of our oldest members and, though she lives in Newark, she wanted her son buried from our church. If you'd care to phone later today . . ."

"It won't be necessary," Cross said. "Our Newark office will be able to locate the family. I thank you very much."

So Lionel Lane had parents in New Jersey. Well, he'd go there right now. Twenty minutes later Cross was in the Pennsylvania Station, hunched over a Newark telephone directory, feverishly thumbing the thin, crisp leaves, searching under L's. Good Lord, here was a long list of names of Lanes: there was an Albert Lane, a Bernard Lane, a Daniel Lane, a Harry Lane . . . and then there came Mary Lane . . . This undoubtedly was Lionel Lane's mother. He jotted down the address and an hour later he was in Newark, inquiring for the street on which the Lanes lived. He was so excited that he had to calm himself when he learned that the street was located in the heart of the local Black Belt: 17 Broome Street in the Hill District. *This* was it!

When he reached the bleak neighborhood, he slowed and mapped out his plan of attack. Presuming that he was on the track of the right family, to go to the Lane house directly and ask questions carried a risk. If, when carrying the name of Lionel Lane, something happened to him and caused that name to get into the newspapers, someone might recall that a stranger had been around asking vague questions. It would be better if he posed as a social worker or a salesman of some sort and in that way pick up bits of information from neighbors or shopkeepers. What kind of a family were the Lanes? Working class or professional? If they turned out to be a family of prominent citizens, then it would be almost impossible to go to the Bureau of Vital Statistics in a city like this and impersonate Lionel Lane and demand a birth certificate without getting into serious trouble. He first had to get hold of some basic facts.

The Lane house proved to be a ramshackle, wooden affair, sitting unpainted on a run-down dirty, treeless street in a bleak slum area. If Lionel Lane came out of this hellhole, then not many people of any consequence could have known him. But was this the house of the family of Lanes whose son was buried in Woodvale?

At that moment he saw an elderly Negro postman bent under the weight of a mailbag coming toward him over the snowy street.

"Say," Cross stopped him, "have you got a minute? Maybe you can help me?"

The postman paused, spat a stream of tobacco juice into a snowdrift, eyed Cross cynically and mumbled: "That depends on what kind of help you want. I'm on my rounds. But I'll spare you a minute."

"I'm from the Central Credit Bureau of New York City," Cross lied fluently. "I'm trying to track down a young chap by the name of Lionel Lane."

"Lionel Lane?" the postman echoed, smiling ironically. "He owed money somewhere?"

"Confidentially, yes."

"Well, the people who let him have money didn't have good sense," the postman observed, spitting another spout of tobacco juice. "And you got a fat chance of collecting, 'cause that baby's where you can't get at 'im. He's six feet deep with snow in his face. He kicked off three days ago. Had consumption—"

"Did he live with his family?"

"When he didn't have any dough, he did; and that was almost all the time. He holed up somewhere in Harlem, I'm told, with a dame. Didn't want his family to know where he was when he was with that dame. Had to forward all his mail there . . ."

"Can you give me his address in Harlem?"

"Sure; 145 West 147th Street, it was."

"What kind of a family has he got? Do you know 'em?"

"Ain't but one person in that outfit that you could call human, and that's the mother . . . She's solid, religious. But the rest of 'em—I've seen 'em, but I don't know 'em and don't want to know 'em," the postman sought to disabuse Cross of any illusions. "Boy, if you're thinking of giving the Lanes any more credit, then just don't."

"What kind of work did Lionel Lane do?"

"Work?" the postman mocked Cross, chuckling. "He used to work in a laundry, but for the past two years he used all his energy pulling at the neck of a bottle—"

"Thanks, Buddy," Cross said.

He felt he had a chance. He went into a bar, THE FAT MAN, and schemed out his next move over a whiskey. How soon was a death reported to the clerks in the Bureau of Vital Statistics? Lionel Lane had died in

Harlem and it was safe to assume that the Newark officials did not yet know that he was dead . . . When he
approached the clerks about a birth certificate, there
must not be in their minds any doubt whatsoever that
he was Lionel Lane. One blunder and the whole structure he was so carefully building would tumble. How
was he to handle it? He reflected intensely, calling upon
his knowledge of white and black race relations to stand
him in good stead. If ever he could act convincingly the
role of a subservient Negro, this was the time. He
would have to present to the officials an appearance of a
Negro so scared and ignorant that any white American
acting out the normal content of his racial consciousness
would never dream that he was up to anything decep-
tive. But why would any black wastrel be wanting a
birth certificate? Cross was well aware that the American
authorities were chronically watchful these days about
handing out birth certificates, for spies were using such
documents to establish their claim to having been born
in the United States. In the end Cross decided that a
simple, an almost silly reason was the best reason that an
ignorant Negro could have in demanding a birth certificate; it would have to be a reason that whites, long
schooled in dealing with Negroes as frightened inferi-
ors, would accept without question.

    He went to the City Hall and presented himself at the
window marked: DUPLICATE BIRTH CERTIFICATES.
Looking apprehensively about, he took his place in line.
When his turn came to face the young white clerk, he
said in a plaintive, querulous tone:

    "He told me to come up here and get the paper."

    The clerk blinked and looked annoyed. "*What?*" the
clerk demanded.

    "The paper, Mister. My boss told me to come and
get it."

"What kind of paper are you talking about, boy?"

"The one that say I was born," Cross told him as though he, in his ignorance, had to teach this white man what to do.

The clerk smiled, then laughed: "Maybe you weren't born, boy. Are you *sure* you were?"

Cross batted his eyes stupidly. He saw that he was making this poorly paid clerk happy; his pretense of dumbness made the clerk feel superior, white.

"Well, they *say* I was born. If I wasn't born, I can't keep my job. That's why my boss told me to come here and get the paper." Cross let a tiny edge of indignation creep into his voice.

The clerk regarded him with benevolent amusement and turned and yelled behind him: "Say, Jack! Come here and get a load of this, will you?"

Another clerk, somewhat older, came forward and asked: "What's up?"

"This coon clown says he was born somewhere," the young clerk said.

"I *don't* believe it," the older clerk said.

"Oh, yes, sir. I *was* born," Cross said, his lips hanging open, his eyes wide with desperation.

"Can you prove it?" the first clerk said.

"Now, look here, Mister. I ain't done nothing to nobody, 'specially to no white folks," Cross wailed in deep distress, pleading innocent to a charge not even mentioned.

"The worst thing you ever did was to be born," the older clerk said.

"But I ain't done nothing wrong, Mister," Cross protested.

"You are always wrong," the young clerk said. "Say, Jack, what in hell do we do with 'im?"

The older clerk pulled down his mouth and muttered:

"Hell, go ahead and give 'im a certificate if he was born around here. These clowns don't mean any harm."

"If I can't say I was born, I'll lose my job," Cross complained.

"Where do you work?" the young clerk asked.

"Machine Tools Company, in Brooklyn."

"What's the address?"

"I don't know the number, not exactly, Mister. But you take the Fulton Street bus and ride—"

"Can that," the old clerk said. "You were born in Newark, you are sure of that?"

"Yes, sir."

"Wait, Jack. He ought to know something about his job," the young clerk said. "Say, boy, what's your boss's name?"

Cross stared in blank amazement, then he shook his head as though trying to avoid the worst trap of a black man's life.

"Mister, I don't ask white folks their personal business," he told them.

The clerks shouted their laughter.

"Where were you born in Newark?" the young clerk asked.

Cross blinked again, then looked up brightly, as though his memory had returned, and said: "In the Third Ward." He pointed elaborately in the direction.

"Whereabouts in the Third Ward?"

"Over the hill— Why, Mister, everybody knows where that is."

The two clerks howled with laughter. The young clerk asked: "What street were you born on 'over the hill', as you call it? And on what date were you born? And what's your name? You got a name, I suppose?"

"Yes, sir. They gave me a name," he said, falling silent.

"Well, what in hell is it?"

"But you know," Cross said, amazement showing on his face. "They say you got all the names here."

The two clerks bent double with mirth. And as he stood there masterfully manipulating their responses, Cross knew exactly what kind of man he would pretend to be in order to allay suspicions if he ever got into trouble. In his role of an ignorant, frightened Negro, each white man—except those few who were free from the race bias of their group—he would encounter would leap to supply him with a background and an identity; each white man would project out upon him his own conception of the Negro and he could safely hide behind it.

"All right, boy," the young clerk agreed. "We'll give you your certificate if we can find your record. But we've got to have your name and the year of your birth. We're pretty smart here, I admit. But we're not so smart that we can guess your name."

"They call me Lionel," Cross admitted at last.

"Lionel what?"

"What Lionel what?" Cross asked stupidly.

"What kind of work do you do at Machine Tools?"

"I load up trucks."

"Do you carry anything upstairs in your head?"

"In my head?" Cross repeated. "I ain't got nothing in my head. What you mean?"

Laughter spilled out of the clerks.

"Boy, if your brains were baggage, you could ship them by air freight for nothing," the older clerk said.

"I ain't got nothing to ship nowhere," Cross defended himself.

"Now, look, everybody's got a first name and a last name, see? Now, for God's sake, tell us your *last* name—"

"Lane," Cross responded promptly.

"Why didn't you say that in the first place?"

"'Cause you didn't ask me."

The clerks threw up their hands in mock despair. People in the line behind Cross, all of whom were white, had begun to join in the merriment. Cross wondered who was laughing at whom.

"In what year were you born?"

"My mama told me it was in 1924; the 29th of June."

"Give us a dollar and we'll mail you a duplicate certificate," the young clerk said.

"But my boss told me to bring it in the morning, or I ain't got no job," Cross complained, whining a bit.

"Okay. Sit down over there on that bench. We'll see what we can do. We'll look it up," the older clerk said resignedly.

Two hours later Cross had the duplicate birth certificate of Lionel Lane and had left in the minds of the clerks a picture of a Negro whom the nation loved and of whom the clerks would speak in the future with contemptuous affection. Maybe some day I could rule this nation with means like this, Cross mused as he rode back to New York. All you have to do is give the people what they want . . . He knew that deep in their hearts those two white clerks knew that no human being on earth was as dense as he had made himself out to be, but they wanted, needed to believe such of Negroes and it helped them to feel racially superior. They were pretending, just as he had been pretending. But maybe men sometimes pretended for much bigger and graver stakes?

Cross was now as solidly identified as he felt he could be for the time being, and the first desire that sprang into his mind was to try to redress, to some extent, the unintentional wrong he had done to that waiter, Bob

Hunter, whom he had met in the dining car more than two weeks ago. He fished in his pocket for the address, made his way to Harlem, and found the grim tenement where Hunter lived. Climbing six flights of rickety stairs, he squinted in shadows from doorway to doorway until he came to a white card whose printed legend read:

MR. & MRS. ROBERT HUNTER

He pushed the bell and a moment later he was staring into Bob Hunter's brown and nervous face. The man was in his shirt sleeves and held a pamphlet with a yellow and red back in his left hand.

"Remember me?" Cross asked.

"Man, where in hell have you been?" Bob exclaimed, his face breaking in a broad grin. "I've been looking for you everywhere! Come in."

Cross walked into a large, clean, rather bare apartment and Bob led him into the living room.

"You *are* Mr. Jordan, ain't you?" Bob asked to make sure.

"How are you, Bob?" Cross asked, ignoring the question.

"Sit down, man," Bob said. "I ain't complaining, though I got a lot I *could* complain about." Bob's eyes were fixed intently upon Cross's face and the lips held a nervous smile.

Cross felt that he could not deceive the man any longer.

"Bob, I suppose you wondered about me, hunh?" Cross asked.

"Well, I sure needed you, man . . . I went to that address you gave me, but it was a funeral parlor and nobody knew you there. Is your name really Jordan?" Bob asked in an appealing yet venturesome tone of voice.

Cross placed his right hand reassuringly upon Bob's shoulder. "Take it easy, Bob. I'll explain everything. Say, how did you make out in that little trouble you had on the train?"

"Hunh? What trouble?" Bob asked.

Cross knew that Bob was pretending that he had not understood. He's trying to save face . . .

"Did that woman on the train make any trouble for you?" Cross asked.

Bob shrugged his shoulders and laughed, but there was no mirth in his voice. "*Trouble?* Hell, man, I got *fired*! I lost my goddamn job, that's all." Bob's eyes were evasive but he could not hide that he felt that Cross had betrayed him unpardonably. "I ain't blaming you none, man. After all, you did jump up and stop that bitch from hitting me with that water pitcher, didn't you? And if you gave me a bum steer 'bout your name and address— Well, you know your own business."

"But didn't the union help you?" Cross asked.

"Man, I'm too goddamn militant for my union," Bob explained. "I had a hell of a fight with 'em. My union's got a left wing, and I'm with the left. When the company brought me up on charges, the rightists piled in on me, and I was out. Man, only *you*, an eyewitness, could have saved me. How come you fooled me like that? You could've said you didn't want to help me— Maybe I could've found some other witnesses. But I didn't look for any 'til it was too late. I was counting on you . . ."

Bob related how the white woman had sued the company, how the company had charged him with carelessness, how the leftists in the union had tried to defend him, and how, in the end, because he could not get a single witness to establish independent corroboration of his version of the accident, he had lost.

"But what about that priest?" Cross asked.

"I went to see 'im," Bob said. "Told me he didn't want to get mixed up in it. Said his job was saving souls and stuff like that. Then he went off to Rome to see the Pope—"

"I'm sorry, Bob."

"Hell, man, it's nothing," Bob said defiantly. "Me and Sarah's making out."

"Are you working now? I can let you have a loan—"

"Man," Bob's face spread in a wide, glad grin, "I'm working for the biggest outfit in the world!"

"What's that?"

"The Party, man."

"What party?"

"Hell, man! There ain't but *one* Party and that's the Communist Party," Bob explained proudly.

"What are you doing for them?"

"Organizing! What the hell do you think?"

"Do you like it?"

"I'm just crazy 'bout it," Bob confessed with a smile. "I'm going to be a professional revolutionary, working twenty-four hours a day beating these rich white bastards. It makes me feel *good*!"

Bob went into the kitchen and brought out two bottles of cold beer and, opening them, sat them on the table.

"Listen, Bob," Cross began, "I don't trust many people in this world—"

"I know *that*!" Bob agreed. "You lied to me on that train so smooth that I would have died trusting your word. Man, you can *lie*!" Bob's howl of laughter was so infectious that Cross was forced to join in.

"Bob, I'm going to trust you as far as I *dare*—"

"Man, I'm black like you and you can trust me till death. Race means a lot to me. I love and trust my own," Bob swore his fidelity.

"Bob, my name's not Addison Jordan," Cross said.

"Hell, I found *that* out," Bob said, exploding with laughter. "But what is it? You don't have to tell me 'less you want to."

"Lionel Lane," Cross lied.

Bob looked at Cross with skeptical eyes and grinned, a light of admiration showing in his face. "You telling the truth now?"

"Well," Cross hedged, feeling that it was impossible to really fool Bob now. "I'm Lionel Lane for the moment." Cross could not help laughing at himself. "But it's the name I'm giving to everybody from now on."

"You did something to the white folks and they're looking for you, hunh?"

Cross looked away, chagrined. His life had become a vast system of pretense; one act of bad faith necessitated another, and in order to prove the sincerity of a new lie he had to fall back upon lying still further. Bob was asking him if he had committed some act of racial heroism against whites, and the only people he had wronged thus far had been black.

"Something like that, Bob," Cross lied vaguely with an embarrassed mumble.

"Brother!" Bob exclaimed seizing hold of Cross's hand and pumping it vigorously in fraternal friendship. "I'm with you till the curtain comes down."

Cross's teeth felt on edge, but he managed to say: "I feel I made you lose your job. Bob, I want to help you—"

"Just be my friend, man; that's all the help I want," Bob's voice rang with hope, his words pouring out in a gush of forgiving generosity. "Now, *I'll* tell you something, see? I ain't no American, I'm British, see? But I'm black, like you . . . I came to this goddamn country from Trinidad ten years ago . . . Had to run off; was an organizer and they were after me . . . So I got to be careful too."

"Your secret's safe with me, Bob," Cross told him; he now understood why Bob's accent had seemed strange to him on the train.

"Now, tell me what you did," Bob asked.

"Bob, you'll just have to trust me. I can't tell you . . ."

"You ain't no *spy*?"

"If I was, do you think I'd tell you?"

They laughed. Bob was overcome with wonder. Cross's secret loomed in his mind more important and intriguing than any concrete crime.

"You were Mr. Jordan on the train, and now you're Mr. Lane," Bob mused, laughing. "That's all right with me." His eyes narrowed and he stared silently for a moment in deep thought. "Man, the Party could *use* you—"

"Really? Why do you say that?"

"You can be so *many* things at once—"

"Maybe I'm *too* many things," Cross said quickly.

"Lionel," Bob said, his mind working fast, "I'm sorry my wife, Sarah, ain't here to meet you. You'll like her, man. She's down to earth and takes nothing off nobody; she's militant . . . Say, we're having some folks over to dinner tonight. Why don't you come over 'bout nine-thirty and eat with us?"

Cross knew that Bob was trying to recruit him. He had no desire whatsoever to join the Communist Party, but he knew that he would feel somewhat at home with Communists, for they, like he, were outsiders. Would not Communism be the best temporary camouflage behind which he could hide from the law? Would not his secret past make Communists think that he was anxious for their help? To be with them was not at all a bad way of ending his isolation and loneliness . . .

"Who's going to be there?"

Bob's face beamed with a look akin to worship.

"Man, you talk just *like* the Party folks! I *declare* you do!" Bob laughed uproariously, delighted and amused.

"Why do you say that?"

"You're so *suspicious*— You don't want to take a step without knowing *where* you're going . . ." Bob sobered. "They're Party folks who's coming."

"Who are they?"

Bob shook his head with an air of deep approval. "Man, you're sure careful," Bob commended him. "There's gonna be Gil and Eva Blount, friends of mine. Gil's a member of the Central Committee of the Communist Party. A damn nice guy. Man, he's sharp, cold as ice. You'll like him; he's a lot like you— And there's gonna be my goddamn organizer, Jack Hilton. Then there's me and Sarah, that's all. And you, if you'll come."

"It's a deal," Cross said, his eyes deep and thoughtful.

Cross said good-bye, descended into the streets, entered a bar and sat brooding over Bob's believing mind. He found himself amused and a little intrigued at the prospects of meeting some Communists tonight. In all of his cudgeling of his brain to find some disguise for his outlaw existence, he had never seriously considered Communism. But why not? Did not the Communists, like he, have a secret to hide? And what was the Communist secret? Cross felt that at the heart of all political movements the concept of the basic inequality of man was enthroned and practiced, and the skill of politicians consisted in how cleverly they hid this elementary truth and gained votes by pretending the contrary . . . If, by pretending, he could find a hiding place, why, he would pretend that he believed in the Communist pretensions . . . Why not? They are deceivers and so am

I . . . That ought to be fair enough, he thought as he took a long gulp of beer.

But the Communists were shrewd; they'd hardly be taken in by his birth certificate; he would have to buttress his pretensions of being Lionel Lane by some other document. What? By God, he had it! Lionel Lane's draft card . . . ! The postman had said that Lane had died of consumption, and then it was highly likely that Lane had been classified in the draft as unfit for military duty . . .

He paid for his beer and went out into the nervously falling snow. There was a black cop standing at the corner and he accosted him, telling him that he had been six months in Arizona for his health, that he had lost his draft card, and that he had forgotten the address of his Draft Board . . . He gave the cop Lionel Lane's address and in turn the cop directed him to the Draft Board which was located in the basement of a church.

Cross was feeling better by the minute. When he found the church, which was located on West 134th Street, he saw a throng of young men hanging around the entrance. No; he'd not go in now; he'd wait until nearly closing time. He mingled with the boys and learned that the Draft Board did not close until nine o'clock that night. It was now a little after seven. He spent the hour and a half in a nearby movie and at ten minutes to nine approached the church, entered the basement and saw that a young Negro clerk was in charge; there were three or four other young men hanging about. When the clerk came to him, Cross recited his prepared lie:

"Look, I'm listed as unfit for military duty with this Board. I've been in Arizona for the past six months for my health and I'm sailing for France; I'm on my way to Switzerland . . . But I've lost my card. I've got to get a duplicate, or I won't be allowed aboard the ship—"

"What's your name and where do you live?"

"The name's Lionel Lane and I'm at 145 West 147th Street."

The clerk left. Cross was nervous. If Lane's death had already been reported, why, he'd simply bolt for it . . . The clerk returned with a folder.

"We've got your record here," the clerk began. "But how do I know you're Lionel Lane?"

"Here's my birth certificate," Cross said, presenting the duplicate he had gotten in Newark.

"Look," the clerk said, examining the certificate, "I'll fix up a duplicate card for you and I'll have the chairman sign it, but the secretary of the board is the man who gives the final okay and he's not here. You'll have to come back in the morning—"

"But I'm sailing in the morning. I've got my ticket. I'm packed to go—"

"Gosh," the clerk said. "This stumps me—"

"But I got to have that card," Cross insisted.

"But I don't have the authority to give it to you—"

"You're looking at my birth certificate," Cross pointed out.

"Look, anybody can have a birth certificate," the clerk said. "We do things here by routine. The chairman'll sign your card tonight. But the secretary's not in; he won't be in 'til tomorrow morning—"

"Okay," Cross assented to the fairness of the clerk's statement. "But, look, if I was trying to dodge the draft, do you think I'd come here and ask for a duplicate?"

"I guess not," the clerk grinned. "Say, what time do you sail?"

"I've got to be at the boat at ten—"

"Okay. I'll get the card ready, have the chairman sign

it. You be here at nine sharp in the morning and the secretary'll give it to you."

"Is that all you can do?"

"That's all, buddy."

"Okay. Thanks."

The clerk turned to another young man and Cross walked into the corridor. When the office closed tonight, his draft card would be signed and on the desk of the chairman of the board. How could he get that card? If he waited till morning, the secretary might raise questions and cause trouble. He walked along the corridor, thinking frantically. He looked around; the lights in the inner offices had been turned off. He glanced over his shoulder and saw that the clerk was busy, bent over the files. Cross walked quickly to his left, not knowing where he was going. Could he hide in the office? No; that was too dangerous . . . How in God's name could he get back here tonight, after everyone had gone? He had it; yes, he'd open a latch on one of the windows near the ground . . . He advanced slowly and softly into the dark, his hand outstretched to prevent his colliding with unseen objects. He flicked on his lighter and shielded the flame with his hand. Yeah; there was a window . . . But could he reach it easily from the outside? He doused the light, pushed the latch on the window and lifted it slowly. Peering out, he could see that the window gave on to a fetid areaway. This was no good . . .

Footsteps in the corridor made him freeze; through the open doorway he saw that a light had been clicked on in the office next to him. He waited. Maybe he could hide in a clothes closet . . . ? The light went out and he heard footsteps retreating. The clerk had gone into that office for something and had returned to the front . . .

He sighed, crept into another office and at once saw

the dim reflection of a street lamp. This was it . . . He unlatched the window and slid it up noiselessly. Fumbling in the dark, he took out his address book and tore off a page and inserted it beneath the sill, then stood debating. Maybe he ought to leave by this window . . . ? Naw; it was too risky. He closed the window; the piece of paper would help him to identify the window from the outside.

Reentering the corridor, he walked out boldly, feeling that it was better to give the impression that he was not afraid, that he knew where he was going. Outside, he ambled along in the drifting snow, scanning the street in both directions. There were not many passersby, but he saw lights shining through the stained glass windows of the church on the first floor. If a service was about to begin, all the better; it would mean that no one would be prying around in the basement. He walked on till he spied the bit of paper jutting from the window sill. Lights still blazed in the draft office. Sheltering himself in a doorway, he waited.

Ten minutes later the lights in the draft office winked out, one by one; finally, the clerk, flanked by two other men, emerged. Was it safe to enter now? Yes; he'd try it. He stood beneath the fluttering piece of paper and lingered till the street was empty; then, in one quick movement, he hoisted the window, climbed into the office and dropped to the floor amid a shower of heaped-up snow from the sill. He closed the window, pushed the lever of his lighter and peered about. The office was deserted. He went into the corridor and looked into all the rooms . . . Now, where was the desk of that Draft Board chairman . . . ? He approached a big, shiny desk that had a swivel chair and saw a neat pile of manila folders. He grabbed them, thumbed quickly through them. Yeah; goddammit, *here it was!* He detached his

draft card; it was signed. He then read the items describing the physical appearance of Lionel Lane and
grew thoughtful. Lionel Lane had weighed 158 pounds
and he weighed only 148 . . . Well, he could always say
that he had lost ten pounds, could he not? That's what
tuberculosis did to you, didn't it . . . ? But this other
item was more difficult; Lionel Lane was listed as being
five feet six inches in height and he was five feet eight. It
was a little thing, but it might cause him trouble . . .
Oh, yes; he could fix that . . . He looked about for a
typewriter; he would type an "8" over that "6"! He uncovered a machine; holding his lighter in his left hand,
he inserted the card, jiggled it until the figure "8" coin-
cided with the "6" and hit the key. There . . . He put
the card into his billfold, doubled the folder, stuffed it
into his inside coat pocket. Now, get out of here . . .

He stood, thinking. Soon the death of Lionel Lane
would be reported to the board and the personnel
would be wondering what had happened to the folder
of Lionel Lane . . . There would be some sort of inquiry . . . A solution clicked in his mind. Yes, *all* the
files should be destroyed. If *his* file alone was missing,
questions would be raised; but if *all* the files were missing, then he had a chance . . . And he noticed that each
manila folder was wrapped in cellophane and cellophane
burned like hell . . . He opened a window so that a
draft would feed the fire, then bent forward and ignited
a folder; he watched the cellophane smoke, curl, leap
into flame. He backed away, seeing the flames grow,
spread from folder to folder; soon the top of the desk
was one blazing, red sheet with thick, acrid smoke
billowing ceilingward. He opened the door and hurried
out, then stiffened in his tracks. Good God! His lips
parted in stupefication. He heard the surging of a lusty
hymn coming from above! He had forgotten that

he was in a church! But there was no help for that now . . .

He left the door of the office open so that a current of air would sweep into the room; then he went down the dark corridor to a stairway and mounted to the street level. The singing came loud and sonorous:

> *Let the lower lights be burning!*
> *Send a gleam across the wave!*
> *Some poor fainting, struggling seaman*
> *You may rescue, you may save.*

He hurried into the street and looked back at the church, then up to the tall steeple which was faintly visible in the frantic flakes. He walked on slowly to the end of the block, wondering when the smoke or the flames would show. He saw a fire alarm box and paused. A man passed. Then a child. He waited until the street was empty, opened the box, pulled the lever, then walked briskly to a corner drugstore, entered, perched himself atop a stool where he could watch the front of the church. He ordered a cup of coffee, sipped it, waiting.

Suddenly he saw a man hurry from the church; then a small knot of men came out; soon a throng of people was pouring from the church door. A moment later he heard the sound of distant sirens.

"Looks like there's a fire somewhere," the clerk behind the counter said.

"I see some people running out of the church down the street," Cross said casually.

The clerk went to the window. "By God, you're right! Fire's coming out of the basement window of the church!"

He joined the clerk at the window. Yes, the draft office was blazing . . .

"How much is this cup of coffee?" he asked.

"Hunh?" the clerk grunted.

"How much is this coffee?"

"Ten cents."

Cross left a dime on the counter and walked calmly from the drugstore. He had a dinner engagement to meet some Communists.

A quarter of an hour later Cross climbed six flights and pushed the bell of Bob's flat. Bob himself opened the door and grabbed his arm.

"Man, give me your coat and hat— Sarah's here and raring to meet you," Bob said, guiding Cross straight to the kitchen where Sarah, a brown-skinned woman with a strong, hard face was cooking dinner. "Sarah, honey! C'mere! I want you to meet Mr. Lane!"

Sarah was bent over a table busily flattening dough with a rolling pin; she glanced up at Cross, then quickly back to her biscuit board.

"Just a sec," she answered placidly.

She was solidly built without being fat, yet her soft, pliable muscles seemed as strong as any man's. She had black hair, a well-shaped mouth and a firm chin. Her movements were deft as she cut the thin spread of dough into biscuits and placed them swiftly into tin pans and shoved them into an oven. She wiped her hands on a dish towel, turned and smiled. Then her face grew solemn as she came toward Cross and stared with eyes full of surprise. The memory of his recent attacks of dread returned and Cross's muscles grew rigid. Had Sarah seen him before? Maybe he had known her in Chicago? Because she was staring at him, he stared at her. Sarah advanced to within a few inches of Cross and broke into a wide grin.

"What's the matter, Sarah? Can't you say hello?" Bob exclaimed.

Sarah cupped her right palm under Cross's chin, cradling it gently. Then a wild roar of laughter spilled out of her; she bent double, unable to control herself. She sobered somewhat and, still holding Cross's face in her right palm, she said:

"Look at that face— *Lead Kindly Light* . . . And he's meeting some Communists tonight, hunh? Honest to Pete, man, you got the *sweetest* face I ever saw!"

She turned from Cross, ran to a chair, flopped in it, flung back her head and yelled at the top of her lungs. Bob joined in, but more sheepishly than Sarah. Their laughter filled the corridor. Maybe they were getting even with him for his having deceived Bob . . . ?

"Don't be mad, man! You got to get used to Sarah— She just blabs out what pops into her mind, that's all," Bob explained.

Cross had had the illusion of feeling at home with these outsiders, but now he felt himself being pushed more than ever into that position where he looked at others as though they were not human. He could have waved his hand and blotted them from existence with no more regret of taking human lives than if he had swatted a couple of insects. Why could he never make others realize how dangerous it was for them to make him feel like this? He lowered his eyes and stared at them, a tight smile hovering on his lips. He trembled to do something, but he clamped his teeth and reined himself in. He knew that he had the kind of face that would always look much younger than his age, but never in his life had another person grabbed hold of that face with their bare hands and made blatant fun of it. What kind of life had Sarah lived that made it possible for her to laugh so openly at him? Pity for her came into his mind, but he banished it, realizing that it was hard to hold pity for someone who most likely did not want it.

Sarah's breasts heaved and tears rolled down her cheeks; and Bob, more restrained—maybe because he had worked around whites and had learned more fear than Sarah—laughed a moment and, seeing that Cross was not angry enough to resort to action, started to laugh again, more uproariously than before, beating his palms against the walls of the hallway and stomping his feet on the floor.

"Okay," Cross said finally. "Maybe I look funny to you."

"Naw— You ain't funny!" Sarah spluttered. "You're just out of this world— And you want to be a Bolshevik! Why, child, they'll eat you for dessert!"

She could laugh no more; in fact, she had laughed so hard that her lips hung open and she breathed orgiastically. Bob stood before Cross, both of his hands resting lightly on Cross's shoulders to show that Cross must not be angry, and he laughed with such a wide mouth that Cross could see the back of his red throat.

"Sarah—stop it! You're *killing* me!" Bob moaned.

Cross sank into a chair and stared at a print of the Moscow Subway that hung on the wall. He had conquered his impulse to anger now; he did not respect them enough to be angry. In his eyes their value as human beings had gone; if they existed, all right; if they did not exist, that was all right too . . .

"Okay. Don't you think I deserve a drink for all that?" he asked them in tones of mild reproof.

"All right, honey," Sarah said at last. "I'm gonna show you my heart's in the right place. I'm gonna give you a *whole* glass of whiskey— You had whiskey before, ain't you?"

"You'd be surprised," Cross told her.

"Know one thing," Sarah said, pouring whiskey into a tumbler. "I'm laughing, but I wonder about you—"

"Why?" Cross asked.

"I see now how Bob made a mistake to trust you on that train," Sarah said soberly. "But I wouldn't've trusted you. No, sir! That nice suit you got on, that nylon shirt, that woolen handmade tie—all that don't mean nothing to me. I'd trust that face of yours as far as I could throw an *elephant*, and you know that ain't far! What you reckon the Communists gonna make out of you?"

"I don't know," Cross answered.

He understood now. Sarah and Bob felt that Communists ought to look like Communists; that is, ragged, desperate, with an air of something slightly crazy. Of course, there were exceptions: white men of cold, sharp minds who sat in dim offices and who ran things, the intellectuals. But Sarah and Bob never expected to see a black intellectual and did not know one when they saw one.

"When did you join the colored race?" Sarah asked, sniggling.

"I never joined," Cross said.

Sarah went off into the kitchen, shaking with laughter. Bob stood near him and kept his right hand on Cross's shoulder. Cross took a long swig from the tumbler; he needed it.

"Don't be mad, man," Bob said. "If we laugh at you, it's 'cause we like you, see?"

"I'm not angry," Cross said in a far-away voice that made Bob sober quickly.

The doorbell rang and Cross was glad. If white guests were arriving, Sarah and Bob would desist in their laughing at him. Repressing his chuckles, Bob went to the door.

"Gil and Eva! Come in! I got somebody here I want you to meet," Bob greeted his guests.

A stolid white man and a tall, blonde white girl came in. Cross rose to meet them.

"I'm Gilbert Blount," the man said, extending his hand, holding a fixed smile on his face. The man's eyes were hard, watchful, grey, and bulbous.

"How are you, Mr. Blount?" Cross asked.

"I'm Gil to my friends," Blount said.

"I'm Lionel," Cross lied.

"And I'm Eva," the girl said and extended an incredibly soft, white hand.

"Here's something in here to wet your throats!" Bob called to them to come into the living room.

It was clear that Bob intended to leave them to talk together and Cross sensed that the meeting had been arranged. What had Bob told Gil about him? Had he led Gil to believe that he had done some great stroke of racial retaliation against whites? It would be like Bob to do such. All right, he'd let these Communists look him over and he would look them over.

But he did not like Gil; there was about the man, even before he had found more valid reasons for his aversion, a rigidity of bodily pose that irked him. Gil was thin without being wiry, tall without being big, aged without being old, and intellectual without partaking of the processes of thought. He spoke in a manner that seemed to indicate that he had difficulty getting the words out of his mouth. Life to Gil was a stubborn, humorless effort that revealed itself in the stiffness of his lips that barely moved as he spoke and a kind of mouthing of his huge teeth when he laughed, which was not often. And back of this was a kind of cold hunger in the man that Cross could not name, a waiting, calculating consciousness whose ends seemed remote.

Gil caught Cross's elbow in a firm grip and said: "Bob told me you were coming here tonight, and I'm glad you came. Whatever your background is, you can feel at home with us."

Cross smiled a smile that he hoped would be interpreted as gratitude. How quickly they work together, Cross thought with wonder. Gil had swallowed the lies he had palmed off on Bob and his reference to his background delighted him. What would Gil think if he really knew? Two strange backgrounds are meeting tonight, Cross told himself. I'm just as complicated as they are . . .

"I'd like to talk to you," Gil continued, guiding him into the living room. "Let's sit over here."

Yes, they've discussed me and they're losing no time. They feel that my being wanted by the police will make me rest my weary head on their red pillow . . . A slow tide of confidence and curiosity was seeping into Cross's consciousness.

"Sure. Whatever you like," Cross said, allowing himself to be led to a sofa in the corner of the room. Gil was going to try to recruit him, all right. But this baby doesn't know what he's got hold of tonight, Cross mused ironically. I've got as many fronts as he's got . . .

Gil sat opposite Cross and Eva pulled over a chair and sat at the side of her husband. Bob came in and poured drinks, handed each of them a glass and left.

"What are you doing now?" Gil asked him bluntly.

Cross smiled and spread out his hands. "Frankly, nothing."

"How do you live?"

"From hand to mouth," he lied; he had almost seven hundred dollars in cash in his pocket.

"Where do you live?"

"On 116th Street in a rented room."

"Are you married?"

"Well, I was once—"

"That's all right. We're not prudes or moralists. That's your business. I just wanted to know if you are free—"

"I'm quite free," Cross said readily. He doesn't know how free I really am, Cross mused. If he knew how free I was, he'd jump out of his skin . . .

He was not a little shocked at Gil's colossal self-conceit. He acts like a God who is about to create a man . . . He has no conception of the privacy of other people's lives . . . He saw Gil's eyes regarding him steadily, coolly, as though Gil was already seeing to what use his life could be put.

"You don't mind my questioning you like this, do you?" Gil asked with a cold smile.

"No. Why should I?" Cross lied with friendly unctuousness.

"We Communists do not admit any subjectivity in human life," Gil said with a slow, even smile, as though proud that he could utter such a horrible statement with such lightmindedness.

"I see," Cross said, striving to keep his voice neutral.

He was seething with resentment at Gil's effrontery. Who in hell does he think he is? He had to brace himself to keep from taking issue not only with Gil's statement but with the whole attitude toward life implied in it. Cross felt himself slowly coming awake, feeling the real world about him. Here was a challenge the measure of which might meet his needs . . . Keep still, he told himself.

"Do you know anything about the revolutionary movement?"

"I know it sketchily in general outline, from 1917 onwards—"

"Where did you pick it up?"

"From books, of course. What do you think?" Cross had difficulty keeping irritation out of his voice.

"Accounts written by counter-revolutionary historians, no doubt," Gil pronounced placidly. He brought out his pipe and began to fill it leisurely with an aromatic tobacco.

Cross had come by his account of the Russian Revolution from the pens of Russian Bolsheviks themselves, but he did not bother to correct Gil's assumption. He sensed that accuracy was not the point here. Gil was trying to impress him, not with learning, but with some attitude of scorn so deep that argument was futile against it. Instead, he took advantage of Gil's silence to observe Eva who sat with her shapely nyloned knees close together and regarded him with wide, enigmatic eyes. When his gaze met hers, she smiled and looked off. She seemed tense, yet rigidly contained. She was a fragile girl of about twenty-four; her attitude was so distracted that one could feel that she would never speak frankly what was really on her mind. Despite this, she seemed kind, impulsive. Her eyes were a clear hazel; her nose small and straight; and her mouth, which was only slightly rouged, was almost severe in its sharpness. The overall aspect of her face, despite the shadow of a smile that flitted over it now and then, was one of tortured, organized concentration. Cross wondered how on earth had she come to be married to a coarse, inhuman character like Blount. Cross now shifted his gaze to Gil and was chagrined to find that Gil had been observing his observation of Eva. Gil smiled tolerantly and Cross found himself boiling with rage. *He thinks I've never met a white girl before . . .*

Something decisive was transpiring in him regarding Gil. He knew that Gil did not take his inner life into account and he felt compelled to do the same with

Gil. This damn thing's catching, he told himself. You have to descend to their level if you are to deal with them . . . There's no other way out . . . But he really liked this; there was an absoluteness about it that appealed to him, excited him. To grapple with Gil would involve a total mobilization of all the resources of his personality, and the conflict would be religious in its intensity.

"What do you think of the position of the Communist Party on the Negro Question?" Gil asked him.

"I know nothing concrete about the Communist position on the Negro," Cross replied. "I know that you fight for Negro rights—"

"I'm surprised," Gil said rudely, ignoring what Cross had been about to say. "How can a man of your intelligence afford not to know the most important contribution on the Negro question that has yet been made?"

"Look, Gil," Cross said in spite of himself; he had not met this provocative kind of argument before and he felt a desire to plead extenuating circumstances. "I've not come across this question in a way that would make me want to go into it that deeply. I'm twenty-six years old and I've not paid much attention to politics."

"The whole of human life is politics, from the cradle to the grave," Gil said, sweeping Cross's explanation into a heap of dust. "For those who don't know this, so much the worse for them. In England and Germany the ruling classes start training their future rulers when they are mere boys. The Party does the same. That's why Communists have something to say about what happens on this earth. Men are not born masters; they are made into masters. We Communists understand that. And, my friend, it's time that you understood it too. History will not respect you nor forgive you for not knowing it.

How can you sit there and be indifferent to the forces that shape and control your destiny? It's your job to find out how this world is run, Lionel. What do you know about dialectical materialism?"

Cross knew a little about the theory, but he knew that his scanty knowledge would never satisfy Gil, so he answered: "Nothing."

"Too bad for you," Gil said; there was no pity in his voice; he spoke as though a man as ignorant as Cross did not deserve to live.

Cross looked at Eva whose eyes flitted at once from his face. He clenched his teeth to keep down his anger. His feelings were bridling so that he found himself picking nervously at his lips with his fingernails. Goddamn this cool, brash man who, though in a different way, was treating him as Bob and Sarah had. How easily he could kill Gil with no regret; Gil was making him feel that he was his enemy, not his personal enemy, but his enemy in general and in principle. And at the moment he could think of no words that he could ever muster that would convey to Gil the depth of his rejection of him. Cross recalled that he had once wished to be a rock that could feel nothing; well, he had met a man who had apparently tried to turn himself into one . . .

Bob passed the open door, poked his head in, grinned, and asked: "Everything's all right?"

"We're doing all right," Gil told Bob.

You conceited sonofabitch, Cross told Gil in his mind.

Gil leaned back and stared at the ceiling, puffing gently at his pipe. Yes, they are definitely trying to recruit me, Cross mused. But I need them, just as much as they need me . . . Then, why not? He could always leave them when he wanted to, couldn't he? And in the meanwhile he would have a chance to establish a new base, a new set of friends . . . As Cross waited on Gil to speak, he did not let his facial expression betray his acute consciousness of Gil's consciousness; through it all he sat listening with a soft, ambiguous smile. But could he, even for the sake of his own selfish ends, stomach this preposterous Gil?

"You must never be a victim," Eva said, stressing the word "victim".

Cross loved her for saying it so sweetly, but hated her assumption of superiority. Yet, in the end it was the soft light in Eva's eyes that made Cross say at last:

"Well, Gil, we're not all lucky enough to be able to keep abreast of events as well as you do."

"I'm not keeping abreast of events," Gil corrected him with imperturbable aloofness. "You learn revolutionary logic by working in the revolutionary movement. Yes, Lionel, you need to stop throwing your life away in individual protests against your exploiters. Pool your strength with your natural allies; get in the revolutionary movement and soak up the lessons of history."

"I'd never try to act before knowing what I was about," Cross told him.

"Look, guy," Gil took his pipe from his mouth and leaned and pointed the stem at him. "I like you, see? I've seen you for about ten minutes and I'm willing to take a chance on you. If I made you a gift, would you accept it?"

Cross smiled and looked at him. These Communists mean business . . .

"My mother used to tell me: 'When somebody gives you something, take it; when somebody takes something away from you, cry'," Cross said.

Gil managed a wry smile, as though he did not approve of the folk-saying because it had not the sanction of Karl Marx; but Eva clapped her hands and laughed delightedly.

"I want to send you to the Workers' School," Gil said, "at my own expense. But there's only one catch to my offer . . ."

"What's that?"

"If I stake you to study, then you'll have to come and live with us."

"Why?" Cross asked, puzzled.

Did this man want him in the same house with a girl as beautiful as Eva? He was crazy . . .

"For many reasons," Gil explained. "First, I'd like to keep track of your progress. Second, I want you to help me in a fight against racism which I'm going to wage in the building in which I live. Third, I want to demonstrate to a certain man, my landlord, who needs to learn a lot, that a Negro is not afraid to live in his building. My landlord's a Fascist, an open Fascist! I want you to move into my apartment. We've a spare room."

Cross looked at Eva.

"We'd be happy to have you," she said; but she did not smile.

Cross sighed. He had not expected this. Well, why not? This man thinks he is cold; well, I'm just as cold as he is . . . Maybe more . . . He is trying to use me, but I'll make *use* of his trying to use me . . .

"I like to gamble sometimes," Cross said, rising. "I'm doing nothing with myself. I'll take you up on this and see where it leads. About the Fascist, lead me to him. I've been accused of many things in my life, but no one has yet said that I was afraid."

Gil rose; he beamed for the first time since he had been in the room and he clapped his hand on Cross's shoulder.

"You're a man in a million! That's the spirit I like to see, boy!" Gil said with stiff, jerky lips.

"The freedom of your people ought to be the most precious thing on earth to you," Eva said solemnly.

Smiling a smile that they thought was acquiescence but which was really irony, Cross stood to one side and watched them. As if at a signal, Bob and Sarah came into the room; there was no attempt to conceal the fact that all of them had discussed Cross previously and had decided to make the offer that Gil had tendered him. Bob was jubilant, slapping Cross on the back and telling him:

"You ain't got no worries now, boy. The Party'll take care of you . . . From now on, the Party's going to be your mother and your father."

Sarah whispered to him, grinning and struggling to repress her laughter: "You're something new, something special. You can go far with that face of yours. Nobody'll think you're up to anything."

Why do they have to crow so openly over me? Cross asked himself. Though he had agreed to give Gil's offer a try, he could not avoid feeling cheapened at the way they boasted of how they had been wise enough to know a "good man" when they saw one. I'll show 'em how good I am, Cross told himself.

Sarah turned and looked at the clock on the mantel; then she and Bob looked at each other.

"Where's Jack?" Bob asked.

"My dinner's being ruined," Sarah complained.

"I say let's eat," Bob said defiantly. "He knew what time we were eating."

"Ditto," said Sarah. "I don't like slaving over a hot stove cooking a good meal and letting it get cold. That Jack Hilton's always doing that. Who does he think he is?"

"He's held up at a meeting," Gil said.

"Come on, folks," Sarah called, beckoning. "Go into the dining room and sit down."

Cross detected in Bob a feeling of hostility toward the absent Jack Hilton and he wondered about it. He joined the others at the dinner table, but even the deliciousness of Sarah's cooking could not banish his sense of their regarding him as a strange fish that they had hauled up out of the sea. Gil downed his food wordlessly, his attention far away. Eva gossiped with Sarah, and Bob ate lustily, now and again looking proudly at Cross. They were eating dessert when the doorbell rang.

"That's Jack," Sarah said with disgust.

"I'll let 'im in," Bob said, rising and going to the door.

Cross heard Bob greet the new guest: "Hey, Jack! You're late. We're eating dessert."

There was a low rumble of voices in the hallway and then Cross saw a slender man of about thirty enter the dining room with his overcoat still on. Flakes of melting snow clung to his hat, and a faint haze of vapor, precipitated by the warm air of the apartment, rose from his clothing. His eyes were dark brown, limpid, deep-set, and stared almost unblinkingly. The face was emaciated, the lips thin and hanging slightly open; the mouth was wide, a little loose. He had a shock of blond hair and his skin was sallow. Under his arm he carried a roll of papers which was slightly damp from the weather outside and he held both of his hands, which had no gloves, clasped tightly in front of him, as though his strained nerves had to have something to hold onto for sake of support. Cross had the impression that the man was under severe nervous strain, and that perhaps a slight emotional push would set him going.

No one save Bob had spoken to him and so far he

had said nothing to anyone. All waited for him to speak. He glanced at Sarah and said dryly:

"I'm sorry I couldn't come in time to eat. But I was detained at the control commission."

Sarah forced a smile and mumbled: "That's all right, Jack."

"The Party comes first," Bob agreed.

"Sit down and have a drink, won't you?" Sarah asked him.

"I don't want a drink," he said. "I can stay but a minute. In fact, I've come on an important errand to speak to Bob."

"We can go into the bedroom," Bob suggested.

"No. I can say it right here," Jack Hilton said in hard, cold, precise tones.

He paused and Cross noticed that Hilton's shoes had cracks in them. The man's feet must be frozen . . .

"Bob Hunter," Jack Hilton began in a tone that sounded as though he was declaiming a prepared speech, "the Party has decided that you must not proceed any further in your attempt to organize any cells in the Dining Car Waiters' Union. The Party does not wish to see that task undertaken at this time. You must forthwith desist from all and any activities in that direction. For further instructions, you will report to your Fraction Cell. Is that clearly understood?"

The man's voice had gradually risen to a high pitch of oratory before he had finished; Cross felt that the importance of the message did not justify such a method of delivery, but he sensed behind the manner of speaking an attempt to impose a respect for higher authority.

"But, man," Bob protested, "what are you saying to me? I'm working at it night and day."

"Then stop it!" The words shot from Hilton's mouth.

"But, Jack," Bob yelled, "I already sent out the letters for a meeting—"

"Then send out letters and cancel the meeting!" Hilton said.

"But— Man, you don't know what you're doing! I declared myself to 'em in public as a Party member—"

Hilton took a step closer to Bob, and, taking the papers he had held under his arm, he doubled them in his right fist and slapped them against his leg to underscore each word he spoke.

"Hunter, when will you ever learn to respect a decision of the Party? You don't discuss decisions of the Party. You *obey* them!"

"But what am I gonna do?" Bob wailed. "I want to organize my union like the Party told me."

"The Party has altered its decision!" Hilton stated flatly.

"Jack," Sarah spoke in a low, calm tone of voice, "listen, this is not as easy as you think. Bob has exposed himself as a member of the Party in order to recruit for the Party. Now, if he drops this work, what is he to do? He can't work for the union and he can't work for the company . . . And now you're telling him he mustn't go on working for the Party—"

"This has *nothing* to do with *you*," Hilton told Sarah. "This decision is between Hunter and the Party—"

Sarah leaped from the table and confronted Hilton. "It *has* something to do with me!" she blazed. "Bob's my husband, and what concerns *him* concerns *me*!"

"Not in the Party it doesn't," Hilton said.

"Then Bob's *not* going to obey any such damned decision!" Sarah shouted. "You wanted Bob to organize the waiters on the dining cars. Now, he's doing that. Then you say stop. Now, why, *why*?"

"The Party is not obliged to justify its decisions to you or anybody," Hilton said.

"I'm gonna keep on organizing," Bob said uncertainly to Hilton.

"Then you will be disciplined," Hilton said.

"What discipline? What can you do to me?" Bob asked, his eyes wide with wonder and anxiety.

"You can be expelled," Hilton told him. "And the Party will blacklist you throughout the labor movement. The Party will kill you. You can't *fight* the Party! *Understand* that?"

There was silence. Cross looked about the dining room. Gil leaned forward, listening, sucking contentedly at his pipe, his elbows resting on the table. There was a quiet twinkle in his eyes as he looked from Bob to Hilton and back again, following their dialogue. Eva was pale, stiff, and seemed not to be breathing; her eyes were full of a look that seemed to be protest. Sarah's eyes were blazing and her chest rose and fell rapidly; Cross could see the throbbing of a tiny vein in her neck. Bob stood bent forward a little, his lips hanging open, his eyes wide and glassy. His stance was a combination of subservience and aggression; it seemed that he was about to bow to Hilton's demands and yet at the same time he could have been ready to leap forward and grab Hilton's throat. Cross wondered if it occurred to Bob that he was trying to drag him into an inhuman machine like this . . . ? Maybe Bob's mind did not possess enough elasticity to bring such ideas to his consciousness . . . ?

"But what can I do?" Bob finally asked in a wail.

Gil rose and walked around the table to Bob and pointed the stem of his pipe into Bob's face.

"You're going to be a Bolshevik and obey the Party," Gil spoke with jerky authority.

"But my fellow workers'll think I'm crazy if I change my mind like that," Bob pointed out.

"That does not matter," Gil said. "You are an instrument of the Party. You exist to execute the Party's will. That's all there is to it."

"But I *feel*—" Bob began.

"Goddamn your damned feelings!" Gil spat. "Who cares about what you feel? Insofar as the Party is concerned, you've got no damned feelings!" Gil paused a moment; there was a look of wild exasperation in his bulbous eyes. "Bob, there's a hell of a lot you don't understand. What do you think men like Molotov do when they get a decision? They carry it *out*! Do you think the Party exists to provide an outlet for your personal feelings? Hell, no! What do you think the Party would be if such happened? We are not Socialists . . . We are *Communists*! And being a Communist is not easy. It means negating yourself, blotting out your personal life and listening only to the voice of the Party. The Party wants you to *obey*! The Party hopes that you can understand *why* you must obey; but even if you don't understand, you *must* obey. If you don't, then the Party will toss you aside, like a broken hammer, and seek another instrument that will obey. Don't think that you are indispensable because you're black and the Party needs you. Hell, no! The Party can find others to do what it wants! Is this asking too much? No. Why? Because the Party needs this obedience to carry out its aims. And what are those aims? The liberation of the working class and the defense of the Soviet Union. The Party, therefore, does not and cannot ask too much of any comrade. It's logical, is it not? The Party is conducting this fight on your behalf and you must fit into it. Is that clear?"

Bob nodded his head affirmatively and then Gil turned and stared at Cross. And Cross felt that a better demonstration of what he was in for could not have happened even if it had been arranged.

"Lane," Gil said, "you are looking at a Party problem. Do you understand it?"

"I understand it," Cross said.

"I must go," Hilton said; he turned and without another word walked out of the room. No one had moved to open the front door for him; Cross heard it slam shut. He looked at Gil and was astonished to see Gil watching him and smiling.

"Do you understand what I mean, Lane, when I say you can't learn this out of books?"

"Yes. But, listen, I see here two points of view. I see—"

His eyes caught sight of a gesture of Gil's hand, a motion that meant for him to remain silent; Cross knew that Gil did not want him to discuss Bob's Party problem in front of Bob.

"It's late," Gil exclaimed. "We must be going, Eva."

"Oh, dear, yes," Eva said. She turned to Sarah. "Darling, thank you for the wonderful dinner."

"It's nothing," Sarah said; she could not lift up her eyes.

Gil asked Cross, when he was close enough to him to talk in a whisper: "Can I give you a lift to 116th Street?"

"Sure," Cross said. He longed to talk to Bob, but felt that it would be better to do so out of the presence of Gil. He rose, burning with protest at what he had seen and heard.

Bob pretended to be brave; he grinned, wagged his head, and crooned: "Boy, the Party's tough, hunh? It's a great Party—"

"That's the spirit," Gil said, going for his overcoat.

"I don't like it," Sarah said, taking a pile of dirty dishes into the kitchen.

"She'll be all right," Bob sought to apologize for her.

"I *won't* be all right!" Sarah shouted at him, her face twisted with anger.

"Darling, let's go," Eva said.

Cross shook hands with Bob and went to the kitchen door to say good-bye to Sarah. The door was closed and when he pushed it open he saw Sarah sitting with her head bowed. Her shoulders were shaking; she was weeping. She had not heard him open the door, and Cross closed it softly and joined the others. He followed Gil and Eva silently down the stairs to the street. Not a word was spoken until they had all gotten into the car and were rolling over the lumpy drifts of snow. Cross was next to Eva and his nostrils were full of the delicate perfume that she wore. He stared straight ahead of him, feeling that his life had at last touched something that stirred him to his depths . . . He was not angry or outraged, just deeply thoughtful, full of wonder. He had witnessed a scene of naked force in which obedience had been exacted through fear and the intensity of the emotions involved shook him.

"Well, what are your impressions, Lionel?" Gil asked, smiling and looking ahead of him.

"It's interesting," Cross said; he did not want to talk now.

"Is that all?" Gil asked, chuckling.

"It's impressive," Cross conceded.

"I didn't expect you to see that tonight," Gil said soberly. "I'm just wondering if you understand it correctly. If you got the right interpretation?"

"I got the right one," Cross said tersely.

"You have a big future ahead of you," Eva said in a

neutral, far-away tone that made Cross wonder what she meant.

"You'll be all right," Gil said.

"Here's 116th Street; you can drop me here," Cross said, relieved.

The car slowed and Gil and Eva looked solemnly at Cross.

"Well, Lionel, have you changed your mind?" Gil asked.

"Absolutely not!"

"Then we can expect you?"

"When do you want me?"

"Tonight. Now. Tomorrow. This week . . . Whenever you want to come," Gil said.

"Give me the address," Cross said.

"It's 13 Charles Street, second floor," Gil said.

"I'll be there about ten in the morning," Cross said. "I've one suitcase, that's all."

"Right," Gil said.

"Good night, Lionel," Eva said.

Gil waved his hand and the car moved off through the dim, snowy streets. Cross stood a moment, looking at its red taillight disappear. He mounted to his room, undressed, and lay on his bed. There was a smile on his face as he stared up into the darkness. They think I'm a little child, he told himself. I don't mind the way they act in organizing . . . I don't mind the wild way they give out their decisions . . . I don't even mind their self-righteousness . . . But that naked force . . . Why? At the mere recollection of Hilton's biting tones, he sucked in his breath. They didn't *have* to treat Bob that way . . . Bob'll follow *any* strong person . . . You can take his hand and lead 'im . . .

He sat on the side of the bed; sleep was far from him. "Once you get that kind of attitude structuralized in an organization that goes on from year to year, how can you ever get it removed . . . ?" he asked out loud.

Cross felt that he was at last awaking. The dream in which he had lived since he had fled Chicago was leaving him. The reality about him was beginning to vibrate: he was slowly becoming himself again, but it was a different self.

Finally, toward dawn, he turned over on his side and slept like a rock for the first time in many weeks.

BOOK THREE

DESCENT

For that which I do I allow not: for what I would, that I do not; but what I hate, that I do.

—ST. PAUL

CROSS WAS AWARE of every echo of meaning surrounding his decision to live with the Blounts. He had accepted their invitation in bad faith which was now almost a congenital condition with him; but he realized that his adversaries were also acting in bad faith, a bad faith of which they were cynically proud. Bad faith, though reprehensible and regrettable, was not unknown to Cross; not only had he been long guilty of it in his personal relations, but he was convinced that bad faith of some degree was an indigenous part of living. The daily stifling of one's sense of terror in the face of life, the far-flung conspiracy of pretending that life was tending toward a goal of redemption, the reasonless assumption that one's dreams and desires were realizable—all of these hourly, human feelings were bad faith. But when Cross saw bad faith being practiced as a way of life, when he saw men mobilizing the natural hopes and anxieties of other men for their own selfish ends, he became all but hypnotized by the spectacle.

He had no illusions regarding the complexity of the situation into which he was voluntarily entering. His past life had prepared him for participating in such compounded duplicities. His temperament made him love to understand those who thought that they were misleading him and it was fun to use his position of being misled to, in his turn, mislead them into a position where they thought that he was misunderstanding them. He knew, of course, that such complicated games carried a risk of *his* misunderstanding those whom he was supposed to understand, but he was willing to shoulder such handicaps. Perhaps we might both misunderstand each other, he mused.

Need for money was not pulling him into this. He had no hankering for publicity, for to be known might mean the return of Cross Damon from the grave, and that would blast his life anew. Also his was not the itch to right wrongs done to others, though those wrongs did at times agitate him. And, above all, he possessed no notion of personal or social wrongs having been done to him; if any such wrongs had existed, he felt fully capable of righting them by his own lonely strength and effort.

It was an emotional compulsion, religious in its intensity, to feel and weigh the worth of himself that was pushing him into the arms of the one thing on earth that could transform his sense of dread, shape it, objectify it, and make it real and rational for him. Logic was guiding his sense of direction, but his emotional needs were dictating the kind of directions he chose.

His affinities with the turbulent instincts of Gil and Hilton were undeniable; he was, in a manner, their brother, just as Houston was his. His difference lay in his intractability being at bottom sharper and more recondite. Too full he was of personal pride to regard himself as an exploited victim; his was not the demand that he be given his share of a mythical heritage. His was a passion to recast, reforge himself anew, and he was certain that Gil and Hilton had once in their lives felt what he was now feeling, that his reaching out for another pitch of consciousness had haunted them just as now it plagued him. But they had resolved their tangled emotions in the rigid disciplines of Communist politics, thereby ejecting from their hearts the pathos of living, purging their consciousness of that perilous subjective tension that spells the humanity of man. And now they were warring to slay in others that same agony of life that had driven them to the wall.

What malevolently psychological advantages were theirs in the waging of their war! Who best could track down criminals than reformed criminals! Gil and Hilton were spiritual bloodhounds on the trail of men whose spirits had not yet been broken as theirs had been. Since they had been defeated, they had decreed that defeat be the lot of all . . .

It was not the objective reality of the revolutionary movement that was pulling so magnetically at Cross; it was something that that movement had and did not know it had that was seducing his attention. It was its believing that it *knew* life; its *conviction* that it had mastered the act of living; its *will* that it could define the ends of existence that fascinated him against his volition. Nowhere else save in these realms had he encountered that brand of organized audacity directed toward secular goals. He loathed their knowledge, their manners, their ends; but he was almost persuaded that they had in a wrong manner moved in a right direction for revealing the content of human life on earth. He knew that their bristling economic theories were simply but vastly clever fishing nets which they dragged skillfully through muddy social waters to snare the attention of shivering and hungry men; but many men, the best of them, would not yield their allegiances on purely economic grounds and he knew that the Party knew this.

While packing his suitcase, he was struck by an idea. Suppose Gil was right in assuming that the Party was justified in coercing obedience from others purely on the basis of its strength? What was there, then, to keep an individual from adopting the same policy? Apparently nothing save cunning and ruthlessness . . .

"Gil'd want to kill me if he knew how I felt," he chuckled, lumbering down the stairway with his suitcase.

A yellow sun was flooding the buildings with a pale light that had no warmth. He headed for the subway and had gone but ten yards when the image of Bob's face rose before his eyes. Yes! How was Bob making out? Had he kept the Party's decision? Instead of going to Gil's place, he rode uptown and made his way to Bob's apartment. Bob answered the door.

"Speak of the devil!" Bob greeted him. "Come in, man. We were just talking 'bout you. You got your suitcase— Going to Gil's, hunh?"

"Yeah." Cross looked searchingly at Bob whose face wore a mask of cheerfulness. "You seem all right after what happened last night."

"Yeah, man," Bob boasted. "That ain't nothing—"

"The hell it ain't!" Sarah's voice boomed from the living room.

"Man, Sarah's mad," Bob said, becoming crestfallen at the sound of her voice. "Go on in."

Bob followed him and the moment Cross stepped into the living room he saw Sarah's angry face.

"Hey, Pretty," Sarah greeted him in cold tones.

"I thought you were going to laugh at me today," Cross said.

"I ain't laughing at no sonofabitch today," Sarah replied.

"She don't understand that the Party has to have discipline," Bob explained. "Women think we men can do as we like—"

"You joined the Party to organize, didn't you?" Sarah demanded.

"Yeah; sure, Sarah. But listen— Lemme explain—"

"You ain't explaining nothing!" Sarah overrode him. "A white man held out a stick to you and said, 'Jump!' And, by God, you jumped, just like any nigger—"

"Listen, woman! This is the *Party*! This—"

"But it's a *white* man's Party, ain't it?" Sarah demanded.

Bob turned to Cross and shook his head helplessly.

"Why don't they want you to go on with your work?" Cross asked Bob.

"He don't know," Sarah answered for Bob. "They walk in here and tell 'im what to do, and he hates it, but he *obeys*! They don't even tell 'im why, but he *obeys*!" She glared at Bob. "Even in the South when the white folks lynched you, they told you *why*! You didn't agree with 'em, but, by God, they told you *why*!"

"Sarah," Bob began, "the Party's an army—"

"Goddamn your Party!" Sarah blazed, leaping to her feet. "What in hell did I marry, a Marxist or a mouse? Listen, nigger, you're going to *organize*, you hear?"

"Baby," Bob whined. "Look, Lionel's new to the Party—"

"Let 'im hear it all!" Sarah yelled. "Let 'im know what he's getting into." Bitter tears filled her eyes; she turned to Cross. "All my life I've seen niggers knuckling down to white people. I saw my mama knuckling down when I was a child in the South. And nothing hurt me so much as when I saw a white man kick her one day . . . Know what I mean? *Kick* her! I said kick her with his *goddamn* foot. I was 'bout six; mama was serving in the white man's house; I was watching from the kitchen door. Mama tripped and fell with the tray and boiling soup splashed all over her. But the white man wasn't worried 'bout that. Hell, naw! He was mad 'cause his dinner was spoiled, so he *kicked* her. It'll stay in my mind till my dying day . . . And everywhere I've looked since I've seen nothing but white folks kicking niggers who are kneeling down . . . Know why I don't go to church, Lionel? 'Cause I have to *kneel* in front of that white priest, and I'll be goddamned if I'll do it. Now, we're in the revolution and the *same* goddamn white man comes along. But he's in the Party now."

"Baby, it's different," Bob wailed.

"Don't tell me it's different; it's the *same* damn thing!" Sarah sat heavily in a chair and her head dropped; she seemed ashamed of her outburst. "Maybe the Party wanted you to expose yourself that way," she began again in a reflective tone. "You're no good to the union, you're no good to the company, and, if you don't obey the Party, you're no good to them. They got you trapped—"

"Sarah," Bob spoke solemnly. "A good Bolshevik obeys. Lenin obeyed, didn't he? Molotov obeys—"

"Then, honey," Sarah sneered at him, "I want you to be one of them who tells the *others* to obey, see? Read your Marx and organize. Hunh? *That* scares you, don't it? They done put the fear of God in your soul!" She rose again, trembling with anger. "Listen, I'm working and helping to support you to *organize*! I'm feeding you to *organize*! Now, you either *organize* or *go*!" She whirled to Cross. "The Party scared the pee out of him this morning. He went to the Control Commission to find out why they didn't want him to go on with his work. When he got back here, he was sick—"

"I *wasn't* sick," Bob protested, ashamed that Cross should know.

"You looked *green*," Sarah said. "And when a man as dark as you looks *green*, he *sick*!"

Bob grabbed his head with his hands, sank into a seat; his body began to tremble. He was suffering, a wet rag billowing between the blasts of Sarah and the Party. Cross was unable to look at him; he stared out of the window.

"What are you going to do, Bob?" Cross asked patiently.

"Hell, man. I don't know," Bob sighed.

"What do you *want* to do?" Cross asked.

Bob's eyes searched Cross's face as though seeking an answer there; he licked his lips and mumbled despairingly:

"I want to organize Negroes—"

"Well, why don't you?"

"You reckon I could do it? Reckon I ought to?" he asked sheepishly.

"You ought to do what you want to do," Cross told him.

Sarah watched Bob with the cold eyes that only a woman can have for her husband. Cross knew that Bob would never win. Bob was too scared to act alone; he had to have a master. The Party had sunk its hold deep in Bob's heart and, if Bob left the Party, he would have to find another . . .

"I'm gonna stick to my own people," he said heavily, his eyes glistening. He had run from one master to another: his race. "That's what I'm gonna do."

"Then, *do* it, Bob," Cross said. "I'll help you."

"You want to help organize Negroes?" Bob asked eagerly, jumping to his feet.

"No. I want to help *you*," Cross told him in clipped tones.

Bob was puzzled; he brushed the meaning in Cross's

words aside. He paced nervously with eyes full of anxiety. "One thing's got me worried," he mumbled. "The Party knows I'm illegally in this country—"

"So what?" Sarah asked.

"Supposed they turn me in to the Immigration folks to get rid of me—?"

"The *Communists*?" Cross asked.

"Sure, man," Bob said. "When the Party fights, they fight with everything."

"They wouldn't dare," Sarah said.

Cross felt that Bob's worries were farfetched. After all, was Bob that important to the Party? He rose to leave and Bob grabbed his hand in gratitude. Sarah followed him to the door. As Cross descended the stairs he wondered why some men wanted to be free and some did not, why some needed freedom and others did not even feel its loss when they did not have it.

After witnessing Bob's turmoil, he had doubts about going to Gil's. Was not Gil but another Hilton? And why did the Party demand abject obedience? He recalled Bob's having told him that the Party was "now your mother and your father", which meant that if he obeyed, the Party would take care of him, but, if he disobeyed, the Party would destroy him. And he had not the right to know *why* he was obeying . . . Why blind obedience? Yet, upon reflection, he found some cynical merit in the Party's demand for it. If no reasons are assigned for a given command, then you cannot criticize, for you do not understand what you are doing. And if obedience without reasons is demanded for little things, it would hold, as a matter of ingrained habit, for bigger and more dangerous things . . . But why had the Party chosen that procedure? Had they found that men would *not* obey otherwise? That could hardly be true, for each day millions of southern Negroes obeyed southern whites; millions of South African natives obeyed the white powers above them; millions of Germans had obeyed Hitler; and in most cases these millions had been given some fantastic excuse to justify the command of obedience. The Nazis tried to win the loyalty of their subjects by conferring upon them ornate titles, noneconomic rewards of various sorts, and by devising schemes of sport and joy. But the only motive that Hilton had held out to Bob was fear. Did the Communists *prefer* fear? He sighed and glanced out of the subway window just in time to discover that the train was slowing for his stop. Well, the answer to his questions was in Gil's apartment . . . .

The Blounts lived in a sparsely furnished, seven-room apartment on the second floor of a red brick building on Charles Street. Eva was not in and Gil received Cross with determined stolidity. The questions that had thronged Cross's mind were now informing his sensibilities. If there was something here to understand, then he, Cross, would get it.

"How are you?" Gil asked him offhandedly.

"Fine."

"Follow me," Gil said, heading down a narrow hallway.

Gil showed him a small room overlooking a depressing stretch of straggling wooden fences separating backyards.

"Will this suit your needs?" Gil asked.

"Most certainly."

"Leave your suitcase and let's have some beer," Gil said and left.

Cross placed his suitcase in a corner and walked slowly down the hallway, passing first what was obviously Gil's bedroom, then Eva's bedroom, and next the dining room, the living room, and finally coming to the kitchen in which Gil stood pouring beer into two tall glasses.

"You get the layout of the place?" Gil asked without looking around.

"Yes; I see it." *He knows I've looked the joint over . . .*

"The bathroom is next door," Gil said. He pointed to a rear door in the kitchen. "That's Eva's studio. She paints, you know."

"Oh; I didn't know," Cross said.

"She's a good painter," Gil told him. "Now, follow me."

Gil took the glasses into the living room and sat one glass for Cross and another for himself on the end tables of two easy chairs. Cross noticed the slow precision with which Gil moved.

"You are observant," Gil observed.

"Just a habit," Cross said.

When they were seated, Gil studied Cross silently for some seconds, took a swallow of beer, lit his pipe and puffed the bowl to a glowing red. He held the burnt-out match delicately in his fingers, then laid it aside carefully in an ashtray. *Why does he act like that?* Cross asked himself. *Or, maybe he was observing the man too closely? He acts like he wants to mesmerize me; if he does, he certainly picked the wrong subject . . .*

"Did anyone see you come up?" Gil asked.

"Not a soul. Why?"

Gil did not answer; he acted as though he had not heard.

"I'd like for you to sit around a week, go to meetings, listen a bit before you start your lessons in the Workers' School," Gil said.

"Just as you say," Cross agreed.

Gil rose and went to his bookcase and took down a

volume, parted the leaves to a certain page, and stood reading for some minutes, puffing slowly on his pipe. He finally sat and spoke while looking out of the window.

"We are going to launch a campaign against realtors who discriminate against Negroes here in Greenwich Village," Gil explained. "There is no law against Negroes living anywhere in this city they want to, but landlords have banded together and made codes against Negroes. One of the leading supporters of this code is the man who lives downstairs; he is my landlord."

Gil's attitude began to assume a pattern of meaning. Cross recalled that Gil had asked him if he had been observed by anyone on his entering the building, and when he had told Gil that no one had seen him and had asked Gil to explain why he had asked such a question, Gil had remained silent. It was clear that Gil was jealously reserving to himself the right to tell Cross the facts in his own way, to paint the entire picture, put in the shadings, the interpretations, the sense of direction. And the words Cross heard would constitute a law which he had to memorize carefully . . . But *why?* Cross asked himself. Let him come out and say what he wants . . .

"This'll be a tough fight," Gil went on. "We'll be attacking the most deeply entrenched money interests in this city. The man downstairs is called Langley Herndon; he's an ex-real estate broker; he's now retired. He's a dyed-in-the-wool Negro hater. He has told me that if he had his way, he'd kill every Negro he could lay his hands on . . .

"Now, here's our strategy. He's going to know soon enough that you're living in my apartment, and the moment he knows, trouble will start. Just enter and leave the building normally. Maintain a polite attitude toward everyone you meet. We mustn't let any side issues develop here; we mustn't give anybody a chance to say that you were rude or insulting to them; understand? Be reserved. If this Herndon should speak to you, and he will, just act as if you were not aware of trespassing his racial boundaries. Let him take the offensive in every instance, that is, up to the point of violence. Now, Lionel, I have a lease . . ." He paused and pulled a batch of papers out of his inside coat pocket. "It's drawn between you and me. The lease I hold with Herndon gives me the right to sublet in whole or in part. Now, the lease I want you to sign was drawn up by a Party lawyer. This whole plan has been most carefully mapped out. Your staying here is perfectly legal; not only human and decent, but *legal*.

"Now, armed with this lease, Herndon has no real recourse to law to throw you or me out. But, of course, he has his goons, his tough boys who may try to waylay you. The cops will be on his side; make no mistake about that.

"Now, let me tell you the kind of man this Herndon is. I mentioned last night that he was a Fascist. He is. I'm not understating it. Herndon began his life as a Texas oil man and he made piles of money. He has the old-fashioned American racist notions, all of them, right up to the hilt, including the so-called biological inferiority of the Negro. He even claims that he has found a philosophical basis and justification for his racial hatred. Understand? He hates not only Negroes, Jews, Chinese, but *all* non-Anglo-Saxons . . . And he is smart enough to give you a mile of specious arguments, gotten out of crackpot books, for his anti-Semitism, anti-Negroism, etc. All of his arguments boil down to this: God made him and his kind to rule over the lower breeds. And God was so kind and thoughtful as to arrange that he be paid handsomely for it. Of course, he has conceived this God of his in the image of a highly successful oil or real estate man, just a little more powerful and wonderful than he is. Herndon is quite anxious to collaborate with God by shouldering a rifle, if necessary, and helping God to defend what God has so generously given him. Herndon feels that God was absolutely right in giving him what he's got, but he does not completely trust God's judgment when it comes to his keeping it.

"As soon as he knows that you're in the building, the entire neighborhood will know it. That ought to happen within the next few hours. From that moment on, you'll have to watch out. Now, I'm getting you a gun and a permit to carry one . . ."

"I've got a gun," Cross told him. "But no permit."

Gil frowned and studied the floor. "How long have you carried a gun?"

"A few weeks. Especially when I travel—"

"You carry it on you?"

"Yes."

"May I see it?"

Cross tendered Gil his gun and Gil broke it, copied down the serial number and returned it.

"A Party contact will help get you a permit," Gil continued, but the tone of his voice had changed.

He's worried about the gun, Cross thought. Otherwise, I've acted in a way to make him trust me, to make him feel that he is the boss; but my having a gun makes him feel that I might have a will of my own . . .

"If and when Herndon moves against us," Gil resumed, "we'll break the case in the *Daily Worker*; we'll break it in England, in France, in China, and the Soviet Union—"

"You don't think a court would uphold your lease?" Cross asked.

Gil seemed annoyed. He gazed down at the figures in the carpet for a moment.

"Lionel, courts are instrumentalities of bourgeois law," he said slowly. "We are going to try this case in the public mind. Above all, this case must serve the Party's organizational interests."

Cross was worried. What would the publicity mean for him? Ought he tell Gil that he could not risk that? No; he would wait; he could always disappear if things went in the wrong direction . . .

"Are you in agreement with this plan?" Gil asked.

"Of course," Cross lied.

"Then tell me what would you think of anyone who tried to defeat this fight for Negroes to live where they wanted to?" Gil asked slowly.

"Why," Cross stammered, "he would be a sonofabitch, to say the least."

Gil did not react to this definition. He stared straight at Cross and then leaned back in his chair. His pipe had gone out and he relit it. Suddenly Gil's eyes seemed to become unseeing.

"He would be a counter-revolutionary," Gil pronounced at last. "And he would deserve to be destroyed by the Party."

Gil's words made Cross at last understand what had been bothering him all along. It came in the tone of Gil's words, in the chilled promise of cold vengeance that edged his voice. *Power!* This was power he saw in action. That was why Gil had evaded answering his questions; Gil had made him assume a position of disadvantage, of waiting to be told what to do. The meaning unfolded like the petals of a black flower in the depths of a swamp. That was why fear was used; that was why no rewards of a tangible nature were given. It worked like this: Gil could lord it over Cross; and, in turn, as his payment for his suffering Gil's domination, Cross could lord it over somebody else. It was odd that he had not sensed it before; it had been *too* simple, *too* elementary. His mind worked feverishly, analyzing the concept. Here was something more recondite than mere political strategy; it was a *life* strategy using political methods as its tools . . . Its essence was a voluptuousness, a deep-going sensuality that took cognizance of fundamental human needs and the answers to those needs. It related man to man in a fearfully organic way. To hold absolute power over others, to define what they should love or fear, to decide if they were to live or die and thereby to ravage the whole of their beings—that was a sensuality that made sexual passion look pale by comparison. It was a noneconomic conception of existence. The rewards for those followers who deserved them did not cost one penny; the only price attached to rewards was the abject suffering of some individual victim who was dominated by the recipient of the reward of power . . . No, they were not dumb, these Gils and Hiltons . . . They knew a thing or two about mankind. They had reached far back into history and had dredged up from its black waters the most ancient of all realities: man's desire to be a god . . . How far wrong were most people in their appraisal of dictators! The popular opinion was that these men were hankering for their pick of beautiful virgins, good food, fragrant cigars, aged whiskey, land, gold . . . But what these men wanted was something much harder to get and their mere getting of it was in itself a way of their keeping it. It was power, not just the exercise of bureaucratic control, but personal power to be wielded directly upon the lives and bodies of others. He recalled now how Hilton and Gil had looked at Bob when Bob had pled against the Party's decision. They had enjoyed it, loved it!

"Do you understand?" he heard Gil asking him.

Cross sighed, looked up and met Gil's eyes with a level stare. "Yes, I understand," he said.

He understood now why Gil had moved so slowly, why his manner was so studied. He had been giving Cross a chance to observe! And he remembered that Gil had been watching him to see that he was watching! The heart of Communism could not be taught; it had to be learned by living, by participation in its rituals.

He heard a key turning in the lock of the door.

"That's Eva," Gil said.

A moment later Eva, wind-blown and cherry-cheeked, with an armful of packages, rushed into the room. Her face held a bright, fixed expression of cheerfulness.

"Welcome," she sang out in her nervous, high-strung way.

Cross stood and smiled at her and wondered if her strained manner was covering her distaste at his presence in the apartment . . . There was something in her attitude that bothered him.

"Thank you," he told her. "I'm here and we're planning—"

"And you'll get action," Eva promised him self-consciously. "If Gil planned it, it's really planned. Hunh, darling?" She bent and kissed Gil lightly on the forehead. "I must get lunch ready now." She turned to Cross. "Just make yourself at home."

"Oh, Eva," Gil called. "I'm not eating lunch in. In fact, I must leave now. Why don't you eat with Lionel? I've got to make a speech at the Dyers' Union. I'll be in for dinner."

"Very well, Gil," Eva said; her face showed no expression.

Gil turned to Cross. "Keep your eyes open, boy." He laughed for the first time. "The fight is on!"

Eva walked slowly into the hallway and a moment later Cross heard her rattling pots and pans in the kitchen. Gil got into his overcoat and left. Cross went to his room and stretched out on his bed, thinking, mulling. His was the hungry type of mind that needed only a scrap of an idea to feed upon, to start his analytical processes rolling. This thing of power . . . Why had he overlooked it till now . . . ? Well, he had not been in those areas of life where power had held forth or reigned openly. Excitement grew in him; he felt that he was beginning to look at the emotional skeleton of man. He understood now the hard Communist insistence on strict obedience in things that had no direct relation to politics proper or to their keeping tight grasp of the reins of power. Once a thorough system of sensual power as a way of life had gotten hold of a man's heart to the extent that it ordered and defined all of his relations, it was bound to codify and arrange all of his life's activities into one organic unity. This systematizing of the sensual impulses of man to be a god must needs be jealous of all rival systems of sensuality, even those found in poetry and music. Cross, lying on his bed and staring at the ceiling, marveled at the astuteness of both Communist and Fascist politicians who had banned the demonic contagions of jazz. And now, too, he could understand why the Communists, instead of shooting the capitalists and bankers as they had so ardently sworn that they would do when they came to power, made instead with blood in their eyes straight for the school teachers, priests, writers, artists, poets, musicians, and the deposed bourgeois governmental rulers as the men who held for them the deadliest of threats to their keeping and extending their power . . .

He saw now that those who, in trying to rationalize their fears of Communism, had said that the practice of Communism was contrary to human nature were naïve or blind to awful facts which they had not the courage to admit; for, as Cross could see, there was not perhaps on earth a system of governing men which was more solidly built upon the sadly embarrassing cupidities of the human heart and its hunger to embrace the unembraceable. Of course, this system of sensualization of the concept of power did not prevail alone in the Communist or Fascist worlds; the Communists had merely rationalized it, brought it nakedly and unseemingly into the open. This systematization of the sensuality of power prevailed, though in a different form, in the so-called capitalistic bourgeois world; it was everywhere, in religion as well as in government, and in all art that was worthy of the name. And bourgeois rulers, along with the men of the church, had forged through time and tradition methods of concealing these systems of sensual power under thick layers of legal, institutionalized, ritualized, ideological, and religious trappings. But at the very heart of this system were the knowing and conscious men who wielded power, saying little or nothing of the real nature of the black art they practiced, the nameless religion by which they lived.

He knew instinctively that such subjects could not readily be explored in discussions with others, for its very victims—if, in strict sense it could be said that they were victims—would deny its reality perhaps more vociferously than those who held in their hands the reins of this system of power. Cross's insight into the functioning of the emotions of a Gil or a Hilton enabled him to isolate his own past actions and gain some measure of insight into them; it had been the blind coercions of a hungry sensuality that had made him try to hug delusions to his heart when he had suspected the malevolence of the innocent and had tried to posit upon the unknowing motives that they could not possibly have had. He rolled over and sat up in bed, his mouth open. He was seeing a vision, but at long last it was not an unreal one. This vision made reality more meaningful, made what his eyes saw take on coherence and depth. For the first time since that snowy evening in Chicago when he had decided to flee, when the waters of desire had drained off the world and had left it dry of interest, meaning began to trickle back again in drops, rivulets . . . He was, in his mind and feelings, isolating this central impulse of informing action by which he and other men lived. There was a hunger for power reaching out of the senses of man and trying to say something in symbols of action. What message, if any, was written in those hieroglyphics of energy? That these actions were far more basic than the mere arrangements of economic relations obtaining between rival social classes, he was convinced. Maybe . . .

A light knock came upon his door.

"Lionel!" It was Eva calling.

"Yes?"

"Lunch is waiting—"

"Coming."

He washed up and went into the dining room and sat at the table, facing Eva who now, though friendly, still seemed to avoid his eyes.

"I don't know what you like to eat," she said, smiling.

"Anything'll do me, Eva," he told her, seeing her now in the light of his ponderous reflections of a moment ago.

"I suppose you and Gil went over a lot today. You'll see that Gil has a grip on life," she said in a strained matter-of-fact tone devoid of any boasting.

"He has indeed," Cross agreed merely to keep the talk going.

As she served him he studied her and was amazed to find that she looked even younger without rouge on her lips and artificial coloring on her cheeks. How did this child—for there was an undeniable childishness about her—fit into his dark broodings and interpretations of Gil's politics? He longed to ask her how she had come to marry Gil, for every move she made and every word she uttered belied her being his wife.

"Are you a native New Yorker; that is, born here, I mean?" he asked.

"Yes; I'm one of those rare ones. I was born about three blocks from here," she said, laughing, keeping her eyes down.

"Did you grow up in the Communist Party?"

"Oh, God no. I was an orphan . . . I encountered the Party when I met Gil." She still did not look at him.

"Oh, I see."

"Do you like music?" she asked.

He had hoped that she would discuss politics; but either she did not want to or she evaded the subject because of its lack of interest for her.

"It's the one thing I know least about, I'm ashamed to admit," he confessed. "I've heard some classical music and liked it; but my level is jazz and folk songs, I'm afraid."

"Really?" She was surprised and thoughtful for a moment. "The reason I asked is that we have stacks of symphonic records over in the left-hand corner of the living room and you are free to play them if you like."

As the lunch progressed, she spoke in a quietly melodious voice of her love of music, painting, poetry, and the beauty of France which she had seen last summer.

Without seeming to, she avoided all mention of herself and made no political observations whatsoever. The simplicity of her manner made him doubt the validity of the theory he had hatched out a few minutes ago. Yet she lives in this communist world and she must know, he thought.

"Say, what was behind that little scene at Bob's last night?" he asked boldly.

"What scene?" She looked startled.

"I'm referring to Hilton's laying down the law to Bob—"

"Oh, *that* . . ." She frowned and murmured, "I'm afraid that Gil will have to explain that."

Either she did not know or she did not want to tell. He did not wish to create the impression that he was fishing for information and he quickly assumed an attitude of naïveté.

"There's so much to learn," he said wistfully. "I must be patient."

"I was *once* as bewildered as you are," she said meaningfully.

It was definite that she was evading him; he sensed reserves of emotion in her and he cast about for a way to make her open up.

"Look, don't think I'm nosey, but are you active in the Party?"

"Not exactly," she said. "I paint." She was frowning.

"Oh, really? Social subjects?" He encouraged her to talk.

A flicker of dismay darted across her face. She's afraid to talk, he thought. She bit her lips and her long eyelashes shadowed her cheeks. She took up a slice of bread, broke it nervously, then put it aside as a sudden impulse came to life in her.

"No. I'm a nonobjective painter," she said modestly.

Cross stared. The wife of a Communist leader painting nonobjectively?

"You don't like nonobjective painting, do you?" she
asked, putting a soft challenge in her voice.

"But I do; absolutely," he answered honestly. "Say,
I've a theory about it—"

"You have?" she said, but she did not look at him.
She was evidently struggling with herself. Then impulsively: "I'd like to hear it."

"Well, you see, maybe my notion is kind of farfetched," he began, glad that they had at last found
some common ground. "Nonobjective painting ex-
presses the dominant consciousness of modern man . . .
Sounds corny, hunh? But I mean it." He hesitated,
wondering what approach would get beneath her reserve. "Modern consciousness is Godlessness and nonobjective painting reflects this negatively. There is really
no nonobjective painting without either a strong assumption of atheism or an active expression of it,
whether the nonobjective painter realizes it or not . . ."

"We agree so far," she said as though thinking of
something else.

"I mean Godlessness in a strict sense," he argued.
"There is nothing but *us*, *man*, and the world that *man*
has made. Beyond that, there's nothing else. The natural
world around us which cradles our existence and which
we claim we know is just a huge, unknowable something or other . . . We may find out how it works, discover some of its so-called laws, but we don't know it
and can't know it . . . Nature's not *us*; it's different. A
part of us is nature, but that part of us that's human and
free is opposed to nature. What there is of the natural
world that seems human to us is what we have projected
out upon it from our own hearts. We created cities,
roads, factories, etc. Sunsets, waterfalls, and landscapes

are but a few accidental aspects of nature that we happen to like, that somehow reflect moods of ours . . . So we are prone to forget all of the other phases of nature that are terrible, inhuman, alien to us . . . Now, my notion is that since this is true, that the world we see is the world we make by our manual or emotional projection, why not let us be honest and paint our own projections, our fantasies, our own moods, our own conceptions of what things are. Let's paint our feelings *directly*. Why let objects master us? Let's take forms, planes, surfaces, colors, volumes, space, etc., and make them express ourselves by our arrangement of them. It's an act of pure creation . . ."

"You've said it," she exclaimed looking fully at him for the first time. "I'm surprised."

"Why?"

"Not many people feel like that," she said. "I'd not have thought that a colored person would like nonobjective art. Your people are so realistic and drenched in life, the world . . . Colored people are so robustly healthy."

"*Some* of us," he said.

"And you're not? How did that happen?"

"It's a long story," he said. "Some people are pushed deeper into their environment and some are pushed completely out of it."

"Do you feel *that* much aloneness?" she asked in surprise.

"Yes; and you?"

"Yes," she said simply and was silent.

"I'd like awfully to see your work."

"All right. But . . ."

"But what?"

"I'd rather you didn't tell Gil we talked about this," she said, reddening.

"I see," he said. What's she afraid of . . . ?

After lunch she took him into a cluttered, dusty room behind the kitchen; it reeked of oil and turpentine. She stood timidly behind him as he looked at walls covered with canvases; more were stacked in corners. The power of her work was immediately apparent; a bewildering array of seemingly disassociated forms—squares, cubes, spheres, triangles, rhombs, trapezes, planes, spirals, crystals, meteors, atomistic constructions, and strange micro-organisms—struggled in space lit sombrely by achromatic tints. Cross advanced to the canvas upon which she was evidently working and which rested upon a huge easel. Between irregular volumes and planes was a feeling of tremendous tension created by points of quiet and steady light, a light that seemed hardly there, yet tying all of her space into one organic whole. Out of a darkly brooding background surged broken forms swimming lyrically in mysterious light stemming from an unseen source. The magical fragility of this light, touching off surprising harmonies of tones, falling in space and bringing to sight half-sensed patterns of form, was Eva, her sense of herself . . . In her work she seemed to be straining to say something that possessed and gripped her life; she spoke tersely, almost cruelly through her forms. Her painting at bottom was the work of a poet trying to make color and form sing in an absolute and total manner. There was a blatant brutality about her volumes, some of which were smashed, cracked, and presented a tactile surface carrying an illusion of such roughness that one felt that the skin of the hand would be torn by touching it . . . He wondered what life experiences made her paint such images of latent danger . . . ?

"Have you exhibited?"

"Yes; last year. Just before I married—"

"You have enough for another exhibit now."

"I shan't exhibit again soon," she said.

"How was your work received?"

"Very well," she muttered.

"And why aren't you going to exhibit again soon?"

"Oh, Lionel, I must go," she said hurriedly, ignoring his question. "Stay and look at them as long as you like . . . Here are the keys to the apartment; one's for the downstairs and the other's for the front door up here. I'm off to do some shopping and then I'll do a concert." She flashed him a quick smile. "Come and go as you like. But watch out for Herndon downstairs . . ."

She left him and a few moments later he heard the front door open and close. She had not wanted to talk to him, but what she had seemed too shy to say in words shouted and pled for her in images. For two hours he looked at every canvas in the room, placing them in the light, examining them from far and near. He had the illusion, while studying them, of standing somehow at the center of Eva's ego and being captured by the private, subjective world that was hers, a world that was frightening in the stark quality of its aloneness; and he knew that it was out of a sense of aloneness that these bold, brutal images, nameless and timeless, had come with the force of compulsions. At least she's lucky to be able to say her terrors and agonies in form and color, he said a little enviously to himself.

With a cigarette glowing in his lips, he went back into the apartment and wandered aimlessly from room to room, probing and idly searching. He smiled, feeling the presence of Eva and Gil as he spied among their belongings. Why did they have two separate bedrooms? Twin beds were all right, but two bedrooms? He recalled the little, pecking kiss that Eva had given Gil when she had come in from her shopping and he was certain that there was something wrong between them.

He ended up in Eva's bedroom, prowling in drawers and desks. At the bottom of a pile of dusty sheets of music lying on the floor of a clothes closet he came across a stack of bound notebooks; he opened one. They were Eva's diaries . . . Ought he risk peeking a little into one? He glanced guiltily over his shoulder. When would she be back? To be surprised reading her intimate diary would be awful . . . He stepped into the hallway and saw that there was a safety night-chain on the door. Yes; he had it . . . He would put the night-chain in place and if Gil or Eva returned suddenly, he could always say that he had put it on in order to be on guard if Herndon came up . . . He chained the door and went back into Eva's bedroom and picked up a volume of the diary that dated back six months of that year. He began reading the small, clear, schoolgirlish handwriting:

"June 10th

"—I'm at last in Paris, city of my dreams! What a wedding gift from Gil! Poor dear, he's too busy with Party work to show me the beauty of this wonderful Paris; his assignments keep him going from morning 'til night . . . But I do manage to see it for myself. The art exhibits, the artists' studios, the sense of leisure, the love of beauty—will I ever be the same again after all this?

"Notre Dame! Rising nobly in the warm summer night like a floodlit dream— The tourist bus is crawling away, taking me from this vision of beauty, remote, fragile, infused with the mood of eternity. At the next stop I got off the bus and walked back to Notre Dame; I could not keep to the schedule of a tourist bus! I sat on a bench and gazed at Notre Dame 'til almost dawn . . . How quiet the city is . . . A lonely, shabby man is pushing a handcart through the city streets. Lines, space, harmony softened by dark mists . . . Dusk of dawn kissing the pavements with tenderness . . . I doubt if Gil would understand feelings like these, yet they mean so much to me, to my heart . . . Mine is the glory of those angels against the background of that pearly, infinite sky . . .

"June 15th

"I'm so numbed with shock that I can hardly think . . . Is this my honeymoon? Is it possible that Gil has betrayed me so cruelly, so cynically? For days now I've pretended to be ill to avoid having it out with him, but in the end I must do it. It all began one afternoon when I went to see a Left Bank art exhibit. I stayed behind and got to talking to some of the younger artists, both American and French, all of whom were complete strangers to me. One young man, an American expatriate, obviously a Trotskyite, began a violent tirade against the Party, charging that membership in the Party was death to artists. I told him that I was a painter and did not think so. He then told me not to be naïve like that silly but gifted Eva Blount girl who had had such a stunningly successful exhibit in New York last spring . . . He did not know who I was, and I asked him what was so naïve about Eva Blount . . . He said that it was being whispered about that Gil Blount had been ordered by the Party to marry her, to get her into the Party for prestige purposes. He went on talking of other instances where such had happened . . . I was silent; I felt cold, dead . . . To stand in a crowd of people and hear them talk of you like that!!! He said that it was common knowledge in the labor movement that Gil Blount had been told to recruit Eva Blount . . . I asked him how did he know this, and what right had he to spread such foul gossip about people he did not know . . . He then went on to tell of facts which only someone close to the revolutionary movement could know . . . He said that Gil's secretary, Rose Lampkin, was his mistress and had been for years, and that at the same time she was spying on Gil . . . I could not contradict him . . . His words suddenly opened up a vast vista of understanding which I fought against desperately. Am I so naïve . . . ?

"To hear one's private life spoken about so brutally, in public! God, can this be true? Yet his words explain so much! Is that why Gil is away from home so much? Is that why he never comes to me except when he's drunk? Oh, God, I feel I've no ground under my feet anymore— I must confront Gil with this . . . But how? Ought I run off? But to where?

"And that Rose Lampkin woman, Gil's secretary . . . Is that his mistress? Is that why he insisted that she accompany us to Paris? The more I think, the sicker I get! I try to tell myself that this cannot be true, yet in my heart I know it and feel it . . .

"June 17th
"Gil has all but said that it's true! Which means that when I confronted him, he would not say anything!!! He raves at me, telling me that I'm trying to undermine his Party position! That I'm slandering him! I asked him to send Rose back to New York, and he said that it was the Party's decision that Rose remain with him . . . And Rose, when she came to the hotel this morning, had a cold smirk on her face. She knows that I know! According to Gil, I must accept this betrayal and be loyal to the Party; to be loyal to my feelings means betraying the Party! I don't know what to do— I feel that everybody's laughing at me, that everybody knows— *I could kill Gil!*

"June 18th
"I must be calm— I've only my work left; that's all. I tell myself all day long that I must give my life to my work. If I make a sudden, hysterical move and lose grip on myself, run off, the Party can always say that I deserted and degenerated! Gil has predicted as much! Can there be betrayals as intimately cynical as this? I'm a fool to wonder, for it is true, it stares me in the face . . . But I don't want to believe it. That's what makes it possible; no one *wants* to believe it . . . What coldness people are capable of! I walk the streets all day to keep thoughts of suicide from filling my head—

"June 19th

"Can I work now? My whole life seems tainted, unclean . . . I've asked Gil to take me back to New York; he says he will as soon as his duties with the French Party are over. I begged him to give me fare, and he says no . . . I'm alone again, just as I was in the orphan home. I didn't lose heart then and I mustn't now. I won't; I can't give up; I must work, work, work, paint . . . But can I paint again? The Party lifted me up in its hands and showed me to the world, and if I disown them, they'll disown me . . . What a trap!

"Gil warned me that I must not talk of this! He demanded to know who told me about the Party deciding that he was to marry me . . . He accuses me of having anti-Party friends!

"I'm afraid. If I stay with Gil, I'll loathe myself; if I run off, the Party will attack me publicly, branding me a renegade. All of my friends are Party people and they would no longer speak to me . . . Night and day Gil demands that I be loyal to the Party. But I owe myself some loyalty too. How can I face myself in the years to come, knowing that I have been bought, and in such a shameful way? Gil says that my personal feelings do not count . . . Doesn't he know he's killing me . . . ?

"June 20th

"I've been hurt; there's no doubt about it. I stand before my easel and cannot paint. I'm numb; my love of work is gone. When Gil comes into the hotel room, I begin to tremble with shame and rage . . . And he tells me that I *must* not, *cannot* talk to anybody . . . If I protest, the Party will destroy me . . . Last night he relented a tiny bit and said that I could be free only if I let the Party choose a husband for me . . . It seems that I'm now guilty not because of what I've done, but because of what I know . . . Goddamn this deception!

"June 21st

"I've begun to notice things that I've never noticed before. Is this because of what Gil and the Party have done to me? I feel like a victim and everywhere I look I think I can see other victims in the making . . . I've just come from a movie where I saw mothers with their young children. It was a horrible gangster film with a tense, melodramatic atmosphere. How can mothers take their children into such places? I should hate to have my children getting used to sights of violence, death, brutality . . . When for years a child has seen men hitting other men, killing or getting killed, he gets used to it. In time it does not impress him any more . . . He gets used to it, and death, betrayal, deception become just unimpressive facts of life, just 'one of those things' . . .

"June 23rd

"Gil came in at 2 A.M., drunk. He's ashamed to face me when he's sober. I understand it: drunk, he's still a free Communist; sober, he's still a slave of his boyhood upbringing in the Bronx and is ashamed of what he's done . . . To every argument I raise, he has one answer: 'You don't understand!' I've got a knife with which I cut canvases and I sleep with it under my pillow. Gil will *never* touch me again, drunk or sober . . .

"My eyes are red and raw from weeping and sleeplessness. Never did I dream that I'd be brought to this! Before this the world was a sad place, but now it's sad *and* dangerous . . . The worst part of all this is that I've no preparation for it; there was no warning. There's nothing I've ever read or heard that could have prepared me for this . . . After father died when I was six, I lived in that orphan home; but even there life seemed rational. Hunger, cold, study; making sacrifices to attend art school—all of that was rational. When I began to win scholarships, all the deprivations were redeemed. But this deliberate deception—? Where does it fit in?

"Gil is sullen, silent; a cold wall— He has his friends; I've none; I'm alone— I've no friends unless I consent to accept what has been done to me! I must be a partner to this crime in order to be forgiven! I see it now; there can be no crimes like this unless there is the consent of the victim! My fear to talk, my silence makes this possible! But dare I speak? Who would believe me? Who'd care? How can I go on like this . . . ?

"June 24th

"I'm afraid my loneliness and melancholy are making me morbid . . . Injustice has always been merely a word to me, now it's a reality. Gil and the Party have opened my eyes and I see . . . In the Paris Metro today I saw something that made me sad. In front of me, on one seat, sat a young mother, middle-class, her face well done-up and glowing with motherly pride; she was holding a little girl of about two years of age on her knees. And that sweet little baby girl, all dressed up in delicate, lacy things took a liking to a pale little boy of about nine or thereabouts. He was filthy, badly dressed; he seemed too mature for his age; he sat next to a huge, vulgar, toothless, harsh-voiced woman—no doubt his mother. Both the little children were at once keen on each other, but the big woman kept telling her son to stop looking and smiling at the baby. The little girl's hands tried to take hold of those of the boy and the boy was enjoying it. The young mother did not like it, but she was too well-bred to want to hurt the little boy's feelings. Maybe the big woman was afraid of what the smartly dressed young woman would say? Anyway, the two women got terribly nervous and finally the young mother pried the tiny, playful, rosy little fingers out of the boy's dirty hands . . . The baby cried and I wanted to cry too— I wonder if Gil realizes how awful people can feel when something happens to them that they cannot understand? I've sworn that Gil will never touch me again . . . I'll die first!

"July 10th

"We're back in New York. My friends are asking me about my honeymoon and I'm forced to smile . . . God, how can I keep up this deception any longer? I'm noticing other victims now. I've become aware of colored people. God, how they take it! Compared to their deception, mine is nothing . . . Yet they manage to go on living, even smiling. How do they do it? They must be strong, healthy, unspoiled by the lies of the white man's world.

"July 12th

"My world has failed me and everything in it . . . What Gil and his Party have done to me is ruining my life, making me possess fantastic notions. My loathing of Gil has gone so far that I cannot any longer abide the color pink. I no longer want to paint in reds and blues and greens . . . They now remind me of Gil's deception. That's why I'm beginning to adore colored people; I could live my life with sunburnt people; I wish I was a warm, rich, brown color—

"July 18th

"I've begged Gil for a little money to start out for myself and he says no; the Party says no; it's no everywhere . . .

"We're in a new apartment and the landlord is truly a Fascist! This morning I met him on the stoop and said good morning to him. For some reason I asked him if there were any black people in the neighborhood. He must have thought that I objected to them, for he said: 'Oh, no; nothing like that around here, lady. But there's a Chinese laundry down the street—' 'But Chinese are not black,' I said. 'Oh, lady, you don't know. They're *almost* black . . . These colored people are all the same . . . God's marked 'em all red, yellow, brown, and black so we could know 'em . . .' Good God, what a world we live in . . ."

Cross smiled and flipped the pages of the diary and began reading the last entry:

"March 3rd

"Bob Hunter, one of the Party organizers, came rushing in to see Gil. When I told him that Gil was out his face fell and he pouted like a child. I like him because he is so open about his desire to fight and free his people from oppression. Bob told me to tell Gil that we must be sure to come to his apartment for dinner tonight— Bob bubbles over with the news of his finding a new, wonderful recruit for the Party. He is a young Negro living under an assumed name, a fugitive from southern racists. He is, according to Bob, who swore me to secrecy, a bright young Negro intellectual who had some dire trouble with whites and committed some crime and is in hiding to save his life. Bob met the young man on a train and he is certain that he has killed a white man and that there is a price on his head . . . It sounds so exciting, terrible, pitiful . . . And they're bringing him into the *Party!* Another victim? I wish I could talk to him and tell him something . . . Colored people are so trusting and naïve . . . He's going to be misled by Gil, just as I have been . . ."

Cross closed the diary; now that he had learned something of Eva's life, he did not want to read any more. He knew enough to make a numbing sense of recognition go through him. Impulsively he wanted to run to her and talk to her, to tell her that she was not alone. But that was foolish. Secrecy was how the world was run. Millions felt alike, but were ashamed to admit it. Here was a lost, brave woman who had enough sensitivity and intelligence to understand what he had to say. She was a victim like he; the difference was that he was a willing victim and she was an involuntary one . . . She protested and he said yes. And a world yawned between his yes and her no . . .

But, Christ, how could she go on living that life? Her tense, artificial manner was now clear. She did not want to talk about politics; she was afraid of what she would say . . . She wanted to help him; and he wanted to help her . . .

And Gil was trusting him because of Bob's foolish stories! Yes; that was rich. Bob had led the Party to feel that it had found a real victim of race hate! Well . . .

He felt sluggish; he replaced the diary and decided to take a walk. He went out of the front door, listening to hear a harsh voice challenging him. But nothing happened. He walked to Washington Square and stood looking at the pigeons fluttering around the treetops, alighting in the snowy grass. He went past the bookshops on Fourth Avenue, browsing here and there. It was cold; he would go home.

He was entering the building when the door of the apartment of Langley Herndon opened. Cross saw a white face watching him from behind thick spectacles. He shut the door to the street, taking his time, then turned and started up the stairs.

"Hey, *you*! Wait a minute!"

It was the voice of a man who was used to issuing orders. Cross paused, turned his head, and registered a look of make-believe surprise.

"What do you want here?" the man asked, coming up to him.

"What do you mean?" Cross countered. "I'm going up to my room."

"Your *room*? Are you *living* here?" Herndon demanded.

"Of course. And who are you? Why are you asking me all this?"

"I just happen to own this goddamn building, that's all," Herndon said with rough irony. "I say who can and can't live here!"

"But I'm not going into *your* apartment," he pretended to misunderstand. "I live upstairs—"

"I don't give a good goddamn *where* you live!" Herndon snapped. "You can't stay in this building—"

"Now, wait a minute! I've signed a lease with Mr. Blount—"

"You can't talk to me that way!"

Herndon advanced and Cross doubled his fist.

"Watch out! You're old and I don't want to hurt

you!" He saw Herndon pause and blink his eyes. "If you want to talk to me, all right. But don't touch me, see?"

Herndon was short, grey, flabby, with a wide mouth. His eyes were reddish and teary at the inflamed corners. His hair was black and slicked flat to the crown of a large, partly bald skull. He was violently agitated and seemed not to know what move to make. His face grew brick red.

"How long have you been in this building?" Herndon asked finally.

"For almost a week," Cross lied.

Herndon looked Cross over, his eyes traveling from Cross's necktie to his shoes.

"Say, come in here," Herndon said suddenly. "I want to talk to you."

Cross knew that the man had changed his tactics. He's going to try to scare me in another way now . . . He stepped into a nicely furnished room which had a large desk. A wood fire burned in the grate and shadows danced along the walls. Herndon studied Cross for some seconds.

"Listen," he began in a tone of voice that indicated that he was stooping to give advice to someone who he doubted had sense enough to profit by it. "You are being misled. For thirty years I've had a strict policy about renting, and nobody's going to make me change it. This lease you're talking about— It's nothing. Forget it. The quicker, the better for you. I'm going to see Blount tonight and give 'im hell. Get me straight. I don't give a good goddamn about what happens to you, see? I could crush you, if I wanted to. Now, go upstairs and pack your stuff and get the hell out of there! You're black and you don't belong there and you goddamn well know it."

"Thanks," Cross said in a low, clear voice. "I'm stay-

ing here as long as Mr. Blount says I can. It's your
move."

"So, you're a Communist, hey?"

"No, I'm not."

"Oh, yes, you are, and you think you're being smart,"
Herndon's voice was rising. "I can take care of your
kind. You Reds think you—"

"I told you that I'm not a Communist; I'm *anti*-
Communist!" Cross said sternly.

"I don't give a good goddamn *what* kind of a Communist you are!" Herndon shouted.

"I didn't think you did," Cross said quietly. "That's
why I insisted on telling you. I'm black and that's
what's riling you. But I will not move from here."

Herndon, his lips quivering, yanked open a drawer of
the desk.

"Be careful, man," Cross warned him, ramming his
hand into his coat pocket. "I'm armed. If you pull out a
gun, I'll shoot you!" Cross was bent forward, his entire
body tense, his eyes not blinking.

Herndon slammed the drawer shut and came to the
side of his desk.

"Get out of here, you black sonofabitch!" he shouted,
his body trembling with rage. "Get out of this house!
Get out of this building! Get out of my sight! If I see
you again, I'll kill you, you hear?"

Cross did not move; he stood towering over Herndon whose mouth held flecks of foam at the corners. '

"I'm going, but I never turn my back on a man who's
yelling at me," he said slowly.

Herndon's lips moved soundlessly. Cross kept his
eyes on Herndon and moved backwards to the door,
still clutching his gun. With his left hand he groped for
the knob, turned it, and pulled the door open.

"Mr. Herndon, whenever you're in my presence, be

careful," Cross said. "You've threatened me and I won't forget it."

He went through the door and shut it. Things would happen fast now. He smiled as he went upstairs. The encounter with Herndon had given him a lift, had almost made the last shred of dreaminess leave him. This thing'll be decided tonight one way or the other, he told himself as he entered the apartment.

Eva returned an hour later. He had to be careful in her presence; he must not let her feel that he had spied on her intimate life.

"Oh, Lionel!" she called.

He went into the hallway and saw Eva still wearing her coat; her cheeks were red and excitement was in her eyes.

"Yes?"

"Herndon says he wants to see Gil as soon as he comes in," Eva said breathlessly. "What happened? Did you have a run in with 'im?"

"We had it," Cross said.

"Did he get rough?"

"He wanted to pull a gun, but I told him I had one, too."

"Oh, Lord—" She leaned weakly against the wall. "Poor Lionel . . ."

Her eyes were full of pity, and Cross knew that she felt that he too was a victim of the Party, that the Party was using him for bait. I'm tougher than you think I am, he said to himself.

"It's nothing," he said. "I like his kind."

"Oh, dear! Where's Gil?" She was trembling.

"Now, Eva, don't worry," Cross tried to soothe her. "Nothing's going to happen for the moment, anyway. His next move will be to try to scare Gil, and I don't think Gil scares easily."

"Don't you want a drink or something?" she asked, looking at him as though she expected to see him collapse.

"I never refuse a drink," he said.

She brought out a bottle of cognac.

"I brought this from France last summer," she said, "feeling that I might need it sometime. And, now's the time."

Cross looked at her and smiled. Bless her; she's feeling good because she feels that she's of some use to me . . .

"Look," he said, pushing the glass she had filled to her. "I think you need this more than I do."

She drank from the glass and poured one for him.

"What do you think will happen, Lionel?" she asked in a whisper. "That Herndon's capable of anything— Oh, God, Lionel, do you think it's *worth* it?"

Cross could see that she was on the verge of telling him to ditch the Party, to get out, to save himself. At that moment he heard Gil's key turning in the lock of the door and a pall of anxiety came over Eva's face. Cross could see Gil hanging up his coat in the hallway. As Gil entered, Eva turned as though to speak to Cross, but checked herself.

"Hello, everybody," Gil said placidly.

"Tired, Gil?" Eva asked; she was trying to act natural.

"Not especially," he said, shrugging. He drew his wallet from his coat pocket and extracted a paper from it, saying: "Here's the permit for your gun, Lionel. The Party had a lawyer pull some strings . . . But be careful, guy."

"Thanks," Cross said. "I can tell you that this permit comes just in time. I met Herndon today."

"Really? And how was it?"

"Rugged."

Eva rushed forward and she caught hold of the lapels of Gil's coat. "You mustn't let Lionel get into this," she spoke hysterically. "Herndon said he wanted to see you the moment you came in . . . And he's already threatened Lionel with a gun—"

"Let Lionel tell me what happened," Gil said, gently pushing Eva to one side, struggling to master his annoyance.

"Well," Cross began. "I was returning from—"

"Just a moment," Gil said. He took out his pipe and began to fill it with tobacco; then he paused and looked intently at Eva. Eva stared; she seemed on the verge of speaking, but controlled herself.

"I must see about dinner," she mumbled, flushing red. She left the room and Gil lit his pipe, sucked at it.

"I'm listening," he said.

Cross related what had transpired, leaving out nothing. Gil made no comment; he rose and stood at a window looking out, smoking silently. Then he turned, sat at his desk and began writing upon a pad of paper. Eva came on tiptoe to the door, peered in apprehensively, then left. Cross lit a cigarette and waited. I'll make him guess at what I'm feeling just as I have to guess at what he's feeling, he told himself.

The doorbell pealed. Gil paused in his writing, lifted his hand from the page, then began writing again. Eva came to the door, her eyes round with fear.

"Gil," she called timidly.

"Yes," Gil answered, but not turning or looking at her.

"Maybe it's Herndon— Shall I answer?" she asked in a whisper.

"You're always to answer the door," he said calmly.

As though seeking support, Eva looked at Cross.

"If it's Herndon, do be careful," she said.

"Eva!" Gil barked at her.

"I'll answer it," Cross said.

"No, Lionel. Eva will answer the door," Gil said in slow, heavy accents of authority.

Cross wanted to rise and take the man by the throat. Why does he act like that? Then he tried to dismiss it from his mind. After all, I'm no angel, he mused. It's really none of my business . . . He was now sorry that he had read Eva's diary; his knowing her as he did made it impossible for him to regard her with detachment. Eva lingered a moment longer at the door, then vanished.

"Oh!" Eva's frightened voice came from the hallway a moment later.

"I'm sorry, Eva— Did I scare you? Is Gil home? I got to see 'im quick— It's awfully important—"

"Come in, Bob— But what's the matter? You look sick or something— Did you have some trouble downstairs?"

"Trouble? Yes. But not downstairs . . . What do you mean? Is Gil here?"

"He's in the living room," Eva said.

Gil had stopped writing, his pen poised over the sheet of paper. His eyes hardened as Bob, his face twitching, his eyes bloodshot and staring, appeared in the doorway.

"Hey, Lane," Bob called to Cross; there was no heartiness in his voice.

Gil whirled in his seat and demanded: "What do you want here, Bob?"

Bob acted as if he had not heard; he sank weakly into a chair. He looked at Gil and forced a sick grin that faded quickly and his face went lifeless, his eyes staring at the floor in a kind of stupor. A large drop of mucus formed at the tip of his flat, brown nose, hovered there for a second, then dropped to his upper lip. He licked at it, unaware that he did so.

"Gil," he begged, "you've got to help me."

Eva stood in the doorway. Cross sat watching. Gil was looking at Bob with half-turned body. Bob turned to Cross.

"Lane, you got to talk to 'im for me—"

"Bob!" Gil shouted, his tone full of dangerous warning. "Lane has nothing to do with this, and you damn well know it! What are you trying to do? Disturb his faith in the Party? You've said enough already to be brought up on serious charges!"

"I just want to talk to 'im—"

"You're trying to influence Lane!" Gil shouted again, leaping to his feet. "You're organizing against the Party right *here* in my presence!"

"No, no, Gil—"

"You're trying to turn Lane against the Party right under my eyes!"

"Oh, God, no! No, Gil!"

"You are guilty right now of ideological factionalism!"

"What's that?" Bob asked incredulously.

"You are trying to get Lane to support your ideas," Gil accused Bob.

Bob sighed; he had come to plead innocent to one crime and now he found himself accused of still another crime. Cross felt certain that Gil did not want him to witness this.

"I'll go to my room," he offered.

"No; stay right here," Gil ordered.

And Cross suddenly realized that Gil wanted him to see what was happening. Gil's chastisement of Bob could either be a warning or an object lesson. How efficient this is, Cross marveled. Not a single word or gesture is wasted. By observing this, Cross, too, could learn how to break and ravage the spirits of others, or he could see what would happen to him if he disobeyed. Eva remained in the doorway, her eyes fixed upon Bob's face. Gil was looking at Eva with eyes full of warning, but Eva was not aware of his gaze. The moment, however, she saw it, she blushed and hurriedly left the room.

"Now, what's the matter with you, Bob?" Gil asked at last.

Bob had not taken off his hat or his coat. Dirty snow melted on his shoes and tiny rings of water were forming on the carpet. Bob spoke in a broken whimper:

"The Party voted to expel me, Gil—"

"I know that," Gil said calmly.

"But Gil, I don't wanna leave the Party— You got to help me— My life's in the Party— The Party's all I got in the world— I made a mistake—"

"Tell that to the Party," Gil said, turning and sitting again at his desk.

"Oh, please, Gil— You don't understand— I don't even want to say it, man— You *know* my problem—I'm British— Only the *Party* knows it!" Bob rose and went to the back of Gil and whispered despairingly: "Listen, an hour ago the Immigration men came to my flat, see? Lucky, I didn't go to the door—Sarah went. She told 'em in a loud voice that I was out— I heard 'em talking to Sarah and I slipped down the back stairs— I came here, to *you*, Gil— You're my friend— Gil, for God's sake, don't let 'em do this; don't let the Party do this to me—"

"How do you know it was the Party?" Gil asked.

"But *only* the Party knew!"

"But how do you *know* the Party did it?" Gil demanded.

"Listen, I once heard Hilton threaten another West

Indian Negro like me— He said he could drop an un-signed note to the Immigration folks if he didn't be-have—"

"But have you any *proof* that the Party told the Gov-ernment?" Gil demanded.

Bob shook his head; his eyes were blank and empty. Cross saw the point; if Bob had no proof, what harm could Bob's accusation do?

"Naw; I ain't got no proof . . ."

Gil rose and stood over Bob.

"Are you accusing the Party of playing the role of a stool pigeon?" he thundered.

Bob winced as though he had been slapped.

"No, no, no!"

"Then what in hell *are* you saying?"

"Gil, listen to me. Ten years ago I had to run off from Trinidad to keep the British from putting me in jail for Party activity— If I go back, they'll snatch me off the boat and take me straight to jail for *ten* years— Ten years in jail in the tropics is death— I mean *death*, man— Don't you understand?"

"I understand," Gil said, nodding his head. "But that doesn't explain why you fought the Party."

"I didn't know I was *fighting* the Party . . . I don't want to fight the Party . . ."

"You took a position *against* the Party! That's counter-revolution! And for counter-revolutionists the Party has no mercy!" Gil told him.

"Gil, you got to tell 'em to give me another chance . . . The Party can *hide* me . . . Let me go to Mexico, anywhere—"

"Who are you to *defy* the Party?"

"I ain't nobody, *nothing* . . ." Bob slid from his chair and lay prone on the floor. "This is *too* much, Gil— Please, please, don't let 'em do this to me! I was wrong!

I confess! And I'll do anything you say, Gil! You're on the Central Committee and they'll listen to you. I been to Headquarters and they won't even talk to me—"

Cross was stunned. He wanted to rise and place his foot on Bob's neck and cut off the flow of whining words. Gil watched Bob with calm, placid eyes and Cross wondered how many men and women Gil had seen in such prostrate positions of penitent surrender to enable him to stare at Bob with so aloof and yet engrossed a passion.

"Did you meet anybody when you came up here?" Gil asked suddenly.

Bob blinked his eyes bewilderedly. "Meet anybody? No; I saw nobody . . . Gil, *please!*"

"All right, Bob. You can go now."

Bob's body galvanized itself to a sitting position on the floor; his hand went to his mouth in dismay.

"Where?"

"I don't care *where* you go—"

"But they'll *get* me, Gil! Look, I'll give my *life* to the Party!"

"The Party doesn't want your life." Gil smiled.

Cross closed his eyes. His anger was centered against Bob for his weakness. No wonder Gil would not give in! The more merciless Gil was the more Bob would yield. Eva came to the door, her eyes avoiding Bob. Cross could see her legs trembling.

"Gil, dinner's ready."

"Go ahead and eat, Lionel. I'll join you later," Gil said.

Cross rose and went out of the room, his eyes avoiding Bob who sobbed on the floor. He had no appetite, but he sat at the table and Eva served him. As he chewed his food, he heard Gil's voice rising in accusation, then Bob's voice falling in meek pleas. Then came a pause during which Bob coughed loudly. Finally there was a sound of footsteps in the hallway. Gil was saying something to Bob at the door, then the door closed. Cross looked at Eva; her eyes were full of fear, and her hand shook slightly as she ate. Gil came briskly to the table, sat, keeping his eyes in front of him. He volunteered no information and acted as though he knew that no one would dare ask for any.

"God, I'm hungry," Gil said pleasantly and reached for the platter of roast beef.

After he had served himself generously, Gil turned to Cross and asked: "Say, did you see who won the chess tournament in Moscow? I was too busy to buy a paper."

"No, I don't know who won," Cross said, slightly nonplussed.

"Do you play chess?" Gil asked.

"No."

"You ought to learn. It's wonderful for relaxation," Gil advised him.

As dinner proceeded in silence, Cross was aware that a feeling of tranquility had descended upon him. In his mind Gil had receded far off until he had become a tiny, little luminous figure upon which all of his attention was focussed. It was as if he was squinting his eye along the barrel of a rifle toward some distant and elusive target and at long last the center of the target had come within the hairline of the sight.

After he had drained his cup of coffee, Gil chuckled softly and asked: "What time is it?" He looked at his wrist watch. "Hummm . . . Ten past nine— I'd better get down and see Herr Herndon."

"Do you want me to come with you?" Cross asked.

"Why?" Gil asked, lifting his brows in surprise.

Cross said nothing. Eva sat stiff, staring with protesting eyes into her empty coffee cup. Then she lifted her eyes to Gil and Cross saw the light of protest die. God, she's scared, Cross thought. If she's that afraid of him, how she must hate him . . . !

Gil stood and went into the hallway, then out of the door. Eva rose suddenly, as though feeling that she had to drown her anxieties in activity, and began clearing the dishes from the table.

"I'll help you," Cross said, taking a stack of plates and starting for the kitchen.

"No, Lionel—"

"Why not?" he said, continuing to clear the table.

"You don't have to, you know," she said.

"I want to," he said. He wanted to be near her.

Then they both were still. Coming from downstairs were loud voices. Cross could distinguish the voice of Gil, then that of Herndon. They were at it strongly. The dishes slid from Eva's hands to the table with a clatter, then she clutched the back of the chair till her knuckles showed white.

"Do you think I ought to go down?" he asked Eva.

She shook her head.

"No. If he said no, then don't. He'd be awfully angry, and when he's angry he doesn't speak for weeks—" She caught herself; she had said more than she had intended. "Lionel, really, don't bother with the dishes. Do what you like . . ." Irritation was in her voice.

He knew that he was making her more nervous; she did not want him to see her state of mind.

"Okay."

He went to his room and the voices were clearer; he put his ear to the floor and heard shouts that carried sounds of hot anger, but no words were distinguishable. He lay on his bed, then jerked upright; there had come a sharp snapping as of wood breaking, then a dull thump, and all was silent. The door of his room flew open and Eva stood there, clasping her hands in front of her, staring at him with eyes filled with terror.

"What was that?"

Cross stood and went to her; she clutched his hands tightly.

"Don't you think I ought to go down?" he asked.

"Yes," she agreed impulsively. Then her body flinched and she shut her eyes in desperation. "No; no; he'd be angry. He'd think that you thought he couldn't handle it—" Tears leaped into her eyes and she turned from him. "If he gets hurt, he'll wonder why we didn't do something. He'll think I did it on purpose—"

"On *purpose*?" he asked.

Yes; she was fighting against a wish for something to happen to Gil; she was longing for someone to put him out of her life . . .

A hoarse scream came from downstairs.

"I'm going down," Cross said suddenly.

"Yes, Lionel," Eva breathed; she was pale, trembling.

He went quickly into the hallway. He realized as he went down the steps that he was acting more as a kind of proxy for the feelings of Eva than his own. *I* really don't care, he thought. When he reached the landing of the first floor, he paused. There came to his ears the sound of grunts, scuffling feet, and the thud of blows. He crept on tiptoe to the door and placed his ear to the panel. Yes, they were fighting . . . Was the door locked? He turned the knob; the door swung in and Cross looked at the two men grappling with each other. Gil lashed out with his right fist, bashing Herndon a crushing blow on the ear and sending him reeling backwards. Herndon collided with a table and when he turned Cross could see that he had the fire poker in his right hand. Cross looked quickly at Gil and saw what he had not seen when he had first looked into the room. Gil was bloody, his face covered with reddish streaks where the fire poker had ripped into his flesh.

Both men were oblivious of Cross who stood in the doorway with a bitter smile on his face. Cross could barely contain his bubbling glee as he watched the bloody battle. Which man did he hate more? Many times during the past twenty-four hours he had wished both of them dead and now he was looking at them batter each other's brains out . . . Let 'em fight it out, he said to himself.

He spun round at the sound of footsteps behind him on the stairs. Eva was descending with wild eyes, her hair flying behind her. He grabbed her shoulders and held her, wanting to keep her out of the room. Eva twisted loose and ran to the doorway. Cross followed and stood behind her. Eva grabbed hold of both jambs of the door and screamed as she saw Gil sinking to the floor under the blows of Herndon's fire poker.

Herndon turned and stared at Eva, still clutching the poker in his right hand. He had the look of a man struggling to awaken from a dream. Then Cross saw the muscles of Herndon's face twitch as he advanced menacingly toward them.

"Get out, or I'll kill you both!" Herndon growled.

Eva screamed again, backed violently into Cross, then turned and ran up the stairs. Before Cross could move, Herndon was upon him and he ducked in time to save his head a swishing blow from the poker which caught him on his right shoulder, leaving a searing line of fire in his flesh. He leaped aside and watched Herndon stumble toward the rear of the hall. Cross felt for his gun, then decided that he would run. It was not fear for Herndon that was making him abandon the fight; he was hoping that Herndon would reenter the room and battle again with Gil . . . He took the stairs four at a time and was halfway up when he heard another scuffling lunge behind him; he paused and glanced back. Gil had rushed out of the room and had grabbed Herndon; the two men now wrestled for possession of the fire poker, rolling, clawing, going from Cross's sight as they fell through the doorway back into the room. Cross caressed his bruised shoulder and looked upward; the door of Gil's apartment was open and he heard Eva's frantic voice.

"Don't you understand? I want the police! For God's sake—"

Cross entered the hallway. Eva thrust the telephone into his hands.

"Lionel, here; call the police . . . I can't make the operator understand anything."

"Okay," he breathed.

"Are you hurt?"

"Not much . . ."

He picked up the telephone, placed the receiver to his ear and heard the metallic hum of the line. He jiggled the hook, then paused, turning his head as another burst of sound came from downstairs. Eva sprang through the doorway, heading for downstairs.

"Eva!" he called after her.

Good Lord, what ought he do? She'll get hurt down there with that Fascist . . . Her sense of guilt's making her overreact to help Gil . . . He left the phone and ran after her, catching her on the landing and dragging her back into the apartment.

"No, no," he told her. "You can't go down there . . . *You* call the police—"

"I don't know what to do," she whimpered.

"I'll go down and help Gil," he said.

Eva stared at him helplessly, her body moving indecisively. He thrust the telephone into her hands and ran from the room, stumbling down the stairs. In the lower hallway, he stood, hearing the sound of the fight. He debated: yes; he *had* to help Gil . . . What would Gil say if he did not? His failure to go to Gil's aid would be something he could never explain . . .

Again he stood in the doorway of Herndon's apartment. They were still fighting. Herndon was rushing at Gil again, the poker raised to strike. Gil backed off, his hands lifted to protect his face and head. Herndon crashed the poker into Gil's hands which seemed to wilt under the blow. The poker flew from Herndon's fingers and clattered to the floor. Gil snatched it up quickly and, with it, charged into Herndon, his face livid with fury; he whacked two telling blows home to Herndon's head and face and Cross heard the tinkling of glass shards as Herndon's spectacles broke and showered from his eyes.

Cross watched, disdainful, detached. He saw that there was a broken table leg lying near the fireplace; someone had no doubt been sent crashing into the table and the heavy oaken leg had snapped in two near the top of the table. Teeth bared, Gil now lifted the poker once again to send another blow to Herndon; but, as his arm was about to descend, the tip of the poker caught in the glass chandelier swinging from the ceiling. There was a musical storm of falling crystal and the ceiling light went out, leaving the room lit only by the leaping shadows of the fire. The force that Gil had put behind that swooping blow now carried him headlong to the floor, the poker bounding free once more.

Catlike, Herndon was on it and before Gil could rise Herndon was raining deadly blows upon the head and face of Gil.

Suddenly a fullness of knowledge declared itself within Cross and he knew what he wanted to do. He was acting before he knew it. He reached down and seized hold of the heavy oaken leg of the table and turned and lifted it high in the air, feeling the solid weight of the wood in his hand, and then he sent it flying squarely into the bloody forehead of Herndon. The impact of the blow sent a tremor along the muscles of his arm. Herndon fell like an ox and lay still. He had no doubt crushed the man's skull. Tense, he stood looking down at Herndon, waiting to see if he would move again. He was concentrated, aware of nothing but Herndon's still, bloody form. Then he was startled; he whirled to see Gil struggling heavily to his feet, blood streaming from his face and neck, clotting his eyes. Cross stared for a moment. He was not through. The imperious feeling that had impelled him to action was not fulfilled. His eyes were unblinkingly on Gil's face. Yes, this other insect had to be crushed, blotted out of existence . . .

His fingers gradually tightened about the oaken table leg; his arm lifted slowly into the air. Gil was dabbing clumsily with his handkerchief at the blood on his neck and cheeks. Cross let go with the table leg, smashing it into the left side of Gil's head. Gil trembled for a split second, then fell headlong toward the fireplace where flames danced and cast wild red shadows over the walls. Cross's hand sank slowly to his side, the table leg resting lightly on the floor, its edges stained with blood. There was silence save for the slow ticking of an ornate clock on the desk.

He filled his lungs and sighed deeply. For perhaps a minute he did not move; his sense gradually assumed a tone of anxiety and he stared more intently at the two bloody forms stretched grotesquely on the smeared rug. Then he sucked in his breath and whirled toward the door. Oh, God, it was still open! Had anyone seen him?

He rushed to it and closed it; then turned back to the room and the two inert forms over which red shadows of the fire flickered. Were they dead? He touched Herndon's shoulder; the man was still; the wide, thin lips hung open; blood oozed from one corner of the mouth. Cross hesitated a second, then lifted the table leg and chopped again into the skull. The body rolled over from force of the blow.

Cross now turned to Gil whose head lay near the fire. He caught hold of one of Gil's legs and yanked the body from the fireplace into the center of the room where he could get a better chance to deliver another blow at the head. Again he lifted the table leg and whacked at Gil and he knew that Gil would never move again.

The universe seemed to be rushing at him with all the concreteness of its totality. He was anchored once again in life, in the flow of things; the world glowed with an interest so sharp that it made his body ache. He had had no plan when he had dealt those blows of death, but now he feared for himself, felt the need of a plan of defense. He knew exactly what he had done; he had done it deliberately, even though he had not planned it. He had not been blank of mind when he had done it, and he was resolved that he would never claim any such thing.

He took one last quick look about the room. One of the drawers of Herndon's desk was open and Cross could see the butt of Herndon's gun half-pulled out. He could almost reconstruct what had happened between the two men. Gil had no doubt grabbed Herndon just as Herndon had been about to seize the gun. And after that they had fought so desperately that neither of them had had a chance to get the gun, or they had forgotten it . . .

The plan sprang full and ripe in his imagination, his

body, his senses; he took out his handkerchief and quickly wiped the table leg which he held in his hand, making sure that no trace of his fingerprints would remain. He went to Herndon, holding the table leg with the handkerchief so that his hand would not touch it, and forced the fingers of Herndon's right hand about it several times so that the man's prints would be found . . . He was breathing heavily. The winking shadows of the fire flicked warningly through the room. Still holding the leg with the handkerchief, he went to Gil and closed Gil's loose fingers about it, letting the wooden leg trail uncertainly about the lifeless hand. He took the fire poker, wiped it clean and inserted it in the fingers of Herndon's right hand . . . No; he changed his mind; he'd let the fire poker rest a few inches from Herndon's hand . . . That was more natural . . . He looked swiftly around to make sure that he was leaving no marks of his having been in the room. He had to hurry . . . The door? Fingerprints on the knob . . . ? No; he would not bother about them. After all, if he made things *too* clean, the police would get suspicious . . . And he had been down here talking to Herndon earlier this afternoon . . . Sure . . . His prints had a right to be on the door. Go up to Eva . . . What would he tell her? There would be questions from the police, from Party leaders, from Eva, from everybody . . . The newspapers . . . ? What would they say? Well, he was just a Negro roomer who had gone down at the suggestion of Mrs. Blount to see what was happening and had seen them fighting . . . .

He opened the door; the downstairs hallway was empty. He caught hold of the door handle and was about to shut it when an idea came to him. Suppose someone came to see Herndon and found both Herndon and Gil dead? Ah, yes; it was better to push the tiny lever on the lock and let the door lock itself. The door would be locked when the police and the Party leaders arrived. That was the trick. They would have to knock down the door. *And he, on his second trip down, had not been able to see what was happening; he had only heard sounds* . . . He adjusted the lock and pulled the door to, hearing it catch. He tried the handle; it was locked. Now, what motive on earth could he have had in killing the two of them? Let them figure that out . . .

He started up the stairs, then paused and looked down at himself. Was there any blood on him? He looked at his hands, his coat, his shoes. He could see nothing. Oh, yes; his handkerchief; it was bloody from where he had wiped the fingerprints from the fire poker and the table leg . . . He would have to burn it. Yes; he'd put it into the kitchen incinerator the first chance he got. And, to be absolutely sure, he would ditch the clothes he was wearing. The police had scientific ways of examining particles and arriving at damaging conclusions. He stood in front of Gil's apartment door and composed himself. Yes; he had to act hurriedly and frantically now. He grabbed hold of the doorknob and rattled it brutally. It was locked.

"Eva!" he yelled.

"Is that you, Lionel? Is Gil with you?"

"It's me; Lionel! Open the door quick!"

He heard the night-chain rattling; she had locked herself in. She opened the door and backed fearfully away from him.

"Did you call the police?" he asked her.

"No. I called Jack Hilton; he's calling the police—What happened?"

He searched her face; her eyes were bleak and frightened. Would she be glad that Gil was dead? Didn't she want him dead so that she could be free?

"The door down there is locked and I can't hear a thing," he told her. "Gil's still in there . . ."

"Oh, God," she whimpered.

He longed to know what was going on in her mind. Was she hoping that Gil was dead? And was she feeling guilty because she was hoping it? If so, then she'd act violently now; she'd try to ease her burden of guilt.

"The door's locked?" she repeated in a quiet voice.

"Yes."

"I'm liquid with fear . . . Look, Lionel, call Jack Hilton again and tell 'im— He thinks maybe Gil's all right now—"

Her voice died in her throat and she had spun around and was out of the door before Cross could grab her. He debated: he had a wound on his shoulder to prove that he had tried to help Gil and maybe it would be a good thing for Eva to see that the door was locked. Then, Eva, panting and whimpering, came rushing in again.

"He's there!" she gasped. "He's coming up here . . ."

"Who?"

"Herndon— I saw 'im on the stairs— He has his gun—"

Was she crazy? Herndon was dead. Eva ran past him into her bedroom. Cross approached the door and looked out; he heard footsteps mounting the stairs on the floor above him. Ah, Eva had thought she had seen Herndon, but she had mistaken another man for Herndon . . . He shut the door and put on the night-chain. Yes; that was something that could be used in his favor. Eva had thought that she had seen Herndon coming up the stairs! *That meant that her testimony would indicate that Herndon was still living after he had come up to the apartment for the second time . . . That could mean that Gil and Herndon killed each other!*

By God, *that* was the plan! He would stick to that story . . .

"Eva!" he called to her. "Give me Hilton's phone number!"

When she did not answer, he went to her. She was lying on the floor of her bedroom; she had fainted. He lifted her to her bed, got a wet towel from the bathroom and patted her face with it. Her eyelids fluttered.

"Give me Hilton's phone number," he asked her.

"My purse," she murmured.

He got her purse and took it to her; she gave him an address book and whispered: "Find the number there, under H . . ."

Cross thumbed through the book, found the number, then walked slowly toward the telephone. His mind clearly grasped the entire situation and every muscle of his body was relaxed. Now, I'd like to see them figure that out, he told himself with a grim smile. I killed two little gods . . . He paused, frowning. But they would have killed me too if they had found me like that . . . Yet, he could not get it straight. Just a moment ago it had all seemed so simple. But now it was knotted and complicated. There was in him no regret for what he had done; no, none at all. But how *could* he have done it? He too had acted like a little god. He had stood amidst those red and flickering shadows, tense and consumed with cold rage, and had judged them and had found them guilty of insulting his sense of life and had carried out a sentence of death upon them. Like Hilton and Gil had acted toward Bob, so had he acted toward Gil and Herndon; he had assumed the role of policeman, judge, supreme court, and executioner,—all in one swift and terrible moment. But, if he resented their being little gods, how could he do the same? His self-assurance ebbed, his pride waned under the impact of his own reflections. Oh, Christ, their disease had reached out and claimed him too. He had been subverted by the contagion of the lawless; he had been defeated by that which he had sought to destroy. He sank listlessly into the chair by the side of the telephone. Yet, no matter what happened, he had to call Hilton; he had to phone that little god . . . ! He was limp. What was the matter with him? He was, yes, he was trapped in the coils of his own doings. He had acted, had shattered the dream that surrounded him, and now the world, including himself in it, had turned mockingly into a concrete, waking nightmare from which he could see no way of escaping. He had become what he had tried to destroy, had taken on the guise of the monster he had slain. Held to a point of attention more by the logic of events than by his own reasoning, his consciousness charged with a sense of meaninglessness, he bent toward the telephone and dialed . . .

BOOK FOUR

DESPAIR

The wine of life is drawn; and the mere lees
Is left this vault to brag of.
— SHAKESPEARE'S *Macbeth*

THE SEDUCTIONS of vanity have lured countless men to destinies that have confounded them, left them straitened and undone. After an arduous journey of experience it is not good to stare in dismay at a world that one was creating without being aware of it, and there is no chastening of the spirit so severely sobering as that rankling sense of guilt that springs from a knowledge of having been snared into the mire of disillusionment when one thought that one was soaring on wings of intellectual pride to a freedom remote from the errors and frailties of the gullible. At times there comes into the lives of men realizations so paralyzing that, for the first time, their hands reach out fumblingly for the touch of another human being.

In Cross's despair it was upon Eva's trapped and deceived heart—into whose depths he had stolen a criminal glimpse—that he now instinctively leaned, his wounded pride groping toward that one shelter where he hoped waited someone who loathed cruelty and yearned to place a kiss of fraternity upon the betrayed and victimized. And, as much for a dawning reverence for her as for the protection of his own self-love, he tried desperately to shield her from the shock of rough events that he knew would be soon sweeping on tidal waves toward the both of them. Many despairs and regrets later, via his acutely developed habit of reflection, when he had reexamined his behavior following his bloody snatching of the lives of Gil and Herndon, he could find nothing remiss in how he had deported himself. To an important extent the logic derived from a mixing of his temperament and gratuitous opportunity had determined his attitude. To have fled immediately upon his gory acts would have been to confess his guilt openly, and to have tried to explain either to the police or to the Party the complex composition of the elementary judgment-feeling that had spurred him to such acts of ethical murder would have been to succumb to a gesture of sheer naïveté of which he was far too intelligent to be capable. He reasoned that it was much safer to lie, to dodge, to blend with the changing hues of the foliage of the landscape for safety in eluding his pursuers.

In talking to Hilton over the telephone, Cross was careful to assume the role of a subordinate, a humble outsider, a man speaking for a temporarily incapacitated woman.

"But Eva phoned and told me that you'd gone down to help Gil," Hilton said in a baffled tone of voice.

"But the door was *locked* this time—"

"Did you try to get in?"

"Yeah. I banged and knocked and hollered—"

"And Herndon didn't answer?"

"No."

"And did you hear anything?"

"Fighting, like I told you—"

"Did you try to get help from anywhere?"

"Eva called you—"

"And the first time you went down, he hit you?"

"Yes, with the fire poker—"

"Where's Eva now?"

"She fainted. She's lying down."

"You hear any noise now?"

"Nothing; nothing at all."

"And Herndon ran Eva back into the apartment, hunh?"

"Yes; I was trying to phone you and she ran out—"

"He had a gun?"

"She said so. I didn't see him. I bolted the door when she came running back in."

"Did Gil seem badly hurt?"

"Gosh, I don't know. I only got a glimpse of 'im," Cross was purposefully vague. "Look, you ought to come over and I could explain it all. I just moved in this morning, see? This Herndon jumped me at sight, told me to get the hell out, wanted to pull a gun on me, said he'd kill me—"

"Where was Gil when you first looked through the door?"

"He was lying on the floor."

"Herndon knocked him down?"

"Seems like it. Herndon had the fire poker in his hand—"

"Did you *see* him strike Gil?"

"Yes."

"Was Gil conscious?"

"I don't know—"

"And you're sure that Eva saw him on the stairs a few minutes ago?"

"Sure; she said so."

"Okay. Now, listen, don't let anybody into the apartment until I come, unless it's the police or somebody from the Party, see?"

"All right."

"That's all. I'll be right over." The line clicked.

Not once had any emotion entered Hilton's voice as he questioned Cross over the telephone, but Cross noticed that throughout Hilton's inquiries had run a theme that puzzled him. Ah, he knew now! Hilton was already trying to establish the fact that Herndon was the *aggressor*. Cross, knowing that Gil was dead, decided that his own defense could be best served by his feeding the Party's hunger for a martyred hero, dead or alive. He marveled at how instinctively Hilton was reacting in terms of the Party's organizational needs. If, in describing what he had seen when he had looked into the doorway, he said that Gil had seemed to be getting the worst of it, that Herndon had been standing over Gil with the fire poker, then the Party would claim, when it found that Gil was dead, that Herndon, the fascist beast, had killed him, and had later died of wounds which Gil, in self-defense, had inflicted on him during the course of the struggle. And then there was that fantastic windfall of luck of Eva's thinking that she had seen Herndon after Herndon had been killed and after the door had been locked! Cross knew that he had to be careful in relating what he had seen, had always to keep sternly in mind that he must do no interpreting at all, that the Party and the police had to weigh what had happened and place their own assessment and value upon it. His aim would be to establish in the minds of the police and Party leaders that Herndon had been alive when he had last looked into the room, that Gil had been hurt, unconscious, maybe dying, and after that the door had been locked . . .

And would not Eva be his unconscious ally? He was convinced that her actions had been determined by an awful sense of guilt toward Gil. Her fantasy of seeing Herndon with a gun on the stairs was but her own feeling that Herndon ought to kill her now that Herndon had done her secret bidding by killing Gil . . . And Eva no doubt felt that he was, like she, a victim of the Party's complicated duplicities . . . Yes, he had a chance to stand clear of suspicion as long as he could manipulate or count upon the guilt-feelings of others.

Cross took a deep breath and tried to keep the facts straight in his mind. This thing had come upon him so suddenly that its reality had not sunk home to him in all of its fullness. Had he killed them or was it a teasing fantasy? He was counting on their both being dead, or his whole plan was crazy. Or, if Gil lived, he was in trouble, both with the police and the Party. He longed to creep downstairs and make sure that they were both dead, but he feared complications would ensue if he broke open the door and looked in . . . And suppose someone saw him in the lower hallway now? But those men *must* be dead. God knows he had pounded them hard enough. Gil would have to be a superman to live after the many slashes that Herndon had rained down upon him and the heavy whacks he had showered upon his defenseless head at the end . . . Of Herndon he could be certain; that Fascist was dead . . .

"Lionel . . ." Eva's voice was calling.

"Yes?"

He went in to her; she was half leaning on her elbow in bed and she looked at him with eyes brimming with fear and guilt.

"Did Gil seem badly hurt?"

"I don't know," he answered her softly.

"What did Hilton say?"

"He said for us to stay here; he's on his way over now. He's phoned the police and the Party."

"But we should try to do something for Gil—"

"The door's *locked*, Eva—"

"Oh, God," she wailed, "I wish Hilton'd come. You hear anything down there now?"

"No," Cross said. "I was listening in the front hall, but I couldn't hear anything."

She broke down again and began weeping. "I can't stand this life— This deception— This everlasting violence— Is there no way to be human any more . . . ?"

Before he could stop her, she had sprung from the bed and was running on swift feet down the hall to the door.

"Gil! Gil!" she was screaming.

"Eva!" he yelled and started after her.

"He'll blame me if we don't help 'im," she sobbed hysterically. "And the Party'll want to know *why* we didn't help 'im . . ." She sobered quickly and stared at him, realizing that she was trying to explain something that he could not possibly understand.

Yes; she, like he, was wondering if Gil was really dead. A wounded Gil, a living Gil, would be a calamity for the both of them. He longed to put her at peace, to tell her that she was free. But he could not. He caught her on the landing, about to descend the stairs. He grabbed her shoulders.

"Herndon's dangerous," he argued. "And Hilton said for us to *keep* from down there—"

"Gil may be hurt," she whimpered. "We could help him—"

"The door's *locked*!" he insisted. Yes, he would stress that she must be loyal to the Party, something which she feared more than she feared Gil. "The Party will perhaps make a test case of this, see? We *can't* interfere . . ." A better idea leaped into his mind; she felt that he was a victim of the Party and he would try to exploit her delusion. That's it . . . "Look, Eva," he argued solemnly, "this is complicated. The reason that Hilton doesn't want me to go down there is that I'm *colored*, see? You know the police . . . They'd try to frame me . . ."

She wilted, turned, and buried her face on his shoulder. Hers was a world ruled by fear. He led her back into the apartment and bolted the door; sweat stood on his forehead. He guided her steps to the bed and gently helped her upon it. They were silent; there came the sound of footsteps in the hallway. Eva strained, lifting herself almost to a sitting position. Could that be the police or Hilton? Cross heard the footsteps mount the stairway. No; it was somebody who lived upstairs.

"The Cushmans," Eva whispered. "They're anti-Party."

Cross stared at her in amazement. To her the world was either Party or anti-Party, and all in between did not count. He sat on a chair at the side of the bed. Eva was shaking; he could hear her teeth rattling. He longed to take hold of her and soothe her, but dared not.

"You think they'll blame us if Gil's badly hurt?" she asked in a whisper.

The Party ruled her not only positively but negatively. It was not only what she did that would make her guilty, but also what she did not do . . .

"We did what we could," he told her. "This was not our idea, Eva. They should have sent someone to help Gil . . . And he wouldn't let me go down with 'im . . ."

Her sense of guilt was a hot bed of coals and she was squirming on it. Cross rose and Eva reached impulsively and grabbed his hand and clung to it.

"Don't go," she begged.

"I was going to try to listen at the door—"

"Don't leave me here," she pled in a whisper of panic.

He sat again on the edge of the bed and felt nervous tremors going through her body. If only he could tell her that she was free! But, no . . . If he told her that he had killed, the horror she felt for the Party would be transferred to him . . .

He was aware of her slim, willowy figure on the bed, the legs that tapered with such a long, slow curve, the suggestively dramatic roundness of her hips, the small but firm breasts, the long and delicate neck, and the hazel pools of her eyes now dark and anxious with dread; and desire for desire rose in him for her for the first time. Oh, God, he must not think of that now . . . He felt the soft pressure from her thin, almost transparent fingers on his hand and she became woman as body of woman for his senses. The depths of him stirred as he realized that she was now alone in the world and did not know it; in a peculiar sense she was at his mercy. What he did or did not do, what he said or did not say would affect her more profoundly now than anything that would ever happen to her. Already she was his in a deeper sense than the sexual, in a sense that included the sexual. At this moment she was again an orphan; she had only him to depend upon and he could now, like Gil had done with Bob, ravage her entire being without any resistance from her. From the poignant pages of her diary and from the fact that Gil was dead and she did not know it, he possessed a comprehension of her existence that she had not the capacity to imagine. Would she suspect him? *Could* she suspect him? She believed that colored people were caught up in life, healthy, untouched and unspoiled by the cynical world of political deceptions . . . Had she not referred to "us" when she spoke of her fear of the Party?

For the first time since he had killed, he felt guilty. It was not a guilt for his having murdered; it was because he now saw that he held over the life of Eva a godlike power and knowledge that even Gil or the Party had not held. He had killed Gil and Herndon because they had wanted to play god to others, and their brutal strivings had struck him as being so utterly obscene that he had torn their lives from them in a moment of supreme conviction that he and he alone was right and that they were eternally wrong. And now Gil lay still and dead downstairs amid the trembling red shadows and he sat here holding Eva's hand, desiring her body. And the wall of deception which he had begun to erect to conceal the nature of her husband's death would throw her, perhaps, into his arms . . .

If the actions of Gil and Herndon were monstrously inhuman, then was not what he was doing also devoid of humanity? If there was a valid difference, just where did it lie? Was the innocence of Gil and Herndon the less because they had millions of supporters, because time and tradition, law and religion had mounted a shield of justification before them? And his guilt, was it the more because he was alone and had no counsel but his own? If Gil or Herndon had done what he had done, would it have worried them? Was not his worrying proof that he was wrong? Did he not need about him the sanctioning buttress of the faces of his brothers in crime to make him feel at home with his deed?

His sense of despair deepened and he yearned for the first time to be free of this circling, brooding that filled his skull, this elusive shadow of himself that tortured him. To go on killing would only sink him deeper into these quicksands of guilt which he wanted so much to avoid. What way was there out of this? The desperately naïve idea of confessing everything to Eva came to him. Might not she, being another victim, understand and help him? *No!* That was crazy . . . She believed him an *innocent* victim, not a *guilty* one! No; he could talk to no one now; he had to tread this guilty treadmill alone . . .

He recovered himself as the fingers of Eva's hand tightened about his own.

"Are you frightened, Lionel?"

"No."

"What can we tell them?"

"The truth. We'll tell them what happened . . ."

He knew that, childlike, she was already thinking that maybe a lie would be a better kind of truth to tell than to try to conceal the guilt that had so long smouldered in her heart. Why was he mulling and hesitating? Ride this thing out and take this lovely girl and live with her . . .

"What are you thinking, Lionel?"

"Nothing," he breathed.

"They'll say we acted wrongly, won't they?"

"How could they?" he asked. "We couldn't do any more than we did—"

"Oh, why did the Party push *you* into this?" she wailed.

"We're in it together," he told her.

"Gil may be wanting us to help him; maybe he's hurt," she began to weep again.

The doorbell rang.

"Go, Lionel!"

Cross ran and let in Jack Hilton and another man. They stared at one another for a moment in silence. Eva came running from the bedroom.

"He's still down there, Jack— Can't you do something?" she implored. "Maybe he's hurt . . ."

Hilton's face turned pale and he spun to Cross.

"But the police? Aren't they here *yet*?"

"No," Cross told him.

"And Gil's *still* down there?"

"Yes."

"And that door's still locked?"

"I guess so," Cross stammered.

"My God—" Hilton said, whirling and going through the door. He halted, turned, and beckoned to his companion. "Come *on*, Menti!"

They thundered down the stairs. Eva followed Menti; and Cross, lingeringly, followed Eva, watching Hilton's movements, wondering what his tactics would be. They paused momentarily in the downstairs hallway. Hilton advanced to the door of Herndon's apartment.

"Is this the door?"

"Yes," Cross told him.

Hilton grabbed the knob and rattled it.

"Gil! Are you there?" Hilton called loudly.

"Gil! Gil!" Eva yelled, hammering on the panels of the door with her fists.

"You'd better break it down," Cross said. "I've called and called—"

Hilton hesitated, then ran to the rear door and tried the handle. He walked back toward them with worried eyes.

"Put your shoulder to it, Menti," Hilton said.

"Okay," Menti agreed eagerly.

Menti, tall, black of hair, with a nervous, too-white face, backed off to the bottom of the stairs, quickly hunched his shoulders and sent himself toward the door and in the second of his body hitting the panels, the door burst in, banging loudly against a wall inside. Menti blocked Cross's vision and he could see nothing; he remembered the room lit by flames and dancing shadows, but the wood fire had died down and, though he had forgotten it, the light on the ceiling had gone out when Gil had accidentally struck the chandelier with the fire poker. Eva pushed past him, then stopped, her face gazing at the floor of Herndon's study.

"Gil! Oh, God, Gil!" she screamed and ran forward.

Cross could now see the dim outlines of Gil and Herndon lying outstretched on the rug. They were as he had left them, the table leg and the fire poker lying near their right hands, their faces darkened with splotches of blood.

"What's happened?" Hilton asked in singsong voice.

"Good Christ," Menti breathed.

"Gil! Gil!" Eva was still screaming, advancing slowly into the room.

Hilton stood without moving, his thin lips hanging open. Eva was now bent over Gil, her hands reaching out as though to touch him, then she closed her eyes and turned her body and leaned weakly against a wall, wailing and sobbing. Cross was observing closely and waiting for questions. Hilton was the first to master himself; he rushed forward, knelt at Gil's side and felt for his pulse. His eyes lifted to Eva's face; then he looked at Cross; he stood slowly, turning and looking at Menti. Only later did he glance at Herndon, then kneel and feel for his pulse.

"Help 'im," Eva begged, staring at Gil as though she expected him to rise and accuse her.

"We better call the police again," Menti said.

"Better call a doctor," Cross ventured.

"Naw; wait," Hilton said, speaking in a vague tone with bated breath, his eyes straying from face to face. "Look, don't touch anything here . . . Let's get upstairs!"

"Get a doctor," Eva begged. "He's bleeding . . . Somebody *do* something . . ." She knelt to touch Gil, but Hilton grabbed her arm.

"Gil's dead, Eva," Hilton told her softly. "Don't touch anything."

"No! No!" Eva screamed, cringed, jammed her fingers against her teeth and sank to the floor. Cross lifted her and held her by her shoulders, conscious that Hilton's eyes were upon him. As he held Eva he knew that now was beginning the time of his drastic test, a test he did not want, for, if he won it, what had he won? Eva? He had not killed to get her. Hilton was still staring at him; then Hilton turned and walked slowly to the hall door. Menti ran to Hilton and grabbed his arm.

"Hadn't I better call the Party again?" he asked.

"We haven't time," Hilton said. "The police'll be here any minute now."

Menti was nonplussed; his eyes narrowed and he stared at Hilton.

"I'm going to call the Party," he said.

"Take it easy, Menti," Hilton said with a slow, ironic smile. "This is more complicated than you think. I'm in charge here. I spoke to Blimin over the phone and he told me to take complete responsibility. *This* is political . . ."

"I see," Menti said, dropping his eyes.

Hilton was now staring at Cross with eyes round with astonishment. And Cross, as he watched Hilton, knew that this was the man he had to cope with, and a slow hatred for Hilton began to surge up in him. He still kept his arm about Eva who was trembling and sagging against him. Why was Hilton staring at him so? Was he already suspecting him? Hilton was a member of the upper circles of the Party and he was no fool. So free were the minds of these Communists that one could not predict what motives would prompt their actions. Cross held himself alert, every atom of him striving supremely to be aware of what was taking place.

"We've no time to lose," Hilton told them roughly. "Everybody get upstairs at once. Stay in the apartment 'til I come."

"No, no," Eva sobbed. "Help Gil—"

"Go upstairs, Eva," Hilton said. "It's too late."

Cross led Eva into the hallway and struggled with her up the steps; Menti helped him, but was looking over his shoulder to see what Hilton was doing. When inside the apartment, Eva clutched Menti and begged:

"Can't something be done, Menti? It's not too late, *is* it?"

"Take it easy, Eva," Menti said. "Hilton's doing everything . . ."

Cross eased Eva upon the sofa of the living room and Menti sat next to her, holding her shoulders. Hilton entered a moment later and Cross could see sweat standing on his forehead.

"He should've broken that door down," Menti told Hilton, nodding to Cross.

"No; he did right," Hilton said. "He's colored . . . This thing is complicated . . ."

"Oh," Menti breathed.

Hilton rushed out of the room and Cross could hear him putting the night-chain on the front door. Hilton returned and knelt at Eva's side.

"Eva," he began in a hurried but composed voice, "can you understand me? Are you fit to be questioned? We don't have much time—"

"But maybe he's not dead, Jack," Eva whimpered. "Try . . . Try to *do* something . . ."

"They're *both* dead, Eva," Hilton explained calmly.

"God in Heaven," Eva sobbed.

"Eva," Hilton spoke sternly. "We've no time for that . . . You must get hold of yourself. You're in the Party. You must rise above all display of personal feeling. There's something of decisive importance to the memory of Gil that I must discuss with you. You hear me?"

"Yes," Eva breathed, trying to still the shaking of her body; she turned wild eyes to Hilton and nodded her head.

"Gil's been killed by a Fascist," Hilton explained. "He was carrying out Party orders when he was killed; he fell in line of duty . . . That must be understood. This is a *Party* matter. The bourgeois press'll try to twist those facts downstairs, and we must see that they don't. I'm sure that Gil, if he were with us now, would agree emphatically to that."

"Yes," Eva said, nodding her head slowly; she glanced at Cross and buried her face in her hands.

Cross grasped the approach; it was as he had hoped it would be. But they had not questioned him yet; that was to come.

"Now, Eva," Hilton was saying, "tell me quickly what happened . . ."

"Ask Lionel . . . I only saw him beating Gil," she said.

"You were not in the room at all?" Hilton asked Eva.

"No . . ." Eva sighed.

Hilton rose and faced Cross.

"Were you in the room?"

"No," Cross said. "I was looking in through the door. He came at me, hit me with the poker— Right here—"

"Start from the beginning and tell me quickly," Hilton urged.

Cross sketched the story briefly, telling the facts just as they had happened, but omitting that he had been in the room.

"God, I'm sorry about Gil," he ended up.

"This is war," Hilton said. "We must expect casualties. Gil was brave." He studied Cross. "I saw you at Bob's last night, didn't I?"

"Yes."

"What's your name?"

"Lionel Lane."

"You've got to help us with this thing," Hilton said. "You were Gil's friend . . ."

"I'll do what I can."

"Listen to me carefully, all of you," Hilton began. "The important thing here is who died *first*. Get it?"

"What do you mean?" Menti asked.

"If it's proved that Herndon died first, then they'll want to brand Gil as a murderer," Hilton explained swiftly.

"But Eva saw Herndon alive with a gun . . . He was after her," Cross told him.

"Yes; I know that," Hilton said. "But when you looked into the door and saw Herndon beating Gil . . . Gil was not able to defend himself, was he? Herndon was killing him . . . Do you understand? It's important."

Menti approached Cross and caught hold of his arm.

"Look, guy, Gil was killed by that Fascist," Menti said. "Do you understand that?"

"Gil died fighting for your people, for *you*," Hilton reminded him.

"I know that," Cross said, simulating bafflement; he knew what they were driving at, but he did not want to seem to grasp it too quickly. He squinted his eyes and looked at the floor; he felt like laughing out loud. They were now begging *him* to believe something that he was praying that *they* would believe!

Cross looked at Eva. Though she had stopped sobbing, Cross could see that she could not quite follow what was being said. Cross felt that now was the time to cooperate with the Party, to demonstrate class consciousness, to cast his solidarity with the revolution. He nodded his head, looking slowly from Hilton to Menti.

"When I looked through the doorway, I saw Herndon with his foot on Gil's chest— He was hitting Gil— With the poker— I don't know how many times he hit 'im— Then Eva came down and Herndon saw us. He ran us back upstairs with the fire poker . . ."

"Yes," Eva sighed.

"And Gil couldn't move when you looked into that door?" Hilton demanded.

"No, he was out, unconscious, it seems to me . . ."

Hilton turned to Eva.

"And you saw Herndon *after* Lionel was up here? He was coming to get into the apartment, hunh? You ran back in and shut the door, didn't you, Eva? He had his gun?"

"Yes," she said.

"That is *proof*," Hilton said.

Cross wondered if Eva really believed that . . . Her sense of guilt was making her paint a picture that was helping him!

"Lionel, you just tell the cops what you saw; stick to your story," Menti said. "Cops are your enemies, boy. Look at what they have done to your people . . . Don't forget the lynchings . . . No matter *what* they do to you, say *nothing* but the truth; you hear? Gil gave his life for *you*. Herndon miscalculated; he thought he could scare Gil . . . When Herndon killed Gil, he was really killing *you*; you understand?"

"I understand," Cross answered.

"You better call those cops again," Menti said.

Hilton left and a moment later Cross heard him dialing the telephone. Menti stood looking at Cross and Eva, and Cross could guess what was going through the man's mind. Menti was hoping that Eva would be able to keep him in line, keep him loyal to the Party; and no doubt that same idea was in the back of Hilton's mind.

"Poor girl," Menti said to Cross, nodding toward Eva. "We owe it to her to protect the name of Gil."

"You can depend on me," Cross assured him; the corners of his mouth twitched, for he was wondering just what they would depend upon him for: to lie for the Party or to try to win Eva? And, back of it all, he was protecting his own wild despair of having surrendered to his pride to the point of having killed . . .

Hilton returned to the room absentmindedly puffing at a cigarette. His bony, ascetic face was tensely concentrated. Cross marveled at the self-possession of this man who, twenty-four hours ago, had mercilessly reduced Bob's enthusiasm for organizing to a quivering heap of whimpering flesh, and Cross was certain that no regretful memories or stings of remorse lingered on in Hilton's mind as he now coldly grappled with this new crisis. Men like Hilton did not spend their days scheming how to get hold of dollars; they worked at organizing and exploiting the raw stuff of human emotions. In their being close to the common impulses of men, in their cynical acceptance of the cupidities of the human heart, in their frank recognition of outlandish passions they were akin to priests. Now that he had killed Gil and had elected to remain near Eva, this man was his adversary, an adversary who played a game whose stakes held nothing less than life and death . . . Cross fought feebly against an intellectual pride that was rising in him and making him want to cope with Hilton, to show him that he and his kind did not possess a monopoly of knowledge about the emotional nature of man. And again Cross was dismayed at himself for contracting the ailment he hated. To fight Hilton meant fighting Hilton on Hilton's own ground, just as he had had to kill Gil and Herndon on their own ground, and that in itself was a defeat, a travesty of the impulse that had first moved him . . . Was all action doomed to this kind of degradation? How did one get around that? Or maybe you couldn't get around it? Perhaps he was staring right now at the focal point of modern history: if you fought men who tried to conquer you in terms of total power you too had to use total power and in the end you became what you tried to defeat . . .

Hilton was restless, chronically ill at ease, shifting from foot to foot, as if he feared that if he stood still he would commit some violent act. There was about his face and eyes that same impression of intolerable strain that had been so noticeable to Cross last night at Bob's. Here was a human instrument that had placed the total capacities of its life completely at the disposal of the Party . . . Cross could feel that Hilton, at this very moment, was pondering some question concerning him, for Hilton's wary eyes were fixed upon his face. Finally Hilton said to Cross:

"Come into the kitchen a moment."

"Sure."

Menti was talking to Eva now in low, consoling tones and Cross left her to trail behind Hilton. When they were inside the kitchen, Hilton shut the door and turned to Cross. He smiled and asked:

"How's she taking it?"

"As you see," Cross answered, on guard.

"You think we ought to get somebody to be with her?"

"Gosh, I don't know." He thought the question odd, for Hilton had shown no concern about Eva's state until now. "She can take care of herself. She shows little of what's going on in her."

"*That's* what I'm scared of," Hilton said in a tone of amused wonder. "She might even be glad that Gil is dead when she's over the shock. Gil was a first-class sonofabitch, if ever there was one. He was an absolutely cold fish whom I tried always to avoid, if I could . . ." He caught hold of Cross's arm and squeezed it. "You're not so bourgeois that speaking the truth about the dead bothers you . . ."

"Hell, no," Cross said; he was genuinely surprised. What was the man getting at?

"Gil was snobbish to the point of inciting murder, really," Hilton went on, smiling wryly. "Frankly, I've no sympathy for him. I'm a Communist and a dead man, so far as I'm concerned, is just so much cold meat." He chuckled uneasily. "He never liked me. I'm just an ex-school teacher, but Gil's father was a 1905'er . . . His real name was Bernstein. He grew up in the Bronx with the air of revolution in his home and it always made him feel that he was of the red elite. He hit at me several times politically, but I dodged him. He was widely hated in the Party."

"I didn't know that," Cross said. Why's he telling me this?

"And Eva's a cold one too," he went on in a tone of voice that told Cross that he was now getting to his point. "There was no love lost between Gil and Eva . . . Don't kid yourself. In the Party, we know things."

Hilton looked at Cross curiously. He's worried about Eva and he's wondering how much I know . . . He decided not to tell Hilton that he knew Eva's marriage had been arranged by the Party, and that Eva had been in revolt, had been seething with hatred and despair.

"She knows a lot about the Party, but Gil was her only real link to us," Hilton pursued his theme. His lips moved without emitting words.

"Have you heard her say anything against the Party?" he asked finally.

Cross decided at once that he would defend Eva: their interests were identical.

"Never." He reflected that he was a newcomer and his word would not mean much. "She's never spoken an anti-Party word— In fact, I've asked her about political issues, but she'd never talk. Of course, you know that I'm not yet a member of the Party . . ."

"She likes colored people," Hilton said. He hastened to add: "I'm not saying that in a nasty way. She does. Tell me, do you think she trusts you?"

Cross understood at last. Hilton was asking him to watch over Eva! And he was longing to do just that, but not for Hilton's or the Party's sake. And, no doubt, in the living room Menti was hinting to Eva to keep an eye on Cross . . .

"I don't know," Cross said cautiously.

"From what I see of her reactions, I think she does," Hilton said with a sly smile.

He was angry, but he hid his feelings. He sensed that at some time in the past Hilton must have made advances to Eva and had been repulsed; and now, in the interests of the Party, he was giving her up. What a man . . . ! Cross thought.

"Why aren't you a member of the Party?"

"Well, I just met Gil and Eva last night."

"That's long enough. You are a Negro and you've an instinct for this sort of thing. I don't mean a racial instinct; it's a socially conditioned instinct for dissimulation which white Americans have bred in you, and you've had to practice it in order to survive. Watching and coping with the racially charged behavior of white Americans are a part of your learning how to live in this country. Look, every day in this land some white man is cussing out some defenseless Negro. But that white bastard is too stupid in intelligence and deficient in imagination to realize that his actions are being duplicated a million times in a million other spots by other whites who feel hatred for Negroes just like he does; therefore, he is too blind to see that this daily wave of a million tiny assaults acts to build up a vast reservoir of resentment in Negroes. At night at home Negroes discuss this bitterly. But the next morning, smiling, they show up on their jobs, swearing that they love white people . . . Why? You know the answer. They have to live, eat, have a roof over their heads . . . So they collaborate with people who they feel are their sworn enemies . . . White America has built up something in you that can help the Party now. Defend yourself against these cops who are coming, and, if you do, you are defending the Party and your own interests at the same time. If you are honest in your heart, you cannot deny the Party. What about it, Lionel?"

How astute the man was! The average white American could never drag such simple truths past his lips, and here was a man confessing it with fluent passion. Did the average white American suspect that men like Hilton existed, men who could easily rise above their petty feelings of racial hatred and, instead of allowing the racial phobias of the mob to dominate their lives, could cynically make use of the racially defensive attitudes instilled in Negroes by the ill-treatment meted out by whites, could use such racial consciousnesses as weapons in their own bitterly determined struggle for power by exploiting this racial consciousness in their own behalf? This Hilton knew his country as only a man who had lived in it but not of it could know it. He was a man who, like Houston, like Gil, was an outsider and was free in what he apprehended. But I'm an outsider too, Cross thought musingly. I'll let him use me for what *I* want to be used for . . .

"I have no objections," Cross said softly.

What greater protection could he dream of than this? The Party he loathed was going to help defend him . . .

"Now, when the police questioning is over, I want to talk to you," Hilton said, giving Cross a card with his address upon it. "I don't live far from here—"

"Okay," Cross agreed, taking the card from him.

They shook hands.

"Just look after Eva," Hilton said. "If anything develops, get in touch with me. In fact, I think you'd better stay close to her."

Cross did not trust himself to answer. He simply nodded. Hilton looked nervously at his wrist watch.

"The police are slow in coming," he commented.

They returned to the living room. Eva was stretched out on the sofa. Cross went to her, bent down and asked:

"Can I get you something, Eva?"

She shook her head, forcing a wan smile to her lips. Menti looked at Hilton and winked. Hilton knelt at the knees of Eva and caught hold of her hand.

"Darling, Gil's gone, but the Party's still here. Your Party lives," he said softly, in solemn tones. "I've no doubt but that you're going to be able to do what you're called upon to do. Here's the situation. Herndon called Gil down to make him put Lionel out of the apartment. You heard noises and you and Lionel went down to see what was the matter. Herndon was beating Gil— He drove both of you upstairs, beating Lionel with the poker— You heard more noises— Eva, you tried to phone the police, but couldn't get through. So you phoned me and I phoned the cops; understand? Then you and Lionel heard more noises and screams. You sent Lionel down to help Gil . . . But the door was locked. Lionel came back up to phone the cops and,

Eva, you started down again— But Herndon ran you back up with his gun— You saw 'im on the stairs with his gun— You both then locked yourselves in, see? You phoned me again— I came with Menti— We broke down the door—" Hilton gripped Eva's arm tightly. "Now, listen, we *didn't* tell you what we found down there, Eva . . . You hear? You *understand* that?"

"What do you mean?" Eva asked, baffled.

"I mean this," Hilton explained. "You and Lionel *did not* go down with us— You and Lionel remained *up here*; understand? You don't know that Gil's *dead*, see? When you hear that he's dead, you must *scream*! Your husband's been *murdered*. Herndon's guilty of *murder*; see? That's all. Herndon's the *murderer*. The rest of the burden's on us . . ."

Eva nodded her head, tears streaming again on her cheeks.

"You are a *Communist*, Eva," Hilton emphasized. "We Communists do what we *have* to do. It's our life."

Then the room was deathly still, for, in the distance, came the faintly rising wail of a siren.

"Are you all right, Eva?" Menti asked.

"I'm all right," Eva said, steeling herself.

The police are coming, Cross told himself. If Eva could face them, then, God knows, he ought to be able to. Buttressed by these two men whose profession was based on a defiance of the men of the law, he would have more than an equal chance. For a moment a nostalgic regret seized hold of him. Why was he not *with* them? Especially at times like this he welcomed their support. As an ally against racist white Americans, they had no peers. But he knew that that was not all. He recalled Bob's squirming on the floor, begging for a mercy that the Party would not grant. No; no, he would not swallow that happening to him . . . The sirens were near now, nearer, then nearer still. Suddenly he could hear them no more and he knew that the police were downstairs in the snow-choked streets in front of the house.

Cross knew that another world, Herndon's world, was coming; the police agents of that world were as much against him as the dead man Herndon had been. And Hilton and Menti were his allies and wanted to defend him, whatever their motives. He was black and, in the baleful eyes of the men who were coming, he had no right to be here in a white apartment building in a white neighborhood. He leaned against the wall, waiting, thinking. Why was it like this? As a Negro, he was not even free enough to choose his own allies.

What a cheap price Hilton was paying for his loyalty! And for men like Hilton, detached from impulses of racial hatred, what a trifling effort to expend to capture the allegiance of millions of people! Was not a world that left itself open to such easy attacks a stupid world, a doomed world, a rotten world not worth fighting for or saving? Since Herndon's world considered him only half-human, why did he not, out of spite and in defense of his own human dignity, turn on that world and, with the help of such base and dubious allies as Hilton and Menti, destroy it? But what would happen to him after that world was destroyed . . . ? Would he not be at the mercy of the Hiltons and Mentis . . . ? Hunh? What a black choice . . . !

He was now hearing the slow, heavy tramp of feet on the stairs. There came the sound of a brutal wrenching at the knob of the door, then the bell pealed impatiently. Cross moved to the center of the room, but Hilton waved him back.

"Stay put. I'll get this. I'll do the talking until they ask you something," Hilton said, going out.

Menti sat holding his arms about Eva and looking at Cross. Cross winked at Menti and Menti smiled. He had to give these men some assurance. He heard Hilton open the door.

"What's the trouble here?" The voice was rough and aggressive.

"There's been an awful fight downstairs," Cross heard Hilton explaining. "I think you'd better go down and see—"

"Whose apartment is this and *who* are you?"

"I'm a friend of one of the men downstairs, Mr. Gilbert Blount," Hilton's voice came clear and steady. "But, say, I think you ought to take a look quick—"

"I asked *you* your name?"

"Hilton, Jack Hilton . . ."

"And where do you live?"

"At the Albert Hotel on University Place."

"And what were these men fighting about?"

"Well, it seems that the landlord, Mr. Herndon, objected to a certain tenant—"

"We'll see about that," a flat, brutal voice sounded.

There was silence. Cross could hear voices but could not make out what was being said.

"What are you doing here now?"

"Mrs. Blount, the wife of one of the men downstairs, asked me to come over," Hilton explained. "Look, don't you think you ought to take a look and see what's happened to the men down there—?"

"Where's Mrs. Blount now?"

"In the living room," Hilton answered. "But maybe a doctor could help those men—"

"Look, Mister, we know our job, so don't try to tell us what to do, see?"

"Well, I just thought—"

"We want to see Mrs. Blount," a hard voice insisted.

"Sure. Come in. That way— She's in the living room."

Cross heard feet coming down the hallway. Eva sat up, supported by Menti's arm. Two policemen, tall and seemingly of Irish extraction, came into the room and at once stopped dead in their tracks at the sight of the dark face of Cross. The older of the two policemen stared at Cross, Eva, Menti, then at Hilton, and finally his large, bold, grey eyes rested on Cross again.

"What's the matter with you people? Are you color blind?" he demanded with a faint sneer on his lips.

"Who are you?" Menti asked.

"Lieutenant Farrel. This is Officer Clark, my aide." He turned toward Eva. "Are you Mrs. Blount?"

"I am," Eva whispered.

"What seems to be the trouble, lady," Farrel asked.

"My husband— He's downstairs— I'm afraid he's hurt— He had an argument with the landlord, Mr. Herndon—"

"Who are these people?" Lieutenant Farrel asked, glancing at Menti and then Cross.

"My name's Herbert Menti, a friend of Mrs. Blount. And this is Lionel Lane, who lives here."

"*You* live here?" Farrel asked Cross, lifting his eyebrows.

"Yes," Cross answered.

"Why?"

"Why not?" Cross countered.

Farrel stared, then rocked back on his heels and looked over the people. "Are you *married* to anybody here?" Farrel demanded.

"No. I room here. I'm a student," Cross said.

"Uh huh," Farrel said.

"Is there anything illegal with Mr. Lane's being here?" Hilton asked pointedly.

"No," Farrel said, pulling down the corners of his mouth. "It's legal, just *legal*."

There was silence in the room as the pounding of feet on the stairs was heard. An officer stumbled through the door, panting, his face red and his eyes round with shock.

"Farrel, downstairs—" he gasped. "Quick, man— Wheeew! Looks like they bashed each other to death! It's a regular slaughterhouse, for real . . . You have to *see* it to believe it—"

"*Two?*" Farrel asked, his mouth dropping open.

"Yep. *Two*, no less."

Cross's eyes went quickly to Eva's face. Could she cope with this? He saw her hesitate a second, then rise, her eyes blazing with disbelief.

"No, *no* . . . ! *What* are you saying? Gil, Gil, *Gil*!" she screamed.

"Lady," Farrel called to her.

"Oh, my poor Gil!" Eva cried, running toward the door.

Farrel grabbed her. Eva struggled, trying to break loose.

"Let me go; let me go . . . Gil— Gil—"

She pulled from Farrel's arms and sank to the floor, sobbing convulsively.

"They've killed my poor husband— Oh, God, help poor Gil—"

"Is that his wife?" the new policeman asked.

"Yes," Menti answered.

"You'd better get her to lie down," Clark said.

"Eva, come with me," Menti said, lifting Eva from the floor. "Darling, take it easy— We don't know for sure yet—"

"I want to go to Gil," she cried.

"No, no; you must stay here," Menti insisted. "Lie here on the sofa—"

Cross was transfixed. She had done it. She had conquered her genuine grief and had replaced it with a pretended one, and somehow he felt that the pretended one was more real than the other. It rang with a sincerity that stemmed from a conscious act of creation.

". . . one used a table leg and the other a fire poker, it seems," the cop was explaining to Farrel.

Farrel's eyes widened in wonder.

"Is it too late to do anything for 'em?" Hilton asked, making sure to include Herndon in his question.

"Clark, stand guard here," Farrel said, ignoring Hilton. He beckoned the other policeman. "Come on. We'll have to get the Medical Examiner if what you say is true . . ."

Grim-lipped, Clark towered over Eva, Menti, Hilton and Cross. Sounds of voices and commotions could be heard downstairs now.

"He didn't seem to like you, Lane," Hilton said.

"Look," the policeman on guard held up his hand in a warning. "I must tell you that I can repeat anything I hear you say, see? So be careful."

"I don't give a damn what you do," Hilton shot at the cop. "I've nothing to hide here. None of us has. Now, I say that that damned Lieutenant Farrel made some nasty cracks here about Mr. Lane. He called us color-blind. He wanted to know if Lane was married to anybody here . . . Now, you can damn well repeat *that* to Headquarters, if you want to. If you don't, I will. Mr. Lane has more than a legal right to be here."

The cop reddened with embarrassment.

"I reckon you got something there, buddy," he said in tones of conciliation.

Cross assumed a relaxed, detached air to what was

happening, but he managed to keep a furtive eye on
Eva. He had enough insight into the psychological reactions of white Americans in racial matters to know
that there were possible two main lines of development
in the events under way: the average cop would either
consider him fair game and concentrate upon him as a
Negro, or he would seize upon the Communist political angle for purposes of public exploitation. I'm going
to sit tight and see which way the cat jumps, Cross
mused, feeling proud that he was conscious of their
consciousness. It was, of course, possible, but not
probable, that they might combine the two issues and
whip up a lynch atmosphere. Barring some fantastic
fact coming to light, he did not see how they could
think of him in relation to the deaths of Gil and Herndon. And, even if they did, there were the machinating
temperaments of both Hilton and Menti working to
advance the organizational interests of the Party by
placing the blame for Gil's death on Herndon, and
thereby protecting him.

He noticed that Eva was now as calm as marble. Ball-
ing a handkerchief in her right fist, she sat looking
bleakly in front of her. His eyes caught hers and he saw
in them a glint of recognition. Yes, she's with me. She
thinks I'm a victim too . . . Her sense of guilt was
throwing her on his side; she had long been wanting
to be free of Gil and now that she was free she wants
to unburden her guilt on to someone else, on to Herndon . . .

Lieutenant Farrel came back into the room, puffing
from climbing the stairs; his heavy brows were knitted
in perplexity. Following him was another policeman
with a notebook and pencil in hand. He demanded the
names, ages, occupations, and identification of all
present. Cross accounted for himself as a student and

showed his birth certificate and draft card. Hilton was a
free lance writer and Menti spoke of himself as an un-
employed printer. The room was quiet; no one volunteered any further information. The burden of getting at
what happened fell upon Farrel, and he was a more
chastened man now that he had seen the charnel house
in Herndon's living room.

"Well, who'll lead off and tell what happened?"

There was silence. Menti looked at Hilton and Hilton
looked at Cross. Cross cleared his throat and spoke in
low, polite tones:

"I'm afraid that you'll have to rely upon me for the
details as to how this started."

Farrel was impressed at the manner in which Cross
spoke.

"And what did you have to do with it?"

"Nothing, directly. But I saw Mr. Herndon striking
Mr. Blount with a fire poker . . ."

Under questioning by Farrel, Cross related what had
been agreed upon among him and Hilton and Menti.
He kept his account terse, making no interpretations at
all, leaving the cops to make their own inferences. Farrel
frowned, looking from face to face. Briefly, Hilton related how he had received two phone calls, one from
Eva and another from Lionel. He told of phoning the
police, of picking up his friend Menti, and rushing over.
He related how they had found Lionel and Eva huddled
in fear in the apartment, how they had gone down and
bashed in the door and found the men lying there,
bloody, still . . .

"We didn't tell Mrs. Blount anything . . . We waited
for you . . ." Hilton wound up.

"Madam, do you know of any reason why anyone
would want to kill your husband?" Farrel asked Eva.

Eva rose magnificently to the question; she threw her

hands to her mouth and screamed: "He killed my husband! He killed poor Gil!"

"You mean that *Herndon* killed him?" Hilton demanded, looking at Farrel. "Didn't he?"

"We don't know," Farrel said.

"But there are eyewitnesses who saw Herndon beating Blount . . ." said Menti.

"That's for the Medical Examiner to say," Farrel hedged.

"But where *were* you guys?" Hilton demanded. "I phoned you thirty minutes ago. I got here in ten minutes—"

"We're pretty busy these days," Farrel said sadly. "We got here as soon as we could— This may be a job for the D.A."

Cross was attention. *Ely Houston?* God . . . Would Houston recall his false name? He was certain that Houston had a vivid recollection of the talk they had had in his compartment on the train. Houston was capable of finding out the truth about him, could even *guess* the truth . . . Houston, a hunchback, an outsider, a man whose physical deformity had forced him to live in but not of the normal rounds of ritualized life, knew the demonic feelings of men who played god because he himself was of the demonic clan, having hidden his kinship with the rebellious by publicly upholding the laws and promises that men live by . . . And Cross knew that his crimes were of a nature that Houston would not only find engrossing but challenging. Houston understood those rare-judgment-feelings that made men kill for no motives defined or known in the realms of law. Cross had no real fear of Farrel, or Clark, or the other flatfoots who wandered blunderingly in and out of the apartment, but for Houston he had something akin to terror . . . The cops were baffled, half-scared men who hid their bewilderment by loud-mouthed blustering; but Houston was so placed psychologically in life that he would feel intuitively at home with his crimes, for he was akin to Gil, to Herndon, to Hilton, and to Cross in temperament and outlook; he had the kind of consciousness that could grasp the mercurial emotions of men whom society had never tamed or disciplined, men whose will had never been broken, men who were wild but sensitive, savage but civilized, intellectual but somehow intrinsically poetic in their inmost hearts.

Farrel left the room and made a lengthy telephone call in the hallway; at last he came in with his verdict.

"All of you must consider yourselves under house arrest," he began. "I'm posting an officer at the door of the apartment for tonight. There are a lot of questions that must be answered. In the morning all of you must face the District Attorney and give him your stories and account for yourselves. The Medical Examiner is downstairs working now—"

"But what is the meaning of this?" Hilton demanded.

"We must determine how those men died downstairs—" Farrel said.

"But it's all very simple," Menti said.

"Mr. Lane told you what happened," Hilton said.

"I'm only obeying orders," Farrel said.

"You mean we have to stay here all night—?" Menti asked.

"Absolutely," Farrel snapped.

"But my wife; she'll be upset," Menti objected.

"You got a phone at home?"

"Yes."

"Then call her," Farrel directed.

"And I'll have to stay too?" Hilton demanded.

"I'm afraid so, sir," Farrel said.

"But *why?*"

"Listen, I'm acting under the orders of the District Attorney. He is acting according to the reports he's getting from the Medical Examiner downstairs. If you want to, I can take you to see an Assistant D.A. Maybe you can arrange something with him . . ."

"The hell with it," Hilton said.

Eva was weeping now afresh.

"I want to see Gil," she sobbed. "Please, please—"

"I'm sorry, lady," Clark said. "They've taken his body to the Morgue."

" . . . and it looks like they killed each other," Farrel was saying in a low voice to another officer.

"It's the most freakish thing I ever saw," the other officer said.

Finally Cross, Eva, Hilton, and Menti were alone; the police had gone, stationing a young cop on guard in the hallway in front of the apartment door. For awhile there was silence among the four of them. Eva was weeping noiselessly but earnestly now, and Cross observed that her grief at this moment had none of that spontaneousness of emotion that had characterized the grief she had pretended for the cops. She was free now; her secret wish had come true . . . Was that why she was weeping?

Cross was frantically trying to weigh all the possibilities involved. Could the Party let Eva, with her guilty knowledge, go free? And the Party's attitude toward him? For the moment the Party was his ally, but Communists were not naïve enough to accept him merely on a basis of a declaration of solidarity. They wanted something more . . . And what could that be . . . ? For its own defense, the Party was trying to dump Eva into his arms, knowing that black and white love could find shelter nowhere else so readily as under its red aegis . . .

Well, for the time being, he'd accept the situation as it was, but not for the Party's reasons . . .

Cross watched Hilton. Eva was resting on the sofa with her face buried in the crook of her elbow, her chest heaving. Menti patted her shoulder. Hilton paced the floor, puffing at the inevitable cigarette that protruded from his lips.

"It didn't go too badly," Hilton spoke as though wanting to share his thoughts. "But, of course, the real showdown will come in the morning with the D.A." He looked at Cross. "You did well. Maintain the same attitude tomorrow. We're behind you."

"I'll try," Cross mumbled; he wondered if he ought to tell Hilton that he had already met the District Attorney. He decided not to; there was no purpose in adding items that would inflame Hilton's already suspicious mind. I'll try to take care of it when it comes, he told himself. But Hilton worried him. The man was *too* calm, *too* collected, his face always a tense, blank mask. How *much* of his reactions was he concealing . . . ?

"I'm sleepy," Hilton said, stretching his arms above his head and giving a yawn that was *too* genuine.

"Why don't you and Menti sleep in Gil's room," Eva suggested in a whisper.

"Okay, I'm turning in," Hilton said. But even now he did not demonstrate any feeling of sympathy for Eva. "Good night," he said, and headed for the hallway.

"Is there anything I can do for you, Eva?" Cross asked.

"No. You should rest, Lionel," she said, looking pityingly at him. "We brought you into a mess, didn't we? I'm sorry . . ."

"Good night," Menti called to her.

An hour later Cross was in bed, turning sleeplessly from side to side, trying mentally to cope with the threat of Ely Houston. What would he think of these deaths? Would he not think it somewhat odd that both Gil and Herndon had been men of extreme ideas? Oh, God . . . Cross sat upright in bed with a wild jerk of his body. Jesus . . . *That bloody handkerchief . . . !* He had to get rid of it before the District Attorney showed up in the morning; it had been in the pocket of his pants until now . . . He got out of bed, pulled on his bathrobe, took the wadded handkerchief and put it into the pocket of the robe and quietly opened the door to the hallway. The apartment was quiet and dark. If anybody demanded where he was going, he could always say that he was on his way to the bathroom . . . He stole silently down the dark hallway to the door of the kitchen. He paused, listening for sounds, then turned the knob, pushed the door inward, and went inside. Faint blue light fell through a window, casting a ghostly radiance over the gas stove, the sink, and the refrigerator. Yes, there was the incinerator . . . He could see and would not have to turn on the light. He crossed the floor and lifted the lid and tossed the guilty handkerchief quickly down. He smelt a whiff of smoke; it would burn soon. His tension ebbed a bit. He turned to go to his room and, like thunder, the kitchen light blazed on. He caught his breath; Hilton was sitting in a chair near the wall, the habitual cigarette hanging unlit from his lips.

"I didn't know you were there," Cross breathed, struggling to stifle his panic.

"What's the matter?" Hilton asked. "You can't sleep either?"

Cross thought rapidly. Had Hilton seen him throw the handkerchief away? He did not think so. Then his job now was to act naturally and not rouse Hilton's suspicions.

"I thought I'd get a glass of milk," Cross mumbled. "Ha-ha— I threw my cigarette down the incinerator— I smoke too much." Ought he have said that? Good God, this sonofabitch Hilton . . .

Moving self-consciously, he took a tumbler from a cupboard and went to the refrigerator and poured some milk.

"Aren't you going to sleep?" Cross asked, taking a sip from the glass.

"I never sleep much," Hilton grumbled. "Just sitting, thinking . . ."

"That's a goddamn shame about Gil, isn't it?" Cross felt compelled to say.

"Yeah," Hilton drawled.

"I should've broken down that damned door," Cross accused himself.

"You did what he told you to, didn't you? You've nothing to worry about."

"Yes. But to die like that—"

"A Communist is a soldier, Lane. He's prepared to die."

"I'm so new at all of this—"

"You're not so new. You know what you're doing."

"But I don't understand—"

"You understand enough," Hilton cut him short.

· What was Hilton thinking? The very manner in which he spoke bothered Cross. But what the hell! He was going to sleep . . . Hilton knew nothing yet.

"I'm tired; good night," Cross said.

"Good night, Lane," Hilton said, staring at the far wall.

Had Hilton seen anything? He went down the hall-way, then paused, listening. There were no sounds. No, Hilton had seen nothing; if he had, he surely would have said something about it. Hilton was no bashful boy . . . Now that he felt out of danger, Cross's heart began to pound with excitement. If Hilton had caught him with that bloody handkerchief, he would have been in Hilton's power for the rest of his life. He would either have had to kill Hilton on the spot, or make a break for it through one of the windows of the apartment. To be in the power of a cold little god like Hilton was about the most awful thing that could happen to a man. He would have trampled on me night and day, Cross thought, shivering with relief. He entered his room and, fumbling in the dark, he pulled off his robe and got into bed.

"Lionel—"

It was Eva's voice coming from nearby; it was low and plaintive. Terror flooded him. Maybe they *all* knew what he had done!

"Eva?"

"Yes."

What was she doing here in his room in the dark? Did she know that he had just burned the handkerchief? He reached out to turn on the light and his hand knocked over a book.

"No," Eva whispered.

He felt her fingers seize hold of his hand.

"Don't turn on the light."

"What's the matter, Eva?"

He felt both of her hands now gripping his own, as though she was trying to hang on to him for life's sake.

"I didn't know you were out of your room," she began, her voice catching in her throat. "I knocked and when you didn't answer, I came in . . ."

Cross felt hot tears dropping on to his fingers.

"Lionel, forgive me— But I'm so *scared*— And I'm so much *alone*— You'll never know how alone I am— I'm bothering you, I know— But I can't stay in my

room alone," she sobbed. "Oh, God, I'm no good—
I'm *too* scared—" For a second she was silent. Then she
spoke again in a changed tone of voice: "You're colored
and you're strong. I'll never know how you manage to
face those awful people and never flinch or quail . . .
You're prepared for them and I'm not . . . Have pity on
me and let me stay here near you . . ."

Her breathing filled the black darkness. Her soul was
reaching gropingly toward him for protection, advice,
solace. Cross smiled, feeling that he was listening to her
words as perhaps God listened to prayers . . . A wave
of hot pride flooded him. She was laying her life at his
feet. With but a gesture of his hand he could own her,
shield her from the Party, from fear, from her own sense
of guilt . . .

"You'll be cold," he said softly.

"No, no . . . I'll be all right."

"Here; take my robe . . ."

"All right," she consented.

He heard her moving amid a rustling of garments in
the dark, and then he felt her hands again, her fingers
entwining themselves in his own.

"You don't mind, Lionel? Please, don't send me away
. . ."

"No, Eva."

"I just can't stand fear, and I'm full of fear when I'm
alone in times like these . . . And I've been scared so
long . . ."

"Just rest easy. You'll be all right. Don't worry . . ."

"I thought you'd understand . . . Listen, don't tell
the others I came in here," she begged convulsively.
"I'm ashamed of being so scared."

"No one will ever know," he told her.

"I don't mind so much if I cry before *you*, but I could

never cry before *them*," she whispered. "And I *need* to cry . . ."

Her weeping now was real, different from the pretended weeping for the Party and different from the weeping she had done in front of Hilton and Menti. In front of the universe of white skins, she was too frozen with fear to cry; but with people of color who she felt were victims and, hence, more understanding, she could weep without check. He wanted to lift her from the floor and take her into the bed, but he felt that such would violate her budding trust.

"Lionel," she called in a whisper.

"Yes?"

She controlled her sobbing and was silent for some moments.

"We could have saved Gil," she whimpered.

"But, Eva, how could we know that that would happen?" he asked her gently, trying to purge her of her sense of guilt.

"But the Party might think that we *let* him be killed," she whispered.

She was not confessing to him, but she was near it.

"But, *why*?" he asked in make-believe astonishment.

She wept afresh, resting her head on his shoulder, gripping his hands rigidly, convulsively.

"You don't understand," she said despairingly. "People are worse than you think . . . They treat you bad because you're colored, but me— People like me, they take our *lives* away . . ."

He was silent. He had given his life away. How could he ever tell her that he understood what had blasted her self-confidence?

"You'll be all right," he said gently.

"You shouldn't be in this. You've suffered enough—"

"I'm used to it, Eva."

"Why's there so much cruelty? I want to die; life's *too* much, *too* much . . ." Her breathing came loud and hoarse. "Is it wrong to feel like that, Lionel?"

"We all feel it. But we have to fight it," he told her.

"Did you ever want to kill yourself?"

"Yes."

"Oh, Lionel!"

Her fingers gripped his like bands of steel. Then he felt her fingers disengage themselves from his and a moment later they were touching his lips, eyes, his hair, tenderly, softly.

"Those cops were horrible to you tonight, weren't they?"

"It was nothing."

"I'm so sorry, Lionel," she sighed. "You have it hard enough, and then we drag you into this . . ."

He understood. She was pitying him for his being black and having to take the scoffs and insults of the white world; and, in doing so, she was pitying him for the wrong reasons. But he could not tell her that. Oh, God . . . If only he could find a way of begging her pity for his having killed Gil, for his having let his soul take on the shape of monstrousness, for his having forsaken his humanity. That was the pitying he needed . . . He knew that Eva, too, had been forced to live as an outsider; she, too, in a different sort of way, was on his side. Maybe, in the future, he could tell her, could unburden himself and feel free once before he died?

He felt her moving and then she was sliding into bed with him.

"Just hold me a little, Lionel," she whispered, shivering and clinging to him.

He held her, feeling her hot tears on his face.

"I'm so cold, so scared, so lost," she sobbed.

At last she grew quiet and later he could tell that she had gone to sleep. It was then that he knew he loved her, wanted to try to banish the dread that haunted her, wanted to tell her what he knew of terror and hopelessness. He held in his arms one woman who was willing to understand, whom life had so tempered that he could talk to her, but between them stood a wall not of race but of mutual guilt, blood, and mistaken identity . . .

Pale dawn crept into the room. Cross looked down at Eva's wan face; she slept as one exhausted. He shook her gently, calling softly to her:

"Eva . . ."

Her eyes fluttered open; when she saw him, she buried her face in his bosom.

"Darling, go to your room," he told her. "It's better that way with Hilton and Menti in the apartment."

"Yes; you're right, Lionel."

She kissed him lightly on his lips and whispered: "Thank you, darling."

And she was gone. The more he thought of her the more he began to care about what would happen to him. Could he fight his way through and have this girl? It seemed impossible, yet that was what he wanted. I mustn't think about it, he told himself. He closed his eyes, but he could still smell the faint odor of her hair, feel the delicate pressure of her fingers upon his face, her lips on his . . . He gritted his teeth and mumbled aloud: Oh, goddamn . . .

Hilton roused him at eight-thirty by rapping on the door.

"Lane, come and get some coffee," Hilton called.

Cross tumbled from bed. Oh, yes . . . He would change his suit . . . And at the first opportunity he would get rid of the clothes he had worn when he had struck down Gil and Herndon . . .

When he went into the kitchen, he found that Hilton had set up breakfast. Eva and Menti were already at the table. Cross sat and began sipping his coffee. What about that bloody handkerchief? Hilton was busy making toast and everything seemed normal. He saw Hilton go to the incinerator and dump some waste paper into it. Yes, he was safe for the time being . . .

Menti ate broodingly. Hilton moved quickly about the kitchen like a man who must either do something or become exasperated. Cross let his eyes rest on Eva; she was pale and tired, looking off into space; finally she did glance at him and there flitted into her eyes a sign that she was with him; he felt better.

The doorbell rang and Hilton started nervously.

"This is it, I think," Hilton said.

Hilton left and a moment later, before Cross could prepare himself, the hunched form of Ely Houston filled the doorway. Cross stared unblinkingly. Houston entered the kitchen and paused; his eyes traveled swiftly around the room and at last rested on Cross.

"Well," Houston exclaimed, "what in the world are you doing here?"

Cross stood, smiled, and reached out his hand to Houston who shook it warmly.

"How are you, Mr. Houston?" Cross said evenly. "I live here."

"At last I've tracked you down," Houston said.

Hilton, Menti, and Eva were thunderstruck. Hilton was staring at Cross with an open mouth and Cross could tell that he was thinking that maybe he was a police spy.

"How is it that you know the District Attorney?" Hilton asked softly.

"Mr. Houston and I have met before," Cross explained lightly.

Houston advanced into the kitchen, followed by Farrel and a tall, lean, grey-haired man on whose chest Cross could see a police badge. Farrel too stared at Cross and said:

"Why didn't you tell me you were a big-shot, boy?"

"I'm not," Cross said.

Everyone was standing now except Eva; tension and distrust hung in the air. The tall, lean man stood in one corner and surveyed the faces of Cross, Menti, and Hilton.

"I've asked about you," Houston began, addressing himself to Cross, "but I couldn't get a line on you . . . I'll never forget that talk we had. Know one thing? I made notes on your ideas." Houston seemed to have forgotten that he had come to investigate the deaths of two men; he was excited and seemed in a holiday mood. "Now, what was it you said . . . ?" Houston paused, ran his hand into his pocket and pulled out a notebook. "I've got it right here, you see." As he thumbed the leaves, the tall man stared in bewilderment at Houston, saying nothing. "Ha— Here it is: 'Man is nothing in particular . . .' You see? I don't forget."

"I see you don't," Cross said.

Hilton was so nervous that he could not control the shaking of his hands. Menti stared, but there was a sardonic smile on his thin lips. Only Eva was listening to Houston.

"Well, what is this all about?" Houston asked of Cross, rubbing his hands together. "We can talk about special problems later— Oh, yes— What was the name you gave me?"

"The name is Lane, Lionel Lane," Cross said.

"Lionel Lane," Houston repeated, paused; then went on. "Mr. Lane, this is the Medical Examiner, Dr. Stockton . . ."

Cross nodded to Dr. Stockton and the doctor nodded to him.

"Farrel," Houston demanded. "What have we got here?"

As Farrel outlined to Houston what he had found downstairs, Houston moved with vacant eyes about the kitchen, his lips pursed, his hat in his hand, his hump seeming to follow him. He walked softly, flat-footedly, as if he feared that he would disturb some delicate process of thought by jarring his brain. He began to frown as Farrel described details of the scene of blood and death.

"And these two men, what were their backgrounds?" Houston asked at last.

"That's a damned strange thing, Mr. D.A.," Farrel said. "Gilbert Blount was a member of the Central Committee of the Communist Party of the United States—"

"You're kidding," Houston protested with wide eyes.

"No, sir," Farrel insisted. "It's a fact—"

"And who's the other one?"

"His twin. A Fascist, they say—"

"What's his name?"

"Langley Herndon—"

Houston snapped his finger, as though trying to recall something.

"Langley Herndon . . . ! Ah! I remember him— He used to write for the *Crusader* sometimes," Houston said. "Hunh! A violent baby— Bloodthirsty— Welcomed Hitler and publicly lauded his extermination of the Jews. Said that America should use the Negro as a scapegoat around which to unify the nation—" He looked at Cross and smiled. "Herndon was perfectly cynical. He argued that anything could be done for any reason . . . He had the Negro singled out as a target, a menace, a danger . . . The Negro was America's ace in the hole if the nation ever experienced any real internal stress. You could say that the nigger was the cause of it and get the rest of the nation to forget its problems and unite to get rid of the niggers . . . Ingenious, hunh?" Houston chuckled and turned to Dr. Stockton. "Well, Doc, how does it look to you? What's your verdict?"

Dr. Stockton cleared his throat, advanced to the kitchen table and rested his briefcase upon it. He took out a sheaf of papers and leafed through them. He lifted his eyes at last to Houston.

"Mr. District Attorney, this is either very simple or very complicated . . ."

"Make it simple," Houston said.

"I'll let you decide that," Dr. Stockton said.

"Oh, wait a minute," Houston interrupted him. He turned and faced Eva, Hilton, Menti, and Cross. "Who are these people? Is anybody here related to either Blount or Herndon?"

"This is Mrs. Blount," Cross told Houston.

"Oh, Madam, I beg your pardon," Houston apologized. "If I'd known it was you, I'd not have spoken as I have. I'm awfully sorry . . ."

"It's nothing," Eva mumbled.

"These things are unpleasant, but we have to get these facts straight— Oh, yes; and the other two gentlemen?"

Farrel introduced Hilton and Menti as friends of Eva.

"All right, Dr. Stockton, you may proceed—"

"Well, Mr. District Attorney, I've all the reports right here. What we can make of these reports is quite another matter. Our Pathological Chemist, Dr. Reddick, has submitted a mass of details. I'll begin first with Blount . . ." He began reading from the report: " 'Multiple incised wounds of scalp; congestion and oedema of brain . . .' "

"Dr. Stockton," Houston interrupted him. "Forgive me— Suppose we save all that for the formal hearing, eh? Right now I just want to know if I'm to look for a murderer or not. Give me this wrapped up in a nutshell . . ."

"Right," Dr. Stockton replied, putting his papers aside. "To all intents and purposes, Mr. District Attorney, these two blokes battered each other to death. All concrete evidence points toward that . . . Let's take that aspect of it first . . . And, mind you, I'm leaving out all question of motive for the time being . . . The definite ascertaining of a different motive could alter the entire picture of our findings . . . Now, due to the great disorder of the room downstairs, we've not yet been able to reconstruct exactly what happened. Yet, the concrete evidence we possess points to the fact of an argument that led to a fist fight . . . There's evidence that Herndon attempted strangulation upon Blount . . . Blount must have freed himself, for the next stage of the fight was with the fire poker. Who grabbed the fire poker first, we do not know. Now, here's the strange thing. *Both* men bear evidence of having been hit with the poker, which means that during the course of the fight the poker must have been lost from the possession of one or the other of the men. In other words, they took turns in lamming each other . . . Follow me?"

"You're saying," Houston paraphrased, "that one man could have dropped the fire poker and the other could have grabbed it?"

"Or," Dr. Stockton added, "one could have wrested the poker from the hands of the other. That happens quite frequently in brawls. A man is pounding another man's brains out with a pop bottle. The other takes the bottle away from him and starts in with the bottle upon the aggressor with the aggressor's own weapon . . . Well, that seems to have happened at the beginning of this fight.

"Now, a third stage of the fight comes. The table leg is now used as the weapon. Just how they got hold of it, we do not know. It seems utterly unlikely that either of the two men had time enough to stop the fight and break that leg off the table. We surmise that one of them crashed against the table in falling and broke the table, the leg coming off, breaking in two . . . The first man who saw that table leg dived for it and took it as his weapon.

"At the present moment, with what we've got to go on, we surmise that Blount got hold of the leg first—"

"How do you figure that?"

"It's a guess," Dr. Stockton said. "The most single powerful blow dealt with that table leg was against the forehead of Herndon . . . That blow could have caused death, not at once, but certainly Herndon would have died of it eventually. Most certainly he was stunned by it and we further surmise that he kept on his feet and continued the fight . . . Now, here's another strange fact in a strange case. *Both* men bear marks of that table leg on their heads . . . That can only be accounted for, too, on the basis that the table leg, like the fire poker, changed hands during the course of the fight, which is highly likely . . . *But,* and this puzzles me, was Herndon *able*, physically *able* to deliver such death-dealing blows upon Blount's head *after* he had received that crushing blow to his own forehead . . . ? Yet the facts point to such. It's possible . . . Men have been known to possess remarkable strength just before dying; men have been known to aim and fire a gun with sharp accuracy and then die straightaway . . . *If* Herndon was able to deal a death-dealing blow to Blount, after having received such a blow himself, then the case is simple."

"Is there any way of telling, Dr. Stockton, how much *time* intervened between these blows?" Houston asked.

"That's impossible," Dr. Stockton said. "Our impression is that those blows were all delivered at approximately the same time. At the most, a half hour could have intervened, but we think the whole fracas took place in about fifteen minutes."

"In other words, you don't think that one man could have been knocked out, could have come to, and resumed the fight . . . ?" Houston asked.

"That's highly speculative," the doctor said. "It *would* explain how Herndon was able to deal such hard blows after he had been mortally wounded. There are some 'ifs' here . . . But these 'ifs' only make the whole picture more complicated." Dr. Stockton paused and pulled forth a batch of photographs from his briefcase. "This is how they looked when the officers arrived . . ." He handed the photographs to Houston.

Rocking on his heels, Houston looked at the photographs and his eyes bulged with suppressed horror. Cross could see a slanting glimpse of the pictures and at once there leaped into his mind the image of that red room with its flickering flames and the two still, bloody forms stretched out on the carpet, drenched in their own blood . . .

"Lovely," Houston commented softly, returning the photographs to Dr. Stockton. He turned to look at Eva. "Would the lady mind excusing herself?" Houston asked.

"Not at all," Eva said; she rose and left the kitchen.

Cross's eyes followed her with anxiety as her wan, tight face went from view.

"There's no use in her hearing this sordid mess," Houston mumbled. He rubbed his hands together, glanced about the room, and then spoke in a loud, sonorous voice:

"Perfect setup. Two extremes meet. A plus and a minus— And they cancel each other out . . . And who could hate each other more than two men like that? It's the Russian-German war all over again, eh? Could be . . . Sounds like it. It fits, doesn't it? Motives? Dr. Stockton, you spoke of leaving out motives . . . Why? You have all the motives on earth here, my dear doctor. These two men were totally opposed to each other in all aspects of life. You might call such motives *natural life* motives . . . Oh, I know that there is no such thing in law as that. But there will be one day . . . I'm sure of it. We might call such motives jealousy. But it's total jealousy. The kind of jealousy the Bible speaks of when it refers to God's being a jealous God, hunh?" Houston looked around the room and smiled.

Cross was trembling; he felt that maybe Houston knew that he was guilty and was mocking him. Was Houston teasing him by speaking his *own* ideas out loud, testing them on the people present? Whose ideas belonged to whom? What crazy luck he had in having this hunchback, the one man he had ever met who understood him, to track him down? Did Houston know how maddeningly close he stood to the truth?

"There's another possibility," Dr. Stockton's voice sounded patiently.

"There are millions of possibilities," Houston said, waving his hand. He looked at Cross. "Of course, there's this problem of Herndon hating to have Negroes in his building, but I take it that that was simply a tiny aspect of his total jealousy toward Blount—"

Hilton and Menti were silent, tight-lipped, staring

first at Houston and then at Cross. Cross waited, wondering what other versions of the crime did the Medical Examiner have in mind.

"So they killed each other," Houston went on. He turned to Farrel. "According to you, Herndon killed Blount, hunh? Yes, he was seen standing over Blount with the fire poker . . . He was strong enough to chase Mrs. Blount up the steps with a gun . . . That fits. He later dies of wounds that Blount had inflicted on him. A double murder, or double manslaughter, whatever you want to call it." Houston faced Dr. Stockton. "Is that more or less your opinion?"

A trace of hesitancy showed in Dr. Stockton's eyes; then he shrugged and said:

"More or less."

"More or less?" Houston was astonished. "What's your reservation?"

"Somebody could have come upon them while they were fighting and killed them both," Dr. Stockton said somewhat sheepishly; he was obviously embarrassed at the farfetched nature of his theory.

Cross felt suspended over a bottomless void. He had thought that Houston would have arrived at that solution first; but, no, it was Dr. Stockton who had put his finger on the truth.

"Good Lord!" Houston exclaimed. "Why can't you fellows take facts just as you find them? Why do you want to make life more complicated than it is, and it's damn well complicated, if you ask me. Now, Dr. Stockton, what motive on earth could anybody have in coming upon those two men fighting and then killing the both of them?"

"I don't know." Dr. Stockton shrugged his shoulders.

"I don't know either," Houston said. "The damned thing's simple. Two hotheads met and had a fight over their total views of life. They fought. One died and then the other died. And for my money, there's something of poetic justice in the whole damn thing."

"Is that the official interpretation, Mr. District Attorney?" Dr. Stockton asked.

"Oh, Dr. Stockton, I'm not trying to encroach upon your duties," Houston said, smiling blandly. "If not this interpretation, then what have you to offer?"

"I don't know," Dr. Stockton said. He turned to Cross and stared at him for several seconds. "You're the young man who saw them fighting?"

"Yes, sir," Cross answered.

"What time did Blount go down to see Herndon?" Dr. Stockton asked.

"It was about ten past nine o'clock," Cross answered.

"How do you know that?" the doctor asked.

"Just before leaving the dinner table, Mr. Blount looked at his watch and told the time to us, and said he had to leave."

Houston came forward and stood in front of Cross. Cross felt that his feet were resting on air, that he could sink right down through the floor.

"How long was Blount gone from the apartment before you went down there?" Houston asked.

Cross frowned, thinking. He felt that it was not really a matter of time; either they found a motive, *his* motive, and accused him or they did not. So he could tell the truth.

"That's really hard to say . . . It's better to tell you what happened. Mrs. Blount was worried. I was too. I offered to go down with Blount, to help him, defend him if anything happened . . . But he wouldn't hear of it. He was a proud man . . . And Mrs. Blount warned me not to interfere. She said he'd be angry, wildly angry if I did . . . I was helping Mrs. Blount clear away the things from the table. Then we began hearing loud voices. We knew that they were quarreling. I offered to go down and Mrs. Blount said no, that he'd be angry. I went to my room and was lying on my bed . . . It was then that I heard that loud noise, like something breaking, a big piece of wood . . . That was the table, maybe . . ."

"No doubt," Dr. Stockton said. "Go on . . ."

"Mrs. Blount came running to me. She was terribly upset. It seems—"

"How long were you in the room before Mrs. Blount came running to you?" Dr. Stockton asked.

"I don't know," Cross said truthfully. "Maybe five minutes; maybe longer . . ."

"And Mrs. Blount asked you to go down?"

"Well, not exactly . . . She didn't seem to know what to do . . . So I offered to go down. But she said no. Then we heard a scream—"

"Could you tell who it was that screamed?"

"No," Cross said honestly. "This time I said I'd go down, and she agreed . . . But she was still afraid. You see, really, she was more afraid of Blount himself than of anything happening to him. The moment I got downstairs in the hallway, I knew a fight was going on . . . I ran to the door, opened it, and saw Herndon beating Blount with the fire poker . . . Blount was on the floor and Herndon had his foot on his chest and was lamming away. I didn't hear Mrs. Blount come down, but all at once I felt her hand touching my back. She started screaming and Herndon saw us . . . He came at us with the fire poker . . . I blocked him just long enough for Mrs. Blount to run upstairs, and Herndon swiped me across the shoulder with the poker . . ." Cross paused, pulled off his coat, opened his shirt and showed his shoulder.

"Why didn't you call the police?" Houston wanted to know.

"When I got upstairs, Mrs. Blount was calling the police . . . She didn't seem able to get connections . . . She asked me to call, then she ran out of the room to go downstairs again . . . I was scared she'd get hurt, so I ran after her, caught her on the landing and brought her back to the apartment. We kept hearing the fighting; there were shouts, screams . . . Mrs. Blount asked me to phone the police—"

"And didn't you phone?" Houston asked.

"No; I wanted to try to help Mr. Blount . . . I told her to phone and I ran downstairs. But I found the door locked this time. I rattled the knob— I called, yelled— I could hear 'em fighting—"

"Whose name did you call?" Dr. Stockton asked.

"Mr. Blount's name. I didn't know what to do. I went back upstairs and—"

"How long were you downstairs the second time?"

"I don't know. Maybe five minutes, maybe longer . . . When I went back to tell Mrs. Blount, she told me that she'd phoned Mr. Hilton and that Mr. Hilton was phoning the police. You see, she thought surely that Mr. Blount was coming up with me. And when I told her that he was still down there, she went really wild . . . I was trying to call the police when she ran out of the door again. This time she came flying back. She said Herndon had his gun and was on his way up . . ."

"Did you see 'im?" Houston asked.

"No. I barred the door. Mrs. Blount fainted and I put water on her face . . ."

Dr. Stockton turned to Farrel, frowning.

"Where was Herndon's gun, Lieutenant?" Dr. Stockton asked.

"In the drawer of his desk," Farrel explained. "The

drawer was half-pulled out. Seems like somebody had just tossed it in there. Might have been the last thing Herndon did before he died."

"Perhaps," Dr. Stockton said slowly.

Cross was still as stone. He could feel that they were not satisfied with this interpretation, but they could find no other that would explain the facts. Houston seemed inclined to accept the picture that Cross had painted. Good. Let the doctor and his scientists discover something else, if they could. Things were not going so badly. But he had to be careful of this man Houston; after all, he may be stalling just to see how he would react. The doctor had hit upon the right solution, but he had no background of ideas to make it stick, no understanding or grasp of the range of motives that could explain it all. And Houston had that, but he seemed not to care to bother with it. Was Houston playing a game?

Dr. Stockton began putting his papers and photographs back into his briefcase.

"Well, I'll have to leave the motives to you, Mr. District Attorney," he said. "My findings are as follows: double murder or double manslaughter . . . The two men died so close together that I'd not like to say who died first, so—"

"Mr. District Attorney," Hilton spoke up for the first time. "There's more to this than you gentlemen are admitting. A man has been murdered. That man was Gilbert Blount. The murderer was Langley Herndon. Now, allow me to identify myself a little more before I continue. I'm a member of the editorial board of the *Daily Worker*. I was a colleague of Gilbert Blount. I want to protest against the light-handed manner in which this case is being handled. The issues here are basically social, and you gentlemen are playing around with probabilities and psychological facts. I'm insisting that some measure of responsibility be shown here. This case has a background of politics, sir. I said *politics*, and I mean it. And you do not want to look into that phase of it, yet the only real motives can be found there. We have *proof* that Herndon killed Blount. Mr. Lane here is an eyewitness . . . He saw Herndon striking Blount with a poker about the head . . . Herndon later struck Mr. Lane with that same fire poker. I'm speaking of the moral side of this case . . . You saw that frightened little woman who just left this room. Herndon chased that poor woman with a gun, terrorized her! Now, I maintain that it's unfair to leave the impression in the public mind that her husband was a murderer—"

Dr. Stockton had his briefcase in his hand.

"Mr. District Attorney, I must be off . . . The rest is up to you. There is no possibility of my giving you an opinion as to who died first. From a clinical point of view, we've nothing to go on. Good morning, gentlemen."

Dr. Stockton walked briskly out of the room. Hilton's thin face turned livid; he whirled to Houston and began to shout:

"Mr. District Attorney, it's but fair to warn you that the *Daily Worker* and the labor movement will fight you about any interpretation of this case that points to Blount as a murderer. He was defending his life against a fascist attack! He was defending his home, his wife, his friend against a man who has publicly advocated the extermination of all racial minorities. Herndon *sent* for Blount to come and see him. Mrs. Blount will testify to that. And Herndon was wildly angry when he did it . . . He later pulled a gun on Mrs. Blount herself . . . There was but one issue in this thing: Could Mr. Lane, a Negro, remain in this apartment? Now, you know that that is true, and so do I.

We all know it. Only yesterday morning Herndon threatened the life of Mr. Lane here . . ."

"Look, Mr.— What's your name?"

"Hilton. John Hilton."

"I see your point, Mr. Hilton," Houston said. "In this particular investigation our aim is to determine *who* died first. And that is something for the Medical Examiner to find out. I asked him who died first, and he says he doesn't know. He has thrown in the sponge. He says that they died so close together in terms of time that it's anybody's guess—"

"But there's another angle to this," Hilton was persistent. "Look, Mr. District Attorney, this Herndon has threatened Mr. Blount many times. He threatened Mr. Lane here. He had the *intent*. Now, there is a *real* difference."

"But no proof," Houston said.

"Yes, there is proof," Hilton overrode Houston. "This man's writings are fascistic. He has advocated the extermination of non-Anglo-Saxon minorities—"

"Oh, Christ, man!" Houston exploded. "That's far-fetched. If you're going to bring that up, why not cite all the Communist arguments and threats against the bourgeoisie? That would make Blount the guilty one, wouldn't it?"

"No," Hilton said.

"Why not? If you're going to be fair, you'll have to admit it," Houston insisted. "Now, look, here is how things stand. We don't know which man died first. We are not going to call this case an instance of double murder. What right has anybody to make Blount a murderer in the eyes of his wife? And, by the same token, what right has anybody to make Herndon a murderer in the eyes of his relatives even if they are not here to protect his name? All right, in the light of what the Medical Examiner has said, I'm going to call this double man-slaughter . . ."

"And we'll call it just plain murder!" Hilton's voice rose in shrill denunciation. "You're taking the side of property in this investigation—"

Cross listened with amazement. Yes, sane men did misread reality. Just as he had once had fantasies, so now he was looking at men who were passionately arguing about their own fantasies, trying to decide which fantasy was to be taken for reality. No one in the room knew the truth of what had happened but he, and yet they were ready to fight and kill, if need be, for what they thought was the truth.

"I beg your pardon, sir," Houston said.

"This is an issue of property versus the individual and his freedom!" Hilton shouted.

"I'm taking no such stand," Houston maintained.

"You're giving the benefit of the doubt to capital!" Hilton charged.

"I'm abiding by the decision of the Medical Examiner," Houston corrected him. "I'll deal with facts and facts alone . . . You're trying to read your class conscious ideas into this investigation, and the law will not accept it."

"We will charge *murder*," Hilton hissed.

Cross had his fists doubled. He wanted to scream at Hilton to stop agitating. Let sleeping dogs lie . . . The more Hilton pressed his case for a class conscious interpretation of the facts, the more dangerous it was for him. Damn Hilton . . . He was trying to prove something false anyhow. And so was Houston. Cross could see that Hilton's attack, though rejected, had somewhat disturbed Houston who was staring thoughtfully off into space. So far Houston had accepted what seemed like a straightforward and normal account of the facts, but if Hilton kept on plugging away in that dogged manner of his, why, Houston might really start thinking; and if he started thinking, there was but one other real direction for his mind to travel. And that damned Houston, if he had the will, could find out the truth . . .

"Farrel, ask Mrs. Blount to come here a moment, will you?" Houston asked.

"Yes, sir."

Farrel left the room and a moment later Eva appeared in the doorway.

"Mrs. Blount, I'm sorry this has to happen in your home," Houston began. "I must question each person here separately. I'd like the use of your living room, if I may."

"Of course," Eva answered in a lifeless manner.

"Now, Farrel, in about ten minutes, send me these people one by one," Houston instructed. "Begin with Mrs. Blount— You are well enough to answer questions, aren't you?"

"Yes," Eva whispered.

Houston went out of the kitchen.

Hilton sidled up to Cross and forced a smile.

"You are some fellow, Lane." Hilton pulled down the corners of his lips in a scowl.

"What do you mean?"

"How did you get to know *him*?"

"So you think I'm in the pay of the police, hunh?" Cross asked, laughing. "I met him once on a train. That's all." A look of doubt was still in Hilton's eyes. "If you don't believe it, then I can't help it. You can check my statements, if you like. After all, how did I know that I'd ever meet him again?"

His words seemed to have some effect, for Hilton was now a little easier in attitude.

"Just the same, I'd like to know more about that," Hilton said.

"Sure," Cross said. "Whenever you like. I've no secrets."

The hell with him, Cross thought. Only one thing worried him about Hilton. Would the man try to poison his relations with Eva? Anger rose slowly in him. He would fight for Eva. He tried to catch her eye, but she was sunk in deep thought, staring blankly before her. He longed to be at her side when she was with Houston, but he knew that that was impossible. What was to be his relationship to her now that Gil was dead? Did it mean that he would have to move from the apartment? After the police had gone, he would talk to her about it. He would tell her, openly and frankly, that he did not ever want to leave her.

Farrel came to the door.

"Mrs. Blount," he called.

Eva rose and followed Farrel into the hallway. Hilton at once closed the kitchen door and turned to Cross.

"What are your plans, Lane?"

"I have no plans," Cross told him.

"Do you intend to stay here?"

"I don't know."

"If you don't, who does?"

"I'm going to speak to Eva about it," Cross said.

"When?"

"Look, I can't very well bother her *now*," Cross protested.

Hilton paced the floor. This man is after me, but why . . . ? He thought of Bob's squirming on the floor, weeping; he thought of Bob's dodging the Immigration authorities and again he was drifting into that state of danger where he was judging others with supreme and final contempt. What right had Hilton to say

who could live and who could not live? Damn him . . .
Hilton must have sensed his mood, for he came close to
Cross and clapped him on the shoulder.

"You're okay, Lane," he said. "We just have to be
careful, that's all. But I must see you sometime, *soon*. As
soon as this is over."

"Sure," Cross said.

At some time in the future, he had a score to settle
with this little god and it filled him with anger to think
of it; then he was angry with himself for getting angry. I
must keep cool, he told himself. Farrel came to the door
and beckoned to Hilton who strode out with defiance in
his eyes and manner. A moment later Cross could hear
Hilton's strident voice rising in vehement argument
with Houston. Why didn't the damn fool let well
enough alone? If he kept hammering at Houston,
Houston would, in the end, start wondering about the
case, start trying to find new theories he could make fit
into it. He strained to hear what was being said in the
living room, but could not make out any words. He
looked at Menti and Menti smiled.

"He's tough, that Hilton," Menti said, nodding ap-
provingly.

"Yes," Cross agreed.

"Eva likes you," Menti said.

"She's a wonderful person," Cross said.

Cross thought that Menti was a weak man who followed Hilton's lead. Could he placate Hilton a little
through Menti? He would try.

"Hilton seems suspicious of me," Cross said. "Is it
because I know Houston?"

"Well," Menti drawled, pulling at his ear and smiling
with embarrassment, "knowing cops is not exactly in
our line, you know."

"But I've no relations with this man," Cross defended

himself. "I met him simply and honestly in the dining car of a train some weeks ago." He recalled that Bob had witnessed their meeting and he added: "Look, I remember now . . . Bob saw it happen—"

"Bob? Bob Hunter?"

"Yes. You know Bob?"

"Let me give you a tip," Menti said, jerking down the corners of his mouth. "From now on, it's not wise to give the name of Bob Hunter as a reference in the Party."

"Why?"

"He's a counter-revolutionary," Menti said simply.

Cross blinked. He had blundered. He felt that he had become entangled in moving shadows.

"You're new to all this," Menti told him kindly. "I believe you're solid. But Hilton trusts nothing and nobody but the Party."

Cross decided to beg and wheedle a bit; he wanted to remain near Eva and the Party had the power to take her from him.

"Look, I've been in connection with the Party for only twenty-four hours," he argued. "I've worked for Hilton, so far . . . I'd like to set his mind straight. What does he think I'm after?"

"What *are* you after?" Menti demanded.

That shot caught Cross squarely unawares. "You distrust me too?"

"We distrust everybody," Menti said.

"Why do you distrust me?"

"We don't know you."

"All right," Cross said, feeling trapped. "Tell me what I should do in order to be trusted by the Party—"

"You have to belong to the Party," Menti said.

"I'm going to join—"

"I don't mean that."

"What *do* you mean, then?"

Menti chuckled cynically, scratched his chin, and looked quizzically at Cross.

"You have to *belong* to the Party," Menti said.

Then Cross understood. The Party would have to have some hold on him before it could trust him; the Party would have to own him morally. And Menti had spoken of it as casually as if he had been reciting the number of inches in a foot . . .

"Do you *belong* to the Party?" Cross asked softly.

"Yes. I've no life except that of the Party. I have no wish, no dream, no will except that of the Party," Menti confessed.

Cross stared in disbelief. Menti had willingly submitted himself to be ravaged and violated by others. And Cross felt that he could never surrender that completely to anybody or anything.

"I don't understand," Cross murmured.

"I know you don't," Menti said indulgently.

"But suppose the Party told you to do something you didn't want to do?"

"That's unthinkable," Menti said stoutly.

"Even unto death?"

"Even unto death and beyond," Menti maintained.

"Beyond?" Cross echoed. "Do you believe in a beyond?"

"In a sense, yes," Menti answered. "If, after I'm dead, the Party wanted to make use of me, wanted to place some interpretation upon my life or death, upon any of my actions for organizational or propaganda purposes, it has the right."

"But, Menti, don't you feel that you've got some value that's yours and yours alone?"

"In the eyes of the Party, no."

They both started at the vicious slamming of a door

down the hallway. Hilton stomped into the kitchen, his face distorted with anger.

"That goddamn sonofabitch," he railed.

Farrel came into the door, beckoned to Menti and said: "You're next."

Hilton took hold of Menti's arm and hissed: "Tell him to go to hell for me!"

"Take it easy, guy," Farrel warned.

Alone with Cross, Hilton changed his attitude quickly.

"When you go in there, stick to your story, see?"

"You can depend on me," Cross assured him.

"We'll see."

"Look," Cross could no longer hold himself in, "you make me feel that I'm guilty of something. You don't trust me. Okay. Distrust breeds distrust. Now that I feel that you don't trust me, I wonder if I ought to trust you—"

"You want to change your story to the D.A.?" Hilton asked.

"Hell, no! Why should I? My talking to the D.A. has nothing to do with it. But, hell, man, don't make me feel I'm dirt under your feet. I don't like it."

Hilton grinned and relented.

"Lane, there's only one thing I want to ask of you—"

"What's that?"

"Take care of Eva."

"I'll do my best."

"I *know* you will," Hilton said and went abruptly out of the kitchen and out of the apartment.

What had he meant? Cross's hands twitched. I'd like to ram that bastard's head against a wall, he muttered to himself.

A few moments later Farrel tapped him on the shoulder.

"You're the last."

When Cross entered the living room, Houston was sitting smoking a cigarette.

"There you are," he greeted Cross. "Sit down."

As Cross sat Houston rose and began to pace the floor, chuckling, now and then tossing a glance at Cross. Had Houston changed his mind? Was he about to spring a trap?

"Tell me, Lane, what do you make out of all this?"

"I hardly know, really, Mr. Houston."

"I wonder how many men in this land refuse to acknowledge the laws of our society?" Houston mused out loud.

"That would be hard to find out, wouldn't it?" Cross asked.

"Yes. And that's just why I'm asking," Houston continued. "Farrel, like the Medical Examiner, keeps mumbling about how somebody could have come upon those two men while they were fighting and killed both of them. That's possible, but highly improbable. What kind of motive could such a killer have? That's what's puzzling me."

Cross was silent. Houston had returned to this dangerous ground. Why? He had to watch himself now. If he disputed such a theory, Houston might think that he was afraid of it. But if he acted casually, nonchalantly about it, would not that make Houston think that he was disinterested, had no emotional connections with it?

"I thought you had accepted the idea of their having killed each other," Cross said, simulating surprise.

"Maybe yes, maybe no," Houston mused. "I'm just playing with this idea. Now, such a killer could not be either a Communist or a Fascist, could he?"

"Why not?" Cross asked.

"Why would a Communist want to kill another Communist in the presence of a Fascist?"

"I draw a blank there," Cross answered.

"And, the other way around, why would a Fascist want to kill a brother Fascist in the presence of a Communist?"

"I couldn't think of a motive."

Cross thought he saw a way of confusing the issue and he put in quickly: "Suppose a Communist came upon two men fighting . . . Suppose Blount was killing Herndon and his brother Communist helped Blount finish him off and then killed Blount too?"

"Why?" Houston asked, stopping and staring.

"I don't know," Cross said. "I'm just exploring possibilities. Now, suppose a friend of Herndon showed up under the opposite circumstances? Suppose he helped to finish off Blount and then killed Herndon—?"

"Why?" Houston demanded again.

"I don't know."

"I don't know either," Houston said. "But while we're on this theory of a third man, suppose either Blount or Herndon killed one another and a third man came upon the victor and killed him. Why? No, your theory is wrong. If there's anything in a third man showing up, after you left, and joining in this fight— and I doubt this—he'd have to be somebody psychologically akin to either Blount or Herndon and yet somehow outside of them. I can't see either a Communist or a Fascist acting in that way."

"Come to think of it, I'm inclined to agree with you," Cross said, trembling at how close to danger he was; only a shadow of a thought separated him from being considered guilty in Houston's eyes.

Houston paced the floor again, sucking at his cigarette.

"Such a killer, if he existed, would have to, for psychological reasons, be akin to both of them, wouldn't he? At least he'd have to *understand* them . . ."

"Why?" Cross asked, smiling.

"Only a brother absolutist would have any motives for killing them on purely ideological grounds," Houston went on. "Let us suppose a normal person came upon those two men fighting . . . What would he do? He would do what you did when you looked into the room. You called the police, or you had Hilton call the police. Now, we've checked the time. It *is* possible that after you left the door, somebody did go into the room and find them fighting. But, in order to kill the two of them on ideological grounds, this killer would have to have the support of a *third* set of ideas . . . We've checked Herndon's apartment; nothing has been stolen. He had plenty of enemies, but they were nowhere near that apartment last night. Now, who is that *third* man with the *third* set of ideas?"

"And what is that *third* set of ideas?" Cross asked.

"That no ideas are necessary to justify his acts," Houston stated without hesitation.

Cross felt a spasm go through his body. Yes, at last Houston was on the right track. But such a track did not lead to proof. He gave a gentle laugh to cover his terror.

Houston continued: "Now, let's see. Just for the sake of argument let us say that Blount, a Communist, hence an outlaw like you and me at heart, has his gang, that is, the Party on his side . . . Now, this Herndon is an outlaw too, but an *old* one. Tradition backs him . . . When he needs it, he has the law on his side, certain sections of society, money, the owners of property . . . Now, both of these men feel that it is beneath their dignity to obey the rules and laws made by what they would choose to call 'others', see? Now, this strange, dream-killer that lives on neither land nor sea, must be some-how akin to these two men, or he would not suspect that they are laws unto themselves. Only this outside killer who does not as yet exist knows that force and force alone guarantees the safety of these two tyrants. This mythical killer partakes of both their notions of lawlessness. That's what makes it possible for him to kill them . . ."

"Two questions I'd like to ask," Cross interposed. "First, why would he partake of their lawlessness? And why do you think that Communist and Fascist ideas are alike?"

"When did I mention *ideas*?" Houston asked scorn-fully. "Ideas are just so much froth on the top of a mug of beer, my dear boy. Men are inventing ideas every day to justify for themselves and others their actions and needs. What makes these *three* men akin is the identity of the impulses in their hearts—"

It was not lost upon Cross that they were now dis-cussing *three* men instead of two, and all three of these men were psychologically akin.

"Mr. Houston, that's a rather fantastic assumption," Cross said; he hoped that Houston would not suspect how deeply he agreed with him. "How can you *prove* that the same impulse actuates all three men?"

Houston paused in his pacing, turned, looked at Cross and then slowly tapped his broad chest with his right thumb.

"I have proof right *here*, Lane," he said quietly.

"What do you mean?" Cross asked, trying to keep anxiety out of his voice.

Houston did not answer at once; he resumed his pac-ing, his eyes deep with reflection.

"The proof is easy to see, but it is rather a daring kind

of proof. Of course, this kind of proof cannot be introduced into court. It has a psychological basis," Houston explained. "It's an 'as if' proof . . . Know what I mean? It's an intuition; it must first come from your own heart, see? How do I know that all three men feel alike? I know because *I* feel that way . . ." Houston sized Cross up. "And I think you feel that way too; that is, if I recall correctly your attitude on the train. The only difference is this: you and I have not acted upon this impulse of ours. The moment we act 'as if' it's true, then it's true; get it? But we've both *got* it. The proof of that is that we both understand it; that's the proof.

"A lawless man has to rein himself in. A man of lawless impulses living amidst a society which seeks to restrain instincts for the common good must be a kind of subjective prison. How such a man must live and sweat behind the bars of himself! God, the millions of prisons in this world! Men simply copied the realities of their hearts when they built prisons. They simply extended into objective reality what was already a subjective reality. Only jailors really believe in jails . . . Only men full of criminal feelings can create a criminal code. Only an enemy of Christianity, like Saint Paul, could establish Christianity. Men who fear drink want laws passed against drinking. Men who cannot manage their sexual appetites launch crusades against vice . . . Lane, we're outsiders and we can understand these new Twentieth Century outlaws, for in our hearts we are outlaws too.

"Here are the psychological origins of tyranny. Don't kid yourself, boy. Napoleon, Mussolini, Stalin, and Hitler knew what they were doing when they cast their beady eyes upon their subjects . . . When a man stood accused, objective evidence was of no avail. The dictator had but to glance into his own heart, and he knew at once that the prisoner at the bar was guilty! For, he reasoned, had he stood in the prisoner's place, he would have been guilty . . . How in hell did he become dictator without becoming guilty? Without breaking all the laws in sight . . . ?

"Now, let's get back to our *third* man who's realized all of this without acting upon it . . . Two tyrants are fighting in a room and our *third* man shows up. He feels towards those two men as those two men feel towards the masses of people . . . He's playing the same game, but on a much smaller scale. Who knows, maybe he's been hurt by both sides? He kills 'em, and with no more compunction than if he were killing flies . . . That man who kills like that is a bleak and tragic man. He is the Twentieth Century writ small . . . Do you get what I'm driving at, Lane?"

Was Houston teasing him? Or was he only talking? Cross laughed again to still his nervous dread. He told himself that he should keep quiet, that he was a damn fool to talk, yet he felt an overpowering desire to help Houston develop his theory.

"The man you are describing," Cross said slowly, listening with numbed dread at the sound of his own voice, "is one for whom all ethical laws are suspended. He acts like a god."

"Like a god!" Houston almost shouted. "That's the word I've been groping for. That's it exactly. But how can you tell when a man feels like that? You walk along the street and all faces look more or less alike. There's no clue to what each man feels or thinks. Indeed, such a man would be hard to detect, for in normal behavior he would act like all other men, maybe a little more subdued than others. But, above all, this man must feel that he *knows* what's right. Then, all at once, he sees something that violates that sense of right and he strikes out to set it as it ought to be. Then he resumes his cool and

correct manner of living. But that, of course, is purely
external. What must go on in a man like that? He must
be something of an inferno, hunh? Something like the
original chaos out of which life and order is supposed to
have come." Houston paused and stared again off into
space, and when he spoke there was a note of wonder in
his voice: "I wonder if such men have any value? Might
not they be the *real* lawgivers . . . Maybe . . . Who
knows?"

Houston stood in front of Cross and laughed. Cross
joined him in laughter, feeling something creeping over
the surface of the skin of his body.

"Some idea, hunh?" Houston asked.

"Yes," Cross said.

Cross waited to be challenged, to be accused. Houston turned and went to the door.

"Farrel," he called.

Cross held his breath. Had he called Farrel to arrest
him?

"We'll wash this thing up," Houston said over his
shoulder to Cross.

Farrel came to the door.

"Make it manslaughter," he told Farrel. "Double
manslaughter. Any other theory is too fantastic."

"Just as you say, Mr. D.A.," Farrel said.

"Now," Houston began, "let's talk about us. When
can I see you sometime?"

"Any time you like."

"What are you doing now?"

"I'm planning to attend some classes at the university . . ."

Cross was conscious as he talked that he was speaking as out of a dream. A moment ago he had been
positive that he was about to be arrested, and now he

sat here free. The room seemed to sway slowly around him.

"Will you have dinner with me some evening?"

"With pleasure."

"What about Sunday evening at Frank's in Harlem?"

"Sure. What time?"

"Eight. Right?"

"Right."

"And forget this mess about Blount and Herndon," Houston said, winking. "Good riddance, I think."

They shook hands and Houston strode to the door, then turned and said casually: "You'll have to testify, maybe, at a hearing of the Medical Examiner, you know."

"Oh, all right," Cross murmured.

Houston left. Cross sat alone and closed his eyes; he wanted to keep them closed and not look any more upon the sight of the world. He recalled Houston's saying that most lawbreakers longed to be punished and he wondered if such was smouldering in him . . . Why did not this thing rest easily on his heart? Or was he only deluding himself in thinking that he was free? He was suddenly tired. Was it worthwhile going on? Eva . . . Yes! There was a hope that one day he could talk to her. She would understand. She too was a victim. But—suppose she knew what he had done? How would she feel about him then? He leaned his forehead on the palm of his hand and the only answer he could find was no answer . . .

Half an hour later he pulled to his feet and went in search of Eva. The door of her room was open and he saw her lying fully dressed across her bed. He should leave; his staying was no good for her . . . He pictured himself getting his suitcase, hat, and coat and going in search of a hiding place . . . A slight nervousness went through him and he was about to act when he heard her voice.

"Lionel?"

"Yes."

"Come in, Lionel," she said.

He went to the bed and bent to her.

"Are you all right?" he asked.

"I'm numb. Are they gone?"

"Yes."

"What did they decide?"

"It's double manslaughter."

"Poor Gil . . ."

"Listen, Eva—"

"Yes."

"You know that Gil asked me to come and stay here. He wanted to send me to the Workers' School. Now, Gil's gone. I don't know what to do."

She lifted her head and her hazel eyes looked at him.

"Do you want to leave, Lionel?"

"No. I never want to leave you, Eva."

Her eyes fell; he could see her chest heaving with effort. She finally looked at him, reached out her hand and touched him, and said in a low, clear voice:

"If you leave, I shall kill myself—"

"God, no," he said. "I'm here. I want to be here near you— Listen, tell me; have you any money?"

"Money?" she repeated with a bitter laugh. "I've nothing. I've not worked at my painting in six months. All Gil and I had was his salary from the Party. I've not sold a picture in over a year . . . I don't know what the Party thinks of me."

Her voice died and her eyes assumed a scared, haunted look. Cross knew that she was wondering if they would let her wander free with her guilty knowledge.

"Look, I have a few hundred dollars," he said.

"Oh, no, Lionel," she protested. "That's impossible! I can't touch that."

"Why?"

"It isn't right. I must work—"

"Eventually, yes. But right now, you need not worry. Look, after this is over, let's go away somewhere together. The Gatineau Mountains in Canada. It'll be safe there, quiet, far from all this—"

Her eyes shone, then tears clouded them.

"I'm sorry about Gil, but Lionel, I'm glad that you are out of that trap," she spoke softly.

"Trap?" he asked; he could not let her know that he knew.

"There's so much I have to tell you—" She gazed off. "Gil told you he wanted to fight for you. It's true; he wanted to. But he was fighting for something else too. His idea of the world—"

"But aren't the two things one thing?" he asked to get her notion of it. "He's fighting for Russia; Russia needs men like me; so when he fights for me he's hitting at the rotten basis that holds up the world that's against Russia. Isn't that it?"

Eva sighed and shook her head.

"You were only a means," she said. "Lionel, the Party sees facts in motion . . . God, what language! But there's no other way to say it. *Facts in motion* . . . You are a fact to them, not a person. You're oppressed, so, to gain your help, they claim they'll fight for you but only in so far as your fight helps them." She looked fearfully about the dim room, as though afraid that someone was listening. "You must break away from this . . ."

He agreed with her, but where could he go? She

thought him a helpless victim; but, rather, he was what she hated. He had been using the Party in the same manner that the Party had been using him.

"I understand," he lied softly to her.

"I'm free now," she breathed. "But for how long? What will they say to me now that Gil's gone? Will they let me go? Will I be able to work again? Can I find new friends?" A twisted smile was on her lips. "Don't mind me, Lionel. I'll tell you what's worrying me later."

"Tell me now, Eva," he urged her. "It's better for you."

She hesitated; she was struggling with herself. Her life was in crisis.

"Lionel, I've been deceived in a way that you'll never know," she whimpered, trying to keep her lips from trembling. "You're colored and maybe you can understand . . . Perhaps you've lived all of your life with something that I've met only recently . . . When you were a child, you studied the same books I studied in school, yet you knew that what you read in those books did not apply to you; you knew you were colored and that the white world made an exception . . . You could prepare yourself against disillusionment. With me, I believed in the Party, all they told me . . . Then I found that it was make-believe . . . I can't even now tell you what they did to me . . . They've blighted me, my life, my work . . . I'm filled with shame and I want to hide . . . Where can I hide, Lionel?"

"Eva, I'd feel happier than I ever dreamed if I could win your trust. You can believe again in life . . . You *can*! You *must* . . . I shall trust you, and if my trust helps you, then you'll trust me in the end. I know it. You've never really been trusted; you've been told what to do, what to think and what to feel, and when it failed you, betrayed you, you hated yourself and the world. I shall trust you—"

"Oh, God, Lionel, I do so much want to try," she gasped, reaching out her arms and pressing him convulsively to her bosom.

He held her tightly, full of a sense of hot despair. What was he doing? Did he, as lost as he was, have the right to talk to her like this? How could he make promises to her? How could he believe in her when he did not believe in himself? Could he tell her of how he had abandoned his mother, Gladys, his three sons, how he had killed Joe Thomas, Gil, Herndon . . . ? Could he tell her that his life was steeped in deception, that he was the essence of the world that she hated and feared? Yet he felt that the cure of his nameless malady lay in winning her trust and love . . .

But could this shrinking and delicate Eva bear the mere hearing of his story? Would she not turn from him in loathing? He felt her tiny, cool hands on his face; he looked into her giving, pleading eyes.

"I want your people to be my people," she said, surrendering her life to him. "I want to feel all the hurt and shame of being black— Let me bear some of it, then I'll feel that I'm worth something. I wish I was black. I do, I *do* — Let me share the fear, the humiliation—"

She was wanting to love him for his being black, and he wanted her love to help him to redeem himself in his own eyes for his crimes! How could this ever be? Could he allow her to love him for his Negritude when being a Negro was the least important thing in his life? He wanted her for reasons which he doubted he could ever tell her, and she loved him for reasons which he did not have. He closed his eyes and rested his head on her shoulder. Yet he wanted that sensitive heart of hers to be his monitor, to check him from sinking into brutality, from succumbing to cruelty, and she wanted to love him for his being black because she thought he was an innocent victim.

"What's the matter, darling?" she asked.

"Nothing," he whispered. "Just tired."

"Poor Lionel . . ."

He was not Lionel Lane. He was nothing, nobody . . . He had tossed his humanity to the winds, and now he wanted it back. He would shatter this poor girl's heart if he took what she was offering. He pulled away from her and walked aimlessly about the room, his eyes unseeing. He needed her if he was to go on living, but would his taking of her kill her?

"Don't worry, Lionel," she smiled at him. "In the future when white men strike at you, they'll see me there at your side."

He buried his face in his hands, closed his eyes and groaned: "God . . ."

She rose and ran to him.

"What's the matter? Don't you want me to be with you?"

"Yes," he whispered despairingly.

"Then why are you so wrought up?"

He must not heap his troubles upon her. He should fly from this room, this girl, this hope of love . . . He seized her face tenderly in his palms and forced a smile to his lips.

"I'll be all right," he said.

"I only want to help you," she said. "For the first time in my life I am beginning to feel I can help somebody—"

Gently Cross crushed her face to his chest to keep her from seeing the bleak look on his face.

"Bless you, Eva," he whispered.

"We'll be together," she pledged herself.

"Together," he repeated wonderingly; but his eyes were gazing toward a distant shore which he was certain he would never reach.

The doorbell rang. Eva broke from him, smiled, kissed him and turned and ran to the door. It was Sarah, grim, gaunt of face, her eyes dark and full of anger.

"Is Hilton here?" she asked without ceremony.

"No; he's gone," Eva told her.

Cross went to Sarah.

"What's the matter? Where's Bob?" Cross asked her.

"I want to see Hilton," Sarah said, ignoring his question. "I'm going to kill him—"

"Oh, darling," Eva wailed. "What's wrong?"

Sarah doubled her fists, lifted them toward the ceiling and bared her teeth in a rage of bitter hate.

"The Party told on Bob— The Immigration men caught him this morning when he came to the apartment for his clothes— Bob's dead— He can't live out those years in that prison in Trinidad— And I'm going to pay off whoever did it— Bob said that Hilton threatened to do it, and only Hilton and the Party knew about Bob's being illegally in the country . . ."

She sank into a chair and sobbed.

"But how could that be possible?" Eva demanded, turning to Cross.

Cross was witnessing the birth of a new Eva. He knew that when she had been with Gil, she would never have been able openly to question or challenge a decision of the Party. And now she was demanding answers.

"It's all my fault," Sarah wept. "I pushed him to disobey the decision . . . He did what I asked and now they got 'im . . . He was screaming when they took him away." She clenched her teeth. "How they fooled 'im. Last night he phoned me and said that Gil had told him that everything would be fixed. He was to go to Mexico—"

"Sarah," Cross took hold of her shoulder. "I have something to tell you. Gil is dead. He was killed last night."

Sarah stared, her lips hanging open.

"What did you say?" she gasped.

"Gil's dead. He was killed last night— He was in an argument with his landlord downstairs . . ."

Sarah rose and stood as though she herself had been condemned. Then impulsively she threw her arms about Eva.

"God, have mercy," she cried.

Cross watched the two women, both of whom had lost their husbands, weep. One husband had died suddenly; the other would die slowly over the years behind the bars of a prison on a hot island.

"I could kill the one who did that to Bob," Eva cried.

Cross's lips parted. That was what he had been wanting to do to Hilton, kill him; but he had fought down the notion. Now Eva was planting it again in his mind. No, no; he would not kill again. Then what did one do when confronted with the Hiltons of this world? Let them trample freely over whom they liked? Never . . . But then what? To kill Hilton was a way of redeeming what Hilton had done to Bob; and also it was a way of lending multiplicity to Hilton's acts, of making them right somehow. To kill him was a way, really, of exonerating him, of justifying him. Yet, what other course was there? To make an appeal to the heart of a man like Hilton was out of the question, for he was beyond any such sentimental considerations. This was a problem the full implications of which only men akin to Hilton and Gil could really see and understand, for they alone knew how far cut off from life one was when one assumed the role of the godlike. Was there no turning back? Once the tie had snapped, was it forever? Cross knew that the only difference between him and Hilton was that his demonism was not buttressed by ideas, a goal. So why should he care? But he did. And he hated Hilton as only one can hate something which is a part of one's own heart.

"Lionel, can't we do something?" Eva asked, oblivious of the gravity of her question. "Let's start *now*! Let's redeem ourselves and help Bob some way, hunh?"

"But what can we do? Bob's gone now—" Cross explained gently.

"It's too late to help Bob," Sarah said. "They've got 'im."

"This has got to stop," Eva cried. "Isn't there some way, Lionel? There must be . . . Men like that should be *killed*!"

She embraced Sarah again and the two women wept for the men they had lost.

He walked slowly from the women and went into the living room and sat down, wrestling with contradictions he could not resolve. Was killing the kind of punishment that Hilton needed? If he killed Hilton, would not someone try to kill him for killing Hilton . . . ? Where did it end? Forgiving the man was out of the question, for a Gil or a Herndon would look upon it as weakness and would use it to establish a crushing defeat upon him who offered forgiveness. Was there not a kind of punishment that could make Hilton repent . . . ? Was that the word: *repent*? Renounce one's aims and go over to the side of the adversary . . . ? But suppose the lawbreaker felt that the adversary had no rights, was so absolutely wrong that he would rather die than submit . . . ?

The pathos of Bob's fate was that Bob had been so

weak, so easily persuaded, so needful of a master that the Party simply had no real need of his liquidation. Cross's broodings suddenly became organized and he went back to Sarah and Eva.

"Sarah, tell me, what Party plans did Bob hurt when he continued to organize?" Cross asked her.

"They were planning to launch a campaign for peace, and if Bob's union had been known as Red—and it was bound to be if Bob had kept on—everybody would have balked at signing any peace appeals. That's all . . . Bob got in their way and they kicked 'im to death." Sarah's eyes narrowed. "The police give you the third degree but the Party gave Bob the fourth degree . . ."

"This must not *be*," Eva said in tones of horror.

Cross wandered restlessly back into the living room. He searched in his pockets and found Hilton's card, then stood staring, holding his wallet in his hand. Yes; if he went to see Hilton, it would be better to leave his money behind. God only knows what might happen . . . He secreted his wad of greenbacks in his suitcase and again stood brooding. Suddenly he moved with purpose; he strode into the hallway and put on his overcoat.

"I'm going down for a bit," he told Eva. He studied Sarah for a moment. "Sarah, why don't you stay with Eva awhile?"

"Sure. I hate being by myself in that empty flat now . . ."

When Cross went down into the snowy street, his gun was nestling close to his hip as he walked. He reached the corner, paused, staring thoughtfully. He should go back and remain with Eva. He was safe then, safe from himself. To mull over Hilton's crimes would unhinge his impulses and make him want to act in that wild, crazy fashion again. But he kept on walking. He

reached University Place and saw the dark red brick bulk
of the Albert Hotel where Hilton lived. Was he in? And
what would he say to Hilton when he found him? He
did not know. Yet he was in the throes of an irrational
compulsion to see Hilton . . . He entered the hotel
lobby and walked to the desk.

"Is Mr. John Hilton in?" he asked the clerk on duty.

"Mr. Hilton, Mr. Hilton—" The clerk turned and
studied the board on which hung the keys of the rooms.
"Room 342 . . . I'm sorry, sir. But he's out."

"Do you know when he'll be back?"

"I'm sorry. I don't know. He left no message."

"Thank you."

Cross went out into the streets again, walking at ran-
dom. It was afternoon and he had not eaten. The day
was grey, sunless; the air was damp, cold. He passed
men and women whose faces expressed the intensity of
their personal concerns. His eyes drifted distractedly
over drugstore windows, the facades of stone and brick
houses, the long green buses pulling through icy streets,
and now and then idly up at some tall, apartment hotel
building. He longed suddenly to be near Eva; but that,
too, was a dubious thing. Why not flee now and start
afresh? But he had once done that and it had led to
nothing, to the nowhere in which he now lived. Running off was no solution, for he would simply take his
problems with him. In any new place he would be
worse off, for Eva would not be there.

He entered a drugstore and ate a ham sandwich and
drank a hot cup of coffee, neither of which he tasted.
Was it that he had gotten himself into such an emotional
state that nothing meant anything anymore, or was it
that *too* much meaning had now entered his life, more
meaning than he could handle? When on the streets
again he came to a tavern and went in and drank a glass

of beer. He saw a pinball machine in a corner; he
dropped a coin into the slot, thumped the tiny little
shining balls with a lever and watched them veer and
jump and bounce amid the flickering lights; he heard
the excited clatter of machinery as the scores flashed in
yellow numbers on a glass screen in front of him and
there was a girl in a scanty red bathing suit and she
danced and leaped and romped on a gleaming and curving sandy beach under tall palm trees . . . He played
twice and did not win. What the hell was he doing? Was
he so lost that he had to resort to this for distraction?
Disgust drove him at last out into the streets again.

Hilton lay like a coiled threat deep in his mind. He
had condemned Bob to ten years of suffering and Cross
was now trying to find some way of getting at him . . .
His anger kept rising. Only the presence of Eva could
evoke in him the drive to forget himself. Yes, he would
make of that girl his life's project, his life's aim; he
would take her hand and lead her and, in leading her, he
would be leading himself out of despair toward some
kind of hope . . . Suppose Hilton tried to take Eva
from him; Hilton had the authority of the Party and
could make endless trouble . . . Hell, he had to have it
out with that man, *now* — He could not go on with
Hilton looming like a black storm cloud over his head.

He turned and made his way back to the Albert Hotel
and entered. "But why ask for Hilton?" he asked himself
in a low voice. Just go up and knock on the door of his
room. Sure . . . He crossed the lobby and stood in
front of the elevator, waiting. Naw; walk up . . . He
turned and saw that no one was observing him and he
took the stairs to the right. Yes; room 342 would be on
the third floor . . . When he reached the third floor
corridor, he looked for the number. He came to the
door of Hilton's room and paused; the door stood open

and he could hear the whirr of a vacuum cleaner. He stepped to one side and waited. Was Hilton married? Or living with some girl? Strangely, he had not taken into consideration that Hilton might not be alone . . . He peered into the doorway and saw the white uniform and the bare, dark brown arm of a Negro maid, then he stiffened as he heard footsteps and he walked quickly away, looking over his shoulder. The Negro maid came out with a pile of dirty linen over her arm and headed down the hallway, leaving the door open. She was, no doubt, going to dump the soiled linen into some receptacle. Cross thought quickly; there might be a bare chance of his hiding in the room . . . The maid went out of sight and he ducked through the door and looked about frantically. Yes; the clothes closet. He opened it, slid in, and crouched in a corner, smelling the sweetishly sour odor of stale sweat. He pulled the door shut. Footsteps sounded again and he heard the maid humming a spiritual. Then the low whine of the vacuum cleaner came to his ears, and when it stopped there was the musical flow of water in the bathroom. More footsteps, silence. Had she gone? He heard the door slam and all was quiet. A moment later he emerged and looked about; the room was empty, untidy. Books were piled helter-skelter; soiled shirts and socks lay about. A greyish light seeped in through half-closed Venetian blinds. He looked in the bathroom to make sure that he was alone, then turned to the cluttered top of the dresser and studied the comb, brush, and a tube of shaving soap. He began pulling out dresser drawers. Clothing, pamphlets, a scrapbook, a flashlight . . . His breath caught in his throat. *What!* Good God in Heaven! What was this? That *Hilton*! What a tricky man . . . On top of a pair of pyjamas lay the balled and bloody handkerchief which he thought he had burnt by dropping it into the incinerator. The crumpled handkerchief showed burnt spots where it had lain on a pile of hot ashes; in fact, one corner was charred black . . . He stood without moving a muscle, unable to believe what his eyes saw so plainly. So Hilton had known all along! But why had he not said anything? Why had Hilton defended him so ardently before the police? Then he understood . . . Hilton was saving this handkerchief as his trump card; he was trying to *own* him morally . . . Hilton had seen him drop that handkerchief into the incinerator and had pretended that he had noticed nothing; and when he had gone back to his room, Hilton had gone downstairs and had gotten hold of it . . . Had bribed the cop at the door, perhaps . . . Or he had gone down to the basement this morning on leaving the apartment and had raked it out of the ashes. The fact was: Hilton had proof of his guilt! Eva had been in his room last night and maybe Hilton had eavesdropped at his door . . . ? Of course! That was the meaning of that last crack that Hilton had made just before he had left the apartment. Hilton had asked him to look after Eva and when he had said that he would do so, Hilton had said, "I *know* you will."

Gingerly, he stuffed the handkerchief into his pocket, then paused. No; it was not safe to put the handkerchief in his pocket like that. He withdrew the spotted handkerchief and then pulled forth his clean, freshly-laundered one. Yes, he would wrap the spotted handkerchief in the clean one; in that way, if he happened to pull out his handkerchief, he would not run the risk of dangling the bloody one carelessly in the face of some stranger. He tightly balled the bloody handkerchief and then wrapped the clean one around it, squeezing and crumpling the clean one so that it would look

used and natural, so that no one would think that anything was wrong . . .

He rummaged further in the dresser drawers. Ah— A
gun! A .32 and fully loaded . . . He took it and broke it
and emptied the bullets into his palm and pocketed
them. Now, he was ready to face Hilton. Where was he?
Had he gone to the headquarters of the Communist
Party? If he had, why had he not taken the handkerchief
with him? Or did he have some other devious idea in
mind? Anyway, it seemed that Hilton had not acted
against him yet. Well, Hilton had had his chance; he
would not act, not *now*. What a fool he had been! These
Communists were so intelligently tricky that it was hard
to cope with them. When Hilton came, he would have
to be on his guard each second, for the man was dangerous. How calm he had acted this morning! A disciplined
man, cold, precise, farseeing, ruthless. Hilton was free
of such infantile stupidities as racial hatred; he was no
frightened, white American dope worried about a white
girl who slept with a colored boy . . . Hilton was after
power and his keeping his mouth shut about Cross's
guilt was but one more step along the road to getting
hold of a bright young man whose life he would own
and whose talents would serve him in his struggle for
power . . .

Cross looked further in the room and found nothing
of interest. He saw a little radio on the night table at the
bedside. He looked at his wrist watch; it was nearing
five o'clock. Where was Hilton? Had he gone to the
police? No; if he had, he certainly would have taken the
handkerchief with him as evidence . . . He sat in a chair
near the bed and turned on the radio, softly, and listened to the low, surging beat of jazz music. He kept his
hand in his pocket on his gun and waited . . .

Half an hour later he jerked alert. A key turned with a

click in the lock of the door. Cross quickly twirled the knob on the radio, leaving the radio still turned on, going in a soft hum. His hand was on his gun and the gun was jammed deep in his overcoat pocket. The door swung in and Hilton, with a toothpick slanting downward from one corner of his thin lips, came into the room and stopped short, blinking his eyes at the sight of Cross. Hilton's body twitched as from an electric shock; he rushed to the dresser and yanked open the drawer that had held his .32 . . . How quick the man was, Cross thought. He smiled at Hilton, stepped past him and shut the door to the corridor. Hilton was pawing frantically in the dresser drawer, then he was still for a second. He spun around and faced Cross, his eyes bulging, his hands empty and trembling.

"I've got your gun, Hilton," Cross told him matter-of-factly.

Cross pulled out the .32 with his left hand and at the same time he drew his own .38 with his right.

"Say," Hilton began in a whisper. "What's wrong?"

"Are you asking me?" Cross mocked him.

Hilton's face was grey, his eyes like brown, flat discs of metal. He moved nervously, backing away from Cross one moment and advancing the next, his mouth working spasmodically. Cross could see that he was about to give vent to some sound.

"If you shout, Hilton, I'll just have to shoot you," Cross told him, accenting the gravity of his words. "Anything you do to attract attention of other people to this room, will be a sign for me to kill you. Now, man, have some sense. I'm in danger, and I'd not hesitate to shoot, see? I was a fool to underestimate you once, but I'll not do it twice. You're clever, intelligent, and I shall treat you as such."

Cross could almost see the rapid calculations spinning

around in Hilton's brain. He had backed off to a wall now and stared at Cross with parted lips; sweat began to gleam on his forehead.

"What do you want, Lane?" Hilton asked.

"Why didn't you tell me you knew what I'd done?" Cross asked.

"What you'd done?" Hilton pretended amazement. "What are you talking about?"

"Quit stalling, Hilton," Cross said. "Look, I found the handkerchief . . . You got it out of the incinerator—"

"Oh," Hilton said, turning pale.

"You knew what I'd done. Why didn't you tell the cops?"

"Because I was glad that you'd done it," Hilton said promptly, simply. "It solved a multitude of problems for me. Gil stood between me and one of the most important assignments on the Central Committee. Gil is gone and I've already got the job. I've wanted Eva for a long time; you freed her . . . Gil's death was like a gift dropped from the sky."

Ah, Cross recalled how Hilton had spoken of Gil last night . . . But he had not thought that that much hate and cupidity had been behind those casual words!

"And when did you know I'd done it?"

"Your coolness made me suspect you right off," Hilton explained without a trace of emotion. "I'm not so stupid a white man that I cannot tell the difference between fear and self-possession in a Negro. You were self-possessed. The cops thought you were just another scared darky. Okay, Lane. You got the handkerchief. Let's make a deal. Let's be reasonable. You wanted Eva. Well, you got her . . . Okay. Take off and let's call it quits—"

"So you think it was to get Eva that I did it?"

"Hell, yes. She's nuts about you and you're in love with her," Hilton said.

"It wasn't because of Eva," Cross told him.

"Then what was it?"

"You'll never know."

"Another revolutionary group?"

"No."

"You're with the police, then?"

"Hell, no."

"Then why did you do it?"

Cross laughed. Just as every man, perhaps, has his price, so every man, it seems, has a limit to his intelligence. Hilton knew that Cross was sincere and it bewildered him.

"I'll trade with you," Hilton urged him. "I don't know what your angle is, but shooting's not going to help anybody . . ."

"It's not that easy, boy," Cross told him. "You and your crowd are smart. I trust *nobody* now."

"I'll not tell 'em, neither the Party or the police," Hilton swore. "Look, I just left Party headquarters. I'm taking Gil's place, in addition to my other assignment. So everything's settled. I was after getting my hands on a quick boy like you, but, hell, you got away. Okay. No hard feelings. You go your way and I'll go mine. To hell with Gil. I don't care. I know you'll never speak of it, and God knows I won't. After all, I helped you with the D.A., didn't I? I kept making a racket about how Herndon was the murderer, didn't I? And Eva worships you . . . You got what you want, hunh? Things went your way."

Hilton's voice had come in a low, urgent stream of words, all precise and straight to the point.

"What about Bob?"

"Bob?" Hilton blinked. "What the hell do you care?"

Hilton's eyes were round with surprise. "Was he your brother or something?"

"No. You sent Bob to Trinidad, to his death—"

"So what? There are a million Bob Hunters. What do they mean? They don't count . . ."

Cross smiled bitterly. How those quiet words riled him! He had to deal with this man in a way that would make him feel what he felt.

"Sit down, Hilton."

Hilton hesitated; he did not know what was coming; his eyes darted and glittered. He licked his lips.

"Make no mistake, Hilton," Cross warned him. "I'd kill you in a minute. If you've got any tricks in mind, forget 'em."

"I've no tricks, Lane. I want to live . . ."

"So did Bob," Cross said. "Now, sit down . . . In that chair there, where I can see you."

Hilton sat and Cross sat on the edge of the bed and held his gun on Hilton.

"I want to know some things, Hilton," he began.

"Let's be reasonable," Hilton said. "Let's not be foolish about this. There's no sense in being drastic . . ."

The man had begun to plead for his life.

"How is it that you care so much for your life and nothing for Bob's?" Cross demanded.

"And what in hell do *you* care for life?" Hilton shot at him.

Cross smiled bitterly. It was a fair question.

"Who do you think *you* are to kill as *you* did?" Hilton demanded. "Herndon's no loss. But Gil was helping you, wasn't he? He took you into his home, trusted you, didn't he? And I shielded you from the cops, didn't I? What are you kicking about, Lane? Let's call it quits."

"No," Cross said thoughtfully. "There's something here I want to understand . . . I'm caught in these quicksands of compulsive actions, just like you are. But, Hilton, I'm reluctantly in it. I don't like it. I want to get out of it . . ."

"But killing me isn't going to get you out of it," Hilton reminded him eagerly, seizing upon every angle to save himself. "The only way out is to *stop*."

"I won't stop; I can't stop as long as men like you keep playing your dirty, tricky games," Cross said; and there was a genuine despair in his voice. "I won't ever feel free as long as you exist, even if you are not hunting me down. You and men like you are my enemies. Bob Hunters will go on being shipped to their deaths as long as you live . . . And don't give me this goddamn argument about your helping me. You help others when it *suits* you, and when it doesn't, you *don't*!"

"That's the law of life," Hilton stated simply.

"It isn't," Cross contradicted him in a frenzy that made Hilton's face turn still whiter. "Maybe you're trying to *make* it into a law—"

"It's what I've found, Lane; and it's what you'll find too."

"I don't believe it," Cross said, realizing that what Hilton had said was true from the past nature of his own experience. "And even if it's true now, we can change it. We can make it different; it *must* be different . . ."

"Why?" Hilton asked mockingly.

"Because— Because—"

"You're looking for paradise on earth," Hilton told him, managing a soft smile. "You're confused, Lane. You're seeking for something that doesn't exist. You want to redeem life on this earth with so-called meaning— But what you see before your eyes is all there is. Get all that idealistic rot out of your head, boy—"

"I'm *not* idealistic," Cross insisted.

"You are!" Hilton swore. "You're an inverted idealist. You're groping for some overall concept with which to tie all life together. There is none, Lane." Hilton was struggling to master his fear; he was trying to get at Cross's feelings, trying to make him feel that he was his older brother, that they shared basically the same views of life, and that Cross should accept his guidance. "Living in this world, Lane, is what we make it, and we make what there is of it. Beyond that there's nothing, nothing whatsoever, nothing at all . . . To think that there's something is to be foolish; to act as if there is something is to be mad . . . Now, let's do business like rational men. Let's make a deal. You do what you want to do, and I'll do what I want. We'll leave each other alone. I don't give a *damn* what you do . . ."

But Cross was not moved. He still held the gun on Hilton, smiling a little, appreciating Hilton's tactics. Then he shook his head; he could not accept what he had heard. There was an anchorage somewhere to be found. The logic of Hilton reduced all actions of life to a kind of trading in death. And that was not his sense of it; he had killed, but not to exalt that. He had been trying to find a way out, to test himself, to see, to know; but not killing just to live . . .

"You don't feel that there is any real justification for anything, hunh, Hilton?"

"Hell, no! I am here, alive, real. That's all the justification there is and will ever be, Lane," Hilton spoke earnestly, advancing arguments to save his life. "Let's start from that. I let you live and you let me live . . ."

"Why should I, if there's no justification? And suppose we break our contract?"

"Then one of us dies, that's all. What the hell is there so important about men dying? Tell me. We're not like the goddamn bourgeois, Lane. We don't make deals in shoes, cotton, iron, and wool . . . We make deals in human lives. Those are the good deals, the important deals, the history-making deals when they are made in a big way. Sweep your illusions aside, Lane. Get down to what is left, and that is: life, life; bare, naked, unjustifiable life; just life existing there and for no reason and no end. The end and the reason are for us to say, to project. That's all. My wanting to live even in this reasonless way is the only check and guarantee you have that I'll keep my promise."

"That's not *enough*!" Cross shouted.

"You're a romantic fool!" Hilton shouted in turn. "You're a kid! An idiot! You're just going about spilling blood for no reason at all, looking for what doesn't exist!"

"And what do *you* kill for?" Cross asked tauntingly.

"Practical reasons."

"And Bob was betrayed to death for practical reasons?"

"Yes. For practical reasons."

"But they were such trivially practical reasons," Cross protested, remembering the agony on Bob's face. "Couldn't there be—?"

"A pretense? Why? Look at it simply, Lane. Why fool yourself? I'm speaking to you now out of the depths of my heart. You know and understand too much to go about looking for rainbows. Let's trade. I've no proof against you. If anything ever happens to you, I'll help you; I'll remember and will stand by you. After all, Lane, no matter what plan I had in mind, I wasn't going to kill you—"

"That's just it!" Cross burst out. "I might forgive you if you had been going to kill me. But, no; you were going to make me a slave. I would never have been able to draw a free breath as long as I lived if you had had your way. I'd have suffered, night and day. You would have dominated my consciousness. No, no, Hilton, there's more here than you say. Goddammit, there *is*! If not, then why all this meaningless suffering? If you had killed me, that would have been a simple act. Killing Bob might have been in a way merciful. He wasn't happy. But to make him suffer ten long years! Hell, *no*! You say life is just life, a simple act of accidental possession in the hands of him who happens to have it. But what's *suffering*? That rests in the senses . . . You might argue that you could snatch a life, blot out a consciousness and get away with it because you're strong and free enough to do it; but why turn a consciousness into a flame of suffering and let it lie, squirming . . . ? No!" Cross's eyes were unblinking, seeing not Hilton sitting there staring at him, but Eva's diary, those pages telling of deception, of shame, of fear; and, too, he was remembering his own agonies in Chicago. He rose from the bed and looked wildly about the room.

"No, Lane," Hilton was saying. "What are you going to do?"

Yes, he would turn up the radio, good and loud; it would help drown out the pistol shot. He turned the knob up and a leaping flood of jazz music filled the room. Hilton rose slowly, sensing that Cross was preparing to act. Cross kept the gun on him, then he saw the bed. Yes, make him get down there between those mattresses, and the sound of the bullet would not be heard.

"Lane, Lane, you're crazy!" Hilton was saying, his head shaking.

Cross saw that the man was losing his grip, was going to pieces.

"Take it easy, Hilton," Cross told him.

"You can't get away with it, Lane!" Hilton begged.

His hands lifted themselves in a plea. "They'll hear the shot— Somebody will know— They'll catch you— Listen, you want money? I got a few thousand— I'll give you anything— But *don't* do this . . ."

Cross was possessed. He was crouching a little in the knees and his finger was conscious of the trigger. No, not yet; load the .32 and use it . . . That was better . . . He backed off from Hilton, pulled out the .32, and, holding his own gun on Hilton, he took one bullet from his pocket. He took his handkerchief and quickly wiped the bullet clean of his fingerprints and slipped it into a chamber of Hilton's gun, his eyes hard on Hilton's face. His fingers fumbled as he worked, for he expected Hilton to make an effort to overpower him while he was nervously busy breaking the .32 and putting the cartridge in . . .

Trusting, hoping for luck, Hilton rushed at him and Cross met the attack with a sharp blow from the butt of his gun across Hilton's forehead. The man slumped to the floor, still conscious, his eyes filmed with fear.

"No, Lane; no, no!"

Hilton was weeping now, suffering. Cross knew that he had to do it quickly or he could not do it at all. The sight of that tortured face was unnerving him. He stopped, grabbed Hilton by the collar, and yanked him toward the bed. He was surprised at how light the man was; and Hilton, in his craven fear, offered little resistance, as though he thought that being pliable might placate Cross and make him compassionate enough to spare his life.

"No, no, no . . . For God's sake, Lane, don't *kill* me!"

He put his gun in his pocket and now held the .32 in his right hand. He kicked Hilton and muttered:

"Get on the bed!"

He had to act quickly, or this man's wild face would make him stop. Hilton, with glazed eyes, scrambled obediently upon the bed, his hand still held shakingly before his eyes.

"Lane, Lane, listen— *Please!*" he sobbed.

Cross paused. Never in his life had he seen a man so undone by fear. He grabbed Hilton's head and, pulling one corner of the mattress up, he forced it over Hilton's head. Quick, quick, or he could not do it. Hilton's fingers were now clawing at Cross's hand that held his head to the bed. Cross placed the .32 at Hilton's temple and squeezed the trigger; there was a click. Oh, God, four of the chambers were empty; only one chamber was filled. Hilton's mouth was moving, but fear robbed him of the capacity of speech. Cross squeezed his finger on the trigger again and another empty click sounded, then again and there was a spurt of blue flame and a gaping hole showed in Hilton's temple and Cross was aware of the dancing waves of jazz music that swirled around the room. He saw that circling the bloody bullet hole in Hilton's temple were black powder burns.

He dropped the corner of the mattress and lowered the volume of the radio. Hilton's hands still moved; a labored breathing went in and out of the thin lips; there was a groan and the form on the bed was quiet. Cross strained, listening. There were no sounds in the corridor. He had to get out of here . . . The .32 . . . Yes . . . He wiped it clean of fingerprints on the sheet of the bed and tossed it beside Hilton's hand. He paused, then forced the gun into Hilton's fingers.

He looked about. His fingerprints— Suddenly he did not want to try to save himself. What was the use? But he had to. He took a dirty shirt of Hilton's and wiped wherever he thought he had touched. He had to go, had to get out of this room. He was more concerned with getting away from the sight of that grotesquely grey face with its gaping mouth than with saving himself. He went to the door, opened it slowly and looked into the corridor. He saw the retreating back of a man. He waited until the man had turned a corner, then he went out of the room, drawing the door to, and walked toward the elevator. He seemed to be floating along without effort; he was never able to remember afterwards making any attempt to run or hide. But when he got to the elevator, he pushed a button and then seemed to realize that he ought not be seen by the elevator boy. The shadow of the car heaved into view through the glass door of the elevator and he ducked away. He saw a flight of steps leading down; he took them, running, then slowed and walked on down to the lobby. Act natural, he told himself. He walked across the lobby, passing one or two people who glanced casually at him. He came to the newsstand and stopped.

"A *Daily News*," he said.

He paid for the paper and, as he turned to walk to the door, there flitted through his head an idea of a way to establish something resembling a partial alibi for himself . . . Ought he try it? Why not? Holding the paper before his eyes and pretending to scan the headlines, he glanced quickly about. No one seemed to be aware of him. Yes, he would do it. He went casually to the desk and asked the clerk:

"Is Mr. Hilton in?"

"Oh, yes; I think he's in now, sir," the clerk replied; he seemed to remember that Cross had asked for Hilton before. Turning, he examined the board holding the keys, then spoke to a brunette girl who sat facing a switchboard to his left. "Will you ring Mr. Hilton, please . . . ? Room 342."

"Okay," the girl said.

"Who shall we tell him is calling?" the clerk asked.

"Lionel Lane."

"Tell 'im Mr. Lane is calling," the clerk told the girl.

Cross watched the girl plug in on room 342 and jiggle a tiny lever. A young woman with a suitcase came to the desk and Cross stepped to one side and listened as she inquired for a room . . .

"There's no answer from Mr. Hilton," the girl at the switchboard told the clerk.

"No answer?" the clerk asked. "But I saw him go up a few minutes ago."

"I'll try again," the girl said.

"Won't you wait a second?" the clerk asked Cross. "We're trying to locate Mr. Hilton."

"Certainly."

"Did you have an appointment with 'im?"

"Well, yes. He asked me to come and see him as soon as possible. No time was specified," Cross explained.

"She's ringing him again," the clerk said, giving the woman with the suitcase the hotel register to sign. "Won't you sit down?"

"Thanks," Cross said.

He sat. He hoped that his present actions would indicate in any future inquiry that he had not been upstairs. Would a murderer act as calmly and politely as he was acting now?

"There's no response at all from Mr. Hilton's room," Cross heard the girl speaking.

"I'm sorry, sir," the clerk said, "but we don't seem to be able to locate Mr. Hilton for the moment."

"That'll be all right," Cross said, rising.

"Would you care to wait awhile?"

"Well . . ."

"Would you like to leave a message?"

Before Cross could answer the elevator door opened and several people came out into the lobby.

"Just a minute," the clerk said, turning to the elevator boy. "Say, Sam, did Mr. Hilton go up?"

Sam looked blank and shook his head.

"I don't know."

"What's the matter with your eyes?"

"I can't remember everybody who rides in this elevator," the boy complained.

"Maybe he's in the dining room," the clerk said.

"Maybe," Sam said, getting into his elevator to ride another load of passengers up.

"Look," Cross said. "I'll just leave a note."

"Right, sir."

On a pad of paper supplied by the clerk, Cross wrote:

Dear Hilton: I was by to see you twice this afternoon. I'll try again tomorrow morning. Everything's fine. Hope you got some sleep after that
session last night.
                                              Lane.
P.S. Don't worry about anything. Eva's doing wonderfully well.
P.P.S. Since you're so busy, why don't you phone
me instead and let's fix a time?

He folded the note and handed it to the clerk who pushed it into the letter slot, numbered 342, of the key-board behind him.

"Thank you," Cross said.

"You're welcome, sir."

It was not until Cross had gone out into the cold streets that the full reaction to what he had done began to set in. He trembled as he walked. Had he acted nor-mal enough? Could it not now be argued in favor of his innocence that he had asked for Jack Hilton *twice*? As his mind grasped more fully the folly of his having killed Hilton, a sense of nauseous depression seized him. He had killed Jack Hilton for many reasons: to redeem Bob's betrayal, for the sake of Sarah's indignation, for Eva's deceived heart; but mainly it had been to rid himself of that sense of outrage that Hilton's attitude had evoked in him, Hilton's assumption that he could have made a slave of him. He was mired deeper now than ever in the bog of consequences flowing from his compelling acts. He would be caught . . . Surely they would come at him now. To be found on the fringes of *two* crimes would certainly make the police think that something was wrong . . . All right; so what? Was he not already lost anyway . . . ?

But was it as bad as all that? Did he not have an ironical array of invisible allies on his side? Would not the police have a rather difficult job of proving his guilt in terms of motives? What motives could they impute to him? The police would first have to prove that he had killed Gil and Herndon before they could get near his motive for having killed Hilton . . . Lacking concrete evidence, the police would have to fall back upon psychological motives. And in that realm he was certain that even Houston, that old outlaw who had trapped himself with the law, that outsider who was privy to the secrets of the moon's dark side, would find it well-nigh impossible to bring himself to the point of believing him guilty . . . Even if Houston should actually believe him guilty, would he dare express his theories about it publicly? Houston had a passion for toying with daring ideas, but juggling with possibilities and realistically putting one's self in a position to say definitely that a man committed a particular crime because of those possibilities were two wholly different things. And especially when the crime stemmed from such a ghostly set of reasons . . .

Were not the queer motives of his crimes in themselves a kind of ally? Would not Houston, precisely because of his position of public trust, instinctively hesitate to expound an idea that went contrary to the basic tenets of normal and even abnormal actions? (For abnormal actions carried with them an aura of irresponsibility, and Cross considered himself *responsible*!) Would not his accuser have to place himself, in branding him guilty, in a *psychological* attitude that would spell the same kind of guilt that resided in the heart of the criminal? There was an inescapable element of contagion here . . . Who could possibly suspect him of being guilty on the basis of his *real* motives unless he himself had wrestled fatally with the same serpentine motives in his own heart? And if one had so wrestled, might he not, on finding Cross guilty, feel inclined to cross the line of law and arraign himself on Cross's side? Was that not the secret of all the revolutionary "front" groups? You flaunted a program that would appeal to a part of the forces of the enemy; you induced a section of the enemy forces to work with you and, while your enemies were standing at your side and seeing the world as you saw it, experiencing life as you lived it, they could decide that yours was as right as the side to which they belonged . . . Until now Cross had been lucky enough to leave no tangible clues behind, and the only clues open to anybody's inspection so far were only his motives . . .

His crimes constituted so decisive a divergence from the plane of ordinary moral considerations, stemmed from so weird an angle of perspective that he who would find him guilty must needs go so far as to place himself at that same point of vision that he had had while committing his crimes; and that person, his accuser, would automatically and of necessity have to become entangled in the very guilt he would denounce! He who would judge him would have to be as much outside of the canons of normal living as he before his guilt would become evident to that judge!

These were the intangible factors that made Cross, deep in his heart, rely upon Houston, the defender of the law, to condone and protect his breaking of the law. That Houston would track him down in time he was certain, but was Houston psychologically free to act upon what he found? Had not Houston admitted that maybe some men had the right to become lawgivers? Was there not, maybe, in Houston's heart the capacity to *respect* some forms of forceful crime? Had not men respected the crimes of Napoleon, Stalin, Mussolini, and Hitler . . . ?

There was no confusion in Cross's mind about this. He knew well that laws, on threat of dire punishment, enjoined men against certain specific acts; but did not those laws, by their very act of being laws, by describing the crimes they prohibited, represent negative projections of man's consciousness to check his own compulsive urge to commit the very crimes which the laws inveighed against? Was not the secret force of law itself really much deeper than the mere negative injunction against certain acts? Did not the positive aspects of law imply a conspiratorial understanding on the part of vast numbers of men to prevent, in terms of action, certain areas of consciousness from *thoughtlessly* assuming the upper hand in their lives? Was not law a struggle of man against man within man? Men who made and executed laws knew that the specific laws they framed or enforced would be violated, and it was not only to brook these specific violations of the law that they intended when they made and enforced those laws. The real aim of law was to *inhibit* in the consciousness of man certain kinds of consciousnesses which the law had to *evoke* clearly and sharply in man's consciousness, for the law possesses the strange capacity of creating vividly in man's consciousness a sense of the reality of the crime it seeks to suppress . . .

Law, then, by inhibiting man's actions, posits a sense of crime in man; law makes the criminal consciousness of man; law makes crime a sensual object, but it casts about that sensually forbidden object a dark halo of dread . . . Implied in law is a free choice to each man living under the law; indeed, one could almost say a free challenge is embedded in the law: if you are *strong* enough, you can do so . . . But you must *know* what you are doing . . .

Cross shrewdly suspected that Houston, a self-confessed outlaw, knew this, felt it; and it was what had made him become an active defender of the law; he *had* to represent the law in order to protect himself against his own weakness and fear . . .

He turned off Eighth Street and walked toward home. As he neared Herndon's apartment building he became aware that a police car was pulling slowly into Charles Street at the opposite end of the block. Did they know already? Tension waxed in him. Yes, he would act natural, keep his wits about him. A confrontation regarding the death of Hilton would be far more serious than the questions he had answered regarding the deaths of Gil and Herndon. The police would now wonder at the coincidence of his being disquietingly near the scenes of *two* murders in twenty-four hours . . .

Yes, the occupants of the police car had evidently spotted him, for the car slowed and he arrived at the entrance of Herndon's building at the same time that the car did. He feigned to pay no attention to the car

and turned to mount the steps of the stoop. The door of
the car flew open and a cop leaped to the sidewalk, ran,
grabbed his arm, and spun him around.

"Just a minute!"

Cross gaped at the cop a moment in simulated surprise.

"What's the matter? What do you want?"

"We want to talk to you!"

Two more policemen came running from the car and
the three of them surrounded him in the growing darkness of the street. Several people paused and stared. One
of the cops barked roughly:

"Get going— This is none of your business!"

The passersby moved reluctantly on.

"What do you want?" Cross asked.

"You're Lionel Lane?"

"That's right."

"You'd better come with us."

"I'll come willingly, but why?"

"You'll know why soon enough."

He allowed himself to be led, looking in alarm from
one face to the other. He would pretend to be stunned;
he would not talk. As they pushed him into the car, he
glanced up at the lighted windows of Eva's apartment
and wondered if she knew. He was sitting jammed between the policemen when the car jerked into motion
and the siren rose to a wail as the car picked up speed.
Then his breath was knocked out of him as the cops
seized him from both left and right and patted his pockets. They found his gun and snatched it.

"Ah, a Colt .38 . . . So you carry a gun, hunh?"

"Of course . . ."

"What the hell do you mean by 'Of course'?"

The cop broke the gun and extracted the bullets.

"I've a permit to carry a gun," he told them gently.

There was a moment's silence. Cross took his wallet from his inside coat pocket and tendered the permit.

"Jesus! It was issued yesterday," a cop exclaimed.

"Has the gun been fired?"

"Doesn't look or smell like it . . ."

Three minutes later the siren died and the car pulled to a screeching stop and the doors were yanked open. Cross was pushed out and hustled into the interior of a police station and made to sit facing a tough, wide-mouthed, grey-haired policeman who stood behind a desk. Cross noticed that a plaque on the desk identified the man as: Captain Ross.

"We picked 'im up in front of where he lives," a cop reported to the captain. "We grabbed him about two minutes after we got the call. He had this . . ." The cop put Cross's gun on the desk. "Here's his permit."

The captain quickly examined the gun, then eyed Cross intently. He rose and stood over Cross.

"Frisk 'im," the captain ordered.

One policeman held him while another swiftly emptied his pockets and piled his package of cigarettes, his ring of keys, his wallet, his lighter, his loose coins, and his folded newspaper upon the desk. He had a moment of wild panic when the policeman pulled the balled handkerchief from his pocket . . . But the policeman handled it gingerly, as though he was afraid of germs. He had been lucky to have thought of wrapping the bloody handkerchief inside the clean one.

"Okay," the captain said. "Take your stuff. Where do you live?"

"13 Charles Street."

"What do you do for a living?"

"I'm a student."

"Where?"

"Well, I haven't enrolled yet—"

"Where were you going when the officer met you?"

"Home. I was in front of the house where I live."

"Why do you carry a gun?"

"My life has been threatened."

"By whom?"

"My landlord who was—"

"When was this?"

"Yesterday. You see—"

"Have you used this gun recently?"

"No. I haven't fired that gun in over five years."

"Do you know John Hilton?"

"Of course. I just left his hotel—"

"You had an appointment with him?"

"That's right. But why are you asking me all this—?"

"We'll do the questioning. Now, what was the purpose of your visit to Mr. Hilton?"

"He invited me to see him."

"What did you say to 'im?"

The police had not mentioned that Hilton was dead, and Cross knew that they were trying to trap him into some inadvertent admission that he knew that Hilton was dead or that he had recently seen him.

"Nothing. He wasn't in."

"But you *saw* him?"

"No, I didn't . . . What's wrong?"

"Did you have a quarrel with 'im?"

"No. I've never quarreled with him."

"You were good friends?"

"I wouldn't quite say that."

"Why?"

"I just met the man two nights ago—"

"And when you saw him just a few minutes ago—"

"I haven't seen Mr. Hilton since ten o'clock this morning."

"Did he give you an appointment to see him another time?"

"What do you mean?" Cross knew that the captain was still trying to trick him into admitting that he had seen Hilton.

"I mean, when you left him this afternoon, when did he tell you that you could see him?"

"But I didn't *see* him this afternoon, I tell you."

"What did he want to see you about?"

"Well," Cross allowed himself to relax a little. "He wanted to talk politics— Look, you know as well as I that Hilton's a Communist. But I thought it was legal to talk to him."

The captain sat down and pulled from the desk drawer the note which he had given to the clerk in the hotel.

"Did you write this?"

Cross affected to be astonished as he examined the note.

"Yes. I wrote this this afternoon, about forty-five minutes ago; or maybe half an hour . . . But how did you get this? I thought I left it for Mr. Hilton . . ."

"Did you push it under the door of his room?"

"No. I left it at the desk. But where did you get it?"

"We found it," the captain said vaguely.

The police were trying in every way possible to drag him into an area where he would make a damaging admission.

"Then Hilton must have dropped it out of his pocket, or something like that. Or maybe the hotel clerk dropped it, lost it . . . But I could swear I left it at the desk with the clerk," Cross allowed himself to be confused, bewildered. He looked nonplussed from one face to another. The policemen were puzzled. "What's this all about? What do you want with me? Did Mr. Hilton say something to you?"

"Mr. Hilton had an accident—"

"Oh," Cross said in surprise. "Not serious, I hope— An automobile accident?"

"You tried to see Hilton earlier today?" the captain asked, ignoring his question.

"Yes."

"And he wasn't in?"

"That's right."

"Did you see Hilton at any time today?"

"Yes. It was this morning when he left the apartment where I live. But what's this all about? What has that got to do with his being hurt? If you told me what you wanted, maybe I could help you," Cross said.

"When did you see Hilton *after* he left you this morning?" the captain continued to ignore his request for more information. "You saw him?"

"No."

"Did Hilton ever threaten you?"

"No; why should he? Look, let me explain . . . Hilton came last night—"

"We're doing the questioning. You just answer!" the captain reminded him. "Do you know of anyone who'd want to harm Hilton?"

Cross gaped and let his eyes assume a roundness of understanding. This is the closest the captain had come to saying that some *person* had hurt Hilton. Now, ought he try to confuse them by telling them about Bob and Sarah? Bob and Sarah had real, ordinary motives for wanting to kill Hilton and the both of them had airtight alibis . . . So what harm would it do to tell of the row that Bob had had with Gil and Hilton? It would give their literal minds something to chew upon for a few minutes.

"Well, look now . . . Let me think—"

"Don't think! Talk! Tell what you know. This is serious."

"Well, it's kind of complicated and I'm rather a stranger to all of them, you see. These people, you know, are Communists, all of them. They had a hot argument the other night about Party matters . . ."

"What people and where was the argument?"

"Bob Hunter and Hilton— It was at Bob's place—"

"Go on; get to the point!"

His eyes roved from face to face. Yes, they were eager to hear the story. He could turn their minds away from him. Bob was on Ellis Island and had the best of all possible alibis. And no doubt Sarah could prove that she had been with Eva at the time that Hilton was killed. He related to them the tale of Bob's illegal entry into the country, of how Hilton had—according to Bob's way of explaining it—threatened to have him deported to Trinidad if he did not obey the Party . . .

"You see, according to Bob, Hilton was going to tip off the Immigration authorities and have him picked up," Cross said.

"Where's this Bob Hunter now?" the captain demanded.

"He was at Ellis Island the last I heard," Cross said gently. "They picked him up for deportation."

The faces of the policemen showed keen disappointment.

"And his wife, Sarah? Where's she now?"

"At my house, maybe. That is, if she's not gone to her own home by now—"

"Where does she live?"

He gave them the information. He was sure that Sarah could readily account for herself. He was using Sarah to fill out his story, to put his recital in a frame of reference that would make his attitude seem normal and cooperative.

"Lane, did you go up to Hilton's room?" the captain asked suddenly, softly.

"No; I told you he wasn't in."

"Did you ever fire a .32?"

"No. I own a .38. You see my gun—"

"Aren't you associated with Hilton in some way?"

"No. But why do you ask me that?"

"You could have walked up the stairs, you know," the captain suggested.

"What stairs?" Cross asked.

"The hotel stairs. Didn't you walk up to Hilton's room?"

"Good God, no! I told you I didn't *see* Hilton!"

There was silence. The captain turned to his desk and wrote something hurriedly upon a pad, tore off the sheet and handed it to a policeman.

"Check at Ellis Island about this Bob Hunter. Make sure he's still there and hasn't been out . . . And send out a radio call for this Sarah, his wife—"

"Say!" Cross exclaimed. "Look, here—" He pretended to be overcome with contrition. "I didn't mean to get Sarah in trouble . . . She's all upset about her husband. I'm sure that she hasn't done anything to anybody. She'll hate me for making people think that she's done something . . ."

"We'll take good care and keep what you've told us strictly confidential, Mr. Lane," the captain said. "Now, let me tell you that Hilton was found dead a few minutes ago in his hotel room . . ."

Cross lifted his head with a jerk and stared at the captain.

"*Dead?*" he echoed.

"Yeah."

He kept his eyes intently upon the captain's face, then took a deep breath; he looked disbelievingly around the room at the faces and leaned weakly forward and rested his hands on the edge of the captain's desk, as though for support.

"God," he sighed. "And I was trying to see him all afternoon."

"You did not go to his room?"

"Of course not. He wasn't in . . ." He paused. "God, he might've been dead when I was asking for him."

"That's possible," the captain said.

"And only last night his friend, Mr. Blount was killed— What's happening—?"

"Blount? Gilbert Blount?" the captain asked, his mouth hanging open.

"Yes. That was Hilton's friend. I'm living in Mr. Blount's apartment. I just spoke to the District Attorney this morning about all of this—"

The policemen were astonished. He knew that their minds were wandering far from him now.

"Get the District Attorney's office on the telephone," the captain ordered. "We'll see what this is all about."

"Yes, sir," a policeman answered and left the room.

Cross sat and waited.

"How deep are you in this Communist business?" the captain asked.

Cross relaxed a bit; their minds were now working normally, leading them into paths where they could find nothing against him.

"I'm not in it at all," he answered. "I belong to no political organizations whatsoever."

"How long have you known Blount?"

"Two days."

"How did you come to meet him?"

"At Bob Hunter's place."

"How did you meet Bob Hunter?"

"On a train."

"And Hilton? How long have you known him?"

"Two days. I met them both the same night."

"Did you ever hear anybody threaten either of them?"

"No."

"Did Bob Hunter or his wife ever threaten them?"

"They had a hot argument, but nobody threatened anybody."

"By the way, let me see your draft card."

Cross tendered his draft card; the captain examined it, copied down some information from it and handed it back to him.

"Where were you born?"

"In Newark, New Jersey."

"Where did you go to school?"

"In Newark."

"This Hilton, what kind of a man was he?"

"What do you mean?"

"His behavior . . . ?"

"Well, he struck me as being very intelligent. He never said much. He's an ex-school teacher."

"Where did he teach school?"

"I don't know. Look, I hardly know the man. I spoke to him for the first time this morning and for only a few minutes—"

"But he wanted to discuss politics with you, didn't he?"

"Sure; I'll talk and have a drink with anybody. Why not? I'd take a drink with you even . . ."

"No thanks," the captain said, smiling suddenly. "Did Hilton owe you any money?"

The captain's manner made Cross feel that he had given up any hope of linking him with the killing of Hilton.

"No. Not a cent."

"Did you *owe* him something?"

"Nothing."

"Did he have a girl friend?"

"I don't know."

"Any men friends?"

"Yes. He was with a guy called Menti—"

"Menti what?"

"I don't remember his first name. He was just called Menti—"

"Spell it."

Cross spelled out Menti's name.

"Where does he live?"

"I don't know."

"Had he quarreled with Hilton?"

"Not in my presence."

"Now, Lane, account for your movements during the afternoon."

Cross sighed, looked at the ceiling, then at the faces around him. He laughed and said:

"You'll have to let me think a minute—"

"Take your time," the captain said.

He told them of his movements in complete detail, leaving out only the half hour he had been in Hilton's room. He was deliberately shrewd enough to get the sequence of his actions twisted and several times he had to interrupt himself and reorder the chronology of events. He told them of his visit to the drugstore, the bar, of his two visits to the hotel, the newspaper he had bought. He told of waiting in the lobby while the girl at the switchboard tried to ring Hilton; of how the clerk had questioned the elevator boy about Hilton's having gone up to his room. When he was pressed to give a conception of how much time he had spent in each place, he grew vague in a helpless sort of way and would

not commit himself. Instead he tried to recall in concrete detail all the many tiny things he had done or seen.
He even told them of his playing the pinball machine
and he extended the number of times he had tried to
win . . .

"We'll check on all of this," the captain told him.
"Lane, you can go now. But don't change your address.
And say nothing about this to no one."

"Just as you say, Captain. And if I can help you in any
way, I'd be glad to do so. I didn't know Hilton very
well, but I'd do what I could—"

The telephone rang and the captain picked up the receiver and listened.

"Okay," he said, hanging up. "Lane, I'm afraid that
you'll have to stick by. The D.A.'s coming over."

"You mean Mr. Houston?"

"Yes."

"Sure. He's a swell guy. I've got a date to have dinner
with him Sunday evening . . ."

The policemen looked at one another. All of his
words had been designed to lure their thoughts away
from him, but not too definitely; he was assuming that a
mild doubt in their minds was better than a certainty.
His strategy was not to account for himself so cleverly
that they would suspect that he was giving them a
carefully doctored story. It was a sounder policy to
make them wonder a little, search, check, and find nothing . . .

He sat alone in an anteroom waiting for the arrival of
Houston. What would the old hunchback think now?
Even if he *thought* him guilty, what could he do? Would
Houston want to hold him for investigation? But would
he not need the justification of some iota of evidence to
do that? Houston could, of course, put him in the
Tombs and then carry on his investigation. But would

he? Would he not think that these two crimes were of a political nature? That some Communist had become disgruntled and had killed Gil and, having killed him, had to kill Herndon to silence him? Would he not think that maybe the same disgruntled Communist had had to kill Hilton to silence him also? While he waited, one of the cops came to him and gave him his gun and the permit.

"The D.A.'s on his way over," the cop said.

"Thanks," Cross said, pocketing his gun.

Cross saw Houston arrive; a policeman escorted him into the captain's office. They're giving me a going-over in there, Cross thought. Half an hour later Cross was taken into the captain's office to confront Houston. They were alone. Houston was grim, tense. He moved lightly and nervously about the room, more stooped and humped than ever, throwing a darting glance at Cross from time to time. Finally he stopped in front of Cross and said:

"You seem to be getting to know the police pretty well."

"Looks like it, doesn't it?" Cross said.

"Is there anything you want to add to what you've told the captain?" Houston asked.

"No; not that I can think of."

"You were *not* in Hilton's room today?"

"Absolutely not."

"And you are *not* in the Party?" Houston asked.

"No. I'm not a member of the Party nor have I ever been."

"Had they asked you to join?"

"Of course."

"And what did you say?"

"I stalled. I talked with them about general sub-jects—"

"And you did *not* see Hilton?"

"I did not."

"When did you last see him?"

"When he left Blount's apartment this morning."

"Were you in communication with him by phone or in any other way since then?"

"No. There'd be no reason for me to be."

Houston paused and brought his fist down on the edge of the captain's desk.

"I wonder what are these damned totalitarians killing each other about!"

"That would be hard to tell," Cross said softly.

"Lane, you know something about how men's minds work. Now, do you think that what we were discussing this morning could have any relation or bearing on these killings?"

Cross felt dread enter him. Houston was again sniffing around on that highly dangerous ground.

"Gosh, I don't know, Mr. Houston," he heaved a mumbling sigh. "It's all fantastic."

"And nothing like it *could* happen," Houston spoke as though he was protesting against something in his own mind. "It's these Communists . . . They're involved in something. Maybe Blount and Hilton were mixed up in spying . . ."

"And Herndon?" Cross felt compelled to ask.

"Goddammit, it doesn't make sense," Houston sputtered, planting himself in front of Cross. "There *must* be a *third* man involved in this."

"It's beginning to appear like it," Cross said, looking Houston straight in the eyes.

Again Houston was wading in his direction. But could Houston permit himself to accept what he was undoubtedly thinking? Could he bring himself to admit that he was standing and looking at a man who acknowledged no laws? Did not the very thought create a dizzy kind of guilt? He saw the hunchback blink his eyes and shake his head . . . Yes; he's backing off from it; he's scared . . .

"There's absolutely nothing concrete to go on in all of this," Houston said as though he was talking of Cross directly for the first time. "I have to keep fighting myself to reject the one and only theory that could tie all of this together . . ."

"What theory is that?"

Cross held his body so tense that he feared that Houston would notice it.

"Could there be a man in whose mind and consciousness all the hopes and inhibitions of the last two thousand years have died? A man whose consciousness has not been conditioned by our culture? A man speaking our language, dressing and behaving like we do, and yet living on a completely different plane? A man who would be the return of ancient man, pre-Christian man? Do you know what I mean?"

Cross felt his body grow hot. His judgment told him to keep quiet, to pretend ignorance; but his emotions clamored to enter this discussion, to tell what he knew. He drew his breath, pushed his personal feelings aside and, when he spoke, he was discussing himself in terms that were displaced and projected.

"He's a man living in our modern industrial cities, but he is devoid of all the moral influences of Christianity. He has all the unique advantages of being privy to our knowledge, but he has either rejected it or had somehow escaped its influence. That he's an atheist goes without saying, but he'd be something more than an atheist. He'd be something like a pagan, but a pagan who feels no need to worship . . . And, by the nature of things, such a man sooner or later is bound to appear. Since we are speculating about this, why can't we say, in theory, that maybe he is appearing already? Modern man sleeps in the myths of the Greeks and the Jews. Those myths are now dying in his head and in his heart. They can no longer serve him. When they are really gone, those myths, *man* returns. Ancient man . . . And what's there to guide him? Nothing at all but his own desires, which would be his only values."

Cross confessed his crime as much as he dared. Houston stood looking moodily out of a dingy window.

"I don't believe it," Houston muttered at last. "It's the Communists. They know something of this. I'm sure of that." But there was no conviction in his voice. He turned to Cross and spoke without looking at him. "All right, Lane. That's all."

"I'll be seeing you Sunday night at Frank's, hunh?"

"What?" Houston asked; he seemed preoccupied. "Oh, yes. Of course. And keep away from those Communists, boy."

"I shall."

Houston's eyes still avoided him. He was rigid a moment, then he turned and strode out of the captain's office, leaving the door ajar. Cross watched his humped back disappear down a dim corridor. He didn't dare . . . The hunchback had looked right at it and had turned his face away! The captain entered.

"That's all, Lane."

"Good evening, sir."

He went out into the street. Yes, he was going to Eva . . . Out of the corner of his eyes he was vaguely conscious of a man leaning against the wall of a building and reading a newspaper. Ah, I wonder if they are trailing me . . . ? He'd see. He was spent; he needed a drink. He headed toward Sixth Avenue, saw a bar; he paused and looked over his shoulder. Yes; the man was following him . . . He went into the bar and had a whiskey. God, how could he get out of this? He wanted to rise and yell for help. Would it not be better to see Houston and tell him that he had gotten in too deep, that he was afraid of himself? His head felt hot; his fingers were trembling. He yearned for the sight of Eva. If only he could talk to somebody! To wander always alone in this desert was too much . . . Once again he had killed and he feared that this time he would be caught. Maybe I *want* to be caught, he told himself. Is that it . . . ? He didn't care . . . He had done what he had wanted to do, hadn't he? Then why worry . . . He paid for his drink and went out into the streets again. The man with the newspaper fell in slowly behind him. He had to see Eva, yet he feared seeing her. He knew that he had to tell her everything now; he *had* to tell . . .

He walked aimlessly, turning corners. He glanced over his shoulder; the man was still trailing him. The street lamps came on, gleaming through the misty winter night. The traffic was heavy. Eva would be worrying, wondering what had happened to him . . . Yes; go to her, get it over with, tell her . . . He'd throw himself upon her mercy.

He turned toward Charles Street and as he neared the apartment he knew that the man was still following him. To hell with him . . . His hands felt like ice, but his body and his face were burning. God, I must have fever . . . He shivered. He came to the building and stared at the windows of Herndon's apartment. That fool! How much of the world's suffering had been inflicted on men by Herndon and his kind? He was not sorry that he had killed him. He would do it again, if need be . . . He shook his head, realizing that Herndon had felt the same about him. How bewilderingly tangled it all was . . .

He went up the steps and entered the downstairs hall-way; he paused, full of contrition at the thought of Eva. Could he face her? He had to, to keep alive he had to face her. He pulled up the stairs and stood uncertainly before the door. He pushed the bell; the door swung open and Eva was looking at him.

"Lionel, where on earth have you been?" she asked him.

He did not answer; he pushed past her and went stumbling into the living room. She followed him and he did not want to look into her face. He glared about nervously, then turned and went into the hallway again, heading for his room.

"Lionel, what's the matter?"

He flopped on his bed and closed his eyes. He felt her fingers on his face.

"You have a fever," she said in alarm. "You silly boy; why did you tramp about so long in the cold? Listen, the police came here asking for Sarah . . . They wouldn't tell me why. What do you suppose they want with her? Do you hear me? Darling, what's the matter? Sarah fixed some food for us. Are you hungry? Oh, God, you must be ill . . . Open your eyes and look at me! Oh, Lionel, you're *really* ill! Here, let me help get you out of your clothes. You must rest. You're under too great a strain. Lord, what have we done to you— Poor boy— I'll get you some hot tea, hunh?"

He felt he wanted to die. What was he worth in the presence of this girl? He was ill, but not with the kind of illness she thought. He felt her pulling off his shoes, then when she tried to get his coat off, he opened his eyes and looked at her.

"Eva," he whispered.

"Darling, you're exhausted," she said. "Where were you and what were you doing?"

"I don't know," he answered her truthfully.

"Did someone bother you?"

He did not answer. She helped him to undress and he lay under the covers quietly, keeping his eyes closed. Eva pulled down the shades and he could feel that the room had grown dark. She cradled his head in her arms and whispered to him:

"Can I get you something?"

"No."

He was fighting the fight of his life. His lips were tightly clamped, his eyes closed. He knew that he wanted to spill it all out, everything. Yet he held still, hoping that it would not come. It no longer now depended upon his debating if he should tell or not, but upon how much strength he had. He opened his eyes and looked at her. Oh, God, such trust in that face . . . How could he tell her? He pulled himself free and stood up in the darkness of the room, his back to her.

"Lionel, get back in bed! You have a temperature," she wailed.

She caught his arm and led him back to the bed; he allowed himself to be guided by her, his eyes glazed and unseeing. She placed her cool palm on his forehead.

"You're burning with fever . . ."

"Naw," he groaned.

"You haven't eaten—"

"I don't care."

"You've got to take care of yourself— You're worried, that's all. Listen, tramping about the streets in the cold and brooding, what's the good of it? You must take care of yourself. You hear? You stood up to those cops fine, you talked wonderfully . . . Then afterwards you start fretting and you break down . . . You mustn't let them get you like that, Lionel. Now, more than ever, you've got to be strong. We have no gang with us now. No Party . . . We're alone, and that means we've got to fight, fight, and be careful . . ."

He stiffened. He'd scream if she kept expressing her faith and belief in him. He tried to pull away from the tug of her hand.

"Lionel, look at me— Look at me— I love you," she whispered.

He shot from the bed and stood up in the darkness of the room, trembling; his body was hot yet he felt cold.

"Lionel, what's wrong?"

"Everything," he breathed.

"Can't you tell me? Did somebody bother you?"

"No."

"Then what is it?"

He was still, his body rigid. Then he felt his lips forming sounds, heard words issuing from his mouth.

"Eva, I killed Hilton—"

"What?"

"I killed Hilton . . ."

"Lionel, get to bed," she said sternly. "You've got a fever."

"No; listen—" He still did not turn around. "My name's not Lionel Lane. It's Cross Damon. Oh, God, what have I done? I've killed and killed and killed . . . Eva, save me; help to save me—"

He felt her arms about him, tugging at him.

"Get in bed, darling," she begged. "You're sick."

She pushed him back to the bed and held him again in her arms.

"Eva, you must hear—"

"No; don't think, don't talk," she cautioned. "Lie still! Be quiet, honey."

"I *must* talk," he said. "I must tell you— Darling, I killed your husband— It was I who struck both Gil and Herndon down—"

"Oh, *God*, Lionel," she cried. "You're delirious!"

"No, no; I'm not," he cried to her. "I killed Gil—I, I killed him, Eva. And Herndon, too. And Hilton— Just now, I did. And in Chicago, I killed a man— Oh, God—Eva, don't leave me now. I need you, I need somebody—"

He clutched at her arms and she held him tightly, like one holding a child.

"Don't leave me, Eva— Never leave me— Promise me you won't— Promise me," he begged.

"I promise," she whispered.

"If you leave me, it's all over,"

"I'll never leave you, Lionel."

What was this? She was not listening to what he was telling her. She thought him delirious. Mad. Wild.

"Eva, don't you realize what I've been telling you? I, *I* killed Gil, Herndon, Hilton, and another man . . . My hands are wet with blood . . ."

She stopped his mouth with her hand, and then he felt tears, hot and copious, falling on to his face.

"Hush, darling," she said. "You're sick."

She pulled away from him and he lay there, his eyes closed, trying to realize that she did not believe him. He heard her moving softly about behind him, and then he was paralyzed with surprise when he felt her soft, naked body coming into bed and nestling close to him. Her warm arms went about his neck and she pulled his face to hers and he felt her lips clinging to his. Good God, he had told her his horror and had expected to hear her scream and run from him; and now she was surrendering herself, giving her gift to the man she loved, hoping to cure the distraction of his mind by placing a benediction upon his senses. For a moment he was rigid, not knowing what to do. Then the warmth of her reached him, stole into his blood; and he was still, tasting the sweet pull of her clinging lips on his. He sighed, lay still for a moment, then caught her face in his hands and kissed her while there whirled above his head a knowledge of what was happening. She had thought his confession was an eruption of delirium; she had been moved to pity by his state of wild anxiousness. What he had tried to tell her had sounded so fantastic that she had with swift instinct rejected it as unreal, as a figment of a fevered imagination, the irresponsible babblings of a sick man. She would never be able to comprehend that he was a lost soul, spinning like a stray atom far beyond the ken of her mind to conceive. The extremity of his state had unveiled Eva, had made hope and trust rise in her for the first time since her deception. She was with him, close to him, mingling the warmth of her flesh with his, but she did not understand who or what he was or what he had done, could not believe it when she heard it. Yet he needed her. And then he turned to her and took her in his arms and had her so slowly and so intensely and with such a mounting frenzy of sensual greed that they both died the little death together and he lay staring into the dark with wide, vacant eyes, afraid even to think. And then, quietly, as his sense of reality returned, as he felt himself again in the room on the bed with her, something close to a prayer rose up from his heart . . . Show me a way not to hurt her . . . Not to let her know . . . I don't want to kill this sweet girl clinging to me . . . I should not have let it happen . . . And his despair seeped from his hot and tired eyes in large, salty tears . . .

Cross now groped his way through uneasy hours under the protection of the fragile shadow of Eva's colossal illusion. This girl was loving him not for his crimes but for virtues that he did not and could not possess. His happiness was now a kind of terror and he strove in vain to banish from his consciousness the realization that he epitomized the quintessence of all that which Eva most deeply loathed and would flee to avoid. He would clamp his teeth in sterile fury when he saw that though Eva was his kind of woman, he was not her kind of man nor would he ever be. But he begged the grace of nameless powers to let him linger with her for yet awhile before he went to grapple with the dark tides of his destiny. During the next few hours they moved around each other with slow and muted tenderness. He knew that she was unaware that he was cringing in anxiety lest she ask the meaning of those horrible syllables that had been on his confessionally loosened tongue, and he knew that when she did ask him, he would have to push his words past a choking throat and tell her. He ached with anxiety as he watched the flame of love and trust glowing in her eyes, for it was he who had lit that fire with his unintentional deception, and he knew that when she finally gained a knowledge of what he was, it would be snuffed out; and his heart shuddered in fear of her going back into her feminine house and slamming the door on life forever.

Early that evening a bailiff showed up with a summons demanding their presence the following morning at the hearing to be held over the bodies of Gil and Herndon at the office of the Chief Medical Examiner.

"Will it be awful, Lionel?" she asked.

"I'm afraid so, darling. But you must brace yourself for it."

"Lionel," she called.

Tenderly she caught hold of his hand, turned his face to her, smiled faintly, then let her lashes rest upon her wan cheeks.

"Yes, Eva," he prompted her; yet quailing for fear that she would ask him about his confessional eruption.

"Tell me, darling," she inquired in a whisper, "is it wrong to love so soon like this?"

Dismay made his lips tremble. "Trust is the heart of life," he whispered and felt he wanted something to strike him dead. "How can one's trusting another be bad?"

She opened her hazel eyes full on him. "I trust you," she said simply. "I wanted to help you and I saw a way to do it . . ."

"Bless you, Eva," he said, averting his face, feeling a constriction in his throat.

"Sarah'll be here in the morning to help me. I must find a black dress—"

"Will you need to buy any clothes?"

"No, honey. I've plenty. Look, you must rest. I'll handle this," she smiled.

How wrapped up she was in her love! How demurely happy! He wandered into the living room, his hands trembling. Could he let her go on like that? But how could he undo it? He sat, his mind roving back over the deaths of Gil and Herndon and Hilton, his feelings protesting against the whole, wild nightmare; but he could think of no concrete move to make. He recalled having bought a newspaper. Had there been anything in it about the deaths of Gil and Herndon? He found the folded copy of the newspaper jammed into his overcoat pocket. When he had bought it in the lobby of the Hotel Albert right after leaving Hilton sprawled and bloody on the bed, he had been too harassed and frightened to read it. He opened it and was amazed to see an artist's pen-and-ink drawing covering the entire front page under a tall, black headline:

DOUBLE TOTALITARIAN MURDER

The picture showed two tall, popeyed, hawk-faced young men in their shirt sleeves—in truth, both men had worn coats and Herndon had been fifty-eight years of age and Gil had been thirty-six—lamming each other in a savage rage; one was flaying a fire poker and the other was wielding a huge table leg which he held high in the air and was about to crash it down upon the head of the other. Cross's lips twitched in a smile at the expressions of exaggerated hatred which the artist had injected into the facial features of both men; their long, unruly hair was matted and falling almost into their eyes; they were unshaven and their skins were pimply; their teeth were bared, long, and pointed, resembling the fangs of wolves or dogs; and the fingers of their hands were gnarled, lumpy, with long, curving nails suggestive of animal claws. The background depicted by the artist was not the fascist Herndon's chastely furnished study, but a filthy den whose ceiling was cracking and peeling, showing the laths. The corners of the room revealed dense spiderwebs; several empty whiskey bottles lay on the floor. Tacked to the torn wallpaper were several photographs of nude women in various erotic postures, each carrying at the bottom legends such as: FREE LOVE—JOY AND MADNESS—NIGHT OF ABANDON, etc.

Cross blinked in disbelief, not knowing whether to laugh or curse. He lowered the paper and sat in deep reflection. Then he muttered out loud:

"But this is a kind of inverted pro-communist and pro-nazi propaganda. They've so distorted these men that no one could ever recognize their psychological types . . . A Gil or a Herndon might be working at the City Desk of the *Daily News* this very moment . . . What kind of people make up these papers? There couldn't be a better way of disguising totalitarian aims than this."

He lifted the paper again and read the long caption running beneath the drawing:

Hardened Metropolitan police circles were rocked and stunned late yesterday by the Greenwich Village sensationally freakish double murder of a Communist by a Fascist and of a Fascist by a Communist. Though the Medical Examiner has technically dubbed the double crime as double manslaughter, it was learned through unusually reliable sources that these men's diseased brains had been poisoned by the dangerously esoteric doctrines of communal property advocated in the decadent writings of the notorious German author Karl Marx, and the Superman ideas sponsored by the syphilis-infected German philosopher Friedrich Nietzsche who died in an insane asylum. These two rowdy agitators, Gilbert Blount and Langley Herndon, clashed bloodily in a quarrel regarding racial amalgamation theories and both died of their mutually inflicted wounds. (See page 3 for further details.)

Cross tossed the paper aside in disgust; then he remembered that Eva might get hold of it and become upset. He took it into the kitchen and dropped it into the incinerator. He paused; oh, God, that goddamned handkerchief that had brought so much trouble! It was *still* in his pocket! He looked around; he was alone in the kitchen. He took the balled, reddish handkerchief from his pocket and stared at the burns, then once again he dropped it into the incinerator, hoping that this would be the last time he had to get rid of it.

Still brooding over the garbled newspaper story, he went back into the living room. What protection did men have against the Blounts and the Herndons of this world if newspapers could give no better interpretation of what they were after than what he had read? Was it that you could not understand the totalitarians unless you partook of their malady? He understood them; but, of course, he was akin to them, differing from them only in that he did not have a party, the sanction of ideas, a gang to aid him and to abet his actions by the threat of force. Both Gil and Herndon were so much more intelligent than the men who had written the news story that it was pathetic. Did that mean that the future was in the hands of men suffering from this terrible sickness? And that the shape of that future would be determined by which of these monsters would be triumphant . . . ? Did the arrogant confidence of these two monsters stem from their secret knowledge that they knew that those who sought to defeat them would have to become like them, have to turn into the very kind of monsters they wanted to destroy? Was it that the totalitarians *knew* that, historically, no matter if they won or lost battles, that the war against individuality and for the subjugation of freedom was bound to be won by their side? Cross shook his head in wonder.

Could they eventually trace Hilton's death to him? Now that he longed to plot out a future with Eva, he could not let his mind stray too far into the realms of hope; he might be accused at any time . . .

He sighed, rose, strode restlessly about. Eva came in and looked anxiously at him.

"How are you, darling?"

"I'm fine," he lied.

She sat at Gil's desk and began sorting papers.

"You have no more fever?"

"None at all. I'm all right."

She rose and went to him; he knew that she had not come into the room to look for papers, but to be near him, to see that he was not fretting.

"Why don't you relax. It's better for you."

"I'll try, Eva," he said and stretched out on the sofa.

He lay with closed eyes, but relaxation was impossible. Eva knelt at the side of the sofa.

"Come to bed, darling. You need sleep . . ."

"Let me just lie here and think a little—"

"You're not worrying? Tell me the truth."

"I'm not worrying, Eva," he lied despairingly.

She kissed him, gazed long into his dark, brooding eyes.

"Everything'll be all right," she said cheerfully. "You'll see."

"As long as you are there, I'll be all right," he told her.

"I'm all in; I'm going to bed."

"Do that, Eva. I'll be along in a little while—"

"And don't go out into that cold again. We'll soon be free from all this terror . . . We'll be where a big, blue sky stretches over our heads, with the wind blowing through the high pine trees . . . They tell me that the lakes in the Gatineau are blue and deep and clear . . ."

"Yes."

"And all this deception'll be at an end," she murmured hopefully. "Things'll be as clear, as sharp as mountains on the horizon . . ." She sighed. "I want to paint again . . . This time I want to create images com-

mon to everybody, symbols that can link men together . . . Rest now, Lionel."

She was gone. He closed his eyes. Despair was in him
so sharply that he was not aware of the room's four
walls about him. What could he do for Eva . . . ? His
obsession was with him again. How much time did he
have before his foolish world caved in?

Oh, yes; the radio . . . What time did the evening
news come on? He turned the dial on the radio, keeping
the tone barely audible, and listened to the impish notes
of blue-jazz leap and cavort in freedom . . . At ten-
thirty there was a pause in the outpouring of jazz and a
sonorously masculine voice recited a medley of political
news items, and then:

*The second Communist leader in twenty-four hours has
been found shot to death by a .32 calibre revolver under baffling circumstances in a Greenwich Village hotel room late
today. The body, that of John Hilton, 32, ex-school teacher, a
militant Communist leader and a recently elected member of
the powerful Central Committee of the Communist Party,
was discovered by a colored cleaning maid as she was making
her rounds early this evening.*

*John Hilton died as a result of a fatal bullet wound in his
left temple. Death, according to the Medical Examiner, was
instantaneous. The death scene showed no signs of violence or
physical struggle save for a slight abrasion on the forehead of
Hilton.*

*Though all present indications point to suicide, police are
continuing their investigation. Murder has not been ruled
out.*

*Hilton's death comes a few hours after that of Gilbert
Blount, another member of the Central Committee of the
Communist Party, whose place on the Central Committee
had already been taken by John Hilton. In labor circles spec-*

ulation is rife as to whether Hilton was killed by some recently expelled member of the Communist Party.

That was all; Cross switched off the radio and stood up. He had not been mentioned, and whether the police would find some trail leading to him was problematical. He went to the window and stared into the winter night; traces of snow and ice showed on the pavements and sidewalks. A heavy mist hung over the city and the houses on the opposite side of the street were dim and ghostly. Occasionally a man or a woman hurried past.

Now that the news of Hilton's death was public, what would Eva think when she heard it? Would she still believe that he had been babbling senselessly when he had come in earlier that evening? Or would the news of Hilton's death plant a tiny seed of doubt in her mind, a doubt that would grow until she regarded him with fearfully questioning eyes? Though Eva was sleeping, he felt driven to know what she would say; it was much better to learn her reaction now than later. The anxious tension of waiting to see if she would suspect him without his telling her was greater than the dread of what she would say when she knew that at least some part of his incoherent outpourings was true.

As though being guided by some imperious influence, he walked slowly toward Eva's bedroom and stood hesitantly in the partially opened doorway, listening to her quiet, regular breathing in the dark. Would it not be better for her to die now and be spared the pain and shock which he knew he had to bring yet to her? Had he not told Hilton that death was better than prolonged and inflamed suffering? Did he not owe it to her to kill her and thereby guard her from the monstrousness of himself? He advanced to the bed and his right hand lifted itself above her head and hovered there. God, no; no more of this killing whose logic led on and on into the grey, deadening reaches of inhuman meaning . . . ! His damned habit of relentless thinking was mangling the very tendons and nerves of the flesh of life! Eva stirred uneasily on the bed and gave forth a profound sigh, a sigh that told him that the destiny of the soul from which it came could not be encompassed by his churning mental processes alone. As he stood there in the dark straining at a decision, he could see that the grinding mechanisms of man's thought could destroy all of life on earth and leave this watery globe bare of the human beings who had produced the thinking . . .

Living thus tensely in his thoughts, Cross knew that this executing of the sentences of thought on life was a kind of continuous madness whose logical end was suicide. No matter how hot and furious the degree of his thinking, he could not convince himself that to kill Eva to ward off the suffering that the future would bring into the world for her was right. By snatching her life he could stave off the suffering, the pain that *he* thought would be hers, but did *his* insight into what the future held justify his killing her on that basis? The answer to that question was beyond his reach. To slay Gil and Herndon and Hilton in a fit of cold rage because they had outraged his sense of existence was one thing; but only if he were *outside* of life itself, beyond existence, could he make such a judgment about Eva whom he loved. How could he ever be able to tell, after killing Eva, that his judgment had been a correct one? Hate yearned to destroy and sought to forget, but love could not. Love strove creatively toward days that had yet to come. If he killed himself, his processes of thought stopped. Or did they? How could he ever tell after having killed himself that his judgment-act had been the right one . . . ?

His hand was still trembling in the air; he was not feeling, just thinking . . . Logic sustained by love could lift future suffering from her, but love informed by hope could keep her with him to live out the unpredictable chances of life. For life's sake, he would spare Eva. For Eva's sake, he would spare her life. Time alone made this teeming world gush and roar like a Niagara with its richness of unforeseeable events; it was only by plunging rashly onward that one could see at all. And even if a god could exist he would have to be bound to some extent by that . . .

Cross grasped the foot of the bed with his hand to steady his trembling legs. Eva turned over and mumbled something in her sleep and he could see the faint, crystalline sheen of her soft white cheeks glowing like a half-perceived image in the dark. His breath went from his lungs in a long, despairing suspire; he reached out his hand, the fingers still shaking from the throes of indecision, touched her shoulder tenderly, and whispered:

"Eva, darling . . ."

He felt her warm body give a slight start, and then her face turned toward him.

"Yes, Lionel."

"Listen, darling. I've something to tell you . . ."

"Yes?"

"I was listening to the radio and some news about Hilton just came over."

"What is it?"

"He's been killed, shot in his hotel room," he said quietly.

Eva was still as stone for a moment, then she stared at him with a look of wildness in her eyes. Was she considering him guilty? He held his breath and waited. Was she linking up his gibberish with what he was now telling her? She gasped and her hand went to her mouth.

"Oh, God . . . *Why?* Who did it?"

"I don't know," he whispered.

She was silent. Did she know? Why didn't she speak? What was the meaning of that fixed, bleak stare? Yes; her hand was moving now; he could hear the whispering rustle of the bedcovers. Then he felt as though he would fall to the floor as her fingers touched his hand.

"I feel awful," she whispered in horror. "*Only* today I said he should be killed . . ." Her wide eyes glistened in the shadows. Her lips hung speechless; she looked at the faint outlines of the walls of the room, then turned again to him. "Do you think it's the Party? Has he disobeyed them?"

His forehead rested on the edge of the bed and he knelt to her, as though mutely appealing against her judgment.

"I don't know," he breathed.

Couldn't she tell? He heard her breath catching in her throat, then the sound of soft crying came to him.

"Why, why, Lionel, is life like this?" she begged of him. "I feel darkness closing in all around me . . . I'm afraid . . . Hold me . . ."

Her trembling arms groped for him and he held her.

"I'm sorry," he mumbled.

"Hilton always frightened me," Eva whispered. "I never liked him. Why, I don't know. And he had just turned poor Bob over to the authorities . . . It's *wrong* to kill like that, Lionel . . ."

Cross bowed his head; he knew that those words, though she did not know it, were really directed at him . . .

"I'm sorry I had to tell you like this. But try to sleep now," he said. "Try and forget it . . ."

He still held her. Her sobs grew less and finally, as though overwhelmed by too much horror, she slept once more. Cross rose and went into the living room and stood at the front window. Eva's own sense of guilt had protected her from suspecting him; she had recoiled because she too had had the impulse to kill Hilton. Eva was *too* good, believed *too* strongly in life. Maybe this belief in goodness was her life, and once it was gone, what then?

Ought he vanish into the winter night and leave her forever? He had a chance to make a clean run for it before suspicion pointed in his direction. In his deserting her like this she would not know what he had done; there would be a hurt in her heart for awhile, but in the end she would get over it and there would always remain a spot of tenderness in her memory for him. And if he stayed, he would surely have to face the shock of her learning of his monstrous deeds. Was there the remotest hope of her still loving him after she had discovered the reaches and depths of his problem? Again the pages of her diary stood before his eyes and his question answered itself. But where could he run to? And what was he running from? He knew that in any hiding place, under whatever guise he chose to conceal himself, he would be alone with himself to meditate in dismay upon the ungovernable compulsiveness of himself and the loss of his sense of direction in life.

No . . . He had to remain. And if he ran off, would not Houston then be certain of his guilt? He cocked his head, listening; from far off came the wail of a siren so faint that it seemed that he was imagining it. Would those sirens sound for him soon? And if they caught him, what would he do? Questions like that agitated him more than the recollection of his crimes. The shame of having to tell, to explain to strangers was overpower-

ing. That could not happen; he would make use of his
gun on himself first . . .

It was only in relation to Eva that his thoughts could
shape themselves with any meaning. Was not there some
way of telling her and stealing the horror from it as he
did so? Nervously, he rubbed his forehead. He was only
fretting himself into a state of jitters by forever juggling
farfetched possibilities like this. He would go to bed.
Half an hour later he lay down by the sleeping form of
Eva, but he did not close his eyes. He knew her hurt,
but could she ever know his? Was there really no direct
bridge between the subjective worlds of people? Was the
possibility of communication only a kind of pretense, an
arrangement assumed to exist but which really did not?
Was the core of the subjective life of each person sealed
off absolutely from that of another and one could tell
what transpired in another heart only when the contents
of that heart were projected outwardly in some objective
form? He recalled that Eva had not responded to him as
he really was; his life had somehow represented for her
something which she had yearned to embrace; and he
lay here now knowing from having stolen a lawless
glimpse into her diary what she felt, her deception, her
shame, but unable really to touch her heart, feeling that
she was forever beyond his reach. A dizzy terror came
over him. Were we really that much alone in this life?
Were all human hearts encased in this irredeemable isolation and we only had the satisfaction of fooling ourselves that we were together? He groaned softly and did
not close his eyes in sleep until dawn crept into the
room.

A little after eight o'clock he was awakened by the
ringing of the doorbell. Eva was still sleeping. He put

on his robe and went to the door. It was Sarah, ashen of face and shaking with fear.

"Good morning, Sarah," Cross said casually, braced to hear her tell of what experience she had had with the police.

"God, Lionel, did you know that Hilton's dead?"

"Yes; I heard about it on the radio."

"Do you know where I slept last night?"

"No. What do you mean?"

"In the police station," Sarah explained with indignation. "I've been in jail, you hear? When I got home last night, the cops were waiting for me at the door of my apartment . . . They hauled me to jail and grilled me for four hours . . . I'm so glad Bob's in Ellis Island, or they'd have him now, for sure."

"But why did they take you to jail?" Cross asked.

"They had the idea that I killed Hilton because Hilton told on Bob—"

"But how did they find out about that?"

"I don't know. Lionel, what's *happening*?"

"God only knows, Sarah."

Sarah was hanging up her overcoat in the hallway.

"You think it was the Party?" she asked in a whisper.

"Who knows—" Cross knew now that she did not suspect him. "When I came in last night, Eva told me the cops had been here asking for you."

"Here?" Sarah echoed.

"Yes."

"How's Eva?"

"She's sleeping," Cross told her.

He told Sarah to wait while he dressed, and then he brewed a pot of coffee.

"I know it's wrong," Sarah began, drinking her coffee, "but I can't say I'm sorry about Hilton . . . But that can't help poor Bob now. He's gone." She sat down her cup and wept. "Lionel, I still hate Hilton. He's dead and I still hate 'im . . ." She shook her head. "There was something cold about Hilton."

"I daresay Hilton would have agreed with you," Cross said.

"Lionel, what do you suppose Hilton got out of sending Bob to his death?"

"Nothing."

"Then why did he take such drastic action for Bob's little offense against the Party?"

"Hilton was obeying orders, and he believed in the orders."

"But Bob's *human*," Sarah protested.

"To Hilton, Bob was only something to be sacrificed in the interests of a vast design," Cross explained.

"To make a better world?" Sarah asked; her voice was strangely hopeful.

Cross knew that she was now seeking for something to redeem the suffering and death that Bob would inherit.

"No, Sarah. To Hilton and men like him the world is perfect just like it is. They just want a chance to rule that world."

"I don't understand," Sarah sighed.

"It's better maybe not to understand," Cross told her. They fell silent. An idea came to Cross. Eva was deeply attached to Sarah, and would not his case be stronger if he threw the two women together? His position was so weak that he felt he needed the strength and help of a woman whose reactions were as straightforward as those of Sarah.

"What are you going to do now, Sarah?" he asked her. "Bob's gone and you're alone."

"I don't know," she mumbled.

"Look, after the hearing with the Medical Examiner, suppose Eva and I moved up to Harlem with you for awhile?"

Sarah's eyes brightened.

"Oh, I'd like that— I'm so alone up there . . . But what would Eva think of it?"

"I don't know. I haven't asked her yet, but I will."

Sarah's feminine instinct for matchmaking came to the fore in her.

"Eva likes you," she said in a tone of voice that indicated that she approved. "What's she going to do now that Gil's dead?"

"She wants to be with me—"

"Oh!" Sarah pondered a moment, then she smiled. "Old Funny Face—" She was moody again, thinking of her own lonely life. "Some people have all the luck."

The official aspects of the Medical Examiner's hearing, which was a kind of inquest, did not prove to be as much of an ordeal as either Cross or Eva had feared. It fell to Cross to bear the burden of giving the longest and most detailed testimony of all the witnesses, for the Communist Party's able and noisy lawyer strove tenaciously to obtain a verdict branding Langley Herndon as the murderer of Gil. Cross, knowing that the Party, in its own interests, would leap to protect him if the police turned on him, answered repeatedly and emphatically that he had seen Herndon beating Gil with the fire poker and he even went so far in his lies as to testify that Gil had not seemed to be in a condition to defend himself.

Eva testified of having seen Herndon with his gun on the stairs; she told of her running back into the apartment and of Lionel Lane's bolting the door against him. But Eva's and Cross's testimony was not strong enough to influence the studied, scientific opinion of the cool

Medical Examiner who contended that both men died in point of time so close together that he could not honorably or justifiably entertain any verdict save that of double manslaughter. In so far as Cross was personally concerned, the hearing was a success; he had managed to deflect all thoughts of guilt from himself.

The most frightening phase of the hearing came after the verdict had been rendered, for newsmen crowded around to get photographs of Eva. Cross was glad that he was forgotten, for he dreaded having his face appear in the press under the false name of Lionel Lane. Sarah hurried Eva to a waiting car provided by the Party and they managed to get away with but a few flashbulbs exploding in Eva's anxious, drawn, and veiled face. Menti had been assigned by the Party to accompany them, and he drove the car. Back in Charles Street, in the lower hallway of the building, they had run into another battery of newsmen and Cross's admiration for Menti rose as he watched the man unhesitatingly and ruthlessly dispatch the reporters and photographers. At last they were in the shelter of the apartment and Cross fastened the night-chain on the door. Sarah took Eva to her room and Cross paced to and fro, preoccupied, conscious of Menti hanging on for no apparent reason. Menti's presence irked Cross; he had nothing in common with this lackey and wished that he would make himself absent. Menti was a hireling, an errand boy, a white-collar by-product of the American industrial world who had offered his meaningless, self-despised existence to the Party to be used, ravaged, dominated, and filled with a purpose, any purpose as long as the burden of the responsibility of his own life was lifted from his quaking shoulders.

"You seem nervous, Lane," Menti commented, smiling and sucking at his cigarette. "What's the matter?"

"Just restless," Cross answered.

"You know, the Party's interested in you," Menti said in a voice that carried a multiplicity of meanings: ironical, teasing, threatening, warning . . .

Cross paused and studied the servile mask of geniality that always served to hide Menti's real motives. Was Menti spying on him for the Party? Cross felt that it was safe to assume that he was . . .

"Why?" Cross asked.

"The Party's interested in intelligent men, and you are intelligent," Menti said in tones of flattery, as though bound to give even Cross, an outsider, his due.

"But I know so little about these matters, Menti," Cross protested, knowing that he knew more than Menti would believe.

"Too bad Gil couldn't've lived to coach you until you were seasoned," Menti said in a tone of wistful regret. "Gil told Hilton before he died that you had the makings of a real Bolshevik: outlook, temperament, and all . . . You liked Gil, didn't you?"

"Of course, Menti," Cross lied in a full-bodied tone. "Gil was my friend."

"And I reckon you liked Hilton too, didn't you?" Menti asked slowly, watching Cross's face.

"Of course," Cross lied. "But I didn't know poor Hilton very well . . ."

"Too bad. He was a brilliant guy. He could have been a damn good friend of yours if they hadn't killed 'im . . ."

"Has the Party got any line on who did it?" Cross asked.

"No," Menti said. "But they'll find out. The Party never sleeps, boy. Once they get an idea into their heads, they *never* give up."

"What idea have they got?"

"How do I know?" Menti said, smiling and studying Cross.

Cross restrained a chuckle, then resumed his striding to and fro. He could handle this Menti. He was certain that Hilton had not taken Menti into his confidence. But did Menti himself suspect him? Cross grew irritable. It was wearying to give the attention and strain necessary to keep track of the motives of Party people. The hell with Menti . . . But in his heart he hoped fervently that no other fool would pop up to threaten him; he was sick of the thought of murder.

"Say, Menti, have the police found any clues as to who killed Hilton?" he asked.

"Nothing. But we know he didn't kill himself," Menti said.

"Really? How do you know?"

"We just know. He didn't have any reason. Say, Lane, could I ask you a question?"

Cross turned and stood in front of Menti, his hands deep in his pockets. Just try to figure me out, boy, Cross mused.

"Sure. What is it?"

"What school did you say you came from?"

"I didn't say," Cross told him; yes, Menti was digging at him now.

"But you told the D.A. that you came from Fisk . . ."

So this clown was not so dumb after all. The Party had checked with Houston and Menti had been informed. Cross's eyes narrowed.

"Why are you asking me this, Menti?" Cross countered softly. He was determined not to let this man see him in any way rattled.

"To find out the truth, of course," Menti said.

"Did the Party ask you to?"

"Yes," Menti answered honestly, looking boldly at Cross.

For the first time the reality of Menti broke through to Cross. There was a shy fanaticism in the man's deep, brown eyes, an apologetic inferiority in his demeanor, an ingratiating humility even in the way he talked—all of which hid something that Cross could not fathom. What was this man up to? That the Party trusted Menti was obvious. But how far would Menti go? Cross blamed himself for having not gotten to know Menti better.

"You knew Hilton well, didn't you?" Cross asked him.

"Better than he knew himself," Menti smiled and hung his head, a sheepish look coming into his eyes.

Then Cross knew. Menti had been spying on Hilton! And Hilton had suspected it, but had not been certain of it. That was why Hilton had not told Menti about his finding of the bloody handkerchief! How complicated it was! What a system of life! Spies spying upon spies who were being spied upon! Imagine a society like that! It would be an elaborate kind of transparent ant heap in which the most intimate feelings of all the men and women in it would be known, a glass jailhouse in which the subjective existence of each man and woman would be public each living moment . . . And if an alien happened to show up in that ant heap, it would at once become evident because that alien would be at once opaque and, hence, known as alien. And for his spying in this ant heap, each spy would derive, as his reward, a satisfaction from the godlike position which he could assume in relation to his neighbor. This spy would not be a complete god, of course; being a complete god would be reserved for the distant dictator. But being a little god was better than being no god at all . . . It was perfect, giving each spy something for his pains and hopes, and supplying each with an explanation for his suffering should he fail . . .

Cross admitted that he had made a psychological mistake; he should have observed Menti closer. Intuitively he sensed an almost organic servility that would make this man lend himself to any use by those whom he respected and loved. He had now to try to get to this man, for he felt that the influence of the Party on Menti's mind now caused Menti to regard him as an opaque object that had to be accounted for. He studied Menti's too-white, sensitive face, almost a woman's face; he looked wonderingly at the deep, brooding eyes that never let you hold their gaze for long; at the bluish tint that always showed just beneath his dead-white, close-shaven skin; at those long and tapering fingers that were sensitive without being in any way delicate . . . The man seemed like an empty, waiting vessel that could be easily filled with either a frightened acquiescence or a strident brutality; or, if necessary, a combination of both.

Cross sat next to Menti and asked him:

"Menti, what have you got against me?"

"Personally, nothing." Menti's voice was affable.

"What do you think I'm up to?"

"I don't know."

"Have you seen me do anything that would make you suspicious of me?"

"No."

"Then why are you prying into me?"

"We don't know you," Menti said without anger.

"What do you want to know about me?"

"Everything."

"What do you call 'knowing' somebody, Menti?"

Menti smiled, crushed out a cigarette, and lit another one.

"It's possible to know enough about a man to know when he would or wouldn't do certain things," Menti said.

"You talk about people as if they were machines, something *made*," Cross protested. "How can you predict behavior?"

"By a man's convictions," Menti said. "By where he stands in the context of a concrete situation."

"So the Party can tell in *advance* if a man will be guilty or not in any given instance?" Cross asked. "You mean to say that?"

"Just that," Menti said. "The logic of a position will make a man act in a certain way. Given a man with a given set of convictions, and given a situation, the Party can tell what that man would do."

"And you could condemn him in advance of his deed?"

"Certainly. It's logical, isn't it?" Menti asked earnestly.

Cross knew that Menti was reflecting the attitude of the Party.

"What are you trying to find out about me?"

"Who you are and what you are doing."

Menti was fluent in his answers and Cross knew that the Party would soon know that he had asked these questions. He would try to send back a human answer.

"I'm a Negro, Menti; I'm trying to learn," Cross lied.

"Learn *what*?"

"How to live."

"Hunh. You mean how the *Party* lives?"

"Hell, no. Have I ever asked you anything about the Party?"

"No. But you got Eva—"

"But Eva's not a political person, Menti. You know that."

"She was Gil's wife."

"So what? Are you moral?"

"The Party is not moral," Menti answered, declining to assert his personal opinion. "You love Eva, don't you?"

"Yes, I do."

"Why?"

"She's a woman, one I've been seeking all my life."

"And she happened to be a wife of a member of the Central Committee—"

"She knows nothing of politics," Cross protested.

"You found that out, didn't you?" Menti demanded.

"Yes."

"Why?" Menti demanded in insolent tones.

It was hopeless. Goddamn this dirty spoon in the hands of the Party! Cross rose. This man would not, could not believe that there existed men who could, at some moments of their lives, be honest as Cross was now honest with him about Eva. Indeed, Cross could feel that his love of Eva would assume baffling guises in the Party's mind. The simpler and more human a thing was, the more the Party feared it . . .

"Listen, Menti, if the Party wants to know anything about me, let 'em come and ask me," Cross said. "They don't have to go licking around the District Attorney . . ."

"They'll come to you; don't worry," Menti assured him. "They went to the D.A. because you know 'im."

And what would Houston think of their asking? Cross felt that he was in danger, but it was not acute yet. Yes, he would move Eva out of this apartment tonight. His real hope was that he could get Eva to trust

him and run off somewhere with her. But what explana-
tions could he give her for such a drastic move? The
only reasons he could give her would be of a nature that
would guarantee her not coming . . . Menti stood and
put on his overcoat; he paused, a cigarette smouldering
in his lips.

"The Party's checked at Fisk University and has found
that you never went to school there," Menti came to the
point at last.

"So?"

"Then why did you tell the D.A. that you went
there?"

"Must I tell the D.A. the truth?" Cross hedged.

"Tell me, what do you plan to do now?"

"Nothing."

"You got any money?"

"Not much."

"You're staying with Eva here?"

"If she lets me," he said.

"She'll let you," Menti said.

Cross was angry, but he knew that he had invited that
crack. He held his peace. But it was clear that the crux
of the Party's attitude was his relationship with Eva.

"I'm blowing, guy," Menti said and left.

Cross sat and brooded. If the Party checked up on
him, they would run into a blank wall, and then what
would they do? Just because his life was not transparent,
would they get suspicious? The secret side of him was a
handicap in the Party's eyes . . . The more they probed
into his background to uncover his identity, the more
inflamed would their suspicions become. But what
would they be suspicious of? And suspicion was not
proof of murder. They would have to peel off layer after
layer of pretense, uncover front after front of make-
believe and where would it lead them in the end?

Eventually, of course, the police could trace him by his fingerprints back to his Post Office identity in Chicago. But what would that really prove? They would run into a truly bewildering set of facts . . .

Sarah came out of Eva's room.

"She wants to see you, Funny Face," Sarah said.

Sarah looked lost, piqued; he could see that she was losing weight. And Eva's happiness was exciting her jealousy.

"I'm going to ask Eva to come to your place," he told her. "We'll all chip in together on the expenses, hunh?"

"I could use some money," Sarah told him flatly. "I've no work now. I got to look for something."

"Don't worry," Cross told her.

He went in to Eva who lay pale and limp on the bed. She summoned a smile for him. He took her hand and they were silent for a long time.

"Eva, I've an idea . . . Until Gil is buried, let us go and live with Sarah in Harlem. It'll take you away from this apartment, those reporters, and you'll be in different surroundings," he explained.

She was thoughtful for a moment, then nodded her head in assent.

"That would be nice. I've always wanted to live there. Is it all right with Sarah?"

"She loves it."

"And we can be alone there, Lionel," Eva said with a sense of relief.

Life in Sarah's sixth-floor walk-up apartment eased the sense of strain in Cross, but it did not free him from the probing presence of Menti who came the next morning, expressing great astonishment at the fact that they had moved. He had gone to the Charles Street apartment, he said, and rang and rang and no one had answered the door.

"Then I knew that if anyone would know where Eva was, it would be Sarah," Menti explained.

He had come, he told them unctuously, to bring Eva news of the Party's elaborate arrangements for Gil's funeral. All Sunday morning Gil's body would lie in state in a union hall, guarded by Communist militants, and in the afternoon it would be shipped to Gil's family in the Bronx for burial. As Menti described the reaction of the Party to Gil's death, Cross could see that Gil's dying was being used to excite admiration for Party leaders in general. Gil had already, in Party circles, been deified as a kind of god who had laid down his only life as a sacrifice on the altar of freedom. Menti then, with measured movements which were supposed to be consonant with death and grief, hauled from his pockets a huge batch of messages of condolence which had come from as far away as Moscow. But Cross observed that Communists were not good when it came to paying respects to the dead; there was something embarrassingly self-conscious about Menti's manner as he sought to convince Eva of the touching solicitude of the Party for her in her bereavement. It's hard to pretend something about death that you really don't feel, Cross thought.

"Now, Eva," Menti went on, smiling slightly. "Don't think the Party has forgotten you. The Party never forgets its own." He drew forth from an inner coat pocket a big envelope and handed it to Eva.

"What's this?" she asked.

"It's for you. Look at it and see," Menti urged.

Cross was standing behind Eva when she tore open the envelope; it was filled with greenbacks.

"But why?" Eva asked, her eyes round with surprise.

"It's yours," Menti said. "You're Gil's widow. The Party will look after you . . ."

"But I can work," Eva's voice faltered. "I'm an artist—"

"Do you spurn the sympathy of the Party?" Menti asked.

"Oh, no . . . It's not that, Menti," Eva said. "But I've never worked for the Party. I was only Gil's wife . . ."

"You helped Gil, you comforted him; you enabled him to keep up his hard pace of work for the Party . . ."

Eva's eyes filled with a look of terror and she sank to the floor and sobbed, shaking her head. Cross knew what was going through her mind. All that Menti had just said about Eva's relationship to Gil was blatantly untrue; Eva had not helped him because she felt she had been deceived and turned into an object, a thing, a means . . . Then what was the meaning of this gesture of the Party? It was a threat wrapped in kindness . . . They were seeking a way to keep a hold over Eva, trying to buy her loyalty, laying the basis for future demands. Cross could feel that the Party was delicately making its first moves against him. He felt alarm, but he knew that he had some time yet before things would become serious enough to warrant his taking action.

"But why are you crying so, my dear?" Menti asked. "Are you surprised?"

"But I shouldn't take it," Eva evaded his question. "I've no right to it."

"The Party is loyal to you," Menti pointed out.

"Yes," Eva gulped.

"And don't you want to be loyal to the Party?"

Eva did not reply; she turned her fear-filled eyes questioningly upon Cross's face, seeking his guidance. And Cross noticed that Eva's appeal for his advice was not lost upon Menti's smilingly observant eyes, eyes that traveled cryptically from Eva's face to Cross's, and then back to Eva's again . . .

Cross found himself paraphrasing a Biblical passage:

"Thou shalt not depend upon others, nor trust them: for this your Party is a jealous Party, visiting the suspicions of the leaders upon the members unto the third and fourth friends of the friends around the Party . . ."

He was now sure that Menti was reporting back to the Party every nuance which he could observe between him and Eva. He hated the money that the Party was offering, but he could not afford to tell Eva not to accept it. He must make them guess at what he knew and felt.

"Why not, honey? It's for you . . ."

"But I don't *want* it, Lionel," she whispered; she was still afraid that the Party would try to dictate her life.

Cross cursed himself. Each step he took carried him deeper into a morass of lies and deceit.

"The Party feels an obligation," Cross said, trying to make his lie sound genuine. "If you refuse, they'll wonder what reasons you could have."

"Exactly," Menti said.

Cross did not believe what Menti had said, and he knew that Menti knew that he did not believe it.

"Oh, all right," Eva sighed. "But I'm young and I have my painting!"

"As soon as you're rested and settled, the Party wants you to paint," Menti told her hurriedly. "Now, tomorrow's Sunday. I'll pick you up in the morning at nine and take you to the union hall, hunh?"

Eva nodded her head. Menti shook hands with her and left. Sarah, who had overheard it all from the back of the room, came forward with a tight and angry face.

"Well, I'll be goddamned," Sarah swore.

"What's the matter?" Eva asked.

"They pay you, but *me* . . . ? I lost Bob, but do they give me one red cent? They took Bob from me, but do they *care*?" Bitter tears welled in her eyes.

"Oh, Sarah," Eva protested guiltily. "Here, you take this money. You need it." She held out the envelope with a gesture of childish generosity.

"I don't want it!" Sarah shouted.

"But, Sarah," Eva wept, "I didn't *ask* the Party for it . . ."

"I ain't mad at you," Sarah stormed. "I'm mad at them! I'm convinced that there's something fishy behind this. They don't give a good goddamn about what happens to you. They're trying to buy your loyalty for some reason." Sarah turned to Cross. "What do you think, Lionel?"

"I don't know, Sarah," he lied helplessly; he agreed with Sarah, but he could not tell her so, at least not yet.

Cross wondered if he was underestimating the Party. Though the Party was not an official adjunct to the police department, it did have wide powers of an effective and peculiar nature; it had its own underground apparatus and special methods of investigation. But what could they do with their findings? And he was convinced that he would have more than ample warning of their movements before they got too close to him.

Late that evening, immediately following dinner, Cross knew that the Party was adamantly on his trail, for Menti showed up accompanied by a short, dark Negro who hovered silently behind him, keeping on his hat and overcoat. This man, known as Hank, had a black, blank mask for a face, a greyish scar that went diagonally across his lips and chin, eyes that held a look of chronic hate whose origin seemed to go back to some inaccessible past. Cross knew that the Party had given

Menti assistance in the form of this thug to help in spying upon him and Eva. This meant that the Party had not acted because it had not quite made up its mind. But what were the leaders thinking? Did they regard him as a spy? If so, for whom? And would they ever be able to fathom his motive in killing Gil? Or would they in the end just create some imaginary crime and try to brand him with its guilt? He knew that they were fully capable of that . . .

Menti pretended that the Party had asked for papers of an urgent political nature that Gil had left behind in his desk. Eva willingly surrendered to Menti the keys of the apartment on Charles Street. Cross had no fear of the Party finding anything incriminating in Eva's apartment, for he had brought his only suitcase with him. Before leaving, Menti lingered at the door, smiling, looking thoughtfully off into space. Hank stood behind Menti, morose, his eyes darting about.

"How are you getting on, Lane?" Menti asked.

"Oh, so-so," Cross said.

"Only so-so?" Menti asked. "You need money?"

"No."

Hank was listening so intently that his eyes glittered.

"The Party's curious about you," Menti said.

"You've told me I'm under suspicion," Cross said. "But you haven't told me what I'm suspected of."

"Say, where were you born?" Menti asked suddenly. "I want to know."

"You mean the Party wants to know— Tell the Party folks to come and ask me what they want to hear—"

"I'm the Party; I'm asking—"

"You think I'm with the police, don't you?" Cross evaded him.

Menti laughed, then playfully slapped Cross on the shoulder.

"Hell, Lane, we're not children," Menti said. "You've no connections with the police; we've investigated and we know . . . Say, tell me, when did you last see Hilton?"

"I tried to see him yesterday afternoon. But he wasn't in."

"What time was that?"

"Gosh, I don't know," Cross smiled. "Is it important?"

"Could be." Menti was baffled at Cross's casual manner. "Can you *prove* you didn't see 'im?"

"I haven't bothered to think about that," Cross said.

"The hotel clerk said a guy of your description asked for Hilton around four o'clock," Menti told him. "That must have been you, hunh?"

"Maybe. There are many Negroes who look like me," Cross said; he knew that they were trying clumsily to link him with Hilton's death.

"Not likely," Menti said. "At least they don't act like you. The hotel clerk remembers you because you acted self-assured, like a man who knows his way around."

"I know my way around," Cross laughed.

"Good-bye," Menti said suddenly.

They left. Cross shut the door and at once Sarah came out of the living room and Cross could see that she had overheard the conversation.

"What are they after you for?" she asked.

"They are crazy," Cross told her, laughing. "You know, they are trying to build up a case . . . They want to accuse me of killing Hilton . . ."

"Good God!" Sarah looked stunned. "Could it be because you're living with Eva? But the Party isn't interested in things like that. They're trying to put their finger on you for something and they're going about it slow and easy. They know you're here with Eva and won't run off—"

"You think so?" Cross asked to test her intuitions.

"I *know* it; I *can* feel it . . ."

Cross forced a laugh and shrugged his shoulders.

Just before going to bed that night, when they were alone together, Eva came demurely to him with a package wrapped up in heavy brown paper. He saw a look of devotion and trust in her tranquil, hazel eyes. She knelt at his feet and caught hold of his hand.

"Lionel," she whispered.

"Yes, darling."

In her attitude was a mute giving of her life to him that sprang from a sense of her newly gained freedom.

"Lionel," she began, "I'm going to let you know something that I once swore that I'd never divulge to anyone on earth. I want you to know the Party you're dealing with . . . They deceived me with Gil. Darling, here in this package are my diaries. They contain my hope and my despair . . . You must not let them make you a victim, too . . . They're clever. Menti's hounding you for something . . . Read these diaries and know the world in which I once lived . . ."

Cross's eyes fell; he tried to keep his sense of shame from showing.

"You must know the kind of woman with whom you've elected to go through life," Eva continued bravely, her eyes full upon his face. "Life has made me akin to you. The world has treated me as it has treated you. You'll see that when you read this . . ."

Cross was a riot of impulses; he wanted to tell her that he had already read them; that he was not worthy of what she was doing; that he too had a past to tell of; that it was to her that he ought to kneel and not she to him . . . One impulse canceled the other and he said nothing; then he seized her and crushed her to him in an outburst of despair that was so deep and sharp that it seemed to stop his breath.

"Until death, Lionel," she whispered.

"Yes; until death," he sighed and bit his lips. He clung to her and hid his face; he did not want her to see the tears that stood stingingly in his eyes. When she pulled herself free, she laughed and wiped his eyes with the tips of her fingers.

"You silly-billy," she said.

"You make me feel that way," he told her truthfully.

"Look, let's go to a midnight movie," she suggested. "I'm tired of being cooped up."

"Okay."

No sooner was he upon the street with Eva than he saw Menti and Hank lurking in a shadowy doorway near a corner. And he knew that Menti had seen him, for the man lowered his head and walked off quickly, pulling Hank after him. He did not call Eva's attention to Menti, feeling that it would only worry her. With Eva clinging to his arm, he moved on over patches of snow and ice, wondering what the Party knew and when it planned to act.

He was now under twenty-four-hour surveillance. Did they think he was going to run off? Were they working with the District Attorney? He felt that he could handle the Party, but Houston was another matter. He damned the day he had met the man who knew so well the spiritual malady that had plagued and undone him—the dilemma of the ethical criminal, the millions of men who lived in the tiny crevices of industrial society completely cut off from humanity, the teeming multitudes of little gods who ruled their own private worlds and acknowledged no outside authority. Hating that part of himself that he could not manage, Cross must perforce fear and hate Houston who knew how close to crime men of his kind had by necessity to live.

After the movie they returned to the apartment to find that Sarah was not in. Eva was worried; it was past two o'clock in the morning and she lamented that they had not had the foresight to invite Sarah along with them, and Cross agreed with her, but for reasons of his own. He suspected that Sarah was with Menti . . .

Sarah arrived around three o'clock accompanied by Menti, Hank, and another elderly, portly, white-haired, well-dressed man. Sarah, slightly tipsy from drink, came straight to Cross with a knowing look in her eyes. They've been pumping her, Cross thought.

"Lionel, I want you to meet Menti's friend, Mr. Blimin," Sarah said.

"How are you?" Cross said.

"I'm glad to meet you, Lane," Blimin said.

They shook hands. Menti at once went to Blimin and Hank and took both of them by their arms.

"Say, you two wanted to find that little room, didn't you?"

"Oh, yes," Blimin said, looking around the room at Cross, Eva, and Sarah. "Will you excuse me?"

Menti herded the two of them into the hallway. It did not look natural. Cross knew that Menti had gotten Blimin and Hank out of the room in order to say something to them of a confidential nature. The moment Menti's footsteps had ceased to sound in the hallway, Sarah rushed to Cross and Eva and burst out in a loud whisper:

"You should have heard what they were asking me about you—"

"Yes? Tell me," Cross urged her.

"Blimin wanted to know your age, your background,

how you spoke, who your mother was, who your father was, what school you came from, what organizations you belonged to . . ."

"Good God!" Cross forced himself to laugh.

"But, *why*?" Eva stood and indignation blazed in her eyes.

"I don't know," Sarah said.

Eva turned to Cross and said: "What do they mean? You've got to tell them off, Lionel."

"I'll do that," he said.

"If you don't tell them, I will," Eva swore with anger.

"But this just started today, honey," he reminded her. He had to keep this thing to normal proportions in her mind. "I'll see them as soon as the ceremony for Gil's over."

"And tell them to keep out of our life," Eva demanded.

"But, wait— I haven't told you everything yet," Sarah said. "That Blimin wanted to know what kind of books you read, what kind of mail you received, if you spoke any foreign languages, if you had any secret appointments, if a lot of telephone calls came for you, how large were the bills you spent, what kind of people came to see you, if I could hear you typing late at night, if you mailed any big envelopes . . . Lord, he was like a lawyer."

"Don't worry, Sarah," Cross told her. "They're worried about Gil and Hilton and they're trying to find out who killed them."

"But why are they snooping around *us*?" Eva demanded.

"Listen, Lionel," Sarah said with deep care. "I hope to God that you're not like Bob. Don't have a past for them to dig into. This is exactly how they were acting before they turned Bob over to the Immigration author-

ities . . . Oh, God, I hate those people, I *hate* 'em!"
Tears of rage blinded Sarah.

"But there are others who are worse than Communists," Cross told Sarah. "The Communists are kittens; but there are tigers in the jungle."

"What do you mean?" Sarah asked.

"Communists are trained and organized; but there are men, their equals, who have never been broken. *They* are more dangerous than Communists!"

"Well, I hate 'em, *hate* 'em *all*!" Sarah hissed.

"If you hate them, then you'll never understand them," Cross explained.

"Why in hell would I want to understand them?" Sarah demanded.

The doorknob turned and Menti, Blimin, and Hank reentered the room. Blimin came straight to Cross and went to work.

"Say, they tell me you were a friend of Gil," Blimin said.

"That's right," Cross answered.

"And you knew Hilton?"

"Not as well as I knew Gil."

"Is this your first time to become acquainted with the Party?"

"That's it."

"What do you think of our Party?"

"Well, I doubt if I know it well enough to form a worthwhile opinion," Cross hedged.

"Could I ask you a direct question?"

"Of course."

"Lane, are you now, directly or indirectly, verbally or organizationally, by proxy or on your own behalf engaged in anti-Party activity?" Blimin let the words roll neatly off the tip of his tongue.

Cross rose from the side of Eva and faced Blimin.

How could he tell this man something that would set his mind at rest, and yet not leave in him the impression that he was evading anything.

"You don't have to answer unless you want to, Lane," Blimin said.

"I'm hesitating in order to give full weight to what you've asked me," Cross said.

The Communists were at last boldly leaping into an area where the police had feared to tread. His relation to the Party was the reverse of his relation to Houston. The essence of the Party was an open lawlessness and it could smell lawlessness in others even when it could not identify it correctly. What tactic could he use here? His first move should be to find out how much they suspected and the degree and intensity of their seriousness.

"Mr. Blimin, I suppose this is as good a time as any for us to have a showdown," Cross began. "What are you suspecting me of? Why are you posing all these vague and roundabout questions?"

"Blimin's not a man to play with," Menti reminded Cross.

"We're careful in the Party, Lane," Blimin said. "And we don't know who you are. You are a close friend of Eva; Eva is close to us, and so you are close to us, but we don't know you. I'd like to see you account for yourself, to put it frankly. We've been trying to get a line on you, and the more we try, the less we find. You don't add up. What do you think of things? How do you feel? To our Party, these questions are of paramount importance. Our Party is under attack from many quarters. You show up suddenly on the scene, and two of our best leaders die under questionable circumstances and you are nearby . . . Naturally, the question arises: *Who is Lionel Lane?* What organization does he belong to? What are his interests? Who are his friends? What ideas does he hold? Now, Lane, I'm here to listen to you. I'm an old man and I'm a pretty good judge of men. If you're honest and on the up and up, I'll be able to tell it, feel it. If you're hiding something, I can tell that too. Is what I'm asking fair?"

"It's fair," Cross conceded.

"Are you willing to talk?"

"Of course," Cross laughed. He knew that Blimin could not drag his secret from him; his past was safe; his past was himself. "I know nothing of the ideology of the Party."

Blimin's face changed; he stood; his eyes grew hard; when he spoke his words were strident and underlined with a tinge of viciousness.

"I'm not talking about ideology. You're a man with the ability to grasp situations. I know that . . . You know goddamn well what I'm wondering about you."

"Well," Cross drawled, "I know you know I'm a stranger—"

"No; no!" Blimin slapped his hand through the air with a gesture of disdain. "I mean this— Your appearance in our midst coincides with death and violence! I'm talking to the point now . . . In the eyes of the Party you are under *suspicion*."

"You suspect me of what?" Cross asked boldly.

"Of almost anything and everything," Blimin stated his case.

"And what do you expect me to do about that?" Cross egged him on.

"Clear yourself of suspicion, or we will take measures to see that you do not remain longer in our midst," Blimin said.

"This is vague," Cross argued. "I'm guilty, you say; but you don't say what I'm supposed to be guilty of—"

"You're dodging, Lane! Right now you're guilty of

evading my questions— Look, you can't play 'possum with us. You're dealing with experienced men. You are supposed to have a background that would make you acceptable to us, but you've not revealed it. We don't understand you, and we don't like to be with people we don't understand. The world in which we live is much too dangerous for us to tolerate you a moment longer."

"Look, for Christ's sake," Cross begged. "I've not had a chance to say anything to anybody yet . . . Gil died suddenly; he was the only high-ranking member of the Party I'd talked to."

"Lane, stop trying to make me believe that you are naïve!" Blimin shouted. "I'm *serious*!"

Eva rose; anger shone in her eyes.

"Comrade Blimin—"

"You keep quiet!" Blimin ordered. "This is no time for you to speak!"

"But—" Eva protested.

"You'll get your chance to speak to the Party later about all this," Blimin said, waving a fat forefinger at her.

"Mr. Blimin, what do you want to know?" Cross demanded of him. "You must tell me, for I refuse to relate my entire life to you and let you pick out what part of my life you want and then brand me with it."

"I don't understand all this," Sarah mumbled uneasily.

"This is no concern of yours!" Blimin snapped at Sarah. His anger fully roused, he whirled on Cross. "Lane, what the hell ghastly joke is this you're pulling on the knowingest people on earth, the Communists? Who the goddamn hell do you think you *are*? What are you *doing* here? When we try to check on you, we run into a maze that leads nowhere. That's no *accident*. Are you a spy? Frankly, we doubt it; we thought so at first, but you've not been close enough to us to get hold of any information. Don't you think, now, that we are scared of you. If we were, you'd not be breathing now . . . But we want to know . . ."

"Know *what?*"

"Are you a *killer?*"

"No!" Eva screamed.

"God in Heaven," Sarah gasped.

The room was silent. He had at last been accused. Now, he had to act. First, he'd let the Party know that he knew what the score was in the world. He'd make them feel that maybe they could use him despite all the vague clouds of suspicion around him. He would make use of Blimin's urging him to talk to make a bid to them.

"We've no evidence, you might say," Blimin went on with his charge. "That's right; we haven't. But *you* are evidence. You come—death! *Why?* Lane, I'm accusing you of EVERYTHING! Now, *talk* for your *life!*" Blimin pronounced a provisional death sentence.

Cross laughed softly, went to the sofa and sat down, lit a cigarette, lifted smiling eyes to Blimin as he drew smoke deep into his lungs.

"Do you think I'm crazy enough to try to defend myself against a charge about which I know nothing? You say you don't understand me. Well, I'm going to talk, and *you're* going to listen. I'm not the kind of fool who'd let you push him into a position of defending himself against a charge of something he's never even dreamed of doing— If you make me do that, why, I'd really be somehow guilty—"

Cross rose, went to the center table and poured out a glass of water; he acted slowly, methodically, taking his time. I'm acting like Gil acted when he was trying to impress me, he told himself. He drained the glass, turned to Blimin, and he confessed not as Blimin wanted him to, but as he felt it. It was as though he was not only speaking to Blimin, but to and for himself, trying to clarify his predicament in his own eyes.

"Now, Mr. Blimin, I take it for granted that you are a member of the Central Committee of the Communist Party, or you would not be here talking to me tonight, or rather this morning. It's half past three . . . Oh, no; you needn't bother to affirm or deny it. I assume you are here for your Party. Let's let it go at that. I'd like for you to take back a straight message to them. They may not like my answer, and I'm not going to try to couch it in terms that will please them. My answer is just simply my way of looking at things, my slant, if you want to call it that.

"One way, among a variety of others, of looking at what is happening in this world today is to view all modern history as being tied together by one overall meaning. And that meaning is this: to a greater or less degree, all human life on this earth today *can* be described as moving away from traditional, agrarian, simple handicraft ways of life toward modern industrialization. Some nations, owing mainly to their historical backgrounds, have already made this journey, have already, so to speak, exhausted their industrial potentials of development and are industrially overripe. I'm referring to nations like England, Japan, Germany, etc. In these nations the problem of the future structure of society and the question of what kind of faith will sustain the individual in his daily life constitute a kind of chronic spiritual terror."

"Lane," Blimin accused him, "you're evading my question—"

"You asked me what I thought and felt about things," Cross shot at him. "Do you want to hear it or not?"

"But get to the point," Blimin insisted.

"Are you in a hurry?" Cross asked. "If so, I'll talk to you some other time—"

"Get to the point, Lane," Blimin said.

"This *is* my point," Cross said. "Now, Mr. Blimin, as I said, other nations, such as China, India, and the vast stretches of Africa have hardly begun this journey toward industrialization. The human and physical resources of these huge nations, comprising as they do more than one half of the human race and more than one half of the territory of the earth, have been stimulated as much as retarded by the impact of Western imperialism; they were retarded inasmuch as they were captive peoples in the hands of the industrialists of the West who needed their physical labor and the natural riches of their soil to keep the giant industrial machines of the West going . . . They were stimulated to leave their tribal, ancestral anchorages of living by being sucked into the orbit of industrial enterprises operating under the management of whites in their homelands under their own eyes . . . The hands of the West reached out greedily for the natural resources of these quaint peoples, but, in reaching, they awakened black, red, brown, and yellow men from their long slumber and sent them, willy-nilly, hurtling down the road of industrialization . . .

"During the past seventy years, America, under the ideological banner of free enterprise, fought a bloody civil war and defeated its agrarian provinces and launched itself, with no pre-history and practically no traditions to check it, upon a program of industrialization the equal of which, in terms of speed and magnitude, the world has never seen. From my point of view, this industrial program could have been accomplished under any dozen different ideological banners. The ideas were not as important as people thought they were; the important thing was the fact of industrialization. Of course, and it is understandable, the defenders of this industrial program justified their dazzling progress by claiming that an organic relationship obtained between their ideas and industrialization. But, really, there was none . . .

"Now, during the past thirty-five years, under the ideological banner of Dialectical Materialism, a small group of ruthless men in Russia seized political power and the entire state apparatus and established a dictatorship. Rationalizing human life to the last degree, they launched a vast, well-disciplined program of industrialization which now rivals that of the United States of America in pretentiousness and power . . . Again I say that what happened in Russia, just as with what happened in America, could have happened under a dozen different ideological banners . . . If you lived in Russia and made such a statement, they'd shoot you; and if you lived in America and made such a statement, they'd blacklist you and starve you to death . . . Modern man still believes in magic; he lives in a rational world but insists on interpreting the events of that world in terms of mystical forces. The simple fact is, the social cat can be skinned in many different ways. The coming history of the many new nations now launching their industrial programs will prove this to be true . . ."

"So!" Blimin exploded, "you sneer at our ideology? You ignore the role of the working class, hunh? You see no difference between Russia and the rest of the imperialist powers?"

"Mr. Blimin," Cross said patiently, "I'm talking to you as one man to another. I'm propaganda-proof. Communism has two truths, two faces. The face you're talking about now is for the workers, for the public, not for me. I look at facts, processes—"

"You're slandering—"

"Don't impute motives to me," Cross insisted. "Am I condemning you and men like you for what you've done? You did what you did because you had to! Anybody who launches himself on the road to naked power is caught in a trap . . . You use idealistic words as your smoke-screen, but behind that screen you *rule* . . . It's a question of *power*!"

"I'll not tolerate your reducing the noble aims of Lenin to a power-hungry man," Blimin raged.

"But Lenin admitted it," Cross told him. "Lenin repeatedly chided his comrades for lacking the will-to-power . . . Again, Mr. Blimin, if you want to talk to me, please understand that I'm not naïve. Your propaganda is *not* for me . . . Do you get that? Now, let me get back to my point . . .

"You may like industrialization or you may hate it. You may think that the process of industrialization ought to be stopped, that it has done great harm to mankind. Or you may feel that it is best to flee from this industrial machine and find haven in some tropical island. (Those little islands, too, are being caught up in the global tide of industrialization and soon there will be no hideaways.) Neither attitude really has anything to do with the basic reality of industrialization itself, which is a neutral process. Industrialization is simply an efficient way of making and doing things, labor-saving, a life-saving way of living. Industrialization is simply a hammer or a saw which has grown infinitely complex and, in itself, is not evil and cannot be evil . . . We can either find ways of controlling this complex hammer or saw and make it serve us, or we can simply drift, let industrial life bog us down, as we have already done. In any case, the sweep of industrialization has gone so far, its spirit has entered so deep in the hearts and habits of men, that we cannot stop it now even if we wanted to. It is a part of us and we are a part of it; if we go on, it goes on, so organically is it a part of our living . . . It cannot be stopped unless we all die or revert to a manner of living which would reduce our lives to a kind of Old Testament simplicity, which is highly unlikely.

"Quickening the process of industrialization was the marriage of scientific knowledge and industry. The interaction between the two progressed like a game of leapfrog. The more society became industrialized, the more men learned about the nature of the world in which they lived, and the more knowledge they gained from that world, the more skill they had in applying their knowledge to the methods of industry . . .

"Now, had this global tide of industrialization consisted only of this, we'd have no problem at all. Indeed, the world would be piled high with products and this earth would be the long-dreamed-of goal of mankind.

"What I've described becomes interesting only in the light of one question: What kind of a queer animal is this being called man who embarked—and without quite knowing it!—upon this program of industrialization? Well, his most dominant characteristic is an enormous propensity toward fear. He is the most scared and trembling of all the animals, and I'm not forgetting those wild ones who live in jungles . . . Learned men have long declaimed upon the thinking and loving capacities of man, but we have yet to hear of man's fears. It might well be that the most important part of human existence is fear itself . . .

"Primitive man, naked and afraid, found that only *one* thing could really quiet his terrors: that is, *Untruth*. He stuffed his head full of myths, and if he had not, he might well have died from fear itself. How many people on this earth die from fear is something we've yet to find out; but that is another story . . .

"The degree and quality of man's fears can be gauged by the scope and density of his myths, that is, by the ingenious manner in which he disguised the world about him. Man was afraid of the clamoring world of storms, volcanoes, and heaving waves and he wanted to change that world. His myths sought to recast that world, tame it, make it more humanly meaningful and endurable. The more abjectly frightened the nation or race of men, the more their myths and religions projected out upon the world another world in *front* of the real world, or, in another way of speaking, they projected another world *behind* the real world they saw, lived, suffered, and died in. Until today almost all of man's worlds have been either pre-worlds or back-worlds, *never* the *real* world . . . (The ancient nations today we call great are the ones who left behind them those towering monuments of fear in the forms of their so-called cultures!)

"That real world man did not want; he was not stouthearted enough to endure its dangers and uncertainties . . . In making his pre-worlds, he always saw reality as a wonderful drama enacted for his special benefit; there were gods and counter-gods locked in deadly conflict the outcome of which spelled good or evil for him, all shaping his destiny. In making his back-worlds man was vain enough to believe that this real world could not be all, that there was another world into which he could somehow escape when he died. Entrance into that back-world depended upon how faithfully he observed certain compulsive rituals which he, in his fear and anxiety, had created over eons of time to placate his sense of dread.

"Man cringed even before the ordinary workings of his own mind; he would not even dare admit the authorship of his own fantasies. He found himself so complex that he fled from himself. That which transpired in his heart he projected out into the skies, or else he would not have been able to sleep at night . . .

"War, famines, earthquakes, epidemics, and social upheavals made no impact upon man's myth-worlds; indeed, calamities served but to strengthen them, for man felt that he was somehow guilty when he was overwhelmed with disaster, had somehow failed to pronounce the magic talisman correctly when catastrophe descended upon him. One thing, however, did get at those myth-worlds, did gnaw at them until they fell from man's eyes and left him staring in dismay at the real, natural, workaday world from which he had for millions of years tried to hide.

"The ravaging scourge that tore away the veil of myth-worlds was science and industry; science slowly painting another world, the real one; and industry uprooting man from his ancestral, ritualized existence and casting him into rational schemes of living in vast, impersonal cities. A split took place in man's consciousness; he began living in the real world by the totems and taboos that had guided him in the world of myths . . . But that could not last for long. Today we are in the midst of that crisis . . . The real world stands at last before our eyes and we don't want to look at it, don't know how to live in it; it terrifies us. All of the vast dramas which man once thought took place in the skies now transpire in our hearts and we quake and are moved compulsively to do what we know not . . ."

"You deliberately and consistently omit to mention the role of the working class," Blimin pointed out, smiling. "It was oppression that awakened man from his slumber . . ."

"Oppression was simply an added irritant," Cross said. "Even if man had not been oppressed, this crisis would have taken place, and you know it. Oppression was a part of the process of industrialization—"

"And wars? You omit war altogether," Blimin said.

"When used as it was used," Cross told him, "industrialization was a kind of war against mankind. That same war might be going on in Russia today, for all I know . . . But let me get on.

"Now, this real world in which we live today has a strange tone and aspect. We Twentieth Century Westerners have outlived the faith of our fathers; our minds have grown so skeptical that we cannot accept the old scheme of moral precepts which once guided man's life. In our modern industrial society we try to steer our hearts by improvised, pragmatic rules which are, in the end, no rules at all. If there are people who tell you that they live by traditional values and precepts—such as the English sometimes pretend—then they are either lying to you or to themselves; maybe they are lying both ways . . . There is no modern industrial nation on earth today that makes decisions based upon anything remotely resembling the injunctions of the Old or New Testament; this holds true in their domestic as well as in their foreign policies.

"Of course, the historical transition from the unreal myth-worlds of yesterday to the bleak, terrifying world of today was not sudden, did not take place all at once. Acting as a brake upon the hot winds of scientific knowledge and the tidal waves of industrial erosion was a group of wonderful people, unhappily now extinct, called liberals. Full of the juices of human kindness, these people decided that they were going to be good, honest Christians without believing in Christianity which their logical minds found offensive. Let reason prevail, they declared. But these kindhearted atheists got scared. They went so far down the godless road that they could see a black nothingness looming as its final end. They retreated in fear. They helped to undermine the old world, but they discovered that the building of a new world was much harder than they had suspected. They called for new systems of ideas, and when no valid ones were forthcoming, they demanded new myths that would not insult the intelligence of man. For their pains they got programs for wars and revolutions . . .

"But one must not overlook the fact that, had it not been for these liberals, the full flood of a senseless existence would have long since broken through the myths of progress which have sustained modern man so far. They did an impossible job with great skill, those liberals. Future history will regard the liberals as the last great defenders of that which really could not be defended, as the last spokesmen of historical man as we've known him for the past two thousand years.

"All of this brings us to one central, decisive fact: the consequences of the atheistic position of modern man, for most men today are atheists, even though they don't know it or won't admit it. They live, dream, and plan on the assumption that there is no God. The full implications of this are enormous. It means that God no longer really concerns us as a reality beyond life, but simply as something projected compulsively from men's minds in answer to their chronic need to be rid of fear, something to meet the obscure needs of daily lives lived amidst strange and threatening facts."

"At least we agree on *something*," Blimin muttered, eyeing Cross askance. "You see the central fact, so why don't you admit the rest? Only the Party can save this world, give it guidance, direction—"

"Mr. Blimin," Cross overrode him, "since religion is dead, religion is everywhere . . . Religion was once an affair of the church; it is now in the streets in each man's heart. Once there were priests; now every man's a priest. Religion's a compulsion, and a compulsion seems to spring from something total in us, catching up in its mighty grip all the other forces of life—sex, intellect, will, physical strength, and carrying them forward toward—what goals? We wish we knew . . . Compulsions exist as much in the individual as in society. Lucky is the man who can share his neighbor's religion! Damned is the man who must invent his own god! Shun that man, for he is a part of the vast cosmos; he is akin to it and he can no more know himself than he can know the world of which he is in some mysterious way a part . . . Blessed is the artificial man, the determined man, the social man . . .

"Mr. Blimin, I'm not even an atheist. To me it's just too bad that some people must lean on imagined gods, that's all. Yet I'd not have it otherwise. They need religion. All right; let them have it. What harm does it do? And it does make for a greater measure of social stability. But I object if somebody grabs me when I'm a defenseless child and injects into me a sedative—the power of which lasts for a lifetime!—which no one would ever be able to tell if I'll ever need or not!

"Now, what does this mean,—that I don't believe in God? It means that I, and you too, can do what we damn well please on this earth. Many men have been doing just that, of course, for a long time, but they didn't have the courage to admit it. They pretended that they were following higher laws, practicing virtue, etc. But such clumsy games exposed themselves before long.

Naïve governments allowed historical records to be kept! Imagine the British, past masters of exploitation and duplicity, allowing a Karl Marx into their British Museum to pore over and unravel the pretensions and self-deceptions of British banditry! Such records of blatant chicanery served thoughtful and astute men as guides in the building of new, scientific, and more efficient methods of deception!

"Today governments, democratic or totalitarian, are much wiser. It is better, they feel, for mankind to be unconscious—or ignorant, which is the same thing—than knowing. They regard the writing of history as the most supremely important of all tasks. Modern governments today watch their history and since men seem to have developed a habit of wanting to know what has happened, they doctor up events, rewrite the past, improvise limited myths and give those myths to the masses of men. But this history is a simple, inspected history, fumigated, purged, and sterilized of all contagious ideas that might lead to the illnesses of independence, freedom, and individuality. Mankind is coming of age . . .

"Those few strong men who do not want to be duped, and who are stout enough in their hearts to accept a godless world, are quite willing, aye, anxious to let the masses of men rest comfortably in their warm cocoons of traditional illusions. Men are more easily and cheaply governed when they fear ghosts more than guns! The real slaves of the Twentieth Century are not those sharecroppers who wince at the stinging swish of a riding boss's whip; the slaves of today are those who are congenitally afraid of the new and the untried, who fall on their knees and break into a deep sweat when confronted with the horrible truth of the uncertain and enigmatic nature of life . . .

"It is the strong at the top, however, who represent modern man. Beyond themselves, their dreams, their hopes, their plans, they know that there is nothing . . .

"Now, the next point, Mr. Blimin— Most of the decisive historic events that happen in this world are not known until *after* they have happened. Few are the people who know the meaning of what they are living through, who even have an inkling of what is happening to them. That's the big trouble with history . . .

"Now, Mr. Blimin, keep that point in mind while I remind you of what is happening in the great cities of the earth today—Chicago, Detroit, Pittsburg, London, Manchester, Paris, Tokyo, Hong Kong, and the rest. These cities are, for the most part, vast pools of human misery, networks of raw human nerves exposed without benefit of illusion or hope to the new, godless world wrought by industrial man. Industrial life plus a rampant capitalism have blasted the lives of men in these cities; those who are lucky enough not to be hungry are ridden with exquisite psychological sufferings. The people of these cities are lost; some of them are so lost that they no longer even know it, and they are the real lost ones. They haunt the movies for distraction; they gamble; they depress their sensibilities with alcohol; or they seek strong sensations to dull their sense of a meaningless existence . . .

"Now, Mr. Blimin, above these so-called toiling masses, for whom I have some sympathy but not as much as you'd expect, are the few industrialists and politicians who yell night and day about freedom, democracy, high wages, etc. These are the exploiters of the millions of rats caught in the industrial trap. That they make great profits out of the exercise of their lordship is perhaps the least of their crimes—"

"Oh, you're showing your true colors," Blimin

snorted. "Are you defending *exploitation* now? Next you're going to tell me what wonderful philanthropists these capitalists are—"

"Not at all. It just so happens, Mr. Blimin," Cross explained, "that I think that their crime is a blacker one than mere exploitation. The end-results of their rule is that they keep the lives of their rats pitched to a mean, sordid level of consciousness. It's right here where you and I disagree deeply. Your wonderful trade unions for a quarter of a century have been fighting for so-called standards of living for workers, fighting for higher wages . . . Had I had anything to say about the goals of those trade unions, I'd have insisted that their fight be to escape completely the domination of the capitalists . . . Not that the workers become richer, but that they become more human, freer . . . You don't want that, Mr. Blimin, and the capitalists don't want it. Why? Because you cannot dupe free men who can think and know . . .

"Now back to my theme . . . The point is not so much that these capitalists despise their rats, but that they despise themselves and all mankind. To keep their rats contented, they strive to convince them that their rats' lives are more glorious, better, richer than at any time in history, and, in the end, they come to believe in their own lies. Consequently today the content of human life on earth is what these cheap-minded men say it is. They are jealous and uneasy, these men, of anyone who tries to lure their rats away. They preach to their rats that their nation is the best of any of the nations, and that as rats they are the very best of all possible rats. They even have I-Am-A-Rat days . . . As long as this works, it's wonderful. The only real enemies of this system are not the rats themselves, but those outsiders who are conscious of what is happening and who seek to change the consciousness of the rats who are being controlled. In situations like this, public consciousness is the key to political power . . . The essence of life today is psychological; men may take power with arms, but their keeping of it is by other means . . . Get me so far, Mr. Blimin?

"Now, rising up from time to time from the pools of restless millions in these vast cities are men who seek to head new movements. Their appearance is much rarer than is popularly supposed, just as genuine revolutions on this earth are rare, few and far between . . . These men who rise to challenge the rulers are jealous men. They feel that they are just as good as the men who rule; indeed, they suspect that they are better . . . They see the countless mistakes that are being made by the men who rule and they think that they could do a more honest, a much cleaner job, a more efficient job. For simplicity's sake, let's call them the Jealous Rebels—"

"Lane!" Blimin thundered, rising in anger. "You *are* cynical, that's all! How can you say Lenin was jealous? He had the fate of mankind close to his heart! We love people—"

Cross was tempted to tell of what Hilton had told him just before he had shot him; but no, he couldn't do that.

"Mr. Blimin, *please*, be honest," Cross begged. "You must assume that I know what this is all about. Don't tell me about the nobility of labor, the glorious future . . . *You* don't believe in that. That's for others, and you damn well know it. You and men of your type are convinced that you know how the game goes and you've thrown down the gauntlet to the capitalists, conservatives, socialists, etc. You Jealous Rebels are intellectuals who know your history and you are anxious not to make the mistakes of your predecessors in rebellious undertakings. You feel that life has become crummy and meaningless and you feel you can give it more meaning than the clumsy men who now rule.

"The thinking of the revolutionary is a cold kind of thinking; he has a realistic insight into history; he has, above all, a sense of what power is, what it's for, both as a means of governing other men and as a means of personal expression. That absolute power is corrupting, à la Lord Acton, is something revolutionaries laugh at. These Jealous Rebels would much rather be corrupted with absolute power than live under the heels of men whom they despise.

"In order to test themselves, to make life a meaningful game, these Jealous Rebels proceed to organize political parties, communist parties, nazi parties, fascist parties, all kinds of parties—"

"No!" Blimin roared. "You cannot equate or confound Communism with Fascism! They are *different*!"

"I admit they are different," Cross conceded. "But the degree of the difference is not worth arguing about. Fascists operate from a narrow, limited basis; they preach nationality, race, soil, blood, folk-feeling and other rot to capture men's hearts. What makes one man a Fascist and another a Communist might be found in the degree in which they are integrated with their culture. The more alienated a man is, the more he'd lean toward Communism . . ."

"Toward rationality," Blimin stated.

"No," Cross corrected him. "Communists *use* rationality. I admit that the Communists are more intelligent, more general in their approach, but the same power-hungry heart beats behind the desire to rule! I'm on pre-political ground here, Mr. Blimin. And you know I'm speaking the truth.

"Now, where do these Jealous Rebels get their programs . . . ? Out of books? From Plato's *Republic*? No! Their programs are but the crude translations of the daydreams of the man in the street, daydreams in which the Jealous Rebels do not believe!

"In order to catch their prey, they deliberately spin vast spiderwebs of ideology, the glittering strands of which are designed to appeal to the hopes of hopeful men. Yes, there are men who think that ideas will lead them to freedom and a fuller life, and these are the men who are the natural victims of the Jealous Rebels who do not feel that to dupe others in this way is immoral; it is their conviction that this is the way life is and only the naïve think to the contrary . . .

"Their aims? Direct and naked power! They know as few others that there is no valid, functioning religion to take the place of the values and creeds of yesterday; and they know that political power, if it is to perform in the minds and emotions of men the role and efficacy that the idea of God once performed, must be total and absolute. These Jealous Rebels are sustained by a sense of the total meaning—or lack of meaning!—of human life on this earth. Their courage is derived from the fact that, win or lose, they are making history, that what they do is decisive for mankind. Caught up passionately in such a realistic myth, what will not an ardent man do . . . ?

"These men are free from petty prejudices. They have to be free from such, for it is precisely the prejudices of *others* that they seek to manipulate for their own uses. They will commit any crime, but never in passion. They work slowly, deliberately, with refinement even. And whatever natural terrors of life there are in the hearts of men, whatever stupid prejudices they harbor in their damp souls, they know how to rouse and sustain those terrors and prejudices and mobilize them for *their* ends.

The mere act of hoping, believing, of being alive makes you a prospective victim for these knowing men! Modern life is a kind of confidence game; if you dream, you can be defeated unless you are careful that you do not dream a dream that has been set up for you!

"I'm not so naïve as to believe that these men want to *change* the world! Why, they love human nature just as it is! They simply want their chance to show what they can do with that world and the people in it. To their minds human life on this earth is a process that is transparently *known*! They are out to grab the entire body of mankind and they will replace faith and habit with organization and discipline . . . *And they feel that they have a chance to do it!*

"Since God as functioning reality in men's minds and hearts has gone, since the death of the gallant liberal, every event of the modern world feeds the growing movement toward the total and absolute, making the Jealous Rebels believe that they have allies everywhere . . . Wars, by mobilizing men into vast armies to fight and die for ideals that are transparently fraudulent, justify this drift toward the total and absolute in modern life. Industrial capitalism, whether it operates for profit or not, herds men around assembly lines to perform senseless tasks—all of which conditions men toward the acceptance of the total and absolute in modern life. Implicit in all political and speculative thought are the germs of ideas that prefigure the triumph of the total and absolute attitudes in modern life. Communication, inventions, radio, television, movies, atomic energy, by annihilating distance and space and the atmosphere of mystery and romance, create the conditions for the creation of organizations reflecting the total and absolute in modern life. Commercial advertising, cheapening and devaluing our notions of human personality, develops and perfects techniques which can be used by political leaders who want to enthrone the total and absolute in modern life. Even anti-communists and anti-fascists must, by fighting the totalitarian threat by using the methods of the totalitarians—and there are no other methods, it seems, to use—guarantee and make inevitable this surge toward the total and absolute in modern life.

"There is no escaping what the future holds. We are going back, *back* to something earlier, maybe better, maybe worse, maybe something more terrifyingly human! These few hundred years of freedom, empire building, voting, liberty, democracy—these will be regarded as the *romantic* centuries in human history. There will be in that future no trial by jury, no writs of habeas corpus, no freedom of speech, of religion—all of this is being buried and not by Communists or Fascists alone, but by their opponents as well. All hands are shoveling clay on to the body of freedom before it even dies, while it lies breathing its last . . .

"There are some people today who sincerely but mistakenly believe that by going to war against a totalitarian nation that they can save the past of which they are so deeply fond. Unwilling or unable to believe that the crisis is as serious and deep as it really is, these people want to launch vast armies and smash the evildoers and reestablish a reign of peace and goodwill—the right to exploit others without interference!—on earth. What these sincere people do not realize is that Communism and Fascism are but the political expressions of the Twentieth Century's atheistic way of life, and that the future will reveal many, many more of these absolutistic systems whose brutality and rigor will make the present-day systems seem like summer outings. The most ludicrous and tragic spectacle on earth is to see a powerful nation bleeding itself white to build up vast heaps of armaments to put down a menace that cannot be put down by military means at all . . . Wars will but tear away the last shreds of belief, leaving man's heart more naked and compulsive than ever before. Can atom bombs correct a man's sense of life? Can ultimatums alter the basic beliefs or nonbeliefs of millions of men? Can you shoot attitudes?

"Mr. Blimin, if you believe that I believe what I've told you, how do you think I'm a menace to your Party? True, I may not believe your Party's aims, but I know enough about politics to know that I could not change your Party, or, as an individual, fight it. So what are you scared of in me? I give you my word that I do not belong to any political party on this earth, and I don't think I will ever join one.

"Now, you asked me what am I doing? Knowing and seeing what is happening in the world today, I don't think that there is much of anything that one can do about it. But there is one little thing, it seems to me, that a man owes to himself. He can look bravely at this horrible totalitarian reptile and, while doing so, discipline his dread, his fear and study it coolly, observe every slither and convolution of its sensuous movements and note down with calmness the pertinent facts. In the face of the totalitarian danger, these facts can help a man to save himself; and he may then be able to call the attention of others around him to the presence and meaning of this reptile and its multitudinous writhings . . .

"That's all, Mr. Blimin. I'm not really anti anything."

There was a long silence. Blimin sat looking at the floor, lifting his eyes now and then to Cross's face. Blimin's eyes were serious; he seemed not to know if he should believe Cross or not; or, if he did believe Cross, then in what way . . . ? Finally Blimin rose, laughed, stared at Cross and said:

"You've answered my question, but I'm afraid that you've raised more questions than you've answered. Frankly, Lane, it's dangerous for a man knowing and feeling what you know and feel to hang around loosely on the peripheries of our Party . . ."

"I came in contact with the Party in quite a natural manner, Mr. Blimin," Cross told him. "I was eating in a dining car one morning and met the late Mr. Bob Hunter . . ."

Blimin reddened. Bob was enroute to Trinidad and the Party had helped to speed him on his way. Blimin covered his embarrassment by shrugging and laughing.

"Well, I won't bother you any more tonight, Lane," he said.

"It's no bother," Cross said.

Hank still stood in the background of the room, his hat and coat still on, his eyes intent upon the face of Cross. Menti had been impressed by what Cross had said; he stared, grinned, winked, and said:

"With a gift of gab like that, you ought to be on the Central Committee."

"No," Cross said. "You don't want men in your Party who can think."

"It all depends," Blimin mumbled; he was leaving the door open.

Yet, Blimin was worried. Cross had tempted him, made him feel that maybe he would work with them, that maybe he could be persuaded . . . *Maybe* . . . Blimin and Menti left with cryptic smiles, but Hank was not moved; his face still held that blank, stolid expression as he went from sight.

"Lionel, I'm worried," Eva confessed. "How could

they think that you, knowing what you know, would stoop to killing . . . ?"

"They can't find who killed Gil and Hilton, so they've got to get a scapegoat," Cross said in a cool, level tone.

"Oh, God," Eva moaned.

Cross watched her closely, wondering if she remembered his confessional babblings. For a moment her stare was full on him, then she looked at the floor. Suddenly she reached for his hand and squeezed it tightly.

"These Communists are mad!" Sarah exclaimed. "I think some spy with a grudge against the Party killed Gil and Hilton."

"If they really knew Lionel, they'd never think he would do anything like that," Eva said.

Cross was numb in his heart. Couldn't they tell he was guilty? Yes, it was their own innocence that kept them from seeing his guilt; they identified themselves with what they hoped he was, and, since they were innocent, he *must* be innocent.

"Now, don't go worrying about foolishness like this," he gently chided the two women, forcing a smile.

Back in the bedroom, he pondered and weighed his chances. Had he spoken too much to Blimin? But how else could he have behaved? He had given vent to his feelings in a way that he hoped would take some of the pressure of the Party off him. Would a normally guilty man have spoken like that? No. The Party knew now that he was not with the police; they knew also that he was not spying for another political party. What motive, then, could he have had, from their point of view, for killing . . . ? They'll think I did it because of Eva! No; Communists were not unintelligent; they could not seriously think that. There was one thing of which he was certain: They would never credit him with as much freedom to act as they had. A certain psychological blindness seemed to be the hallmark of all men who had to create their own worlds . . . All other men were mere material for them; they could admit no rivals, no equals; other men were either above them or below them.

Long after Eva had gone to sleep in his arms, he lay awake wondering if he could ride out this trouble and keep her with him. He was suffering this torturing surveillance of the Party only to keep near her. It was dawn before he managed to close his eyes in sleep.

The next morning Cross eagerly searched the Sunday papers in vain for further mention of Hilton. Nor was there any news on the radio. Maybe things would quiet down for awhile? But he knew that the Party and the police were still hunting, probing, observing. Dread was still with him; he lived in the anticipation of another sudden confrontation that would send him hurtling down the path of blood again . . .

After breakfast Menti and Hank came with a car and took them to the union hall. Long queues of workers were entering the doors and filing slowly past the dark, shining coffin in which Gil lay with ashen and upturned face. Huge wreaths of flowers were banked about the coffin which was surrounded by Communist militants standing stiffly at attention. Cross was impressed by the soberness of the shabby men and women who had come to pay their tribute to Gil. It's better than spending their time playing pinball machines, seeing movies or drinking in bars, he admitted musingly to himself.

Eva was sobbing quietly as he led her by the arm to the coffin. Why's she weeping? he wondered. Was it for grief over Gil? That could hardly be, for she had hated him. Was it because her life had been blasted? Or was it because she was on the verge of freedom? Maybe it was simply because she was overwhelmed . . .

Cross stood looking at Gil's cold and tired face which seemed now somewhat shrunken, but still retaining its lines of rigidity of character. There lies a modern man, Cross said to himself sadly. He lived as reasonlessly as he died . . . Life, to him, was a game devoid of all significance except that which he put into it. Life was a game and he played it with all of his skill to the bitter end. Cross was convinced that Gil, in an abstract sense, could not have disagreed with the manner in which he had met his death. Gil just experienced a sudden transitional leap in the dialectical materialistic development of life, that's all . . . Cross repressed a wry smile as he gently led Eva from the side of the coffin.

After the Party had had its last say over the body of Gil, Gil's sister, Blanche, a greying woman of forty-odd from the Bronx, deeply religious and sharply color-conscious, took charge and began to make arrangements for the shipment of Gil's remains for proper religious ceremonies and burial. Cross kept discreetly in the background while Eva and Blanche, who were strained, cold, and distant toward each other, discussed the disposition of Gil's books, furniture, and other personal belongings.

Blimin accosted Cross cordially at the back of the union hall.

"I've been thinking over your analysis of last night," Blimin said. "With a little discipline, we could do something with you."

"And?" Cross prompted him to talk.

"Why do you shun us when you understand so much?"

"I'm not shunning anybody," Cross told him.

"I can see why Gil wanted to train you," Blimin said.

"Why have you changed your mind? You accepted Gil's offer—"

"I've been so busy coping with suspicions that I've had no chance to think of anything," Cross said.

"Lane, is there anything you *want*?" Blimin asked.

"What do you mean?"

"For a man of your ability, the Party can make exceptions," Blimin explained. "Or maybe you've *got* what you want already?"

Cross stared. This was the nearest the Party had come to hinting that he had perhaps killed Gil to get Eva! And Blimin had implied that if he would surrender, the Party would consider forgiving him for even that! But that meant giving up Eva . . . !

"Blimin, I don't like talk like this," Cross said.

"It's easier and simpler when we know what a man wants," Blimin went relentlessly on. "But with you, we don't know what you want. Well, good-bye." Blimin turned and walked off briskly.

Menti, still accompanied by the sullen Hank, was restrained, cordial, and noncommittal as he drove them back to Harlem. The nervous tension of the ceremony had given Eva a headache for which she took some aspirins and went to bed. Cross loitered in the living room, mulling over his dinner engagement with Houston. What had the Party said to him? And how much weight would Houston give to what the Party had said? He knew that the best proof of Houston's suspiciousness would be for Houston to begin straightaway prying into his past. And it was too late now for him to fabricate a new past for himself. Every lie he told now would only increase his difficulties. Ought he to slip out of the apartment and vanish? Such an act would declare his guilt, and it would mean losing Eva forever.

He left the apartment early to keep his dinner appointment with Houston; he wanted a chance to breathe some fresh air and organize his thoughts prior to confronting a man whose mind he feared. Houston knew what power was and loved it, or else he would not have stood to be elected to a public office. Would he, if he had Cross dead-to-rights, ravage him as he had seen Gil ravage Bob and Eva? Such was possible . . . Cross knew in his heart that the first man, from the police or from the Party, who could sense intuitively what his psychological state was would know that he was guilty. But in order to know that they would have to have courage enough to admit the character of the world in which he and they both lived; and he seriously doubted if Houston really had that much courage.

Reluctantly he made his way toward Frank's Restaurant on 125th Street through the cold wintry air. About him neon lights shimmered in red and blue and green and rose. For the first time in months Cross could see the sky stretching above the tenement roofs. A few clusters of brittle stars winked in a blue-black luminosity. Cars whirred over the icy asphalt pavement with sticky whines. He tramped grimly past towering Negro churches from whose doorways rolled softly, almost apologetically, the plaintive spirituals of his people. How lucky they were, those black worshippers, to be able to feel lonely together! What fantastic blessings were theirs to be able to express their sense of abandonment in a manner that bound them in unison! But with whom could he join in howling his loneliness?

When he came in view of Frank's Restaurant, he paused, dropped his cigarette and stomped out its glow with his heel. Then his body jerked; out of a corner of his eyes he saw two white men approaching. He lifted his head and looked at them. There was a light of intentionality in their eyes that gripped him and his lips parted slowly.

"Are you Lionel Lane?" one of the men asked.

"That's right," he answered.

One of the men pulled his right hand from his coat pocket and pushed his outstretched palm under Cross's nose; in that palm gleamed a police badge.

"I'm Detective Hornsby, attached to the District Attorney's office," he said.

"Yes?" he said and waited.

"You had an appointment, I believe, with the District Attorney here at eight o'clock?"

"That's right."

"The District Attorney cannot make it. We tried to see you at your apartment, but you had gone," Hornsby said.

"I'm sorry," Cross mumbled and waited; there was something else he knew that these men had to tell him.

"The District Attorney asked us to bring you to him," Hornsby said.

Cross noticed that the other detective had his hands jammed into his overcoat pockets and he had not spoken a word or moved.

"Am I being arrested?" Cross asked softly.

"We cannot answer any questions, I'm afraid. Will you come along with us?" Hornsby asked.

So this was it at last. The dinner engagement was resolving itself into an official confrontation. What did they know? Ought he make a dash for it? No; he could not get away; they might have other armed, plainclothes men nearby. He did not move and they had not moved. He was suddenly tired. The face of Eva flashed through his mind; he would lose her. And if he lost her, what else mattered? He sighed, nodded his head.

"All right," he said quietly.

"Are you armed?" Hornsby asked.

He hesitated, then smiled. "Yes."

"Where's the gun? Don't move. Just tell us and we'll take it from you."

"It's on my right hip," he said.

They were efficient; they relieved him of his gun without attracting the attention of a single passerby.

"The car is that black sedan at the curb. Walk toward it between us and get in," Hornsby said.

Cross did as he was told; when seated in the car he leaned back and sighed. His despair drained off him in one second and he felt that he wanted to sleep. And in the next instant he knew exactly what he had to do. He would do nothing, say nothing; there was nothing that he could really say. Let them make their case; he would not help or hinder them. He would bear it as though it was not he himself who was undergoing it. The car moved off into the night, heading downtown, and he lay back, his heart locked against the world. I'll see what they can make out of me, he said to himself.

BOOK FIVE

DECISION

. . . Man is the only being who makes promises.
— FRIEDRICH NIETZSCHE

CROSS FOUND HIMSELF in the uniquely ironic position of comprehending far more keenly than his captors the nature and meaning of the situation confronting him. Even while the car in which he sat huddled between the two detectives bore him toward the office of the District Attorney, he could anticipate the general methods and approach of the police. They had first to prove who he was. Well, let them; that was their business, not his . . . He wondered how much of his path of blood and deception had they uncovered; but his wonderment was devoid of any desire to erect a strategy of legal defense for himself. That did not concern him at all; his preoccupations were more basic and recondite.

He knew that he had cynically scorned, wantonly violated every commitment that civilized men owe, in terms of common honesty and sacred honor, to those with whom they live. That, in essence, was his crime. The rest of his brutal and bloody thrashings about were the mere offshoots of that one central, cardinal fact. And for the crime of his contemptuous repudiation of all the fundamental promises that men live by he intended to make no legal defense for the good and ample reason that he well knew that no such defense was possible. And he was staunchly resolved to face his would-be judgers with a tight mouth from which not one word to help clarify his emotions or motives would issue. He would compel them, by a challenging silence, to identify his attitude.

And Houston . . . ? Was he still juggling ideas or had he found the courage to put two and two together? Houston, of all the officers of the law, could put the "finger" on him, could brand him guilty in a psychological sense. But had he dug up enough proof to make a legal charge stick? And would Houston dare explain his conception of this guilt to his colleagues? Would not a man in so responsible a position run the risk of losing public confidence by merely putting such notions into words . . . ? Cross barely suppressed a smile as he glanced furtively at the stolid faces of the two detectives who sat to either side of him.

The moment he entered the police car he knew that his search was over. There were to be no more of those torrid promptings of his heart to make him confess his horrible deeds and then wrestle and sweat to restrain his urge to kill the recipient of his confession. The burden of what was to be proved would fall upon those who had brought him to heel. His crimes had carried a stamp of the absolute and if they wanted to nail him down, their actions and attitudes would have to carry a stamp of the absolute against him. Let them haul up all of his bloody doings and turn them this way and that and see what conclusions they could come to . . .

There were two immediate dangers threatening him. The District Attorney could, if he were so minded, remand him for psychological observation at Bellevue; all right, he was confident of being declared sane. The other danger was more indirect, more difficult. Suppose the police had unraveled all that he had done and suppose the general public felt so revolted that they would want to drag him into some dirty alley and take his life and be done with it. He understood that reaction and feared it; it was the same cold fury he had felt against Herndon and Gil and Hilton . . . Should such now fall to him, he would be watching his own compulsions in reverse! If he could avoid those two pitfalls, he was prepared, willing even, to undergo whatever inquisitions they could serve up.

At some point in his past life, while living the normal ritual of days allotted to us all, he had come to a consciousness of having somehow fallen into a vast web of pledges and promises which he had not intended to make and whose implied obligations had been slowly smothering his spirit; and, by a stroke of freakish good luck, he had been able to rip the viscous strands of that web and fling them behind him. As always he was honest with himself; he knew, of course, that his commitments had been no more galling or burdensome than those which other millions of men and women about him shouldered so uncomplainingly every day; yet he knew that deep in the hearts of many of those millions was the same desire—shamefaced, inarticulate, and impotent—to have done with them as he had. It was not because he was a Negro that he had found his obligations intolerable; it was because there resided in his heart a sharp sense of freedom that had somehow escaped being dulled by intimidating conditions. Cross had never really been tamed . . .

He felt that at the time of his making his promises,—it had started in his childhood, before he had even been able to talk!—that his true and free consent had not been asked or given and that he had not been in a condition to understand the far-reaching nature of what he had been asked to pledge.

What was the question with which he, in his silence, would confront them? It was this: If he was to be loyal, to love, to show pity, mercy, forgiveness; if he was to abstain from cruelty, to be mindful of the rights of others, to live and let live, to believe in such resounding words as glory, culture, civilization, and progress, then let them demonstrate how it was to be done so that the carrying out of these duties and the practicing of these virtues in the modern world would not reduce a healthy, hungry man to a creature of nervous dread and paint that man's look of the world in the black hues of meaninglessness.

To be sure, accident had made possible his decision to dishonor those unwritten vows that he had been circumstantially made to promise, but his eagerness in embracing the opportunities presented by that subway accident had robbed that accident of its element of contingency, and the rest had flowed naturally and inevitably.

The assumptive promises he had welched on were not materially anchored, yet they were indubitably the things of this world, comprising as they did the veritable axis of daily existence. He, like Gil and Hilton, but for radically divergent reasons, had not been concerned with the buying and selling of corn, bonds, machines, paper, or steel. It had been the naked, irreducible facts of sentient life itself that he had tried to grapple with in his snapping asunder the ties that bound him. It was the restrictions of marriage, the duties to children, obligations to friends, to sweethearts, and blood kin that he had struck at so blindly and—gallantly? For Cross had had no party, no myths, no tradition, no race, no soil, no culture, and no ideas—except perhaps the idea that ideas in themselves were, at best, dubious!

What made him wonder so anxiously about how much they knew of his past was that he was desirous of being put at once in the center of what was about to happen to him. He detested surprises. To be confronted continuously with the unforeseen when his movements were restricted would deprive his attitude of coherence and balance, and it was an evenness of deportment that he wanted to cling to now above all. For Cross was proud and was proud of his pride and knew it.

And Eva—? His memory of her made a dart of wincing pain go through him. He had at last found a recollection which he could not reduce to some impulse projected out of his hungry heart, for Eva's loneliness as expressed in her life and in her painting had become identified with the deepest regions of his being. He could have shared so much with her; they could have walked together through life; he could have been an anchor to her and she to him. But all chance of that was now gone . . .

The police car pulled to a stop and Cross looked curiously at the entrance of a huge building.

"Is this the District Attorney's office?" he asked.

"Yep," Hornsby said.

The detectives guided Cross out and escorted him through a wide door, across a deserted, spacious lobby, and stood to either side of him as they were lifted up in an elevator to the tenth floor. He was marched down a white-tiled corridor and into the anteroom of an ornately furnished office in which two uniformed policemen stood guard. Hornsby pushed open a door and Cross was ushered into the presence of Houston who, flanked by two other men, sat behind a large desk staring solemnly at him.

"Here's your man, sir," Hornsby said, saluting, turning, and leaving with the other officer.

Cross stared at the three men wordlessly. He was not going to say anything. Theirs was the burden. Houston, leaning back in a swivel chair, both watchful and relaxed, stroked his chin. Cross knew that he was in the presence of men sworn to punish those who did not obey the mandates formulated to protect lives and property, and toward them he felt no bitterness, no hate; he did not regard them as his enemies. He understood the origin of their power and authority and the scope of their duties, and he did not look upon his being hauled here as an act of injustice. Had the situation been different, he would not have hesitated to have sat down and talked with them, tried to show them that really his so-called crime was derived basically from the fact that he saw and felt the world differently than they did; he would have even tried, had he had the chance, to make them see and feel it as he did. But he knew that was useless now; it was too late . . . But he would not help or hinder them; theirs was the power, theirs the initiative.

Houston finally pulled himself erect and came from behind his desk on those softly padded feet of his, his body moving slowly and stiffly, his hump seemingly more prominent than Cross could ever remember having seen it. Houston's face was tensely concentrated, his eyes deeply absorbed with inner considerations. His long, dangling arms and his pointed, strong fingers swung grotesquely at his sides. He turned and studied a pile of papers on his desk for a moment, then whirled to Cross and said:

"I hardly know where to begin with you. I wish to God I hadn't met you on that train, or hadn't talked to you. It would make my task easier . . ."

"I'm sorry if I'm embarrassing you, Mr. Houston," Cross smiled as he spoke.

Houston stared, then glanced at his two aides and again at Cross.

"Do you know what this is all about?" Houston asked; he acted as though he was puzzled as to what line to take.

"I know nothing whatsoever," Cross replied affably.

"I'd been looking forward to having dinner with you, then these reports began to flood in here," Houston sighed.

The other two men, both standing, were youngish. One, the younger, was lawyerish in appearance. The other was tall, grey at the temples, and had the air of being a high-ranking police official, though he was dressed in plain clothes.

"Is there anything you want to say before we begin questioning you, Lane or Damon or what the hell your name is?"

So they had found out who he was! Well, good . . . But what else did they know?

"I have nothing whatever to say," Cross answered.

"Do you acknowledge the name of Cross Damon to be your real, your own, your true name?" Houston asked.

"I acknowledge nothing," Cross replied.

The three men looked at one another.

"Listen, you're intelligent enough, of course, to realize that I cannot force you to answer my questions. You also know that you have the right to counsel. You know too that what you tell me I can use against you in court. I can't force you to incriminate yourself. But whatever it is you're hiding, it would be better if you told me; it would be easier for you in the long run."

Cross smiled. He would at once set Houston straight about that.

"You may question me, sir," he said, hoping that Houston would question him, for that was the only way in which he could tell how much Houston knew, "but I reserve the right to answer what questions of yours I please. I might as well tell you that I'm not concerned with incriminating myself. I'm a perfectly free agent and if I elect to remain silent to some of your questions, it is for reasons of my own."

"Right," Houston said, staring thoughtfully at Cross. He then went back to his desk and sat. "Sit down."

"I prefer standing for awhile, if you don't mind," Cross said; he felt better on his feet to face what was coming. He was alert, tense, but free of all dread and compulsions. He was focussed to a point of supreme self-defense.

"If you like," Houston muttered. "Now, let's start at the beginning. You worked until about a month and a half ago as a clerk in the Post Office in Chicago, did you not?"

"I don't affirm it or deny it," Cross said.

"But, Damon, we've *proof* of who you are," Houston said.

"We got your fingerprints out of Mrs. Blount's apartment and the FBI has at last identified you."

Cross did not answer; his facial expression did not change.

"Do you now persist in denying your identity?"

"I affirm or deny nothing," Cross repeated.

Houston frowned, then he turned to the elder of his two aides. "Bring in that secretary of the Postal Union, Neil," Houston ordered.

"Right, sir," Neil answered, going to a door and beckoning.

Finch, with whom Cross had negotiated his eight-hundred-dollar loan, walked slowly into the room. He stopped and stared at Cross; Cross returned Finch's gaze with level eyes.

"Is this man known to you as Cross Damon?" Houston asked.

"Yes, sir. That's him, all right. I'd know him in a million," Finch said eagerly. "Hello, Damon."

Cross kept his eyes steadily on Finch's face and did not answer.

"Are you in trouble, boy?" Finch asked cordially.

Cross was silent, but his lips twitched in a slight smile.

"You'd swear to this identification in court?" Houston asked.

"Of course, I would," Finch said.

"Well, that's all, Mr. Finch. Thanks for your cooperation."

"Not at all. Are you through with me, sir?" Finch asked.

"Yes; for the time being."

Finch started out, turning and straining his neck, his baffled eyes remaining on Cross's face until he collided with the edge of the opened door. Neil had to grab Finch's arm to keep him from falling. Cross's face broke into a wide grin; he watched Finch vanish down the hallway, holding his hand to his forehead where he had bumped it against the door.

"Are you crazy?" Houston's voice came to him.

"I'm sorry, sir," Cross said.

"What are you laughing at?"

"Finch was so amazed that he did not see the door," Cross explained soberly.

"*You* may be the amazed one before I'm through with you," Houston snapped. "You are presumed to be dead, you know that?"

"I know nothing," Cross said.

"You were in a subway accident. Do you acknowledge that?"

"I acknowledge nothing, sir."

"Good God, man!" Houston exploded. "Maybe you're an amnesia victim. Do you recall being injured in the subway accident?"

"I've nothing to say."

"You say you *don't* remember?"

"I say *nothing*, sir."

"If you say you don't remember, it simplifies things—"

"I say nothing," he repeated.

He doubted now if Houston knew of the hotel in which he had met Jenny and had killed Joe Thomas. So far nothing of a damaging nature had come to light. Some of his past was known. So what?

"We'll see about that," Houston said; he was plainly annoyed. "It's just possible you're telling the truth. You may have been injured and don't recall anything . . ."

Cross knew that Houston was now toying with the idea that he *was* perhaps an amnesia victim; but no one knew for sure that he had been in the subway accident and he loathed anybody's thinking that his conduct had been influenced by any injury.

"May I state quite clearly and plainly, Mr. Houston, that I've never at any time in my life sustained any injuries of whatever nature that would cause me any lapse of memory," Cross said.

Houston was momentarily rattled and his mouth gaped: the two men behind him blinked their eyes. Yeah; they'd been planning to bait me with that amnesia approach, he told himself.

"What is this, a game?" Houston demanded.

"That depends upon your interpretation, sir."

"What are you hiding, Damon?"

"I affirm or deny nothing."

"You know of that accident," Houston spoke in a puzzled tone of voice. "You admitted it by implication. But you don't want to take advantage of that accident to justify anything you've done." Houston had spoken in a tone of voice that showed that he was thinking out loud, trying to find a way to get at Cross. He rose and walked close to Cross and stared into his face and said in a low, charged voice: "Damon, I've some very bad news for you."

"Yes," Cross said, holding tense and ready for surprises.

"Damon, your mother died in Chicago yesterday. She was astonished that you were still alive. It is believed that she died of shock, the shock of what you had done to her . . ."

He held still. Was this true? Or was Houston lying, trying to break him down? He was aware that Houston was watching every flicker of his eyelids. His mother was over sixty; she had been in frail health for a long time, and he was inclined to believe that what Houston had said was true . . . And the shock of what he had done had killed her? A churning wave went through his stomach, but he steeled himself against emotion. Well, he had already grieved over her once, and so it made no real difference now. A slow sigh went from him. He saw again his mother as he had seen her that last time, walking with faltering steps over the snow in front of the church, going to get into the car that was to bear his supposed body to the cemetery for burial . . . How bent and frail she had looked! How lost, uncomprehending, and weak . . . But not a facial muscle moved as he gazed into the eyes of Houston. Houston turned and walked slowly back to his desk, glancing at his aides as he did so. He sat and resumed his watching of Cross's face. He's waiting for the news to sink in, Cross thought. He felt that he ought to be sorry, but he could not summon the necessary degree of emotion. Had she suffered much? Then the truth of it dawned upon him; his mother had been dead for him for years, and that was why he had been able to reflect upon her so coldly and analytically while she had still been living . . . To him his mother's reality was that she had taught him to feel what he was now feeling. He was at this moment living out the sense of life that she had conferred upon him, a sense of life which, in the end, he had accepted as his own. It had been her moral strictures that had made him a criminal in a deeper sense than Houston's questions so far could admit.

"Did you hear what I said, Damon?" Houston asked softly.

"Certainly."

"And what's your reaction?"

"Nothing."

"You're not even curious as to how she died?"

Cross struggled with himself; yes, Houston was using the tactics of Gil and Hilton. Houston was attempting to bring him repentantly to his knees, trying to rule him through the deep conditioning that all men felt in common for their parents.

"No," he said, the words coming softly from his lips.

Houston shook his head in disbelief.

"Damon, do you deny meeting me in the dining car of a train on the 8th of February last?"

"I affirm or deny nothing."

"Do you belong to any organizations whatsoever?"

"I belong to nothing."

"Do you subscribe to any political philosophy?"

"I subscribe to nothing."

"Are you working for any foreign government?"

"No."

"Have you ever made any public speeches?"

"No."

"Did you ever write under your own or an assumed name in any periodical or newspaper?"

"No."

"Have you ever been in jail?"

"I've nothing to say."

"Did you ever commit a felony?"

"I admit nothing."

Houston leaped to his feet and walked with long strides toward Cross.

"Damon, did you kill Gilbert Blount?" Houston thundered.

"I've nothing to say."

"Did you kill Langley Herndon?"

"I affirm or deny nothing."

"Did you kill Jack Hilton?"

"I affirm or deny nothing."

Houston had reached the important questions, but he had not mentioned Joe Thomas yet. Did that mean that he did not have to worry about Joe? Surely, Houston would have thrown it at him if he had known . . . He was not absolutely certain about Joe Thomas, but he was reasonably sure . . . What could have happened there? Perhaps the Chicago police had marked it "Unsolved"? Now, what evidence did they have against him in relation to Gil and Herndon and Hilton . . . ? Houston's eyes were wide and intent as they stared at his face, but Cross knew that those eyes were reflecting processes of thought far removed from the questions that Houston had asked so far.

"Do you hate Communism, Damon?" Houston asked softly, suddenly.

Now, Houston had gotten to the point. This is where

I must be careful . . . Houston had now entered territory known well to both of them.

"What a strange question to ask me," Cross stalled.

"I'm asking you do you hate Communism?" Houston
insisted.

"How can one *hate* Communism?" he asked, smiling.

"Then you love Communism?"

"No."

"Are you a member of any so-called revolutionary
party?"

"No."

"Were you *ever* a member of the Communist Party?"

"No. And I've never been a Fascist either."

"I know that—"

"How *could* you know that?" Cross asked.

Houston blinked, pulled down the corners of his
mouth. "You're a Negro—"

"Negroes can be Fascists too," Cross told him.

"Are you a Fascist then?"

"No."

"The Fascist angle is not important; they wouldn't
take you in anyhow," Houston said with a tinge of satisfaction.

"Fundamentally, Fascism has nothing to do with
race," Cross told him.

"Are you bragging about that?"

"I'm stating facts to you, sir."

"Do you believe in Communism?"

"How can one believe in Communism?" Cross countered again.

He saw that Houston resented his question; he knew
that Houston was seeking for a motive for the deaths of
Gil and Hilton, and Houston knew that he knew it.

"Isn't Communism something that one believes in?"
Houston asked.

Cross drew a deep breath. Ought he wade out into this? Why not? If he did, he would isolate himself so sharply in a psychological sense that Houston would be bound to get a faint clue, but a psychological clue only. And there was a vast distance between psychological clues and concrete proof.

"It's true that there are some people who do believe in the ideology of Communism," Cross explained. "But real Communist leaders do not believe in its ideology as an article of faith. Such an ideology is simply in their hands and minds an instrument for organizing people. A real Communist would have a certain degree of contempt for you if you passionately believed in his ideology. He would accept you as a follower, but not as an equal. The real heart of Communism, Mr. Houston, is the will to power. And you know that, sir, as well as I do."

"Would you use such an instrument in organizing people?"

"I wouldn't touch such an instrument with a ten-foot pole," Cross said earnestly.

"Why?"

"I think such an instrument is an insult to human life and intelligence," Cross said.

"Well, what kind of instrument would you use in organizing people?"

"I don't know, sir."

"But you agree that people ought to be organized?"

"Certainly, sir."

"Why?"

"Human life on this earth must proceed on some rational basis, sir."

"Then, what organizational instrument would you advocate?"

"None. I've not discovered any to my liking, sir."

"And still you feel that human society needs organization? That it stands in urgent need of such, in your opinion?"

"Yes; of course. It's self-evident."

"You feel that the inability of men to form stable governments in the nations of the world proves that, don't you?"

"It's self-evident, sir."

"You know that if America pulled its support from Europe, Europe would collapse?"

"Yes."

"Are you willing to see that support pulled out?"

"No."

"You agree with that support?"

"No."

"You think it's bad?"

"Yes; it is very bad."

"But you do not advocate its being pulled out?"

"No."

"Why?"

"It's better than nothing, sir."

"But it's bad?"

"Yes."

"Why?"

"It doesn't answer their needs, sir. It's a stopgap."

"Would Communism answer their needs?"

"No. Of course not."

"What, then, would answer their needs, in your opinion?"

"Really, Mr. Houston— You are aware as well as I am of the complex nature of human needs, especially the needs of modern man . . . We've been over this ground once. Maybe there's no answer to their needs—"

"Do you support the Red Chinese?"

"I don't support 'em or fight 'em; they're just

Red Chinese, sir. It's the way they've organized themselves."

"Don't you think they could have organized themselves our way?"

"Why should they?"

"I'm asking you do you think they ought to have done it our way?"

"I could not say yes to that unless, first, I felt that ours was the system that they should have, sir. Second, I'm the kind of man who simply cannot feel that kind of godlike imperiousness to impose my will on others."

"But you feel that all of this unrest on earth today is because man is seeking for an organization of his social life?"

"He urgently needs one," Cross said stoutly. "I'm guilty of thinking and believing that, sir."

Houston blinked, sighed. His eyes roved restlessly about the room.

"Yes, you told me that on the train when I first met you. But I'm not accusing you of any such—"

"I know it, sir," Cross said jovially. "I was just making a little confession to you."

"It's no crime under our laws to believe that something or other ought to be done in society—"

"I beg your pardon, sir. In my opinion, it is right *there* where the real crime is," Cross maintained. "A man today who believes that he cannot live by the articles of faith of his society is a criminal and you know it, even though Congress has not gotten around to making such into law. You know that as well as I do, sir. We've talked about that."

Houston threw up his hands. Cross was amused. Houston was looking right at his guilt, and would not admit it. Houston stared at him with wide, startled eyes, then, glancing guiltily at his aides, sat again at his desk, poring over his stack of papers. Cross wanted to laugh. What did papers have to do with this? Houston looked at Neil, nodded to him, and Neil hurriedly left the room. He's executing something previously agreed upon, Cross said to himself. He waited. Houston looked up suddenly.

"Damon, suppose you come upon a man attempting to organize human society in a way that was supremely offensive to you, what would you do?" Houston asked in a slow, loud tone.

He was asking indirectly if he had killed Gil and Herndon and Hilton.

"I decline to say."

"You don't like Communists, do you?"

"No."

"Which do you hate more? Communists or Fascists?"

"Well, I'm afraid I hate the Fascists more, sir."

"Why?"

"Well, they've more real support. Of course, this is a debatable question. Maybe I feel like that because I'm a Negro and Fascists are dead against us."

"If you saw an opportunity to send two of them to their graves in one blow, would you do it?"

Cross looked at Houston and laughed.

"Would *you*?" he countered.

"Will you answer the question?" Houston demanded.

"I decline to answer, sir," Cross said.

"Why?"

"Because you know the answer."

"You would kill them, wouldn't you?"

"I decline to answer."

"Goddammit, I'll break your spirit yet!" Houston raged.

The next face that showed in the doorway made Cross feel that he should have been sitting down, because, for a moment, he felt like falling. It was Gladys. She was smartly dressed. Her face was pale with apprehension and her movements stiff with shock. She was clutching a pocketbook and staring at Cross. Houston looked quickly from Gladys to Cross. Gladys reached out a trembling hand and caught hold of the edge of the desk for support. Cross was furious; he gritted his teeth. What point was there in Houston's dragging Gladys into this? Yes; Houston, too, liked to play at being a little god, liked to ravage the souls of others. That was why he was District Attorney . . . And Cross vowed that Houston would never see him humbled, unnerved, or weeping. Houston had thought that the sight of Gladys would make him break down and talk. Well, he would not react. He would show Houston that he had miscalculated. Then Cross sucked in his breath sharply; from the open door behind Gladys, being led by Neil, came his three sons, Cross, Jr., Robert, and Peter. He whirled to Houston and saw an expression of sensual excitement upon the hunchback's lean face. That sonofabitch . . . Cross, Jr., his eyes wide and his lips parted, stared at his father, then clutched his mother's hand, whimpering:

"Mummy, is he *Daddy* for real?"

Cross felt the muscles in his calves aching. Robert and Peter stood close to Gladys, staring; then they, too, began weeping, the flow of their tears being caused more by fear and uneasiness than any understanding.

"Why did Daddy come back, Mummy?" Peter asked.

"It's *not* Daddy," Robert said emphatically, indignantly, still crying.

Keep still, Cross told himself. His body was rigid. He had often imagined many kinds of confrontations, but he had never dreamed of this. To let his sons see him standing mute, stony . . . ! He could *kill* Houston! His anger was so hot that he could not permit himself to look into Houston's face.

Gladys, blinded by tears, her mouth distorted with silent weeping, groped for her children and huddled them clumsily about her, trying to keep her face averted. Cross returned the stares of everyone in the room without allowing his face to betray any expression whatever. Then he could hold it in no longer.

"Why are you doing this?" the words broke from him in a spasm of rage.

"At last I got a rise out of you, hunh?" Houston asked, wetting his lips with his tongue, reveling in deep satisfaction. "I had your wife and children flown here this morning from Chicago . . ."

Cross could tell that Houston was trying to justify his actions.

"I didn't want to make any mistake about identifying you, Damon," Houston said.

But Cross was not be be fooled; he knew that Houston loved this, just as he too sometimes loved lording it over others. But that look of sensual triumph on Houston's face had already sent Cross scuttling back to his shell of iron reserve, to his stance of defense. All right, suppose they were his sons? He had given them up, hadn't he? He would make a supreme effort and remain cold, hard. Sentiment must not subvert him now. He was lost, that much was true; but he must not let human claims drag him into a position where Houston could crow over him . . . Nothing could so undo him so easily now as Houston's gloating or bragging. Those frightened, little brown-faced boys were his sons, flesh of his flesh; they were the future of himself and he had rejected that self.

"Damon, I realize that you and your wife did not get along together," Houston said. "She told me that. But, man, here are your children . . . They need you. Go to them."

Cross made his face a mask.

"Damon, can you stand there and look at the bewildered faces of those children and say nothing?" Houston demanded.

Cross shut out the sight of the world and tried not to hear.

"You can redeem yourself with them, Damon," Houston was saying. "Are you going to let them remember you all of their lives like *this*? Boys love to think of their fathers as strong, wise men," Houston went implacably on. "To many a son the image of his father is what lifts him up in life. A father can make a boy feel that he has a sure foundation under him, can give him confidence . . ."

Cross summoned all his control and pushed Houston's words away; he would not react; he would not be human; he was shunt of these claims and he would die shunt of them . . .

Houston turned and looked at Gladys whose face was hidden by her crumpled handkerchief; the woman's body seemed so rigid that if one touched her ever so lightly she would fall prone.

"Mrs. Damon," Houston began in a loud, clear voice, "do you recognize this man standing there?" Houston pointed at Cross.

Gladys slowly turned her face and stared at Cross with wet, red eyes. Then she quickly bowed her head; both of her hands convulsively covered her face in one shuddering motion and her chest heaved as she wept in dry gulps. Houston gently grasped her shoulder and led her to a chair.

"I'm asking you: Do you recognize this man as your husband, Mrs. Damon?" Houston demanded.

Gladys was still, then she shook her head with a slow, dreamy movement, shook it negatively and at once Cross knew that Gladys was not shaking her head in answer to Houston's question, but was asserting her right to reject him as he had once rejected her! Gladys was protesting his presence on earth. Houston's face showed astonishment; he did not understand what was transpiring in the woman. He had thought that a storm of words would have poured out of Gladys, and that he, Cross, would have been moved to pity. Cross knew that Gladys would rather have had him dead.

"Mrs. Damon, I *asked* you if that is your *husband*?"

Her cheeks wet with tears as far down as her chin, Gladys finally nodded her head affirmatively. Houston blinked in bewilderment.

"Now, *which* answer is it, Mrs. Damon," Houston demanded. "Is he your *husband*, or is he *not*?"

Cross burst into a gale of laughter that made the bodies of everyone in the room jerk. Houston gaped at Cross, then his face settled into a mold of anger. Cross knew that there was a conflict in Gladys. Her first reaction had been to say that she did not know him; then she had wanted to be honest with the District Attorney and had said yes. And now she was more confused than ever and she shook her head again, negatively. It was an identity deeper than that which Houston was asking for that Gladys was denying.

"Mrs. Damon, again I ask you, is this your husband, Cross Damon?"

Gladys rose, turned her back on Cross, nodded affirmatively to Houston and murmured brokenly: "Yes; it's he—"

She ran to the door, turned, snatched wildly at her children, grabbing them by their clothes and pulling them into the other room.

"But, Mrs. Damon, you—" Houston was trying to speak.

"No, no, no!" Gladys screamed and wept and the little boys joined her in crying, crying because they saw their mother unnerved and bitterly hysterical.

"Help her, Neil," Houston said; comprehension was now in his eyes.

The two men assisted Gladys into the next room and finally the door closed. Cross still stood, his face impassive.

"You are the lowest sonofabitch I've ever seen in all of my life," Houston said savagely.

"I return the compliment," Cross said. "What on earth did you gain by dragging her in here?"

Houston did not answer and Cross knew that he could not. Houston ran his spread fingers through his hair and sat again behind his desk, glaring at Cross.

"Damon, I'll get to the point. The Communists have been badgering me night and day to take action against you. They are charging that you killed Blount, Hilton, and Herndon," Houston told him.

"And what are *you* charging me with?" Cross asked.

Houston did not reply.

"How can you charge me merely on the insistence of Communists who are suspicious and frightened of me?" Cross demanded.

"*Why* are they frightened of you?"

"Ask them."

"Are you a member of any anti-Communist group?"

"I'm not a member of *anything*, Mr. Houston."

"Are you anti-Communist even as an individual?"

"I'll tell you as I told them: I'm not anti anything."

"But you don't support them, do you?"

"Hell, no. And millions of other men don't either—"

"But you are like them in your reactions. That much

I know," Houston said. "And the motive is right here."

"You think so?"

"The strongest motive on earth—"

"There are millions of men with the same motives—"

"I've no evidence against you, Damon, or Lane; if I had, I'd tell you so. I'm straight in this office. But I had a right to find out who you are," Houston explained in a tired voice. "There's another motive you could have had—"

"Yes?"

"You wanted Mrs. Blount. Men have killed for women before—"

"Mr. Houston, I don't believe that you really believe that," Cross told him. "Before Gil died, I never touched his wife, never so much as looked at her with desire in my eyes. Now, for the rest of this mess, you will have to prove your case against me."

"You started living with Mrs. Blount right off, before her husband was even buried," Houston charged.

"What law did I violate in doing that?" Cross countered. "And don't forget that I was living in the apartment *when* he died."

"You took her to Harlem—"

"That was to get her away from the press."

Cross was now convinced that Houston had no evidence; he had thought that Cross would have collapsed at the sight of Gladys and his sons and would have made some fatal mistake, some slip that would have helped him to build his case.

"The Communist case against you is as follows," Houston told him. "They claim that you went downstairs that night to see if Blount was all right. You saw him wounded. You finished him off. Then Herndon came upon you and you had to kill him. Hilton found out about it in some way, and you had to kill him to keep him silent."

"I've no comment to make on that."

Houston stood again and Neil and the other assistant reentered the room.

"I was thinking of remanding you for a psychiatric examination," Houston said.

"What purpose would that serve?" asked the youngish man who had stood silent through all of this.

"Sending me for psychiatric observation would be as good an excuse as any to hold me on," Cross told him placidly.

Houston sat down heavily in his chair.

"Hell, *no*!" He turned and stared exasperatedly at the youngish man who had spoken. "I'm not going to play games with this man. I've run this office straight so far, and I'll continue. If the police and the Medical Examiner cannot dig up enough evidence, I'll be damned if I'll hold him 'til they cook up something."

Cross realized that the youngish man was no doubt a psychiatrist.

"No opinion that we could give you from the hospital would be of any legal use in relation to what I've heard so far. The man seems to be orientated and is defending himself," the young man said.

Houston stood and smiled shyly at Cross.

"That's all for tonight, Lane," he said.

"You mean you are through with me for the time being?" Cross asked.

"For the time being, yes. You may go."

Neil held open the door for him and Cross slowly walked toward it; then he paused, his mind filled with an impish notion. He turned to Houston.

"The best way to get a victim is to find an innocent man," he told the District Attorney. "An *absolutely* inno-

cent man. Such a man is *free* to be charged with anything. An innocent man is overwhelmed when he is
falsely accused and he is at a loss for words. He doesn't
know how to defend himself," Cross went on, teasing
the District Attorney. "You don't really need much evidence at all to charge an innocent man. The bigger the
charge, the more likely people are to think that that man
must have done something, or else no one would have
charged him. The way to make a man guilty is to attack
him without cause, without reason. The logic there is: if
he was not guilty, no one would have dared to charge
him. I was innocent to the extent that I didn't have a
good name that would stand up under investigation. I
had a secret name and you found it, ergo, I'm guilty of
something. Good night, sir."

He walked down the corridor to the elevator and
dropped to the street, thinking, I've got to see Eva . . .
He grabbed a taxi and shot uptown. He knew that
Houston was not through with him yet. But I *dare* him
to admit what he knows . . . He already knows, but of
what use is his knowledge . . . ? But the Party . . . ?
That was another thing. They did not have to be certain
to brand you guilty. If they could not *understand* you,
then you were guilty! Yes; he'd have to take Eva away at
once, take her out of New York. He'd ask her to come
away tonight . . .

He paid the taxi and looked up at the windows of
Sarah's apartment. Lights were blazing through the curtains. Were Menti and Hank up there? He grew hot
with hate. He'd send them packing, those fools! He'd
take Eva with him right now . . .

He bounded up the steps and pushed the bell of the
door. Sarah opened it almost at once. Her face was
tense with fear and curiosity.

"Did the police find you?"

"Yes. Where's Eva?"

"But what have you done, Lionel? What did they want?"

"Nothing. But where's Eva?"

"She's gone. With Menti and Blimin— But what are the cops after you for?"

"It's nothing— Where did Menti and Blimin take Eva?"

"I don't know. They just asked her to come with them. But are you in some kind of trouble?"

He sighed. Then whirled as the doorbell rang.

"Maybe that's Eva now," Sarah said, hurrying.

It was Eva. She came quickly and excitedly into the hallway. She was a little stooped, as though bent with dread; she stopped at the sight of Cross. Her face went white and her eyes held a wild, scared look. *She knows something* . . . The Party had told her; he could feel it. He ran toward her.

"God, Eva, what's the matter?"

She backed away from him, stumbling against a wall, her eyes transfixed with terror.

"Eva, let me tell you everything!" he cried.

She looked at him with an opened mouth and shook her head.

"Darling, listen. I've been wanting to tell you—"

"Your name's not Lionel . . . You're married, aren't you?"

"Yes," he sighed.

"Why didn't you tell me?" she demanded in helpless despair.

"I'll explain everything . . ."

"Oh, God, the Party's accusing you of *everything*— All night I've battled and fought and wept and screamed to save you— To protect you— And they say I'm wrong; they say you're guilty of something—

Why didn't you tell me this . . . ? Where's your wife?"

"She's here in the city somewhere; but you and I are together—"

"Does she love you?"

How like a woman to think of those little things first!

"No."

"Do you love her?"

"No."

"You have three small sons—?"

"Yes."

"You deserted them?"

"Yes, Eva."

"And you know that your mother died yesterday?"

"Yes."

"Then you're really the man who ran off from Chicago, leaving his family—?"

"Yes."

"You don't love your family?"

"No."

His answers had come automatically; he was staring at the floor, waiting for her to question him further. Eva covered her eyes with her hands and leaned against the wall. She sighed in despair.

"What kind of a man are you?" she asked in a whisper.

He had confessed a part of it; now he had to tell her all. She had to believe in him, help him, understand him . . .

"Eva, come into the room," he begged her. "I must talk to you—"

"I feel dead," Eva whimpered. "*Why* did you fool me?" She choked and wept for a moment. "Nothing you ever told me was true . . . And Lionel's not your name! Oh, God!"

Sarah was staring from one to the other with an open mouth.

"What's happened?" she asked.

"His name's not Lionel Lane," Eva sobbed.

Sarah backed away from Cross as though he had become a leper.

"You mean you gave us *another* false name?" she demanded indignantly. "You gave Bob a false name the first time you met him . . ."

"I must talk to you, Eva," he said. "Come into the room. I love you. This *can't* break us up. It *mustn't*. I'll explain everything. You'll see."

Sarah stepped between him and Eva.

"What are you doing to her? Leave her alone— She's scared to death—"

"I've *got* to talk to her, Sarah. I'll explain everything to you later," he said, taking Sarah's arm and pushing her to one side.

He was clinging to a thread of hope. He knew that in spite of all, she still believed in him. But what was he to tell her? Her staunch confidence in him had helped her to weather the storm she had met at the Party headquarters, and now she had come meekly to him for confirmation of what she had fought for, and he could not give it to her. He took her gently by the arm and led her down the hallway and into their bedroom. He could feel the tension in her body as she moved, pulling jerkily but feebly against his hand. He wanted more than anything on earth to keep her, and yet he did not know how; he had no notion of what to say. He closed the bedroom door and turned to her.

"*What's* your name?" she asked him softly.

"Cross Damon," he answered, but he could not look her in the eye.

"*Why* didn't you tell me this before?"

"I was afraid to, and I was ashamed," he told her truthfully.

He glanced at her now and what he saw filled him with frenzy. There were other and bigger questions looming behind those clear, hazel eyes, and those questions condemned him more crushingly than anything that Houston could have said to him. He saw her lips move several times, but no words came from her. She turned from him and leaned against the wall, sobbing softly.

"I gave you my diary to read," she whimpered. "I thought you'd be honest with me . . . *You've* deceived me too!"

"I was frightened of telling you everything, of telling you the truth," he said. "I was afraid that you'd run off from me."

"Lionel—" She paused and cried afresh. "I don't even know what to call you now . . ." She went to the bed and sank upon it, staring in bleak dismay before her.

Yes, she wants to ask me about Gil . . . She wants to know . . . Oh, God! He went to his knees and clutched his arms about her legs. He would beg and plead for his life. He waited in agony for her to ask, and he felt that he could scarcely draw his breath into his lungs.

"Eva," he begged. "It's not too late. If you love me, it's never too late. Remember that. You told me you loved me, and I need you now. If you turn from me, the world collapses . . ."

"So— S-s-so it w-was *true* . . . What you told me that night? When you came in?"

He hung his head and could not answer.

"You were trying to tell me something— You were all mixed up and you spoke of killing men— Oh, God—! I thought you were delirious, ill. I thought you were talking out of your mind because of fever and worry . . ."

She had asked him directly at last! And he could not lift his eyes to look her in the face. He tightened his arms about her legs, afraid to let go of her.

"Eva, I love you; I love you," he mumbled frantically. "You must remember that. I'm crazed with fear and worry now. Don't leave me . . ."

"You *did* it, then? What the Party said?"

"What did they say?"

"They said you killed Gil to get me . . ."

He was tempted. Ought he tell her a lie and let her think that? Would it not touch her heart and make the look of the world seem less strange and hostile to her? Would it not make her love him the more? But would he not be locking himself up again behind the wall of himself if he lied to her again? What would lying solve now? Nothing . . . And what made it so hellishly difficult was that when he lifted his eyes he could see in her face that she was expecting to hear him say that he had killed Gil for her, to get her, out of his love for her.

"Nooooo," he breathed. "I killed Gil . . . But it was not for you—"

"Oh, God in Heaven! Why *did* you kill him, Lionel?"

"I don't know," he whispered.

"*Why?* There must be some *reason* . . ."

He shook his head; his body was trembling all over.

"You *must* know; you *say* you did it," she said.

Could he ever tell her? He had to try. He had to talk or he could not go on living. He had to try to get for once in his life from behind himself, to walk out of his house as she had once walked out of her house to meet him.

"Eva," he whispered hoarsely, still clutching her legs. "It goes way back . . . God, help me to explain . . . I *want* to explain . . ." He felt hot tears rolling down his cheeks. "You see, Eva, I don't *believe* in anything . . ." He spoke in a tone of voice that he knew sounded unreal, not convincing. But how could he make it sound otherwise? How did one *tell* these things?

"What had Gil done to you?" she asked in a whisper that carried an overtone of hope.

"Nothing," he sighed and felt that he would choke. "Oh, God, he did nothing to me . . . Eva, I'm praying to you to try to understand me . . . *Somebody* must understand me . . . I'll die if you don't understand . . . Look, when you can't believe in anything, when you're just here on this earth and there's nothing, *nothing* else . . . Oh, Christ, I can't explain it! You have to *feel* it! You have to *live* it! It has to be in your blood before it can become real to you . . . I feel like I'm talking to you from another world . . . Trying to talk to you through a glass wall . . . I know you can't understand . . . But, Eva, you must love me and trust me!" He shook his head in bewilderment. "If you understood, you'd suffer too like I did . . . Oh, no; you'll never understand this . . ." Despair was full in him. "I didn't ever want to tell you like this . . ." All of his hope had gone and he was talking to her out of a sense of futility.

"When did you kill him?"

"When I went down to see what had happened . . . They were fighting . . . God, I can't explain how I felt . . . When I looked at them, I suddenly hated them both . . . They'd done nothing to me . . . They weren't even paying any attention to me; they were fighting so hard that they didn't even know that I was in the room . . ." He knew that what he was saying did not sound convincing to her. And the knowledge of it maddened him; he stood and began shouting: "Don't you *understand*? You've been scared, haven't you? You know what it means to live senselessly? When every day is a foolish day? And when I stood in that room I saw more senselessness and foolishness right before my eyes and I felt a way to stop it! I hated what I saw! And I hated myself because all my life I was unable to do anything about it . . . I tell you, I *hated* it. It insulted me . . . I wanted to blot it out, wipe it from the face of the earth . . ." It seemed that he had forgotten that he was speaking to her; his hands and arms made gestures as he stood in the dim room before her and reenacted his crime. "I took the table leg and battered Herndon down, killed him . . . I did it; yes . . . I wasn't angry with him personally; not then . . . I'd been angry with him before, but I felt no anger then . . . I killed 'im because I didn't think he had a right to live . . . Did you ever feel like that about anybody? No; you couldn't feel that . . ." He paused and rubbed his eyes; then he seemed to remember that he was telling her about what had happened. "Then I hit Gil . . . He wasn't expecting it . . . I was mad with them . . . No; not personally mad. Don't you know what I mean . . . ? I can't say it right, goddammit, I *can't* . . . I wanted to live so badly; I wanted a good life so terribly much that what I saw made me mad, *mad* . . . And I killed them . . . Eva, *believe me* . . . It was that that made me kill them . . ." He looked at her and there was no light of comprehension in her eyes. "Oh, God, you don't *believe* me . . . You *can't* believe me . . . But you *must*, Eva; you *can*; you of all the people in the world can understand . . . I *know* it . . ." His voice died away in a whisper. Then he resumed, reciting his words as though he was reliving the scene of the murder and blood again. "I kept hitting them until they were dead . . . I wasn't sorry . . . I knew I was right . . . Then I wiped off all the fingerprints . . . I didn't want to be caught; I didn't want to be punished . . . Then I came up to you . . . That's what I did, Eva. Now, can you understand that?"

She was white as a sheet; she seemed not to breathe.

"And Hilton *too*?" she asked in a whisper.

"Yes," he sighed.

"Because he knew?"

"No; not exactly. No."

"Then *why*?"

"Mainly because of what he did to Bob . . . And because of what he wanted to do to me," he said, speaking mechanically.

She was still as a block of ice. Her eyes stared unseeingly into the shadows of the room. Then he saw her body jerk as some idea came into her mind.

"That night when you were trying to tell me," she began in a whisper. "You spoke of Chicago . . ." She shook her head helplessly, then bit her pale lips. "You said you killed somebody else . . ."

"Eva, Eva . . . Please, I need help . . . If ever a man needed your love, I need it . . . I've killed and killed . . . Have mercy on me . . . Pity me, but not for what has been done to me, but for what I've done to others and myself . . . You be my judge; you tell me if I'm to live now . . . Can you tell me . . . ?"

She was edging away from him; her eyes reflected horror.

"But I thought you were against brutality— I thought you were going to tell me what Gil had done to you— I thought you hated suffering—"

"I do!" he shouted. "That's why I did it! I couldn't stand the thought of it, the sight of it . . . !"

She did not believe him; she could not believe him. She was a reluctant victim and he was a willing one . . . He stared fully at her and reached out his hand to touch her. She leaped away from him, gasping, and scrambled to her feet.

"Eva," he pleaded.

She ran from him, to the door. He started after her, frantic, his bloodshot eyes glistening.

"Eva, please try to understand . . . It's hard . . . I know . . . But try, *try* . . . I can redeem myself . . . Let me be with you . . ." He was praying to her.

She gave a short scream and ran out of the room. He followed her out of the door. Sarah came rushing down the hall.

"What's the matter?"

"Sarah, Sarah, help me," Eva wailed.

"Lionel, leave her alone," Sarah yelled.

Eva clutched Sarah and clung to her, her body shaking.

"Lionel, what have you done to her?"

Then abruptly, Eva twisted around in the arms of Sarah and looked at Cross and while she was looking he saw the light go out of her eyes. She seemed stricken, not knowing where she was; she pulled away from Sarah and ran on down the hall until she came to the door of the living room. She paused, looked wildly about her, then ran into the living room and slammed the door. He rushed to the door and heard the lock click.

"Eva, for God's sake, listen . . ."

"What did you do to her?" Sarah wailed.

"Leave me alone, will you!" he told her savagely.

"But, Lionel, you're driving her crazy . . ."

The front doorbell pealed and Cross stood wondering who it was. The hell with whoever was coming . . . He pounded on the door of the living room with his fists as Sarah went down the hall to the front door.

"Eva, let me come in and talk to you," he begged her, but deep in him he felt that she never would.

Menti came through the front door; Sarah was holding the door open for him. Behind Menti was Hank, sullen, his hands thrust deep in his overcoat pockets. Menti paused, sensing that something was happening.

"What's the matter here?" he asked.

"Eva's locked herself inside and won't come out," Sarah said.

"What are *you* doing here?" Menti asked Cross.

"The hell with you," Cross snapped at him. "I've a right to be here."

"I thought the D.A. had grabbed you," Menti said.

"He did, but I'm free now," Cross told him. "Your Party's trick didn't work, Menti."

"Be careful of what you say about the Party—"

"Oh, God, don't fight in here," Sarah begged.

"Eva," Cross called through the door. "Open the door, honey!"

Cross felt his legs trembling. What could he do? If he could only talk to her, quiet her down, he might make her see what had happened to him.

"Eva!" he called again.

Cross turned and looked appealingly at Sarah.

"Don't you have a key to this door?"

"No," she said, shaking her head.

Cross put his ear to the panel of the door; he could hear no sounds. God, what could she be doing?

"Eva! Eva!" He took hold of the doorknob and rattled it furiously.

He was conscious that Menti was looking at him with a sardonic smile. That sonofabitch . . . ! But maybe Menti could help make Eva open the door.

"Menti, call her. Tell her to open the door."

"Why? Leave her alone . . . What can I do if she runs away from you?" Menti said, chuckling.

"Damn you!" Cross growled. He saw Hank staring at

him with tense hatred. "And you too!" Cross spat at him. He turned to the door again. "Eva!"

There came a loud, heavy pounding upon the front hall door. Sarah started toward it, then paused, looking at Cross. The pounding came again. Then a hoarse voice yelled:

"Say, open up in there!"

Sarah opened the door and backed away as a tall, black man rushed into the hallway, his eyes wide with excitement.

"Say, wasn't it from this apartment that a woman jumped from a window . . . ?" he asked, looking from one to the other of them.

Sarah, Hank, Menti, and Cross—all of them were silent, standing open-mouthed, staring at the black man's face. Cross, for a moment, could not think; his feelings froze; he was not even aware of his surroundings. Then a realization of what the man had said came to him in the form of a flashing image of Eva's frail body hurtling through the icy air of the night outside. The words clanged in his mind as though someone was shouting in his ears: Oh, God, it's Eva . . . ! For a split second the world was blotted out; then he was running and stumbling through the doorway, falling and sliding down the dark, winding flights of rickety stairs. He reached the street panting and aching from where he had knocked himself against the walls and bannisters on his way down. He leaped clear of the steps of the stoop and saw that a crowd of Negroes had already begun to gather in a knot near the edge of the sidewalk. He sprinted to them, plowing them aside. Yes . . . There was Eva . . . She was lying half on her stomach with her face to the pavement, her body twisted so that the toes of her shoes were pointing upwards and her face was hidden in the snow. Already blobs of blood had seeped from her head and Cross could see where someone had stepped on a loosened lock of her blonde hair, crunching and burying it in the dirty snow. *Eva!* The word rang so loud in his mind that he was not conscious of what went on about him. He had lost. She had fled from him forever; she had taken one swift look into the black depths of his heart, into the churning horror of his deeds and had been so revolted that she had chosen this way out, had slammed her door on life.

He knelt, turned her gently over, stared at the bruised and shattered face, the gaping, defenseless mouth, the flattened nostrils from which blood streaked and stained his trembling hands.

"Eva, Eva," he whimpered and cradled her head in his arms.

He looked up at the looming circle of dark faces for the first time, his eyes pleading for help.

"Get a doctor," he begged.

"Better get the police," someone said roughly.

"Did he *kill* her?"

"Maybe a car ran over her . . ."

"Naw; somebody pushed her out of a window—"

"I heard her hit the sidewalk; it was like a pistol shot!"

"Look, she's a *white* gal!"

"What *she* doing up here in Harlem?"

"Get some help, please," Cross pleaded. "Somebody— Somebody *do* something— She's hurt!"

An elderly Negro with white hair bent to him and whispered: "I sent in an alarm for the police."

"Did she jump outta a window?"

"It was from up there— One, two, three, four— Lord, she fell *six* floors— She's dead or she'll die—"

Cross held his breath and stared directly in front of

him, holding Eva against his chest; he was afraid to look down at her broken face and her half-opened eyes . . . He knew that he had to look and a sigh went from him as he saw those hazel eyes now filmed and unseeing. She was limp in his arms and her body felt terribly light, as though her substance was dwindling as her life ebbed. He bent closer and saw that under the waving, tumbling coils of her blonde hair the top of her skull had been bashed in bloodily. His lips trembled as he realized that it was hopeless. Gently, he eased her body back to the snow-packed pavement and felt for her pulse; she had none. He hardly knew what happened after that. He kept kneeling, staring at her, repeating softly:

"Eva, Eva . . ."

At last Menti was at his side, and there was the dark form of Hank looming menacingly in the background. Sarah, her eyes bulging, her fingers twisting nervously, stood whimpering. And then there came to his ears the distant sound of sirens, the sirens he had so long feared, sirens that rose to a hysterical scream on the winter air. They were not sounding for him, those sirens, but for the only woman he had ever loved. He was now locked in loneliness.

"Why did she do it?" Menti asked.

Cross glanced at him and did not answer. He saw that Menti's face was calm, composed, alert, devoid of grief or shock, his eyes glowing with the intense, detached curiosity of a man long schooled in disaster. To those hard, disciplined eyes the sight of Eva's crumpled body was a thing to be expected, was something that fitted inevitably into life's dark design.

"Did somebody push her out?" a man's voice asked.

"No, no," Sarah said. "She jumped. I was there . . ."

"*Why* did she do it, Lane?" Menti asked again, softly, insistently into Cross's ear.

Cross looked into Menti's eyes without making any sign that he had heard him. The sirens were wailing closer now; then he saw the police cars turn the corner with screeching brakes; there was a swish of tires on ice and snow as the cars skidded to a stop. Blue-coated officers leaped out and ran forward. Cross saw Menti rise, detach himself stealthily from the crowd, walk down the sidewalk and slink into a candy store. Yes, Menti was going to call the Party and report. Cross envied the strength and self-possession which Menti derived from his total submissiveness to the Party; it was the Mentis of this earth that made power possible, that made leadership possible; silent Menti was, enduring, uncomplaining, obscure, humble, dutiful . . . Without the Mentis of this world, men could not move in concerted action, whether they wished to move to left or right, toward slavery or freedom, toward war or peace . . . The millions of obedient Mentis were the foundation of human life, society, mankind . . . What was the meaning of Menti? What did he want? What could buy his loyalty? What did he need? One thing was certain, no government on earth today was really offering Menti what he really wanted . . . Maybe no government could . . . ? Cross sighed.

"My God," a young white cop said as he bent forward, "what's she doing in Harlem?"

Another cop felt for Eva's pulse.

"Call for an ambulance, *quick*!" he said.

"Now, what happened?" another cop demanded.

"She jumped from the window of my apartment," Sarah managed to say.

"*Who* are *you*?"

"Sarah Hunter. I live up there on the sixth floor— Where you see the lights in the window," Sarah explained in halting tones, pointing. "I don't know what made her do it . . . Her husband was killed two days ago . . . Maybe that's why— But she didn't seem worried or anything— It was suddenlike—"

"What's her name?"

"Mrs. Eva Blount."

"Where did she live?"

"At 13 Charles Street, but she was staying with me . . ."

"Hunh?" the cop grunted, looking at Cross, then at Menti who had come back. He turned and addressed a young cop. "You better get hold of the Medical Examiner's office . . ." The young cop rushed off to the police car.

Cross stood up. He could feel Menti's elbow touching him. The cops were now asking the names and addresses of those who had seen Eva fall, what time she had fallen, and who had seen her in the neighborhood before. Cross gave his name and address, so did Menti and Sarah.

"You three," the cop said, indicating Cross, Menti, and Sarah, "will have to come to the station with us."

Cross did not care; it was over for him. Eva was gone; she had slipped through his clutching, clumsy fingers . . . He had botched it and Eva's crushed and mute face told him that this was hell: this swooping sense of meaninglessness, this having done what could never be undone . . . He had in him to the full the feeling that had sent him on this long, bloody, twisting road: self-loathing . . .

"She's gone," he heard a cop say.

"Really?"

"Yep."

From the throat of the night another siren screamed. That must be the ambulance . . . Eva was dead and now in recollection he knew her for what she had meant to him; already he was feeling what he had been grasping for in his loving her. That capacity in him to suffer had seized upon this lovely, frail girl as the representation and appearance in life of what he felt had to be protected and defended. To that frightened heart he had made, out of his compulsive need for companionship, out of his hunger for solace, a promise that he had not been able to keep, that he had *known* he could not keep, and, as the intensity of his lying promise had swollen, so had her distance from him widened until at last she was forever beyond his reach. Self-love as well as self-hate had dogged him to the end and he had not been able to outwit the predetermined molds of his destiny. And his too-keen habit of self-reflection would not permit him to hide from himself what he had done. Between him and Eva a mutual selfishness had entwined itself, each feeding greedily on the other and on itself, and, in that reciprocally devouring passion his falsely pledged promise had been the single element that had broken the unity, smashing it beyond all mending, all recall, for eternity.

Two internes pushed past Cross. An ague seized him as he saw them lift Eva's limp body and place it upon a stretcher and march with it to the ambulance and shove it into the rear door. The motor roared; the ambulance started off and the siren rose to a screaming pitch . . . Eva . . . Eva . . . He was alone.

"All right, folks— Break it up, now— Move along— Get going—" the police were saying.

Cross, Sarah, and Menti were jammed into the back seat of a police car and driven to a nearby police station where they had to wait in a dirty anteroom for hours. It was the Party again that tried unwittingly to come to Cross's assistance, for Menti, bending to him and whispering, said:

"Tell 'em nothing. Just say she jumped, but nobody saw her, see? But nothing else. We don't talk to cops."

Cross and Sarah nodded. He saw a look of wonder in Sarah's eyes as she stared at him. Yes, Sarah was silently asking what it was that he had said to Eva that had made her so wildly hysterical, had made her lock herself in the room and jump . . . And Cross was aware that Menti now regarded him with mounting hatred; his eyes were harder than agate as they rested on Cross's face. I'm glad that Sarah was there when Eva jumped, he told himself. Menti would like to accuse me of pushing her out of the window . . . The Party would be more suspicious of him now than ever. The hour was approaching when he would have to flee New York and try his luckless fortune elsewhere; that is, if Houston did not first place a fatal finger upon him.

They were questioned in relays, and when Cross's turn came, he obeyed Menti's injunction to the extent that he told a simple story of a girl whose husband had just been killed; he said that grief, maybe, had made her jump out of the window. But he thought better of Menti's advice and felt that he ought to tell the impersonal captain who was questioning him that he had just been interviewed by the District Attorney, for they would most surely discover it after he had gone and they would come rushing to question him again, thinking that he had for some reason tried to conceal it.

Complications arose at once; the puzzled captain telephoned Houston and Cross was instructed to go back home and remain there until further notice, and he was informed that a police guard would be placed at the front and back doors of the apartment.

When he emerged from the police station, Sarah and Menti had gone. He walked back to the apartment alone, climbed the steps and found a cop on guard in the hallway.

"You live here?" the cop asked.

"Yeah."

"If you go in, you can't come out 'til the D.A. says so," the cop informed him.

"I know that," Cross said.

The cop let him pass. He let himself in and went straight to the room he had shared with Eva and stood staring at her comb and lipstick on the cluttered top of the dresser. A few strands of her blonde hair still clung curlingly to the bristles of the hairbrush. There was her purse, an ashtray of cigarette stubs whose tips showed the rouge she had worn, a delicately scented handkerchief, a crumpled wad of face tissue . . . His throat ached and he fell upon the bed, burying his face in the pillow and lay as still as death, longing for oblivion, for the world to close in on him and swallow him forever.

He started when the door opened. It was Menti; he had not bothered to knock. Resentment flooded Cross and he did not care to rise to receive him. Menti left the door ajar and came to the bed and sat upon it, a few inches from Cross. These sonofabitches! They presumed they owned him, that they could come upon him when they liked, that he had no inviolate, private world of his own into which they could not penetrate at will. He clenched his teeth and kept his eyes averted and waited for Menti to speak. Then he was forced to look at Menti, for Menti gave forth a series of low, contented chuckles.

"You *are* an important man," Menti said.

"What the hell are you talking about?" Cross demanded.

"The whole Central Committee is meeting just about you," Menti informed him. "You sure bring trouble.

You've been in this city just a few days, but wherever you show your face, death's not far behind . . ." Menti rubbed his chin meditatively and continued: "Why did Eva jump?"

"You ought to be telling me," Cross hedged; he wanted to know what had been said when the Party questioned Eva. "She was terribly upset when she came in. She said she'd been to a Party meeting—"

"Did she tell *you* that?" Menti asked.

"Sure. Why not?"

"She was instructed *not* to."

"By whom?"

"The Party—"

"But why?"

"Well," Menti said, ignoring Cross's question, "she was never really a Bolshevik, you know." Menti shook his head in wonder. "She was a self-centered bourgeois artist . . . Say, do you know that the Party estimates that only about thirteen percent of all artists and intellectuals ever make the grade with us?" Menti smiled, indicating that Eva was no great loss. He continued: "Eva broke a decision when she talked to you. But what did she say . . . ?"

Cross saw an opportunity to sow confusion in Menti's mind by interpreting Eva's words to his advantage.

"She was horrified," he said. "She said that the Party was trying to convince her that I'd killed Gil to get her— But she knew that that wasn't true. I'd never said a word to Eva until after Herndon had killed Gil— It was Eva who made the advances. She came to my room that very night—"

Menti was impressed; he nodded his head.

"Hilton told the Party that," he admitted. "I don't get this."

"I didn't kill Gil to get Eva," Cross went on. "Anybody who thinks that is crazy. You and your Party are looking for the wrong *motives*, Menti . . . I ought to be hopping mad at you and your comrades for putting the D.A. on me. But he's no fool. Do you think a guy walks into a man's apartment and that very night kills him to take his wife? Good Lord, Menti, *think* a little. Do you think I'd risk my neck doing a thing like that? All right, maybe someone *did* go in there and kill the two of them. But how do you know they did it just to get Eva? Think of the many people the Party has wronged . . . They might have had a motive . . . A woman could have done it . . ."

"What woman?" Menti asked slyly.

"Look, Menti," Cross said shrewdly, "don't think everybody's naïve. Eva was a victim . . ."

"How do you know that?" Menti demanded. "What kind of a victim?"

"The Party tricked her into marrying Gil—"

"Who told you *that*?"

"Eva did," Cross lied readily. "Even Eva had a motive for killing Gil . . . But, of course, she was with me when Herndon killed Gil—"

"And you were with her when Hilton was killed?" Menti asked, fishing.

"No."

"Where were you then?" Menti tried to tie him down.

"In a bar. I've accounted for myself with the police," Cross maintained. "Look, I'm just as worried about the motive that could have made anybody go in there and kill Gil and Herndon as you are . . . But to say that getting Eva was the motive . . . Why, that's underestimating people, Menti . . ." Cross could barely repress a smile as he argued gently. "Maybe Gil had enemies with strange motives, motives which only the Party could understand . . . Did you ever think of that?"

Before Menti could answer, Cross saw the form of Blimin come through the door and head for the bed. He understood why Menti had left the door ajar; it was to give Blimin a chance to eavesdrop on their conversation.

"I see I won't have to repeat what I've said," Cross said to Blimin.

Blimin smiled coldly, planted himself in front of Cross and studied him for some time. Cross met the stare calmly, waiting.

"Well, at last we know *who* you are, Damon," Blimin said.

"So?"

"What are you up to? What's your game?"

"I'm trying to live, Mr. Blimin—"

"Do you want to join our Party?"

"Frankly, no."

"Menti says you promised Hilton that you would."

"That was before I'd met you, sir," Cross said.

"What did you tell Mrs. Blount?"

"Nothing," Cross said, looking Blimin straight in the eyes.

"Tell me, have you ever been outside of the continental boundaries of the United States?" Blimin asked.

"No. I've not been to Russia, Italy, Germany, Mexico, Argentina, or Spain . . ."

"Now that Mrs. Blount's dead, what do you intend to do?"

"I don't know."

"May I ask what arrangements did you make with the District Attorney?"

"None. He put me through the paces, but he had no evidence to hold me on," Cross explained good-naturedly.

"Don't you consider it an honor to be asked to join the Party?" Blimin was smiling now.

Cross had watched Blimin's mood change; the man had assumed a debonair attitude, as though all of his previous questions had not been as important as he had pretended. But Cross was not to be taken in by this belated pretense of cordiality; he knew that it meant simply that the Party was more baffled about him and his motives than ever; and they were trying to get closer to him in order to learn more about him. How free these men were! How they could turn, change; how they played make-believe with human emotions! They sensed, as Houston had, that in some as yet unknown and oblique way he was related to them and, being of their moods and temperament, he could too sense this in them. One had to be sensitive here; one had to realize that one was to some extent understood, and one had to act in a way that would not completely kill their trust; yet, at the same time, one had to be in a position not to let them make one pledge more than one was willing to yield. If he refused to promise to join the Party now they might suspect that his finality and abruptness had back of it something fatally serious; yes, he would make his attitude more equivocal . . .

"If you're not anti-Party, then why do you so flatly refuse to consider the Party's invitation to become a member?" Blimin asked.

"Look, man," Cross protested. "I've just undergone a prolonged grilling at the hands of the District Attorney . . . And it was you and your friends who egged the D.A. to pin something on me . . . Now, I ask you:

don't you think I'm right when I hesitate to embrace you? Haven't you a sense of balance?"

"Come now, Lane or Damon," Blimin chided him unctuously. "We admit we put you through the paces. But we were trying to protect ourselves. Can you really blame us for that?"

Cross bowed his head in thought. He wondered why Menti and Blimin had been allowed to enter the apartment and talk to him? They must be trying to get information from me for the police, he reasoned. He could not trust anyone now . . .

"I can't give you an answer now," he hedged, leaving the door open. "I'm just too tired and upset. I've got to get my bearings— Look, as soon as I hit this city and touched the Party, my life's turned upside down—"

"I understand," Blimin said softly.

Cross did not believe that Blimin understood, and he knew that Blimin knew that he did not believe it; they had reached that point where mutual lies made further communication impossible. But at least they had arrived at a truce. Cross smiled and said:

"Can't we talk about this later?"

"Of course," Blimin agreed readily, his mind busy elsewhere. "You're staying here?"

"Yes."

"Then we'll see you, hunh?"

"Of course."

Menti and Blimin left. They've gone straight to the police to report, he assured himself. They had been gone barely two minutes before Sarah came to him.

"I know there ain't no use asking you what it's all about, 'cause you ain't gonna tell me," she protested tearfully.

"Sarah, I'm tired; sit down, though," he said, lying back on the bed.

"What happened to Eva? And what is your name? You make me scared . . ." She let her voice trail off in confusion. Then, as though she did not expect him to answer, she said: "I'm sick of all this. I'm alone. I'm thirty-five years old. And what have I got? Nothing. Bob's gone; they took 'im from me. The Party? The hell with it. I'll never work with them again. Listen, Lionel, you know what I'm gonna do? I'm gonna do what my mother told me to do when I was sick and tired and didn't know where I was going—"

"What are you going to do?"

"I'm going to confession."

"Are you Catholic?"

"Yes," she said. "I ditched the church 'cause I felt they were doping me . . . But, now—I give up . . . I'm lost; I don't know if I'm going or coming . . . Bob and Gil and Hilton and now Eva . . . Why? It scares me . . . Only God can answer all this . . . Don't you think so?"

She was completely rattled. Her eyes had that restless, desperate look of one tired and confused and unable to support the feeling of it any longer.

"What are you talking about, Sarah? Only God can answer what?"

"These killings . . ." She groped for words. "Life doesn't make sense any more; it's crazy . . . People getting killed and nobody even sorry about it . . . It ain't *right* . . . I can't understand it. You know, Menti really laughed about Eva?" she stated in a half-questioning tone.

Poor Sarah . . . She was crushed and scared. She had to rest, to find support, a master; she was yearning to submit.

"What are you going to do, Lionel . . . ?" She paused, shook her head and looked at him with wonder.

"Your name's Cross; that's what Menti said. I don't like it; I like Lionel better . . ."

She was reacting to him now as woman; she knew that he was alone and she was wondering if she, maybe, could somehow team up with him. How movingly simple this woman was! She, like Eva, would recoil in horror (or maybe laughter; who knows?) if she knew the kind of man she was letting her dreams mull over.

"Forget me, Sarah," he told her directly.

"But what must I do?"

"What do you want to do?" he asked her.

"Oh, no," she murmured, shaking her head in fear. "You asked Bob that question just before they took him away. You told him to do what he wanted . . . No; no; I don't want to do that. Look what it brings!"

She did not want the responsibility of her life any longer. Why was life given to man if man could not handle it?

"Sarah, what I'm trying to ask you is this: What helps you most? What makes you feel better, good, 'sent' as you call it?" he asked her gently.

She brooded a bit, her face soft with memory.

"When I was a child I was happy," she mused. "At least, I thought I was . . ."

Cross wanted hotly to dispute that; he was convinced that there were no happy childhoods, that the myth of the happy childhood had been invented by middle-class people to show that their parents had had money when they were children, or by people whose memories of unpleasant days were so defective that they could delude themselves into believing that they had come into this world "trailing clouds of glory". Anthropologists, sociologists, psychologists, and the best accounts of childhood in all the serious and responsible literature of mankind depicted the child as coming into the world as a nasty, stinking little criminal savage (charming because it was harmless!) wholly intent upon the gratification of its own egoistic pleasures and satisfactions. Its criminality became subjective in relation to the checking of its unbridled impulses, and it was not until its imperious will had been subdued that it became civilized in some sense. And enough of the child-criminal had survived in Cross to make him know that criminal-consciousness, which is another name for childhood, could never be happy.

But why argue with Sarah about all of this? Her case was urgent and truths of this nature would serve but to make her more unhappy.

"And what do you think made you happy when you were a child, Sarah?"

"I don't know for sure," Sarah sighed. "But I didn't keep wondering about things like this . . . I believed in God . . . I went to Mass . . . Everything was simple . . ."

"And you want it to be simple again," he said. "I know . . . Well, do what you were doing when you were a child and see if it makes life simple again. Now, what do you really want to do? Look at me and tell me . . ."

"I want to find a man . . ."

"Can you? Be honest."

"I'm pretty old for that," she sighed, bit her lips. "I'm fat now. And I've no confidence in myself anymore," she let her voice die in her throat and tears began to well into her eyes. She bent forward and cried: "I'm going to Confession . . ."

Well, why not? All the church had to do was predict that life was terrible, that man would become overwhelmed with contradictory experiences. They could drill this simple, elementary truth of life into the hearts of impressionable children. Then the Fathers of the church could sit back and watch the generations of the sons and daughters of men grow up and go forth on their little voyages of proud, vain desire, could watch them with soft, ironic smiles, for they knew that sooner or later they would come crawling back to the faith of their childhood, seeking solace, whimpering for mercy, for forgiveness. Cross rose and paced the room, looking at Sarah now and then, smiling compassionately at her. Sarah leaped to her feet, her face wet with tears and her eyes hard with outrage.

"Are you laughing at me?" she demanded. "Then you *must* be crazy, like Menti said . . ."

"So, Menti said that, hunh?"

"And, by God, now I'm beginning to believe he's right!"

Cross went to her and placed his hand tenderly on top of her head.

"It might be better for you if you did believe that," he said.

She stopped crying and stared at him, not understanding. "Why do you say that?"

"You need rest, Sarah," he said. "Take your burden to God and lay it down . . . Remember, He said: *'Come unto me all ye that labor and are heavy laden, and I will give you rest . . .'*"

"But you don't *believe* that," she protested, baffled, half-scared. "I know you don't. *Do* you?"

"No," he could not resist telling her the truth.

"Then why do you tell *me* that?"

"Perhaps God uses the Devil to guide people home," he told her impishly.

Sarah blinked, then she ran to him, her lips curling

with hate and scorn; she began hitting him with her doubled fists. Cross ducked his head and burst into prolonged laughter.

"Don't, Sarah," he protested good-naturedly.

"You *bastard*! You're making *fun* of me! I could kill you, kill you . . . I swear, I could! You hear, I could kill you . . ." She paused, thinking, blinked her eyes. "Maybe you *did* kill them like Menti said . . ."

"It's you who're talking about killing me," he reminded her. "When did I ever say I wanted to kill somebody?"

"You're laughing, but you can't fool me," she said, her eyes lit with intuition. "I saw something crazy in you the first time . . ."

"Oh, no!" Cross protested, chuckling. "You laughed at me. Remember how you laughed?"

"I didn't know you then—"

"My dear, you don't know me now," Cross told her. "But look, in all seriousness, I tell you that you ought to go back to your church. You *need* it."

She did not know what to think. She saw that Cross was both serious and amused. The expression on her face told him that thoughts were clashing violently in her mind. Her mouth hung open, then her lips became compressed.

"You are a *devil*!" she burst out bitterly. "You're making fun of me and it ain't *right*! It ain't *good* to laugh at people for things like *that* . . . You like to see suffering . . ."

"I do not," he said.

"You do; I see it in you—"

"Sarah, what I feel does not concern you; forget it," he told her. "You asked my advice; I say you ought to go back to God."

"And what are you going to do?"

"Nothing," he said simply, quietly, looking at her with eyes that twinkled for the first time in many weeks.

She gazed at him, then looked away. She went to the door, pivoted; her mind was made up.

"I don't like you!" she shouted in a sudden rage and went out, slamming the door.

Yes, Sarah was going back to the church. What did it matter that the church had no answer for the ills of this earth? The priests could at least tell her to stop hoping for anything in this life, to curb and deny her desires, to forget her humiliating color consciousness, her poverty, that all of that was as nothing in the eyes of an eternal God. And for those who were weak, was that not right, fitting, necessary? Was it such a bad world, after all? The only trouble was that he and his kind were restlessly envious of the priests, the churches, the Communists, the Fascists, the men of power . . . That was it. He would have to live without that green foam of jealousy welling into his eyes and blinding him to how weak he was in relation to their organized strength. Render unto church that which is the church's, and render unto the Party that which is the Party's . . . But where would *he* stand? Was there no neutral ground?

He sat on the bed, looking at his suitcase. He ought to pack his things. Yes . . . He moved about listlessly, absent-minded, slowly filling the suitcase without conviction that he would ever have the right to move about again in freedom. Oh, yes; there was something he really wanted to do; he would take Eva's diaries with him, keep them as a memento . . . He pulled out the dresser drawer and saw that they were not there. He looked through all the drawers, under the bed, in the clothes closet. Now, where had he put them? Maybe Eva had taken them back when she had heard the Party's suspicions? But he did not believe that she would have done that without first telling him; it was not like Eva's transparent honesty. Then where *were* they? *The Party!* He would bet his life that Menti had taken them . . . Goddamn him! He had wanted those diaries . . . Well, if Menti had stolen them, they were gone. To argue with the Party about them was useless.

Through the closed door of his room came the faint tinkling of the front doorbell. He stood still, waiting, wondering whom it could be. Was it Menti again with his everlasting Hank? He placed his ear to the door panel and listened.

"Is Lane or Damon in?"

It was Houston's voice. Had he dug up any new evidence against him? Was he coming finally to arrest him?

Sarah's voice sounded cold and clipped: "He's in his room . . . There . . ."

Houston's footsteps echoed down the hallway and died in front of his door. Cross sank upon the bed. He would let Houston take the initiative. Eva was dead and there was no fight in him. A series of sharp knocks sounded on the door.

"Come in," he called.

The door swung open and there was Houston and behind him loomed a tall, blue-coated officer. Under Houston's arm was a bulky package wrapped in brown paper. Houston turned to the officer and said: "Wait down the hall."

"Yes, sir."

The officer left and Houston came in and closed the door softly behind him. He approached Cross, smiling vaguely. Houston had a relaxed, confident air and Cross felt that his time had come. He *knows* now . . . All right; if this was the end, then he did not care . . . Houston looked around, found a chair, dragged it to the bed and eased his deformed body on to it, some two feet from Cross. Cross felt sweat breaking out over his chest and he cursed himself for being unable to control his physical reactions. Well, why didn't the hunchback sonofabitch speak? Why did he sit there with that goddamn gloating smirk on his face? He longed for his gun; if he had it in his hands he would shoot the hell out of that little triumphant god even if he burned for it . . . All right; he had lost, but Houston would see that he could take his defeat without flinching.

"Damon, I've solved it. You're guilty. You killed Blount, Herndon, and Hilton . . ."

Houston's voice rang with finality. Cross waited; his role was to say nothing. Let Houston carry the ball. Slowly Houston unwrapped the brown package and there lay the set of thin angular notebooks: the diaries of Eva . . .

"You're a lucky, blundering fool," Houston spat at him. "The only witness I could have put in the box against you was Eva Blount, and she's dead. If she hadn't leaped from that window, you'd be on your way to the electric chair . . . If she had lived, she would have told me what you told her, and what you *told* her made her kill herself. I've found out that much, Damon." Houston rubbed his hands nervously across his eyes. "Goddammit, I was your unwitting accomplice for seventy-two hours! I just couldn't bring myself to admit what I knew in my heart to be true! And no doubt you were banking on just that. What made that girl kill herself was what made me unable to admit that you were guilty. I wonder if you planned it like that? No; I don't think you did. It was too perfect to be planned. You depended upon the human heart rejecting a horror of that magnitude and you were almost right, almost successful . . ."

"How did you get those diaries?" Cross asked him. "From the Party?"

"No. An officer took them from this room when you and the others were in the police station," Houston said. "I've read them and I understand it *all* now."

"Did she mention me in there?" he asked, feeling that he had to know at once.

"Only a little, toward the end— What she said did not matter. It was what she *was* that mattered," Houston told him. "She said that she loved you, but that was all. But what a victim was that Eva Blount!"

Houston carelessly tossed the notebooks upon the bed, at Cross's side. Cross was surprised, wondering why Houston was returning the books to him.

"It was all very simple when at last I'd found the key," Houston began in a slow, measured tone. "And the key was this deceived woman, Eva Blount . . . Look Damon, I'm an honest man; I'm not going to brag or lie to you. Right off I want to confess that I was haywire in the beginning. That damned Communist Party pushed me off on the wrong track. That paranoiac Blimin was at my office day and night, demanding action, yelling that you had killed Blount and Herndon because of Eva . . . The Party claimed at first that you were a Trotskyite, then they swore that you were a government spy. In the end they screamed that you saw an opportunity to kill Blount and take his wife and you took it . . . Funny, isn't it, how they misread things? Every man, it seems, interprets the world in the light of his habits and desires. The Party shouted at me: 'He sold out to get the girl!' Their own slogans blinded them. They argued that you had to kill Herndon because Herndon had seen you kill Blount; further, they claimed that Hilton had found out somehow and that you then had to kill him . . . Despite the fact that they could not offer any evidence in support of this, I, at first, felt that it did sound rather plausible. But deep down I was worried; it was *too* pat; it did not suit your character, did not fit what you told me that morning on the train. Remember? 'Man's nothing in particular . . .'

"What a baffling chase you gave us! In the first place, you seemed so innocent, *too* innocent; we made only the most perfunctory investigations . . . When we began to feel that you *must* know something, we checked your draft card and, lo and behold, a fire had destroyed the records! I wonder if you could have had anything to do with that? You won't answer? All right; it isn't important . . . Then, for twenty-four hours, we made no new moves against you. But Hilton's death told us that we were up against something sinister. We decided to track down every lead, no matter how trivial . . .

"It was not until we, almost as an afterthought, tried to verify your birth certificate that we began to think of you seriously as a possible murderer. What a joke that certificate was! In Newark the clerks in the Bureau of Vital Statistics remembered you, but we thought that we were surely on the wrong track when we heard their description of you! Boy, what an actor you are! You should have been on the stage . . . When at last we were certain that you were Lionel Lane and that Lionel Lane was dead, we were back where we started from. It was decided that you had assumed this man's name, and we swung then toward thinking that you were in some Communist opposition group. But that fizzled. No political group in America had ever heard of you . . .

"Then we began checking your fingerprints and we ran into another stone wall. For the second time we discovered that you were dead . . . Cross Damon, Negro postal clerk of Chicago: *dead* . . . Killed in a subway accident. The FBI flew to Chicago to make sure. They reported to me that you were no more . . . They even exhumed the other Negro's body, but that didn't tell us anything. Then the police started checking with the Missing Persons Bureau. We found that a man of your height and description had been reported missing the day after you were *supposed* to have been killed . . . Who was this man? He was a cleaner and dresser of chickens in a meat market . . .

"Finally we had to rely on comparing descriptions of you that we got from Chicago with what we could observe of you here in New York, then we knew that we had the right man. We knew you were Cross Damon, no matter how many dead men you were hiding behind . . .

"But was it possible that Cross Damon was doing all of this killing. But why? That was the most baffling aspect of all. You'll never know how I struggled against accepting your guilt. *I didn't want to believe it.* After having isolated you, identified you, we faced a riddle. Nothing in your entire background had touched politics. Then I had a brainstorm. I wired Chicago to send me a list of the titles of the books you'd left behind in your room and when they wired back a long list I was delighted . . . That was the first real clue. Your Nietzsche, your Hegel, your Jaspers, your Heidegger, your Husserl, your Kierkegaard, and your Dostoevsky were the clues . . . I said to myself that we are dealing with a man who has wallowed in guilty thought. But the more I pondered this thing, the sorrier I felt for you. I began to feel as though I'd killed Blount, Herndon, and Hilton myself . . .

"And when I read those diaries and saw into the deceived heart of this little Eva, I knew damn well that you did not kill to get her. She was hysterically waiting for some man to ask her to run off from that impossible

Blount and his Party . . . I visited her studio and looked at those powerful projections of nonobjective horror she had painted; then I read her diaries and I knew you'd love her, understand her; she was a sensitive artist and represented in her life and work a quality of suffering that would move a heart like yours. In spirit, Eva was your sister. Both of you were abandoned, fearful, without a form or discipline for living; and, therefore, you were both a prey to compulsions. In the face of life, she shrank, but you advanced. But here, attack or retreat, is a form of fear. No; you didn't kill to get her; you didn't have to. You'd want to lead her, remake her, save her, and at bottom you'd be wanting, in doing this, to save yourself . . . And she was ripe to respond on the same basis; she wanted to *help* you . . .

"Damon, last night you said something that hurt me. When I had the cops pick you up and bring you to my office, when I was putting the heat on you, you told me— Well, you implied that I was a kind of monster for confronting you with your wife and children— No, Damon, I'm not that kind of a man. If I were a sadist, I could have had you locked up in the Tombs days ago for investigation, but I didn't." Houston smiled ironically. "I wouldn't deliberately torture anything or anybody on this earth. But, of course, I do so live that I find myself in situations where people are suffering. After all, why did I become a District Attorney? But, hell, that's another story.

"No; I wasn't torturing you last night. I was trying to identify you; I had to be absolutely certain that you were Cross Damon, postal clerk of Chicago, supposedly dead, married, etc. But there was another thing I wanted to know. I had to see how you would react when I told you of your mother's death, how you would react when you saw your sons . . . I'm a District

Attorney, Damon; I was tracking down emotional clues; I was doing my police work . . .

"You were so inhuman that I would not have believed it unless I'd seen it. Today many sociologists say that the American Negro, having been stripped of his African tribal culture, has not had time to become completely adjusted to our mores, that the life of the family of the Western World has not had time to sink in, etc. But with you, you are adjusted and more . . . You've grown up and gone beyond our rituals. I knew that you were beyond organized religion, but I didn't suspect that you were already beyond the family. Last night you stood there in my office and committed the greatest and last crime of all. You did not bat your eye when I told you that your mother was dead. It hurt you, yes; I could see it, but you rode it out. Boy, you had killed your mother long, long ago . . . You must have known your mother well, understood her both emotionally and intellectually; and when one can see and weigh one's mother like that, well, she's dead to one . . . And when you saw those three fine sons of yours! They tugged at your heart and memory and you were wildly angry and ashamed; but you rode out that too; you overcame it . . . And I said to myself: 'This man *could* have killed Blount, Herndon, and Hilton . . . Only *he* could have done it. He has the emotional capacity—or *lack* of it!—to do it.'

"Then I sat down and thought. After all, Damon, as I told you on the train that morning, I'm close enough to you, being a hunchback, being an outsider, to know how some of your feelings and thought processes *must* go. In a sense, I'm your brother . . . We men are not complete strangers on this earth. The world changes, but men are always the same. And especially the various basic types of men—and you are an ancient, fundamental type—run the same.

"When I first talked to you in the Blount apartment, how you must have laughed at me! I walked all around you and could not see you! And then Hilton started his crazy, class-conscious pressure. Strange, the Communists had access to this insight as well as I and they didn't want to see . . ."

Cross was still. Yes; he was caught. But where was the *proof*? Eva could not witness against him. Had Houston, then, some hidden evidence? If this was the best that Houston could do, why, he would simply walk into court and keep his damned mouth shut and let him see if he could convict him.

"Damon, you are an atheist," Houston resumed, "and that is the heart of this matter. You know what convinced me that you were guilty? No; I didn't find any clues you'd left behind . . . It was in a realm far afield that I found conclusive proof. Where?" Houston lifted his arm toward the window. "Right out there in those teeming streets . . . Damon, you act individually just like modern man lives in the mass each day.

"You see, hopeful men seize upon every tiny incident and read the dreams of their hearts into them. Each hour of the day men are asking: 'Do you think we'll have peace? Don't you think what General So-and-So said means we'll have war? Don't you think that the White House pronouncement means that prices will be lower?' Or maybe he observes that his neighbor is reading a radical book and comes to the conclusion that he is a spy and ought to be killed? And, Damon, that was the way you were living. The only difference was that your compulsions were negative, had no direction . . .

"In the old days we were concerned with mobs, with

thousands of men running amuck in the streets. The mob has conquered completely. When the mob has grown so vast that you cannot see it, then it is everywhere. Today the compulsive acts of the lynching mobs have become enthroned in each individual heart . . . Every man now acts as a criminal, a policeman, a judge, and an executioner . . .

"But to come back to this individual mob-you who is called Cross Damon. What an atheist you are! You know, real atheists are rare, really. A genuine atheist is a real Christian turned upside down; God descends from the sky and takes up abode, so to speak, behind the fleshy bars of his heart! Men argue about their not believing in God and the mere act of doing so makes them believers. It is only when they do not feel the need to deny Him that they really do not believe in Him." Houston rose in his excitement and paced the floor, as though he had forgotten the existence of Cross. "*You went all the way!* You have drawn all the conclusions and deductions that could be drawn from the atheistic position and you have inherited the feelings that only real atheists can have. At first I didn't believe it, but when you stared so unfeelingly at your sons, when you laughed when your poor wife could not summon enough strength to identify you, I knew that you were beyond the pale of all the *little* feelings, the *humble* feelings, the *human* feelings . . . *I knew that you could do anything!* Not in a towering rage, not to save falling mankind, not to establish social justice, not for glory . . . But just because you happen to feel like that one day . . .

"You are a free man. Ideas do not knock you off your feet, make you dizzy, make you fall down and serve others. You always suspect that ideas are in the service of other people . . . Oh, I *know* you, boy! Blimin told me about your ideas."

Cross hovered over a vast void. Was this man making fun of him or was he sympathizing with him? What he had feared most had come; there was nothing he could hide from Houston. He kept his eyes on the floor, afraid to look up at Houston's passion-inflamed face.

"You felt that you were right, but not in the sense that you had to insist upon it. No! Does one explain when he says he wants three teaspoons of sugar in his coffee instead of two? You don't have to justify that, do you? You had risen—or sunk!—to that attitude toward the lives of those about you . . .

"But, Damon, you made one fatal mistake. You saw through all the ideologies, pretenses, frauds, but you did not see through *yourself*. How magnificently you tossed away this God who plagues and helps man so much! But you did not and could not toss out of your heart that part of you from which the God notion had come. And what part of a man is that? It is desire . . . Don't you know it? Why didn't you just live a quiet life like all other men? That's the correct way of being godless. Why be restless? Why let desire plague you? Why not conquer it too?"

Houston was questioning Cross in a kind manner, like a brother would question him.

"Desire? Why does man desire? It's crazy, for it's almost certain that he'll never get what he desires . . . Is desire not a kind of warning in man to let him know that he is limited? Is desire in man not a kind of danger signal of man to himself? Desire is the mad thing, the irrational thing. Damon, you peeled off layer after layer of illusion and make-believe and stripped yourself down to just simply naked desire and you thought that you had gotten hold of the core of reality. And, in a sense, you had. But what does one *do* with desire? Man desires ultimately to be a god . . . Man desires *everything* . . .

Why not? Desire is a restless, floating demon . . . Desire tries to seize itself and never can . . . It's an illusion, but the most solid one! Desire is what snared you, my boy. You felt that what brooked desire could be killed; what annoyed, could be gotten rid of . . .

"Only a man feeling like that could have gone down into that room and seen those two men fighting it out, and then killed the *both* of them! Not taking sides . . . Not preferring the lesser evil . . . Just a sweeping and supreme gesture of disdain and disgust with the both of them! And only a man akin to them could have hated them that much, and you know it, Damon! You slew them just because they offended you . . . It was just like taking a cinder out of your eye because it stings a bit . . ."

Houston paused in front of Cross and chuckled, his eyes bright and mischievous. Cross looked at him and said to himself: That must have been how I looked when Sarah saw me laughing at her! Sarah had gotten angry, had leaped to her feet and had tried to beat him with her doubled fists, had shouted and cursed him; but he could not afford to act that way with Houston. Pride held him still. To show resentment would give the game away. No; he would sit and take it all.

"How you must have felt in that awful room! I wish you'd tell me! Did you calculate every movement? Or did you act without knowing it? Did you realize what you were doing? Or did you invent the idea of it afterwards? How did those two men look to you? And which one did you kill first? I'll bet a million dollars that, even though you're a free man, you killed Herndon first, eh? You're a Negro and you know what Fascism means to you and your people. Even a man like you cannot be as indifferent as he would like . . . Your feet, Damon, I'll bet, were of earthy clay and you killed

Herndon first . . . Won't you tell me? No? All right . . . I'll not press you; these are unimportant details . . .

"Ha-ha-ha! Of course, I don't believe that Eva Blount saw Herndon on those stairs. I can't *prove* that she didn't, but I don't believe it. She was wrought up; she wished Blount out of her life, wanted him dead . . . She imagined she saw Herndon. And I'll bet you you seized upon her fantasy and tried to fool us all with it . . .

"I know that Blount would not have touched you. He thought he had snared you into his ideological spider-web and that you were his slave, his moral slave, the slave who believes in the ideas that are given to him . . . But, if you killed Blount first, Herndon would have killed you the next instant, wouldn't he? I'm right, hunh? Ha-ha-ha! I'm clever, boy, when I get my sights at last leveled on the right target. And you must certainly have gotten a rich, deep satisfaction out of killing that nigger-hater, Herndon. And Blount's face must have been a study in amazement when you suddenly turned on him . . .

"Then you wiped off all the fingerprints; there was none of yours in the room except on the door. And they had a right to be there, for you had been in the room talking to Herndon that afternoon, hadn't you?

"All right . . . Now comes a gap that I can't fill—I don't know how Hilton found out that you had killed the two of them . . . Did you tell him? Hunh? No; you don't want to answer? All right. You can tell me . . . No; you must not. Then I'd be bound by my oath of office and I'd have to use it against you . . . Ha-ha . . . Get the point, Damon?

"But I don't think you told Hilton anything. You're much too clever for that. Anyhow, he found out someway . . . These Communists eat and breathe suspicion. He had his eyes on you from the beginning, according to the Party, but not for any reason, just in general . . . And he caught you in your little godly game . . .

"You went to see him. You must have known that he knew. I must admit that I'm a bit foggy about this part of it. He had asked you to come and talk to him about joining the Party . . . But I can't believe that you went there for that. *That* might have been your excuse . . . But that was not your purpose. After all, Damon, I'm only human. I can't know all. I'm not a god and do not claim to be one, or want to be one. Ha-ha-ha . . . I curb my desires, you see?

"But, if I know the Hilton type, and I do to some extent, I'd expect a deal to be made. Damon, why wasn't there a deal, an understanding arrived at between you and Hilton? Maybe the reality of this beautiful Eva had begun to enter the picture to some extent then? Maybe you two just hated each other naturally because you were so much alike? You little gods who traffic in human life, who buy and sell the souls of men, why couldn't you have not made a trade?

"Well, I guess that maybe you couldn't trust each other, hunh? That's the big trouble with gods when they get together. Gods cannot share power; each god must have all the power or he's no god. Logical, hunh? For, what's a god if he has a rival? So damn much jealousy enters, hunh? Look at Hitler and Stalin . . . Boy, if they could have been reasonable, they could have divided this whole earth up between them. But, no; each felt that he and he alone had to have the whole earth. So they chewed each other up. When gods fall out, little worms can live . . .

"But, joking aside . . . You killed Hilton with his own gun and you didn't leave a clue. How did you get into the hotel? You were at the hotel desk early that afternoon, but no one remembers seeing you there after that, either entering or leaving. Of course, they have a rather racially liberal policy at the Albert Hotel and Negroes leaving or entering would not be the occasion for anybody's noticing, would it? And sometimes I suppose all things work together for the loves and desires of little gods?"

Cross felt dead. How could this man lay open his life with such decisive strokes? With such mocking cynicism? Goddamn him to hell!

"Now, these diaries . . . This girl deceived by the Party . . . This naïve child made the mistake of thinking that she had found in you something clean, pure, something her heart had dreamed of. In *you*, of all the men on earth! She looked upon you and your people as her brothers and sisters in suffering . . . What irony! Hurt, deceived, she projected out upon you her desires! Afraid of deception, she embraced a fount of deception! Full of timid, feminine desire, she flings her arms about a furnace of desire and is consumed in it . . . Then you, in your desert of loneliness, must have told her what you had done. She'd fought the Party for you, told them upon her life that you were an innocent man . . . And, in a sense, she was right; you were innocent of what the Party was charging. But, for a reason I do not know, you told her and she leaped . . . That's how I figure it. What you told her was too much for her. You made her feel that she could no longer trust any person on this earth. She leaped from that window to escape the kind of world you showed her! You *drove* her out of life. What you told her was the crowning horror of all the horrors! The apex of deception . . . And you *had* to tell her; you wanted her help. But did you tell her that Gil had not done anything to you? Did you tell her that you killed Gil for *nothing*? Boy, did you, could you go that far? I wonder . . .

"Damon, those diaries told me that you were guilty, and that girl's leaping from that window was proof of it. Will you admit it? No? Your silence is a confession! Your inability to challenge me is proof! I'm waiting . . . *Speak!* Tell me I'm wrong . . . You *can't*!"

Houston turned, opened the door of the room and went out. Cross lay watching the door swing a little to and fro on a squeaky hinge. Well, Houston was going to get the cops and they were going to take him to the station now . . . This was the end. But what evidence did Houston have? What facts to buttress all of this? So far he had cited nothing but psychological facts. Come to think of it, they were not even psychological facts. They were feelings, lightninglike intuitions which only a man who had lived long on that lower (or was it a higher?) level of life could know. He heard Houston's footsteps coming back. He braced himself.

Houston entered the room with a glass of water in his right hand. He stood looking at Cross a solemn moment, then he lifted the glass to his lips and drained it thirstily, his humped body resembling that of a huge, waiting spider.

"I was thirsty," Houston confessed in the voice of a man who had satisfied a physical need. He sighed. "I haven't spoken so much since I was last facing a jury a month ago."

Cross could bear it no longer; his lips trembled.

"Get it over with! If you think you'll drag one word from me, you're crazy!" he shouted.

"Now," Houston spoke in a soothing tone, "don't spoil it all. You were playing your role so well . . ."

"You're gloating over me! Okay, start your damned wheels turning to punish me . . . !"

"Hold on, my friend. I'm not through yet," Houston said with a feeling of deep relish in his voice. "You'll be punished, but not in the way *you* think. Ah, I know . . . You have visions of lashes, third degree sessions, blinding spotlights in your eyes, questions popping at you for hours on end. You may even think of mobs, for all I know . . . And all of this because the cops want you to confess. But, Damon, you've confessed already . . ."

Hot tension leaped in Cross. Had he overlooked something silly that would send him to the chair? Had he left some foolish thing undone that would make him look like an adolescent boy stealing apples from a neighbor's orchard?

"Confession?" he stammered. "What do you mean?"

Houston threw back his head and laughed. "You confessed to *me*, just to *me*, to *me* alone. See? I've no concrete evidence to use in court against you . . ."

Was the man crazy? What was he getting at?

"Listen, Damon, you made your own law," Houston pronounced. "And, by God, I, for one, am going to let you live by it. I'm pretty certain you're finished with this killing phase . . . So, I'm going to let you go. See? Yes; just go! *You're free!* Just like that." Houston snapped his fingers in Cross's face. "I'm going to let you keep this in your heart 'til the end of your days! Sleep with it, eat with it, brood over it, make love with it . . . You are going to punish yourself, see? You are your own law, so you'll be your own judge . . . I wouldn't *help* you by taking you to jail . . . I've very little concrete evidence to haul you into court on anyhow; it's likely I couldn't convict you . . . And I'll not give you the satisfaction of sitting in a court of law with those tight lips of yours and gloating at me or any jury while we tried to prove the impossible. What the hell could a jury of housewives, like the simple-minded Sarah Hunter, make out of a guy like you? I'll not give you the chance to make that kind of a fool out of me, Damon! No, sir! I'm much too smart for that.

"These killings will be marked unsolved. And, in a sense, they are. Even now I cannot say why you killed in a rational manner, in a manner that would persuade others . . . I've not told anyone of what I've found about you." Houston tapped his head. "It's all right here. And it'll stay there. You're trembling . . . Oh, yes; I understand now. You thought that I was going to get the cop to arrest you when I went out for that glass of water . . . ? Ha-ha-ha! Oh, you're sweating, hunh? Boy, you'll sweat tears of terror, night and day. That's the lot of a little god. Didn't you know that gods were lonely? When you eat, a part of you will stand back, shy and embarrassed. When you make love, a part of you will turn away in shame. From now on, there will be a dead hand holding life back from you . . . Will you find your way back? I doubt it. To whom could you tell your story, Damon? Who will listen? A psychoanalyst? You have no respect for them, and what the hell could they do for you? They'd be frightened of you; they'd rush out of their consulting rooms, their hair standing on end, screaming with terror. No; they are not for you, my boy. It's between *you* and *you*, you and yourself."

Houston stood looking down with musing eyes at Cross. And Cross felt sweat running down his face; it was on his chest, seeping down his arms. Even his legs were wet. Suddenly he wanted to beg this man not to leave him. He could not believe that it was like this that it was to end . . . But he could make no move.

"That's all," Houston said. "Whatever nameless powers that be, may they have something like mercy on your tormented soul."

He turned and strode out of the room. Cross could

hear him speaking in low tones to Sarah, then there came the echo of his footsteps along the hallway; then he heard the front door open and close. He was alone. He felt like screaming for Houston to come back, to talk to him, to tell him what to do. But he clamped his teeth and held still. I'm alone, he said to himself. He felt dizzy. Terror wrapped him around in a sheet of flame and his body wept tears . . . The prop had gone; Houston had gone; the world against which he had pitched his rebellion had pitied him, almost forgiven him . . . The thing he had been fighting had turned its face from him as though he was no longer worthy of having an opponent and this rejection was a judgment so inhuman that he could not bear to think of it.

He had broken all of his promises to the world and the people in it, but he had never reckoned on that world turning on him and breaking its promise to him too! He was not to be punished! Men would not give meaning to what he had done! Society would not even look at it, recognize it! That was not fair, wasn't right, just . . . The ludicrous nature of his protest came to him and he smiled wryly at his own self-deception. Always back deep in his mind, he had counted on their railing at him, storming, cursing, condemning . . . Instead, nothing, silence, the silence that roars like an indifferent cataract, the silence that reaches like a casual clap of thunder to the end of space and time . . .

He had to talk to somebody! But to whom? No; he had to keep this crime choked in his throat. He, like others, had to pretend that nothing like this could ever happen; he had to collaborate and help keep the secret. He had to go forward into the future and pretend that the world was as tradition said it was . . .

His head dropped senselessly to the bedcover and he drifted off into that state of bleak relaxation that comes after an exhausting strain. He was not sleeping, not fully awake; he was existing with an alien world looming implacably over and against him. But all of his compulsions were gone, leaving him empty of even desire . . .

He did not stir from his room until late the next morning, and when he did emerge, it was to go into the kitchen with Eva's diary. Since Houston had laid his self-hate and his self-love so mockingly naked, he felt that he no longer had any right to keep the diary and he was resolved to burn it. He opened one of the notebooks and tore out a sheet; just before touching the page to the flame of his lighter, he let his eyes stray listlessly over the lines, reading:

"March 3rd

"Last night was in Harlem and had dinner with Bob and Sarah Hunter. A tall, sensitive young Negro, Lionel Lane, was there; he was tense and seemed to be seeking for something in life. He struck me as one who would leave no stone unturned to find his destiny. Gil was taken with him and asked him to come and live with us awhile . . . Will he too be 'used' as I have been? How can I warn him? I dreamed of him after going to bed— I thought he asked me to come and see him and I was afraid because he lived in Harlem— Then I became so ashamed of my fear that I decided to go anyhow. I dreamed that when I got to Harlem there was, for some reason, a huge crowd of people waiting to see me and I felt quite embarrassed and lost . . . I was trembling, fearing to be asked to explain why I was in Harlem. Lionel came and rescued me; he was so magnificently himself, so self-assured among his own people who loved and respected him. The moment he arrived the crowd changed its attitude toward me . . . Then he took my arm and led me down the street; he was smiling as we passed in front of the masses of strange people. A wave of happiness flooded me and I fainted . . . Is not all virtue with the oppressed who are not corrupted? I must find some way of saving this boy from the muck in which my life has become bogged . . . But how can I do it?

"*March 4th*

"Lionel is now in the apartment and I'm filled with a sense of dread. I'd planned to remain in all day, but since he is here, I've decided to go out. I'll go to a concert in the afternoon. That is as good an excuse as any to get away . . . But I must try to save him from his own naïveté . . . He is so quiet, trusting, sensitive . . . What is he thinking all the time? I see him sitting and brooding and his eyes hold the most self-absorbing look I've ever seen in a human being . . . God, he must be suffering . . . ? Is he mulling over the past wrongs done to him and his people? I wish I could help someone like that."

Cross crumpled the sheet, held it to the flame, and watched it burn. Once he turned his head sharply, feeling that Eva was standing near, watching him . . . Slowly he burnt the pages, dropped the charred remains in the sink, ran water over them and flushed them down the drain. When he finished he lifted his eyes and looked out of the window.

Bright sunshine was flooding the world with warm, yellow light and he became aware that he could hear the soft, faint sounds of water dripping. Yes, a thaw had set in. The ice was melting; the snow was dissolving and flowing from the roofs . . .

He heard the front door of the apartment open and close; a moment later Sarah came into the kitchen. She had been out into the streets and was still wearing her overcoat.

"I knew you were tired and I didn't want to awaken you," she began without ceremony. "But now you are up and I can talk to you."

"Yes, Sarah. What is it?"

"I want you to move." She did not look at him as she spoke.

"Of course. What do I owe you for our staying here . . ."

"Nothing." Her voice was bitter.

"I can pay my way." He wanted to help her, but he did not know how.

"I don't want your money," she said. "I'm starting a new life . . . I went to confession this morning." Her voice was metallic, cold.

"I'm glad for you," Cross said. He was suddenly resentful of the fact that Sarah had failed to see that he, of his own accord, was about to move. "Is your telling me to move so bluntly your first act of Christian charity?"

Sarah's eyes hardened.

"This is *my* apartment—" she began.

"I don't dispute that," Cross told her. "But I thought your practicing religion again would make you a little kind . . . I'm all packed to go. I've enough money to take care of myself for a bit . . . And for that, I'm damned lucky. I'm glad that I'm not at your mercy . . ."

"I don't want to argue with you—"

"You won't. I'll get out in five minutes."

There was no communication between them. Couldn't they part as friends who had a little sympathy for each other? Cross looked at her and knew at once that there was no way. Sarah desired too much. Only a great promise could lift her up and help her to live again. Promises . . . ? Could he ever make promises again? And he could not promise anything to Sarah; she had already received from her church a promise covering the whole of her life on this earth and the life to come . . . He turned from her, entered his room, picked up his suitcase, and went into the hall. Sarah stood in the kitchen doorway, looking at him.

"Good-bye, Sarah."

She did not answer; he saw her face reflect a struggle. He started toward her and she burst into tears, whirled, turned into the kitchen and slammed the door. He pivoted on his heels and walked on down the hall, opened the door and went out.

The streets were wet under the glare of a bright sun. He paused on the stoop; he had no notion where he was going. He heard water gurgling in the gutters, running toward the conduits of the sewers. He walked toward Seventh Avenue, thinking: Was it possible that all he had learned in the last few weeks would remain locked forever in his heart? Would he ever be able to say anything about it? And Eva . . . ?

He became aware of someone following him and he turned. It was Menti and behind Menti was that sullen, inexpressive Hank whose hands were jammed as always in his overcoat pockets, his eyes staring hard at Cross from beneath the brim of a dirty hat.

Cross stopped and waited for Menti to catch up with him. "Are you following me, Menti?"

"Where are you going?" Menti asked, grinning.

"I don't know. Tell the Party that I said I didn't know."

"Leaving town?"

"I don't know."

"How can one get in touch with you?"

"You can't."

"You won't have an address?"

"Maybe not."

"Well, I'll be seeing you," Menti said. "Don't forget the Party."

"How could I ever forget the Party?" Cross asked him.

Menti grinned and turned away. Cross kept on to the end of the block. He was moving again among people. But how could he ever make a bridge from him to them? To live with them again would mean making promises, commitments. But he had strayed so far that little commitments were now of no avail. He would have to start all over again. And it was impossible to do that *alone* . . .

He checked his suitcase and went into a cinema and sat looking at the moving shadows on the screen without understanding their import. Two hours later he came out and had lunch. Once again he stood upon the sidewalk, will-less, aimless. Then he was agitated. There was Menti down at the far end of the block, and Hank was behind him. They were watching him. Goddamn them . . .

He came to Lenox Avenue and headed toward downtown. He saw another movie house. He looked over his shoulder; Menti and Hank were moving toward him . . . Quickly he paid his admission and ducked into the sheltering darkness of the cinema, looking now and then to see if Menti or his man was near . . . He could not find them.

When he emerged three hours later, stiff and thirsty, Menti and Hank were not to be seen. Had he ditched them? Maybe . . . Dusk was falling upon Harlem. Neon lights gleamed in the deepening mists. He went into a bar and sat in the rear, facing the door, keeping watch. He downed several whiskies which he could not feel or taste. What was he going to do? Find another room or leave town . . . ?

Once more on the sidewalk, he looked for Menti. Suddenly he longed for the shelter of a well-lighted place, something like a huge hotel lobby with throngs of people and hard, glaring electric bulbs shedding clarity and safety upon everything . . . He found himself facing Central Park. He paused at a street corner till the red traffic light turned green, then he crossed and walked alongside Central Park, heading toward downtown.

He glanced over his shoulder, feeling that he was being followed; but there was no one to be seen on the night streets behind him. An occasional car whizzed past, its headlights illuminating the foggy night about him for a moment, then leaving him alone in the dark once more. Ahead he saw a young couple coming toward him, engrossed in each other . . . A sense of Eva flashed through him and he knew that the bleakness he was now feeling came from the desire he had had of having her with him . . . This homelessness would not have been so difficult to bear if he had not based his hopes on being with her.

Again he paused and glanced over his shoulder. Yes; there were two dark forms lurking in the shadows about a block away. Menti and Hank were after him . . . And he was in a bad spot here next to Central Park. He was in danger; he looked around him in panic. He had to hide somewhere, quickly . . . If he could dodge them tonight, he would leave the city first thing tomorrow morning . . . A taxi? But there was none in sight. If only he had the shelter of the home of a friend in which to hide . . . Who? Oh, God, yes . . . *Hattie!* He'd quite forgotten her. He had run off from her and left her to fend for herself with her confidence men. How had she made out? He would call her now, and if she was in, he'd go right over . . .

Ahead of him, across the street, were the lights of a drugstore. He looked again over his shoulder and saw the dark forms of Menti and Hank standing, watching. He crossed the street and entered the drugstore, breathing easier amidst the neon lights, the rows of colored bottles, the gleaming mirrors . . . He thumbed through a telephone directory, found Hattie's number, dropped a coin in the box, and dialed. He heard the faint sound of her phone ringing. Maybe she had already lost her home and had moved . . . ?

"Hello." It was Hattie's voice; it sounded tired.

"Hattie?"

"Yes. Who's this?"

"Hattie, this is Jordan. Addison Jordan. Remember?"

There was a pause and he heard her gasp.

"Oh, God! What *happened* to you?" Her voice was cold and distant.

"Look, I want to see you. I'll tell you everything . . ."

"Where are you?"

"In a drugstore, near Central Park."

"Why did you run off like that?"

"Oh, God, Hattie. I know I acted badly . . ."

"What do you want now?"

"I want to see you. Now. Tonight."

"Listen, I'm in a mess. Maybe I can see you next week— Look, you see, I'm in trouble. I'm losing my home . . . You understand?"

He heard her sobbing quietly.

"Did the police ever catch White and Mills?" he asked.

"No," she heaved over the line. "There was no trace of 'em. And today I was supposed to pay $250 to straighten out the mortgage. I didn't have it. I must get out in the morning; the bank is taking over the house . . ."

"You say you need $250?"

"Yes."

"Hattie, I'll let you have it. I've got it with me. Can I see you now?"

There was a moment's silence.

"You mean that really?" she asked, a note of scared hope was in her voice.

"Yes; I tell you I got it with me, in cash."

"Oh, God . . ."

"I'll take a taxi over right now, hear?"

"Oh, God in Heaven," she cried. "But, don't fool me, *please* . . ."

"I'll see you in ten minutes, Hattie."

"Okay. But don't fool me—"

He hung up. He would hide with her until he made up his mind where he wanted to go. He left the phone booth and looked through the drugstore window. Menti and Hank were not in sight. Central Park lay black and silent across the street. He went out and looked for a taxi. There was none . . . Well, he'd walk until he saw one. He swung along the pavement, full of desperate hope . . . He'd give Hattie the $250; it would be worth it to hide himself, and he owed it to her for what he had done by running off . . . How quiet the night was! Had Menti and Hank given him up? There's a taxi . . .

"Taxi!" he bellowed.

The taxi slowed and pulled to a curb half a block away alongside the park. He broke into a wild run, waving his hand to assure the driver that he was coming. He crossed the street and walked with the park flanking him. He was lucky after all . . .

A second later he heard a snapping sound, as of a twig being broken, and then a faint footfall; there was a shower of something like loose gravel and in the same instant he felt tearing through his chest a searing streak of fire and a loud, sharp report smote his ears as his body jerked forward. The next moment he was sprawled flat on his back, having pitched headlong over his suitcase. He was staring toward a sky he could not see. Pain ripped at his chest. He had been shot. Somewhere in the region of his heart was a jumping, pulsing pain. He heard footsteps running. The Party . . . Then his inner world began to turn as dark as that world around him. He heard vague voices.

"You hurt, Mister?"

He felt someone tugging at his arm and pain rose from his chest in one huge red wave and engulfed him.

When Cross opened his eyes again he was aware of a dim light in a partially darkened room. He was cold and tired. As some measure of consciousness returned, he struggled to lift himself upon his elbow, but he felt an alien hand softly restraining him.

"You must be still."

It was the voice of a woman. He struggled to focus his eyes and mumbled: "What happened?"

"You're hurt. Lie still."

The nurse was a foggy blur of white. Yes, he was in a hospital and then he felt again that awful ball of fire in his chest and he was aware that he was laboring in his breathing. He tried to lift his right hand, but it was too, too heavy. They got me, he thought. He felt no wonder, hate, or surprise. He had been going to the taxi and they had shot him . . . A fit of uncontrollable coughing seized him and shadows closed in again.

A long time later, his eyes fluttered weakly open and he saw daylight. The dim figure of a nurse in white leaned over him and beyond her he was vaguely conscious of other people whose presence seemed remote and unimportant.

"Damon," a familiar voice came into his ear. "Can you hear me?"

He heard the question, but it seemed foolish to try to

answer. He attempted again to focus his eyes, but could not.

"Damon, this is Houston, the District Attorney. Can you talk a little . . . ?"

A fleeting smile passed through him, making his lips twitch slightly. Houston! His pal! The old hunchback! The wise old scared outlaw who had found a way of embracing his fear so that he could live and act without being too scared! He longed to see Houston; once more he sought to focus his eyes, but the face looming over him remained a blob of pink.

"Who shot you, Damon? Did you see him?"

How foolish and unessential it was to ask him that now! What did it matter?

"Was it the Party? Can you hear me? Was it the Party folks who shot you?" The voice was insistent.

Yes; he'd try to answer; he struggled to move his tongue and shape his lips and he whispered:

"I don't know. I think so . . ."

"Don't try to talk too much, Damon. Just listen and answer briefly. Save your strength . . . Did the Party find out you had killed Gil and Hilton?"

"No," he whispered.

"Then why do you think they shot you?"

"They guessed . . ."

"You didn't confess, didn't tell 'em?"

"No."

"Did they have any proof? How did they know?"

"They didn't know . . . They didn't understand me . . . And they shoot what they don't understand . . ."

"Listen, if you can give me anything to go on, I'll prosecute them."

Cross sighed. His lips were dry, burning. What silliness was Houston talking? He had been living by a law and that law had turned on him. That was all.

"Forget it," he whispered.

"But if you know anything—"

"Skip it."

Pain seized him again and he felt someone holding his arm; they were injecting a sedative into him to quiet the pain.

"Damon, this is Houston still . . . Look, is there anything you want to tell me? These killings, were there more of them?"

Oh, God, that poor clown of a Joe Thomas . . . !

"Yes . . ."

"Where?"

"One other man . . . In Chicago. His name was Joe Thomas . . . I killed him in a hotel room to keep him from . . . betraying me . . ."

"Is that all?"

"That's all . . . Isn't that . . . *enough*?"

He felt suddenly sleepy and he had to fight against it. He had nestling blackly deep in him a knowledge of his pending end that made him know that he had but a short time in which to say anything.

"Damon, can you hear me?"

"Yes," he managed to whisper.

Houston's voice seemed to be closer now and the tone had changed; it was the voice of a brother asking an urgent, confidential question.

"Damon, listen to me, just listen and think about what I'm asking and then try to answer . . . This is Houston still talking to you . . . Damon, you were an outsider . . . You know what I mean, don't you? You lived apart . . . Damon, tell me, why did you choose to live that way?"

The damned old curious outlaw! He never forgot anything. He was still on his trail . . . Still hunting him down . . . Sure; he'd tell 'im . . .

"I wanted to be free . . . To feel what I was worth
. . . What living meant to me . . . I loved life too . . .
much . . ."

"And what did you find?"

"Nothing . . ." He lay very still and summoned all of
his strength. "The search can't be done alone," he let his
voice issue from a dry throat in which he felt death lurking. "Never alone . . . Alone a man is nothing . . .
Man is a promise that he must never break . . ."

"Is there anything, Damon, you want me to tell anybody?"

His mind reeled at the question. There was so much
and yet it was so little . . .

"I wish I had some way to give the meaning of my
life to others . . . To make a bridge from man to man
. . . Starting from scratch every time is . . . is no good.
Tell them not to come down this road . . . Men hate
themselves and it makes them hate others . . . We must
find some way of being good to ourselves . . . Man is
all we've got . . . I wish I could ask men to meet themselves . . . We're different from what we seem . . .
Maybe worse, maybe better . . . But certainly different
. . . We're strangers to ourselves." He was silent for a
moment, then he continued, whispering: "Don't think
I'm so odd and strange . . . I'm not . . . I'm legion
. . . I've lived alone, but I'm everywhere . . . Man is
returning to the earth . . . For a long time he has been
sleeping, wrapped in a dream . . . He is awakening
now, awakening from his dreams and finding himself in
a waking nightmare . . . The myth-men are going . . .
The real men, the last men are coming . . . Somebody
must prepare the way for them . . . Tell the world what
they are like . . . We are here already, if others but had
the courage to see us . . ."

He felt a weak impulse to laugh. His strength was

flowing rapidly from him. His eyes would not focus. The world that was visible was a grey, translucent screen that had begun to shimmer and waver. He closed his eyes and struggled with his tongue and lips to try to shape words.

"Do you understand what I mean, Damon?" Houston asked softly. "I'm talking about *you*, your life . . . How was it with *you*, Damon?"

His eyes stared bleakly. His effort was supreme; his lips parted; his tongue moved; he cursed that damned ball of seething fire that raged in his chest and managed to get his reluctant breath past it to make words:

"It . . . It was . . . horrible . . ."

There was a short silence, then Houston's voice came again: "What do you mean? What was horrible?"

The effort to keep his heavy eyes open was too much and it was not worth trying. He stopped fighting and let his lids droop and darkness soothed him for a moment; once more he struggled grimly to control his lips and tongue, to still that exploding ball of fire that leaped white hot in his chest; then he said in a softly falling, dying whisper:

"All of it . . ."

"But why? *Why*? Try and tell me . . ."

"Because in my heart . . . I'm . . . I felt . . . I'm *innocent* . . . That's what made the horror . . ."

He felt his dull head falling helplessly to one side. Huge black shadows were descending softly down upon him. He took a chest full of air and sighed . . .

He was dead.

London – Paris, 1952

Chronology

1908   Born Richard Nathaniel Wright; September 4, on Rucker's Plantation, a farm near Roxie, Mississippi, 22 miles east of Natchez, first child of Nathan Wright, an illiterate sharecropper, and Ella Wilson Wright, a schoolteacher. (All four grandparents had been born in slavery. Father was born shortly before 1880, the son of Nathaniel Wright, a freed slave who farmed a plot of land he had been given at the end of the Civil War. Maternal grandfather, Richard Wilson, born March 21, 1847, served in the United States Navy in 1865, then became disillusioned because of a bureaucratic error that deprived him of his pension. Maternal grandmother, Margaret Bolton Wilson, of Irish, Scottish, American Indian, and African descent, was virtually white in appearance. A house slave before the Emancipation, she later became a midwife nurse, a devoted Seventh-day Adventist, and the strict head of her Natchez household, which included eight surviving children. Mother, born 1883, married Nathan Wright in 1907 despite her parents' disapproval, and then gave up school teaching to work on the farm.)

1910   Brother Leon Alan, called Alan, born September 24.

1911–12   Unable to care for her children while working on the farm, mother takes Wright and his brother to live with Wilson family in Natchez. Father rejoins family and finds work in a sawmill. Wright accidentally sets fire to grandparents' house.

1913–14   Family moves to Memphis, Tennessee, by steamboat. Father deserts family to live with another woman, leaving them impoverished. Mother finds work as a cook.

1915–16   Wright enters school at Howe Institute, Memphis,
            in September 1915. Mother falls seriously ill in early
            1916. Grandmother comes to care for family. After
            grandmother returns home, mother puts Wright
            and his brother in the Settlement House, Methodist
            orphanage in Memphis, where they stay for over a
            month. Spends relatively pleasant summer at 1107
            Lynch Street in Jackson, Mississippi, where mater-
            nal grandparents now live, before going with
            mother and brother to Elaine, Arkansas, to live with
            his favorite aunt, Maggie (his mother's younger sis-
            ter), and her husband, Silas Hoskins, a saloon-
            keeper.

1917–18   After Hoskins is murdered by whites who want his
            prosperous liquor business, terrified family flees to
            West Helena, Arkansas, then returns to Jackson with
            Aunt Maggie to live with the Wilsons. After several
            months they go back to West Helena, where mother
            and aunt find work cooking and cleaning for whites.
            Aunt Maggie leaves with her lover, "Professor"
            Matthews, a fugitive from the law (they eventually
            settle in Detroit).

1918–19   Wright enters local school in fall 1918. Mother's
            health deteriorates early in 1919 and Wright is forced
            to leave school to earn money. Delivers wood and
            laundry and carries lunches to railroad workers.
            Family moves frequently because of lack of rent
            money; Wright gathers stray pieces of coal along
            railroad tracks to heat their home. Mother suffers
            paralyzing stroke, and grandmother comes to bring
            the family back to Jackson. Aunt Maggie helps care
            for mother, then takes Leon Alan back to Detroit
            with her; other aunts and uncles help pay for moth-
            er's treatment.

1919–20   Wright moves into home of aunt and uncle, Clark
            and Jody Wilson, in nearby Greenwood, Missis-

sippi, where he is able to attend school. Finds household calm and orderly but his aunt and uncle cold and unsympathetic, and is terrified by episodes of sleepwalking. Returns to grandparents' home in Jackson. Mother begins to show signs of recovery from paralysis, then has relapse caused by a cerebral blood clot that leaves her virtually crippled. Her illness impoverishes the family, already hurt by the rheumatism that makes Grandfather Wilson unable to work.

1920–21   Enters Seventh-day Adventist school taught by his youngest aunt, Addie. Only nine years older than Wright, she is a rigid disciplinarian often at odds with him. Wright rebels against the rules and practices of the religion, including its diet, which forbids eating pork. Finds himself opposed to his family in general, except for his mother, who is too sick to help him.

1921–22   Enters the fifth grade of the Jim Hill School in Jackson, two years behind his age group. Does well, quickly gains in confidence, and is soon promoted to the sixth grade. Begins friendships, some of them lasting into his adulthood, with a number of other students, including Dick Jordan, Joe Brown, Perry Booker, D. C. Blackburn, Lewis Anderson, Sarah McNeamer, and Essie Lee Ward. Takes job as a newsboy, which gives him the chance to read material forbidden at home because of religious prohibitions. Family life continues to be difficult, although his mother's health improves slightly. Travels briefly during summer in the Mississippi Delta region as "secretary-accountant" to an insurance agent, W. Mance. The trip allows him to know better the rural South, but he is dismayed by the illiteracy and lack of education he encounters among blacks.

1922–23   Enters the seventh grade. Grandfather Wilson dies November 8. After many arguments, grandmother reluctantly lets Wright take jobs after school and on Saturday (the Seventh-day Adventist sabbath). Runs errands and performs small chores, mainly for whites. For the first time has enough money to buy school books, food to combat his chronic hunger, and clothing. Baptized in the Methodist Church, mainly to please his mother. Avidly reads pulp magazines, dime novels, and books and magazines discarded by others. Uncle Thomas Wilson, his wife, and their two daughters come to live with the family in spring 1923. Mother's health worsens. Wright works during the summer at a brickyard and as a caddy at a golf course.

1923–24   Enters eighth grade at the Smith Robertson Junior High School, Jackson (a former slave, Smith Robertson had become a successful local barber and a community leader; the school, built in 1894, was the first black institution of its kind in Jackson). Until he can afford a bicycle, Wright walks several miles daily to and from the school. Makes new friends at school, including Wade Griffin, Varnie Reed, Arthur Leaner, and Minnie Farish. Begins working for the Walls, a white family he finds kindly (will serve them for two years). Later remembers writing his first short story, "The Voodoo of Hell's Half-Acre," in late winter (story is reported to have been published in the spring as "Hell's Half-Acre" in the Jackson *Southern Register*, a black weekly newspaper; no copies are known to be extant). Brother Leon Alan returns from Detroit. Wright is initially pleased, but their relationship soon disappoints him. Works for the American Optical Company, cleaning workshop and making deliveries.

1924–25   Enters ninth grade at Smith Robertson Junior High School, and graduates on May 29, 1925, as valedictorian. Rejects graduation speech prepared for him by the principal and instead delivers his own, "The Attributes of Life." Works as a delivery boy, sales clerk, hotel hallboy and bellboy, and in a movie theater. Begins classes in fall at newly founded Lanier High School, but quits a few weeks later to earn money. Leaves Jackson for Memphis, Tennessee, where he boards with a family at 570 Beale Street.

1926   Works for low pay as a dishwasher and delivery boy and at the Merry Optical Company. Reads widely in *Harper's*, *Atlantic Monthly*, *The American Mercury*, and other magazines. Moves to 875 Griffith Place.

1927   Joined by mother, who is still in poor health, and brother; they take an apartment together at 370 Washington Street. After reading an editorial highly critical of H. L. Mencken, long noted as a critic of the white South, Wright seeks out Mencken's *Prejudices* and *A Book of Prefaces* and is particularly impressed by Mencken's iconoclasm and use of "words as weapons." These books serve as guides to further reading, including works by Theodore Dreiser, Sinclair Lewis, Sherwood Anderson, the elder Alexandre Dumas, Frank Harris, and O. Henry. Aunt Maggie, who has been deserted by "Professor" Matthews, joins family in the fall. In December, Wright and Maggie, who hopes to open a beauty salon, move to the South Side of Chicago, while mother and Leon Alan return to Jackson. Sees his aunt Cleopatra ("Sissy"), but is disappointed to find that she lives in a rooming house, not an apartment, and moves into a rooming house with Aunt Maggie.

1928   Works as delivery boy in a delicatessen, then as a dishwasher. Wright finds Chicago stimulating and less racially oppressive than the South, but is often dismayed by the pace and disarray of urban life. Passes written examination for the postal service in the spring, then begins work in the summer as a temporary employee at 65 cents an hour. Rents an apartment with Aunt Maggie and is joined by mother and brother. In the fall Wright fails the postal service medical examination required for a permanent position because of chronic undernourishment and returns to dishwashing. Disputes over money and his reading cause tension with Aunt Maggie. Wright takes another apartment for family and invites his aunt Cleopatra to move in with them.

1929   After undertaking a crash diet to increase his weight, Wright passes the physical examination and is hired by the central post office at Clark Street and Jackson Boulevard as a substitute clerk and mail sorter. Moves with family to four rooms at 4831 Vincennes Avenue, which allows him to read and write in relative comfort. Dislikes the post office bureaucracy, but becomes friendly with many fellow workers, both black and white. Among his friends are schoolmates from the South, including Essie Lee Ward, Arthur Leaner, and Joe Brown. Writes steadily and attends meetings of a local black literary group, but feels distant from its middle-class members. Attracted by the Universal Negro Improvement Association, a group inspired by Marcus Garvey, but does not join it.

1930   Volume of mail drops in decline following the 1929 Wall Street crash; Wright has his working hours cut back before losing his job altogether. South Side sinks into economic depression. Works temporarily for post office in the summer. Mother suffers a relapse, aunt Cleopatra has a heart attack, and brother develops stomach ulcers. Begins work on "Cesspool," novel about black life in Chicago. Enrolls in tenth grade at Hyde Park Public School, but soon drops out.

1931   Reads books recommended by friend William Harper (who will later own a bookstore on the South Side). Wright is particularly impressed by Dreiser and Joseph Conrad, and continues to write. Short story "Superstition" is published in April *Abbott's Monthly Magazine*, a black journal (magazine fails before Wright is paid). Through a distant relative, finds job as a funeral insurance agent for several burial societies. Also works as an assistant to a black Republican precinct captain during the mayoral campaign, and at the post office in December. Becomes interested in views of Communist orators and organizers, especially those in the League of Struggle for Negro Rights.

1932   Sells insurance policies door-to-door and works briefly as an assistant to a Democratic precinct captain. Family moves to slum apartment as Wright is increasingly unable to sell policies to blacks impoverished by the Depression. Asks for and receives relief assistance from the Cook County Bureau of Public Welfare, which finds him a temporary job as a street cleaner. Works at the post office during the Christmas season.

1933   Digs ditches in the Cook County Forest Preserves, then works at Michael Reese Hospital, caring for animals used in medical research. Recruited by fellow post office worker Abraham Aaron to join the newly formed Chicago branch of the John Reed Club, a national literary organization sponsored by the Communist party. Welcomed and encouraged by the almost entirely white membership of the club, Wright begins to read and study *New Masses* and *International Literature*, the organ of the International League of Revolutionary Writers. Writes and submits revolutionary poems ("I Have Seen Black Hands," "A Red Love Note") to *Left Front*, the magazine of the midwestern John Reed Clubs. Elected executive secretary of the Chicago John Reed Club and organizes a successful lecture series which allows him to meet a variety of intellectuals. Gives lecture at open forum on "The Literature of the Negro."

1934   Hoping to consolidate his position in the John Reed Club, Wright joins the Communist party; is also impressed by the party's opposition to racial discrimination. Publishes poetry in *Left Front*, *Anvil*, and *New Masses*. Becomes a member of the editorial board of *Left Front*. Enjoys literary and social friendships with Bill Jordan, Abraham Chapman, Howard Nutt, Laurence Lipton, Nelson Algren, Joyce Gourfain, and Jane Newton. Grandmother Wilson comes to Chicago to join the family; they move to apartment at 4804 St. Lawrence Avenue, near the railroad tracks. Mother's paralysis returns after attack of encephalitis. Wright is laid off by the hospital in the summer, and again works as a street sweeper and ditch digger before being hired to supervise a youth club organized to counter juvenile delinquency among blacks on the South Side. Attends Middle West Writers' Congress in August and the national congress of John Reed Clubs in September. Dismayed by party decision to cease publication of *Left Front* and to dissolve the John Reed Clubs in 1935 as part of its Popular Front strategy. Meets Jack Conroy, editor of *Anvil*. Reading in Chicago by this time includes Henry James (especially the Prefaces to the New York Edition), Gertrude Stein (notably her *Three Lives*, with its portrait of a black character, Melanctha Herbert), Faulkner,

T. S. Eliot, Sherwood Anderson, Dos Passos, O'Neill, Stephen Crane, Dreiser, Whitman, Poe, D. H. Lawrence, Conrad, Galsworthy, Hardy, Dickens, George Moore, Carlyle, Swift, Shakespeare, Tolstoy, Dostoevsky, Turgenev, Chekhov, Proust, Dumas, and Balzac. Lectures on the career of Langston Hughes to the Indianapolis John Reed Club in November and contributes fee to new publication *Midland Left*.

1935   Publishes leftist poetry in *Midland Left*, a short-lived journal, *New Masses* ("Red Leaves of Red Books" and "Spread Your Sunshine"), and *International Literature* ("A Red Slogan"). Family moves to 2636 Grove Avenue. Begins submitting novel "Cesspool" to publishers (later retitled *Lawd Today!* by Wright; it is rejected repeatedly over the next two years, then published posthumously as *Lawd Today* in 1963 by Walker and Company). Wright attends the first American Writers' Congress, held in New York in April. Speaks on "The Isolation of the Negro Writer," meets Chicago novelist James T. Farrell, and becomes one of fifty members of the national council of the newly formed League of American Writers. Works on story "Big Boy Leaves Home." Publishes "Between the World and Me," poem about lynching, in July–August *Partisan Review*. Falls seriously ill with attack of pneumonia during the summer. Article "Avant-Garde Writing" wins second prize in contest sponsored by two literary magazines but is never published. First piece of journalism, "Joe Louis Uncovers Dynamite," describing the reaction of Chicago blacks to the Louis–Max Baer fight, published in *New Masses*. Grandmother Wilson dies. Family, with Wright still virtually its sole support, moves to 3743 Indiana Avenue. Wright is hired by the Federal Writers' Project (part of the Works Progress Administration) to help research the history of Illinois and of the Negro in Chicago for the Illinois volume in the American Guide Series. Discusses influence of Hemingway with fellow writers in federal project.

1936   Publishes "Transcontinental," a six-page radical poem influenced by Whitman and Louis Aragon, in January *International Literature*. Becomes a principal organizer of the Communist party—sponsored National Negro Congress (successor to the League of Struggle for Negro Rights), held in Chicago in February, and reports on it for *New Masses*. Transferred in spring to the Federal Theatre Project, where he serves as literary adviser and press agent for the Negro Federal Theatre of Chicago and becomes involved in dramatic productions. Finishes two one-act plays based in part on a section of his unpublished novel. In April, Wright takes a leading role in the new South Side Writers' Group (members will include Arna Bontemps, Frank Marshall Davis, Theodore Ward, Fenton Johnson, Horace Cayton, and Margaret Walker). Takes an active role in the Middle West Writers' Congress, held in Chicago June 14–15. Because of what he later describes as a Communist plot against him on the Federal Theatre Project assignment, Wright returns to the Writers' Project, where he becomes a group coordinator. Story "Big Boy Leaves Home" appears in anthology *The New Caravan* in November and receives critical attention and praise in mainstream newspapers and journals.

1937   Publishes poem "We of the Streets" in April *New Masses* and story "Silt" in the August number. Breaks with the Communist party in Chicago, basically over the question of his freedom as a writer. Brother finds job with the Works Progress Administration and assumes some responsibility for support of the family. Wright ranks first in postal service examination in Chicago, but turns down offer in May of permanent position at approximately $2,000 a year in order to move to New York City to pursue career as a writer. Stays briefly with artist acquaintances in Greenwich Village, then moves to Harlem; by mid-June he has a furnished room in the Douglass Hotel at 809 St. Nicholas Avenue. Attends Second American Writers' Congress as a delegate and serves as a session president; stresses the need for writers to think of themselves as writers first and not as laborers. Becomes Harlem editor of the Communist newspaper *Daily Worker* and writes over 200 articles for it during the year, including pieces on blues singer Leadbelly and the continuing Scottsboro Boys controversy. With Dorothy West and Marian Minus, helps launch magazine *New Challenge*, designed to present black life "in relationship to the struggle against war and Fascism." Wright publishes "The Ethics of Living Jim Crow—An Autobiographical Sketch" in *American Stuff: WPA Writers' Anthology* (essay is later included in the second edition of *Uncle Tom's Children* and incorporated into *Black Boy*). In November, publishes influential essay "Blueprint for Negro Writing" in *New Challenge*, criticizing past black literature and urging a Marxist-influenced approach that would transcend nationalism. Lacking party support, *New Challenge* fails after one number. Befriends 23-year-old Ralph Ellison. Wright's second novel, "Tarbaby's Dawn," about a black adolescent in the South, is rejected by publishers (it remains unpublished). Learns that story "Fire and Cloud" has won first prize ($500) among 600 entries in *Story Magazine* contest. Wright joins the New York Federal Writers' Project (will write the Harlem section for *New York Panorama* and work on "The Harlems" in *The New York City Guide*).

1938   Rents furnished room at 139 West 143rd Street. Engages Paul Reynolds, Jr., as literary agent. Reynolds makes arrangements to place *Uncle Tom's Children: Four Novellas* ("Big Boy Leaves Home," "Down by the Riverside," "Long Black Song," and "Fire and Cloud") with editor Edward Aswell at Harper and Brothers, beginning Wright's long association with Aswell and Harper; book is published in March and is widely praised. Sends Aswell outline of novel about a black youth in Chicago. Announces plans to marry daughter of his Harlem landlady in May, but then cancels wedding, telling friends that a medical examination had revealed that the young woman has congenital syphilis. Moves into home of friends from Chicago, Jane and Herbert Newton, at 175 Carleton Avenue in Brooklyn. Story "Bright and Morning Star" appears in May *New Masses*. Writes about the second Joe Louis–Max Schmeling fight in the June *Daily Worker* and July *New Masses*. In June, replaces Horace Gregory on the editorial board of the literature section of *New Masses*. Works steadily on new novel; often writes in Fort Greene Park in the mornings, and discusses his progress with Jane Newton. Asks Margaret Walker to send him newspaper accounts of the case of Robert Nixon, a young Chicago black man accused of murder (executed in August 1939). Moves in the fall with the Newtons to 522 Gates Avenue. Congressman Martin Dies, chairman of the House Special Committee on Un-American Activities, denounces "The Ethics of Living Jim Crow" during an investigation of the Federal Writers' Project. Finishes first draft of novel, now titled *Native Son*, in October and receives $400 advance from Harper in November. "Fire and Cloud" wins the O. Henry

Memorial Award ($200). Travels to Chicago in November to research settings and events used in *Native Son*. Moves with Newtons to 87 Lefferts Place.

1939   Meets Ellen Poplar (b. 1912), daughter of Polish Jewish immigrants and a Communist party organizer in Brooklyn. Completes revised version of novel in February and shows it to Reynolds. Awarded Guggenheim Fellowship ($2,500) in March and resigns from the Federal Writers' Project in May. Discusses black American writing with Langston Hughes, Alain Locke, Countee Cullen, and Warren Cochrane during meeting of Harlem Cultural Congress. After Newtons' landlord evicts them, Wright moves to Douglass Hotel at 809 St. Nicholas Avenue in May, renting room next to Theodore Ward, a friend from Chicago. Becomes close to Ellen Poplar and considers marrying her, but also sees Dhima Rose Meadman, a modern-dance teacher of Russian Jewish ancestry. Plays active role at Third American Writers' Congress. Finishes *Native Son* on June 10. Ward dramatizes "Bright and Morning Star." The story is included in Edward O'Brien's *Best American Short Stories, 1939* and *Fifty Best American Short Stories (1914–1939)*. Begins work on new novel, "Little Sister." Marries Dhima Rose Meadman in August in Episcopal church on Convent Avenue, with Ralph Ellison serving as best man. Lives with his wife, her two-year-old son by an earlier marriage, and his mother-in-law in large apartment on fashionable Hamilton Terrace in Harlem. Attends Festival of Negro Culture held in Chicago in September. Moves to Crompond, New York, to work on "Little Sister" (it is never completed).

1940   Visits Chicago in February and buys house for his family on Vincennes Avenue. Has lunch in Chicago with W.E.B. Du Bois, Langston Hughes, and Arna

Bontemps. *Native Son* published by Harper and Brothers March 1 and is offered by the Book-of-the-Month Club as one of its two main selections. In three weeks it sells 215,000 copies. Wright delivers talk "How 'Bigger' Was Born" at Columbia University on March 12 (later published as a pamphlet by Harper, then added to future printings of *Native Son*). *Native Son* is banned in Birmingham, Alabama, libraries. Takes his first airplane flight when he accompanies *Life* magazine photographers to Chicago for an article on the South Side; tours the area with sociologist Horace Cayton, beginning long friendship (article is later canceled). Sails in April for Veracruz, Mexico, with wife, her son, mother-in-law, and wife's pianist. Rents ten-room villa in the Miraval Colony in Cuernevaca. Takes lessons in Spanish and studies the guitar. Reunited with Herbert Kline, friend from the Chicago John Reed Club, who is filming documentary *The Forgotten Village* with John Steinbeck; Wright travels with them through the countryside and takes an interest in the filming. Signs contract with John Houseman and Orson Welles for stage production of *Native Son*. Marriage becomes strained. Wright leaves Mexico in June and travels through the South alone. Visits his father, a poor and broken farm laborer, in Natchez, but is unable to make anything other than a token reconciliation with him. Goes to Chapel Hill, North Carolina, to begin collaboration with Paul Green on stage adaptation of *Native Son*. Meets producer John Houseman and drives to New York with him. Travels to Chicago to do research for book on black American life featuring photographs selected by Edwin Rosskam. Wright and Langston Hughes are guests of honor at reception given by Jack Conroy and Nelson Algren to launch magazine *New Anvil*. Returns to Chapel Hill in July to continue work with Paul Green. Elected vice-president of the League of American Writers. Harper reissues story collection as *Uncle Tom's Children: Five Long Stories* with "Bright and Morning Star" added and "The Ethics of Living Jim Crow" as an introduction. Starts divorce proceedings. Moves in with the Newtons, now at 343 Grand Avenue in Brooklyn; in the autumn Ellen Poplar moves into the Newton house. In September Wright is elected a vice-president of American Peace Mobilization, a Communist-sponsored group opposed to American involvement in World War II. Works with Houseman on revising stage version of *Native Son* (both Wright and Houseman think that Green has diverged too much from the novel); Houseman agrees that Orson Welles, who is finishing *Citizen Kane*, should direct. Story "Almos' a Man" appears in *O. Henry Award Prize Stories of 1940*.

1941   In January the National Association for the Advancement of Colored People awards Wright the Spingarn Medal, given annually to the black American judged to have made the most notable achievement in the preceding year. Rehearsals for *Native Son* begin in February. Marries Ellen Poplar in Coytesville, New Jersey, on March 12. They move to 473 West 140th Street. *Native Son*, starring Canada Lee, opens at St. James Theatre on March 24 after a benefit performance for the NAACP. Reviews are generally favorable, though the play is attacked in the Hearst papers, which are hostile to Welles following *Citizen Kane*. Production runs in New York until June 15. Welles' striking but costly staging causes production to lose some money, but it recovers during successful tour of Pittsburgh, Boston, Chicago, Milwaukee, Detroit, St. Louis, and Baltimore. Wright asks the governor of New Jersey to parole Clinton Brewer, a black man imprisoned since 1923 for murdering a young woman, arguing

that Brewer, who had taught himself music composition, has rehabilitated himself (Brewer is released
July 8; Wright had previously sent one of his pieces
to his friend, record producer and talent scout John
Hammond, who arranged for Count Basie to
record it). Begins novel "Black Hope" (never completed). Introduces Ellen to his family in Chicago
during visit in April. Signs appeal of forty members
of the League of American Writers against American intervention in the war that appears in *New
Masses* May 27, and publishes "Not My People's
War" in *New Masses* June 17. After Germany invades
the Soviet Union, June 22, American Peace Mobilization changes its name to American People's Mobilization. Wright travels to Houston with Horace
Cayton and John Hammond to accept Spingarn
award from NAACP convention on June 27. Delivers enthusiastically received speech, in which his
criticism of Roosevelt administration racial policies
is muted in response to Communist party pressure.
Lectures at Writers' Schools sponsored by the
League of American Writers. Wrights move to 11
Revere Place, Brooklyn, in July. At John Hammond's request, Wright writes "Note on Jim Crow
Blues" as a preface to the blues singer Josh White's
Southern Exposure, an album of three recordings attacking segregation. Hammond then produces re-
cording of Paul Robeson singing Wright's blues
song "King Joe," accompanied by the Count Basie
orchestra. *12 Million Black Voices: A Folk History of the
Negro in the United States,* with photographs selected by Edwin Rosskam (one taken by Wright),
published by Viking Press in October to enthusiastic reviews. Wright reads *Dark Legend,* a psychoan-
alytic study of matricide by psychiatrist Frederic
Wertham, then writes to Wertham about Clinton
Brewer, who had murdered another young woman
within months of his release. Wertham intervenes in

the case and helps save Brewer from execution (Wright and Wertham begin close friendship, and Wright becomes increasingly interested in psychoanalysis). Finishes draft of novel "The Man Who Lived Underground." Signs petition "Communication to All American Writers" in December 16 *New Masses*, supporting America's entry into the war after the December 7 Japanese attack on Pearl Harbor.

1942   Mother and Aunt Maggie rejoin Addie in Jackson, Mississippi (brother remains in Chicago, though house on Vincennes Avenue is sold two years later). Daughter Julia, Wright's first child, born April 15. Wrights move in summer to 7 Middagh Street, a 19th-century house near the Brooklyn Bridge shared by George Davis, Carson McCullers, and other writers and artists. Excerpts from "The Man Who Lived Underground" appear in *Accent*. As the sole support of his family, Wright is classified 3-A and not drafted. Unsuccessfully tries to secure a special commission in the psychological warfare or propaganda services of the army. *Native Son* returns to Broadway in October (runs until January 1943). Publishes "What You Don't Know Won't Hurt You," article describing some of his experiences as a hospital janitor in Chicago, in December *Harper's Magazine*. Breaks quietly with the Communist party over its unwillingness to confront wartime racial discrimination and its continuing attempts to control his writing.

1943   Accompanied by Horace Cayton, Wright goes to Fisk University, Nashville, in April to deliver talk on his experiences with racism. Strong reaction from the audience leads Wright to begin autobiography *American Hunger*. Neighbors and associates are interviewed by the Federal Bureau of Investigation. (Files obtained under the Freedom of Information

Act in the 1970s show that the FBI began an investigation in December 1942 to determine if *12 Million Black Voices* was prosecutable under the sedition statutes. Although the sedition investigation is concluded in 1943, the FBI will continue to monitor Wright's activities, chiefly through the use of informers, for the remainder of his life.) Wrights move in August to 89 Lefferts Place in Brooklyn Heights. Helps organize the Citizens' Emergency Conference for Interracial Unity in response to widespread riots in Harlem following the wounding of a black soldier by white police in August. Finishes *American Hunger* in December.

1944   Writes film scenario "Melody Limited," about group of black singers during Reconstruction (scenario is never produced). Becomes friends with C.L.R. James, a Trinidad-born historian and Trotskyist, with whom he plans a book, "The Negro Speaks," and a journal, "American Pages" (neither of these projects appear), and his wife, Constance Webb. Writes series of radio programs on the life of a black family for producer Leston Huntley and is frustrated when Huntley is unable to place the series, in part because of criticism by middle-class blacks. Attends party held in honor of Theodore Dreiser on June 2, where Wright and Dreiser discuss the influence of life in Chicago on their attitudes. Deepens friendship with Dorothy Norman, New York *Post* editorial writer and editor of *Twice a Year*, who introduces him to existentialist philosophy and literature. Book-of-the-Month Club tells Harper that it will accept only the first section of *American Hunger*, describing Wright's experiences in the South; Wright agrees to this arrangement. Changes title to *Black Boy*. (Second section, telling of Wright's life in Chicago, is published as *American Hunger* by Harper & Row in 1977.)

Wrights vacation in August outside Ottawa and in the nearby Gatineau country in Quebec. Excerpts from second section of autobiography appear as "I Tried to Be a Communist" in *Atlantic Monthly*, August–September, making public Wright's break with the Communist party. He is denounced by various party organs, including *New Masses* and the *Daily Worker*. Helps the Chicago poet Gwendolyn Brooks to place her first book, *A Street in Bronzeville*. Expanded version of "The Man Who Lived Underground" is published as a novella in *Cross Section*.

1945   To circumvent racial discrimination, Wrights form the "Richelieu Realty Co." and use their lawyer as an intermediary in buying a house at 13 Charles Street in Greenwich Village. (Residence is delayed by their waiting for a Communist tenant hostile to Wright to leave and by redecorating.) Reviews books for *P.M.* newspaper; his highly favorable review of Gertrude Stein's *Wars I Have Seen* leads to correspondence with her. *Black Boy: A Record of Childhood and Youth* published by Harper and Brothers in March to enthusiastic reviews. The book is number one on the bestseller list from April 29 to June 6 and stirs controversy when it is denounced as obscene in the U.S. Senate by Democrat Theodore Bilbo of Mississippi. Takes part in several radio programs, including the nationally influential "Town Meeting," where he argues the negative on the question "Are We Solving America's Race Problem?" In the summer, Wrights vacation on island off Quebec City, and Wright lectures at the Bread Loaf writers' school in Middlebury, Vermont. Writes long introduction to *Black Metropolis*, a sociological study of black Chicago by Horace Cayton and St. Clair Drake. Befriending a number of younger writers, white and black, Wright helps the

20-year-old James Baldwin win a Eugene F. Saxton Foundation Fellowship. Publishes a favorable review of Chester Himes's first novel, *If He Hollers Let Him Go*, and lends Himes $1,000. In the fall, Wrights move to an apartment at 82 Washington Place in Greenwich Village to be closer to a school for Julia. Wright undertakes four-month lecture tour but stops after six weeks because of exhaustion.

1946   Serves as honorary pallbearer at funeral on January 12 of poet Countee Cullen, attending service at Salem Methodist Church in Harlem and burial at Woodlawn Cemetery in the Bronx. By January 19, *Black Boy* has sold 195,000 copies in the Harper trade edition and 351,000 through the Book-of-the-Month Club, making it the fourth best-selling nonfiction title of 1945. Wright, his psychiatrist friend Dr. Frederic Wertham, and others found the Lafargue Clinic, a free psychiatric clinic in Harlem. Meets Jean-Paul Sartre in New York. Receives invitation to visit France, but requests for a passport meet with opposition. Wright goes to Washington for an interview and enlists the aid of Dorothy Norman (who appoints him co-editor of *Twice a Year*), Gertrude Stein, and French cultural attaché, anthropologist Claude Lévi-Strauss, who sends him an official invitation from the French government to visit Paris for a month. Wright leaves New York on May 1. In Paris, welcomed by Gertrude Stein and by almost all the important French literary societies and circles. (Stein dies on July 27 after operation for cancer.) Meets Simone de Beauvoir and André Gide, whose *Travels in the Congo* has impressed Wright, as well as Léopold Sédar Senghor of Senegal, Aimé Césaire of Martinique, and others in the *Négritude* movement. Assists Senghor, Césaire, and Alioune Diop of Senegal in founding the magazine *Présence Africaine* and attends its first board meeting at the

Brasserie Lipp. Donates a manuscript to an auction for benefit of experimental dramatist Antonin Artaud. "The Man Who Killed a Shadow" published in French in *Les Lettres Françaises* (first appears in English in 1949 in magazine *Zero*). Leaves Paris in late December and travels to London.

1947   Meets the Trinidad-born intellectual George Padmore and dines with members of the Coloured Writers' Association, including its president, Cedric Dover, author of *Half Caste*, and the colored South African journalist and novelist Peter Abrahams. Returns to New York in January. Moves with family into their Charles Street house in Greenwich Village. Helps to welcome Simone de Beauvoir to New York in the spring. Refuses offer from Hollywood producer to film *Native Son* with character Bigger Thomas changed to a white man. Wright's works are being translated into French, Italian, German, Dutch, and Czech. Decides to return to Europe permanently with his family, partially in response to the racial hostility they are encountering in New York. Sells Greenwich Village house in June. Vacations at a cottage at Wading River, Long Island, owned by a friend. Buys an Oldsmobile sedan to take to Europe. Wright, his wife, and daughter reach Paris in August. They rent rooms from a friend, Odette Lieutier, in her apartment on the rue de Lille, then move into an apartment at 166 Avenue de Neuilly. Albin Michel publishes French translation of *Native Son* in autumn.

1948   Begins to read more deeply in existentialism, including Heidegger and Husserl. Sees much of Sartre and Simone de Beauvoir. Wright is particularly impressed by Camus' *The Stranger*, and begins work on an existentialist novel, eventually titled *The Outsider*. Gallimard translation of *Black Boy* wins French

Critics' Award. Wright establishes friendships with the Reverend Clayton Williams, pastor of the American Church, and with Harry Goldberg of the American Library. Becomes unofficial spokesman for African-American colony in Paris, which includes James Baldwin. Visits Italy for the publication there of *Native Son*. Meets with Carlo Levi and Ignazio Silone, who later introduces him to Arthur Koestler in Paris. Interviewed by his Italian translator, Fernanda Pivano, Wright says he likes to read *Metamorphosis*, *Moby-Dick*, *Ulysses*, and *The Sound and the Fury*. Travels through Belgium to London, where he sees a performance of *Native Son* and renews friendship with George Padmore, who stirs Wright's interest in the question of colonialism in Africa. Moves with family to 14 rue Monsieur le Prince in the Latin Quarter in May. Ellen returns to New York in June to select furniture and other possessions for their new life in France. Wright is beset by recurring sinus problems and influenza. His tonsils are removed. Aids Sartre and Camus in the leadership of the Rassemblement Démocratique Révolutionnaire (RDR), an organization of intellectuals critical of both the Soviet Union and the United States. Wright plays prominent role in its writers' congress, held in Paris on December 13, delivering lengthy speech (translated by Simone de Beauvoir). Spends $6,000 to buy Paul Green's share of film rights to *Native Son* in hopes of making screen version with French director Pierre Chenal.

1949   Daughter Rachel born January 17 at the American Hospital. Wright travels again to Rome and to Switzerland, for the publication of *Black Boy*. In April, James T. Farrell and Nelson Algren visit him in Paris. Suspects socialist David Rousset of trying to shift the RDR toward a more pro-American, anti-Soviet stance. Refuses to attend large RDR rally held on April 30 (organization soon splits and dissolves). In May, visits London to consult with Richard Crossman, who is including "I Tried to Be a Communist" with similar essays by Koestler, Gide, Silone, Stephen Spender, and Louis Fischer in collection *The God That Failed* (published later in year, book is widely reviewed). Continues work on his existentialist novel. Assists George Plimpton and others in launching of *Paris Review*. James Baldwin's essay "Everybody's Protest Novel," attacking Stowe's *Uncle Tom's Cabin* but including criticism of *Native Son*, sours relationship between Wright and Baldwin. Wright writes screenplay for *Native Son*, adding several dream sequences to the story, then revises it with Chenal. After Canada Lee withdraws from project because of new commitments and worsening health, Wright undertakes to play the main role of Bigger Thomas. Sails for the United States in August, briefly visiting New York before going to Chicago for filming of exteriors for *Native Son*. Sees old friends Horace Cayton, St. Clair Drake, and others. Leaves New York in September for Argentina, where film is being made (Chenal had worked there during World War II, and political pressure had blocked access to French studios). Makes brief stops in Trinidad, Brazil, and Uruguay before arriving in Buenos Aires in October. Loses 35 pounds in preparation for the role by following strict diet and exercise program. Continues working on screenplay with Chenal.

1950   Production is delayed by financial problems. Wright finds atmosphere of Argentine life under the Perón dictatorship oppressive. Filming ends in June. Wright leaves Buenos Aires in July. Stops briefly in Brazil and Trinidad, spends two weeks in Haiti, then returns to Paris by way of New York, where he visits Frederic Wertham and the Lafargue Clinic. In

Paris, begins work on screenplay about Toussaint L'Ouverture of Haiti. Works with Aimé Césaire on "Revelation of Negro Art," an exhibition that includes works from the Musée de l'Homme and song and dance performances at the Cité Universitaire. Vacations in the fall in the Swiss and French Alps, visiting Basel, Zurich, and the Aoste Valley, where he is a jury member with Paul Eluard, Louis Bromfield, and others for international San Vicente literary prize. Founds and becomes president of the Franco-American Fellowship, intended to protest official American policies and oppose racial discrimination by American companies and organizations active in France. Fellowship members take precautions when meeting in anticipation of surveillance by the American government (files released in the 1970s show that the Fellowship was monitored by informers employed by the Central Intelligence Agency and the FBI).

1951   Lectures in Turin, Genoa, and Rome in January. *Sangre Negra* (the film version of *Native Son*) opens to acclaim in Buenos Aires on March 30. American distributor cuts almost 30 minutes from film under pressure from New York state censors (original length was approximately 105 minutes); shortened version opens in New York on June 16 to unfavorable reviews. (Several states ban the film, but it is shown in Beverly Hills and, in spring 1952, in Mississippi, where members of Wright's family see it.) A partially restored print is warmly received at the Venice Film Festival in August. The Milan press praises Wright's acting; in general, his performance is deemed sincere but awkward, especially by American critics who compare it with Canada Lee's stage version. Wright visits the sociologist Gunnar Myrdal in Geneva, beginning a long friendship. With Jean Cocteau, inaugurates the Cercle International du Théâtre et du Cinéma. *New Story Magazine* accepts excerpts from Jean Genet's *Our Lady of the Flowers* on Wright's recommendation. Baldwin's essay "Many Thousands Gone," an explicit attack on Wright in *Partisan Review* (November–December), leads to painful break between the writers. Submits screenplay about refugees forced to choose between sides in the Cold War to the French Association of Film Writers.

1952   Travels to England in February. Spends several months in London and Catford, Surrey, completing the first full version of *The Outsider*. Vacations with his family in Corrèze at the end of August and continues to revise and cut novel. Refuses suggestion by John Fischer, his new Harper editor, that he come to the United States for the publication of his book, citing the risk that he would be subpoenaed by an anti-Communist congressional investigating committee. Begins work in December on a novel about a white psychopathic murderer, based in part on his experience with Clinton Brewer.

1953   Begins correspondence with Frantz Fanon. *The Outsider* published by Harper and Brothers in March. Reviews are mixed; sales are initially brisk but eventually disappointing in comparison to *Native Son* and *Black Boy*. Wright composes an introduction to *In the Castle of My Skin*, first novel by the young Barbados writer George Lamming. Friendship with Sartre cools as Sartre moves closer to Communism. Wright's circle of friends remains wide, including Americans such as Chester Himes and William Gardner Smith, but he begins to withdraw from official organizations and to avoid formal gatherings. He is a regular at favorite cafés such as the Monaco and Tournon, where he entertains a steady stream of visitors from America, including

Elmer Carter, Dorothy Norman, Nelson Algren, E. Franklin Frazier, and Louis Wirth. Discusses treatment of Algerians in France with Ben Burns, editor of *Ebony* magazine, during his visit. Wright tells Burns that he avoids criticizing French policies for fear of being deported. Ellen Wright begins work as a literary agent with Hélène Bokanowski, a prolific translator of Wright's work. From June to August, Wright travels in the Gold Coast (then a British colony with limited self-government, after 1957 the independent country of Ghana) to collect material for a book on Africa. Boat stops briefly in Freetown, Sierra Leone, en route to Takoradi; from there travels by road 170 miles to Accra, his main stop. Meets Prime Minister Kwame Nkrumah and other members of the pro-independence Convention People's Party, as well as Osei Agyeman Prempeh II, king of the Ashanti, and other traditional leaders. Excursions take him from Accra to Cape Coast, Christianborg, and Prampram; visits slave-trading fortresses and dungeons. Travels almost 3,000 miles in a chauffeur-driven car, touring the interior through Koforidua to Mampong, and the Secondi-Takoradi to Kumasi regions. In general, Wright is fascinated by Africans but is reinforced in his sense of self as a Western intellectual. Visits England to discuss his impressions with George and Dorothy Padmore before returning to Paris in September to begin work on book about his trip. Undergoes surgery for hernia.

1954   Revises book on Africa. Decides to write an account of Spanish life and culture. Drives his Citroen almost 4,000 miles between August 15 and September 9 on a route that includes Barcelona, Valencia, Saragossa, Guadalajara, Madrid, Córdoba, Seville, Granada, and Málaga. On September 16 State Department and FBI officials interview Wright in

Paris about his relationship to the Communist party when he goes to renew his passport. *Black Power: A Record of Reactions in a Land of Pathos*, about his African trip, published by Harper and Brothers September 22. Receives mixed reviews in America, but is widely praised in France. *Savage Holiday*, novel about psychopathic murderer, is published as a paperback original by Avon after having been rejected by Harper. Book attracts little attention in the United States but is well received as *Le Dieu de Mascarade* in France. Visits Geneva with Gunnar Myrdal for further research on Spain at the United Nations library. Lectures on Africa in Amsterdam in October, where he meets Margrit de Sablonière, his Dutch translator, and begins an important friendship with her. Returns to Spain on November 8. Hires a driver and travels through Irun and on to Madrid, where he stays before returning to Paris in mid-December.

1955   An old Chicago friend, the cartoonist Ollie "Bootsie" Harrington, arrives to live in France. Wright secures funding for his attendance at forthcoming conference of non-aligned nations in Bandung, Indonesia, from the Paris office of the Congress for Cultural Freedom, an international alliance of anti-Communist intellectuals. Returns to Spain February 20, and spends several weeks there, including Holy Week in Granada and Seville. Leaves Spain on April 10 for Indonesia. At Bandung, Wright shares room with missionary Winburn T. Thomas. Leaders attending conference include Nehru (with whom Wright speaks), Sukarno, Sihanouk, Nasser, and Zhou Enlai. Remains in Indonesia at home of Thomas until May 5, working on notes of his impressions, then returns to Europe via Ceylon and Kenya. Begins writing an account of the conference. Spends July to October with family at their new country home, a small farm in village of Ailly in eastern Normandy. Plans series of novels dealing with the conflicts between individuals and society (including one set in Aztec Mexico), but abandons the project on the advice of Reynolds and Aswell (now with McGraw-Hill). Returns to Paris when daughter Rachel falls ill with scarlet fever, then goes back to Ailly when her continued quarantine makes work at home difficult. *Bandoeng: 1.500.000.000 hommes*, French translation of book on non-aligned conference, published in December.

1956   Prepares manuscript of book on Spain in February and March, often living alone at Ailly, where he enjoys hours of gardening. Fearing deportation, remains silent on Algerian war of independence while in France (will offer guarded criticism of war when in other European countries). *The Color Curtain: A Report on the Bandung Conference*, with an introduction by Gunnar Myrdal, published March 19 by World Publishers in America and receives favorable reviews. Revises and cuts book on Spain. Adapts Louis Sapin's play *Papa Bon Dieu* as *Daddy Goodness* but is unable to have it produced. First Congress of Negro Artists and Writers, sponsored by *Présence Africaine* and which Wright had helped plan, meets in Paris in September, attended by delegates from Africa, the United States, and the Caribbean. Wright speaks on "Tradition and Industrialization: The Tragic Plight of the African Elites" and participates in several sessions. Suspects that *Présence Africaine* is being secretly taken over by the French government through anti-nationalist Africans and considers withdrawing from its activities. Lectures in Hamburg on "The Psychological Reactions of Oppressed Peoples" and tours the city with Ellen. Attends a meeting in London of the Congress for Cultural Freedom, organized by Arthur Koestler.

Travels alone to Stockholm in late November for the Swedish publication of *The Outsider*; it sells 35,000 copies in four days (*Native Son* had sold 75,000 copies and *Black Boy* 65,000). Lectures in Sweden, Norway, and Denmark before returning to Paris in early December. Agrees to help found the American Society for African Culture, inspired by the French Société Africaine de Culture. Returning to native material, Wright begins work on novel set in Mississippi.

1957   Aunt Maggie dies January 20 in Jackson, Mississippi, where she had been taking care of Wright's mother (Wright has continued to help support them through the years). Mother moves in with a niece, then goes to Chicago at the end of June to live with Leon Alan. *Pagan Spain* published by Harper in February to good reviews but weak sales. Works at Ailly on new novel. Travels throughout Italy with Ellen during the spring. Visits West Germany in July to interview black American servicemen stationed there. *White Man, Listen!*, a collection of essays drawn from Wright's lectures, published October 15 by Doubleday (where Edward Aswell is now an editor). The book is especially well-received by the black press in the United States.

1958   Finishes *The Long Dream*, Mississippi novel, and begins "Island of Hallucinations," sequel set in France. Seeking to renew his passport, he is again compelled to report to the American embassy in February and sign a statement admitting his past membership in the Communist party. Becomes increasingly alienated from the black community in Paris, which is torn by suspicion and dissension; finds himself the object of resentment, including rumors that he is an agent of the FBI or the CIA. Depressed and isolated from other blacks, Wright suspects that he is being persecuted by agents of the U.S. government. Takes part in a session of the Congress for Cultural Freedom, and in seminars on American literature sponsored by the American Cultural Center in Paris. Supports Sartre and Simone de Beauvoir in their opposition to the new regime of General de Gaulle. Works on new novel at Ailly during summer. *The Long Dream* published by Doubleday in October to often hostile reviews and flat sales. When Leon Alan telegraphs that their mother is seriously ill, Wright is forced to borrow extra money from Reynolds to send to his brother. Edward Aswell, his long-time editor, dies November 5. Considers moving to England and enlists aid of Labour member of Parliament John Strachey, who obtains assurances from the Home Secretary that Wright's application for residence will be fairly considered. Wright distances himself from various organizations he had previously supported, including *Présence Africaine* and the Société Africaine de Culture.

1959   Mother dies January 14. Wright sends the manuscript of "Island of Hallucinations" to Reynolds in February. Later in the month, he spends a day with Martin Luther King, Jr., who is passing through Paris en route to India. Timothy Seldes (Aswell's successor at Doubleday) asks for major revisions in "Island of Hallucinations"; Wright puts book aside (it is never completed). Discouraged by financial worries, weak reviews, poor health, and frustrating state of his novel, Wright continues to curtail his public activities. Declines to attend the second Congress of Black Writers and Artists in Rome. Plans a study of French Africa. After Doubleday promises a $2,500 advance, Wright asks the American Society for African Culture for an additional $7,500, but is turned down; believes CIA infiltration of the organization is responsible for his rejection. Tired of what he considers to be growing American political and cultural influence in French life and in the wake of increased attacks by other expatriate black writers, Wright prepares to leave France and live in England. Sells farm at Ailly. His play *Daddy Goodness* is produced in Paris in the spring. Wright falls ill in June with attack of amoebic dysentery, probably picked up in Africa. Illness persists despite treatment at American Hospital. Vacations at the Moulin d'Andé near Saint-Pierre du Vauvray in Normandy. With daughter Julia now at the University of Cambridge, his wife Ellen and daughter Rachel establish themselves in London. Ellen works there as a literary agent and looks for a permanent home for the family. Wright begins writing haiku (eventually completes some 4,000 pieces). Harassed by British passport officials during visit to England in September. Sees George Padmore, who dies not long after Wright's visit. Wright returns to England for the funeral. Tries to obtain resident visa from the Home Office, but is denied one without explanation. Alone in Paris, he sells home on rue Monsieur le Prince and moves to a two-room apartment on rue Régis. Recovers from dysentery but continues to have intestinal problems. Among his close friends at this time are Michel and Hélène Bokanowski, Colette and Rémi Dreyfus, Simone de Beauvoir, Ollie Harrington, and the Reverend Clayton Williams. "Big Black Good Man" is included in *Best American Stories of 1958*.

1960   *The Long Dream*, adapted by Ketti Frings, opens on Broadway February 17 to poor reviews and closes within a week. Translation of *The Long Dream* well-received in France, but earnings are not enough to quell Wright's deepening anxiety about money. In April, driving his own Peugeot, Wright accompanies his gastroenterologist, Victor Schwartzmann, and Dr. Schwartzmann's father to medical conference in Leiden, Holland, where he visits Margrit de Sablonière. Selects and arranges 811 haiku for possible publication. Declines offers from Congress for Cultural Freedom to attend conferences on Tolstoy in Venice and New Delhi, believing that the organization is controlled by the American government (the Congress is later shown to have received substantial covert funding from the CIA). Records series of interviews concerning his work in June for French radio. Spends much of summer at Moulin d'Andé, where he begins new novel, "A Father's Law." Falls ill on return to Paris in September. Julia Wright decides to study at the Sorbonne and visits her father before returning to England to pack her belongings. In September, Dorothy Padmore comes to visit. Later, old Chicago friend Arna Bontemps makes his first visit to Paris. Wright delivers lecture on November 8 at the American Church on the situation of black artists and intellectuals. Accuses the American government of creating and manipulating dissension among them through spies and provocateurs. Continues to suffer from intestinal difficulties and dizzy spells. Finishes complete proofreading of collection of stories, *Eight Men* (published by World Publishers in 1961). Welcomes Langston Hughes to his home for a brief but enjoyable visit on the morning of November 26, then enters the Eugene Gibez Clinic for diagnostic examinations and convalescence. Dies there of a heart attack shortly before 11:00 P.M., November 28. Cremated, along with a copy of *Black Boy*, at the Père Lachaise cemetery December 3, where his ashes are interred.

Note on the Text

This volume presents the text of Richard Wright's *The
Outsider* from the final typescript of the novel, submitted to his publishers in October 1952. This is the last
version of the text that Wright prepared without external intervention by his publisher. A great deal of material pertaining to the publication of this work, including
typescripts, proofs, and correspondence between Wright
and his publishers, is in the James Weldon Johnson Collection of the Beinecke Library at Yale University and in
the Harper and Brothers archive in the Firestone Library at Princeton University.

Wright began making notes for the novel that became
The Outsider in 1948 while living in Paris. In February
1952 he went to England to do intensive work on the
manuscript, and by April or May he had finished a first
draft and sent it to his agent, Paul Reynolds, who suggested some revisions. Wright sent him a second typescript in July (now in the Johnson Collection at the
Beinecke Library, catalogued as JWJ Wright #854).
Reynolds then had the revised typescript delivered to
Jack Fischer, who had replaced Edward Aswell as
Wright's editor at Harper and Brothers when Aswell
left the firm. Both Reynolds and Fischer sent Wright
lists of suggested revisions, but the kinds of changes
they asked for were very different. Paul Reynolds sent
Wright specific factual questions and raised issues of
plausibility and continuity. Jack Fischer, on the other
hand, relying on a reading by a consultant who remains
unidentified, asked Wright to cut the novel by one-third
(from 220,000 to 150,000 words), to eliminate the beginning through the subway wreck, to drop the Joe and
Jenny sequence, to cut the entire Hattie episode, and to

shorten or eliminate passages involving stream-of-consciousness and philosophical monologue. If followed, these revisions would have produced a very different novel from the one Wright had written. Fischer was interested in scheduling the novel for publication the following March, and he asked Wright to supply the final manuscript by October 1. Fischer also proposed to make the cuts and revisions at Harper, with Wright to see and approve the changes, but Wright declined the offer, preferring to make the revisions himself.

Wright worked on the novel through August and September, making revisions in three stages. He used the typescript returned from Fischer (JWJ Wright #854) to mark his revisions, then incorporated them onto a re-typed master-copy (JWJ Wright #856) that showed the old page numbers from the previous version; and finally he prepared a clean copy (JWJ Wright #858) incorporating some further revisions. This typescript was submitted to Harper and Brothers early in October. Wright did shorten the novel from its original length of 741 typescript pages to 620 pages by compressing certain passages, but he resisted Fischer's suggestions to eliminate entire sections of the novel. (Letters and typescripts now in the Johnson Collection at the Beinecke Library and in the Harper and Brothers archive in the Firestone Library of Princeton University reveal that Wright had a less than ideal working relationship with Fischer.) Wright incorporated, on the other hand, many of the revisions suggested by Paul Reynolds, whose advice he appreciated.

Wright submitted his final manuscript within days of when Harper and Brothers had requested it in order to meet the scheduled March 1953 publication date. However, in November 1952, after another reading by the unidentified consultant, Fischer again requested that Wright cut out the Hattie sequence. Wright had already shortened it to some extent and now reluctantly shortened it further. He was forced to use his master-copy (JWJ Wright #856) as a guide, since he had sent both the ribbon and carbon copies of the final typescript (JWJ Wright #858) to New York for the publisher's use. Wright prepared unnumbered pages of copy to show how the cutting should be done and sent these to Fischer. These pages were inserted by Harper and Brothers into the final typescript (JWJ Wright #858), replacing the pages that had previously contained the scene. In addition, two other pages and many whole passages and words were removed by a copy-editor for the publisher without Wright's knowledge (the pages that were removed are not known to be extant). Wright was later informed that some minor cutting had been done in house, but that he would be able to restore the cut material, if he wished, when correcting galleys. (For examples of the larger cuts made by the publisher, see the notes to this volume.) Because of the rush to produce books for March publication, however, he was allowed only 48 hours to read the galleys that incorporated the changes made by the publisher. Wright received galleys on December 20 and returned the first portion on December 21 and the remainder by December 23. These galleys are not known to survive, but there are some variants between the published book and the copy-edited typescript. A few of them seem to be instances where Wright attempted to restore his original meaning, but the time allotted was too short to allow him to do very much. In order to meet the schedule for publication, Wright had agreed that further reading of proofs be done by the publisher.

The Outsider was published by Harper and Brothers

on March 18, 1953. Wright received advance copies in late February, and on March 17 he sent Fischer a list of 12 typographical errors, followed by another list of four errors several weeks later. Though Fischer included 13 of these corrections in a list of changes he sent to the printer, there is no evidence that any of these corrections were ever made in later printings or subsequent editions. Of the 16 corrections requested by Wright, only five apply to the text printed in this volume; these have been incorporated at the following places: at 76.30, "on to her" has been changed to "onto her"; at 107.20, "come in" has been changed to "come out"; at 244.31, "hold on to" has been changed to "hold onto"; at 459.18, "condolences" has been changed to "condolence"; and at 564.34–35, a sentence has been added: ". . . Blimin told me about your ideas.'"

In order to eliminate the effects of the unauthorized copy-editing done by the publisher, this volume prints the text of the final typescript of *The Outsider*, submitted by Wright in October 1952 (JWJ Wright #858), ignoring the editorial markings, and uses Wright's master-copy (JWJ Wright #856) for those pages removed by the publisher from the final typescript at the following places: pp. 149.6–150.5, 180.16–194.8, 310.6–311.2, and 579.26–581.21.

This volume presents the proof and typescript texts chosen for inclusion without change, except for the correction of typographical errors. Spelling, punctuation, and capitalization often are expressive features and they are not altered, even when inconsistent or irregular. The following is a list of the typographical errors corrected, cited by page and line number: 7.31, "Say; 15.7, walking; 15.18, walking; 17.30, Moreoever; 26.23, whom; 29.19, quiet,; 33.20, what're they; 33.21, what they're; 34.25, scarda; 37.26, harrassed; 38.8, wore; 39.25, identing;

42.34, damned; 46.10, said; 48.27, beserk; 48.34, there was; 49.11, said; 51.20, halldoor; 51.33, proceded; 62.21, tussel; 62.33, scene of; 68.27, penicillen; 77.18–19, existence; 79.7, musn't; 80.7, six years; 81.8, than; 81.10, childrens'; 82.8, divising; 83.25, "Hello,"; 87.1, said,; 89.27, eight-hundred dollar; 89.35, everyday; 91.16, would'nt; 91.31, Assistand; 94.34, mightly; 99.13, Absolutely; 103.15, *occured*; 103.30, *26 year-old*; 105.17–18, rammified; 106.35, very day; 112.10, to a; 113.16, accroutrements; 114.7, starting; 120.33, Be; 126.17, irresistably; 126.27, Gladys, his; 134.15, Joes; 146.18, accomodations; 149.15, it; 149.22, non-exsitent; 153.34, that saw; 155.32, priest;; 162.34–35, raising of; 173.11, particular'",; 174.20, simple; 181.31, an an; 184.5, $100,000-apartment; 185.4, $100,000-apartment; 185.8, subtly; 187.34, "I; 190.17, white; 191.5, "She; 191.10, feling; 191.13, grapsed; 192.15, him; 192.17, Crosd; 193.11, back; 197.22–23, emminent; 197.24, facist; 204.33, decollete; 205.28, everyday; 206.18, twelve years; 208.30, realtives; 210.17, heared; 214.5, was not; 215.29, worse; 216.17, worse; 222.1, Jordon; 237.16–17, unctiousness; 238.30, obervation; 239.22–23, want to make me; 243.10, tended; 243.26, mantle; 243.33, let; 245.20–21, precede; 246.25, had; 247.23, agression; 248.26, indispensible; 249.5, said.; 250.16, was rolling; 261.14, five-room; 264.19, made; 267.27, virgins;; 271.17, were written; 274.1, wife a; 280.9, get?; 282.10, becomes; 284.33, told him; 287.24, whom; 287.26, mislead; 292.34, mucous; 298.1, saw that the; 298.34, sharp,; 300.22, advance; 302.15, tingling; 308.21, yes,; 309.4, destory; 310.13, dissillusionment; 313.23, interpretating; 315.9, down to; 317.17, effect; 318.15, lay; 318.35, trod; 320.32, chandalier; 326.35, in back; 331.11, whom; 335.10, Who's; 335.25, downstairs; 343.21, spontanenousness; 343.22, her grief; 349.7, whom; 359.25, his; 362.20, Corss; 362.23, moment,; 362.30, Blount saw; 364.5, Cross as; 368.8, Housten;

370.8, sometime; 371.28, We; 377.1, "others"; 379.25, that's; 380.2, externel; 388.8, in a; 391.32, any more; 392.16, would; 393.11–12, receptable; 393.19, whines; 402.17, reason; 403.17, shame of; 405.33, Hilton; 406.11, ralize; 407.1, Whom; 411.23, enveighed; 411.31, know; 412.25, wit; 414.26, this; 415.13, Or; 416.17, effected; 417.22, We're; 421.11, tended; 423.12, telepone; 433.16, keen; 437.19, Supermen; 437.20, syphillis; 442.26–27, but it was; 446.28, irredeemible; 454.34, "knowing"; 459.5, unctiously; 464.35, your; 466.24, four hour; 466.30, — dilemma; 468.23, dollar bills; 473.19, you; 478.19, the products; 478.20, long dreamed; 480.31, out; 484.19, sterlized; 486.2, philanthrophists; 486.21, capitalist; 486.33, its; 487.6, Blimen; 488.26, alieniated; 490.6, naïve to; 492.28, to others; 495.26, Communists; 498.6, dead to; 501.4, NEITZSCHE; 502.21, was to; 503.20–21, committments; 503.23, everyday; 504.4, question which; 504.6, it he; 504.21, flowed as; 504.30, sentinent; 505.4, desirious; 505.30–31, a ornately; 506.33, wished; 508.34–35, eight hundred dollar-loan; 509.5, known; 519.16, sucked his; 523.5, and and; 526.5, Attorny; 531.5, legs afraid,; 535.1, gasping; 535.20, strickened; 535.31, whomever; 538.4, words; 538.20, Someone; 541.4, What; 547.12, sometime; 547.30, Now,; 548.2, on me; 549.4, unctiously; 550.9, I'm; 551.20, "sent"; 555.30, momento; 556.8, tingling; 557.4, sonofabtich; 557.29, backing; 557.32, I was; 562.3, believe; 562.27, it.; 574.20, "used"; 580.9, Addision; 581.18, Hatte; 584.34, anything?; 586.21, softly,.

Notes

In the notes below, the reference numbers denote page and line of this volume (the line count includes chapter headings). No note is made for information available in standard desk-reference books such as *Webster's Collegiate* and *Webster's Biographical* dictionaries. Footnotes in the text are Wright's own. For more biographical background than is included in the Chronology, see: Michel Fabre, *The Unfinished Quest of Richard Wright*, translated from the French by Isabel Barzun, (New York: William Morrow & Company, Inc., 1973); Addison Gayle, *Richard Wright: Ordeal of a Native Son* (Garden City, New York: Anchor Books/Doubleday, 1980); Constance Webb, *Richard Wright: A Biography* (New York: G. P. Putnam's Sons, 1968). For references to works by Wright and to other studies, see: Charles T. Davis and Michel Fabre, *Richard Wright: a primary bibliography* (Boston: G. K. Hall & Co., 1982); and Keneth Kinnamon, *A Richard Wright Bibliography: Fifty Years of Criticism and Commentary, 1933–1982* (Westport, Connecticut: Greenwood Press, 1988).

v.1–2   *For Rachel . . . soil*]   Added by Wright in proof stages.

xxxi.1–5   *Cruelty . . .* BLAKE]   "The Divine Image," stanza 1.

1.3–6   Dread . . . —KIERKEGAARD]   From an 1842 entry in *Journals*. The translation is by William Lowrie and appears in his introduction to Kierkegaard's *The Concept of Dread* (1944). Wright condensed the last part of Lowrie's translation, which reads: " . . . for one fears, but what one fears one desires."

3.1–4   *If the . . . come up*]   A common refrain, variations of which appear in several blues songs.

4.15–19   Tiny . . . snow.]   Cut for the book edition. This note and others like it give some examples of cuts and revisions made by Harper editors without Wright's knowledge.

4.21–24   Joe sobered . . . chuckled.]   Cut for the book edition.

27.16–20   He shuddered . . . depress him.]   Cut for the book edition.

28.33–29.9   "Son, . . . Cross?"] Cut for the book edition.

36.10   5743 Indiana] In 1935, Wright lived with his family at 3743 Indiana Avenue.

40.28–34   It was . . . first time.] Cut for the book edition.

53.29–31   He felt . . . attacks.] Cut for the book edition.

53.32–34   He would . . . overcome.] Cut for the book edition.

54.8–11   They knew . . . as man.] Cut for the book edition.

58.20–27   "Did . . . role.] Cut for the book edition.

71.31   Cross.] In the book, a sentence was inserted here: "Until now he had managed to keep up his classes at the University, but he lost heart for study and dropped out of school."

92.4–5   Tribune Tower] Ambitiously planned by the owners of the wealthy Chicago *Tribune* newspaper, and built finally as a Gothic tower directly influenced by medieval European cathedrals, the tower was formally opened on July 6, 1925, on Michigan Avenue in downtown Chicago.

122.24   faces] During preparation of the book edition, "faces" was changed to "thought" by an editor at Harper. In the proof stages it was changed again and appears in the book edition as "image."

127.18–23   "What . . . cynically.] Cut for the book edition.

145.26–30   spilled . . . phlegm;] In the book edition, cut to read: "spilled over a flattened grapefruit hull; . . ."

147.5–9   When Joe's . . . Jenny.] Cut for the book edition.

149.3–5   As silent . . . CRANE] From "Legend." Written in 1924, the poem was first published in 1930.

149.6–150.5   CROSS'S . . . sustain himself.] Cut for the book edition.

164.28–165.1   "After . . . conscious of it.] Cut for the book edition.

165.6–7   For those . . . drama . . ."] Cut for the book edition.

170.10–12   The American . . . coward.] Cut for the book edition.

178.4–8   His morbid . . . reality.] Cut for the book edition.

180.16–194.8   What stalled . . . out of the room.] Cut for the book edition.

196.31–197.32   Because Cross . . . man Cross] Cut and revised for the book edition to read: "Cross's heart was full of a longing to search for himself and create a future . . ."

198.23–31   Another sign . . . asterisks.] Cut for the book edition.

208.24–26   "Looks . . . mumbled.] Cut for the book edition.

217.20   "They . . . Lionel,"] In the book edition, changed to: " 'They call me Lionel Lane,' . . ."

217.21–218.7   "Lionel what?" . . . at whom.] Cut for the book edition.

230.7–10   Let . . . save.] From the hymn composed by the Pennsylvania-born religious singer and composer Philip Paul Bliss (1838–76).

232.2–5   Then a wild . . . right palm,] In the book edition, revised to read: "Then she began to laugh, still holding Cross's face."

232.6   Lead, Kindly Light] Hymn (1835), words by John Henry Newman, then a minister in the Church of England (later a Roman Catholic cardinal).

232.9–10   flopped . . . lungs.] In the book edition, revised to read: " . . . laughing even louder."

233.1–8   Sarah's . . . floor.] Cut for the book edition.

233.14–20   She could . . . Bob moaned.] Cut for the book edition.

251.16   13 Charles Street] The address of a house in Greenwich Village that Wright and his wife bought in 1945.

253.3–5   For that . . . PAUL] Romans 7:15.

265.31   Daily Worker] The newspaper, based in New York City, was first published in 1924 by the Communist party and served for some time as its official organ. Chronically plagued by financial problems as well as editorial and political pressures, the newspaper officially closed in 1957.

274.5–275.16   "Say, . . . "Why?"]   Cut for the book edition.

276.9–10   atomistic . . . micro-organisms]   Cut for the book edition.

276.13–16   Between . . . organic whole.]   Cut for the book edition.

276.24–33   she spoke tersely . . . danger . . . ?]   Cut for the book edition.

277.24   bold, brutal]   In the book edition, revised to read: "haunted . . ."

279.18   silly but gifted]   Cut for the book edition.

279.35–37   His words . . . naïve . . . ?]   Cut for the book edition.

280.6   But how? . . . to where?]   Cut for the book edition.

280.28–29   run off . . . degenerated!]   Cut for the book edition.

281.8–10   The Party . . . trap!]   Cut for the book edition.

281.31   Goddamn this deception!]   Cut for the book edition.

301.24–27   he called . . . help Gil . . .]   Cut for the book edition.

310.6–311.18   The seductions . . . pursuers.]   Cut for the book edition.

316.21–23   The Party . . . do . . .]   Cut for the book edition.

328.10–12   There was . . . Bob's.]   Cut for the book edition.

339.25–29   . . . Her sense . . . Herndon . . .]   Cut for the book edition.

356.30–357.5   "You're saying," . . . this fight.]   Cut and revised for the book edition to: " 'Right,' Houston said."

367.14–368.6   "I beg . . . truth . . .]   Cut for the book edition.

372.14–34   Cross stared . . . Party, no."]   Cut for the book edition.

376.27–377.22   Houston continued . . . psychologically akin.] Cut for the book edition.

389.20–390.4   He walked . . . and Eva.]   Cut for the book edition.

408.1–12   Before . . . passengers up.]   Cut for the book edition.

410.1–412.19   Were not . . . fear . . .]   Cut for the book edition.

421.18–32   "This Hilton, . . . money?"]   Cut for the book edition.

422.1–16   "No. . . . presence."]   Cut for the book edition.

423.20–28   All of . . . nothing . . .]   Cut for the book edition.

436.31–437.5   He lowered . . . this."]   Cut for the book edition.

461.4   Biblical passage:]   Cf. Exodus 20:5 and Deuteronomy 5:9.

488.8–9   That absolute . . . Acton,]   "Power tends to corrupt and absolute power corrupts absolutely," from a letter to Bishop Mandell Creighton, April 5, 1887. John Emerich Edward Dalberg (1834–1902), first Baron Acton, was a leader of liberal Roman Catholics in England who questioned the doctrine of papal infallibility enunciated in 1870 by the First Vatican Council.

501.3–4   . . . Man . . . NIETZSCHE]   Cf. *The Genealogy of Morals* (1887), "Second Essay, 'Guilt,' 'Bad Conscience,' and the Like," parts 1–2.

540.9–24   Cross envied . . . sighed.]   Cut for the book edition.

551.32   "trailing . . . glory"]   From stanza 5, line 7, "Ode: Intimations of Immortality from Recollections of Early Childhood" (1807), by William Wordsworth: "But trailing clouds of glory do we come / From God, who is our home."

551.32–552.10   Anthropologists, . . . happy.]   Cut for the book edition.

553.26–28   *'Come . . . rest . . .'*]   Matthew 11:28.

579.26–581.21   Who? . . . him up?]   Cut for the book edition.